LEGACY OF BRICK & BONE

TAINTED DOMINION
BOOK 2

KRYSTLE MATAR

ALSO BY KRYSTLE MATAR

Legacy of the Brightwash (Tainted Dominion #1)

Tainted (A Tainted Dominion Novella)

Anthologies

Alchemy of Sorrow (featuring The Paperweight Watch)

Anatomy of Fear (featuring Baby Teeth)

AUTHOR'S NOTE

Dear Reader,

Thank you for joining me here in the Dominion. Tashué's story depicts scenes containing and/or discussing instances of domestic violence, miscarriage, addiction, drug and alcohol use and/or abuse, prisoner abuse, police brutality, racism, and torture. There are also instances of animal death.

I tried to depict what it's like to try to love in a world that's terribly bleak, and that meant portraying that bleakness. It also meant portraying love, found family, hope, passion, courage in the face of overwhelming odds.

It's a rough world out there, and it's a rough world in here. Here's to trying to muddle through it all and finding love in the darkness.

Take care of yourself. Even if that means skipping this book.

Love,

K

For Stella
For teaching me how to survive

ACKNOWLEDGMENTS

Once again, I am reminded how it takes a village to support a writer. Where do I even start?

Karem, you deserve first billing, if only because you've survived living with me while I vacillated rapidly between despair, threatening to give up, and hyper focus. Thank you for companionship, support, surprise beer deliveries, and way too many late night burgers. You're my King.

The obligatory nod to the late great David Gemmell, without whom I would never have taken this writing business seriously. Another vital nod to Dennis Lehane, who never ceases to inspire me.

And now, the village. I can't count the number of friends I've met on Twitter, and in various other indie circles. There's something really special about the way readers and writers get to come together and share in the deep love for storytelling. All of you have been so special to me, in ways that are hard to full articulate. Thank you for making an awkward hot mess of a writer feel connected, seen, and loved. Thanks to everyone who bought, reviewed, boosted, everyone who's stuck with me through endless babbling (here I am, at it again) and all the delays it took to get this book out. I want to thank you all by name, but I'll write another 50k and then I won't be able to fit this book in print!

Specifically, thanks again to Nick, who started me on this journey by pulling me into the indie crowd.

I love my Before We Go Blog family especially. And now I call myself a member of the FanFiAddict family, too, and I am honoured. Thank you, Beth and David, for everything. You've built pillars of this wonderful community, holding us up so we can reach as many people as possible with our stories.

To my frogicorn brethren and sisteren, I love you all. Jenn, Tim, Kerstin, Holly, Ben, Fletcher, Clayton, Lauren, Taya, Christopher—it was an honour to stand with you in SPFBO 7. Here's to the wildest ride of my professional life, and here's to the companionship that got us through it. And Jenn specifically, here's to the wildest story about minotaurs I have ever witnessed.

Thanks again to Fletcher, for slogging through the hot pile of garbage I sent you and helping me to find the gems. (Everything bad that happens in this book is his fault and angry mail should be sent to him.)

Thank you to Connor, my hero. I can't wait to watch the rise of your career. You're going places, kid.

Sara, my whisker, what can I even say? Thank you for being so interesting and thank you for being like family.

Special love to Dan and Fiona. Thank you both for helping me ground my own feet in who I am, and for giving me the courage to just be that person, come what may.

Adrian, thank you for taking the time to teach me how to tattoo myself safely! Your company through what was a very hard stage of my life in general helped keep me close(ish) to sane.

Thank you to Ryan Cahill and Carissa Broadbent for inspiring me to reach for the stars.

Saving the very best for last, thank you to Ronkwahrhakónha again, because without you, Tashué wouldn't be the man he is. I wouldn't be the person I am, either. You make us both a little bit more complete and I am forever grateful for the time and the friendship.

And once again to you, dear reader. For trusting me to lead you somewhere worth going. For letting me reach out to you, so that we can go there together. Without you, I would probably still be writing, but it would definitely be a lot more lonely.

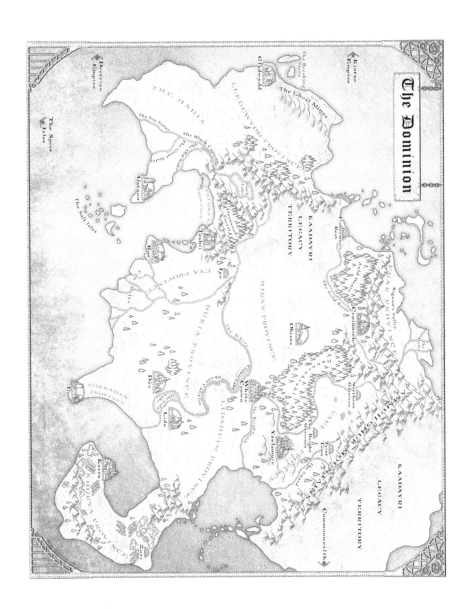

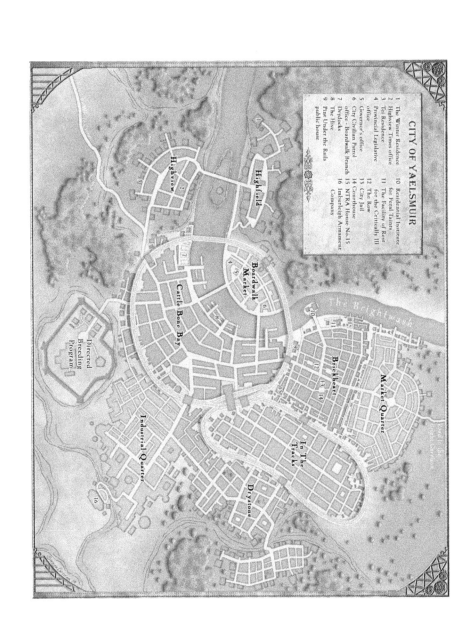

CITY OF YAELSMUIR

1   The Winter Residence
2   Highview Times office
3   Tel Residence
4   Provincial Legislative
    office
5   Governor's office
6   City Civilian Patrol
    office - Boardwalk Branch
7   Drydocks
8   The Hive
9   Pint Under the Rails
    public house

10 Residential Institute
    for Feral Taints
11 The Facility of Rest
    for the Critically Ill
12 The Row
13 City Jail
14 Courthouse
15 NTRA House No.15
16 Imburleigh Armament
    Company

Highview

Highfield

Boardwalk
Market

Cattle Bone Bay

The Brightwash

Directed
Breeding
Program

Brickheart

Market Quarter

In The
Tracks

Industrial Quarter

Drytone

WHAT CAME BEFORE

AKA "SO, THIS IDIOT—"

Day 1 Tashué Blackwood finds the body of a dead child on the bank of the river. Her arms and legs have been removed before death, and there is a tattoo on the back of her neck, showing a series of numbers. Tashué tries to encourage the investigation, but ultimately he has to surrender the girl's body to the crematorium and return to his own job. As a Regulation Officer for the National Tainted Registration Authority, he has to monitor a number of people with Talent. One, Glaen Forsooth, has been seen 'fraternizing' with another tainted without Authority permission, and Tashué gives him a warning that this is breaking the law. After Glaen, Tashué visits his son Jason, who is a prisoner at the Residential Institute for Feral Tainted and Non-Compliant (the Rift) for refusing to register his Talent. He asks if Jason has ever seen anyone in the Rift with a tattoo like the girl had, but Jason doesn't know anything. Jason asks Tashué to check in on his mother. Stella Whiterock, hiding as a 'whisperer' at the Facility of Rest, takes over the hospice care of a young boy who is dying.

Day 2 Tashué starts the paperwork necessary to visit Jason's mother, Keoh, who is housed at the Breeding Program. At his job, he takes over Stella's file. Nathaniel Wolfe (the mayor), Illea Winter (the governor's wife), and Rainer Elsworth (the head of the Authority) enlist Tashué to be a spokesman for the Authority, as support for Governor Myron Winter's reelection campaign.

Day 4 The boy in Stella's care is getting better—she's been healing him instead of assisting with his hospice care. Back at her home, Tashué visits her on behalf of the Authority, asking questions about her and her daughter, Ceridwen. As an aside, he asks Stella about the child he found, wondering if she saw the child at the Facility, but Stella has no information to give him. Tashué meets Illea at a tailor's shop, to be fitted for a formal suit since he's to attend a banquet Illea is hosting in honour of the Queen.

Day 6 The boy in Stella's care is recovered enough to go home. She takes Ceridwen to the Market, where they meet Tashué by chance. She's intrigued by the new suit and offers to help Tashué get ready for the banquet. Jason, meanwhile, gets into a fight with other prisoners. In the struggle, he breaks through the layer of suppression that keeps all the inmates of the Rift separated from their Talent. He tries to escape, but the suppression is restored and he's beaten badly by the other inmates. On the way to the banquet, Tashué stops in an illicit fight hall to meet Lorne. He asks for Lorne's help in finding information about the girl. People in the hall notice Tashué's Authority badge and pick a fight. He breaks a man's jaw with an ashtray, getting blood on his suit. Powell Iwan puts a stop to any more fighting and declares Tashué welcome in the hall any time. At the banquet, Tashué tries to keep up with talk of politics and manners, but he's out of his element. When the guests sit down, someone notices the blood on Tashué's clothes. Illea takes him upstairs to change, where she reveals her hopes that he'll consider running for mayor when Wolfe's term is up, and she intends to derail Myron's career as governor. Things get heated and they have sex, and then return to the banquet after Tashué puts on a new suit.

Day 7 After staying the night with Illea, Ishmael brings Tashué to Wolfe's house, where they confirm their hopes that Tashué would be interested in running for Mayor. Myron is only a puppet for Rainer, and they don't trust him. Tashué is worried Jason will become collateral damage if he moves against Rainer and Myron. Wolfe asks Ishmael to figure out how to protect Jason, implying Ishmael could get Jason out of the Rift. Stella is worried that she's been in the city too long and is concerned about how close she's getting to Tashué, especially considering he's with the Authority. She finds a barge in the Market and books passage out of the city, beginning preparation for leaving. Tashué is tracked down by Allie Tei, a reporter. She also found the body of a dead child and is looking for answers. They compare notes and promise to contact each other if they find anything.

Day 9 Tashué meets Lorne, who has information for him—Glaen has been seen fraternizing still. He also found information about the girl and brings Tashué to see a woman who claims she escaped from the Breeding Program. She says she saw the Authority take the children and remove their arms and legs, breaking their minds to turn them into vessels of Talent that the Authority calls 'energy units.' She gets scared and runs away, and Tashué sends Lorne after her to talk her down. Tashué meets Kazrani at their usual pub. Someone tracks her down because one of the cases she manages is causing a scene in the street. Kazrani and Tashué go to try to settle things, but the man panics, shoots someone, and escapes. Tashué and Kazrani give chase, but the man escapes and blows up a barge carrying a load of thermite, causing a massive fire in the Market.

Day 10 Someone from the Authority visits Jason, asking him to register so he can be transferred to the Breeding Program. They're impressed by the strength of his Talent. Jason declines.

Day 14 After days of fighting the fire and searching for survivors without sleeping, Wolfe sends Tashué home to rest. Stella walks him home, where they kiss, but Stella leaves before things progress.

Day 15 Lorne found some information that suggests the dead girl is connected to the Army of the Red Dawn, so he asks Vasska Czarny if it's true. Vasska tells Lorne to leave the Red Dawn alone before he gets hurt.

Day 17 Tashué and Kazrani attend a formal gathering at a large gun factory, where the Authority is running promotions. Tashué is promoted to Station House Commander, and receives a medal of honour for his efforts in fighting the fire. He resents all the pomp and speeches; he doesn't like being a part of Myron's campaign and he's been questioning his role in the Authority, especially since Kazrani's case went so tragically wrong. He uses his leverage, though, asking Rainer for permission to see Keoh, thus skipping the long paperwork process that stopped him before.

Day 18 In spite of his reservations, Tashué takes over his station house as Commander. Rainer wants to organize the press to come with Tashué on Glaen's arrest, and delivers the paperwork that allows Tashué to see Keoh. At the Breeding Program, Keoh seems to be falling back into opium addiction. Tashué asks her about the woman who escaped, but Keoh doesn't know her. After, assembles a group to arrest Glaen and

Gianna—the woman Glaen was fraternizing with—as per Rainer's wishes. Glaen goes peacefully, but Gianna tries to escape. Duskan Hill-braun shoots her, and Tashué can't stop the bleeding in time to save her life. Stella goes to Tashué's apartment to check on him that evening. Tashué talks about what happened to Gianna and his doubts about the Authority and the laws it upholds. Stella still intends to leave, but doesn't tell him. She spends the night, when she tells him that she can feel his Talent, which is much bigger than he thought but dormant.

Day 19 Stella's boss at the Facility tracks down Tashué, since he's her officer. He asks about Stella's Talent and explains that a fair number of her patients have healed enough to go home, which is unusual for hospice care. He wonders if she had been improperly assessed, and should be reassigned as a healer. Rhodrishi, a healer, visiting Tashué, explains that it's not possible to heal someone by accident. It takes a great amount of skill and training, and it's painful. He encourages Tashué to talk to Stella and really listen. She's packing to leave the city when Tashué arrives. He asks about her Talent and she confesses she's hiding with fake paperwork. When Tashué sees the tattoo on the back of Cerid-wen's neck, he realizes Stella is running to protect Ceridwen, who is from the Breeding Program. Stella admits she's planning to leave, and Tashué signs forged paperwork for her to transfer to a job in another city.

Day 20 Stella admits that she's running from the Authority, specifi-cally a man named Siras Duncreek who has been hunting her for years. Tashué gives her his gun to shoot Siras if she sees him.

Day 22 Lorne gets the shit beaten out of him at the fight hall.

Day 23 Tashué visits Jason, trying to convince him to register so they can leave the city once Jason is out of the Rift. When Jason refuses, Tashué breaks a chair and punches a guard who tries to restrain him, getting himself banned from the Rift. He goes to the Breeding Program to see Keoh again, but the staff inform him she's died of an opium over-dose. They give him her paltry belongings and her remains, cremated in an urn. At his home, Powell is waiting for Tashué with Lorne, who's in bad shape. Powell explains that someone from the Red Dawn is respon-sible for the deaths of the children. They also asked to have Lorne beaten to get him to stop asking questions. Powell gives Tashué the name of the man who killed the children: Edgar Hale.

Day 24 Tashué goes to meet Stella at the Facility, but he finds her collapsed and unresponsive. Ceridwen is with her, safe. He carries Stella to the nearby hospital, where Rhodrishi is working with the survivors from the Market fire. Back at the Station House, Tashué asks the other officers for help finding Siras, who attacked Stella but got away after she shot him. Duskan quips that Siras is doing them a favour—one fewer case for them to deal with—and Tashué loses it, beating Duskan until the other officers drag them apart. Kazrani walks Tashué out, and Tashué explains everything that's happened.

Day 25 Lorne visits Jason, and delivers the news that Jason's mother has died. Jason reveals there's a possibility of getting out, and he's going to take the chance. Tashué tracks down Edgar Hale and questions him about the children. Hale confirms the children were mutilated when they came to him—the Authority does this and calls them energy units—and admits he killed them. He alleges it was someone else's idea, a man named Davik Kaine. Tashué kills Hale as per Powell's request. Tashué goes to Allie to tell her Hale's story, but when he arrives at her office, she's being attacked by an unknown assailant. She shoots her attacker, killing him, and in the confusion shoots Tashué, too. They flee the scene, heading back to Tashué's apartment where Rhodrishi is taken care of Stella; he's able to help heal Tashué's wound enough to keep him stable. Stella is awake and she tells Allie everything: Ceridwen is a child from the Breeding Program, who Davik Kaine stole 'to make people see what the Authority is doing.' Stella couldn't bear to let Davik kill a child, so she took baby-Ceridwen and ran. She's also running from her husband, Bothain, who was abusive and the Provincial Administrator of the Authority up north, where Stella is from. He sent Siras after Stella to track her down and kill her. Her real name is Ffyanwy Rhydderch. Tashué brings Allie to Wolfe's house, hoping Wolfe can protect her while they all figure out what to do next. They tell him everything, including who Stella really is. Tashué tracks down Powell Iwan, delivering the empty bullet casing from the bullet that killed Hale. He's figured out that Powell considers Davik a threat, and offers to 'stand in the gap' left by Davik's death when Powell finally moves against him. In exchange, he asks Powell to get Jason out of the Rift.

Day 26 Tashué returns to his apartment. Kazrani offers to go with Stella and Ceridwen to protect them on the road. On Keoh's urn, Tashué notices her Breeding Program number, which identifies her as the mother of the girl Tashué found in the river. Judging by the girl's age, Tashué guesses her to be Keoh's second child (and thus the first for the Breeding Program.)

Day 27 Tashué escorts Stella and Ceridwen to the hospital to meet

Rhodrishi, who has agreed to guide everyone through the wilderness. He wants to know what Tashué is going to do next, and Tashué doesn't know exactly, but he doesn't want to play a part in the Authority anymore.

Day 33 Illea has spent the night at Wolfe's house. She's pregnant and beginning to feel the first symptoms of illness. She's restless about Myron's career and asks Wolfe for help getting rid of him. Before they can discuss anything further, Rainer shows up to remind Illea that she's expected at the official opening of the hospital, which has become a political event for Myron. Tashué shows up at the event as expected. What's not expected is that he's been drinking, and he's carrying Keoh's urn. He confronts Rainer about the children. Rainer admits the children are mutilated to make them lighter and easier to transport, and he doesn't consider them human at all. They are assets, to be bred and refined for maximum efficiency. The economy depends on them. Tashué draws his gun and considers shooting Rainer, but Wolfe and Ishmael stop him. They walk away, and Tashué brings Keoh's urn to the river at the same place he found the girl. He spreads her ashes in the water—but is arrested for threatening to shoot Rainer.

And so, this idiot is in a lot of trouble.

PROLOGUE

I shmael,

    I hope this letter finds you well.

    I'm writing to ask for your advice. Things in Yaelsmuir are sliding out of my control. The election is fast approaching, and I fear we aren't as prepared as we'd hoped. Miss Redbone isn't polling as well as we expected by now, and we're concerned that Myron is going to pull ahead again and take another Governor's term. Should that be the case, Rainer will push the the Provincial Police Force through to legislation. Whether or not a unified police force rather than city-based Civilian Patroller organizations would be beneficial is still perhaps up for debate, however I know with certainty that Rainer controlling a second body of law will be disastrous for Dominion stability.

    Illea is currently privy to some of the planning since Rainer believes she's on board for Myron's career, as she was in previous years. There's talk of the Queen stopping in Yaelsmuir after she returns from the Commonwealth, and Illea will be hosting a banquet in her honour. Myron will likely announce his candidacy then to gain the Queen's approval.

    Thanks to Illea's reconnaissance, we know Rainer is talking about having some kind of spokesman for the National Tainted Registration Authority. His intention, as I understand it, is to have the individual parade around on the campaign trail to somehow bolster Rainer's stance about how successful the Registration Program has been, probably to give credibility to the police force.

    I am also still at a loss as for who will run for the Mayor's office after me. I cannot sustain a career divided between the Mayor's duties and the Queen's Voting Council. The Council has been taking advantage of the fact that I can't travel to White Crown as often anymore and schedules votes for when I can't possibly make it down. Since I'm so close, they won't let me vote in absentia. If I withdraw from the Council, I can't imagine who will fill my seat after me. A Crowne loyalist, no doubt. One of Maes's boot lickers. We must hang on to provincial autonomy. We can't let the Crowne take back what we've fought so hard for. They still haven't filled General Deri's seat. I think they're waiting to squeeze me out so they can fill both seats at once and obliterate all our work once I'm gone.

I don't know what your plans were or how long you were supposed to be stationed away. I know it's been difficult for you since Deri died. I worry I'm somewhat to blame for this mess, for travelling west when I did. I felt one of us should go pay our respects to the Deri family, and it seemed unlikely you would have the time in the near future. Sadiya sends her regards. She has some things that belonged to Deri that she would like to give you. She hopes you'll eventually make your way out west, but if it's not possible, she'll make arrangements to meet you in Yaelsmuir. She understands, of course, how restricted your time is. The division waits for no one's grief.

I hope there is some arrangement that can be made to see you home soon. If that isn't possible, I understand. Any insights you have for boosting Miss Redbone's chances would be incredibly valuable.

I'm sorry I didn't listen to you sooner. I should have known things would be complicated.

Nathaniel

G *eneral,*
I've filed for furlough. I should receive it; I haven't requested furlough since my father died. Hopefully it will see me back in Yaelsmuir in time to help you with the election, but in case it doesn't, this is what I want you to start with.

Firstly, a large portion of the population who are voting for the name Winter are in fact voting for Illea rather than Myron. Yaelsmuir loves Illea, and her notoriety has served Myron's career in the past. If the pair of you are serious about preventing Myron from winning the popular vote, then Illea needs to join Eirdis's campaign efforts this year. Her silence in past years has always been received as assent—the time for silence is over.

Secondly, the wealthy vote goes to Rainer rather than Myron; people with money don't trust Myron with a bent copper crown, but they know Rainer controls Myron's decisions and they're willing to back Rainer's ambitions. You need to undercut his message of stability. Attack his finances, his credibility, bring to light his past failures.

He'll be campaigning on the promise of stability, which is why the Provincial Police Force has gained popularity. It sounds like security. You need to make people paranoid he'll use it to silence and suppress his enemies. You need people to be afraid of the idea of him having that much power.

Thirdly is your star, Eirdis. She's going to base her campaign in the Bay, yes? She needs to be wary of stirring up that population too much, or the rest of the city will feel threatened, and it will be harder to keep people from voting for the Police Force. She needs to spread her influence to the rest of the quarters. A campaign fundraiser that pulls together as many quarters as possible, minus Highfield and Highview—they'll just try to steal the show if they're involved. Whatever happened to the pugilist club Powell Iwan was promising? Has it launched yet? The city loves a good sporting event and it gives the Bay more substance to offer the city beyond its usual debauchery.

You should marry Eirdis. I know you're probably frowning already and muttering something about privacy and propriety, but if you and Eirdis are married—she can keep the name Redbone if she likes but technically your family name has more social capital—then people will be voting for the pair of you and it will increase her overall popularity.

Finally, if Illea is still working with Rainer and able to influence his decisions, you should have her suggest a candidate for the NTRA mascot so it looks like her idea. Put up someone you would be willing to back for Mayor when the time comes. Let it be their political debut. The NTRA is filled with officers with a military background which, on the surface, will look good for Rainer, but hopefully you'll be able to pull on their loyalty. A veteran would likely be your best bet; you need someone resolute, strong, unflinching, charming enough, the sort that won't be intimidated by Myron, Rainer, or Powell Iwan. A veteran—even one with a badge—is more likely to connect to you than Rainer Elsworth, who did not serve at all. If you find someone handsome with a good military record, the more medals the better, Rainer will believe it was Illea's idea. Don't leave it until the Mayoral election year, or you'll be scrambling again like you are now. After the lucky tinman takes the stage, Illea can throw her weight behind Eirdis. It'll be too late then for Rainer to get rid of his spokesperson.

Get started there and keep me posted.

Ishmael

I shmael,
       While I appreciate the political value of a Redbone-Wolfe marriage, I am not taking any advice on the matter at this time.

Illea and I are looking for candidates as you suggested, but the process is slow. We can't well shift through the National Tainted Regulation Authority personnel files without alerting Rainer to what we're doing. Hopefully we can find someone in time. Rainer intends to debut his 'face of the Authority' at the banquet for the Queen, probably to try to impress the Queen with his political savvy.

You're missed around the house. Hattie has been preparing your room in anticipation of your arrival and I think Cook is planning a bit of a banquet in your honour. He's dug out the old recipe cards you made. Take care of yourself, and safe travels.

Nathaniel

1

ISHMAEL

DAY 6

Fucking Yaelsmuir and all its fucking rain—of all the nights for Ishmael to be caught in a storm, of course it was when he was trying to climb up the side of Illea Winter's house. Queen Leony liked it when they lied and snuck around; she was thrilled by him and his various abilities, intrigued by the way his career was cloaked in secret even from her. When he came up with the idea of climbing up to her window, he'd only thought about the easy pleasure of seeing her eyes glitter with delight. And not about the weather.

It hadn't been raining this hard when he left the banquet. Just a drizzle when he met Illea's head cook in the greenhouse to smoke hashish. Savvas always had the best hashish, and they'd only smoked a little. Savvas got to bask in another job well done as the rest of the staff cleaned the kitchen of the wreckage his brilliance left, and Ishmael could kill a little time while the last of the guests left so Leony could maintain her privacy by retreating to the guest suite alone. Wasn't until Ishmael started climbing that the clouds really opened up.

In a strange way—probably because the hashish chipped off the edges of his good sense—the rhythm of the raindrops on his body muffled the usual tumult that existed in his mind. It didn't go away, of course. It rarely did. Complete silence was usually only obtained with amounts of opium that made his priest nervous, so he'd given up on the idea of achieving that much peace. Reducing everything to a dull thrum was the best he could hope for.

But the rain was dangerous—it sluiced off the roof and poured down Ishmael's back, the cold making his fingers so numb that he could barely move them anymore. Every hand- and foothold became treacherously slick, and he cursed his self-indulgent stupidity with every moment he was on the side of the house in a storm. It felt a little bit like he was going to fucking die to get his prick wet.

He'd only gotten home a few days ago. In time to try to help Eirdis Redbone get elected, or at least try. In time to offer Tashué up to the meat grinder that was Yaelsmuir politics. The poor bastard was the perfect choice for what Wolfe needed—steadfast, loyal to Wolfe over Elsworth, ferocious when he needed to be—but he probably had no idea what he'd agreed to. And he'd fallen so perfectly into all of it, letting Illea tempt him so Elsworth and Myron would dismiss Tashué as another of Illea's playthings while Ishmael and Wolfe prepared him for a political career behind Elsworth's back. It all went better than Ishmael expected. Illea's antics had the Queen's approval, which may well be the death knell of Myron's career. If the people of Highfield thought Myron had fallen out of favour in the eyes of the Crowne, Rainer was likely fighting a losing battle to get his re-election. Eirdis might finally have a chance to move Myron out of the Governor's office.

If it was anyone other than Illea, Ishmael might have left the table to join them—to hell with Dominion prudishness, especially if Illea had left her own table first. But Ishmael didn't trust Illea, and their relationship would only get more complicated if he started sleeping with her. Besides, he knew the Queen would call for him if he left his evening open, and whatever gossip she had would be worth far more than a roll with Tashué and Illea.

He shifted his weight too fast—his hand slipped and his heart lurched and his stomach wrapped itself around his throat—but he caught himself. Fucking hell, he should have been paying attention.

A giddy laugh bubbled up from his chest. Of all the idiotic ways he'd almost died, this one had to rank among the best and most ridiculous. He could imagine the wild rumours that would burn through Yaelsmuir if he was found dead on the paving stones outside Illea's manor. Although it was fitting, given that most of the people in this country who knew his name thought of him as a useless drunk. He shifted his weight slowly, moving laterally along the house until he stood on the ledge of a windowsill, his shoulder pressed against the cold glass. Rain soaked into his clothes, but he stood a moment, savouring the strain in all his muscles and the way his heart buzzed even with the hashish in his system to slow him down. He'd been emotionally numb often enough in his life that he could enjoy the very particular *oh fuck I almost died* rush that filled his body. It didn't matter how complicated things felt in this moment. It didn't matter who he longed for or was trying to grieve. Scheming for Wolfe and Illea felt incredibly small and far away. He'd almost fallen, and he was alive. The ugly Yaelsmuir rain hadn't conquered him this time.

Once the tremble in his arms had settled, he resumed his climb.

He hauled himself over the edge of the balcony outside the Queen's suite of rooms. The door to the balcony was unlocked by prior arrangement, and he let himself in. He shook the water from his hair, giving Illea's furniture a wet spray that gave him a petty sense of satisfaction. All the oil he used to tame his wild curls to fashionable smoothness would probably leave little stains on the upholstery.

The Queen's staff populated the sitting room, a few servants to see to her needs through the night. One of them came forward to help him out of his coat, peeling it off his arms to hang it by the hearth to dry.

"Mr. Saeati," Leony said, her voice light with her joy. The hashish billowing through Ishmael's body caught the sound of her happiness and sent it ringing through his bones, chasing away his melancholy. She stood in the doorway between the two rooms, stripped of all the banquet finery —makeup and jewels and layers of structured clothes had all been removed. Instead, she wore a long, silk dressing gown, the hem pooling on the floor around her feet, her hair assembled in a single plait. She was a handsome woman. Strong lines in her face. Broad shoulders and a long, athletic build. "You made it."

"Of course, Your Majesty," Ishmael said, pushing his hair out of his face. He stalked across the room to her, leaving wet footprints across Illea's rug. "I serve at my Queen's pleasure. Who am I to refuse when my liege lady calls for me?"

Leony smiled, retreating slowly into the bedchamber and glancing back at him as she went. "Such a humble servant you are. So very sacrificing, indulging me and my whims. You should come and warm up— your clothes look terribly soaked. I imagine you'll want to get out of your wet clothes as swiftly as possible. I'll get a wonderful show out of it, too."

Ishmael grinned, following her to the bedroom. "You know me so well, your Majesty, and you are most gracious. So considerate to allow me a moment to get more comfortable."

Leony retreated all the way to the bed, sitting on the edge. She crossed her ankles demurely in front of her, like she couldn't ever escape her training as to how to present herself to the world, even when she was indulging in secret sexual encounters.

His cold, hashish-numb fingers were slow as they rifled through his pockets, but he still took the time to pull all his things out, lining them up on the mantle. Yaelsmuir had officially entered 'best not carry anything important in your pockets' season. The thin-bladed knife that Deri gave him years ago was fine, of course. He'd had a bag of candy, but fortunately it was empty by the time he got stuck in the rain. The bag was soaked through. He unclipped his pocket watch from its chain to set it aside—he'd check on it later. This was why he didn't carry emotionally significant watches anymore. Anything he was attached to was on display at the watch shop in the Boardwalk Market.

He wriggled out of his jacket, a servant helping by dragging the wet wool off his arms. The heat permeated his clothes, making his cold skin tingly and alive. It was almost painful, the rapid transition from cold to hot. But the pain helped ground him in his body and in the moment, just like the rush of fear had. His waistcoat next—the thin white linen of his shirt was soaked through and it showed the lines of his body and his tattoos, and he could feel Leony watching him. She'd seen them all before, but they still held her fascination. He opened his trousers and fought his way out of them, adding more things to the mantle: his cigarette case, a box of matches, a few spare crowns. Leony's eyes settled on the tattoo on his thigh. The skyline of the Black Mountains in the Derccian Empire, with the moon hanging between the peaks and sand dunes trailing down toward Ishmael's knee. Of all his tattoos, it was his favourite. It represented the most painful of his assignments, only the second time in his life he'd been to the mountain range his people named themselves after—the Qasan. The whole objective went sideways. But at least he'd helped his people. Not as much as they needed. Not enough to make the Qasan safe again. But he'd helped a little, even though it went against Crowne interest.

Gods, he needed to stop. He was here for fun and gossip, not to feel sorry for himself, and thinking about those mountains never led him anywhere good.

"Can I get you anything, Mr. Saeati?" the last servant in the room asked.

"Thank you, no," Ishmael said, hanging the trousers from the coat tree beside the fire.

The servant glanced at Leony, who nodded. The servant retreated, pulling the bedroom doors closed behind her, leaving Ishmael and Leony in the closest thing the Queen ever got to privacy. Her staff would still listen from the other side of the door. They'd come at the slightest indication that the Queen needed anything. But for now, there was no one else in the room.

"This might be my last chance to entertain you, Mr. Saeati." Leony's voice betrayed the weight the statement carried. She hadn't mastered the skill of hiding her emotions, especially when she felt them keenly, and Ishmael could only imagine how miserable that made her life at court. Being the Queen wasn't the same as being the most powerful person in the room. "My family is getting increasingly impatient for me to find a husband and begin making heirs for the Crowne."

"Surely they can't force you," Ishmael scoffed, stripping out of his shirt, hanging it from the hook beside the hearth. With luck, Leony would indulge his presence until morning, and his clothes would be dry by then. "There are laws that allow you to select an heir if you can't produce children."

Leony sighed, very softly, and arranged her features into a stiff smile. "Yes, Mr. Saeati, I'm very much aware of the laws."

Ishmael grimaced. Maybe luck had less to do with whether she'd let him stay the night, and the deciding factor would be whether or not he could avoid insulting the Queen's intelligence. The fire gave a loud pop, throwing embers out onto the floor in front of the hearth. Ishmael stepped on them, his socks so soggy with rainwater that the embers didn't stand a chance—they hissed as they died out.

"Of course, your Majesty. I didn't mean to sound like I was *telling* you —I was asking what excuse they are giving when the law supports your right not to."

Leony shrugged, looking down at her hands as her fingers traced the intricate embroidery on her dressing gown. The style was vaguely Derccian, with carefully layered geometric patterns, rather than the depictions of flora and fauna as was the usual Dominion fashion for silk. "They insist that it's only meant to be used in the case of a monarch being *unable* to produce an heir. And since I am not yet wed nor have I tested my capabilities to conceive rigorously, the exception does not yet apply."

"Sounds like a pile of shit," Ishmael muttered, sinking down on the chair near beside the fire to peel off his soggy socks. He tossed them toward the fire to dry.

Leony laughed. "Would that I could present 'this sounds like a pile of shit' as a legal argument, but alas I must pay a solicitor to fight it. Or cave and marry someone. It would probably be less emotionally devastating to marry someone than to pay a solicitor who knows they've been hired by the Queen's purse."

"The amount of emotional devastation you'll get in the marriage depends entirely on who you choose, I suppose," Ishmael said, rising to peel off his drawers next. If his socks and his drawers weren't dry by the time he left, he'd just as well leave them behind rather than struggle back into them.

The full-length mirror in the dressing room caught his reflection, turning his body to long lines and dark forms on the silver-painted glass. He hadn't noticed the mirror before—he must have stepped into its angle when he retreated to the chair. Catching sight of his body dragged the melancholy back. The scars and the tattoos held so many memories, snagging old pain and holding it in memoriam. More than that—he'd lost a lot of weight while he was away this time, because grief once again took up physical space in his gut and he hadn't eaten nearly enough. His bones pushed too insistently at his skin, and his face looked haggard and worn and older than he felt. He had to constantly remind himself that he was well into his thirties, even approaching forty. Time went faster than he could feel it, especially with all the travelling he did for the diplomatic division. Even more so after the news reached him that his mentor, his handler, his lover, Gwilym Deri had died in White Crown. And Ishmael was expected to keep working, keep serving the Dominion, because individual grief was nothing in the face of sovereign stability and General Maes's ambition.

The letter from Wolfe asking for help may well have saved Ishmael. Filing furlough and coming home—even if home was a damned mess of politics and unprocessed grief—gave him something to hang on to.

Leony was watching him, like she was waiting for him. How long had he been frozen in the moment, trying not to look at himself? He wasn't sure. The hashish made time harder to track—and it made him more self-pitying than he'd realized.

"You haven't any new tattoos this time." Leony smiled when she said it and he knew she was biting back the urge to ask what they meant, what they were for. People loved to ask what they were for. "And you've lost a lot of weight."

Ishmael shrugged, sliding a hand over his chest, over the snake tattoo up his ribs, mouth open and ready to strike. When was the last time he was naked for the Queen? He couldn't even remember for sure. It had to be while Deri was still alive, so more than two years. "Nothing struck my fancy while I was away." He didn't say anything about his weight. Leony knew him well enough that she'd be worried if he said something flippant about not being hungry. "Any good candidates? For your emotionally devastating marriage, I mean."

Leony smiled—she'd been waiting for this, clearly, and she was excited to deliver her answer. "The best so far is Raheem Deri."

Ishmael almost choked on his own tongue. He tried to breathe and speak and swallow and curse and praise the gods at once but the abrupt shift in mood made his mouth too clumsy to keep up and he was left spluttering. Leony smiled. She was clearly enjoying the reaction she was getting.

"A Qasani King," Ishmael finally said.

"Yes." Leony lifted her chin like she was practicing the defiance she needed to make a move this audacious happen. "A Qasani King in White Crown. The first in Dominion history."

"There hasn't been a Qasani King *anywhere* since the Derccian Empire swallowed the Qasan," Ishmael blurted. The fire heated his back, his legs turning his skin tingly and finally dry. He pushed his hands through his hair, the shock passing through him in rapidly shifting waves. "The Deri family, good gods. The whole brood is exactly as tenacious and intelligent as you would need from a husband. Raheem specifically borders on ruthless, judging by his career. I'll wager that's because he had to eat a lot of shit from his colleges and his superiors to climb up to General. He was so angry that Deri wouldn't commission the General rank for him. Deri tried to explain that his name wasn't as beneficial as Raheem thought it would be, given his rocky history with the military, but as you've probably already gleaned, Raheem's always leaned rather idealistic and stubborn until reality grips him." He was babbling, but he couldn't stop. A Qasani King, gods, what a gift. "Deri was so proud when he got word that Raheem earned his stars on the battlefield. No one could dispute he *deserved* those stars. I don't think they got the chance to see each other in person since then, but Deri talked about it endlessly. This calls for a toast or something, your Majesty. To commemorate the moment and all that."

"A toast?" Leony asked. She rose to her feet, eyes drifting up and down Ishmael's naked body. "A lovely idea. I'll send for something—sparkling wine or something harder?"

"If you like," Ishmael said, flashing his most mischievous grin. The one that made Leony blush every time, especially if he looked her in the eye. And it worked again—she blushed so hard she pressed her hands against her cheeks like she could make them stop giving her emotions away. "Certainly Illea has a fine selection of wine from every region imaginable. But Savvas sent me away with the good Ibeh hashish, and if there's one perfect way to celebrate a marriage in the Deri family, it's with a cloud of smoke."

Leony laughed, shaking her head. "Well, I defer to your expertise, Mr. Saeati. Since you know the family so well."

Ishmael went back to the mantle, snatching up his cigarette case and his matches. Both were metal and sealed well enough to protect their contents from the rain. Savvas had given him a few hashish laced cigarettes in exchange for the best gossip about Agrion, the country his parents left behind to find a 'better life' in the Dominion. Ishmael's deployment in the region had been short and blessedly bloodless but wildly stressful with the Queen in the area as an arbiter for the latest peace accords. Avoiding being seen—and thus recognized—by her and her massive entourage had stretched the very limits of his skills. He'd wondered more than once if Maes had sent him there hoping he'd burn his confidentiality, which would finally give Maes an excuse to get rid of Ishmael. Maes and Deri used to split control over the diplomatic division, which gave Ishmael some measure of protection. But it had been two years now since Deri died, and the diplomatic division—arguably the most powerful military branch in the Dominion—didn't yet have a second administrative General, leaving Maes in full control.

Even as he lit the cigarette and took the first drag of oily smoke, an echo of dread rolled through him. The thing about people who shifted the balance of power was that doing so always made the people who held the power very angry. And the Deri family had powerful enemies already. He blew the smoke out toward the fire, watching it mix for a moment with the twisting flames before disappearing up the chimney.

"General Maes will be furious."

Leony shrugged. "I am very aware of Maes's inclination to throw temper tantrums, but Raheem has gold stars. He has served with honour and distinction. Maes wouldn't dare question Raheem's credentials out loud, so he'll have to seethe quietly." She padded across the room, taking the cigarette from Ishmael's fingers. "We've thought about putting Raheem forward as the second diplomatic division General, but then this idea seemed like a better move for Crowne stability."

Ishmael almost laughed as Leony took her first drag of smoke. "I think Maes would sooner chew off his own leg than allow another Deri into the division. Especially Deri's son. But King—he can't stop that, not legitimately anyway. Which leaves…" Unease slithered down his spine. If Maes couldn't publicly oppose a King he didn't want, he would resort to what he did best—scheming quietly and destroying things secretly. "A lot of illegitimate tactics."

"Why Ishmael," Leony scoffed dramatically, putting her free hand to her chest. "Are you implying that General Maes is the sort of man who skirts around the laws when they don't suit him?"

Ishmael let go of a laugh that time, letting it fight the looming unease. Maes was a power-hungry murderer, but if the Queen had proof of it, she would have arrested him by now. And though Ishmael was reasonably sure Leony had nothing but distrust for Maes, speaking the truth was still a slippery slope. Talking about the ways Maes broke the law came dangerously close to talking about how Deri also broke laws. Even though he was dead, there were still plenty of people who could be held accountable for smuggling illegal goods, for the murder of Dominion citizens, and for interfering with Dominion politics when it was technically extremely illegal for members of the diplomatic division to do so. Never mind the plain old murder charges; it was against Dominion law for any branch of the foreign deployment army to engage in military action on Dominion homeland soil, and since the diplomatic division was created to shape the politics abroad by any means necessary, simply advising in an election cycle like Ishmael was doing for Wolfe was technically sedition and treason.

Leony turned back to the bed, bringing the cigarette with her, leaving a line of smoke twisting behind her. Ishmael followed, grabbing an ashtray off one of the tables near the fireplace.

"If ever General Maes wanted to shift careers," Ishmael said finally, resting the ashtray on the bedside table, "I'm sure he would do very well as a solicitor, finding loopholes in the law for the highest bidder."

"That's a very measured answer," she said, letting Ishmael pass her to get into the bed first. She took another drag from the cigarette, smoke curling around her face as she raised an eyebrow at him. Her tightly coiled shoulders were relaxing already. "I'm impressed."

Ishmael shrugged. He sank down into the bed, breathing a slow sigh of relief. The blankets were deliciously warmed by the coal pan down near the footboard, and the hashish made his own body feel a little bit liquid, especially the places that were tired and sore from the climb and the almost fall. Leony rested the cigarette in the ashtray so she could shed her dressing gown, sliding under the covers next to him. She ran her fingers over the sheaf of wheat tattoo that swept across his chest, bowing over his right collarbone like the stalks were bent in some imaginary wind.

"It's generally regarded as career suicide to speak ill of General Maes," Ishmael muttered. He reached past her to grab the cigarette again, taking another slow drag, in and out, sending it up to the canopy over the bed where it danced beneath the silk. It was a good thing he'd only smoked a little with Savvas. "I try to keep my skills at avoiding honest answers as sharp as possible, even in company as trustworthy as yours, your Majesty."

She frowned, propping herself up on her knuckles so she could look down at his face again. "Do you think that's what happened to Gwilym?"

Ishmael sighed. This grief wouldn't let him go. It didn't seem to matter what he did—whether he let himself think about it, or he numbed himself with whatever substances he could get into his body—it was stuck in his chest, half-realized, trapped by anger and too many unanswered questions. Two years on, and this was actually the first time he had the chance to talk to someone who'd been in the capital when Deri died. Ishmael had been deployed when it happened. He'd talked to Wolfe plenty, getting every detail the last time he was home, forcing Wolfe to repeat everything he knew more times than could be considered healthy. But Wolfe only had second-hand reports, and so it didn't matter how many times Ishmael examined the details, he still knew pieces were missing.

"The official story is that he had a heart attack," Ishmael said slowly. "I find myself wondering if someone was instructed to lie about how he died. Of all the ways I expected him to meet his end, sudden heart failure wasn't on the list. Unless the heart failure was caused by something like too much opium at a party, which seems entirely more plausible. He was forty-six."

Leony slid her fingers through Ishmael's still damp hair, watching his expression again. Hers looked sad—her mouth turned down in the corners, her eyes soft around the edges. "Are you asking me if I asked someone to lie to save Gwilym's reputation?"

"I don't know, your Majesty," Ishmael admitted. "Usually I'm good about accepting that some things will never have answers, but—I don't know. It's harder to accept unanswered questions when the person you lost…"

"Meant so much?" Leony supplied.

Ishmael nodded. He didn't trust his voice enough.

"His healer was with him," Leony supplied. Her fingers drifted across all the tattoos on his left shoulder, her whole hand sweeping across the intricate whorl of small tally marks that made a swirling pattern like a mosaic on his skin. She didn't know the weight of the ink she touched, but Ishmael felt it, like those black lines sank past muscle and bone to hook themselves on his soul. He offered the cigarette to her so she'd stop touching them. "The Kaadayri man, with tattoos on the backs of his hands."

"Eilas Kheir?" Ishmael asked. "I thought he'd retired."

Leony nodded, blowing out another line of smoke. "He has, as I understand it. He was passing through White Crown, so he was staying with Gwilym when it happened. He's the one who reported the death to us. I asked him to tell me the truth, at least—whatever story he wanted to offer to protect the dignity of the Deri family, I didn't mind, but I wanted to know if it was something else. The healer swore it was heart failure. The poor man was so distraught over the whole situation."

Something uneasy took up residence in the back of Ishmael's throat, bitter tasting and impossible to swallow. What was Eilas doing in White Crown? Their job taught them never to believe in the appearance of coincidence. So why was Deri's most trusted but retired healer in White Crown when Deri was experiencing sudden and catastrophic heart failure? The last words Ishmael remembered from Eilas were *if I never touch another fucking unhinged diplomat until my next lifetime, it will be ten lifetimes too soon.* He must have been helping Deri with something, but what?

"I understand he escorted Gwilym's remains back to the west coast," Leony continued when Ishmael didn't speak. Her words lost their clipped edges, coming more freely, as they always did when they smoked together. More than once, Ishmael had wondered if she was the sort of person who enjoyed chatting but at some point convinced herself the inclination was dangerous, giving too much away, so tried to stop. "Gwilym's wife wrote to me after, thanking me, although I couldn't imagine what for. She said they gave his remains to the ocean because it's the Lledewyddyd way, and they also had a Qasani priest to send the gods their prayers. I thought maybe you would like to know that. She said his conversion was meaningful to him. I have to admit, I was surprised. I never imagined Gwilym Deri to be the sort of man who would turn to faith."

"Why?" Ishmael asked, a bit of a smile pulling at the corners of his mouth as he took the cigarette back. "Because he was irreverent?"

Leony shrugged, rolling toward him. She folded her hands together on Ishmael's chest and rested her chin on her knuckles. "Among other things, yes. Irreverent, indulgent, stubbornly independent."

Ishmael turned his face away from her, blowing smoke toward the window. "And you think those things made him unsuited to prayer? Those same words describe me."

Leony laughed, her face losing the last of its tension. "It isn't easier to imagine *you* praying, Ishmael Saeati."

Ishmael grinned. He shifted one arm under the blankets so he could slide his hand down her back until he found the bottom of her chemise. He dragged it up, letting his fingers dance over her skin. She bit her lip, a soft groan rumbling from her throat, her back arching deliciously toward his touch. This, at least, was comfortable and familiar. This, he was good at. Touching another person, reading the cues their body gave, basking in the satisfaction of someone else's pleasure. "That's because you're imagining stuffy, boring Sisters of the North Star, your Majesty. They tend to pray quietly about how grateful they are for everything. I think the people of the Dominion have forgotten what it's like to pray to squabbling gods—the North Star and the Ash Child are liberators, of course, but ultimately they were just people, standing against the terrible might of the Godking. Qasani prayer is more... expressive, which seems to be how it was here in the Dominion before the Godking destroyed all the temples your people had. Our prayer is rather like an argument with the gods. At times, enough of a spectacle to draw an audience." Another breath of smoke, in and out. He flicked ashes from the cigarette toward the fire, but they landed on the rug instead, sinking into one of his wet footprints. "And it involves opium for grieving and khat for celebrations and hashish for coping now and then."

"Is that what we're doing?" Leony grinned, taking the cigarette back.

"'Coping,' the pair of us?"

Laughter rolled light and easy through Ishmael's chest. He pushed his hand into Leony's hair. He wanted to shake it loose of its plait so it would hang all about him in an auburn curtain, but Leony wouldn't enjoy that. Maybe when the election was over, Ishmael would head west. Find the poppy farm and whichever Deri children still lived there, and pray with the Im-Aqi who served the whole family. Grieve there, with them, so that he could feel it properly instead of living his life half convinced Deri would show up at any minute to pull him out of this whole mess.

"It only counts as coping if there's a priest around," he said, sending the words into the lavender scent of her hair. "Let's call this adjusting."

"Adjusting to what?"

"To all this cold weather," Ishmael grunted. "I keep coming back during shit weather instead of coming back when it's nice."

Leony laughed. She rolled off Ishmael to rest beside him, sprawling her limbs across the bed. The wind blew rain against their window as if to demonstrate the ferocity of Yaelsmuir weather, and Leony blew a line of smoke at the glass in defiance. "That's because the terrible weather lasts most of the year in this part of the Dominion. There are two months to the year where summer is in full force, and it reminds me of the Salt Isles of the Southern Commonwealth, but mostly it's just rain and freezing rain and snow."

The rain made twisting lines down the glass and dancing shadows on her face, making it seem like she was a part of the storm. Like the weather was trying to snatch them out of this comfort. But they were secure in the bed, the curtains of the canopy waiting to be pulled closed to block out the whole world. The hashish and the warmth of the bed unwound the tension from him, bit by bit. She offered the cigarette back to him, but he shook his head. Savvas's hashish was strong, and he didn't want to render himself fucking useless—all his fatigue was creeping up on him, settling in his joints, in his spine. It would be too easy to close his eyes and drift on the smoke a while, hover between sleep and wakefulness, sunk in half-numb oblivion, but that was a damned waste of a perfectly good night. He needed to talk, or move, or something.

"It's a good idea," he said, dragging himself back up out of the listlessness. "Dangerous and bold and audacious and borderline rebellious, but good. People will never stop complaining, though. It won't be an easy life for either of you."

Leony shrugged at that, taking a slow drag of smoke. "It never has been."

"You should marry him in secret," he said. "As soon as possible, preferably before anyone even notices he's arrived in White Crown. That way, Maes can't argue against it or conspire to send Raheem away on some far distant deployment. Is he in the Dominion?"

"He is," Leony said. She stretched out toward the bedside table, crushing the cigarette in the heavy brass ashtray. "He's in Teshii, ready to travel east if we come to a final decision."

Ishmael rolled toward her, wrapping his arms around her and pressing his whole body against her back. She was so warm, her thighs strong and soft as she angled herself back toward him. She melted into his arms, leaning her head back against him, letting him press his face into the thickest part of her hair. "Is there any reason *not* to go through with it?"

Leony shrugged at that, her shoulders pressing against Ishmael's chest. "'Any' reason? Sure. There's a small hoard of the usual reasons. I never thought I would get married. I never thought I'd take the throne, either, so it doesn't matter what I think. I don't like being backed into a corner like this, and I resent the implication that my only valuable contribution to the future is making more Crowne babies. I worry about the lives I'll upend. Raheem, for all his courage, probably doesn't realize the scale of what he's getting himself into. As you said, he seems rather stubbornly idealistic. Everything about his life will change, and I can't promise him the change will be for the better. I'm not sure he understands the gravity of it. Not just for him, but for his siblings and his mother, who will suddenly become the Royal Family. Is it true they're all adopted, the Deri children?"

"Refugees from the Qasan," Ishmael said with a nod. "Sadiya works with a charity that helps to direct refugees into established communities here so they have a safe place to settle. Sometimes children are orphaned by the journey over, or earlier in all the chaos—she finds them homes, too. Sometimes that home is hers."

Leony rolled toward Ishmael, draping her arm over his shoulders. Her eyes were heavy-lidded and content, her fingers tracing lazy circles on the sensitive skin between his shoulder blades, making his skin tight with gooseflesh. "Was it ever... strange? You and him, and then his wife."

"Strange? No." Ishmael leaned down to kiss her shoulder, right beside the hem of her narrow sleeve. Her skin was deliciously soft beneath his lips, stirring him up out of the slow, melancholy mood, igniting his insatiable appetite. "Sadiya and Gwilym married for business. By the time I knew them, they were like-minded allies who cared for each other very deeply. Maybe it was challenging to figure out when they were younger—you know how young people are, all that passion and no sense—but by the time Deri and I started sleeping together, they had their boundaries well sorted. It's not unusual for Qasani marriages to be layered like that. Some choose more than one zawraj—spouse-mate. Or some, like Deri and his wife, only have each other, and they've all their adopted Qasani children, and Deri puts his cock where it suited him."

A fresh spasm of pain seared through Ishmael's soul. Saying *wherever it suited Deri* should have been the right thing to say. The pair of them made a career of pretending not to be overly attached to people. But the truth was so much more complicated than that, as heavy truths were wont to be. Reducing their relationship to *wherever it suited Deri* made him feel empty and alone, even with someone in his arms.

"He was your teacher, wasn't he?" Leony asked.

Ishmael nodded. He kissed her lips to try to reignite the fire before the grief could catch hold again and ruin the evening. She leaned into the kiss, lingering like she was savouring the taste of him. Her mouth tasted like smoke, but also sweet, like dessert wine and tart fruit, the lingering flavours of Illea's banquet. Savvas really was brilliant. "He was. He recruited me from the Academy, and he trained me in everything we do as diplomats. People make assumptions about him because I was young, but... Well. I'm very persistent when I want something."

She laughed at that, her head tilting back to reveal the long sweep of her throat. He kissed it, feeling her pulse race, the sound of her laughter chasing the last of the melancholy away. "You are very persistent indeed."

Her body was so wonderfully warm in his arms, reminding him that he wasn't alone at all.

He propped his head up with one hand, rising up out of the comfort of his pillow so he didn't fall asleep. He let the other find her skin, wandering down far enough to reach the hem of her chemise again and then wandering back up, dragging the silk with him so he could run his fingers over the curve of her hip and then the dip her waist made while she lay on her side, and then her broad chest. She gave a little gasp, hooking her thigh over his hip. Each moment stretched out deliciously, the flames behind his back making her eyes sparkle, the hashish rolling through him to make everything blend together. His hand moved almost without his thought, back down between her thighs. He groaned at the wetness that greeted him. He wanted to touch it more, wanted to put his mouth on it, wanted to devour her. He shifted closer to her, until his cock pressed against her leg. A little groan escaped her throat, and her hand came down, fingers sliding across the underside of him and he kissed whatever skin he could reach. Her shoulder, her throat, the sweep of her jaw. The head of his cock pressed up against her but he couldn't quite slide into her at the angle and it made his whole body ache for her. It was incredible the difference between her now and how stiffly she held herself only a few moments ago. It made him wonder, not for the first time, who she might have been if deaths in the family hadn't forced her to take the Crowne. But that was a dangerous line of thought because he'd start applying it to himself—how might life have been different *if only*.

Better to focus on this moment. Her skin was creamy and smooth and so indulgently warm. His fingers found the hem of her chemise again, pushing it up, up, his heart hammering with anticipation. How long had it been since he'd fallen into another person for company and pleasure and the thrill of release? He couldn't even remember if he'd fucked anyone while he was away this time. Maybe he'd drifted through that whole deployment, only half-alive. Focused on the objective while pieces of him withered under the pressure of his grief and anger. But now here he was, with a familiar partner, and she was working toward a future he could almost hope for, and for the first time in a long time, he could say he was excited about something. It made him want her more. He wanted to turn this room into a shrine to her pleasure. But his treacherous, restless mind was still twisting through the future and all the ways the Dominion would change if she really married Raheem.

"You know they're all provincialists, every last one of them. It's writ in their bones. It'll be the biggest argument people will use against the whole idea."

He didn't dare say the rest—that Deri wasn't only a provincialist. He was a Crowne abolitionist, who thought the nation would be better off without royalty at all. At least some of his children agreed with him, though Ishmael wasn't sure who exactly. And so did Ishmael, for all that he liked Leony specifically. The Crowne was a monument to a past that the Dominion had evolved beyond, and progress demanded governance by the people and not some family bloodline. Maybe once, Voth the Liberator had held the Dominion together after the Godking was destroyed. Revolution had a habit of making a country unstable, and Voth's strong rule kept things relatively peaceful. But now? The Crowne no longer held the interests of the whole Dominion. Leony tried her best, but the things she said at the banquet highlighted her biggest blindspot. The Talented.

"Depends on which branch of the Deri family," Leony said, her voice gone breathy and unfocused, but the politics of it all had her, too, and the words tumbled out of her even as he slid a finger into her. Gods, she was so wet, and it took all the self-control he had to go slowly and let her speak. "Gwilym's brood are provincialists, but his family history lies in privateering for the Crowne. It will help smooth things over, I hope. The intention is that we can strike a balance between Crowne authority and provincial autonomy—and what better way to demonstrate it than with a marriage to the most famous provincialists in the Dominion?"

"Most infamous, I should think." He pushed his face into her neck, kissing the spot where he could feel her pulse racing, sliding his tongue across the hollow beneath her jaw to taste her sweat. "I have to admit, I'm surprised you're so eager to ally yourself with provincialists. I would have imagined the head wearing the Crowne would lean rather more toward Crowne loyalists."

"A weathered eye looks toward the future, Mr. Saeati," Leony said. The hashish and the pleasure ravaged their way through her usual prim enunciation, and her words went breathy and less distinct. "And the easiest way to predict the future is to pay attention to the shifting politics of other countries. Power structures are shifting away from monarchies as self-governance grows in popularity. To try to fight the shift is to invite rebellion, and no one wants that. I want to pave the road to the future without the horrible bloodshed that comes with unrest. I'm hoping, by crowning Raheem Deri as King, the pair of us can strike a balance that maintains Crowne sovereignty while allowing provincial autonomy to stabilize and grow, for the benefit of every province."

She was right, of course. The collapse of the monarchy would be bloody and ugly, even if he thought it was *right*. It felt so treacherous, contemplating it while his fingers were wet from her, his Queen, whom he was sworn by his military career to protect at all costs. She was gasping in his ear, and he was contemplating the dissolution of the monarchy. But this marriage, it could protect her, the most compassionate monarch the Dominion had seen in a long time. So, maybe it wasn't such a terrible thing for her to secure her position by marrying Raheem. Maybe Raheem and Leony together could steer the Dominion toward a more equitable future without the terrible bloodshed of a coup or a civil war.

It thrummed in him with all the excitement he had early in his career, all the heady rush of shaping the world for the better, before all the cynicism and exhaustion caught up to him.

Ishmael pulled his face out of her neck so he could look her in the eye. "Have there been whispers of war?" he asked, probably too innocently.

Deri had been convinced that war was coming, but sometimes it was hard to gauge which of his opinions came from cynicism and which came from real threats. *Just because I'm cynical,* he'd grumble, *doesn't reduce the fact that the world is actively shit.* Deri had been convinced that something was coming, something big and ugly, something that made him restless. Ishmael had thought they were in everything together, but at the end, it seemed like Deri was trying to protect him from something. And then he died. The fact that his healer was there when it happened only made him suspect that Deri was right.

"There's always whispers," Leony said. Ishmael hated the answer, but it was true. "I'm sure you know that. But ideally this keeps them at whisper levels instead of giving them fuel to grow into more imminent plans."

Fucking Myron and this stupid election felt like a minor distraction compared to *this.* Maybe he would find time to slip down to White Crown and witness the wedding. Shake Raheem's hand and look him in the eye and warn him about how bad his life was about to be while also congratulating him for taking the burden on himself. The Crowne family would *loathe* Raheem for this, but surely he knew that. He wondered if Raheem and his siblings had the same fears Ishmael did—that Deri's heart attack was contrived somehow, or a lie to cover the truth that Maes was responsible. Maybe that was why Raheem was willing to accept the weight of the whole country onto his shoulders—maybe he was coming to White Crown to square things with Maes himself.

A shiver ran down Ishmael's spine.

Maybe it would all result in war anyway, even though Leony was trying to prevent it. Maybe Raheem didn't care half a wit for the

Crowne or making peace. Maybe the road he was paving was one for revenge.

"Well," Ishmael said, pushing those thoughts out of his head before he really ruined his mood, "here's to a peaceful marriage and a stable, prosperous country."

"Indeed," Leony gasped. "Here's hoping Raheem Deri is the man he needs to be to withstand the weight of it all."

His whole body buzzed with renewed energy, even as the hashish fought to turn him sedate and too slow. He wanted to ask how long Leony and Raheem had been planning this. Had Deri known? Gods, he would be proud and furious in equal measures, as he usually was when Raheem was involved.

But she kissed him before he could find a coy way to ask more questions. He groaned against her, crushing their bodies together. She broke the kiss first to catch her breath, her whole body tense as she shifted enough to reach between them to touch his cock again, her hands trembling a little. Excitement maybe or anticipation, or the way all this future wound tightly in her bones and spilled around them both the more they talked about it, like their words made all the possibilities more real.

Ishmael rolled away from her, onto his back. She followed him, rolling on top of him without hesitating. Straddling his hips. Kissing him with hunger that hadn't been there before. All the excitement and the hashish had her finally, stripping her out of her cage of demure restraint.

"You should come up higher, your Majesty," Ishmael said. He slid his hands down her back again, dragging her chemise up to her waist. "Let me show you how deeply and enthusiastically I *respect* you."

Leony laughed, the sound lilting and a little wild. She sat up straight, pushing the blankets off her shoulders, that braid of hers so long the end of it tickled his navel as she worked her way up his body. He watched her face as she made her slow way up, watched the way she bit her lip and the way her eyes burned with the lust that crackled in the air between them like a storm, chasing away everything except how desperately he wanted to taste her. He shifted his arm so she could get her legs around his shoulders and settle on his face.

He groaned, sliding his hands up her back, under her chemise, leaning up against her when she didn't fully settle her weight against him. There was no better taste in all the world than that of someone's pleasure. He licked her slowly, listening to the way her breathing changed, the way she settled against him in slow increments. Her pleasure felt so fucking good, making his body buzz, making his cock ache for her. He slid a finger into her as he sucked on her and that made her buck against him with delicious impatience, made her breath and her moans grow so loud that he wondered if the whole house could hear her. If servants gathered out in the hall to listen.

Louder, he wanted to tell her, *louder so the whole fucking city can hear you—*

And his treacherous mind wouldn't let him escape Deri for long—he remembered too well what it was like to share lovers with him, what it was like to devour someone while Deri watched, what it was like to be so surrounded with sweat and passion and Deri's voice in his ear, deep and rumbling and voracious. He could almost feel the weight of the bed shift, as it would when Deri crawled toward him, like the hashish in his mind trapped him somewhere between reality and his imagination, summoning Deri up out of the past to taunt him with something he couldn't have, something he ached for with every shred of who he was.

Don't think about Deri—think about Leony—

Her whole body trembled, rocked, her hands on the headboard above him to keep her weight still half hovering, her orgasm rolling through her in waves until she couldn't handle the intensity anymore and she twisted away from him. Ishmael caught her thighs before he could get too far, kissing her skin, her knee, her thighs, her hips, teeth nipping softly against the sensitive skin to make her gasp and squirm. She laughed again, sweat glistening on her throat, her collarbone.

"You are too good to me," she gasped. "So self sacrificing in your respect."

"It is my *immense* pleasure, your Majesty," Ishmael said.

He nipped her thigh again and tried to ignore all the questions still swirling through his head. He should be satisfied, should be thinking about how badly he wanted to fuck her and make her scream for him, but the politics of it all wouldn't let him go.

She worked her way down his body, biting her lip again, watching his face. He pushed his hands up under her chemise, pushing the hem up higher as his hands climbed her body. Her chest was misted in more sweat, the beads of moisture dancing on her ribcage and along the sweep of her breasts, her nipples still deliciously hard. He sat up as she lowered herself onto him, groaning as he pushed the chemise up higher, bunching it under her arms as she wrapped them around his shoulders to hold their bodies together. His tongue found one hard nipple and she gasped, her hips rocking slowly, dragging across the whole length of him like she was teasing herself, and it took all the self-control he had not to grab her and hold her so he could fuck her harder. She didn't like it, the pain, didn't like control being taken away from her, didn't like when he got rough, so he had to keep himself restrained. The pain was only fun if his partner enjoyed it, too.

But keeping his hands under control only made it harder to control his wandering thoughts. "Is it true you gave gold Captain's bars to the first Jitabvi to ever go to the Officer's Academy?"

Leony laughed, leaning back from Ishmael, but her hips didn't stop. She rocked slowly, holding his shoulders for balance. "Ever the diplomat, Mr. Saeati," she breathed. "Still fishing for the best gossip."

Ishmael grinned, sliding his hands down her back, grabbing her ass with both hands so he could guide her just a little faster. And the hashish trapped the pleasure, sending it through him in repeating waves that didn't obey the laws of time. "I've been away a whole year. I have to catch up somehow."

Leony groaned, so deliciously loud, her head tilting back and making a long line of her neck. "You're lucky I enjoy your company so much."

"Yes, your Majesty," Ishmael said. He squeezed her ass harder, pulling their bodies together and shifting his weight so he could buck his hips into her and kiss her throat, tasting the rush of her heartbeat and the salt of her sweat. She wouldn't let him kiss her on the lips until he washed his face but he could kiss her everywhere else. "I am exceedingly fortunate. The most blessed man in the Dominion."

She groaned and closed her eyes, clinging to him. Sweat gathered on both of them, the fire crackling beside them. "It's true. Tevir Mahalouwan—one of Raheem's men, and Raheem insisted it was time. I think he wrote me a hundred letters, vouching for Mahalouwan's prowess. And he was right. Mahalouwan's test scores were nearly perfect. Some people tried to accuse him of cheating, but there was never any evidence. He's a brilliant man and he'll be an invaluable asset to the Foreign Deployment." She pulled him closer, pushing her face into his hair as she moved faster. "Does that satisfy your curiosity, or do you have any more questions?"

"Ah—no more questions," Ishmael laughed, laying a kiss on her collarbone, her sweat dancing under his lips. "I promise."

"Good."

She pressed her hands against his chest and he leaned back, settling his head on the pillow. She finally lifted her chemise over her head, revealing all her skin and her scars and the beautiful deep hue of her nipples that he wanted to put his mouth on, but she rested her hands on his chest like she wanted to keep him pinned. As if that would keep him quiet.

He couldn't stop thinking, couldn't silence the endless loop of ideas that flitted through his head, but at least he could bask in the simple and fulfilling pleasure of letting the Queen ride him in Illea Winter's house, after that perfect disaster of a banquet where most of Highfield glared at him as if it was a little bit his fault that Illea and Tashué made such a spectacle. The only thing that would have made the moment better was if the people of Highfield knew he was *here*. If they knew that the Queen of the Common Man took him to her bed because he was the most exciting person at Illea's table, if he could watch the outrage and the scandal and the jealousy pass through their eyes.

He wasn't going to last much longer—he closed his eyes and clenched his teeth and tried to measure his breathing to delay the inevitable, but it wasn't working, even though Leony's pace was fading, like she was getting tired. It had been a while since last he fucked, and now he was half drunk and mostly high and sunk into a kind of excitement he hadn't felt in years, something that felt entirely too much like optimism. A Deri, as King. Maes would chew on his own spine with the rage of it.

He caught Leony's hips and held her still, trying to catch his breath. But no. Even that wasn't enough. Leony shifted her weight forward so she slid off him—they'd done this enough together that she knew. He groaned as he came, spilling hot across his own navel, across her thigh, the release rolling through his whole body.

Leony rolled off him, settling on the pillow beside him and dragging the blankets back up to cover them both. Panting, gasping, sweating, pushing her hands through her hair as she tried to catch her breath.

He should say something, maybe, or roll toward her to make sure she was satisfied, but his mind was working too much.

"Whose idea was it?" Ishmael asked.

Leony made an inarticulate noise that was pitched like a question.

"Marrying Raheem. Whose idea was it?"

"Ishmael," she said, rolling away from him but shifting so the curve of her ass pressed against his hip, inviting him to fold himself against her. "Go to sleep."

2

ISHMAEL

DAY 17

It felt strange to be walking through the Bay, wearing his best formal suit. Perfectly cut, especially now that he'd put on a bit of weight, velvet and silk and gold buttons, the best that Bellmore had to offer for his body and his style—but in Cattle Bone Bay. His overcoat cost more than a month's rent. It made him stand out too much. Eyes lingered on him as he passed through the alleys and streets, making his way toward the Hive. If he had time, he would have changed before coming down here, but that meant changing *again* after he left. He had to get to the Imburleigh factory for the cursed Authority promotions. Illea wanted him there because she was still pretending to be an innocent bystander in Myron's career, and Wolfe was all too happy to play along. So of course that was why Powell Iwan wanted to see him *now*. He liked to remind people how very important he was and demand Ishmael's time when he didn't have any to spare.

Or maybe the reason he felt strange was the way the Market fire had set him so completely off balance. It didn't matter how hard he worked to protect people, how carefully he manipulated the politics to try to improve people's lives, how much he advised and plotted and maneuvered, sometimes the whole fucking Market caught fire, and innocent people kept dying no matter what he did. Sometimes, all he could do was dig corpses out of the rubble of someone else's destruction.

Ishmael grabbed newspapers as he walked through the Bay, getting as many different titles as he could. Powell would keep him waiting, and he might as well do some work while he was sitting around. He pulled the crime pages, the social rag, even the one foreign events page in the Bay, which tended to print mostly the salacious details of the sex lives of the royalty in other countries. To hell with foreign policy on the effect it might have on Dominion trade and thus the Dominion economy—which prince had gotten himself in trouble with his cock this time? The Bay was very consistent in their interests.

Powell Iwan stationed himself on top of the Hive, in a room that was half office and half sitting room. Its position at the top of the Hive meant it caught all the warm air rising from the various halls and warehouses below; the fight hall especially generated a lot of heat with all those spectators jostling around the stage and the bar. The furniture in Powell's room was all modest and rather old, nothing to hint at the immeasurable wealth under Powell's name. The man could have moved across the river to Highfield and run his business from a manse on the high side of the city like generations of merchants before him. He'd been in Yaelsmuir for half a century or more, gathering wealth and power to make his name at least as big as Wolfe, Winter, or anyone else on the other side of the river, and he stayed in the Bay by choice.

Ishmael headed all the way up, up the switchback stairs that felt far too flimsy for how high above the river they were. Like a strong gust of wind could knock it all down. Fuck the river and fuck the docks and fuck the Hive especially. Nothing good happened here.

Vasska let Ishmael into the room, giving one of his small, shy smiles. Such a beautiful boy—young man now—with his blond hair and his blue eyes and his mother's fine features. He hid that cunning mind with his little smiles and the way he didn't quite meet your eyes until he had something important to say, and then you saw his lineage in the sharpness that he'd inherited or learnt from his grandfather.

"Good afternoon, Mr. Saeati," he said, stepping aside.

Ishmael checked his timepiece as he stepped into the door, shrugging out of his coat. He was going to be late, and Wolfe was going to be annoyed. "Afternoon, Vasska. How's your grandad these days?"

Vasska shrugged, his mouth twisting to something like a frown before he forced it back to a neutral expression as he took Ishmael's coat. "He's started his winter slide early this year. He had a hard night."

"I'm sorry," Ishmael said. "I know how hard it is to watch it happen and not be able to do anything. When all of this political shit is settled, you and I will go have a drink somewhere, hey?"

"Sure," Vasska said. "When all of this is over, and we magically have nothing else that's trying to fall apart and needs all our attention."

Ishmael laughed and followed through the apartment. "It sounds like you don't believe that day will come any time soon."

"I don't know how you got that impression," Vasska said. "I see you brought plenty of reading material."

Ishmael tucked all the folded papers under his arm. "Of course. A diplomat likes to know the happenings of the world."

"Have a seat," Vasska said, waving Ishmael to the small room with the extra potbelly stove. "He'll be along as soon as he's done testing your patience."

"Naturally," Ishmael said, sinking into a sofa.

There were other rooms up here somewhere, proper offices for Powell to sit and keep track of the news of his quarter and all the paperwork he produced to make the Hive look like it complied with all the city's tax and import laws.

Ishmael flipped through the newspapers as he waited, scanning the headlines, speed-reading through each article. An article about the Imburleigh event Ishmael was supposed to be at by now—the paper roasted the Imburleigh Armament Company for backing Myron, but treated Wolfe more gently. Ishmael couldn't hide from the twinge of sympathy he felt for Mallory. If he knew her, she would be furious about backing Myron again, but the Imburleigh board of investors must be salivating over the arms contract Myron's police force would need. Eirdis Redbone's reporter was running excellent content about Wolfe and Tashué, priming people to talk about them for the next two years while the last of Wolfe's Mayoral term ran out. Nothing about how Tashué got his White Shield story yet, even though Ishmael told Wolfe to run it, but that was probably because the news cycle had been subsumed by the Market fire. Tashué Blackwood the hero, who fought the flames for days.

Another paper scorned Wolfe's involvement in the Market fire, but asked why the tenement fire this morning didn't get any such attention. The whole building was destroyed, but the fire was contained after a few hours and some well-timed rain, which was a good outcome as far as fires were concerned. The article deliberately ignored that the Market fire received so much press because it burned wildly out of control for days. Ishmael made note of the reporter's name—he wondered if the paper was one of Rainer's or not. Or maybe one of Powell's for that matter. Although Powell worked with Wolfe reasonably well, it served his interest to make sure the Bay wasn't *too* loyal to Wolfe.

Another knock on the door had Vasska walking through the hall again. He was stiffer this time, his emotions hidden away—but Ishmael couldn't see the door from where he sat.

"Mr. Kaine," Vasska said. "Thank you for coming."

Tension passed through Ishmael's whole body, burning hot and painful before he forced himself to breathe through it and keep a calm exterior. Davik fucking Kaine. Why was he here, too?

Ishmael did his best to avoid Davik Kaine as much as possible. The man was ambitious, ruthless, hungry for power like everyone else. None of that made him different, really—Ishmael had encountered plenty of dangerous people in his life, and he knew how to anticipate them and their greed. But the thing he didn't like about Davik was the bastard was *observant*. There was always something a little too knowing in his eyes, and now and then he said things that made it seem like he knew things about Ishmael's career. There was no conceivable reason for him to know anything about the diplomatic division. He was just a thug criminal in Cattle Bone Bay who used to be a thug rebel in Cruinnich.

Ishmael kept his eyes down, shaking off the unease before Davik entered the sitting room. Thank fuck for the newspapers. He flipped to the foreign news. There were rumours that a rebel was rising in the desert outside Ibashah, uniting the Ibeh people to rise against the military that had overthrown the monarchy in a bloody coup. The Ghost Queen, they called her—allegedly, she was the murdered Ibeh Queen reincarnated. Ishmael couldn't help but smile a little. He *knew* she would be resilient enough to survive after he'd helped her fake her death. He sent a prayer to the gods that she survived whatever she planned. She might have been Ibeh and not Qasani, but Ishmael thought the Qasani gods could still give people a little shove in the right direction if they so desired.

"What are you smiling about, Saeati?"

Ishmael didn't look up when Davik entered. His voice—a low, buttery northland burr, surely exaggerated because no one from Cruinnich was that heavily accented—was too enticing, and his face was too attractive for his own good. All that charm made it so he was used to a certain amount of attention, and so when Ishmael refused to make eye contact it almost always got under Davik's skin. "The King of Agrion has lost another concubine, apparently. They have a habit of escaping him."

"Maybe if the King of Agrion was better at pleasing his concubines, they wouldn't be so eager to get away," Davik said. He sunk down on the sofa beside Ishmael, stretching his arm across the back, immediately putting himself into Ishmael's personal space. He was an expert at taking up as much space as possible.

"Maybe you could give him some pointers about pleasing concubines even if you've got a small prick," Ishmael said. "I'm sure he would appreciate your experience. Failing that, you could send your girls over to teach his concubines how to lie."

Davik snorted. He rested a hand on his leg and the tattoos on his fingers always caught Ishmael's eye. He couldn't help but wonder if Davik's tattoos were for him or if they were part of his carefully considered appearance—but then, people wondered the same about Ishmael, so maybe he was a hypocrite for thinking about them at all. "It's nice to know you spend so much time thinking about whether or not my cock will please you, Saeati. But even I have standards, so I'll be keeping it to myself."

Ishmael laughed, glancing at Davik. He was dressed almost as finely as Ishmael, his suit of luxuriously soft wool tailored to compliment his athletic build. The colours were muted, the quality of it more subtle than Ishmael's clothes. His beard and his hair were always trimmed and oiled so they gleamed nicely, hairs settling in exactly the right place, unlike Ishmael's unruly waves that defied taming. "Are you trying to imply that I'm too much of a slut for you? That's rich. What's the matter, Davik? Intimidated by experience? Worried I'll know you're boring? The pretty ones like you are always boring. You depend too much on how exciting it is to be *near* you and don't give enough attention to the important things like skills."

Davik winked, and Ishmael wanted to punch him in the face. "Ishmael Saeati, did you just call me pretty? I'm flattered, but my answer is still no."

Ishmael rolled his eyes, looking back down at the newsprint. He scanned through the article about the Ghost Queen again, trying to discern whatever details he could from the rumours, but they were vague and generally indistinct. He shifted through his pockets while he read, finding whatever bag of candy he had so he could keep his hands busy. It took the pressure off sitting still if his hands were moving or he had something to eat. His whole life felt like one big string of trying to find ways to use his energy before the build-up of it drove him out of his mind. Deri was the one who suggested he keep food in his pockets.

The candy was an assorted bag of odds and ends, so Ishmael took whatever his fingers found first. A clove rock, the bright red and white candy infused with clove oil, giving it a delightfully powerful flavour to counter all that sugar. Deri hated the pungent taste of them. And some-how, that was comforting.

"I wasn't expecting you to be here," Davik said. "What do you think this is about?"

"Don't know," Ishmael said, rolling the candy with his tongue so that it sat between his cheek and his teeth, sucking on it as loudly and obnox-iously as possible. "Powell will let us know when he's ready."

Ishmael bit down on the candy, and it shattered in his mouth with a satisfying crunch, spreading clove oil and sugar across his tongue. He flipped through the social pages last. There were strange details about Illea Winter's sex life, which now included Tashué. Apparently he'd been seen with a few of the most beautiful, powerful women in the city since the banquet—like Mallory Imburleigh—which meant clearly he'd slept with each of them since Illea had so memorably entertained him. It was a load of shit. Ishmael would be annoyed that no one speculated about which of the beautiful men Tashué had slept with, except he knew that the editor of this particular paper was especially fixated on heterosexual couples.

Ishmael reached into his pocket, pulling out another candy. A piece of salt water taffy this time.

"Do you share your candy?" Davik asked.

Ishmael smiled sweetly, pulling the wax paper off the taffy. "I only share with people I like."

Davik's mouth quirked with another smug grin. "I love how you play hard to get to try to distract me from how uncomfortable you are."

Ishmael rolled his eyes again, looking down at the paper. Fucking Davik. "Sweetheart, you don't make me uncomfortable. There's nothing about you that's threatening at all. You're just a minor inconvenience while I sit here, waiting for Powell Iwan." He popped the taffy into his mouth. "An unpleasant aroma lingering in the room. Like a fart."

Davik laughed like a man who knew he was far more than a minor inconvenience. Only the *second* most powerful man in the Bay. Powell had the Hive but Davik had his smuggling lines and his feral Talented who came to the Bay for protection. And his pugilist club, a front for all the money he needed to keep those smuggling lines healthy.

He'd built enough power that he was posing a serious threat to Powell Iwan—it was probably the first legitimate rival Powell had faced since before Ishmael was even born. Which meant Powell would be planning to have Davik dealt with any day now.

Vasska stepped back into the room carrying a pot of tea. Steam curled from the spout, smelling of all the herbs that would see Powell Iwan through another winter. Ishmael folded up the newsprints in time to watch Powell shuffle into the room, holding Adley's arm to keep himself steady. He moved slow and had that glassy-eyed look—Adley must be giving him laudanum so he could sleep. Ishmael stood, setting the stacks of newsprint beside him on the sofa so that once Powell was sitting and settled, Ishmael could step around the table and shake his hand. Powell clasped Ishmael's hand in both of his, something he'd started doing in the last few years as his health declined—the tiniest show of affection, or something like it. Or maybe it was an attempt to cling to someone younger and healthier than he was, like he thought it would save him from the inevitability of death.

"Your hands are cold, boy," Powell muttered, but his voice had that raspy quality that it did when he was coughing a lot. No surprise, given the ugly, wet weather.

"They're always cold, Mr. Iwan," Ishmael said, his words a little mangled by the candy still in his mouth—taffy was hard to get rid of quickly, unless he swallowed it. "Even when it's hot outside."

"Sucking on sweets again, are you?" Powell asked. "What've you got?"

Ishmael shrugged, reaching into his pocket and pulling out the paper bag. "All sorts of things this time. I went to the candy store and took a big scoop from the broken candy jar. Got two whole bags for a half-crown."

Powell chuckled. "All that money you get from Wolfe and from your father's watches, and you still spend each half crown like you don't know when you're getting the next one."

Ishmael shrugged again. "Growing up hungry leaves its mark on your bones."

"Aye, it does that. You and I have that in common."

"I have those clove rocks you like," Ishmael said, opening the bag and shaking it around a bit to watch for the flash of white. "Would you like one? I also have sugar coated hazelnuts if you prefer."

"I can't resist those clove rocks," Powell said. "You're good to have around, Saeati. Helps me remember what it's like to be young."

"I try my best," Ishmael said. He fished a clove rock out, the side of it chipped away. "There you are, sir."

"Thank you, son." Powell took the candy and rested it on the edge of the saucer, next to his teacup. "Been home a whole two weeks, and this is the first time you come pay your respects. I expected you would have turned up sooner."

"I'm sorry. It's this fucking election. Keeping up is running me ragged. I hardly have time to think a full fucking sentence, let alone going around to visit. And then the Market fire made everything worse."

"Mmm, is that why you're looking so skinny?"

Ishmael ran a hand down the front of his waistcoat. "Believe it or not, I've been putting weight on since I got home."

Behind Ishmael, Davik sighed. Fucking *sighed* and shifted in his seat, like he wanted things to move along faster. And hell, Ishmael wanted that too, but who sighed at Powell Iwan?

Vasska stepped into the tension, carrying a teapot that curled steam behind him. Ishmael took his chance to sit, sinking back down beside Davik. The other man sat stiffly, his hands folded over his navel, his body coiled as tight as a clock's mainspring.

"There you are, Grandad, a fresh pot," Vasska said, pouring some into Powell's cup. "Can I get you anything else?"

"That's fine, boy."

"You haven't eaten anything today, Grandad—can I make you something?"

"Later." Powell waved Vasska off. "Don't you start nagging me now."

"Yes, Grandad," Vasska said, retreating. But he didn't leave. He lingered in the hall, close enough to listen.

"He takes good care of me, that boy," Powell said. Ishmael wondered if Powell knew Vasska was still hovering nearby. Something about the interaction seemed strange—why was Vasska going through such effort to draw attention to Powell's ailing health when Davik was in the room? Why had Vasska removed himself from the conversation when he could have stayed, and why was he hovering within ear shot like he was hiding? Ishmael glanced up at Adley—did Adley know the interaction was strange, too? If he did, nothing showed on his face. "He'll make a good father one day. I've been hoping he'll start making his children while I'm still here, but he keeps me waiting."

"I think you're right about that," Davik said. The tension in him uncoiled a half measure or so—maybe that was Vasska's intent. If it was, he'd broken the tension rather brilliantly. "About him being a good father, I mean. He's got a lot of love in his heart, doesn't he?"

"He does indeed," Powell said. "How many little ones have you got now, Kaine?"

"Three in all, Mr. Iwan. Rowan's fifteen now, and the girls, are five and seven. They went down the smugglers' road with their mam this summer, since I was going to be so busy getting the club ready."

"Rowan Kaine doesn't want to learn to be a smuggler?"

Davik shrugged. "He wanted to help with the pugilist club. He's been working as hard as anyone else, getting it ready. He's excited for our first pugilist, whenever you find the right man for us."

Powell nodded, ignoring the implied question of when Davik might expect a pugilist for the club. The match for Eirdis was in a few weeks, as far as Ishmael was aware. He wondered what Powell was playing at, making Davik and Eirdis both wait so long for their fighter.

"I hope your boy's got more sense than mine ever did."

"Hard to tell if a fifteen year old has sense at all, innit?" Davik said. "Too much confidence at that age, not enough wisdom or fear."

"Truer words," Powell muttered. "Enjoy the little ones whilst they're still so small. Doesn't last near long enough."

"No sir, it most certainly doesn't. I miss 'em something fierce when they're gone."

"What about you, Saeati?" Powell asked. "Do you have any children?"

No point lying about it to Powell because he'd probably find out eventually—if he hadn't already—and he'd be furious if Ishmael didn't tell the truth. Knowing Powell, he'd known the truth since the day Ishmael's daughter was born. "Just the one, that I know of. She'll be twenty now, or thereabout."

"You think there are a lot you don't know about?" Powell asked.

Ishmael shrugged. It felt strange, acknowledging his daughter in front of Davik. So few people knew. "I try not to make accidental humans anymore, Mr. Iwan. If I can't take care of them, I've no business making them, have I?"

Powell snorted. "I know the reputation you have, boy. You can't honestly tell me it's all lies."

"The rumours are all true, Mr. Iwan. Every single one of them.

Especially the ones that contradict each other. Anyway, I can't make accidental humans in someone's mouth, can I? Or if I fuck men."

Powell shrugged. "You have the opposite problem that I ever did. Wasn't so much interested in all the fucking, but I wanted the children. I got a load of idiots, but at least one of those idiots made Vasska."

"I wanted them. Especially when I was younger," Ishmael said, picking up the newsprint from the sofa and folding them all together, resting them in his lap. He wasn't expecting to talk about children and hopes and dreams, and it all sat heavily in his chest. So many of the things he'd wanted had slipped through his fingers like so much ash. "But the division makes things like a future and a family hard to plan for."

"Boy, life in its entirety makes a future and a family hard to plan for." Powell shifted in his seat, waving a hand like he was batting Ishmael's foolishness away. "All you have is this moment. Your heart could stop right now, or a stroke could destroy your brain, or a feeble old man could decide he's had enough of your shit and have someone open your throat for you. I won't, because your shit is useful to me. And you're good to Vasska and that's about all I care about these days. But you never know what'll happen in a moment. So you want children? Good. Go make them while your cock still works. The way you fuck around, I'm sure you'll double the population of the Bay for me with your little Saeati bastards. But don't for a moment think the future is a thing you can control. All you can do is roll the dice as many times as the world lets you before you find yourself standing in front of the Keeper of the Keys."

"Yessir, Mr. Iwan. Hard to argue with advice like that."

Powell nodded like he was satisfied. "I suppose you'll be getting impatient to hear my answer about Losek."

Who the fuck is Losek?

Davik gave a little shrug. "You know me so well, Mr. Iwan."

Powell lifted his mug and took a few sips. "He's a gambler?"

"Yes, sir, Mr. Iwan," Davik said. "Has a staggering amount of debt with bookies around the city. We thought we would scrub him off quick, make it look like he skipped town."

"Excuse me for cutting in, Mr. Iwan," Ishmael said, "who is Losek?"

"I'm getting there, boy—be patient," Powell said, flicking his fingers at Ishmael like he was scolding a dog to sit. "A guard at the Rift, isn't that right, Mr. Kaine? And your plan is that you'll put in someone else, someone you can work with?"

"It's all taken care of, Mr. Iwan," Davik said. "Once Losek is gone, the people most likely to take his job are people willing to work with me, and then I'll finally be able to get the Blackwood boy out, along with a few of my people."

The words hit Ishmael like a jolt of electricity. *The Blackwood boy—this is about Jason.*

Powell nodded at Davik. "You've put a lot of thought into it."

"Yes sir, Mr. Iwan," Davik said. "I wouldn't waste your time with half-ideas that ain't ready yet. But now that we have this, we need to move quick. The Breeding Program wants him and I can only fuck their paperwork for so long."

Another nod, and then Powell pointed a bony, arthritis-bent finger right at Ishmael. "I want him to do it."

Something hot buzzed in Ishmael's ears. This isn't what he imagined when he asked Powell for help with Jason. "I don't like killing in Yaelsmuir, Mr. Iwan."

"I don't give half a shit what you like, Mr. Saeati," Powell muttered into his cup. "You came to me all in a lather, wanting that Blackwood boy out of the Rift. I'll pay any price for him, you said. I haven't the resources to smuggle him out in a hurry, you said, so please Mr. Iwan, I never ask you for anything, would you please help me."

Ishmael sighed, picking lint off his trousers to keep his hands busy. At least they were steady. They never shook in tense moments like this, thank fuck. "I don't recall being that melodramatic."

"You're right, you weren't," Powell said with a grin. "But I hear what isn't said, don't I? Canny old man, I am, and I know that if Ishmael Saeati comes to me for help, he's got his heart on the line, hasn't he? He can play cool and uninterested, but he's not a man that asks for things unless it means something big. So I'm giving you your something big, aren't I? The Blackwood boy is getting out even though I don't like fucking around with the Rift. It brings too much attention this way if it goes wrong. But I thought about it, and I decided that boy is worth it. And Mayor Wolfe, he must be real invested in those Blackwoods if he's ready to send you tiptoeing around those precious laws of his. So I'll allow it. Our Mr. Kaine here needs to scrub Losek to get it done, fine—but I want it done by you personally, Saeati. I trust you to take care of it the way I like."

"With all due respect, Mr. Iwan, I don't need any help," Davik said. "My people are highly capable, and we've been working on this for a long time."

Powell laughed. "Whenever someone starts a statement with the words 'with all due respect,' I always know I'm about to be disrespected." Powell paused to sip his tea, letting Davik's tension coil up again. "I don't give a single rat's turd what you think your people are capable of, Mr. Kaine. You owe me this, and you'll do it, or you and I will be renegotiating the terms of all our agreements."

"How do I owe you this?" Davik scoffed. "I haven't asked you for anything—"

"Edgar Hale has," Powell interrupted. "And you're responsible for his debts, so yes, sir, you owe me this and more. I'll give Hale what he wanted—my idiot fighter will take his beating and get his nose out of your business. And in return, I take my price from you."

Davik took a deep breath, his jaw clenched tight, but then he exhaled and unwound. "Edgar Hale is an idiot and he doesn't speak for me, Mr. Iwan. I don't even know what fighter you're talking about."

"Then you'd best put a muzzle on Hale, Mr. Kaine, because he seems to think he does. He's a rabid dog, shoving his big ugly face into matters that don't concern him and biting my people. And just like a dog owner is responsible for his mongrel when it hurts people, you're going to settle his debt with me right now. My fighter is going to take his beating like a man because he's got a good, stubborn head on his shoulders, and I trust him to stand, but you're going to pay the healer's bills to save his life when it's over—and Ishmael Saeati is making Losek vanish without a trace so no one will have reason to think the Bay was involved. You're putting my business in jeopardy, fucking around with the Rift."

"We appreciate that, Mr. Iwan," Davik said. "That's why we came to you first, and that's why we put together a solid plan. It will look like he ran from his debts—we'll have someone trash his apartment like they were looking for him, and we'll take things a man on the run might want. It'll be quiet. No one will connect it back to you."

"You're fucking right about that, and that's why I want him to do it," Powell said, pointing at Ishmael again. "He knows what he's doing. Not like your lot, a bunch of rebel malcontents who think they're soldiers. He knows how these things are done quietly in the Bay. It's him or my answer is no."

"And what does a diplomat know about killing?" Davik asked.

"I don't fucking care what a *diplomat* knows, but this boy is born and raised Bay, and he knows how I like things done," Powell said, his voice getting that hard edge he had when he was losing patience.

"Yes sir, Mr. Iwan," Ishmael cut in. "Whatever you say, sir. We'll get it done."

"Good boy," Powell said. "I knew I could count on you."

"Of course, Mr. Iwan."

Powell flicked his fingers at Davik. "You can go, Mr. Kaine. Our Saeati will present himself to you tomorrow so that you can tell him where to find Losek."

"Yes sir, Mr. Iwan." Davik pushed himself to his feet, smoothing out his clothes. He pulled his coat from the hook by the fire, retreating.

"Mr. Kaine," Powell said, of course waiting for Davik to be halfway out of the room so he had to pause and come back, "one more thing."

"Of course, Mr. Iwan," Davik said, his voice clipped, his pretty northland burr fading a little like he couldn't quite hang on to the farce of over playing it when he was so angry.

"It would be a real shame if Edgar Hale skipped town before my people had a chance to balance the scales with him. If he disappears, I'll have to send people looking for him, and I'll be damned if I haven't got better things for my people to do than running around after a wet turd like fucking Hale."

"Yes sir, Mr. Iwan," Davik said, pulling on his coat with short, sharp movements. "I'll make sure Edgar hasn't got any reason to think he needs to disappear."

"Thank you, Mr. Kaine. I appreciate your cooperation, as always."

Davik left quietly, but his anger lingered in the room after he was gone. And Vasska, still listening. Making himself busy so he could over-hear without looking like he was going to intrude.

"How long will it take, do you think, for Kaine to get that Blackwood boy out?" Powell asked finally.

Ishmael shrugged. "I don't know, Mr. Iwan. I only just found out he was the one planning all of that now, when you told me I'm going to help him."

"You'll find out for me," Powell said. "When you talk to Kaine, see if you can gauge how long they're thinking."

"Yes sir. I would say it won't be long, though, not if they actually mean to get Jason out safely. Gossip is that it was Jason who broke the suppression."

"Aye, I heard the gossip," Powell said. "That's why I'm letting this all happen, and that's why I want you involved. I don't want that Blackwood boy in Kaine's hands when this is over. You'll make sure that boy knows who can keep him safe, won't you?"

"Yes sir, Mr. Iwan. I'll make sure he knows that you're the one in control of the Bay." This wasn't exactly what he hoped for when he came to Powell for help with Jason, but it was better than nothing. He'd have to make Tashué understand how things *really* worked in this city, keep Tashué from doing something stupid. But hopefully the prospect of getting Jason out finally would eat through his usual rigid, self-righteous bullshit. "I suspect Jason will be inclined to like what Davik has to say, though. He spent all those years in the Rift because he didn't want to register, and Davik's got all those feral Talented with him—I expect he'll fall in with them all pretty quickly."

Powell grunted. "That's why you'll do Kaine for me, too. After the Blackwood boy is out."

Ishmael stifled a sigh. Just because he'd seen it coming didn't mean he liked it. He didn't want to get involved with Kaine. "You want me to take care of it?"

Powell shrugged, picking up the clove rock and turning it around a few times between his fingers. "Don't pretend you're surprised. The man is too stupid and too arrogant to know when to fall in line. He's outstayed his welcome in my city. His time is running out. And lucky for me, I have this wonderful Qasani boy who is very good at what he does, and he does what I ask. He knows what his purpose is, even though he says obnoxious things like 'I don't like killing in Yaelsmuir.'"

"Yes sir, Mr. Iwan," Ishmael said, even though the words 'he knows what his purpose is' scorched like a hot brand on his soul. Some days, he'd give anything for his purpose to be *anything* else. "How much time does Kaine have left?"

Powell grunted, picking up the clove rock and turning it round and round between his fingers. "We'll see, won't we? He'll get that Blackwood boy out for me, and then we'll see. Tell me: do I have to worry about the father?"

"The father?"

Powell nodded, putting the clove rock in his mouth and sucking on it slowly. "The Blackwood boy's father. He's got the tin. He's getting the brass today at the Imburleigh event you're dressed so pretty for. Do I have to worry about him, or does he understand that he doesn't carry that fucking badge in my quarter anymore?"

"I'm sure Captain Blackwood understands that things are done a certain way around here," Ishmael said slowly. Even though he was certain that the collision of Powell Iwan and Tashué Blackwood would exhaust all of Ishmael's skill. He wasn't Tashué's keeper, and he didn't owe Tashué anything. And yet—for all that Ishmael couldn't be honest with anyone about the details of his career, somehow Tashué still managed to see the shape of all the things Ishmael couldn't say, and that earned him a certain amount of loyalty. Enough that he didn't want to see Tashué devoured by Powell's ruthlessness.

"Does he?" Powell pressed. "Are you sure? Because that big idiot wore his badge into my fight hall a few weeks ago, almost started a riot."

"That'll be the night he broke a man's face with an ashtray, I imagine. I would have loved to see that." Ishmael pulled another candy out of the bag, this time a broken half of a lemon drop. "If I know him, he's learned his lesson."

"You better make sure," Powell said. "Damn fucking sure. I won't have him down here interfering with things, you hear me? I know you have some kind of relationship with him, so maybe you can keep him out of trouble."

Fucking Tashué. Hopefully Ishmael could convince him fast enough to keep him alive, or Powell would send someone else to make his body disappear. "Yes sir, Mr. Iwan. I imagine you want Hale gone, too. Who's taking care of him?"

"Don't you worry your pretty little head about Hale," Powell said.

"Yes sir, Mr. Iwan."

"Good boy." Powell sipped his tea again, nodding to himself. "I knew it would be easy with you. I wish my idiot sons had been half as smart as you, Saeati. It's too bad you offered yourself up to the division. I would have liked to have more of your time."

Ishmael stifled a sigh, giving another shrug. "I thought the Academy would give me what I wanted."

"Oh, and old Powell couldn't get you anything?"

Ishmael spread his hands. "What can I say? I was sixteen and in love with a girl from the other side of the river. I thought if I could get into the Academy, it would be a respectable enough career move that her family would let her marry me."

"And instead that Deri scooped you up, turned you into a diplomat," Powell said.

Ishmael shrugged. "Deri saved me. But he also doomed me, I think. Things never quite go the way we hope, do they?"

"No, they never do," Powell said. "At least I've got my boy, Vasska. Vicious smart, he is, for all his soft soul. You'll watch out for him, won't you? Once I'm dead. He could use a man like you at his shoulder."

"I'll do my best, Mr. Iwan."

Powell nodded. "That's all I can ask, isn't it? Off you go, then. I know the General doesn't like it when you're late. Send him my regards."

Ishmael nodded, pushing himself to his feet. "Absolutely, Mr. Iwan."

Ishmael tucked the papers under his arm and headed for the door. Vasska met his eye—was there panic there, or maybe grief? Maybe not. The look, whatever it was, was too cold a thing. Calculation, maybe. A decision.

"I look forward to when we can have that drink, Mr. Saeati," Vasska said.

"Any time you like, Vasska. Just let me know when."

D avik hadn't left. He leaned against the side of the carriage, while Oskar the driver did his very best to pretend Davik wasn't there at all. Davik nursed a cigar while he waited, blowing smoke into rings that twisted into the wind. He grinned around the cigar when Ishmael approached, a tattooed hand coming up to pull the cigar out of his mouth.

"I thought I'd catch a ride with you, since we're headed the same direction," Davik said, smoke drifting from between his lips as he spoke. "Since we're working together now and all."

Ishmael stifled a sigh. He was too busy and too tired to deal with all the cock measuring that was about to happen. This fucking event—he didn't want to go to the Imburleigh factory and he didn't want to see Illea or Mallory, and he definitely didn't want to see Rainer or Myron. And he didn't want to deal with fucking Davik's ego. He should have retired years ago, when he still had the chance. He could be in his father's watch shop right now, building beautiful things with his hands. Or he could be at the factory in the Industrial quarter, supervising the incredible machines and craftsmen that made Saeati movements to be shipped to jewellers all over the world. Instead, other people were doing those things, and he was stuck forever fighting with politicians and crime lords. He was just fucking tired. Thirty-six was too young to be this eternally *tired*.

"Fine," Ishmael muttered. "At least open the door for me and let me in."

Davik stepped aside, opening the carriage door and giving a bow. "After you, then."

Ishmael stepped up into the carriage, sinking down into the bench. Davik settled with him, blowing smoke out the door before he pulled it closed. Ishmael should have known better than to go to Powell Iwan for help with Jason, but he hadn't seen any other choice—he didn't have the resources to get Jason out, not on a tight timeline, especially not after the rumours about what he'd done with his Talent. If only Tashué had asked him sooner.

"I know you think you're hot shit in this city, Saeati, but I won't have you coming into my business and fucking it up," Davik said. The carriage rattled down the street, the Bay cobbles especially uneven and throwing the carriage around a little too much. "You can do this one, but then I want you gone again."

"It would be my immense pleasure to get myself right back out of your business as swiftly as possible," Ishmael said. "I don't give a shit about you, Davik. I don't give a shit about your people. I don't give a shit what you're doing with that fancy little pugilist club of yours. You can play King of the Talented in your little corner of the Bay, and I truly couldn't care less. Powell Iwan gave me an order, I obey, and that's the end of it."

"Gave you an order, is it?" Davik asked. "And Ishmael Saeati, the good soldier who always follows orders, does what he's told without question. Is that it?"

"That's exactly it."

"So who are those Blackwoods to you, hey?" Davik asked, and the mellow tone of his voice did nothing to put Ishmael at ease. "They must be special if they're enough to make you go asking favours of Powell Iwan."

"It's nothing," Ishmael said. "General Wolfe wanted it, and Powell Iwan was the only person I could think of who could make it happen in a hurry."

"Don't lie to me, Saeati," Davik said, his chin dropping, his dark eyes flaring with the threat.

"Don't take that fucking tone with me, Davik," Ishmael snapped. "I'm not playing games with you, alright? I'll stay out of your business, and you can stay the fuck out of mine and then we'll part ways when we're done."

Davik moved fast, pushing Ishmael into the corner of the carriage. Davik was taller than Ishmael, his body lean and strong, crowding Ishmael easily. His hand closed around Ishmael's throat, squeezing hard on the sides so Ishmael could breathe and speak, but the blood flow to his brain slowed to a crawl. Ishmael caught Davik's wrist, but there wasn't anywhere for Ishmael to retreat to.

"Except you are in my business already, aren't you?" Davik said, the words sliding slowly through his accent. "You've asked Iwan for your little favour, and now you're in the middle of everything, aren't you?"

"Oh, Davik," Ishmael breathed, sliding his hands up Davik's thighs, so close now, the jostling of the carriage making Ishmael's head crash against the wood panelling, driving their bodies even closer together. Ishmael slid his hands up to Davik's hips, his thumbs trailing along either side of Davik's cock, barely brushing it as he went, feeling the outline of it. Let Davik think he was in charge, let Davik think Ishmael was just a slut. "You were pretending to be uninterested in me, but now I *know* you want to fuck me. I love getting roughed up."

Davik laughed, shifting until he was kneeling on the bench between Ishmael's legs, looming over Ishmael, taking up the entire field of Ishmael's vision. "Oh yeah? Are you offering me a good time, Saeati?"

"The best time you've ever had, sweetheart," Ishmael rasped. He leaned into Davik's hand, crushing himself against Davik's palm, and it was enough to make Davik back off a little. And the distance was proof that he was bluffing. Maybe he put his hand on Ishmael, but he still wanted Ishmael to talk, and he didn't want to get in shit with Powell over the business with the Rift and Jason Blackwood.

"You give Tashué Blackwood a good time? Is that why you're so eager to get his son out of the Rift? Is that why you've made it my fucking problem?"

"Wolfe told me to," Ishmael said again. If he had to, if he *really* had to, he'd take Davik by the cock and fucking twist but it would be easier to work with him if he didn't. "I've entertained half this city, Davik. If a good fuck was all it took to get me to interfere with people's lives, I wouldn't have *any* free time left. Wolfe needed it so I did it."

"Why?" Davik relaxed his grip on Ishmael's throat to give Ishmael the benefit of a bit more blood in his brain. "Why does Wolfe give half a bloody shit about Tashué Blackwood and his wee tainted son?"

"It was Blackwood's price for running for Mayor." Gods, let it be enough to convince Davik. "Wolfe wants to retire the next cycle, go back to White Crown a while to be the good hero, fighting for provincial autonomy and all that shit. He wants Blackwood to run for Mayor next, and Blackwood was worried about his son and what would happen if he went against Rainer in this stupid election." Ishmael slid his hand across Davik's cock again. "All this rough play, Davik, I'm starting to get turned on. Are we having fun or what?"

Davik finally broke, slapping Ishmael's hand away. "Touch me like that again, and I'll break your fucking fingers."

"So do it already," Ishmael snapped. "Go ahead. Why stop at breaking them? Why not just slice one right off, hey? There's something real impressive about a trophy like a man's thumb. All you need is a good sharp knife and then you cut right over the knuckle and pop. You've got a new charm to hang around your neck. Then people will know you really mean business instead of this half-assed bullshit with your hand on my throat. I've had lovers that fucked rougher than this."

"How come a diplomat knows so much about killing people and cutting off fingers?" Davik asked.

"It's got nothing to do with diplomacy, Davik, and it's got everything to do with growing up in the Bay. Not everyone has the benefit of rolling into town with a shit load of money and a chip on their shoulder like you. Some of us had to fucking *survive.*"

Davik grunted, letting go of Ishmael's throat and retreating. "Sure, Saeati. Whatever you say."

Ishmael tried to smooth out the silk of his tie, but Davik had crumpled it too much. He worked the knot open, dragging it out of his collar. "I don't know why you're so fucking agitated. You're coming out ahead in this deal. Jason Blackwood has incredible Talent—he's the one that broke suppression. He's the sort of kid you would love, I'm sure. Anti-Authority, stubborn as hell, brave enough to last three years in that place, and powerful. He'll fold right in with your harem of Talented or whatever it is you have going on at that pugilist club."

Davik laughed at that. "Harem, is it? Is that what they say I'm doing?"

Ishmael snorted, shaking out the cravat and smoothing it on his leg. "As if you don't know what people say about you."

The carriage stopped. "The pugilist club, Mr. Saeati."

Ishmael reached out, snatching Davik's cigar from his hand and taking a slow puff, blowing smoke at Davik's face. "Your stop, Mr. Kaine."

Davik slid toward the door, leaving his cigar in Ishmael's hand. "I want you out of my business as soon as this is done. This ain't an open invitation for you to come stick your filthy hands in my club on Iwan's behalf."

"Why's that, Davik?" Ishmael asked. "What are you afraid I'll find down there?"

"I don't give a shit what you find." Davik pushed the door open, unfolding his long body and stepping out onto the street. "I just don't like your smug fucking face."

Ishmael took another drag from the cigar, and flicked it at Davik before he could close the door. It sailed past Davik's head to land somewhere behind him in a gutter, and Davik snorted and pushed the door shut. The carriage rattled down the street again, the horse's hooves clacking against cobbles, shaking Ishmael in his seat.

Fuck everything.

He shook out the tie and folded it again so that the vibrant stripe of plum purple sat down the centre of the knot he was about to make. Quick motions saw it wrapped under his collar, the knot precise and plump below the apple of his throat, the long ends tucked into the front of his waistcoat. It was enough to make him look like he was in control.

But not enough to make him *feel* like he was in control, and not enough to take the weight out of his chest. It was going to be a long night.

3

TASHUÉ

DAY 27

"It's time for me to go," Stella said.

It didn't matter how long Tashué had been preparing himself for this moment; it still hurt to hear her say it. The words slid into his chest, the blade of a knife. He swallowed the pain and any words he might have said. Nothing he could say would help.

"I expect you to come find me," she said. "Don't make me wait too long."

He kissed her face. Buried himself in her hair. Breathed in the scent of her. "I'll come as soon as I can."

To promise anything more than 'as soon as I can' was a lie.

Dawn broke late this time of year, and the sun hadn't made its way up the horizon yet. His room was only partially lit by the brights outside his window, the cold light that washed colour out of his his world. He'd slept all day and all through the night, and a twinge of guilt ate at a part of him. Had she left the bed while he was asleep? Had Kazrani fed Ceridwen while Tashué and Stella lay tangled together in these blankets, their bodies worn and weakened by the trials of the last few days?

At some point, Rhodrishi had come for both of them, his Talent spreading into them so that they were all the same person, their Talent becoming a braid that caught on all the things they had in common. And Tashué tried to push the guilt away. He hadn't slept well since... since he found Stella on the stairs of the Facility. Since then, he'd been shot, he'd killed a man, he'd broken away little pieces of the person he told himself he wanted to be. At some point, he had to stop and sleep.

But he still couldn't help but wish he'd spent a bit more time with Ceridwen and Stella. Before they left.

Tashué rolled away from Stella, finding matches to light the oil lamp. To give them enough light to see by. Stella dressed in travelling clothes that Tashué bought for her in the blur of days since learning she was leaving. Trousers and a linen shirt and a waistcoat made of thick wool with plenty of pockets for all the little things you needed at hand in the wilderness. A button-up knitted sweater and a jacket loose enough to fit over it. All of it colours of the autumn forest; brown and burnt orange and weather-worn tan, so she would blend into the rugged wilderness. She pulled her hair into a simple braid to keep it out of her face. She looked ready to conquer the world. She looked tired. She hung her coat from the back of the door, ready to gather it up when it was time to go. Heavy leather, lined with fleece. Calfskin gloves and a knitted scarf stuck out of one of the pockets.

He'd never seen her in trousers before. They were the natural choice for wilderness travel and sitting astride the saddle, so he hadn't thought much about it when he bought them for her. Three years, she'd been living beside him, but she always wore skirts and bodices—the Facility uniform was structured and formal, and her personal clothes were worn and patched and darned, but always skirts. Three years. He wished he'd tried to know her sooner. Maybe all of this could have been avoided.

He rolled from bed, too, putting a hand to the bullet wound. It was healing well already, but the pain was deep in the muscle tissue, like the body remembered how terrible the trauma was and rejected the possibility that it could be so well healed after so short a time.

"Lieutenant Mahalouwan said she would meet us at the hospital with horses," Stella said softly. The apartment was quiet—Ceridwen must still be sleeping. She passed him his trousers, from one of the Bellmore suits Illea had bought for him because he was supposed to be a politician or something. "And supplies. Rhodrishi said it takes about three weeks in good weather to get up into the mountain valleys. But this isn't good weather, so. We might stop there—he said there's a traveller's settlement that's well hidden. And if we have to wait there for the spring thaw, so be it. We'll be well sheltered, at least."

Her voice trembled and she bit off the last words like she was afraid to let the emotion out. Tashué caught her in his arms, pulling her against his body, the coarse wool of her clothes scratching against his bare chest, against the scabbed knot of the bullet wound. Tashue kissed her hair again, wrapping the braid around his hand to feel the strength of it.

"I've missed the mountains," she said.

"Did Kaz say anything about getting guns?" Tashué asked. "She probably still has her rifle—you said you were better with a rifle than a pistol?"

Stella nodded. "My father taught us both how to hunt game. Aelwyd and me."

Tashué reached for the rifle he kept, the relic of his military history. He hadn't used it much since he'd retired. Shooting clay pigeons outside town with Kaz, teaching Jason how to handle guns. "Maybe this will serve you better than my old pistol. Grab the lamp."

Stella followed him to the kitchen with the oil lamp, shielding her hand in front of the flame to protect it while they walked to the sitting room. He lay the rifle on the coffee table and took the gun oil from the top shelf of his kitchen, grabbing a rag from the counter. Some pressure built itself in his bones as he moved, something vicious and angry, unlocked by the weight of the rifle when he carried it, the cold metal and the wooden stock all so familiar to his hand that it could have been a part of his body. But he wasn't going to use it. It felt wrong. It sent sparks of tension through his marrow. He wanted to go with Stella and Ceridwen and protect them both from the whole world, but he couldn't leave Jason behind.

Stella found his other oil lamps, lighting a few of them and setting them at the table so he could see what he was doing. Not that he needed to see. These movements were as natural to him as breathing.

"The army shipped us these guns when they sent us up to the Black Ridge," Tashué said. His hands didn't need him to think as he went through the routine of cleaning all the dust away, oiling all the moving parts, racking the lever action a few times to make sure it moved smoothly. "The Jitabvi companies were always late getting the newest supplies, but Maddox fought for these repeaters when he found out where we were going. He knew it was going to be shit before we even got there." He used a piece of a mirror to catch the light, shining it into the barrel so he could look down the long metal tube and make sure it was still unobstructed. "These guns saved a lot of lives up there. We wouldn't have been able to hang on as long as we did with the single shot rifles we had before. This holds ten. I know they have

Imburleighs now that hold up to fifteen, but... this gun won't let you down."

"Tashué, I can't take that," Stella said softly. "It's a national relic. Do you know how much a first-round Imburleigh repeater is worth? It belongs in a museum."

Tashué shook his head. "That's what General Imburleigh said when Ishmael told her I still had it. Something about wanting it for the private collection. But it's a gun. And it works. And it might save your life like it saved mine."

Stella reached out, sliding her finger over one of the divots in the wood, where blood had permeated the grain. "Thank you. I didn't mean to sound ungrateful. I know... I know it's probably complicated, letting go of a thing that was with you up on the Ridge."

Tashué nodded. How did she always see him so clearly? "When I find you, you can give it back to me."

Stella sank down on the sofa beside Tashué, kissing him on the cheek. "Thank you."

She took the gun from his hands, resting the weight of it in her lap, the strap hanging over her knees. He slid the box of ammunition closer to her, the old cardboard dragging on his table. She took a handful of shells and slid them through the side gate with a confidence that spoke of experience and practice. She'd mentioned her sister. Her father. Maybe she'd told him to call her Stella still, but maybe she was also remembering what it meant to be Ffyanwy Rhydderch.

The simmering light and dancing shadows from the lamps made Keoh's urn gleam in the darkness, the copper shine catching his eye. And it dragged at something in him, something ugly and filled with shame. Of course he couldn't help Stella; he couldn't help Keoh either. Just like he hadn't been able to help Jason for three and a half years. He'd been stagnant and frozen since... fuck. Since he didn't even know when. Living his life halfway, not quite breathing, waiting for something to make sense along the way, but nothing made sense. Nothing made sense since he retired from the military. That life was shit, and the Ridge had changed things, but at least when he was a soldier he knew his purpose.

The bitterness kept twisting in him as Stella loaded all ten rounds into the gun that saved his life from the worst posting of his career. Nothing made sense because there was no sense. Military structure was an illusion covering the ugly truth of life: there was only life and death and the inevitability of greed. Cruelty. The blood of people who didn't have a choice but to bleed for the rich. Opium smoke to wash away all the pain, and the long lingering echo of mistakes.

Stella touched his hand, dragging him out of the hypnotic dance that Keoh's urn was performing on his kitchen table. "I should wake Ceridwen. We can get breakfast on the way to the hospital."

"Let me. Please?"

Stella nodded.

Tashué pushed the box of shells closer to her. "Load up your pockets with as much as you can carry. I'd give you my gun belt but I don't think it'll fit you. We'll put the rest in your saddle bag when we meet Kaz."

He stood so he could escape the stillness and the heavy feeling that sat in his chest. When he pushed the bedroom door open, the first soft brightness of dawn gave definition to the bed, to the strawberry blond mess of Ceridwen's hair. He touched her foot first, giving it a little squeeze.

"Ceridwen," he said, sitting at the end of the bed to tap her knee. "It's time to get up."

Ceridwen gave a soft groan and rolled over, pulling the blanket up higher over her head. Just like Jason. He never liked getting out of bed on time, either.

"Your mam is ready to go, little warrior. It's time to get up and get dressed."

Ceridwen pushed the blankets down again, turning her face toward the window, toward the light. The sunlight sat differently on her features than they did on Stella. Had he only noticed the differences because he *knew* Stella hadn't brought Ceridwen into the world? He'd never questioned it before. But now he couldn't help but wonder who gave Ceridwen the lovely colour of her hair and the eyes that were hazel instead of green like Stella's, and the freckles that had convinced Tashué they were mother and daughter by blood.

Ceridwen's lip trembled. "Do we have to go?"

"You do, little warrior," Tashué said softly. "I'm sorry. Your mam said we'd get breakfast on our way to the hospital to meet Colonel Kheir. Maybe we'll go see if Miss Muir's is open yet, what do you say? And then Kaz will meet us there with your ponies. You listen to Kaz, alright? She's an excellent rider and she'll teach you everything you need to know."

Ceridwen nodded, pushing the blankets back and swinging her feet over the edge of the bed, resting her toes on the cold wood floor. "Is she a good teacher?"

"She is. She taught me a lot. I already knew how to ride when I met her, but she taught me how to sleep in the saddle. And she taught me how to take care of her son while we were on the march. We took turns sleeping with him during the day, right up on horseback. She taught me how to be a parent. Taught me how to be myself, even before I knew who I was. She'll take good care of you."

"Will she teach me how to fight like she does? She's a warrior, isn't she? A soldier? I'd like to learn how to fight, I think. I'd like to be able to protect Mam if something else happens."

"Oh, Ceridwen," Tashué said. He put his arm around her shoulder and pulled her against his chest so he could lay a kiss in her messy hair. "I'm sorry you feel like you have to protect your mam. Kaz will take good care of you both, I promise."

4

LORNE
DAY 27

Edgar Hale—or, at least, what remained of him—hung upside down from the window of his apartment above a warehouse. A rope was knotted around both his ankles, and his carcass swayed in the wind that came off the Brightwash. Scavengers had peeled layers of him away in the days since he died. A stray dog walked in slow circles beneath the corpse, snarling at anyone who walked too close. It paused, now and then, to lick the old, clotted blood and brain matter from the cobbles beneath Hale, where pieces of him had fallen to the road after oozing out of the massive hole through his skull.

Lorne wasn't sure how long he stood there, watching the corpse swing back and forth. Watching the crows and the turkey vultures gather on windowsills and rooftops, their heads bobbing as they each tried to figure out how to get to the hanging meat.

He'd decided he didn't want to be found for a while. The aftermath of the fight left his ears ringing more often than not, and delivering the news to Jason that Keoh was dead had splintered something in Lorne's soul. Sometimes at night, when he was wandering through the city, looking for a safe place to sleep that didn't cost anything, he looked north up the river to see the ominous glow of the Rift, and he wondered how hard it would be to walk right into that fucking place. Climb a wall or something, just so he could hug Jason again. If he had to be tired and sore and bloody, at least he could do it with Jason in his arms.

But then he'd heard the news about Edgar Hale, and morbid curiosity drew him to the warehouse. He'd been dead two days, and the late autumn cold kept his meat from rotting. If the scavengers didn't finish him off, soon he'd freeze, and he'd likely be there all winter, a hanging weight of meat and bone and ice.

Powell Iwan had asked Tashué to kill this man, and apparently Tashué had found it in him to obey. Lorne told himself he shouldn't be surprised, but he was anyway. He couldn't put his finger on why exactly. Tashué had seemed perfectly at ease that day in his apartment, shooting the shit with Powell Iwan, a man who would have killed them both if Tashué gave the wrong answer to the questions Powell was asking. And yet as long as Lorne had known Tashué, he'd tried to draw rigid lines around reality, talking about right and wrong and laws as if they were an iron code that was easy to follow. But now that Hale was hanging like that, to be picked apart one bit at a time, Lorne wondered if the reason Tashué fought so hard to define himself by lines and laws was because he knew life was a slippery fucking slope. Sometimes it didn't take much to push you down into unimaginable violence. So maybe his insistence that he needed to follow the law was his way of keeping all that capacity for violence under control.

And Edgar Hale had killed that child Tashué found, so maybe sometimes that capacity for violence wasn't such a terrible thing.

Vasska came around the corner. He walked right under the corpse like it didn't bother him at all. The dog snarled at him, but Vasska hissed through his teeth. The dog lowered its head and backed off, but as soon as Vasska cleared the corpse, the dog went back to its post, looking up at the body. It reared up on its back legs, pressing its front paws against the wall like it wondered if it could crawl its way up to a good meal. Lorne thought about leaving, about melting back into the alley and going somewhere else fast. He was tired. He was tired of the Hive and tired of Powell Iwan and tired of thinking about the Army of the Red Dawn. But it was too late. Vasska had already spotted him.

"Your face looks like shit," Vasska said, stopping in the mouth of the alley.

"Oh, hey," Lorne said, as brightly as he could, even though talking still hurt. Hurt his jaw, hurt his lips, hurt his tongue. "Thanks! I appreciate it. I wouldn't have noticed if you hadn't told me."

Vasska sighed. He leaned against the wall and crossed his arms over his chest, turning his face away from the bitter cold wind that came off the river. It caught all his blond hair, mussing it in every direction. The wind stung in all the places on Lorne's face that were struggling to heal. Stella had helped with whatever was bleeding internally, but that still left the mess of his face and his hands and the clumsy stitches he'd placed himself because his lip wouldn't stop bleeding.

"Can we skip the part where you're all furious with me, like I had something to do with all this?" Vasska asked. "I told you, didn't I? I told you not to fuck around with the Red Dawn. I told you they would fuck you up, but you didn't want to listen to good advice. You pushed, and Edgar Hale wanted you dead—and Grandad protected you."

"Protected me," Lorne echoed, his voice going flat with his anger. "That's what Powell Iwan's protection looks like, does it?"

"Yes it does," Vasska said. "Hale wanted you dead, and now look at him. Everyone knows he asked for that fight. And you're still walking around in the Bay with that big fucking chip on your shoulder, so now the whole Bay knows you're *untouchable*. So yes, this is exactly what Powell Iwan's protection looks like. I'm sorry you got hurt so bad, I really am. I'm sorry it went the way it did. But you're in the middle of it now."

"Fuck off," Lorne muttered, pulling his collar up around his face in a poor attempt at shielding himself from the cold. "I'm not in the middle of anything. I'm done. I'm sick of the Red Dawn, and I'm sick of fighting. Maybe I'll take the job General Wolfe's been offering me—go to Highfield and run spies for him exclusively."

Vasska sighed, opening his coat to pull out his cigarillo case. He flicked it open and offered one to Lorne, and habit made Lorne take one, even though he knew the smoke would hurt all the cuts in his mouth. Vasska leaned in real close, using both of their bodies to shield the match as he popped it on the side of the building, huddling low over the flame to light his cigarillo. And then it was Lorne's turn. The pair of them stood so close Lorne could feel the heat of Vasska's body, which only highlighted how fucking miserable it was outside. The wind and the rain and the frost that crawled across everything at night—it was a shit time to be out on the streets. In the summer he could almost forget how bad it was, so long as he found a way to keep hydrated. But the winters killed. He'd never imagined he would still be on the fucking streets of Yaelsmuir this long after landing here, but he didn't regret putting Alys through school. And he didn't regret tying his life to Jason. It's just that it meant his whole life was fucking stuck. Building a life for his sister that he'd probably never get to see, waiting for a life with Jason that would probably never come.

"It's too late to back off now, Lorne," Vasska said, and his voice was softer than before. He'd lost the confrontational edge now that they were standing closer, huddling against the wind and making ribbons of smoke between them. "You stuck your nose in it like I told you not to, and now this is your life. Grandad said whoever won the match was going down to the real fights to be the Bay's first tourney pugilist. You beat Ijaz, so you get to go learn how to box."

"Sure," Lorne muttered. "Sounds great. Sounds like a real treat. Are you going to leave out the part about who's running that pugilist club? Were you going to send me down there and hope I didn't notice I was going to work for Davik fucking Kaine? I thought I was supposed to stay away from the Red Dawn, and now you're sending me right into their headquarters?"

"I *told* you, it's too late for you to stay away," Vasska said. "I was hoping you would go down there knowing exactly who you're working for but also knowing that I've done my best to take care of you in a city that's all too happy to chew up guys like you and spit them out as nothing but gristle and bone. And I was hoping you'd keep an eye on Davik fucking Kaine for me, because I think my grandfather is going to die this year and I think Davik is going to try to kill me once Grandad is gone."

All the layers of information sucked the rage out of Lorne's chest. It took him a moment to parse out each one, separating them like threads in a vicious knot.

"You took care of me, did you?" Lorne asked.

Anger flashed across Vasska's face for a moment, bright and powerful and threatening, twice as potent with Hale's corpse swinging on the other side of the street. "Out of all the things I just said, that's the one you want to talk about?"

Lorne opened his mouth to say something to make it better, but no words came. He hadn't meant it the way Vasska was apparently taking it —it wasn't an argument or a denial; it was surprise. He didn't exactly feel taken care of, but then again, he'd survived this long, and made enough money to take care of Alys, when the Bay was notorious for doing exactly what Vasska said—eating people whole and coughing up the parts that couldn't be consumed so that they were just empty eyes and a body that moved without really being alive.

"Yes, I took care of you," Vasska said. "Yes, I fucking did look out for you. Yes, I did put in a good word with Grandad for you when you turned up to the fight hall, looking for income, and yes, I did make sure people didn't fuck with you while you were coming up. And now here you are, with all that money, and all that ego, like you still think you're alone in this world. But *that's* what happens to your enemies." He turned to face Hale, blowing smoke into the street. "I know you took a shit beating, but fucking look! Hale got his head blown open for fucking with you. So yes, this is what being taken care of looks like in the Bay. I'm sorry it went the way it did. I'm never going to forget what it was like to watch you go down and then keep getting up like you didn't care—I don't know how you do it. Maybe you honestly don't care, but that means the rest of us have to fill in the gaps and care *for* you. Orix had to beat the crowd back while you were still fighting because people wanted to get up there and defend you. Grandad said you had to go down to shut Hale up, so we had to keep people off the stage. And then when you were done, eight people helped Tam drag you down."

Lorne shook his head, touching the tender spots on his face when they gave a dull flare of pain, as if to remind him of the beating. "I don't remember that. I remember Tam helping, but I don't remember how I got there."

Vasska shrugged, flicking ash toward the street. "This quarter loves you, Lorne. People love that you don't take any shit, and you don't back down. They love that you never left the Bay, even though you're making good money in those fights. No one knows the reason you never left is because you're sending all that money to your sister in Teshii, and you feel trapped, and you resent the Bay for it. And it's a good thing all those people who love you don't know how much you hate it here or they'd feel so betrayed. You're their hero—they *rioted* for you. And Grandad let them because he was proud of them for standing up for you. So now's your chance to pay some of that back. Go down to the pugilist club and fight for Davik Kaine, and let the city love you even more. Davik will have a healer to fix you up and you'll get three meals a day of whatever it is that athletes eat to look so good. You'll have a roof over your head this winter, for the first time since when? And all I ask is that you keep an eye on shit. Let me know if Davik is making plans to come for me."

"What makes you think Iwan is going to die?" Lorne asked.

Vasska snorted, looking at Lorne with an eyebrow raised. "Have you talked to him lately?"

Lorne grimaced, and a jolt of pain passed through his lip as it split again. Started to bleed. He sucked the blood off his lip and shrugged. "The last time I talked to him was at Tashué's apartment, when he asked Tashué to get rid of Edgar Hale. I had other shit on my mind than keeping an eye on his health. Did Tashué really kill Hale? I mean, he's obviously dead but—it was really Tashué?"

Vasska turned his face away, blowing a long line of smoke into the wind. "Grandad is collecting new soldiers. I think he's trying to find people who will be loyal to me when he dies. Maybe he's betting on Tashué Blackwood's paternal instincts, hoping some of that ferocity will spread to me since I'm about the same age as you and Jason. Maybe Grandad is hoping that if we get Jason out, Tashué will feel like he owes us. Either way, Tashué promised to stand with Grandad once Davik is dead."

"Is that a yes, Vasska? Did he kill Hale?"

"Don't sound so surprised. The man was a soldier for ten years. You know what that's like. How it leaves a mark on you no matter how much you pretend it doesn't."

A crow fluttered down from one of the windowsills, catching hold of Hale's trousers with both feet. Its beak went searching through a hole in the wool that had been ripped open by some other carrion-eater. All that effort was rewarded by a glistening chunk of thigh meat, red and yellow with blood and fat. Lorne shuddered, turning his back on the corpse so he didn't have to watch anymore. "So Iwan wants to off Davik, but you think Davik is going to kill you and Iwan?"

Vasska didn't turn away. He watched the crow and smoked one leisurely breath at a time. "No, I think Davik is going to let the shit weather kill Grandad, and then once Grandad is out of the way, he'll come after me next. But I don't know for sure. This fucking election is going to go Myron's way, and then we'll have the police force sticking their nose in our shit, and they'll try to get control of the Bay. The best thing for both of us would be working together. I'll hold the Hive, and Davik can hold the Red Dawn, and together we can have the Bay and keep the police force out, just like we kept the Authority out. But I don't know what for sure Davik wants to do. So I'm hoping you'll go down there and keep an eye. For me."

Lorne dabbed his lip, watching the dark blood spread across his sleeve. "How come Iwan doesn't have someone off Davik, if you're so worried?"

"Because Davik is the only person with the resources to get Jason out of the Rift."

Lorne's eyes snapped up to Vasska's face so fast, it made him dizzy. He had to stand still a moment just to let the words sink hooks into him, had to breathe slow to make his heart stop hammering enough that he wouldn't faint.

"There it is," Vasska said softly. "You weren't sure about getting involved for me, but you'll do it for Jason, hey? I guess I can't really be insulted or surprised. It's funny how things kind of draw themselves together, isn't it?"

"What's that supposed to mean?" Lorne asked.

"I still remember the first time Kaine came down to the Bay to make a deal with Grandad. Must have been fifteen years ago, because Rowan's mother was so pregnant she looked like she could burst, but she wouldn't miss the meeting for anything. My mother liked that about her. I don't remember what her name was. I remember watching her struggle up the stairs, wondering if I should do anything. My mother sat with her and they whispered to each other like they'd known each other all along." He shrugged again, like he was shaking off the memory. "They all made a deal that Davik would run his smuggling road through the Hive. Guns, opium, salt, and other sundry life supplies, all headed east across the mountains. My mother pushed Grandad to make the deal, said it was an opportunity to be more than we were. She said Grandad was getting complacent, growing stagnant, and it would be the end of him if he didn't start growing new opportunities. And then all that shit happened up north, and Davik left Cruinnich permanently, and he came down here to keep building."

"All that shit," Lorne echoed. "I heard the Red Dawn set off bombs up north."

Vasska nodded. "That's how the story goes. Bombs and riots. The Authority lined people up in the streets in front of firing squads. They say the Red Dawn chased Davik out of Cruinnich, just to end the violence."

"And then he came here. Why's he still going by Davik Kaine?"

Vasska's eyes wandered across the street to Hale's body. "He built his roots here under that name. And then after he was chased out of Cruinnich, he disappeared for a while, and rumours said he was all over the Dominion. So, when he drifted back here with Rowan, he just kind of folded back in. My mother thought he'd planned it—he knew it was going to get bad up there so he set up his backup plan here. But then she died, leaving a gap. Davik scooped up control of all her whorehouses, and suddenly he was more powerful than Grandad ever intended him to be. Back then they were kind of... in a standoff. Davik acted like he was real fond of me, like him fucking my mother a few times made us something. But if I was *close* to everyone who fucked my mother, well... she had a type. At least Davik is smarter than my father ever was. It left the balance precarious, after she was gone. We've all been holding our breath since, you know? Waiting to see who would fuck up first. Grandad and Adley make their plans, and Davik tiptoes around his side of the Bay. Probably making all sorts of his own plans. But then, a couple weeks ago, Tashué Blackwood finds the body of a little dead girl on the riverbank, and suddenly people are sticking their noses in business that never used to concern them." He glanced pointedly at Lorne, blowing smoke up over Lorne's head. "And all the cracks and flaws and vulnerabilities in the Bay are blown wide open." He snapped his fingers. "Just like that, it could all fall apart."

Lorne glanced back over his shoulder at Hale. Three more crows had joined the effort, one of them ripping open Hale's shirt to peck at the flesh over his ribcage.

"If we don't step carefully, it's going to be war down here," Vasska went on. "Davik's people against the Hive. And the piece in the middle of it all, the thing that keeps Grandad and Davik from finally moving against each other and a lot of blood flowing in the streets of this quarter as they fight each other for power, is Jason Blackwood. A kid that didn't matter last month. No one knew his name. He matters a whole hell of a lot now. And I bet he has no idea."

"Leave Jason out of this, Vasska, or I swear—"

"I can't leave Jason out of this," Vasska interrupted. "That's what I'm trying to tell you, if you'd listen for once. He is the thing pulling everyone together. Wolfe wants Tashué to run for Mayor at the next election, and the price Tashué asked for is Jason's safety. So Wolfe sent Ishmael down here to make a deal with Grandad, except Grandad can't be arsed to fuck around with the Rift. He decided it was worth it to make Wolfe owe him another favour and doubly worth it if Tashué takes the Mayor's office, so he kicked it to Davik because he knew Davik is trying to get a few of his people out of that place. Adding Jason into their plans wouldn't have changed anything, and Grandad gets to offer Davik a way to do Grandad a favour. And for approximately two days, none of it *mattered*. It was just a thing everyone was doing for the politics. We've done it before. The Bay and the Mayor have to work together or none of this works. But then word got out that Jason is the one who broke suppression at the Rift and now he matters so much that everyone needs him. Grandad wants him on my side, Davik wants him in the Red Dawn, the Breeding Program wants him to make tainted babies with that much raw power, just like his mother did. And Tashué made his deal, and Wolfe wants to know why nothing's happened yet. Eventually, Davik will finally get Jason out, and then the fight for Jason's loyalty kicks off. So I think you should be down there. I think you should be involved with whatever Davik's planning, and I think you should be there to hang on to Jason when the storm hits. And since you'll be down there for him, I would appreciate it if you were also looking out for me, so that I can protect both of you when everything goes to shit."

"You'll protect us, hey?" Lorne asked.

"I'll try."

The fight-tremble rolled through Lorne's bones, making everything feel too sharp and too violent even though they were just standing here talking. Talking about war, talking about bloodshed. Talking about Jason. Lorne turned to watch the crows eat Edgar Hale, but that only served to make his heart beat faster and make his head feel too far away. "Why me, then?"

Vasska snorted, flicking ash into the wind, watching it skitter across the cobbles until it hit a puddle that swallowed it whole. "What do you want me to say? That I'm so devoted to you because we've been through too much together? Get your head out of your ass, Lorne. Why you? Because you and Jason and Tashué Blackwood are fucking up my whole damned life, but maybe you'll be the ones who save me."

"Isn't Davik going to know I'm there for you? Isn't he going to want retribution for…" He waved at Hale, whose carcass swung like a clock pendulum as the crows jostled him more and more.

"Probably," Vasska said with a shrug. "But if he kills you, he fucks the balance of the standoff, doesn't he?"

Lorne laughed. "So you're betting my life on the fact that he probably won't fuck up the standoff. Great. Thanks. I appreciate it, Vasska."

"It's worth it though, isn't it? For Jason."

"Fuck you."

"Is that a yes?"

Lorne dabbed his lip again. For Jason. He would do fucking anything for Jason. He would rip his heart out and lay it on an altar for Jason. He would walk into the Rift himself if he thought it would help Jason. And a little part of him resented Vasska for knowing it and using it, but a much bigger part was so fucking relieved that someone was doing something. Finally. And a part of him was guilty that he hadn't been the one to set any of this in motion. He'd been so wrapped up in being *stuck* that he hadn't been able to see any way out.

"How am I supposed to get word back to you if I'm down there learning how to be a pugilist?"

Vasska reached into his pocket again, producing a scrap of newsprint that had been clipped from a larger page. Small and tattered, the ink half-smudged like it had been touched before it had the chance to dry. "Remember this?"

Lorne took the scrap—from one of the Bay papers, about the tenement fire that killed that woman from the Breeding Program. Lorne could almost smell the ash again, hear the screams of the dying. And he could see that woman again, and the wild look in her eye, and the things she told him and Tashué about the children from the Breeding Program. "Yeah. I remember."

"You fought it, people say. You were there, trying to put it out."

Lorne nodded. Fat load of good him fighting it did. It felt like his whole life was him fighting things that wouldn't change. "The rain put it out. What's this got to do with Davik and his club?"

"Nothing," Vasska admitted. "But it's your excuse to come talk to me even though you're training. I heard some rumours about the fire."

"What kind of rumours?"

"Someone set the fire on purpose. I want to know if it's true, and I want to know if anyone saw who did it. So I was hoping you can get your people on it, and maybe we can find out for sure."

Something cold and hollow and heavy rang like a death knell in Lorne's chest. Someone set that fire on purpose—what were the chances it was a coincidence and had nothing to do with the woman from the Breeding Program? Probably fucking slim. It defied reason to think the two things weren't connected. And he'd put her in there, trying to help her, but it only brought death. Death to her and just about everyone else who lived there.

"Yeah," Lorne said. "I'll see what I can drag up. I'll let people know you're looking, and then I guess I'll go down to Davik's club."

Vasska nodded. "Tell him Grandad sent you, like they agreed."

Lorne took a long drag of the cigarillo, wishing the smoke would wash him clean of all the guilt that sat like poison in him, making everything taste foul. "Sure. For you and Jason."

5

LORNE
DAY 27

Davik Kaine's pugilist club stood on the outside of the tracks, at the base of the hill, looking out at the Industrial Quarter. It was a massive building. Higher than the tram line, the footprint extending half the block. Surely the whole thing wasn't just the pugilist club—the western side of the building looked like it was housing maybe. But even it was dwarfed by the Breeding Program, which lay its shadow across the club with its high walls and its solitary position on the hill outside the city limits.

But when Lorne tried to get into the club, the doors were locked.

Lorne tried them a few times and shook them hard and kicked them too, but they were still fucking locked. What kind of pugilist club was locked during the day?

A group of people gathered outside the club, in the field between the road and the looming presence of the Breeding Program. Lorne stood on the steps of the pugilist club a while, watching them. A woman threw plates in the air and a man with a small rifle shot them out of the sky with incredible precision. The plates shattered, raining porcelain onto the field. A bonfire that twisted flames into the wind. People drank and ate and danced near the bonfire, a chaotic cluster of bodies that made Lorne's skin feel too fucking tight. It wasn't the crowd—he'd folded into much more chaos at the Hive. It was the inescapable realization that all of these people could well be Army of the Red Dawn, and he'd spent the last little while being told not to fuck around with the Red Dawn.

Sometimes life did that to you. Sometimes it fucked you over.

The man with the rifle spotted Lorne watching and gave a great, sweeping bow, spreading his arms to the sides. When he bowed like that, it pulled his shirt open, showing the long line of his chest, all lean and wiry. As cold as it was out here, he had his coat open and his shirt unbuttoned like the cold didn't touch him.

"You must be the Lightning!" he said, with a wide grin. "So nice to see you finally. We've been expecting you."

Lorne shifted his weight from one foot to the other. He wasn't exactly expecting a warm welcome. "You've been expecting me?"

"Of course—Mr. Iwan said you'd be our pugilist and we've been waiting for you to show up."

"It's only been a week since I fought Ijaz. You can't have waited that long."

"Well, sure," the man said with a shrug, "but he waited to send us *anyone* 'til the last possible moment. We've been ready for months, and the exhibition match for Redbone is coming up fast." The man swept an arm toward himself, gesturing to Lorne to come closer. "Come over so we don't have to yell at each other! You know how to shoot?"

"Do I know how to shoot?" Lorne echoed. "Sure. I know how to shoot a gun, but I'm supposed to be here to learn how to box."

The man gave another easy grin, dazzling in its charm. "Sure Mr. Lightning, but the door's locked, ain't it? Dav had the floor waxed for the big match, and he said it ain't ready for us to walk on, so he told us to fuck off a while. So you should just come out and play nice, hey? Show me how good you can shoot."

The man turned away from Lorne and nodded to the woman, and she tossed two more plates, one right after the other. The rifle—a .22 from the size and sound of it—was fast and accurate and easy to rack with the pump action, and both plates exploded.

Lorne sighed, heading across the field toward the group. There was something false and shallow about the man's friendliness, something predatory about his grin, charming though it was. It all left Lorne's senses jangly and raw. Lorne walked slow, waiting for the moment when the man racked another round and swung that little .22 on him. Or maybe he was imagining things. Maybe it was everything Vasska said that left him buzzing and tense. He'd left the diplomatic division because he hated shit like this. Hated trying to keep up, hated gambling people's lives against the incredible scale of human greed and corruption. But this wasn't the division, where he made his gambles and his guesses *for the Crowne*. It was all for Jason.

Grass and brush clung to Lorne's trousers as he walked, his boots sinking into the mud of the narrow path that cut across the field. The last rain made everything soggy and by the time Lorne reached the group, his trouser legs and his socks were heavy and cold, the wool soaking up all that old rain.

The man watched Lorne's approach, brown eyes scanning his face with particular attention. "Mr. Iwan didn't get you a healer after your fight?"

Lorne shrugged. "Someone looked at everything inside, but she decided my face wasn't a priority."

"Not a priority?" The man laughed, resting his rifle on his shoulder. "You look like you been trying to kiss barbed wire."

"Took a lot of shots to the face. It's not every day a man gets beaten in public on the order of the Army of the Red Dawn. It's a lot to recover from." Of all the stupid, idiotic, dangerous things to say. He was supposed to be here for Jason, but instead he was apparently here to get himself killed by speaking without thinking.

The man grinned, but something went tense, like a fight was brewing. "Don't know what you're talking about."

The woman tossed a plate up in the air, up over Lorne's head, and the man snapped his rifle up and fired. The porcelain shattered a few feet behind Lorne, the sound sharp and splintering in his ears, but none of the porcelain hit him. But Lorne couldn't flinch. Couldn't back away. He kept fucking walking because he didn't want to turn his back on these people, and he didn't want to give ground. He cursed his idiot mouth with every step he took.

"Ain't no Red Dawn in Yaelsmuir," the man continued. "Authority always says so. Rainer Elsworth himself says it. No organized presence or some shit like that."

Lorne walked closer, toward that gun, toward the barrel. It was too late now to make the words disappear, and he couldn't flinch or they'd know he was on the back foot. He spent his whole life saying he wasn't afraid of dying. And it was true, in a sense—he wasn't afraid of the great, black nothing that would get him, and he wasn't afraid of what- ever came after. But now, with everything laid at his feet, he was very much afraid of not being here when Jason got out. He was terrified of the idea of Davik Kaine and Powell Iwan fighting over Jason and ripping him apart in the process. And what would happen to Alys when his money stopped coming to her account?

"Look, I didn't mean it like that." Lorne looked him in the eye and kept walking until the rifle was pressed into his navel, so hot he could feel it through his clothes, so hot it singed the dirty wool of his coat. "I'm not looking for a fight with any of you. Powell Iwan said I'm your pugilist now, so here I am. Whatever the story is, I'm on board. There's no Red Dawn in Yaelsmuir, and the Red Dawn didn't ask Powell Iwan to have me beaten to make a point. What else? Oh, right. The Red Dawn didn't kill that girl, either. Edgar Hale did that, and he's dead, great luck."

"Yeah, great luck." The man racked a new round into the chamber. "We're all glad he's gone. Big relief. He was a real pile of runny cowshit." The man turned the rifle around to push it into Lorne's hands, breaking the tension of the moment with a smile so broad and bright that the force of it hit Lorne like a physical blow. "You're a cold fucker, hey?"

Lorne snatched the gun from the man's hands. "You're a talkative fucker, aren't you?"

The woman laughed. "He's got you there."

It was warmer over by the fire, at least. The flames whipped in the wind, sending trailing embers that wouldn't catch anywhere because everything was so wet.

The man grabbed Lorne by the chin and leaned in, turning Lorne's face this way and that to examine all the damage. He was taller than Lorne, forcing Lorne to lean his head back to meet the other man's gaze. Warm brown eyes and sandy blond hair and a little spray of freckles on his cheeks that danced when he grimaced at the mess that was Lorne's face. His hands were surprisingly warm considering how cold it was out here.

"Your face really does look like shit. Oh well, we're honoured to have you, Mr. Lightning. That was a hell of a fight, you and the Hammer? Haven't seen anything like that in a long time."

Lorne blinked uselessly, the total shift of energy leaving him off balance. "You saw the fight?"

The man grinned again. He let go of Lorne's chin, but he stayed close like personal space wasn't a concept that existed to him. "Of course I saw the fight. Everyone in the Bay wanted to see that fight. Didn't think you'd win that one, to be honest. Thought for sure the Hammer was going to be our pugilist. Lost some money betting against you."

"Sorry," Lorne said, but felt stupid after he said it.

The man laughed. "Are you serious? Shit, never apologize for fighting like *that*. Money well spent, that was. Wouldn't have believed it if I hadn't seen it with my own eyes. Anyway, I made it all back and then some betting on the fights after, once I had an eye for the way you moved. We'll have to fix up your face, or the league won't let you box. They run things a little tighter in the proper league matches. You'll have to learn all the rules in a hurry, hey? Old man Iwan really wanted us to sweat, leaving it so close to the match."

"So, when will the floors be ready?" Lorne asked, looking back toward the pugilist club. "If I've got so much to do."

"I dunno." The man knocked a knuckle against the butt of the rifle as if to draw Lorne's attention to the fact he was still holding it. "Might as well get to know each other while we're waiting, hey? I'm László, this is my sister Irén, and these idiots are officially your fanbase. Hey! Idiots! Wave to our new pugilist!"

The crowd laughed and swirled and bubbled like a big keg of beer, turning to Lorne to wave.

"If you need anything while you're here, you can ask the idiots, or you can ask me," László said, grinning. "But don't ask Irén, because she's a bitch and she won't do anything you ask."

"Suck my balls," Irén snorted.

László grinned and winked at Lorne. "See? But don't call her a bitch or she'll hurt you, and then we won't have a pugilist. I'm allowed because she's my sister."

"Sure," Lorne said. "I promise not to call you a bitch or ask you for anything."

"Faster learner, you are," Irén said, pushing hair out of her face. "That's a relief. You ready to shoot?"

Lorne nodded.

Irén grinned and threw the plate high and fast, sending it spinning away toward the city. Lorne swept the rifle up, breathing slow, his whole body following that fucking plate. Fire in the still moment when the lungs were empty. The .22 didn't kick hard, and it wasn't especially loud, but it shot straight. Lorne missed anyway.

Lorne racked the slide action, and the empty shell popped out, but there were no more rounds. László took his gun back, and Lorne watched him go through the clearly familiar motion of loading fresh shells. The metal jackets skittered down into place, the sound rattling down the bones of Lorne's spine. It was worse than the actual sound of the gunshots, somehow. A promise of violence, filled with the potential of blood and pain. The splintered plate was a release of the potential—shattered porcelain, no one hurt. But the loading reminded him how fucking stupid he was and how close he'd come to ruining his chance here by saying that idiot thing about the Red Dawn before he even knew anyone's name.

Irén whistled at Lorne, catching his attention again before tossing a plate over the fire. He lifted the rifle and shot. The bullet clipped the edge of the plate and sent it tumbling down into the fire, chipped but whole, but then the flames had the porcelain, and there was no getting it back.

"Too far left," László said. "You leaned into it too hard." He came closer to Lorne, putting his hands on Lorne's hips and slowly guiding Lorne's stance. "Relax a bit, yeah? No one's going to punch you in the face."

Lorne racked a fresh round in, the slide action smooth. "I always assume someone's about to punch me in the face. That way, when people start swinging, I'm ready."

"Sounds like a real exhausting way to live your life, Mr. Lightning."

Lorne shrugged. "Better than getting caught off guard and punched in the face."

László blew out a long breath, his cheeks puffing out and making him look younger. "Well, I am very pleased to inform you that we watch out for each other around here. So you can unclench a little, yeah? Relax and try again. It's just a twenty-two—you don't have to brace for the mule kick of a forty-five. And I know you're always ready to be punched in the face, but you've got a gun in your hands. You're powerful."

Lorne lifted the gun. Relax, fuck. Such a little word, but shit. He couldn't remember the last time he relaxed. Maybe it was before Jason was arrested. Maybe it was on some rooftop in the city, the pair of them staring at the smoke-choked sky, talking about nothing. Certainly he hadn't really relaxed since Jason was arrested. It felt too much like a betrayal when he knew for a fact Jason couldn't fucking well relax in the Rift.

So Lorne didn't relax exactly. He didn't really know how anymore.

He exhaled, long and slow, like he was headed for another fight. That, he could do.

Irén threw another plate. Trigger. Kick. Shatter.

"That's better, hey?" László said, grinning again. All the tension had bled out of him, and he leaned a little closer to Lorne, the necklace he wore swinging out from his open shirt, all of the charms jangling together. One of them was a tooth, maybe, but Lorne couldn't imagine what kind of animal had teeth that big. A predator for sure, with the aggressive hook of it. "You're not bad with my pea shooter. You a fast learner or did you already know what you're doing?"

"Army." Another round, another plate. Trigger, kick, shatter. "16th Infantry." It was easy now, the motions so familiar that it was like his muscles remembered. Rack, trigger, kick, shatter. László was right when he said the .22 didn't have much kick. Army issue .45s could hurt bad if they caught you off guard. But now that he had the feel for it, it was like meeting an old friend. Things fell into rhythm. "Served my three and then got stuck here after I discharged. You do this often? Just stand around the field all afternoon and shoot things and have bonfires?"

László shrugged. "Field's a good place for a fire, ain't it? You can almost believe you've got space out here."

"Except that fucking Breeding Program is right there," Lorne muttered. He couldn't look at it. The walls loomed in his peripheral vision, but he didn't want to turn to it and admit its existence. Jason's mother died in that place. He felt the pain of that as raw and ugly as if it were his own mother. Worse, even, because the one thing he wanted in the whole world was to give Jason a life of stability and contentment but Jason was in the fucking Rift and his mother was dead. Chased the poppy dreams until her body just stopped. Rack, trigger, kick, shatter.

"It sure is," László said brightly, flashing another big grin.

He took the gun back and loaded it up again. Irén with the plates turned and started hurling them toward the Breeding Program walls. László shot three out of the sky before a louder gunshot clapped over the wind, and a plate shattered before László fired. A pair of guards, up on the walls. Bundled against the cold. Irén laughed and kept throwing plates for the guards, and their rifles had a ferocious roar that turned the plates to dust.

This wasn't what Lorne was expecting at all.

A whistle pulled Lorne's attention back to the road. Someone had come out of the club, and they stood on the steps, holding the door open. A young man, still gangly and awkward like he was growing into his limbs, his cheeks attempting to grow facial hair but only producing fuzz.

"Da says you can come in now!"

"Fucking finally," László said, slinging his rifle over his shoulder. "I'm starving. Let's go, Mr. Lightning. We'll show you around and feed you."

"Don't feed him too much," Irén said. "The wild, mangy look suits the first Bay pugilist."

László laughed, throwing his arm around Lorne's shoulders and walking him back along the path. The boy led them up to the steps of the pugilist club, dragging the door open.

"I didn't realize you were hunting for fresh meat, László," the boy said before they could go in.

"Have a little respect, Rowan. This here's our new pugilist."

Rowan met Lorne's eyes like he wasn't especially impressed except he was putting too much effort into looking disinterested, and it just made him look young. A boy, trying to fit in with the hard, dangerous adults around him but not quite bridging the gap. Rowan Kaine, must be, the kid Vasska was talking about. "Sure looks like a pugilist."

"What's that supposed to mean?" László scoffed, offended on Lorne's behalf.

"Means his face looks like pulp, and his eyes look like they've never had a thought behind them in his whole life."

Lorne laughed, trying to match the high, wild, indulgent sound that László made. "That's cute. Adorable. Baby's first insult."

László snorted, and Rowan's face spasmed with surprise and outrage, but Lorne walked past him through the open door. Into the giant warehouse. His new pugilist club.

The air smelled like fresh wax and varnish and potential, the hardwood floors buffed to an immaculate shine. The door swung closed behind them and the place felt too big and too empty and too hot. It was strange to be so hot this time of year, with the winter wind invading the city, with storms roiling on the horizon, promising snow and ice. Their footsteps echoed on the floor, the sound bouncing around under the high ceilings and the pipes that ran above their heads. The club had good equipment, and László rattled off the names of everything like it was supposed to mean something to Lorne. They had a proper ring with ropes to keep the fighters up where they belonged instead of leaving them to fall into the crowd if they weren't vigilant.

Something hot and anxious crawled through Lorne's chest as László showed him around. Somehow outside was easier to forget why he was here and whose company he was suddenly keeping, but now that he was inside, it was all sinking back into his bones. He tried not to think about all the ways this could go wrong, but the list jumped through his head anyway. Maybe Davik Kaine was going to kill him. There was no fucking way that Davik was going to let him walk around after everything. Hale wanted Lorne dead for a reason—Lorne had been snooping around, and now Lorne knew things. He was going to end up like Hale—maybe Kaine would hang Lorne outside the pugilist club to see if the crows would eat Lorne any faster than they were eating Hale.

It was worth trying if it meant seeing Jason again, but fuck if he wasn't certain he was going to screw this up.

He should have said something to someone about his sister. Tashué maybe—he'd help if Lorne asked him to, without a doubt. Lorne should have gone to Brickheart before coming here, explained how to collect all the assets from the various businesses he invested in and told Tashué which bank to send it to in Teshii to fill up Alys's accounts. That way she'd have everything Lorne had to give if he died here.

Breathe.

A man approached, wearing nothing but his shirt and his trousers, sleeves rolled up to his elbows to show his tattoos—intricate knotwork, a scrawl of some words Lorne couldn't quite make out, stacked bricks that circled his left forearm and disappeared under his sleeve. More tattoos on the backs of his hands. His beard was neatly trimmed, salt-and-pepper hair swept back off his forehead. He had friendly eyes. Davik Kaine— had to be. He smiled and it felt like a threat, so liquid and easy. The smile of a man who knew he was handsome and powerful, a man who knew he was in total control. It made Lorne's heart beat double-time, or maybe it was what Vasska said about Davik Kaine getting Jason out. László called him Dav, like they were all a happy family around here.

"You must be the Lledewydd Lightning," Davik fucking Kaine said, his voice low and mellow and rolling in a heavy northland burr. "You look like ripe shite."

"At least we know he can take some pain and he won't quit," László said brightly. "You should've seen that fight, Dav. Mad fucker kept getting back up."

Davik shrugged like he wasn't especially impressed. "Stubborn men aren't exactly hard to come by in this quarter. Are your hands still shite, too? Let me see 'em."

Make this work for Jason. "It's not a big deal, Mr. Kaine. I've fought with hands in worse shape than this."

"Maybe, but you're a proper boxer now, and we've got to get you into tournament shape," Davik said. "Stretch 'em out, laddie, let me see."

Lorne stretched out his hands, and Davik came closer, running his thumb across Lorne's knuckles. "They're only a bit sore."

"You ever break anything?" Davik asked.

"What? Ah—yeah. These two." Lorne touched the knuckle of the middle finger and the smallest. "Different fights, but one right after the other and it hurt for a long time after it was healed. Or maybe it took a long time to heal, I don't know. That's when I got better with my left. That was a while ago, though."

"Aye, you've got a hammer of a left," Davik said. "The bones, they still hurt?"

"In the winter, when it's cold and wet—they ache."

"It's always cold and wet 'round here, innit it?" Davik took his hand, fingers squeezing the bones, the knuckles. Lorne didn't know what he was looking for, exactly. "And your wrists? How are they?"

"I don't know. They're wrists. They move. I haven't broken them, if that's what you're asking. I broke my forearm when I was a kid. The left. Dislocated my shoulder in the military, falling from a tree. Turns out I'm a shit scout. Sprained both my ankles at one time or another. I don't think I've hurt my knees? If I did, I don't remember. I broke my foot when I was a kid, too. The right, I think? I kicked a crab trap, and it fucking hurt. I guess I don't know for sure it was broken, but I couldn't walk on it for months without it hurting. Hobbled around all summer. Does it matter? Hasn't everyone broken something at some point?"

"No, actually," Rowan said. "Some people go through their lives without any broken bones at all, if you can believe it."

"All those breaks make me wonder if you've got fragile bones," László said.

"Or he hits things too fucking hard," Davik said with another shrug. "That's where I'd put my money if we're taking bets. Why don't you take a look, László, see if there's a problem."

"Wait," Lorne said. It was all moving faster than he could keep up with, but of course it was moving fast. He didn't know what else he expected—László said Lorne's first match was soon. "Take a look—what do you mean?"

"National Pugilist League requires a healer for each club, Mr. Lightning," Davik said, crossing his arms over his chest. "Helps reduce casualties and all that, and helps optimizing training to make the best athletes possible. Is that going to be a problem?"

"I just—"

"Let me guess," Rowan interrupted. "You're fucking that Blackwood kid because he's cute and tight, but you're still afraid of the tainted, just like everyone else. Lucky for you, he's locked up so you can pretend to be the compassionate, self-sacrificing hero who's taken up with a *tainted* boy even though you're *clean*, without actually facing the reality that your lover could turn you inside out if he wanted to."

Rage burst so hot in Lorne's chest, he had to bite down on it to keep it from making him say something truly idiotic. He forced himself to wait a moment, chewing on the rage, breathing slow through the fury until it subsided enough to let him speak with some veneer of calm. He turned to Davik instead of Rowan, looking the older man in the eye. "That your son?"

"Aye, he's mine, the idiot," Davik muttered.

Lorne nodded, grinding his teeth together so hard it made them creak before he trusted himself to speak. "You tell your son if he ever talks about Jason like that again, I'm knocking some of his teeth out." He spoke each word calmly, but with sharp edges he couldn't contain. "I'm not usually the type that hits children, but there are some things I won't stand for, and anyone talking about Jason like that is one of them."

"You can tell him yourself, Mr. Lightning," Davik said with a lazy, disinterested shrug. "I been trying to tell him he'd catch a fist with that mouth of his, but folks 'round here let him get away with too much because they think I'll hand out retribution for it."

"I don't think I need to repeat myself," Lorne said, looking over at Rowan. "I think he heard me."

"Did you hear the man, Rowan?" Davik asked, glancing over his shoulder at the boy.

"Yeah," Rowan said, but his voice was trembling—anger or fear or maybe some mix of both. Maybe Lorne had underestimated him because his face looked so young, but maybe he was just as ready to fight as Lorne was. "I heard him fine, Da."

"Great," Davik said, and his voice dropped pitch, and the hard rolling of his rs made the word sound like a primal growl. He leaned in closer to Lorne, and suddenly László was standing too close so Lorne couldn't back up. "He listened to you, and now you're going to listen to me real close, yeah? I haven't got time to fuck around with you and play all these fun little games about whether or not we trust each other. I need this club to work and Powell Iwan fucked me more than a little by making me wait so long for you. We're supposed to put on a good showing for this fundraiser, but all I got is some smart mouth boy that looks like ground beef and doesn't know how to box. So, you need to get to work right now and cut the shit. You think you've got something in that ugly head of yours that I don't already know? Spare me. I know Powell picked you because he figured he knew you'd be loyal, and I'm willing to bet my whole fucking club that they lured you over here by telling you about getting the Blackwood kid out of the Rift, so you understand what's at stake around here, yeah? Whatever you promised Powell, I don't give a ripe shite."

"I didn't promise Powell fucking anything," Lorne said.

Davik hissed air through his teeth, the same way Vasska hissed at that stray dog, and held up a hand. "I ain't done talking, laddie. So you're going to shut your mouth and keep listening."

Lorne clenched his fists so hard the scabs on his knuckles split and oozed blood that dripped like hot acid from the wounds, his back ramrod straight and his eyes locked on Davik's face. "Sure thing, Mr. Kaine."

"Good boy, you're a fast learner. So here it is, the one and only time I'm going to threaten you. You can either cooperate and work the hardest you ever worked in your fucking life and suck your little feelings right back into your chest and let László fix your hands and your stupid face, or I'm going to put your body in the Brightwash and put one of my own people as the pugilist for this fight. Understood?"

"I'm not afraid of dying, Mr. Kaine," Lorne said.

Davik made the hissing sound again, and it took all of Lorne's self-control not to snap his head forward and break the motherfucker's nose. "Son, you misunderstand me. I don't need you to be afraid. Whether you're scared of meeting the Keeper of the Keys or not, you'll still be dead, and I'll be running my club the way I want. I need you to know I won't be letting some crusty wank stain of a *boy* ruin what I've been building for fucking years. Are we clear, Mr. Lightning?"

"Oh, am I allowed to talk now?" Lorne asked.

Davik smiled, sharp and unimpressed. "Aye, this would be a good time."

"Great," Lorne said, the word grinding out of him like shards of glass. There was something comforting about this much anger, simmering in him, keeping him safe from doubt or worry, leaving no room for anything but the intensity of it. "I was going to save you all the talking, but maybe you like the sound of your own voice, hey?"

Davik laughed. "I like you, laddie. If you're willing to work, I think you'll fit in well here."

"I'm willing to work, Mr. Kaine," Lorne said. "I was going to say I didn't promise Powell Iwan anything, because fuck him. And I know it was your man Hale that set me up for the fight that made me look like ground beef, but I hear someone took care of Hale, so you and me, we don't have any problems. Because Vasska *did* tell me you're getting Jason out, and I want you to understand that it's the only thing I care about in the whole world. He's been in there three years, and you're telling me that you're going to do what I couldn't? What his father couldn't? Fantastic. If I have to box, fine. If I have to walk into the Rift myself, fine. If I have to be bait so you can pull off whatever you've got planned, that's perfect. I'm here for him, and I'll do *anything.*" It wasn't a lie, not really.

Davik relaxed instantly, clapping his hands together and leaning back to give Lorne space to breathe again. "Fantastic. That's what I like to hear, laddie. I like people that are driven by something bigger than they are. These fists are mine now, you hear me? They hit what I tell them to hit. You don't hit anything else. You've got a mean temper, but I've got a lot riding on your fists so they're mine."

"Yeah, sure," Lorne said. "My wrists belong to you, too? Is that why you were asking about them? Am I allowed to jerk off or are you worried I'll sprain something?"

László barked fresh laughter that chased all the tension out of the room.

Davik grinned. "Son, if you're going to sprain something by jerking off, your cock is bigger than you deserve, or your wrists will need more work before we put you in the ring. Let me know which it is since we haven't got much time to get you ready."

Lorne shrugged, fighting to unclench his fists, but *fuck* they hurt. "My wrists are fine."

László dropped his arm around Lorne's shoulder, pulling them together like he'd decided they were best friends. "I like him, Dav. Can we keep him?"

"Aye, I think we can. I think you'll fit in great around here, Mr. Lightning. My people haven't any quit in them, either. You've good fists, boy. Good swing. Good reach. Natural movement and all that. We should be able to shape you just fine."

Lorne shrugged. "I just hit people for money."

"So what are we doing first, Dav?" László asked. "We're getting started right away, yeah?"

"Yeah," Davik said. "Do you know how to use a skip rope?"

People filtered into the massive space, settling at the bar, throwing themselves at the equipment, filling the big, empty space with bodies and noise. It wasn't any better than when the place was empty because now he was aware of how many people could fit in this building—there weren't that many yet, or at least it didn't feel like it with the way the building sprawled across half the block, but Lorne's imagination could fill the empty spaces with the crush of people that would show up for the match he was supposed to box in. And he wondered if every single one of them would be Red Dawn.

"A skip rope?" Lorne asked. "Sure. Why?"

"I need to watch you while you exercise to see how your body uses energy and how best to get you to peak performance," László explained. "And if we're worried about your bones, I guess we'll look at them, too. See how they take the impact. And your joints for that matter. We'll be using Talent to do that."

"We?" Lorne asked.

"Me and Rowan," László said. "I'm your healer, but I'll be teaching him how to take care of you, in case I can't always be here. You won't feel us doing anything. I'll try to stay out of your mind, but sometimes there is a bit of…" László shrugged, searching for the right word. "Bleeding. From your thoughts, into mine. It's a myth that healers can go digging around in your thoughts and memories. We only see what's on the surface—what you're thinking about in the moment. And feel your emotions. You can think about things you don't mind me seeing. But, you should know, I've seen it all. I don't think there's anything in that skull of yours that will shake me up. Give me your wrist."

Lorne blinked at him. "My what?"

László motioned to Lorne's hand. "Your wrist, darling. That thing you need to jerk off that giant cock of yours."

A flush spread hot and fast across Lorne's face and László grinned again. Lorne thrust one arm out and László held him strangely, pressing two fingers against the underside of Lorne's wrist and then he stood a moment with his eyes closed.

"Your resting heart rate is fast, but we'll call that stress, hey?" László said, letting go of Lorne. "Might as well get started."

Davik waved someone forward to take Lorne's coat, and László thrust a skip rope into his hand. Everyone moved back to give him space. Lorne got tangled in the rope a few times while he got used to the particular length and weight of it—it was too long for him, so he wrapped it around his hands a few times to get it right. The exertion of jumping made his heart beat faster and his lungs ache and his legs burn and his arms hurt. And it all felt almost good, comforting, this all-consuming body ache. Easier than the ache that settled in his soul when he thought about how long it had been since he'd been physically intimate with the single person he loved most in the world. The burning panic that tried to squeeze the air out of him when he wondered what would become of him if Jason died before getting out. Died in the process of getting out. Died in the inevitable chaos that would explode across Yaelsmuir when all those people broke out of the Rift. How was Davik going to get Jason out? Fuck.

Stop thinking about Jason in the Rift, behind that metal grate, small and tired and crushed by the weight of his ugly reality.

Think about Jason in the Bay, the first time they met. Scared, maybe, but luminous. Intimidated by life and by Cattle Bone Bay but alight with his own inner glow. Short-tempered and brave and funny.

Jason in Brickheart, trying to decide what to do about his Talent. Whether he'd keep hiding it or if he'd register.

The feeling of Jason's Talent, like a breeze across Lorne's skin. Like a kiss on his beating heart, the most intimate thing he'd ever experienced in his life. And then a real kiss on the mouth, the kind with lips and tongues and heavy breathing, and instead of a breeze on his skin, it was Jason's hands. There was hardly any space at all in Jason's small bed, but it didn't matter because their bodies pressed so close together that for a while, it was like they occupied the same space.

That was the last time they got the chance to touch each other so much. They fought the next morning because Jason didn't understand why Lorne wouldn't settle in Brickheart, why Lorne felt he needed to stay in the Bay. Stay homeless, drifting. Lorne needed to work, needed to keep his expenses low. Needed to send every crown he had to Alys's account so she could stay in school and have a life that was better than the way Lorne floated from one infuriating existence to another. But he wasn't good at talking about Alys, and he wasn't good at explaining himself at all, so Jason thought Lorne didn't want to settle *with him.*

And then Jason was arrested.

Processed to the Rift.

It was summer when Lorne went back to the apartment on the Row to find Tashué drunk in his living room and breaking things. Because none of the things Tashué tried to do had worked, and now they had nothing to do but wait and see if Jason would register to get himself out.

Three and a half years. Waiting for Jason to register, or figure out something else.

And now, 'something else' was here, and somehow Lorne learning how to box was going to help.

"That's plenty, Mr. Lightning," László called. "I don't see any real problems, Dav. He used that rope a long time, and when the pain started, his thinking went internal and he ignored how much it hurt—I think he just doesn't pay attention to his limits."

Now that he'd stopped, the pain came rolling in, his lungs burning, his legs aching. Sweat crawled under his clothes. "So my bones and joints and heart and lungs are all fine," he said, once he'd caught his breath enough to string so many words together, "but my head is fucked up?"

"Sounds like it," Davik said. "You'll fit right in around here."

6

STELLA
DAY 27

It was a bad time to travel across open ground, with winter coming fast and bringing rain and ice to Yael province. But then life didn't always leave nice things like *choices*.

By the time they met Rhodrishi at the hospital, and then found Kazrani in the livestock market, it was already past noon. Ceridwen's grief at leaving Tashué behind was tempered by the horses, at least. Shaggy Hitjurgavit ponies, since Kazrani said she couldn't find any Jitabvi ponies on short notice, not with whatever coins she had in her pocket and no connections in the Yaelsmuir livestock trade. The shaggy island horses from the north were hardy and fleet-footed and strong enough to carry them across the wilderness. Rhodrishi's horse was bigger than the ponies, a majestic roan mare with deep scars on her flanks. Stella could scarcely imagine what kind of switch or whip had made marks like that. But then, she was no stranger to a rough hand, so maybe she could imagine.

There were only a few hours of daylight left once they hit the road, but everyone felt the same urgency to keep going instead of delaying any more. So, with Ceridwen seeming more layers of wool and leather and fur than she was an actual human child, and Stella carrying the big rifle Tashué had given to her—loaned to her—she followed Kazrani and Rhodrishi out of the city, away from the closest thing she had to a home since leaving Cruinnich. Away from the first person she'd shared so much of herself with since...

Best not to think about the last time she thought she was falling in love. Those years, those people, that version of herself, were all long gone. And any happiness or comfort she might have found in those old memories would be like water from a poisoned well, for they would only lead her to thinking about everything that came after. The ways that Davik Kaine fell apart, the people she lost. Bothain. Siras.

Best not think of the past at all, or she would have to admit to herself she was running from Davik almost as much as she was running from Siras and Bothain. Running from their history and the inexorable pull of him. She counted herself blessed by the North Star that she didn't know he was in Yaelsmuir until she was ready to leave. She might have gone to find him if she knew, only to be drawn back into his web of lies and empty promises. It was better to think about Tashué and the low, gentle tones of his voice as he sat in his living room and told her about how many times the old Imburleigh rifle saved his life. Despair tried to tell her that she'd never see him again, but she was heading out into the wilderness with his gun and the people he loved, so maybe it wasn't too much to hope he'd come for her.

Kazrani, for her part, seemed undaunted by the prospect of the journey, sitting straight and tall in her saddle. She kept Ceridwen's little pony —the smallest of the three, with a shaggy grey coat and a wild shock of a mane that fell in front of her eyes—on a guide rope, giving Ceridwen constant and encouraging instruction. Heels down, back straight, head up. Keep your eyes on your surroundings, and keep a hand on the pommel of your saddle, just in case.

They didn't make it far up the road before Rhodrishi led them to look for a place to camp for the night: a hollow in the face of one of the many rocky hills that sprawled around the city. Trees growing among the rock made an overhang into a shelter with a roof and a wall of twisting, sinuous roots. They didn't bother setting a fire—they were too exhausted to cook, anyway. They passed around chunks of smoked sausage and whole carrots, feeding the green tops to the horses.

Stella struggled to get comfortable on the bed of stone, softened only by her bedroll, which wasn't nearly thick enough to cushion her hips or her shoulders. Sleep eluded her even though she was so exhausted she couldn't think. The cold air wrapped around her body like a lover she didn't want, seeping into her skin. It didn't seem to matter how many layers she swathed herself in, the cold and the damp made her ache.

She was never cold when she was with Tashué Blackwood.

Such a short time they had together, but everything about him was so warm—his bed and the feeling of being lost in his big, beautiful arms, of being crushed against his body because he burned for her, and he couldn't seem to bear the idea of leaving so much as an inch of space between them. His hot eyes, the deep rumble of his voice, his big hands on his rifle, his agitation barely contained as he handed the gun over to Stella. Nothing about that man was cold at all.

Sleep took her eventually, pulling her down into dreams of him. His chest pressed against hers, and the way he kissed her face. She dreamt of his scars and his tattoos. She dreamt of his strong hands wandering her body and the calluses that scraped her skin. She dreamt of his mouth on her skin, between her thighs, his tongue, his fingers, the heat of him setting her on fire—

But something changed. He was hurting her. He pried her knees apart even though she told him no. He bit her shoulder and held her tight so she couldn't twist away from him. The cruelty made her weep. She didn't expect it from him, not Tashué. She wanted to leave, to escape this next man who used her so cheaply like so many others before him—but she didn't want to be alone in the world, drifting and hollow again. When she looked at his face, he didn't look like Tashué anymore. His mouth was the wrong shape, his eyes looked too blue, his hair was an ashy blond. Bothain—he looked like Bothain. Or maybe he looked like Siras, maybe those eyes were the emerald green of a summer day but filled with so much resentment that she knew the summer hated her simply for being untouchable.

If she could only remember what Tashué really looked like, he would stop being so cruel and would return to the man she was falling in love with, the man who kissed her tears and gave away pieces of himself to keep her safe. If she could only remember what colour his eyes were. They weren't blue like Bothain's, or green like Siras's.

She woke with a start.

Her cheeks were wet—had it been raining? No, her face was tight and sore. She'd been crying in her sleep.

The dread of the nightmare clung to her, but at least as she lay in the darkness beneath the stone overhang, she could remember what Tashué looked like. Amber eyes. Brown hair. Beard that was reddish, thick. An earth spirit, built of clay and loam—that's how she thought of him. The day she brought him fragrance of citrus and mint, the day she helped him dress because his scarred hands were too clumsy for the tiny buttons on that beautiful Bellmore suit. Hanging on to the details of reality helped chase the nightmare away.

Rhodrishi moved quietly around the little camp. He sparked a match, the snap of the sulphur breaking through the quiet, the flare of light drawing Stella's eye. Shredded cedar bark took the flame eagerly, and Rhodrishi fed twigs into the growing heat. Stella wanted get up and help —she didn't want to go back to sleep now and risk seeing Siras again, even if it was just a dream. But she was so tired. So incredibly exhausted. She couldn't summon the strength to get up, not yet, even though her bed of stone was so uncomfortable. The lingering effect of the healing process, perhaps, her body begging her for more time to rest. She didn't even know the internal injuries she was recovering from—she didn't dare look. She didn't want to know what Siras had done to her. And it didn't matter when Siras was still after her. She had no idea if her shot had killed him or not, but him being dead felt like too much to hope for. There was no time to rest.

They travelled a few hours on the second day, and then Rhodrishi led them off the road again, through the red-twig dogwood that grew in a wild tangle. He cut vibrant red branches off the shrub as their horses navigated through. Rhodrishi stripped the bark from the dogwood branches as he rode beside Ceridwen, prompting her to help in his low, gentle voice, showing her how to strip the twigs. Good for a fever, he said, and to travel with winter chill coming was to invite fevers.

Kazrani and Rhodrishi took turns leading Ceridwen's pony with the guide rope they'd tied to the pony's bridle, teaching Ceridwen to be confident in the saddle. Ceridwen held onto the pommel, and she battered Kazrani with questions—what's this part of the saddle called, is it true Jitabvi can sleep in the saddle, is it true Jitabvi children can ride before they walk, is it true Tashué Blackwood was a war hero, is he Jitabvi too?

And Kazrani answered each question with a boundless patience. She had Ceridwen memorize every name of every piece of tack: bridle, bit, reins, girth, saddle, pommel, on and on. And the horses—mane, withers, tail, fetlock, pastern, hoof, frog. Yes, it's true you can sleep in the saddle, you hook one leg around the pommel like this and lean back and trust your fellow riders won't let your horse wander off. Yes, the children learn to ride before they can walk, because parents take their babies into the saddle with them from the day they're born. Yes, Tashué Blackwood is a hero, he saved the company on the Black Ridge. Iris Company, of Mad Maddox's 8th. No, he's not Jitabvi, but we adopted him into the ashrab, and that made him family.

In the afternoon, Kazrani peeled away to study their back trail and watch for Siras Duncreek.

The questions Ceridwen had for Rhodrishi were different, and some of them cut Stella to the core. Ceridwen tried to whisper those questions, but she wasn't very good at whispering at all.

"Why does Mam have the Wrath?"

"Because your mam worked very hard to protect you both, and it stretched her Talent too far. It hurts the mind, to stretch Talent like that. It leaves… scars, making Talent harder to control."

"Will she get better?"

"I hope so. I'll try to help her once we're settled. Hopefully we can retrain her Talent to flow more naturally. But for now, so long as she stops using her Talent, she won't get any worse."

"When will my Talent wake?"

"It's waking already. Can't you feel it?"

"I don't know. What am I supposed to feel?"

"The whole world, stretching out all around you, and the ebb and flow of its energy—like standing in a stream and feeling the current wash around you."

"Then yes, I think I do feel that. If I use my Talent, will I get the Wrath like Mam?"

"No, my girl. The Wrath comes from stretching yourself beyond your limits and from using Talent without regard for the effects it has on your mind. Once we're safe and settled, I'll teach you to respect it, and you'll understand yourself and your mam better. For now, leave it be. We don't know who might feel you using it."

Stella pressed her lips together hard instead of mentioning exactly who might feel them, who might be tracking them even now. Ceridwen didn't need to hear Siras's name any more than she already had.

"Yes, Colonel Kheir."

"Can I tell you something about myself, Ceridwen?" Rhodrishi asked, his voice dropping to a conspiratorial half-whisper that wasn't necessary considering they were riding alone across the wilderness, but it captured Ceridwen's attention completely. "It's not exactly a secret—but it's something I only talk about with my friends."

"Yes!"

"I don't like being called Colonel Kheir. I would rather you call me Rhodrishi."

Ceridwen went quiet for a whole half-minute at least—an incredible stretch of time for her—as she considered the revelation. "Why don't you like being called Colonel Kheir?"

"It's not my name. My people don't have second names the same way yours do; we only have the name our parents gave us. But the Dominion, they always insist we have a second name for their paperwork, especially if we want to register or serve in the military. Sometimes, we choose names with some meaning, but even so they aren't really our names. It's just one more thing the Dominion and the Authority force us to be."

"Oh." Ceridwen's brow furrowed into deep lines, making her look older. Her hands tightened on the pommel of her saddle, and the horses plodded on. The weight of Rhodrishi's answers had taken the speed out of her rapid fire questions, and if Stella wasn't so exhausted, she might have been amused by the sombre consideration on Ceridwen's face. "Why does Lieutenant Mahalouwan call you Colonel Kheir? Does that mean she's not your friend?"

Rhodrishi sighed. "No, I still value her friendship. It's just—some people understand how burdensome it can be to change yourself for the Authority. Like your mam, she understands. But some people don't. Lieutenant Mahalouwan is a fierce and loyal soldier, but she knew me in the military. It can be hard to break military habits."

The silence stretched even longer this time.

"What does Kheir mean?" Stella asked. Ceridwen's curiosity was apparently infectious. "Why did you choose it?"

"Kheir is a word for hands in one of the old languages of the early Dominion settlers," Rhodrishi said. "People in the cities look down their noses at people who work with their hands, but the work we do with our hands is some of the most important. Someone gives birth to a child, and the first thing we do is hold it in our hands. We reach out and touch those we love with our hands. We gather, sow, harvest and prepare food with our hands. A healer puts their hands on a person, and they can see all the broken places and hopefully how to fix them. Our hands are a gift."

A gift indeed. It made her think of Tashué's hands, of how big they were, how rough they were with scars and calluses. She wondered where those calluses came from. His work as a Regulation Officer was mostly paperwork and speaking to people, but then he must do something physical to keep his body so fit.

But thinking about Tashué's hands only made her think of the dream from the night before.

It had been a long, long time since she'd even mentioned Bothain's name. So long that she had almost convinced herself that part of her life —Ffyanwy's life—was gone, cut away from this new person she was as sure as she cut pain away from the people she tended to as a whisperer named Stella Whiterock. But speaking the names of her past, feeling the shape of them for the first time in years, reminded her that she was *both* women at once. Stella would not have come to be were it not for the choices Ffyanwy had made and the pain that pushed her in that direction.

Not only pain, she reminded herself, glancing at Ceridwen. There was also hope. One day, perhaps she'd explain to Ceridwen how their lives came together. But not out here. Not now, when they were plunging into the unknown.

Somehow, she would have to reckon both versions of herself. Did she want to go back to being Ffyanwy, after nearly a decade of being Stella? Or had she seen and endured too much to ever go back, like she told Tashué when he asked her the same thing?

She didn't know. And she was too tired to figure it out. All she could do was stay in the saddle and let the little pony carry her farther away from Tashué. Farther into the wilderness.

7

STELLA
DAY 29

On the third day of travel, they stopped at a little cottage. Abandoned and worn down, with holes in the wall and no windows or doors to keep the wind out. But there was a wood store built up alongside one wall, where the roof between the barn and the cabin proper protected it from the weather. The centre of the roof was caved in, but the chimney was in good shape so they could lay their fire in the hearth and position their bedrolls beside it to catch the heat. Creeping five-leaf ivy covered most of the walls, leaves turned deep red by the cold, bare vines starting to peek through as the leaves rapidly fell away, leaving a red carpet. There was even hay in the barn for the horses and wood stacked to feed their fire, even though the building was clearly abandoned.

"It's the way things are done out here," Rhodrishi said softly, by way of explanation. "This cabin is a safe place to hide from bad weather for folks who can't follow the paved road and use all the roadhouses."

A massive storm rolled over them as they settled, battering the cottage with wind and heavy rain, building puddles in the field. Rain came in the hole in the centre, but there was enough roof left in the corners to shelter them.

"Winter isn't a good time to head into the mountains," Rhodrishi said, watching the water pour down from the broken roof. At least it drained away from them—the hearth seemed to stand on a high spot and the floor sloped downward from there. "The good trails may be washed out already."

"We take the next best trails, then," Kazrani said. "Or we go back."

"No, there's no going back," Rhodrishi said, shaking his head. "Ceridwen's Talent is quickening. It's massive, as we would expect from her. She isn't safe in Yaelsmuir."

"You can feel it?" Ceridwen asked. "My Talent?"

"I can, sweet child," Rhodrishi said. "It hangs in the air like the changing of the atmosphere before a storm."

Fear simmered through the layers of exhaustion. Stella knew all to well the hazards of a strong Talent quickening in a young body. Another name she hadn't uttered in too long, and perhaps it was the name that weighed most heavily on her. Stella had no son. Stella only had Ceridwen. But telling herself that didn't lessen the pain—it only made it worse, like she'd spent the last near decade trying to erase poor, doomed Rhion. Her son deserved more than a mother who couldn't speak his name because she was pretending to be someone else.

"She's young for quickening," Stella said, fighting for control of her voice.

Rhodrishi only shrugged and the lack of concern from him was comforting. "A little young, but not dangerously so. She might have quickened earlier, but you kept it in check. She's old enough and strong enough now, we can guide her through it if it becomes overwhelming. It could have been worse, considering..."

Considering she was a Breeding Program child. Considering she was *bred* to be powerful, to be a source of energy. Perhaps compared to other children born to the Program, she was quickening late. Thanks to Stella knotting her Talent, Rhodrishi seemed to imply. Ceridwen didn't know any of it, and Rhodrishi left it unsaid.

"Why do you braid your hair?" Ceridwen asked, using a stick to stir the embers of the fire. Stella didn't know if she was relieved or worried that Ceridwen changed the subject away from Talent. She didn't want Ceridwen to be afraid of her own strength, but it would be a long and exhausting conversation. "It always looks so lovely with the silk and the braids. What's it for? And how come the braids are different now than when we were still in the city?"

Kazrani's hands went up to her hair, sliding a finger around one braid. "It tells the story of my life. My ashrab, my unit, my family. The colours tell where I come from. The shape of the braids tell what I've done. And these braids I have now, they're for the march. Keeps everything out of my face so that if things get…" *Violent,* she was probably going to say, but she stopped herself and glanced at Ceridwen. So many words floated in the air between the adults, left unsaid for Ceridwen's sake. Stella was drowning in all the words, all the things she was afraid of but couldn't talk about. "If things get hectic, it's one less thing for me to worry about."

"How did your parents die?" Ceridwen asked. "Mr. Blackwood said you were young when it happened. The same age as me. And that's how you got to be glass."

"Glass?" Kazrani echoed.

Ceridwen pulled her bag of marbles out of her pocket, the glass clinking together in the muslin. "Glass is made of sand, but fire is what makes it beautiful instead of just sand. That's what he said. He said we're like sand—and then bad things happen, and it's like the fire that makes us into glass. Mam getting hurt was my fire. And Mr. Blackwood said losing your parents was yours."

Kazrani sighed, turning her face to the hearth. The light of it played in the wrinkles on her face, turning them to deep lines that made her look so beautifully experienced now that her face was relaxed. "My father was taken by the Wrath. Killed my mother and my brother."

"Not everyone with the Wrath is dangerous," Stella said, the weariness making her speak before she could think better of it.

Kazrani's brow furrowed, her eyes going tight and flinty, the peace disappearing so quickly, it made Stella wonder if she'd really witnessed it or if she'd imagined it. "I know that."

"The Wrath only advances when people continue to use their Talent," Rhodrishi said before Stella could apologize. "Miss Whiterock has stopped. Besides, her Wrath was only ever a danger to her."

"I know that!" Kazrani snapped. "I wouldn't be here if I didn't know that! Ceridwen asked me about my father, and I answered honestly. Am I wrong to still feel the pain of losing my whole family in one night? The pain of being outcast from my ashrab because no one trusted the daughter of a Wrath-twisted tainted man after that? I was a child, alone in the wilderness, with no kindly friends to watch over me. So yes, I curse my father for what he did, and I curse the tainted parts of him for ruining his mind, and I curse the very Talent in me because it comes from him and I can't bring myself to trust it. But I am here, protecting Ceridwen and Stella both, because I understand they are not my father. I would have hoped you understood me better than that, Colonel. After how many years I've known you, I would have thought you wouldn't question my loyalty so easily."

"I don't question your loyalty, Lieutenant," Rhodrishi said softly. "I know how deeply you love him, over everything else."

Kazrani took a deep breath, and tears gathered in her dark eyes. She swiped at them quickly, turning her face away from all of them.

"I'm sorry." Ceridwen dropped her stick beside the hearth and went to Kazrani's side. She sank down beside the older woman, giving a shy hug. "Please don't fight. I didn't mean to ask a question that made you angry."

"Ah, Ceridwen." Kazrani took another deep breath and returned the hug, laying her cheek atop Ceridwen's head. Such a gift, that child had, bringing comfort to everyone. "I'm not angry. Not with you, or Colonel Kheir. It's part of being hotblood, isn't it? Getting riled up easily."

"What's hotblood?"

"It's a way of life," Kazrani said simply. "Hotblood or coldblood— it's how we build our lives, how we make sense of a world that casts us in all different forms."

"Does he mean Mr. Blackwood?" Ceridwen asked. "You love him, too?"

"Yes, child," Kazrani breathed. "I love him very much. He's like my brother, but more than that, because we found each other at a time when we both felt a little lost."

"He has a knack for that," Stella said. "Of finding people when they're lost."

Kazrani nodded. "I promised him I would keep you all safe. I mean my word, when I give it. It's not right, the Authority sending a man like Siras to hunt you down. I'll protect you with my life. I'll see you safe so that he can come find you."

She dreamt of her house in Cruinnich. Of high ceilings and comfortable rooms, furniture and paintings and photographs everywhere. She dreamt of the little clockwork train her father bought her. He'd built the track himself and commissioned the train from an incredible artist in Yaelsmuir. There was a crank at the back of the engine, and winding it up sent it round, round, round the track. If she cranked it to its full tension, it would run on its track for almost an hour.

It should have been a happy place, that house. It should have been where she could raise her family.

But she'd married Bothain, and he'd invaded her house and her sense of identity, stripping pieces of her soul away with his cruelty. And Siras Duncreek was always around. Leering at her from a distance, edging closer when he thought she wasn't looking at him. But she always knew where he was. To lose track of him meant letting him sneak up on her, meant seeing the predatory smile he had when he made her jump. Sometimes she felt his Talent brush against her, like he was checking her heart, listening to her breathing.

"What's the matter?" he asked. "Are you afraid of me? Do you think you're too good for me, Ffyanwy Rhydderch?"

Best to say nothing when he started asking questions like that. Best to ignore him, to keep busy, because anything she said would make him taunt her more.

"What can I do to convince you I'm not that bad?" he asked, sliding a finger down the back of her bodice, along the line of buttons. His grimy hands would leave stains on the white lace. "I promise, I'm quite charming once you get to know me."

"I'm married, Siras."

He snorted, leaning closer. "I'm sure that doesn't stop you. Do you still fuck Davik Kaine? What about your Pashibé slut? Are you still hiding in the corner of your little hospital so you can fuck her? I like that. I like the sounds you make when she slides her fingers into you, Ffyanwy. One day, I want you to make those sounds for me. Just once—I'm not greedy. Once will do."

"Siras." Bothain's voice cut across the dream, as commanding and powerful as it had been in life. "Leave her be."

"I promise I won't tell him," Siras whispered. "It'll be our secret. We tainted have to stand together."

She woke that night to the sound of Kazrani cursing. Under her breath, in her Jitab tongue, the curses were rough and round and hissed through her clenched teeth. And for a moment, there was nothing but relief that someone had woken her and saved her from that dream—but then she realized Kazrani was leaning over Ceridwen, peeling away some of the blankets, and terror burned through her.

"What?" Stella asked, kicking back her blankets and staggering from her bed roll. "What is it?"

"She's so warm," Kazrani breathed.

"No," Stella gasped, but her legs went weak. How cruel, how terribly cruel, that they should leave Yaelsmuir to keep Ceridwen safe only for her to catch some ugly sickness out here. They'd been so careful, keeping Ceridwen warm and dry. She hadn't shown any symptoms of sickness, either—no cough or chills. How had it come on so suddenly? Stella dropped to her knees at Ceridwen's side, pressing a hand into her forehead. She was warm, and Stella's hands were so cold and damp that the dry heat of Ceridwen's body made her skin ache. "Rhodrishi!"

He came out of his bedroll next, but he didn't have any panic in him. "She's not ill, Miss Whiterock. She's fine."

"What's the matter?" Ceridwen asked, coming awake slowly, blinking at them all. "Why is everyone up? It's still so dark."

"It's only that you're so very warm, Pigeon, and the rest of us are half-frozen," Stella said. Rhodrishi sounded so sure, and Ceridwen sounded mystified, so perhaps things were fine. "Do you feel ill?"

"Ill? No." Ceridwen pulled the blanket up to her chin. "I'm sleepy."

"Remember I told you not to use your Talent, Ceridwen?" Rhodrishi said.

"My Talent? I didn't do anything," Ceridwen whined.

Talent—yes—that was the answer. How had Stella missed it? Rhodrishi had described it as pressure in the air yesterday, but now it was more like a source of heat, bleeding into Stella and warming her from the outside in. "You're supposed to wait, Pigeon. Remember?"

"I didn't do anything, Mam," Ceridwen repeated. The fatigue gave her voice an edge of petulance, and Stella could hardly blame her. The adults had woken her in the middle of the night and were interrogating her. "I only *wished* to be warm, and then I was, and was dreaming about you making bread, Mam. I miss fresh bread. Can we bake bread again when we get to the legacy territory?"

"You wished to be warm, did you?" Rhodrishi asked. "That's your Talent, sweet girl. No more wishing, for now."

"Yes, Rhodrishi." She rolled over, eyeing the hole in the roof where the rain was coming down. "If I can't wish, can we add more logs to the fire?"

Stella didn't sleep anymore that night. It went against all her instincts to be so fearful of Talent. But then, using Talent had a way of shaping the mind—maybe her fear was a scar, like Rhodrishi said, an effect of using her Talent to knot her strength as well as Ceridwen's all these years. Whatever the source, the anxiety kept her awake. Sleep was no refuge anyway. Her dreams seemed determined to keep her vigilant, a constant reminder that Siras was out there.

She listened to the storm for the rest of the night, waiting for it to blow itself out, but it didn't. It was still raining when the sun tried to rise, halting their progress. It was too cold to go out in the rain, so they hunkered down to wait it out.

Panic crept into Stella's mind—what if Siras was right behind them, coming closer, too stubborn to camp during the storm? She tried to relax and enjoy the day of rest; her thighs and her back were certainly thankful for the break from the saddle. But her mind twisted into circles she couldn't control, remembering every miserable encounter she'd had with Siras up until the moment he stepped from the streets in Yaelsmuir and invaded her body with his burning, crushing Talent.

By the time the storm passed, it was too late to venture out. The cottage had hidden bounties, at least—and old herb garden had grown wild, but there were treasures in the tangle. Rhodrishi sent Ceridwen after all manners of medicinal things; his knees and his back were too sore for him to go digging around in the dirt, he said, and the task kept Ceridwen occupied. She looked like she was enjoying the instruction, the mud, the field, the weak efforts of the sun. Rhodrishi pointed her in this direction and that, harvesting mint, comfrey, chamomile. A stand of coneflower yielded withered purple petals and drying seed pods.

A field of vines and withered leaves offered acorn squash, rainwater sitting on their thick green skins. They gathered up as many as they could, bringing them back to the cabin, and then went back out again with a blanket-turned-basket to collect more. As many as they could carry.

They turned the ponies and Rhodrishi's mare out of the barn and into the field beside the cottage, letting them graze.

Rhodrishi rolled a few squash into the fire, the green skin turning black, curls of steam twisting up through cracks as they formed. Stella sank down onto her bedroll, looking at her hands, muddy from cleaning the squash before packing them away in their saddle bags. She couldn't remember a time when she was this exhausted—even working nights at the Facility wasn't this bad. Was it the recovery, the days in the saddle, the hard nights, the emotion, the cold? Or an avalanche of all of it, crushing every last shred of strength from her?

Kazrani came into the cottage, tracking mud across the floor. She didn't look tired. But for the show of emotion last night, Stella had never seen Kazrani look anything other than *ready*. "Do you know what Siras Duncreek looks like?"

"Of course," Stella said, forcing the words past the panic that made it hard to breathe.

Kazrani motioned for Stella to follow and headed back out. Kazrani had a pair of binoculars, and she handed them to Stella as she headed down the road.

"We're going to head up this rise, but before we get to the top, I want you to drop to your stomach," Kazrani said. "And then we'll crawl up the rest of the way. But we have to be quick before we lose the light."

Stella nodded and followed. The wilderness made short order of her travelling clothes' appearance of being *new*—everything was all stained approximately the same mud colour already, and crawling up the hill only served to set the stains better. At least the coat was thick and comfortable, the leather tough enough to survive the rough handling. It occurred to her she'd never had a leather coat before. Her life in Cruinnich meant finer fashion, even when her family was travelling up to the Hand. And her life since she named herself Stella meant she had to spend her coins carefully lest they run out, and a leather greatcoat of such durable construction was prohibitively expensive. It seemed such a stupid thing to think about now, but thinking on the quality of the leather took the bitter edge out of her panic.

"You should see a hill, a few hours away to the south, the one with dogwood on it," Kazrani said. "Do you see it?"

Stella fought to swallow the fear. Her hands shook as she lifted the binoculars to her face, making them impossible to look through. Three days—they'd only been out of the city for three days and Siras was already coming—she shouldn't have left. She'd dragged Ceridwen out into the wilderness for nothing. She should have stayed with Tashué—

Kazrani rested a strong, steady hand on Stella's shoulder, giving it a squeeze. "It's fine, Stella. If it's Siras, I'll stay right here with my rifle and I'll shoot him as soon as he's in range. These old Imburleighs are good to a few hundred yards, and I've always been a steady shot. And then it's over. All I need is you to look and tell me if it's him or not."

Would be that easy—could things could really end here and now? If

Kazrani killed Siras, what would they do next? Go back? Keep pushing toward the mountains?

Didn't matter—first she had to find whoever was following them. It took some struggling to find the hill, the way the slightest shift of movement sent her looking way off course making the binoculars a frustrating tool. But then, yes, she had her eyes on the dogwood again, bright red bark on the backdrop of muted colours. It was unusual for the brushy plant to grow on high ground like that; it was as if these bushes didn't know they were meant to be lowland shrubs and had crept up the hill to get a better view of the world.

"Yes," Stella said finally. "I see it."

"Just past that, there's another hill. You should see something moving —a man, on a horse. The horse is paint: white, brown, and black. Do you see him?"

Stella forced herself to breathe deep and slow, clenching her teeth against the rising wave of panic. She remembered all too well the feeling of Siras's Talent, sliding through her body, burning and squeezing. She'd never felt so hot in all her life, as if he was trying to cook her from within. But she didn't have time to panic. The sun was setting, and soon she wouldn't be able to see so far away, and she needed to know if it was Siras or not.

She found the man on the leggy paint horse. It made her breath catch, putting eyes on a rider out in the wilderness. But—his hair was a curly tangle of black. Even in the failing light, she could find the details of him. His face was broad and tanned, half hidden by his beard, and the collar of his massive greatcoat turned up around his cheeks to protect him from the damp wind. He looked every inch the rugged bushman, his hands scarred, his leather coat stitched with patches on the elbows and the shoulders, his head ducked into the wind, his horse ladened with as many saddle bags as any of their mounts.

"No," Stella gasped, breathing out the tension in a long rush, leaving her body so loose and relaxed, she could have sunk right down into the mud. But then something that felt like disappointment filled its place. It wasn't Siras—so it wasn't over. "That's not Duncreek."

"Are you sure?" Kazrani pressed.

"Positive. Siras Duncreek has red hair, like mine, and his face is angular and sharp. Nothing about this man fits. It's not him—not even if he tried to dye his hair."

Kazrani sighed slowly, tucking her binoculars away. "If you go back to the cottage, I can shoot him when he crests the next hill."

"What?" Stella gasped. "Why? He isn't Siras."

Kazrani shrugged, as if shooting men she didn't know was no great burden for her. "He's following us."

"How can you tell?" Stella pressed. "Couldn't he be merely another man making his way for the legacy territory? People go there to seek refuge from the Registration Authority. Or simply a man with a family somewhere, going home for the winter."

Kazrani shook her head, making her braids dance. "I'd like to believe it is so simple, but he's been trailing us. One man, riding alone on a good horse like that—he should have passed us by now, since he would be able to move faster than we do, even though it's only been a few days. Now it looks like he's headed right toward the cabin."

"That's not reason enough to kill a man," Stella scoffed. "You can't kill him for travelling the same direction as us."

Kazrani gave another long sigh and her shoulders slumped a bit. "I'm meant to keep you safe, Miss Whiterock. Sometimes that means making ugly choices."

"Not this choice," Stella said. "He hasn't done anything. He's just a man on a horse in the wilderness."

"Back down to the cottage, then," Kazrani said. She sounded strangely deflated. Perhaps part of her had longed for an easy answer— one bullet and it was over. "We'll deal with him when he catches up."

8

STELLA
DAY 29

They heard the horse first.

It called to the ponies in the barn, who responded loudly.

Soup simmered in the hearth, and Ceridwen waited eagerly for her meal—Stella half wished Ceridwen would settle in her bedroll and be asleep when the travelling man arrived, but Ceridwen wouldn't retreat to her bedroll without being fed. Stella spent the evening praying the rider wouldn't come, but all those prayers died with the otherwise merry sound of horse conversation. So much of her emotion since Siras came for her was terror, and it was changing her; day by day, it was stripping away all the pieces of her that once had been capable of bravery, or strength, or peace. Kazrani swept up Tashué's big rifle and pressed it into Stella's trembling hands.

"Sit," Kazrani said, her voice a hoarse whisper. "By the fire, facing the door. Rifle ready, but don't shoot unless you're sure we want to kill him. The forty-five packs a mean punch."

"You're going to kill him?" Ceridwen whimpered.

"Only if he's a threat, Ceridwen," Kazrani said. "Sit behind your mam now, out of the way and quiet. That's a good girl."

The bedroll was no shelter. Kazrani pulled her own rifle from her saddle bag, thumbing back the hammer and moving to the window of the cabin. She stood beside the frame instead of in front of it, so the fire wouldn't silhouette her in the open space. The size of the gun made her look bigger; she was short and wolf-lean, but she carried that big rifle with the same natural ease as Tashué when he took his rifle down from atop his wardrobe and cleaned it before handing it over to Stella. And Stella was accustomed to carrying a rifle, but not like Tashué and Kazrani. Whatever came, Kazrani was ready. Compared to her, Stella felt woefully in-equipped.

"Hello, the camp," the rider said, from outside the cabin.

"I know that voice," Rhodrishi whispered, standing beside Kazrani. He had his rifle out, too—Stella had missed the moment he'd retrieved it in her own panic, and she cursed herself for it. The fire gave only murky light, but she should have been vigilant, watchful, aware of everything. "He runs the smugglers' road west."

The smugglers' road—that brought old memories to the surface, swirling Stella back through time. Once, her whole life revolved around the smugglers' road. Somehow it was comforting. Something familiar, something she was used to thinking about. "What's he doing so far south, then?" Stella whispered. "They don't run through Yaelsmuir."

"They do now," Rhodrishi said, forcing the words out in a rush, his urgency giving him more animation than Stella had seen from him since they started. "Davik Kaine forged a road from White Crown to Yaelsmuir to the legacy territory. It's faster—they move a lot of refugees from the Authority to Taint Town. But it's also more dangerous down this way. The Authority patrols this stretch with more numbers than they could ever muster up north. They call this stretch the Desperate Road."

How fitting that Stella should find herself on the Desperate Road, Siras Duncreek nipping at her heels.

"What's a smuggler road?" Ceridwen asked, even as she pressed her cheek into Stella's back. She was trembling, too, Stella's fear infectious, but the curiosity apparently pushed the question out anyway.

Kazrani shook her head. "We'll explain it later, Ceridwen." Her finger rested on the trigger guard of her rifle, the fire crackling softly to illuminate her features as she peered out the window. "How well do you know him?"

"Well enough," Rhodrishi said.

"I won't ask how you know smugglers, Colonel. I think I don't want to know."

Rhodrishi nodded once, leaving the conversation there as he stepped to the door. "Come in slowly, Ozra Sgèin."

Ozra Sgèin. Stella turned the name over in her head a few times, trying to remember if she'd heard it before. Back when she was Ffyanwy and her hospital was a refuge for the smugglers running the road, where they came in knots to rest and barter for medical supplies. But it didn't summon any specific memory, even though Sgèin was a northern name for certain, the sort of name that sounded like the mountains. Sounded like high peaks and pine forests and callused hands.

Ozra stopped in the threshold of the cabin's door. The fire only lit the edges of him, turning him into a silhouette. Broad shoulders that were made bigger by the fur collar of his leather duster. One fist closed around his horse's reins, the leggy painted gelding right behind him on the other side of the doorway. Ozra held his hands up.

"Ain't no need for guns, Rhodrishi. I'm alone. Just looking for a safe place to spend the night."

"I'm sorry, Ozra," Rhodrishi said. "I told Lieutenant Mahalouwan it wasn't necessary, but she's the cautious sort."

"Aye," Ozra said. He took a half step into the cabin, catching a bit more light so that Stella could see his eyes taking in the details of each of them and their guns. Stella must have been the clearest, since she sat the closest to the fire, her body fuzzy with its warmth. He raised his hands, still holding his reins. "Cautious indeed. Are you folks hunted?"

"We are," Kazrani said, watching out the window a while, "so you'll excuse our caution. Are you alone?"

"Aye," Ozra said. "I said I was. Just me and my bloody loud horse. This crofter's cottage is meant to be kept as a safe place for travellers."

"Are you armed?" Kazrani asked.

Ozra nodded. "I've two pistols at my side and a pair of rifles on my horse. A forty-five and a twenty-two for hunting small things."

"You'll hand them all over if you'd like to camp here tonight," Kazrani said. "It's cold and late, but we've meat in our pot and a good fire in the hearth. If you'd like to keep your guns, you can fuck off."

"Och," Ozra said, shifting, raising his hands higher. "That ain't exactly road etiquette."

"She's new to the road." Rhodrishi slung the strap of his rifle over his shoulder. "And she has good reason to be a bit tense. Come in, and I'll explain as much as I can."

"Sure," Ozra said. "You promise she won't shoot me?"

There was humour in his voice, in spite of all the tension in the air. Like being shot was simply a reality of his life. And maybe it was no surprise, if he was a smuggler. It wasn't an easy life. But he was travelling alone, without any pack horses, which struck Stella as strange. He was either carrying something small—letters, perhaps, or money, stashed away in his saddle bags, although they looked a little light. Or he wasn't carrying anything at all, which begged the question: why was he on so-called Desperate Road in miserable weather?

"I can't make promises, I'm afraid," Rhodrishi said, a smile pulling at the corners of his mouth. "Lieutenant Mahalouwan is rather like a gun with a hair trigger. But it's all for a good reason—you'll understand when you come in."

Ozra stood a while, looking at each of them in turn—Rhodrishi and Kazrani, then Stella again. She tightened her grip on Tashué's rifle, trying to summon the steady courage he would have. Ozra Sgèin. There was a time Stella could have guessed exactly where he was born—or at least where his roots were planted in the mountains—from his last name alone, but all those details were fuzzy after being away from the north for so long. Not only away, but also lying to herself about who she was and what she remembered, so she could lie more convincingly when someone asked details about Stella Whiterock's life.

The intensity of his gaze slid off Stella and back to Rhodrishi. "What brings you out this time of the year? This isn't a good time for making runs."

Rhodrishi shrugged, pointing his gun at the ground. "What ever brings desperate people east of Yaelsmuir?"

"If it's so unusual, then I ask you the same question, Mr. Sgèin," Kazrani said. "Where are you headed so soon after a storm?"

"East," Ozra said.

"Don't let Lieutenant Mahalouwan put you off," Rhodrishi said, coming all the way through the cabin. Dismissing Kazrani's question, apparently, but Stella thought it a good question, and she wanted the answer. "She's quite charming under regular circumstances."

Ozra sighed, taking another small step forward. The horse trailed in behind him. He tossed the reins over his shoulder, like that was all it took to keep his horse with him. With his hands free, he opened the buttons of his coat to reveal the pistols, belted above his hips cavalry style, with the grips pointing forward. "The pot does smell good."

Stella glanced back at Ceridwen as Kazrani set about disarming Ozra. The initial fear had drained out of Ceridwen's features and she looked her usual self again—wide-eyed and curious, her mouth the hard line it made when she knew it wasn't the time for her barely-restrained questions. Was Stella the only person gripped by terror every day? She squeezed her eyes shut, trying to swallow the panic. She couldn't withstand this, this haemorrhage of her surety, but Siras's attack was all she could think about. One moment, she was stepping from the Facility of Rest to meet Tashué, and the next Siras was all she could see, and pain was all she knew. Pain and terrible fear—she was going to die, and no one would protect Ceridwen, and Bothain would win.

That moment left its scars in her, tearing her open time and time again as her mind conjured every possible scenario of things going wrong. Was this simply her reality now? Fear of *everything*?

"He's got a very nice horse," Ceridwen whispered.

Stella forced her eyes open. She couldn't defend herself or Ceridwen if her eyes were closed. "Hush, Pigeon."

"If you're looking for more weapons, I've only got the four guns," Ozra said, drawing Stella's attention back to him. He held his coat open as Kazrani's hands skimmed over his body. His hips, his thighs, his back. Kazrani hadn't taken the pistols yet. And they were smiling, the pair of them. Flirting. "But I've a hunting knife on my belt."

"A very big hunting knife indeed, Mr. Sgèin. I'm impressed."

Ozra made a sound halfway between a cough and a laugh. "You're welcome to it whenever you've need of a big tool, Lieutenant."

"I can handle myself quite well without a man's tools, thank you," Kazrani said easily. She'd been ready to shoot this man earlier in the day, put a bullet through him from enough distance that he probably never would have seen her as he lay dying. And now she was flirting. For all that she scowled when Rhodrishi and Stella talked about the smugglers' road, she would fit right in with any of the smugglers Stella had known. All of them, a little in love with the danger, the rush. All of them a little mad for the fear and the victory and the bloodshed. "But maybe I'll take the knife off you anyway. I don't know you from a pile of horse shit, Ozra Sgèin, so I don't know if I can trust your word."

"His word don't count for nothing?" Ozra asked, nodding toward Rhodrishi.

"Not when I've a job to do." Kazrani pulled his first pistol from its holster at his hip, spinning it on her finger before shoving it into the pocket of her overcoat. She took the second pistol, another spin—but she held it up for a moment, catching the light of the fire to examine it. Even from the distance, Stella could see the incredible detail engraved into the barrels. The wooden grips were worn and stained, but they would have been ornate at one point. "Both Imburleighs."

"Expensive Imburleighs," Stella said, just for the sake of saying *something* into the space. For the sake of being present without cowering anymore. Her own voice gave her courage. A reminder that she could speak.

"Aye." Ozra's eyes flicking toward Stella. "Had 'em a while now. Best guns in the world, they say."

"It's true." Kazrani pushed the second pistol into her pocket, the grip sticking out. "They are."

Kazrani stepped around him, knocking her shoulder into his arm as she passed, as if to remind him that she may have been half his size but she was still very much in charge. And she had all of Ozra's attention—his eyes tracked her, his mouth pulled into a half-smile that looked tired, bewildered, but amused. Kazrani paused long enough to give the gelding a scratch under the chin when he turned to watch her, then pulled Ozra's rifle from the soft scabbard hung from the saddle. She turned it around in her hands so the side gate pointed at his chest, racking the lever action and ejecting the bullet from the chamber, sending it flying at Ozra. His hand snapped up and he caught it. Kazrani racked again, again, and Ozra caught each bullet, hands as deft and precise as a juggler. When the rifle was empty, she slung the strap over her shoulder. She had the same smile. Perhaps the bullet catching impressed her.

"Where's the other rifle?" she asked.

"Do you trust me enough to show you without you shooting me, Lieutenant?"

Kazrani grinned. "Slowly."

"Mam," Ceridwen whispered, pulling on the back of Stella's coat. "Why are you afraid of him? Rhodrishi said he was safe."

"Miss Mahalouwan just wants to be careful, Pigeon," Stella whispered. "Until we know for sure."

"The twenty-two is empty. I only use it for hunting, and I ran out of bullets for it a while back."

"It doesn't match the other three," Kazrani said, turning the smaller rifle toward the light of the fire. Another Imburleigh, probably, but it didn't have any embellishment to it at all.

"The forty-fives are a set. Twenty years old or so."

"Then the rifle would be from the early run of Imburleigh repeaters," Kazrani said, her head cocking to one side.

"We've always had access to good guns up north," Ozra said. "Benefits of being on the smugglers' road."

Kazrani's mouth twisted into a grimace, and she leaned away. Her discomfort pulled Stella out of her own panic. It was funny, the difference—Kazrani was so comfortable with the idea of shooting him, killing him on the road, flirting with him while taking his weapons, casually brushing her hand over the buttons on the front of his trousers as if it was nothing at all. But every time anyone said the word 'smuggler,' she flinched—and every time anyone said the word 'smuggler,' Stella felt a little bit more like... like home was within reach. Ozra Sgèin and his mountain name and his beautiful Imburleigh pistols and the horse that followed him like a massive dog. How long had he owned those guns of his? Depending on what year he got them, they may well have passed through Stella's—Ffyanwy's—hospital, right under Bothain's nose. And if he got them before the hospital, when they were brand new, they probably still passed through Cruinnich, through the hands of the gun runners who used fake paperwork from Rhydderch Stone to protect themselves from scrutiny wherever they travelled.

"Have you had enough fun tormenting the man, Lieutenant?" Rhodrishi asked. "Can he see to his horse now?"

"Of course," Kazrani said, stepping away, her voice clipped and short. "He looks tired."

"Aye, I've been trying to make more progress," Ozra said, turning to his horse and loosening the girth. "But Caraid's turning into an old man these days."

"Is that his name?" Ceridwen asked, the curiosity bubbling over in her. "Caraid?"

"It is," Ozra said. He unbuckled his saddle bags, leaving them against the wall beside the door. "Means 'friend' in Dhu-Vèig. He's been a good friend these last twenty years."

"What's Dhu-Vèig?" Ceridwen asked.

"It's an old northern tongue, a blend between Skairn and the languages of Kishoan and Pashibé," Ozra said. He patted the horse's chest, getting him to back out of the cabin.

"My horse's name is Grippni." Ceridwen sat up straighter behind

Stella, leaning into her arm like she wanted to pass Stella and go visit Caraid the horse. "The horse trader said that means 'good luck' in the land where ponies like her come from."

Ozra glanced back over his shoulder as he stood silhouetted in the doorway, giving Ceridwen a soft smile. "Friends and good luck are good things to have on the road, aren't they?"

Ozra stepped out into the darkness, the details of him falling away as he led his horse out to the barn. Rhodrishi sighed, setting his gun down among his saddle bags, shaking his head. Kazrani stood by the window, watching. The clouds had swallowed the sky, smothering any light of the moon. Rhodrishi dragged the pot from the hearth and lifted the heavy lid. A puff of fragrant steam swirled up, the soup still bubbling with the heat of the cast iron pot. In spite of the fear, Stella's mouth watered. The bounty from the garden plots made their simple road soup smell especially delicious. Garlic and onion and sage, the squash cut into chunks and the last of the dried sausage bobbing in the broth. He served Ceridwen first.

"Eat, girl," he said. "No more gawping. It's getting late, and I'd like to cover a lot of ground tomorrow."

"Yes, Rhodrishi," Ceridwen said, but she seemed to be vibrating with the pressure of her unasked questions.

"You too, Miss Whiterock. You need your strength, and Ozra is no threat to either of you."

"Wait for now," Kazrani said, freezing Stella's hands as she reached for the bowl. "Leave your hand on your gun, Stella."

"This isn't the way things are done on the road," Rhodrishi snapped. "This cabin is meant to be a safe place for travellers and I told you he's trustworthy."

Kazrani blew out a sharp breath, leaning on the window. "I've two people to protect, and orders from my Captain. I won't be jeopardizing their safety in the name of the way you think things should be done."

"It's not the way I *think* they're done," Rhodrishi bristled. "It's common decency."

"There's nothing common about our situation, Colonel. Would that I had a company of soldiers, but I don't. There's only me. And I'm old enough and worn enough to know that the only thing common is the capacity for cruelty in people you'd otherwise think are harmless. So I won't be sorry for doing what I have to in order to follow the orders my Captain gave me. Not on this road or anywhere in the world."

"She's right, Rhodrishi," Ozra's voice came from outside. "She doesn't know the road, and she doesn't know me—and she's got the wee one to think about. For whatever it's worth, if I were standing in her boots now, I wouldn't trust me either."

Rhodrishi grunted. He rested the bowl on the floor, near Stella's leg. It curled steam up toward her, asking for her attention, but her hands closed harder around Tashué's rifle. If only he were here. Maybe it wouldn't all seem so hopeless if he were here. When had she gotten so dependent on him for courage? She hated herself for it. Hated him a little for pulling her so completely into him and then letting her go. But even that felt unfair—he didn't let her go, he stayed for his son and that, more than anything else, Stella could understand.

"Don't encourage her, Ozra," Rhodrishi said. "She'll just shoot you to prove she's right."

Ozra laughed at that. He paused in the cabin door and kicked mud off his boots before he hefted his saddle bags and slung them over his shoulders. The simple motion took the last tension out of Stella's chest. The floor was warped, and the rain had left leaf litter and rotten thatch across the floor, but he still paused in the doorway to try to get rid of the mud caked on his boots, and he kicked the thatch out of the way like he wanted to sweep it up but hadn't the tools. It showed more care for the run-down old cabin than she expected.

"I'm hoping that since she's taken all my guns, the inclination to point weapons at me will subside. But it doesn't seem to be working just yet. You should eat, miss. I'll keep my distance."

Stella left her rifle across her lap but took the bowl from the floor where Rhodrishi left it. She needed to eat; they were both right about that. But though the soup smelled so inviting, it tasted of ash when she tried some. Her stomach turned to a hard pit. The fear had released its grip on her, and her hands weren't trembling anymore, but it lived in her gut instead, like she'd swallowed it to get rid of it and now there was no room for food.

"Where are you from, Ozra Sgèin?" Stella asked instead of eating, saying his name slowly and testing the shape of it.

He shrugged, taking the bowl Rhodrishi offered him with a nod of thanks. "I'm from Cruinnich."

"Not with that accent, you aren't," Stella said, shaking her head. "You're from farther north than that, but I can't tell where."

Ozra smiled, resting his bags down and settling on the floor near the hearth, as far away from Stella and Ceridwen as he could get whilst still sitting somewhere dry. "Aye, you caught me. I grew up fishing the Hand. I usually say Cruinnich since no one south of the Gold knows anything about Riguan. I should have heard it in your voice though—faded though the accent is. Whereabouts are you from?"

"From Cruinnich," she said. "Born and raised in the city. But I've travelled some."

"What brings you down this way?" Ozra asked. He ate slowly, savouring each bite, the fire-light painting the expression of perfect bliss on his face. And Ceridwen's strain of curiosity burned to life in Stella—how long had he been travelling? Alone, no less. His hands were ingrained with dirt, and his knuckles were cracked from hard use and dry skin, but he kept his beard reasonably trimmed. What skin on his face that wasn't covered by hair had that tanned and weathered look of a face exposed to elements all year round, making it impossible to guess how old he was. Where was he going, alone, in weather such as this? The question would bother her until she got a satisfactory answer. "If you had a mind to head for the legacy territory, it would have been safer to go 'round up north."

"My daughter and I have been living in Yaelsmuir for a time," Stella said softly. "And now we aren't."

Ceridwen made a noise in the back of her throat, pushing her face into Stella's shoulder again. Perhaps Stella shouldn't have asked and opened the door for Ozra asking in return. She twisted, putting her arm around Ceridwen's shoulders, tugging her closer.

"Whatever the reason is, I'm sorry," Ozra said before Stella could think of some way to fill the silence. "I know it ain't easy, leaving behind what you know."

"So then, you understand why we're so guarded," Kazrani said. She was still by the window, like she half expected someone else to turn up. "It's time to tell us why you're following us."

"It's just that I saw you folks headed off the road, and I wondered if you needed an extra set of eyes on the trail," Ozra said. "You can ask Rhodrishi—I make my living out this way, and I've travelled with him more than once."

"That's exactly my problem," Kazrani said. "You make your living by breaking the law. You're a criminal and a smuggler, helping people escape from whatever reckoning they deserve. And yet, here you are, without any goods to smuggle, in weather you said wasn't fit for travelling, without any people to guide—you're lying about something, Ozra Sgèin. Which comes as no surprise, not to me. People like you aren't to be trusted."

"People like me—" Ozra scoffed.

"Lieutenant, none of this is necessary," Rhodrishi said, cutting over Ozra's outrage. But he sounded angry, too, or at least frustrated, his voice straining more than usual.

Anger rushed hot through Stella's veins, pushing words out before she could think better of it. Kazrani was protecting her, but— "Only someone who doesn't understand the purpose of the law would assume that someone who breaks it can't be trusted."

"The law is for keeping people safe," Kazrani said.

"How could you say that?" Stella snapped. "How could you *possibly* believe that after—" She bit off her words before she could finish that thought, glancing at Ozra. As a smuggler, he probably knew exactly what the law was for. But he didn't know about Ceridwen and what Stella was running from—and Ceridwen didn't know the truth of her parentage, either. One day perhaps Stella would have to explain it all, but North Star help her, not *now*. Not like this. "After everything."

"Right," Ozra said. "I can tell when I'm causing problems. I'll move on. I'll see you next season, Rhodrishi. Best of luck to you. If you'd do me the favour of leaving my guns behind like you said, I'll come fetch them after you're gone."

He turned to go, leaving his bedroll behind and everything—maybe intending to sleep with the horses—surely not under the sky, without shelter, with the weather so foul and wet?

"Ozra, I'd rather you stayed," Rhodrishi said, half rising, but he winced and froze, catching the wall to keep himself steady. "You're right, we could use another pair of eyes on the trail."

"No," Kazrani said. "It's not necessary. I'll leave your guns behind. And if I see you on our back trail again, I'm going to shoot you."

"Kaz—" Stella said.

"Wait!" Ceridwen cried, standing before Stella could even finish a thought. "Please don't shoot him."

"Hush, Pigeon!" Stella half rose, but it was too late, Ceridwen was already moving like she was trying to catch Ozra. She tried to catch Ceridwen, her arm, her hand, her sleeve, anything, but Ceridwen was too fast, too nimble, dodging Stella's grasp like she'd expected it.

And Talent crackled in the air around Ozra like a storm, an angry winter gale.

"Wait!" Ceridwen said again, putting her body between Kazrani and the fearsome muzzle of her rifle, and Ozra's back. "He isn't here to hurt us. I can feel it."

"Ceridwen." The name left Stella's mouth like a breath, a prayer. She didn't dare move too fast in case Kazrani overreacted and fired—in case Ozra and that Talent of his were doing something terrible. "Please, Ceridwen, just come back!"

Ozra turned back to them. That Talent, still crackling, out of control, like some invisible force dragging Ozra and Ceridwen closer together—what was he doing?

Some figure drifted in the Talent. Another person. Except it couldn't be another person, because Ozra was alone, and if Talent had been hiding a whole human body, Stella would have felt it before now, wouldn't she? It was a suggestion of a form, a billow of cloth, a lock of hair. And then it was gone, sunk back into the wild tangle of energy. The storm subsided so completely it was like it had never happened. No one else seemed to notice—Rhodrishi didn't say anything.

"It isn't polite to be rustling around in a man's mind without his permission, wee girl," Ozra breathed. His hand clutched at his own chest like it was hurting him, and some old instinct made Stella's own Talent twitch—was his heart hurting him? Was it a thing that Ffyanwy Rhydderch could have healed? But she held it back. She didn't dare reach out to him, not after the fury she saw in his Talent.

"I never touched your mind," Ceridwen said, her whole eager face pointing up at him. Unafraid of the Talent or the ghost in it—if she had even felt it. Had Stella imagined it in her fresh surge of fear? "I could feel it, coming from you. You aren't here to hurt us, are you? You're here to help."

Ozra's mouth twisted, and Stella didn't know him well enough to begin to define what sort of expression it was. But his eyes, glittering in the light of the fire, looked sad. "I'd like to help, aye."

"Step out of the way, Ceridwen," Kazrani said. "It isn't safe, putting yourself in front of a gun like that. Go on now, go sit with your mam."

"First, promise you won't shoot him," Ceridwen pressed. "He doesn't deserve it. He didn't do anything bad."

Kazrani scowled. "I promise I won't shoot him unless he deserves it. Now sit down, between your mam and Rhodrishi."

Stella took a half step, then another. A sob caught in her throat. If she could get close enough, she'd grab Ceridwen and drag her. Away from Kazrani's gun, away from Ozra and that wild, angry Talent of his before it billowed to life again. Ozra saw her coming and took a step back, giving ground, backing halfway out of the cabin door.

Rhodrishi rose next, slowly, his face pulling with strain. But once he was up, he was imposing, a man who stood with perfect confidence, a man who knew what he was capable of. He put himself in front of the gun next, standing in the middle of them all. Did he not feel the Talent? Had he not seen the figure in it? Perhaps Stella was simply going out of her mind, seeing faces where there were none, the constant fear addling her brains.

Rhodrishi put his hands on Ceridwen's shoulders, pushing her gently. "Go sit now, Ceridwen. You're giving your poor mam a fright, standing in front of a gun like that."

Ceridwen dug in her heels, her hands turning to white-knuckled fists like she was hanging on to the very air around her. "I don't want Miss Mahalouwan to shoot Mr. Sgèin. Why can't he come with us? He wants to come. I can feel it. Can't you feel it? He doesn't mean us any harm."

"And why does he want to come with us, Ceridwen?" Kazrani pressed. "Can you tell that?"

"I don't know. I don't know what he's thinking. Just what he's feeling. Can't you feel it too, Mam?"

"No, I can't," Stella said. "I saw his Talent, though. Did you see it? It's immense. Please, come over here, out of the way, while Kazrani and Rhodrishi and Mr. Sgèin sort themselves out."

"I ain't here to cause any harm," Ozra said, shaking his head. He took another half-step back, but Kazrani's arms twitched like she might just lift that gun and blow a hole through him, and he froze. "I'm sorry if my Talent startled you, miss. I've the Wrath, is all. It isn't any danger to anyone but me. I drift too far from my body, too far out of my own mind. I think one day I'll drift so far that I won't come back, and my body will die without me in it."

"My mam has the Wrath, too," Ceridwen said. "And Rhodrishi said he'd help Mam. Maybe he can help you, too." She swung to Rhodrishi, grabbing his sleeve. "Can you feel it, Rhodrishi? Can you feel his feelings?"

"I could, if I needed to—but I don't need to," Rhodrishi said. "I know Ozra, and I trust him. He's a good man, with a canny mind and good familiarity with this stretch of land. Go sit down now, over by the fire like you were before. Everyone is going to relax, and Lieutenant Mahalouwan is going to put her guns down, and if you're still hungry, you can have more soup."

"I'm meant to keep them safe, Colonel—"

"Yes," Rhodrishi interrupted, his voice hard again. Hard and exhausted. "You are. You're meant to keep them safe from any threat. But Ozra is not a threat. And I'm meant to guide them across the open ground between here and the legacy territory, and I'm telling you, that job is easier with Ozra's help. You've never been out this way, I'll wager —you don't know yet how hard the going can be. An extra pair of eyes will help."

"He's a smuggler," Kazrani said flatly, but the fight was draining out of her.

"Yes, a smuggler," Rhodrishi said. He reached out and grabbed the barrel of Kazrani's gun, pushing it straight down at the floor. "Whom I've travelled with before, because I smuggled goods back across the mountains, too. More times than I can count, with paperwork forged by Captain Blackwood to protect me and my goods. I shouldn't have to justify myself to you, but I'm going to in the hopes you'll stop insulting Ozra—and me at the same time. The Authority imposes incredible tariffs and restrictions on trade with the legacy territory, so we do what we must to survive. I know you don't understand what that's like—I know you believe in the law. It's not an easy thing, to change the entire way you see the world. But just as Captain Blackwood asked you to keep Miss Whiterock and Ceridwen safe, he asked me to be their guide. Just as you love him like family, so too am I bonded to him in ways I can't possibly explain. And even if I wasn't indebted to him, I would still help because they deserve a chance at whatever safety I can help them find. And I'm telling you, one final time, that I need Ozra's help. It's alright, Stella, you can come take Ceridwen's hand—Ozra won't hurt either of you, and Lieutenant Mahalouwan is going to put her gun away."

Stella's feet were so fast and clumsy that she staggered when she started moving again, but she caught Ceridwen's hand and dragged her out of the centre of the adults that loomed around her. And Ceridwen came willingly, letting Stella pull Ceridwen right up against her, their bodies pressing together so hard it must have hurt, but Stella couldn't relax, not with the fear reborn. Redoubled. Vicious and terrible. Had Rhodrishi not seen the figure in Ozra's Talent? Stella might have believed she'd imagined it except she could still see the details in her mind's eye—hair and cloth and almost features—and blood. Drawn toward Ceridwen, Stella was sure of it. It was no drifting that she saw. It was a presence. Hadn't Rhodrishi seen it?

Ozra exhaled slowly, his hands relaxing from his chest, but he still kept them hovering like he wasn't sure where to put them to keep Kazrani from shooting him. "What's happened, Rhodrishi? What are you running from?"

"My mam was attacked by Siras Duncreek back in Yaelsmuir," Ceridwen said, her voice trembling still, clutching Stella back as hard as Stella clutched her. "He's been chasing her a long time, and I didn't know. And she got badly hurt and I don't want anyone else to get hurt, not like she did, so I don't want Miss Mahalouwan to shoot you."

"That's good of you, Ceridwen." Ozra said Ceridwen's name slowly, like he was testing the cadence of it. He mimicked the way Stella said it instead of passing too quickly over the syllables like Kazrani did. "But I don't need you to protect me. Rhodrishi is right—you shouldn't put your body in front of the business end of a gun. I'm sure Miss Mahalouwan would never hurt you on purpose, but accidents happen, and guns aren't things to trifle with."

"Let's try to get some sleep, Pigeon," Stella said. "It's late, and we've missed a day of travelling. We'll be up early in the morning, won't we? To get further down the road like Rhodrishi said."

"I don't want her to shoot him, Mam," Ceridwen said in that whisper of hers that wasn't quiet at all. "He's here to help."

"I know, Pigeon. You've done a good job protecting him, haven't you? They're going to settle down, all of them, and we'll sleep. And in the morning we'll have it all sorted and we'll get moving again."

S tella lay in her bedroll and listened to Ceridwen's soft snoring, but she listened, too, to the whispering. They were talking about her, the three of them. They kept their voices low and chose their words delicately, explaining to Ozra that they were running from Siras. That Stella was still recovering from her wounds and they could only move so fast. But they needed to move before the weather blocked them. Needed to pray a bit that the weather hadn't blocked them already, trapping them here in this cabin, only a few days' ride from the city.

Kazrani walked away, which must have been the ultimate concession for her. She went out into the night to keep watch, leaving Ozra behind with Stella and Rhodrishi. Accepting that Rhodrishi spoke for his trustworthiness.

Rhodrishi came to her, crouching slowly beside her bedroll so he could whisper to her without disturbing Ceridwen. "Ozra has some things to say about our route, and you should be the one who decides."

Stella nodded, gathering up her blanket to bring it with her to shield her from the cold. She stood too quickly, and all the blood drained out of her head, leaving her listing. Rhodrishi caught her, holding her steady as white emptiness passed in front of her eyes, bright and blind, her hands grasping at nothing because they were so far away she couldn't feel her fingers.

"I'm sorry," Stella breathed.

"None of that, Miss Whiterock," Rhodrishi said. He crouched down to pick up her blanket again, draping it over her shoulders. "My patient won't be apologizing for her body struggling to heal. Take your time."

Stella squeezed her eyes shut until the feeling was gone, moving slowly, placing each foot gingerly. They didn't go far, at least. Ozra stood in the overhang that connected the barn to the cabin.

"I'll only ask you to hear Ozra's opinion with an open mind—he knows this stretch of road better than I do. After that, the decision is yours. I'll stay true to my word to help you wherever you decide to do. And I'm certain Lieutenant Mahalouwan will protect you, no matter what. But since it's your future, and Ceridwen's, I thought you should be given final say about which direction we go."

"Alright," Stella said. She looked in Ozra's general direction, not that it did her any good with the darkness so thick. But she could hear his low, steady breathing and feel the general presence of him. "I'm listening, Ozra Sgèin."

"Rhodrishi said he was hoping to get you folks to Taint Town, and you'll cross the mountains there, into the legacy territory."

"That's my understanding, yes," Stella said. "Rhodrishi wanted to go home, and he was very kind to guide us."

Ozra sighed, and Stella could hear the creaking of his leather coat as he shifted his weight. "Trick with getting to Taint Town from Yaelsmuir is getting past the Bright Garrison. They run patrols, trying to catch folks out in the open. Rhodrishi chose this route 'cause it's fast, but it ain't safe. Especially with the wee one. She's plenty brave, that's for damned sure, but Rhodrishi said this is her first time on horseback and, well... Best way to run the Desperate Road is to ride like a wildfire's chasing you. Fast as you can, sleeping in the saddle, only stopping when the horses need rest. No cook fires, no camps."

The words opened yawning dread in Stella's chest. It wasn't hot and wild like the panic. It was cold, precise, and sure. She didn't know exactly what was wrong with her, but she knew she wouldn't survive any more than a few days of travel like that.

She shook her head, but Ozra surely couldn't see her. "I can't—"

"I know," Ozra interrupted, his voice gentle and sad. "Rhodrishi explained it. There's no shame in it, Miss Whiterock. We go at whatever pace you and the wee one can manage. That's why I was wondering if we ain't better off going another route. Best way is to go 'round. Through the Dunnenbrahl, until you're north of the Garrison, and then cut east. Or hard east from here until you're in the mountains proper, and then wind your way south or north to the good passes."

"That's the way I usually go," Rhodrishi supplied. "Hard travel. And neither route is fast. A few weeks in good weather. More this time of year, especially with how wet it's been."

Weeks. The prospect was almost as bad as riding hard and fast. Weeks in the insufficient bedroll, weeks of camping and thin soup made of forage. That would take them well into winter. Weeks of rain, then snow and ice.

"In all likelihood, we'd be snowed in before we made it far," Ozra said, following the same line of thought that made Stella so cold with despair. "Winter's as good as here. It's only a matter of time before the first big snow storm hits, and then we'll be stalled wherever we are until it's clear enough to travel again. But that ain't such a bad thing, really. Surviving winter is slow going, aye—but it takes patience. Finding good shelter, stocking up supplies while we can still see the ground."

"What are you suggesting, then?" Stella asked. "That we stop somewhere, or that we push on?"

"Well, that's why I'm askin' you," Ozra said. "It's all for you and your girl. We can risk the Desperate Road, move as fast as the pair of you can manage. Or we can slow down, take the long roads. Or we stop somewhere for the winter. There's good places on this side of the river, you could hunker down and last all winter on forage and trade if you'd rather be alone out here. Or there's plenty of logging camps in the Dunnenbrahl—I work a good camp every winter, and we'd find 'em in about a week if the weather is kind to us and we turn around now. Two weeks if the bloody rain keeps hitting us. But compared to months? Old Callum runs a safe camp, and your Ceridwen would have other children around. The wee ones, they do laundry and help cook and take care of the chickens and learn to repair tools—all the small jobs that lets the rest of us work the bush."

"Did Rhodrishi tell you about her Talent?" Stella asked. She couldn't tell if the thought of spending the winter with other people was comforting or terrifying. Perhaps she was too tired to feel anything that required that much intensity. "It's quickening, and I can't hide it anymore. Anyone with Talent will feel her strength."

"Aye, he told me. You needn't worry about the folks in the logging camp. Callum... well. He don't ask too many questions. Neither does anyone else."

Clouds drifted, revealing the face of the moon. Its light danced on the thatched roof and the wooden walls of the cabin, the barn. On Ozra's shoulder and the fleece collar. On Rhodrishi's iron grey hair. For a moment, Stella let herself believe that this was the extent of her reality. People reduced to only the vaguest of details, close enough to touch if she wanted but so far away.

"They say the Dunnenbrahl is haunted," Stella said.

"Aye, they say that. The wise logging camps work carefully."

Stella tried to focus on the details of Ozra's face, but the darkness kept them hidden. "What about Siras? It's only a matter of time before he finds me again. And if we're only going as far as the Dunnenbrahl, that time will be short."

Ozra sighed again. He kicked something on the ground and Stella could hear it skitter off into the darkness. "I know Siras, curse my foul luck. His Talent isn't especially strong. He won't be tracking you with Talent—he'll have to use bushcraft for that."

"Is that supposed to comfort me?" Stella asked. Something like anger and resentment flared to life, but it was half-numb and far away. Was this her Wrath, whispering her emotions right out of her, turning her empty? "I imagine bushcraft is one of his skills. The Duncreek is a hard place to live, and he's travelled plenty, hunting folks for Bothain Clannaugh. And he's an excellent shot. If he had any discipline, he'd be a marksman for the military, but Bothain never expected him to follow rules of decency like the military would, so he took his Enquiry badge. I once heard him boast that he prefers killing up close. He likes to watch people's eyes when he's hurting them." Laying each fact out felt terribly like reciting an incantation spell for her own doom. She closed her eyes again so she didn't have to see pity or horror in these men's eyes as she hurled out of numbness and back into her sharp panic.

"I know all that Miss Whiterock," Ozra said gently. "My point was more that I agree with you—he'll find you eventually. He won't stop at the borders of the legacy territory just 'cause the laws say the Authority can't cross those lines. Borders ain't never been much of an obstacle for the Authority. They want someone bad enough, they'll chase you to the other side of the world. So, why not go somewhere with other folks who ain't got no regard for the Authority? Somewhere not all that far away, where folk'll protect you when Siras comes into camp looking for you."

"Why would they do that for me? They don't know me."

Ozra shifted, leaning against the wall. The moonlight caught the hair of his beard, tangled black and weather-worn. "Loggers take care of their own. If you work the camp, they'll protect you. And then in the spring, if you still want to head east, I'll lead you."

"And why would *you* do that, Ozra Sgèin? You don't know me either."

"Why would I protect two people from Siras Duncreek? Because it would be an honour, Miss Whiterock."

Stella turned back to the moon. Wisps of clouds passed in front of its glowing face, rubbing the details away for a while. Dimming the light. Near a decade ago, she'd made a decision to run alone. To fold herself into the anonymity of Stella Whiterock and disappear. Any number of people would have come with her if she'd told them she was running. She could have lived on the smugglers' road. But she'd made the choice to go alone. She couldn't bear the thought of other people getting hurt for her. Couldn't bring herself to look people in the eye and admit to them everything that was going so horribly wrong. The burden of shame was too heavy, making it impossible to explain to the people who loved her how all her hopes and dreams had turned to dust under Bothain's cruel hands.

But now she was surrounded by people anyway. After so many years of being alone, she'd gathered something like a family to herself by accident, by falling in love with Tashué Blackwood. She didn't know Kazrani or Rhodrishi, but they loved him and that love was gifted to her by extension. And Ozra came along with Rhodrishi, apparently.

Sadness swept through her, though if someone asked her why, she couldn't explain it.

"We told Tashué we were heading east," she said, her voice barely above a whisper. If she talked about him too loudly, the sadness might swallow her whole. "That's where he'll go, if he follows."

That *if* was too awful a word.

"If you decide to settle somewhere, one of us can go down to Yaelsmuir," Rhodrishi offered. "Myself or Lieutenant Mahalouwan. Or even Ozra. He knows his way around Yaelsmuir." The moon shone on his shoulders enough to show his shrug. "We'll sort it out once you've made a decision and you're as safe as we can make you."

Stella turned away from them both, looking west. Toward Yaelsmuir, toward the sprawling Dunnenbrahl. If she let Ozra turn her around, would she ride straight back to Yaelsmuir? Back to Tashué. The entirety of her body screamed yes. Go. Run right back to him. It was a mistake to leave. The entirety of her body screamed no. She had to get away from Siras. Had to protect Ceridwen.

"Can I give you my answer in the morning?"

"Aye," Ozra said. "Sleep on it."

Sleep. If only that would be how she spent her night.

She stepped out from under the overhang, watching the west a while. The moonlight danced on the road that led them to this little cabin. The same road that led Ozra to them.

"I was worried about you, Ozra," Rhodrishi said. He didn't try to pitch his voice low. He didn't mind Stella overhearing or reminding her that they were still there in case she needed them. "No one saw you on the road this summer. Some folks were wondering if you'd gotten yourself killed finally."

"Ah—no. I brought some folks up north, to the outpost south of Cruinnich. They're always looking for more hands, and that family needed a place to go that's more permanent than the logging camps. I can take you and Miss Whiterock that way in the spring if you want. If you still want to make it across to the legacy territory, crossing north of the Gold is safer. It'd be a long journey, though. Took me a few months to come back down this far."

North of the Gold. Sweet North Star, how she longed to be north of the Gold again. Maybe it was time. Kazrani could go back to Yaelsmuir and tell Tashué where to find her. She'd been gone ten years—so long as she stayed out of Cruinnich proper, she probably wouldn't find anyone who recognized her as Ffyanwy anymore.

"What brought you all this way back down?" Rhodrishi asked. "I thought you were from up that way."

"I am but… well. I don't stay up there anymore. I don't know why I came this far," Ozra said. "Couldn't explain it if I tried. Usually I'm looking for Callum by now, but here I am. Just felt like the right thing to do. Like I was being pushed this way, or pulled."

Stella looked back over her shoulder, watching the moonlight kiss the pair of them. "Don't let Kazrani hear you say that, Mr. Sgèin. She'll shoot you for certain."

Ozra laughed. "Wouldn't be the first time. Although with that big Imburleigh she's got, it'd probably be the last."

"Are you always so cavalier about getting shot?" Stella asked.

Ozra shrugged again, stepping out of the overhang and turning his face toward the moon. It smoothed his features, making him look younger than she'd first guessed. "I don't know. Life ain't exactly what I expected. More than once, I looked death in the eye, thinking it would be the end of me. But instead, I just keep living. I ain't always sure what to do with the time I've got."

Stella didn't know what to say to that. The realization that she could relate came in slow, uncomfortable layers. Were it not for Ceridwen, she wouldn't know what to do with her time, either.

"When you were up north, did you pass through Cruinnich?" she asked instead of thinking about time. Talking about Ffyanwy again reminded her how much she missed that city.

Ozra shook his head. "I ain't been to Cruinnich in years."

"My youngest son has settled there now," Rhodrishi said. "Or somewhere near it. He won't say exactly where, at least not in his letters. He was out west on a Qasani poppy farm for years, but something happened. They were forced to leave. He says revolution is coming."

Ozra kicked another stone, sending it skittering through the soggy grass. "Everyone always says the revolution is coming. Wishful thinking, mostly."

"I know," Rhodrishi said. "I've been around a lot longer than you, and I've heard it a thousand times over. But travelling for the military means I've also seen it. The growth of it and the way it consumes a country. I think, in some way, it's already started here. In the shadows and on the smugglers' roads. In the places the Authority can't quite reach and so they resort to wanton cruelty. My son has seen it, too. He probably knows even better than I do, since his career was in politics, rather than healing in the aftermath."

Stella shook her head, heading back into the cabin. She'd listened to talk of revolution her entire life, and it hadn't come yet. Best not to let herself get swept up in the idea of it, not this time. For now, there was only Ceridwen.

9

STELLA
DAY 30

"I thought you were trying to go home," Stella said. She spoke as quietly as she could, to let Ceridwen sleep as long as possible. It was still dark out. Rhodrishi had banked the fire high to get the soup simmering for their breakfast. "That's why you were headed east."

Rhodrishi sighed. He didn't say anything a while, rolling up his blankets to be ready to pack them back into his saddle bags. She watched his hands—the deep age lines in them, the rheumatic swelling his knuckles, the way his ishani tattoos shifted every time he moved. She knew the story of how Tashué and Rhodrishi came to know each other; Rhodrishi had healed Tashué more than once during Tashué's years of service. And yet she couldn't help but wonder how they came to be so tied together, so that they took such risks for each other. Tashué had forged paperwork for Rhodrishi; she had to admit it came as a surprise. She'd thought him so rigid. The moment he'd signed her paperwork had seemed such a terrible burden for him. But there were cracks in that foundation of his already, apparently. Perhaps the strain was less the paperwork and more... everything else. All the ugly truths he'd learned. Her leaving even though something beautiful was coming to life between them.

"Whatever you decide, I'll go with you," Rhodrishi said finally, placing each word slowly into the space between them. He settled on the floor beside her, using a stick to cluster the coals closer to their pot of soup. "You're right that I wanted to go home, but…" He closed his hands into fists, making an old but deep scar stand stark between his knuckles. "I've often wondered about children like her. The very notion of the Breeding Program always sat foul in my heart, but I never imagined how terrible the reality was. And then I heard the things you and Tashué had to say… and here she is. Now's my chance to do something. She's worth it, Stella. Helping her is worth more than dying on the wrong side of the mountain."

"Dying on the wrong side of the mountain?" Stella echoed.

Rhodrishi spread his hands. "I don't know how much time I have—it could be any day now, or it could be a while still. It's all so uncertain."

"What is it?" Stella asked. "Can we help you? Ceridwen's so strong already—is it cancer? Once we're settled, I can try to teach her to help you. I worked in the hospital for years, and I learned so much from the people I've known."

Rhodrishi shook his head. "The arteries around my heart have been thinning. I've been working on it, but… well. I keep trying to repair them, but then they go again, faster and faster each time."

"Healer's heart," Stella said, her stomach sinking. There was nothing to be done for a healer's heart, not really. They could delay the inevitable, but time was already running out.

"What's healer's heart?" Kazrani asked, crouching between them. She was packed already, her blankets and Ozra's guns rolled together and strapped to her saddle bags so she could mount up quickly. The lost day of travel seemed to be driving her out of her own skin, and the clear weather meant she would have been out the door already if Stella knew where they were going.

"It's common when healers get to be old like I am," Rhodrishi whispered. Ceridwen shifted and Rhodrishi glanced at her, but she wasn't waking—her snoring rose in volume as she settled flat on her back. "It's the strain of it all. If we work carefully, it's less likely, but the Army likes things done *their* way, and their way is too… restrictive to allow Talent to flow properly. I worked around their guidelines as much as I could, but…" He shrugged again. "These things happen."

"What a curse Talent is," Kazrani whispered, her mouth pulling into a snarl. "You spend your whole life saving people's lives, and this is what you get in return. A failing heart."

Rhodrishi bristled, anger rising to the surface in an instant, so much faster than last night when they were arguing about Ozra. "What a curse your Authority is, that it's taught people to fear and resent the power to save lives. No one lives forever, Lieutenant. I turned seventy-three this year. If it wasn't my heart failing, it would be something else. But those laws you've trusted all your life, they told you to curse my Talent when it was the only thing that kept scores of people on this side of life. Tashué Blackwood was one of them. If you hadn't brought him to me when you did, none of us would even be here now because he would have died. How old was he in those days? Nineteen? Twenty? My Talent gave him over twenty years so far, years he wouldn't have seen otherwise and a son that wouldn't have existed if he'd died. Don't look me in the eye and curse my Talent. Not after it's given *you* so much."

Kazrani shook her head, turning her face toward the fire. Outrage and compassion warred for supremacy in Stella's chest. She knew that far-away look, when the eyes focused on something long gone and the heart was trapped beating in a time where everything had changed.

Rhodrishi sighed. "He's the same age as my boys, did I ever tell you that? And I remember when you and your Sergeant brought him to me —I wondered where his parents were. Wondered if they knew where we were deployed. I got a letter from my youngest son while I was working on him. Eilas had gone to the Officer's Academy, but he loathed it. All of his letters had become a list of all the ways the Academy misunderstood Talent and Dominion history. I tried to tell him that these were the things we learned to accept—the rest of his brothers went through the Academy, like I did. But he's never been one to accept anything, that boy. Just like his mother." He shrugged, looking down at his tattoos again. "With my son's letter in my hand and Tashué Blackwood in my hospital tent, I wondered how many Pashibé soldiers had been devoured by the Army. There's so few of us. It seemed meant to be. Talent does that. Draws us together without us feeling it work."

"You knew he was Pashibé when you met him?" Stella asked.

"I thought it was possible. His name—One Who Sees. And Blackwood—the land around Yaelsmuir, it used to be called the Black Wood, and so a lot of families chose it as their last names as an anchor to how things used to be. And of course, that Talent of his. I could feel it even back then, dormant in him. Waiting. I knew if it ever quickened, he would be incredible." Rhodrishi shook his head, looking down at his hands, at the ishani tattoos on the backs, at the marriage tattoos across his palms. "There was a time I hoped to die near Yaelsmuir. On the land that was the Black Wood. The hill that the Imburleigh factory stands on was once our burial field. If I died there, I thought I would get to rest among my ancestors, and it gave me comfort for a time. But the more I went back, the more I felt... I didn't want my bones to rest beside the foundation of the Authority. House One, where the worst laws were written. So then, I thought I would go north to Cruinnich. That's where my wife died. Or east, across the mountains—to the wrong side, the only side left to us. Two of my sons have settled there, and they've grandchildren now. I don't feel old enough to have great-grandchildren. But in the next breath, I feel so impossibly tired that death doesn't seem so terrible. Resting. Sinking back into the flow of Talent where my wife has gone before me. We all die eventually, and I miss her. But then, I met you. And her." He looked toward Ceridwen, a bit of a smile turning up the corners of his sombre mouth. "I can't change the past. I can't undo the damage the Authority has done. But I can help to save a gift of a child, who was given a chance at life by a brave young woman who sacrificed everything to save her. And that's something. I mean it very earnestly when I say wherever you go, I'll follow. Make your choice for her. She's worth it. I like to think it would make my wife incredibly proud to know I've finally taken a stand for something."

Stella wiped the tears from her eyes with trembling hands. They'd gathered quietly while she listened to the gentle cadence of Rhodrishi's voice, but this emotion wasn't exactly grief. She couldn't name what it was. But not grief.

The unmistakable sound of someone chopping wood invaded the silence—each strike of the axe snapped through the cabin. Ceridwen stirred again, this time the snoring coming to an abrupt end. Stella turned her face away from the fire, hiding her tears in the long shadows behind her as she fought for her composure.

"Is there soup for breakfast?" Ceridwen asked, rolling from her blankets. "I'm hungry."

"Can't recall a time you haven't been hungry, dear girl," Kazrani said, rising to her feet. Her voice softened when she spoke to Ceridwen, filling with patience and joy. "You're like my boy, when he was your age. No matter how much I fed him, he couldn't ever be filled up to the top."

"You have a son?" Ceridwen asked, rubbing her eyes. "I didn't know that. Where is he?"

"He's in the military now. He was over in the Derccian Empire, fighting for the Crowne, but I expect he'll be rotated home soon. It'd be nice to meet him in the Hadia, if I can. Maybe in the spring, once the pair of you are safe and settled, I'll head out that way."

"Is it far? To the Hadia?"

"It's the other side of the Dominion," Kazrani said. The longing in her voice was all too familiar—it seemed the lot of them belonged to families separated, drawn apart by too much distance and too much time. "But it's worth the trip to see Tevir. Fetch your comb for me, sweet girl, and we'll fix your hair."

Ceridwen nodded, rising to her feet and retrieving her comb from her saddle bag. She settled in Kazrani's lap and it made Stella's entire body ache. Ceridwen had so much love in her little body, so much trust. Where would she be safe? Could Stella find somewhere for Ceridwen to have some measure of happiness?

"How old is your son?" Ceridwen asked.

"Twenty-six," Kazrani said, using the comb to pick tangles out of Ceridwen's hair. A residual knot of stress twisted through Stella at the prospect of someone else fixing Ceridwen's hair, but she fought to ignore it. Kazrani knew about Ceridwen's tattoo and why she had it. That horrible number that Stella had seen so many times that the shape of it was imprinted in her soul—1232-0579-5453. Her mother, her father, her. For the first time since running, there were people Stella didn't have to hide from. She wondered if Kazrani studied the numbers when she combed Ceridwen's hair, or if she ignored them. Pretended they weren't there. "And he's got his daughter with him, too—she's just turned five. A spring baby, like Tevir. Back in the Hadia, they say the babies born in the spring are the ones with the most energy."

"I was born in the winter," Ceridwen said. "What do people say about babies born in the winter?"

"Winter babies are steady old souls. I think that's about right for you, Little Miss Whiterock."

Stella pushed herself to her feet, as slowly as she could. Her joints ached with the incremental movement, but it was better than the dizzy spell she would invite by standing any faster. The sun lit the distant horizon, spilling its first rays down the road and into the space between the barn and the cabin. Ozra's coat and heavy knitted sweater hung from the eaves on the roof between the two buildings. Sleeves rolled up and boots sunk into the mud, he split cord wood with a massive splitting maul and a single downward stroke. His forearms were adorned with tattoos, and more peaked out from his top hem, which hung low around his neck without a collar on his shirt to keep it in place. With the speed of each movement, it was impossible for Stella to discern any details of the ink.

He spotted her watching and paused for a moment, turning toward her to show he was listening even as he set up a fresh round of wood on the chopping block.

"How would we cross the river?" Stella asked. "Do we have to go back to Yaelsmuir?"

"Ah—no. I've always avoided that city as much as I can, so I know my way around it." He brought his maul up, over his head, then down with force and precision. The wood jumped apart as if it had been waiting for the axe to cleave through it. He kicked the smaller piece toward the pile he was making, bending to retrieve the bigger piece. "There's a mill town that runs a barge across. This time of year, they'll be running all day long, getting folks to the Dunnenbrahl side to fill the camps." Up, down, split. Sweat beaded along his collarbone in spite of the cold. He blew out a heavy breath, pushing his hand through his hair to get it out of his face. "I take it you've made a decision?"

Stella sighed, emptying her lungs completely in the hopes it would let the dread out. "I'm putting a lot of trust in you and your logging camp."

"I know." He kicked both pieces toward the pile and grabbed a fresh round. But he paused, resting the head of his maul on the toe of his boot to keep it out of the mud, his earnest eyes sweeping over Stella's face. "It ain't easy, what you've been doing. And I'm sorry you've been doing it so long. Rhodrishi told me—nine years, near all of the wee girl's life. I know it changes the way you see the whole world. Turns everyone into a threat, turns every choice into a terrible burden. I hope I can help you find some peace."

His compassion almost took the air out of her lungs, but it was better to speak than to let herself sink down into emotion again. There wasn't time. Now that the sun was up, they needed to get going.

"How long have you been running?" she asked instead.

"Longer than I expected to," Ozra said. He sank his axe into the chopping block and started gathering up the split logs, stacking them against the cabin wall to replenish what they'd used. "I thought the Authority or the wilderness would have gotten the better of me by now. But I haven't been running as long as you."

Stella nodded. "To the Dunnenbrahl, then. Maybe we'll both find some peace."

"You'll lead the way," Kazrani said, when Ozra explained the route they would take. North for a while, and then west, and they'd cross the Brightwash at the mill town in a few days. When he said it, it didn't sound like such a terrible thing. It didn't sound impossible, like the prospect of the ride to Taint Town. "And if I don't like what I see, I'll put a chunk of lead through your back."

Ozra hauled himself up into the saddle with all the grace of a man accustomed to living on horseback. "What've you got, a forty-five?"

"Yes."

"Aim for the back of my head, then, if you don't mind. That way, short as you are on your wee pony, the bullet will pass through me on an upward trajectory and you won't hit poor old Caraid, too." The leggy paint's ears flicked toward Ozra at the sound of his name, and Ozra patted the horse's neck. "He's a fine old horse, if a touch stubborn at times. He'll serve you well if you decide you're done with me."

Rhodrishi only sighed at them, kicking his roan mare out onto the road, leading Ceridwen's pony with the guide rope. "When you're done threatening the man, Lieutenant, you're welcome to catch up."

Ozra winked at Kazrani before turning Caraid toward the road, kicking the paint into a trot to pull ahead of Rhodrishi. Kazrani gave a shout that sounded like a battle cry, kicking her pony hard and sending it tearing off after him. Caraid took off after her, throwing up clods of mud as both horses pushed to a full canter. Caraid's long legs let him overtake the pony in no time. Rhodrishi's mare tried to follow, but he hauled hard on her reins, drawing her to a complete stop so Stella could catch up.

"I daresay they're made for each other," Rhodrishi muttered, sounding both amused and exhausted in equal measures.

"My mother would say, cut from the same cloth," Stella said. "I think she's starting to like him, in spite of herself."

"If she likes him, how come she keeps saying she'll shoot him?" Ceridwen asked.

"Soldier's humour," Rhodrishi said, kicking his mare into a walk again. "When you've lived a life built around violence, these things don't seem so terrible."

"I hope she doesn't shoot him," Ceridwen said, her voice thin. "I don't want anyone else to get hurt like Mam did."

"I'm sorry, Pigeon," Stella said. "I wish I could tell you it won't happen again, but it's dangerous out here. There's no telling what will happen."

The silence that stretched was terrible, but Stella told herself that offering a hard truth was better than a comforting lie that the world would prove untrue.

Stella lost track of which direction Ozra led them, but he cut across the growing foothills, climbing higher and higher, and then forest swallowed them. The track went up and up, twisting around rock and root, up and down slopes that couldn't seem to decide whether they were mountains or hillocks. They passed more than a few spots where the trail passed close to a sprawling colony of aspen trunks, leaning so low over the track that travellers had gone wide around them, cutting a new track through the forest and abandoning the straighter path to the trees.

The forest was never quiet. The wind passed through branches and the last dry leaves, leaving an ever-present rattling. The air tasted humid and cold and heavy with the scent of all the loam and moss and slowly rotting leaf litter.

On a good flat stretch between hills, they kicked their horses faster, teaching Ceridwen to post to the trot. It took longer than Stella would have liked for her muscles to remember the rhythm of posting. How long had it been since she'd ridden a horse? She bounced miserably for a while, but then, suddenly, she got it—she stood in the saddle as she bounced up, stayed up there for one beat, and then lowered herself back down. She knew her thighs would ache after this, but the speed felt good —felt like they were actually accomplishing something.

"Mam, Mam, I'm doing it!"

"Good job, Pigeon!"

As soon as she said it, of course, Ceridwen lost the rhythm and started thumping miserably against the pony's back. But she found the rhythm again and she looked so natural in the saddle. Kazrani had braided her hair in a more beautiful plait than Stella could ever hope to master, and her back was straight and proud, her heels down like Kazrani had been teaching her. The road twisted east, up a rise, and a forest loomed in the distance, evergreens standing like emerald statues among bone-white branches of the tangled aspen. For this one, beautiful moment, there was no fear.

"Excellent, Ceridwen!" Kazrani called, her pony trotting along behind Ceridwen. Her voice was breathy and bright and so filled with joy. "Tug the reins now. Just a bit at a time. Don't haul on Grippni's mouth too hard, just tug and tug until she slows down. That's a good girl!" Kazrani rode her pony beside Ceridwen, reaching out and rustling Ceridwen's hair. "Well done, Ceridwen. Some people take days before they get the rhythm of the post. You did an excellent job, my girl. You'll be an expert horsewoman in no time at all."

Ceridwen beamed.

They camped next to Greene's Creek—that's what Ozra Sgèin called it. Stella liked hearing him say it, liked the heavy way his r rolled in *Greene's*, lingering on the letter for a long time. She liked the way he said *girl* when he spoke to Ceridwen, breaking the word into two syllables. *Gir-rl*. His voice sounded like the parts of home she had forgotten to miss, the human things that took root among mountains and stone. She missed the streets, the rough cobbles and the shops that lined the boulevard on the way to her hospital. She missed the sound of the river—the Gold was slower and wider than the Brightwash, at least where it passed through Cruinnich, and river traffic was a riot of noise and colour and smells. She missed the festivals for solstices and equinoxes and harvests—they were completely different in Cruinnich, more focused on the cycle of agriculture the people of Cruinnich were so utterly dependant on since they were so far removed from industry and trade. Cruinnich was the largest city in Fuar, and yet it still felt like a small town compared to Yaelsmuir.

She missed the languages she'd left behind. She missed listening to the smugglers speak to each other; Pashibé or Kishoan or the old Skairn —from which Stella's family descended, at least the side that wasn't from Lledewydd—or even the Dhu-Vèig, the hybrid blend of all three of those languages. The streets were filled with musical lilting rhythms of each of them, hawkers and vendors and shop keepers and all the many food carts that bobbed along the cobblestones and floated on the river. She missed the way the Gold froze over all winter and the food stalls switched from boats to little on-ice huts, and people could ice-skate from one to the next, savouring all the flavours of winter.

She missed her house. The one she grew up in, the one filled to bursting with happy memories—her parents, her sister Aelwyd. Kona, the healer's daughter, who lived with the Rhydderch family. They grew up together, Kona and Ffyanwy, their relationship shifting and morphing with time and age until they were some inextricable mix of family, friends, lovers, twin souls.

She missed her son. He may have been Bothain's son, too, but Rhion grew in her body and nursed from her breast, and she loved him more than she ever thought possible. She missed the future she thought she was going to have. She missed the version of Davik Kaine before everything went so horribly wrong. She missed Ffyanwy Rhydderch.

But even if she went back now, so many of those things she missed wouldn't be there. Her parents had died while she was Stella Whiterock. Kona was killed by the Authority, driving her and Davik half-mad with grief. Her son—killed by his own quickening Talent. And Davik, down in Yaelsmuir. Perhaps angrier and more dangerous than ever.

Ozra led them to a stand of trees, and they camped beneath the sprawling branches of a massive weeping willow near the bank of the creek. The yellow leaves made a soft carpet on the ground, and a cleft between a rock and earth and a jutting, gnarled root gave them a place to build a fire that would hide the light from view of the thin farmer's road they'd been following. The relief she felt at climbing down from the saddle was undermined by dread of the dreams waiting for her— Bothain and Siras waiting to torment her with the memories of what they'd done to her, Tashué waiting to taunt her with the reminder of what she'd left behind.

The figure again—she swore she saw it, out of the corner of her eye. Movement in the gathering dark as Ozra busied himself with laying a fire and getting their nightly meal heating up. Someone stood between Ozra and Ceridwen. The energy wasn't wild and angry like the last time. It was simply there, a presence in the air like lingering perfume. But when she turned her face toward it to get a better view, it was already gone.

"Do you have your own pot or kettle, Ozra?" Rhodrishi asked. "Our pot is taken by the soup."

"Aye," Ozra said, finding his kettle among his saddle bags. "Making tisane, then?"

Rhodrishi nodded. "Miss Whiterock could use it, I think."

Ozra emptied his canteen into his kettle. Rhodrishi dropped in the leaves from the nettle plant he'd pulled from the ground, handling them carefully to avoid the sting of them, and then went about peeling the dirty skin off a bundle of dandelion taproots, dropping little chunks of tender root flesh into the water.

"Trying to get more iron into Miss Whiterock?" Ozra asked.

Rhodrishi filled the kettle with his waterskin. "You know herbalism."

Ozra nodded. "My mam's a healer, up north. Always said it was best to use hand and herb if you could. Talent was to be a last resort."

"A wise woman, your mother," Rhodrishi said, brushing his hands together.

"Aye. She's popular with folk up that way. Ain't shy to put a man in his place, ain't afraid to get her hands dirty."

Rhodrishi set the kettle into the flames. "Good qualities for rugged land like the Hand."

"Hope she's still up there helping people. Ain't seen her in years."

"It's a very particular kind of longing, when you haven't seen your family for a long time," Rhodrishi said softly.

"Is Sgèin your mother's name?" Stella asked. "Has an old Skairn sound to it. Maybe it's why I feel like I know you."

"It is, and my mam's family is Skairn like you said, from the old settlers that came up all that time ago. My da's family is Kishoan and Skairn blended. My parents married the Kishoan way, and my mam's got her Kishoan warrior tattoos—fully adopted by my father's folks. They met running the old smugglers' road, same way just about anyone meets up north of the Gold." Ozra shrugged, the firelight playing in the lines on his face, making them look deeper. Making him look terribly sad. Making the air around the camp feel heavy with regret and all the people they all longed for. Even Ceridwen was quiet. "I hope they're still up there."

A particular kind of longing, indeed.

10

STELLA

DAY 31

The prospect of climbing into the saddle for another day of travel filled Stella with dread. Her back hurt, her legs hurt, and the trail wound on and on without an end. It hadn't yet been a full week since they left Yaelsmuir, and it both felt like an eternity and like time was passing too fast—they hadn't gotten far enough in the days they'd been travelling, but Yaelsmuir seemed so impossibly far away. Stella tried to comfort herself with the knowledge that they weren't going much farther. All they had to do was get across the Brightwash, and then into the Dunnenbrahl.

Ceridwen watched Greene's Creek with intensity as they rode. A splash rippled over the surface of the creek, and then another. "Mam. Mam! Is that a fish jumping?"

"I don't know, Pigeon," Stella said. "I didn't see."

Another splash, and Ceridwen squealed with delight, dropping the reins to clap her hands together. "It was! It was a fish! Look, did you see, Mam? A fish *did* jump!"

"Are you wishing again, Ceridwen?" Rhodrishi asked.

"I'm trying not to," Ceridwen said, and her voice wavered. "I was just thinking it would be nice to see a fish, is all, and then one jumped, and I wanted to see another for sure."

"You need to be more careful, Pigeon," Stella said softly. "We don't know who else is out here with us—we don't know who can sense Talent when we use it."

"Wishing, is it?" Ozra asked. "That's some Talent, little Miss Whiterock."

"I didn't mean to," Ceridwen pressed, her voice gone petulant again. She was usually so easy to guide, but the fatigue of travel paired with trying to avoid her wishing was clearly wearing on her patience. "I just wanted to see—"

"Sit up straight, Ceridwen," Kazrani called. Either she didn't hear, or she was looking to shut off the argument. Either way, it felt a blessing. "Heels down, watch the trail. If there's another flat stretch, we'll trot again."

"Yes, Miss Mahalouwan," Ceridwen said, forcing her heels down. "What kind of fish are in the creek? Are they big?"

"Depends on what you mean by big," Ozra said. "Greene's Creek has plenty of brook trout, and they can get mighty big as far as stream fish go. Some of these little offshoots are shallower and muddier, and they'll have brown bullhead. Nothing like in the rivers though—pike and muskellunge, they get proper big. Need good fishing line to catch them. Where we're crossing, there won't be too many big things, what with the river traffic. But we'll follow the Brightwash a while to get to the camp. Maybe we'll go fishing and you'll see, hey?"

Ceridwen only nodded, her attention wandering down to the creek again. Perhaps she was thinking about fish. Trying to convince herself not to wish to see them jump. And it seemed terrible, taking that wishing away from her. Perhaps it was a mistake to tell her to stop. If Siras couldn't feel Talent from long distances, maybe they could teach her a few little things to keep the restlessness at bay.

"What was it like to fish the Hand, Mr. Sgèin?" Stella asked. Perhaps if she started the process of asking questions, it would give Ceridwen something else to think about for now.

"Ah, it was cold," Ozra said. "And there were a lot of grizzly bears."

"Grizzly bears?" Ceridwen asked, swivelling in her saddle, her eyes wide again. It was good to see her so delighted and curious.

"Aye," Ozra said. He pulled a plug of salt beef from his saddle bag and tossed a piece to Ceridwen. "They're attracted to the river when the salmon are spawning. They wade right into the water like we did, scoop the salmon out with their big paws. Or catch them out of the air when they're trying to jump up the waterfalls. You learn to live in peace with them. But carry a big gun, just in case."

"Did *you* ever see a grizzly bear, Mam?"

Stella smiled. "Only from afar. My mam knew how to keep them away, with her Talent. She wouldn't let them get anywhere close to us, but we saw one, with her cubs, fishing in the river. And my sister said the cubs were sisters like us, and she named one Aelwyd and named the other after me."

"I didn't know you had a sister," Ceridwen said softly. "Was it nice, having a sister? Is she my aunt?"

"Yes, it was nice, and yes, she is your aunt. If the North Star smiles on us, you'll meet her one day."

"I never had a big family before," Ceridwen said and her voice was thick again. "I always wished for a big family. I wished for a da, and then Mr. Blackwood said he'd like to be my da, but now we're out here and I miss him. I'm sorry, Mam, maybe I shouldn't have wished, but I wanted a da to play with me like Gil's da did, and Mr. Blackwood played with all of us. I thought it would just be so nice to have a big family. I know you tried your best, Mam, I'm sorry—it's just that it was lonely sometimes. And if Mr. Blackwood was my da, then Jason would be my brother, wouldn't he? And you have a sister so I have an aunt, too—I *have* a big family, but I don't get to see any of them and it's not fair."

Stella couldn't breathe. Couldn't think. Couldn't feel her own body, except for the tears that stung in her eyes. She hadn't known Ceridwen was lonely. But of course she was. Stella worked and slept and barely survived because she was so exhausted. So numb. Of course a child as vibrant and energetic and friendly as Ceridwen would crave more.

"Ah, girl," Ozra said, and his voice was smooth and soothing. He rode his horse up beside Ceridwen so he could lean a little closer to her. "I know how you feel. It's hard to be out in the big world sometimes, muddling through. I know things are hard now, but this is only a moment in your life. Life does that—it goes up and down, back and forth. Sometimes things are easy, sometimes things are hard. They're never quite what we imagined, either. But you've been lucky, meeting good people. Maybe you don't have a da like you said, but there are people here for you who love you. Lieutenant Mahalouwan, and Rhodrishi—they're your road family now, and road families are a special kind of family."

"It's true, Ceridwen," Kazrani said. "We're here to take care of you. Captain Blackwood is my family, and so now you are, too. You're been so brave and so strong—you'd fit right in back home on the Hadia. I'm honoured to know you, sweet girl."

Stella squeezed her eyes shut, trusting her pony to follow along. Perhaps she never should have left Yaelsmuir. Perhaps she should have stayed, and trusted Tashué and Kazrani to protect her.

It was too late, now. North. And then west.

———————

"Thank you for what you said to Ceridwen today," Stella whispered. Ozra had harvested sunchokes from a clearing they'd passed, the knobbly little roots holding on to so much dirt they had to wash them in the creek. "I didn't realize she was so lonely. I should have known—she's always been so friendly, even when she was just wee."

"Some folks were built to be around people," Ozra said. "My sister's like that. She was always getting herself into trouble because she wanted to be in the middle of things. Got us into trouble a few times, too."

"How many siblings do you have?"

"There's six of us in all. I'm the eldest, and then I've three sisters and two brothers. The youngest would be coming up on twenty now, I suppose. Wee Brodie. He was still a baby when I saw him last—just turned three, I think. Still had fat cheeks and dimples on his fingers." He shook his head, cupping a hand and darting it across the surface of the creek, sending a spray of water across the shallows. Like he needed to release some tension in his body, needed to watch the water dance. "We all grew up on the smugglers' road. Where we lived was a few days' ride from a big trading post. We did salmon fishing in the autumn, but my da's family, they were all smugglers. Every last one of them. Like they were born with it in their marrow. All us learnt to do our part, one way or another—either running with the smugglers, or helping at the trading post, or harvesting healing supplies from the wilderness with my mam's parents. It's a good life. Dangerous, sure. But this whole country is dangerous for the likes of us."

"Will you ever go back?" Stella asked. "It sounds like there's plenty of people waiting to see you again."

Ozra sighed, scooping up the cleaned sunchokes and setting them aside. "Do you know what threadwalking is?"

"It's like scrying, isn't it?" Stella asked.

"Scrying?" came Kazrani's voice as she approached. Of the entire party, she was the only one who didn't look tired. She walked with such confidence, such energy, springing into her horse's saddle every morning, keeping busy long into the night. "Do you mean to tell us you're a fortune teller, Mr. Sgèin?"

"Kaz," Stella sighed.

"What?" Kazrani asked, crouching beside Stella. "I don't know. Scrying isn't exactly an Authority assignment. How am I supposed to know?"

"It's not fortune telling," Ozra grumbled. "The world and everything in it is woven together like fabric. The ability to reach into the fabric and see the threads and feel the shape, or even change them, is what we call Talent. If you use Talent to make fire, you would reach into the fabric and take hold of a thread of heat and focus it in your kindling until flames caught. The same for all of the things we change with Talent— we're shaping the threads. How much shaping we can do depends on how powerful a person's willpower is, how deeply they can concentrate, how well they understand the world and what they're toying with."

"Sure," Kazrani said. "But that doesn't explain scrying."

"Threadwalking," Ozra corrected. He leaned back, shaking the water off his hands. "Threadwalkers train to see threads and study them. First we learn to see the present. You can stretch across this whole world and see anything if you understand how to see the whole fabric without getting overwhelmed. And then you learn to walk the past. You can follow a thread backward. I could pluck your thread right up, Lieutenant, and walk your whole life. I can see the day you were born, and the day your parents were born. The further you travel, the harder it is to focus on the details. It begins to fall away, the threads blurring together so they become less distinct. I was only starting to learn when the Authority took me."

"So, what, you can look at my whole life?" Kazrani asked, her voice gone stiff and resentful. Stella couldn't blame her. Was Stella's own pain so easily observed? Did Ozra see the moments that lived in her soul like a cancer, changing the shape of her no matter how much she tried to hold on to herself? "Seems a little intrusive, doesn't it?"

"Aye, it does. Which is why threadwalkers are selected carefully and trained to respect the privacy of others before they're taught to walk the threads. And I can't do it now anyway—I've the Wrath."

"Fantastic," Kazrani muttered.

"It ain't a threat to anyone but myself," Ozra said, his voice gone hard. "The Authority learned about the threadwalking, sent me down into the mines to find veins of gold. I went out of my mind down there in all that darkness, all that stillness. I lost myself a bit—bled right up into the mountain until I couldn't feel my own body anymore. Apparently, one day I just started screaming, and they couldn't make me stop. They dragged me out and reassigned me. My Wrath, it don't do anything but make me drift."

"You were going to tell us why you haven't gone home yet," Stella cut in. She didn't dare let herself imagine how ugly things would get if Ozra ever found out Kazrani was a tinman.

Ozra exhaled slowly, blowing the tension right out of his body and flicking the surface of the water again. "Before I was captured by the Authority, I was starting to learn to walk the future. The future is the hardest to walk, because none of it is certain. There's no one thread, so much as everything that came before it splintering into all the possibilities. What we see is open to interpretation. And mood. Threadwalkers spend a long time learning who *we* are as individuals and what scars we carry, so we can understand how we interpret potential threads. I didn't have time to finish my training—I hadn't even finished learning to walk the past. But I look anyway. Or I did, before the Wrath got so bad I couldn't look at all anymore. The Authority took everything from me—I wanted to know if I could go back home, once I got away from them. But any time I walk a thread that takes me home, I see death and pain and the Authority. I don't know. Maybe the Authority follows me north. I had Enquiry Officers hunting me for a time, before I put a bullet in each of them."

"But Ozra, you just said you can't know for certain," Stella said. "And your interpretations change based on what you see. Couldn't it be that you're only seeing your own fears and not the real future?"

Ozra shrugged, wiping his cheeks in sharp movements before plunging his hands back into the creek like the ugly cold of the water was a comfort. "If it was your family, would you go back if there was even a chance your presence could cause them suffering?"

She didn't argue. He was right. She would go back to her sister—the only family she had left—in a moment if she knew for sure that Bothain and Siras wouldn't make them both pay for it.

"Why've you got Enquiry Officers hunting you, Mr. Sgèin?" Kazrani asked. Her voice had lost the hard, judgemental edge, at least. "What have you done?"

Ozra scowled. "They're hunting me because I escaped the evil place they were keeping me. The only things I've ever done were done in self-defence because they don't think the likes of us are human. You won't make me feel guilty for a single bullet, Lieutenant. No matter how much you scowl at me."

"We should get these back to the fire and start on supper," Stella said, gathering up the sunchokes and piling them in her arms "Before Ceridwen withers away from imagined starvation."

Kazrani didn't press the question. She helped Stella gather things up instead, pushing the little roots into her pockets and following Stella away. "You don't want to know where our guide comes from?"

"He come from the Hand," Stella said. "He comes from a place so wild and so dangerous, it sets your bones differently. He comes from a life where Talent is treated as a gift instead of a thing to be ashamed of, and he was caught by the Authority for it. I know all I need to know, Lieutenant."

11

ILLEA

DAY 33

Nathaniel Wolfe's new hospital was a marvel of modern amenities merged onto the ornate architecture of an age gone by, decorated with craftsmanship that was centuries old. It was built when Yaelsmuir was only on one side of the river and Brickheart was the richest quarter. Records showed that the building had been built by the Winter family, and Amias had loved the gothic arches, the gargoyles framing the windows, the incredibly dramatic doors.

Illea watched through the carriage window as they approached the red brick building from behind. The crowds had already gathered in front, so Nathaniel's driver took a circuitous route around to the rear courtyard. The stately brick sent a pang of longing through Illea's chest. Had Nathaniel thought about Amias while the renovations rolled through the building? Perhaps Nathaniel had chosen this building for his hospital because of the link to Amias's memory. Amias would have loved the pageantry of it all. One of the biggest, most ornate buildings in Brickheart—second only to the courthouse a few blocks away—being turned into a hospital that was on target to receive extensive funds for charity work. Nathaniel had been working on this project since Eirdis Redbone was Mayor, inspired, he said, by the legacy of the long missing Ffyanwy Rhydderch.

"The pregnancy is unexpected," Illea said. Nathaniel was adamant that Ishmael needed to know everything so he could help, but it felt strange to say the words out loud. "I'll do my best to keep it. Of course, there's only so much I can do to guard against the whims of fate and my body, even with a healer's help, but this is what I wanted. Certainly not under these circumstances, but this is the hand I've been dealt, as it were, so I'd like to move quickly."

Ishmael watched her with bleary, tired eyes, but there was a sharpness to him even in his ragged state. "You're concerned that it gives Myron a reason to stay if he finds out? A hook to keep pulling more and more from your estate."

Illea nodded. Bless him for understanding so quickly. "It's not his, of course, but since we're married, any child I bear while the marriage contract is still valid is technically his ward and property."

"Whose child is it?" Ishmael asked.

Illea swallowed the reactive fury that tried to bloom. "I appreciate that you're trying to get a full picture before you offer advice, but does it matter? The child is Winter."

Ishmael's eyes flicked to Nathaniel's face, a silent question passing between them. The cart hit an especially deep hole in the road, rattling them all. Ishmael's whole body went too far left and he barely caught himself before his head hit the carriage wall. He grimaced, squeezing his eyes shut. Feeling the pain of his hangover especially acutely, no doubt.

"You could always kill him," he said.

"Ishmael," Illea huffed. "Be serious."

"It ends things rather neatly for you, doesn't it? No more bickering over estates, no more combing over contracts for loopholes. He can't claim custody over your child if he's dead, can he? A nice neat end to this election, too. People can't vote for him if he's dead, and his Deputy Governor isn't popular enough to beat Eirdis."

Illea shook her head, looking to Nathaniel. He usually pulled Ishmael into order when he was being foolish like this. But something dark crossed in front of Nathaniel's eyes, something hard and unforgiving— sweet North Star, was he actually considering it?

Was it such a terrible idea?

The carriage rounded a corner and Oskar, Nathaniel's driver, shouted to a passing carriage, pleasantries of people who knew each other. A timely reminder that though they felt alone in this carriage, there were people on the other side of the thin wooden walls. Perhaps not the best time to contemplate spousal murder.

"Is Colonel Kheir going to be part of the grand opening?" Illea asked, changing the subject as their carriage rolled into the courtyard finally, joining those dropping off other wealthy guests. "Having a Hands of Bronwynn recipient involved would make for excellent press."

Nathaniel gave a small sigh, fidgeting with the ribbons adorning his dress blues. He still looked angry, though Illea couldn't quite guess why. "That was the intention, but unfortunately he had to leave rather suddenly. He's been having troubles with his health, I think. I suspect he's anxious to go home before the weather makes travel impossible."

"How did your grand opening turn into a political event for Myron?" Ishmael muttered. He had his trilby hat tipped low so the brim shaded his eyes, no doubt defending himself against the sun since he was obviously teetering between being still drunk and being hungover. "Shouldn't you have Eirdis running around, being charming and giving speeches? Brickheart will have a lot of votes for her."

"Eirdis will speak after the opening, once people have started drinking," Illea said. "That's her best crowd."

"I tried to keep Myron out of it," Nathaniel grunted, "but since he's Governor, he did technically give provincial money to the project. If he's reelected, I'll have to work with him for the rest of my term, won't I?"

Ishmael scowled. "If you'd campaigned more aggressively against him, you wouldn't have to make so many contingency plans for working with him."

Nathaniel huffed, tapping the head of his cane against the wall beside him. "Let's not do this again, not now. We deal with the reality we have, and not the one we wish for. I didn't know, earlier, how vital it would be to move aggressively against the pair of them, and now we're stuck. If you would be so kind as to climb out of the bottle like I keep asking you, we can talk about all the unexpected problems in front of us."

The carriage came to a stop before Nathaniel could answer. Illea pushed her hands into the pockets of her velvet overcoat to help her resist the urge to lay her hands over her navel. Since learning of the pregnancy, her hands always wandered there, as if she could touch her child.

"I'll meet you out front when it's time for speeches," Nathaniel said.

Ishmael shrugged. "Is Captain Blackwood coming?"

Nathaniel pushed the door open, stepping down first. "He'll be around eventually. Behave yourself."

"Yes, General," Ishmael said, unfolding his long limbs from the carriage, leaving the hat behind. "I'll do my best not to call Myron an idiot to his face."

"Oh, please do," Illea said. "It would be delightful to watch him splutter for a while. Perhaps he'll get so flustered that he'll forget his speech and hemorrhage votes for looking like he's drunk again and then we won't have to resort to drastic measures."

Mallory came through the courtyard, wearing her military dress uniform, sky blue for infantry and a braided black velvet sash for the artillery attachment, the Imburleigh Armament Company logo made into a patch on her sleeve. She looked so natural in it, like she preferred her uniform to anything in the current style for wealthy women. She always looked so stiff in petticoats and bustles and bodices, no matter how flattering they were to her figure, but she wore those dress blues like a second skin.

Mallory linked arms with Illea, kissing her on the cheek. Ishmael was already ahead of them, and Mallory seemed perfectly content to let him walk away without greeting him.

"Did you read the announcement from White Crown this morning?" Mallory asked, her voice flushed with excitement. The best thing about Mallory was her willingness to skip all the insipid greeting rituals and small talk to jump right into business when she had something on her mind. "The Queen sent it out to every newspaper in the Dominion, I hear. All bidding for the rail line is closed already and the Queen will announce the contract in the new year."

"Of course I read it," Illea said. She walked with Mallory into the hospital, where refreshments were being offered in a large event room on the ground floor. It was quieter in the event hall, since it was only open to donors from Highfield and Highview, but the crowd was still thick with the excitement. People had taken rather more interest in political function since Illea's banquet. "I have it memorized. I could recite it word for word, if you like."

Mallory grinned, plucking a glass of chilled apple cider from a circulating tray. Illea took a glass, too. The rich sweetness slid down her throat like velvet, and her stomach seemed pleased with it. The nausea from earlier had passed for now, but she should eat again soon. It was too crowded here for her to afford even the slightest slip in her composure, especially with how people were watching her.

"We should recite it together," Mallory said. "I thought she would have a decision sooner than the new year. Do you know why there's been a delay?"

"You didn't hear this from me," Illea said, dropping her voice low.

Mallory leaned in until there was hardly any space between them, their shoulders pressing together. "Why? What have you heard, Illea?"

Ishmael drifted back with a glass of brandy in his hand, as if it wasn't ten o'clock in the morning. He must have an extra sense for when secrets were being whispered. Illea hooked her arm into Ishmael's elbow, guiding both Mallory and Ishmael out of the busy room and into one of the empty hallways, finding an alcove for them to crowd into.

"Our Queen's health hasn't been... what it was," Illea said softly, glancing down the hall. It was empty for now. "She talked about it some while she was here, but only in confidence. The trip to the Commonwealth was especially taxing on her, and she's been struggling to recover."

"Is that true, or are you trying to start rumours?" Ishmael scoffed. "She seemed perfectly healthy to me."

Mallory huffed. "When did you have the time to examine your patient, Dr. Saeati?"

"After the banquet, General Imburleigh," Ishmael said, smiling sweetly. "She invited me up to her room where I had the opportunity to study her breathing and her heartbeat and her overall energy levels. As usual, I was very pleased to serve my Liege lady."

Mallory's cheeks flushed deep red. "You're a pig."

"You *asked*. What did you expect me to say?"

"Perhaps something a bit more respectful about our monarch instead of acting like she's just another conquest for you to brag about."

"Ah, I see the cause of the misunderstanding," Ishmael said. "You think I'm bragging but I'm only commenting on her health as I observed it when she invited me to her room to entertain her for the night. If I was bragging, I would mention how often and vigorously she orgasmed while she was sitting on my face, but I know conversation like that makes you scowl at me so I thought I'd leave those details out."

Illea leaned against Ishmael, catching his attention. "She's scowling anyway, darling. Perhaps you should behave yourself like Nathaniel asked."

Ishmael rolled his eyes like a petulant teenager, sipping his brandy. He was especially surly today as he often was when he fell into his drinking binges. "What makes you think our Queen is unhealthy?"

"She said as much, and my healer confirmed it," Illea said.

"She honestly seemed fine," Ishmael pressed. "I would have known if she wasn't feeling well."

Illea reached down, catching Ishmael's wrist. He genuinely seemed concerned, which was rather touching. Or perhaps he felt guilty for not noticing anything while he kept the Queen up half the night—her servants had whispered all the details to her after Blackwood left the next morning. They could hear the fuss from the hallways, though they admitted they hadn't been able to hear whatever Ishmael and Leony whispered about when their voices pitched low.

"She's been intent on hiding it, which of course I understand," Illea said.

"If you understand, why are you spreading the gossip?" Ishmael interrupted.

Illea scoffed. "It's not gossip. It's business. If it affects the rail line, my business partner needs to know. And I am certain neither of you will spread what I've said, or have I misjudged you, Ishmael?"

"You're hilarious, Illea. A regular comedian."

"The brandy is making you cranky, love," Illea said. "Perhaps you need to find an empty bed somewhere, and Mallory can tuck you in for your late morning nap."

"Does she have any idea the cause?" Mallory cut in. "She's so young—"

"I know," Illea said. "About the same age as the lot of us. She's been working with her healers to try to discover the cause—Tilde thought her blood pressure was alarmingly low while she was here, but then Leony said she was feeling fine. And clearly none of it was enough to stand in the way of a night of good company."

"Excellent company," Ishmael corrected.

Mallory's flush only deepened and she drank from her glass of cider as if trying to hide, but it was no use. "Ishmael, honestly."

"General Imburleigh, honestly."

"One of these days, Ishmael, you'll have to prove to me that assertion is true," Illea said.

"I'll send over my calendar," Ishmael said, swirling his brandy in his glass. He looked Illea in the eye and something strange crackled in the air—or perhaps that was simply Illea's body, making every waking moment uncomfortable these days. Perhaps it was the way he said *you could just kill him* so casually, and she wasn't as appalled by the suggestion as she knew she should have been. "We'll make an appointment in the earliest availability."

"I'm surprised at you, Illea," Mallory said. "You aren't usually so taken with the antics of men."

"Mallory, the antics of men are endlessly amusing to me," Illea said. "If I surround myself with men people love to gossip about, then everyone is busy talking about my sex life, and no one is anticipating how my stunning proposal for the very first nationally sponsored rail line has already won the bid."

"Oh gods, we're talking about lumber *again?*" Ishmael muttered.

"You're welcome to find yourself some other entertainment, Mr. Saeati," Mallory said stiffly. "The adults are trying to discuss business now instead of your sex life."

Ishmael bared his teeth, his expression surprisingly savage considering it was a usual round of the patented Ishmael-Mallory-bickering. "Have a lovely day, General Imburleigh."

With that, he stalked off, leaving Illea and Mallory alone in the alcove. It was for the best, given his mood.

Mallory forced a smile, smoothing out the front of her jacket to try to hide the way the interaction had rattled her, but her eyes trailed after Ishmael as he slid into the crowd. "Will you be going down to White Crown yourself when the announcement comes down?"

"Of course," Illea said. How far advanced would she be in her pregnancy by then? How long did she have before it started to show? "I would be most honoured if you joined me. I wrote to Miss Rhydderch, too—since she's in Obisza for your factory, she's going to try to make it down to Yaelsmuir in time for the three of us to travel together."

"Alistair is quite pleased with her and her help," Mallory said. "I think he'll be sad to lose her company."

Illea cocked an eyebrow at Mallory. "You think so?"

"Don't look at me like that, Illea Winter," Mallory muttered. "Aelwyd Rhydderch is happily married. Everyone knows she's devoted to Bruce."

Illea rested a hand gently on Mallory's arm. "Would Alistair Imburleigh call himself happily married?"

Mallory sighed, her attention drifting toward the crowd in the event hall. "I think he would, yes. Perhaps not if you asked him five years ago, but now—yes."

Illea took Mallory's hand and gave an affectionate squeeze. "I'm happy to hear it. Truly. I can think of no one more deserving of a happy marriage than you, after everything."

Mallory squeezed Illea's hand right back. They didn't need to speak to *everything*. The city had spent years gossiping about how Mallory and Alistair seemed on the verge of a divorce, and the Imburleigh board of investors had made things worse by hiring solicitors to protect the company if things went that far. Not that Alistair had ever been the type to chase after conflict or money that wasn't his. All the attention on his marriage and his finances had nearly ended things, as Mallory told it. Though she'd never told Illea what the initial source of the conflict was, what had driven them apart in the first place.

Illea followed Mallory's gaze—she was still watching Ishmael. He flirted with a stunning young man Illea didn't recognize, the pair of them standing close together and touching each other's arms in not-so-subtle ways. Ishmael leaned in to whisper something in the man's ear, and the man blushed wildly. Ishmael must have been feeling better now that he'd gotten some brandy into his system, and had the attention of someone who liked his antics.

"Did you sleep with him?" Illea asked. "Is that why he annoys you so much?"

Mallory bristled, glancing up at Illea. "Couldn't it be that his crudeness and his general disrespect irritate me endlessly?"

"I don't know, Mallory," Illea said. "That's why I'm asking. He's rather like Langston, I suppose."

Mallory sighed, leaving the alcove. "There's too much for me to do during every waking moment of the day for me to waste time gossiping about Ishmael Saeati. Even so, I would still say he's nothing like Langston. For all of Ishmael's flaws, at least he takes his family business seriously. They're considering the benefits of building a second factory to keep up with the demand."

"Here in Yaelsmuir?"

"I'm not sure exactly, but Mr. Saan was very interested in our surveys of Obisza."

"Obisza is about to be a boom city," Illea said, her mind twisting away into business prospects. "When's their next election? Do you know?"

Mallory shook her head. "I know they ran a Mayoral election while I was there... hmm. Two years ago? It was the first time we were trying to break ground; I'll check my diary for the exact date. Their Mayor died unexpectedly in a drowning accident and they called an election to replace him since the Deputy Mayor was also rather unwell at the time."

"Isn't Obisza landlocked?"

"It is, but they've an old quarry where they hold harvest festivals and the like. It was a terrible mess."

A familiar voice rolled through the crowd, drawing Illea's attention. Bothain Clannaugh had a natural inclination to making his presence known, even in a room as crowded as the hospital event hall. He looked excellent—he'd put on weight since last Illea had seen him, breadth sitting well across his shoulders and his chest. He had beautiful gold hair and startling blue eyes like Amias, and now he had a military dress uniform and gold General's stars on his chest, but that was where the similarities ended. While Amias had been a beacon of joy, lit from within by energy and scattered dreams, Bothain was stone. Cold, immovable. Passionate in his own way, but never a dreamer. Ruthless. A little dangerous. Exciting.

"I didn't know General Clannaugh was coming," Mallory said.

Illea drained the last of her cider in her glass, eyes searching the crowd for Ishmael. She caught his eye and tilted her head at him, hoping he'd come back. She hadn't expected Bothain to come to Yaelsmuir either, but if he was here, he would probably want to meet Nathaniel, and Ishmael was best at convincing Nathaniel to do things he didn't like. "Rainer never said anything about it—perhaps it was unexpected."

Mallory headed toward the crowd like she was intending to meet Bothain in the press of bodies, but Illea surreptitiously caught her hand, holding her back.

"Stay here," she said, turning her back to Bothain. "Let him come to us."

Mallory smiled, squeezing Illea's hand. "Illea Winter, are you trying to make a good impression on General Clannaugh?"

Illea gave the smallest of shrugs. "It's good to have the attention of powerful people."

Mallory's smile faded. "Be careful with him, Illea. I know he's very charming. But…"

"I know," Illea said. "A missing wife casts a long shadow."

Mallory nodded, but footsteps behind Illea forestalled any answer. "General Clannaugh," she said, standing straighter. "I didn't expect to see you here. I thought you were in White Crown waiting for deployment."

"I've been released to come lend my voice to Rainer's campaign until I'm properly needed with the 12ᵗʰ," Bothain said. And what a voice it was. The deep timbre of it sent a shiver of pleasure down Illea's spine. He shook Mallory's hand with all the reverence Mallory Imburleigh deserved. "And how fortunate I am, to be here in Yaelsmuir with such incredible company. It's a pleasure to see you again, General Imburleigh. I was honoured to have you attend my graduation."

"I have to commend you for receiving the gold stars, General," Mallory said, and she was no stranger to accepting that sort of deference from men who were easily twice her size. She may have been short in stature, but she was unintimidated by men as a general rule. "The testing is most rigorous."

"I was fortunate to have an excellent tutor in General Maes," Bothain said. "I'm sorry I wasn't able to make it in time for the event at the factory a few days ago. I hear you made a rousing speech for Myron's police force."

Mallory forced a smile, but Illea knew her well enough to see the strain in it. Mallory wasn't especially invested in Myron having his stupid police force, but the board had written the speech they wanted her to recite, and she'd had no choice but to get up on that stage and give it her entire support. *The hazards*, Illea's father would say, *of trusting small minds to keep an eye on profits*. He had never liked the Imburleigh board of investors, and when he heard about them fanning the flames of the conflict in Mallory's marriage, his distrust was validated with uncomfortable accuracy.

"Thank you," Mallory said stiffly. "The speech writers on staff are some of the best in the business."

"Of course. But the orator is the one that sells the performance, and I hear you dazzled the crowd—to no one's surprise. And speaking of dazzling." Bothain's eyes fixed on Illea. "It's truly a pleasure to see you again, Miss Winter. It's been entirely too long."

Illea smiled, stepping closer. She had to stand on her tiptoes to kiss Bothain on the cheek, and he bent down to accommodate her. Both his hands rested on her waist, so comfortable there, so natural, that for a moment it seemed like he would pull her against his body and kiss her on the lips, even here in public. But he didn't. He kept enough distance that they were still seemly in the crowd, but Illea could see even more people watching.

"It's good to see you, General," Illea said. "I have to offer my apologies that I wasn't able to attend the graduation this summer, but I am delighted that you've made it up to Yaelsmuir."

"The pleasure is indeed mine, Miss Winter," Bothain said, his voice low and bedroom-soft, and Illea was almost disappointed that Myron wasn't around. He would just about bite off his own tongue to see Bothain so close and speaking so intimately. And Tashué Blackwood was coming, too—hopefully Myron's brain would spontaneously combust and save her the trouble of all the political maneuvering. "You're every bit as stunning as I remember, even so early in the morning."

"You flatter me, Bothain," Illea said. "It's very charming."

"You are easy to flatter, Miss Winter."

"General Clannaugh!" Rainer came from the crowd, his face carefully arranged in a grin that didn't exactly hide the panic in his eyes. Myron must have been drinking already for Rainer to look so perturbed. "You made good time up the river. I'm surprised to find you here at Myron's function."

"I came because I was under the impression that this was General Wolfe's function and I wanted to pay my respects," Bothain said dryly. "Seeing as it's his hospital, after all. I'm surprised General Wolfe gave up credit so easily, considering he's backing Eirdis Redbone's campaign. Is she here? I have to admit, I'm curious to meet her and see what she has to say about her platform."

"I thought you were here to support Myron's campaign, General Clannaugh," Mallory said.

"I'm here to support the campaign in the interest of the police force," Bothain said. "Myron is an unfortunate concession. If Miss Redbone was amenable to the force, I would back her campaign in an instant."

Rainer gave a strangled sound like he wanted to argue but caught the words halfway out his throat. Illea couldn't help but laugh at the way Rainer's eyes goggled and his moustache twitched like it was a nervous, hairy little creature stuck to his top lip.

"General Clannaugh, I know I liked you for a reason," Illea said. "Your company is always so entertaining in new and unexpected ways."

"I take it you're voting Redbone this year?" Bothain asked.

"I may abstain from voting," Illea lied. "While I generally think Myron is an idiot and the bane of my existence, having him in the Governor's office keeps him out of my house for most of the day, and that is its own victory."

"Illea, I think this is better discussed in a private setting," Rainer said. "You know how much influence your vote holds—"

"What about you, General Imburleigh?" Bothain interrupted, sending Rainer spluttering again. "I know your speech was for Myron, but where's your vote going?"

Mallory smiled coyly, keeping better composure than Illea. Ishmael may have been able to get under her skin talking about sex, but this—public relations and political opinions—was her area of comfort. "The Imburleigh Armament Company endorses Governor Winter's campaign and his plans for a provincial police force."

Bothain was not so easily swayed. "And what does General Imburleigh think?"

Mallory clasped her hands in front of herself, taking a moment to choose her words carefully. "General Imburleigh believes in a rather more progressive vision of the future. General Imburleigh would rather money be spent on improving the overall quality of life for people in this province, much the way that General Wolfe and Miss Redbone are so famous for advocating."

"One might argue that a firm hand on crime might in fact do that," Bothain said. "Accountability and justice would keep the streets safer."

"One might argue that," Mallory conceded with a bit of a shrug. "But one might also argue that improving the overall function of this city would reduce crime, since the highest motivator to criminal activity tends to be financial insecurity. Criminalizing poverty will set us back, and I would much rather see provincial funds allocated to improving economic stability for the most vulnerable of our population."

"I hear there'll be a nationally sponsored train line in your future, General Imburleigh," Rainer said quickly before the police force could be debated any further. It was a shame Eirdis wasn't here yet—Mallory's talking points were excellent, and it would have been good for people to see Eirdis and Mallory together in this. Perhaps Mallory would be willing to repeat them after Myron's speech. "Obisza to Yaelsmuir."

"Winter, Imburleigh, and Rhydderch have bid for the contract," Illea said. She rested her hand in the crook of Bothain's elbow, standing close enough to catch the delicious heat of his body. "Though nothing is certain yet."

"I admire your false humility, Miss Winter," Bothain said. "The general consensus in White Crown already says the contract will be yours. Since you're the only lumber supplier on this side of the Dominion, there's no point paying a third party to buy lumber from you. Same for Miss Rhydderch. She'll be the natural choice for stone. I hear she's already in Obisza anyway, helping with the Uhl factory."

"She is," Mallory said stiffly. Illea wondered if she was protective of Aelwyd Rhydderch. Illea could hardly blame her if she was. Bothain hadn't handled himself well when his wife—Aelwyd's elder sister—went missing, and the Clannaugh-Rhydderch fight for control over Ffyanwy's shares of Rhydderch Stone was infamous. Business women of the Dominion felt the horror of watching it all unfold. That Bothain thought himself entitled to a share of the Rhydderch company after everything did not endear him to many people. Bothain didn't know it, but Illea and Mallory had helped Aelwyd find the solicitor that so viciously defended her company from Bothain's ambition. But it was that very ambition that made him so appealing to Illea. "She does excellent work. I would trust no one else with the job."

"Mr. Elsworth says you've a few of the new Uhl rifles with you," Bothain said, wisely pivoting out of the tension. "I would dearly love to try them. I'm dying to know the difference between an Uhl and an Imburleigh."

"The goal was to allow the Uhl line be experimental," Mallory said, relaxing immediately. "There's no doubt that the Imburleigh rifles are the best selling and highest quality rifles on the market, but the Uhl factory will be the cutting edge of innovation. We have Talented technicians at every step to insure uniformity and precision in the craftsmanship of every weapon we produce and experiment with."

Bothain's head cocked to one side, and he glanced at Rainer. "Have you a contract with the Authority for your tainted?"

"We have a directed work program," Mallory said with a proud smile. "Mr. Elsworth was very accommodating and understood my desire to find the best and most brilliant minds myself."

"I thought the directed work program was being phased out," Bothain said, and the frustration in his voice surprised Illea. Perhaps his conflicts with Rainer weren't yet resolved even though he'd finally left the Authority behind. Why, then, had Rainer asked for his help in the campaign? "I thought you had decided that the registry was paramount, and that you wanted to control the assignment of tainted to various businesses. After everything that happened in Cruinnich, I thought it was abundantly clear that the directed work program was a disaster waiting to happen."

"Mallory Imburleigh is no Davik Kaine," Rainer said quickly. "I agree that in *most* cases, the registry is paramount—but I think we can agree that Miss Imburleigh is not most cases. In fact, she's an upstanding businesswoman of this nation with a decorated military career. She can be trusted for her level head in all things, including the handling of her tainted employees."

"I would agree that General Imburleigh is all those things, but Langston Imburleigh is not," Bothain said. "What happens when he begins to interfere?"

"He won't," Illea said. "He won't be touching the Uhl factory at all."

"He's on the Imburleigh board, isn't he?" Bothain asked.

"He is," Mallory said. "But the Uhl line is not controlled by the Imburleigh Armament Company's board of investors."

"Really?" Bothain asked, his head cocking to one side, his interest piqued. "Who controls the Uhl line?"

"We do," Mallory said with a modest smile. "Miss Winter, Miss Rhydderch and I."

"I'm only a silent investor," Illea said, waving a hand. "The Uhl factory is Mallory's passion, and I back her in all her decisions."

"How did that come about?" Bothain asked. "Imburleigh Armament Company didn't want the expansion?"

"The Imburleigh Armament Company's board of investors lack the forward thinking vision to see Mallory's brilliance," Illea said. "They are very much in love with stable profits and can't understand the need for innovation. They are complacent. They don't understand that Imburleigh is the best *because* they dared innovate, all those generations ago."

"We've funded it ourselves," Mallory said. "We have licensed the IAC logo to stamp on everything we produce, alongside the new Uhl logo. The rest is up to us for now."

"It will be a brilliant future for all of you," Rainer said. "Thank you for coming, General Clannaugh—I should go find Myron and make sure he's ready for his speech."

"Make sure he isn't blind drunk, you mean?" Bothain laughed.

Rainer ignored the jab, folding back into the crowd.

"I do have a few of the Uhl rifles here," Mallory said. "I haven't the time to go on a hunting trip, I'm afraid. I didn't know you were coming, otherwise I would have tried to organize something. But I would be delighted to have them delivered to you so that you can try them while you're here. I would be most interested to hear what you think."

"That is incredibly generous of you, General Imburleigh," Bothain said. "I very much look forward to it."

All the talk of guns lost Illea. She would happily talk about the business of *anything* for days, but the function of guns and hunting ranged from simply boring to being deeply painful when it made her think of Amias.

Ishmael came finally, a fresh glass of brandy in his hand. "I thought I knew all of the decorated Generals in Yaelsmuir politics."

"Ishmael, this is General Clannaugh," Illea supplied.

"Clannaugh, as in the Fist of the North?" Ishmael asked.

Bothain turned, offering a tight smile and a handshake. "No longer of the north. Now of the 12th infantry."

"The one with all the fancy medals," Ishmael said, accepting the handshake. "If you're going to go ahead and buy valour, there's no better division to get ahold of."

Bothain laughed. "Ah, to be insulted by the infamous Ishmael Saeati. General Maes warned me about you."

Ishmael smiled, his head cocking to one side. "In that case, send General Maes my disregard. How's the old bastard doing? I haven't been to White Crown since before General Deri died."

"Ornery and hard to get along with, same as ever," Bothain muttered. "But he likes Rhydderch whisky, so I bring him crates of it every time I see him, and that seems to be enough to buy his tolerance."

"I thought you said you were close to him, Bothain," Illea said.

"That's about as close as anyone can get to Maes," Ishmael said, sipping his brandy. "Earning his tolerance."

"I understand you were close to Deri," Bothain said. "A strike against you in Maes's opinion, I'm afraid. But Deri was a solid man as far as I'm concerned."

"He was," Ishmael said. "I was very fond of him. It was quite a blow when he died."

"Yes, 'fond' is the word for it," Bothain said.

"I'm sorry, General, was that too modest for you?" Ishmael asked, giving his brightest, most dazzling smile. His smile beamed most brightly when he was letting his stubble grow in—he hadn't had the time to shave like he usually did before formal functions. "We fucked, often and vigorously. He was an excellent lover. Always knew how to push things to the very edge of my comfort without becoming too violent. I have a few scars that I'm especially fond of. Would you like to see?"

"Ishmael," Mallory breathed.

"What?" Ishmael snapped. "He asked. People keep asking about my sex life and then acting scandalized when I give an honest answer."

"It's all part of his act, General Imburleigh," Bothain said with a smile. "He hides his capabilities quite well under all his outrageous antics. I wouldn't have believed the things Maes said about his brilliance if I hadn't seen his file myself."

Ishmael's composure broke for a moment, a tiny fraction of a second in which his eyebrows rose and his shoulders went tense, and it was so startling, it sent a shiver of empathetic dread down Illea's spine. "I wasn't aware the 12th had clearance for diplomatic files."

"Ah, well, neither does Wolfe, does he? But General Wolfe was quite close to General Deri and that's how he got involved in diplomatic files, isn't it? Was he fucking Deri, too?"

"No, actually, I believe General Wolfe prefers less aggressive company," Ishmael said. "Deri's skills would have been wasted on him."

"Did Deri's wife invite you to the interment on the west coast?" Bothain asked. "I hear his family sent his bones back to the ocean or some such."

Ishmael flinched, and it was painful to witness. He was usually so guarded, like Bothain said, hiding behind the facade of irreverence and vice. The spasm across his face showed the core of him for one vulnerable moment. Mallory reached out to him, her fingers brushing across the back of his hand, some attempt to offer comfort. And Illea wondered, again, why Mallory was so irritated by him, but so quick to come to his defence.

"Yes, I was invited, but no, I didn't go," Ishmael said, and even his voice was thick with emotion. "Deri died while I was deployed and the interment was arranged before I got back."

"To the Commonwealth, wasn't it?"

Ishmael smiled behind his brandy, draining the glass. "Well, you said you've seen my file, so you'd know if it was the Commonwealth or the Derccian Empire or the Kiatze Empire or the fucking moon, wouldn't you?"

"I suppose it doesn't matter," Bothain said with a shrug. "Oh, I have something for you. It made its way to White Crown somehow. Or maybe it never left White Crown? I'm not sure of the circumstances exactly. In any case, Maes wanted me to make sure it got to you and sends his apologies for the delay."

"Perhaps this could be dealt with privately, General Clannaugh," Mallory said.

Ishmael laughed bitterly, the sound so sharp it slid like a knife along Illea's nerves. "No, of course General Clannaugh wants witnesses for whatever he's about to hand me. That way, I can't dispute it was given to me. He's also making a point about how he's got power over me. He wants me to feel it, and maybe sweat a little, and wonder what he and Maes have been talking about down in White Crown. But I already know what Maes thinks of me, so none of this petty manipulation comes as a surprise."

Bothain shifted, pulling his jacket open so he could reach into his breast pocket, drawing out a letter. "You're very clever, Mr. Saeati, but I think your career has made you paranoid. I'm just delivering some mail."

Bothain didn't reach far enough to close the gap between him and Ishmael, giving Illea a moment to catch sight of the back of the letter. The Deri seal—red wax with black swirls, the D flanked by the outline of opium poppies—was broken. Ishmael stepped into the space between them, taking the letter and tucking it into his pocket immediately. He didn't retreat—he stayed close to Bothain and Illea, the air hot with tension, looking Bothain in the eye. So much for Bothain and Ishmael making a good impression on each other.

"Does General Maes make a habit of opening other people's mail?" Ishmael asked.

Bothain shrugged. "He's known to keep an eye on his enemies."

"Even after they're dead?"

"You can write Maes your thoughts if you feel particularly put out." Bothain gave an expression of his that was *like* a smile but was too tight and aggressive. "Although it's not especially out of the ordinary for the military to read their troop's mail, isn't it? To keep an eye out for any breach in confidentiality."

"Ishmael, darling, we should go out front and wait for Captain Blackwood," Illea said, catching Ishmael's hand and giving it a squeeze, desperate to get out of this moment so she could regroup. She'd hoped that Ishmael would help smooth things over with Nathaniel—who made more than a few loaded statements about Bothain's propensity for violence when news broke that he'd left the Authority—but clearly that wasn't to be. "He won't know to come inside to find us, will he?"

"No, you're right," Ishmael said. "He won't, and Captain Blackwood deserves the very best treatment, doesn't he? Lead the way, Illea."

"It was a pleasure to see you, General Clannaugh," Illea said, letting go of Bothain's arm. "I leave you in General Imburleigh's highly capable company. I'm sure the pair of you will happily talk about guns for the rest of the day."

Bothain leaned down to kiss Illea's cheek. Ishmael's face was reassembled into a mask, but Mallory still showed the ripples of her shock. Ishmael being abrasive was generally unsurprising, but Bothain had deftly fired the first volleys of that conflict, making his scorn a tactile presence that hung in the air. Illea almost felt bad for leaving Mallory with Bothain, but the hospital was crowded and Mallory knew how to talk to powerful men.

She led Ishmael away, and she could feel the way Bothain watched them both go, the sensation sending a shiver down Illea's spine. Was Bothain watching Illea, or Ishmael? The interaction hadn't gone the way she'd expected at all, and she cursed herself for the oversight. She'd known that Bothain had ties to General Maes, and that Maes and Deri were enemies, but she'd underestimated how close Ishmael was to Deri, apparently. He fucked so many people, how was she supposed to know they were actually emotionally involved?

Perhaps she could convince Eirdis to have Bothain campaign with her, instead. It would give firm backing to Eirdis's presence; it would help sway the wealthier quarters to see Eirdis standing with military power, especially the famous 12th. Eirdis was pragmatic and power hungry. Maybe Illea could convince her that endorsing the idea of a police force would help her steal the election from Myron, and if that happened before news of Illea's pregnancy broke, perhaps he'd finally leave.

"What the fuck is Bothain Clannaugh doing here?" Ishmael snapped, his voice pitched low as they made their way through the halls of the hospital toward the front entrance but still charged with fury. "Is he here for the election?"

"I don't know," Illea admitted. "It's a pleasant surprise."

"What did you do?" Ishmael asked.

"Excuse me?"

Ishmael grimaced, shaking his head. He stepped out into the bright open space of the main steps. Out front, the crowd from Brickheart and the Market and In the Tracks milled in the street, which was closed to carriage traffic for the day. Kegs of light cider or beer were available, and someone was serving thick slices of bread dripping with butter. The atmosphere was entirely different, more chaotic, more crowded, but also more joyous, voices rising in a cacophony that made her head ache.

"What did you promise him?" Ishmael asked. "How did you lure him into this?"

"I didn't promise him anything," Illea scoffed. "He came up of his own volition, and he didn't tell me he was coming. And even if I did, so what? He's a boon to our cause. He knows things about Rainer—if he decided to back Eirdis, he could destroy Myron and Rainer's campaign once and for all."

"What things?" Ishmael asked. "What does he know?"

"I'm not sure exactly. He doesn't trust me that much. Not yet, in any case. With luck, I can draw him in now that he's here and we're ostensibly on the same side in all this."

Ishmael leaned closer, his whole body vibrating with his new wild tension. "Why did he leave the Authority, do you know that?"

Illea lay a hand on Ishmael's chest, torn between the desire to push him back to get more space and the desire to pull him closer to draw more secrets out of him. "He was irritated with Rainer—he thought Rainer was making mistakes, and he felt his career had progressed as far as Rainer would allow. When Maes wrote to him to tell him the previous General of the 12th was retiring, he jumped at the chance to switch tracks. That's when he told me the Authority was doomed to collapse. Something about secrets, about Rainer over reaching. I don't know. He never gave me specifics."

"Where is he staying while he's here? With Rainer?"

"I think so."

"So Rainer doesn't know Clannaugh has turned on him?"

Illea shook her head. "Not that I'm aware. Not yet."

Ishmael grimaced, his gaze sliding across the crowd. It was too late for any more questions—she spotted Tashué coming down the street. He was in his beautiful cavalry dress greens and carried something under his arm. The White Shield on his chest caught the light, the white enamel positively glowing. Ishmael sucked in a fast breath as if he were bracing himself to dive under water. The sharpness melted away until his movements were loose again. Was he pretending to be drunk for the sake of his reputation?

But Bothain's words echoed in Illea's mind. *If I hadn't seen his file myself* —how many of those secrets might he be inclined to share with Illea?

She almost felt treacherous for thinking it, but how many layers existed in Ishmael's career? And could she use any of it now?

They intercepted Tashué in the chaos, and Illea stood on her tiptoes to kiss him on the cheek. He smelled like stale whisky and cigarillo smoke and rage, his whole body simmering with something ugly.

"Mr. Blackwood, you made it. You look so good in your dress uniform." She slid a hand along his chest, and she could *feel* his heart hammering. What was he planning?

"Thank you, Miss Winter," Tashué grunted. "Is Rainer here yet?"

"Of course. He's been waiting for you. He's around the side of the building, with Myron. Shall I bring you to him?"

"Please," Tashué grunted.

Illea nodded, turning, leading the way. Ishmael fell in step beside Tashué, the pair of them trailing behind Illea. What a strange day, so many pieces of it moving in ways she didn't expect. Her own body swept itself away in all the excitement, making her hands tremble.

"Why do you have an urn?" Ishmael asked.

"It's Keoh."

"Oh, well, that explains everything," Ishmael muttered. "Are you drunk?"

"Probably."

Ishmael nodded. "Me too, I think. Didn't get the chance to sleep it all off yet."

Illea glanced over her shoulder at both of them, grinning. Except now she knew Ishmael was lying about how drunk he was because she'd seen him fold into it. The air crackled with so much potential for chaos. "Excellent. All the best scandals start with drunk men."

12

TASHUÉ

DAY 33

"Is all that shit true?" Ishmael asked. "The things you said to Rainer?"

"Fucking hell, you're useless when you're drinking, aren't you?" Tashué ran a hand over his face. "I told General Wolfe all of this already."

"I told you, I wasn't working," Ishmael muttered, reaching into his pocket and pulling out a handful of dates. He offered some to Tashué, but Tashué waved them off. "What are you going to do next?"

"I'm going to find a way to fucking prove it." Tashué stood, but all the whisky seemed to hit him in the face like a punch, making his knees weak. He sank back down, closing his eyes as the world tilted and spun.

"Easy there, Captain. Don't start puking, or I'll fucking join you and all that whisky will be wasted."

"It's all so fucked. How did I not know any of this? I worked for the Authority for nineteen fucking years, and I didn't know. I have to fix it..." He ran both his hands over his face, trying to scrub away the slow, foggy feeling in his brain. Shit, they'd finished that bottle too damned fast. "If I can find proof, maybe I can fix it. I can make it fucking stop. Energy units, for fuck's sake."

"Tashué Blackwood."

Tashué turned, looking over his shoulder. A half-dozen Patrollers were standing behind him, clustered in close. A few of the younger ones had the pale faces and trembling hands of youths fearful of their first action, but the older ones had grim and unrelenting expressions.

"Shit," Ishmael breathed. "Tashué, don't fight it. No matter what they do, don't fight them, or they'll kill you. Just do what they tell you."

Something buzzed in Tashué's ears—tension building in his muscles, crawling over his bones.

"Look at me, you bastard! Don't fight it!"

"Put your hands behind your head, Mr. Blackwood," the Patroller said. "You're under arrest for uttering threats against the Chief Administrator of the National Tainted Registration Authority."

Jason—the thought struck him so hard he needed a moment to catch his breath. If he was arrested and he had as much Talent as Stella said would he be processed to the Rift?

The possibility drained all the anger out of him. Maybe he should have been afraid, but seeing Jason again—maybe together, the pair of them could find a way to get out of that place. He could hold his son again. He could apologize for all the ways he'd been *so wrong* all these years.

"Don't do anything stupid," Ishmael said.

Tashué lifted his hands slowly, lacing his fingers behind his head. Jason was worth it. Every other thought slithered through his mind too slowly and too far away, but that realization hit him with perfect clarity. He'd go to the Rift with Jason and figure shit out from there. And he wouldn't have to wait for Powell Iwan anymore. He could make it happen himself, like he should have years ago. "I'm not going to do anything stupid."

Ishmael put his hands up, too, but he twisted his body to show his palms to the Patrollers. Tashué fought against the urge to stand, to move. He hated it, sitting there, all those guns pointed at his back, all those nervous trigger fingers hovering, all the gunpowder waiting to do its job and ignite. He'd been on the other side of a moment like this often enough to know that getting up now was a mistake. Someone would take it as a threat, and he'd get shot. Just sit. Just wait. It was worth it for Jason.

He locked his eyes on the whisky bottle sitting in the shale by his feet. Empty. And Keoh's urn, sitting beside him, water pooling in the bottom. All of Keoh's ashes were gone, into the Brightwash. How fast did that water flow? Would her ashes make it all the way out to sea, or would they settle at the bottom of the river before that? That fucking urn had brought him to this moment. Staring at it on his kitchen table, keeping company with it day and night, feeling the weight of its judgement and his failure. That weight had driven him to drink way too much. Just to try to get away from it. But of course escape was impossible. The whisky made him angrier. And now here he was.

One of the Patrollers shifted. Whispered, "He's a big fucker. I hope we don't have to take him down."

"Captain Blackwood has a pistol and a large knife in a holster under his jacket," Ishmael said. "I'm going to take them out and set them aside so there aren't any problems. How does that sound?"

A moment, stretching—Tashué's heartbeat pounded through his whole body. The river, the city, it all rose to an incredible roar.

"Do it," another Patroller said. "Slowly."

Ishmael released a long breath, his shoulders relaxing a little. "Sit up straighter so I can reach, Captain. Don't do anything stupid."

"You said that already," Tashué said, straightening his back, taking in a deep, slow breath, filling his lungs full to bursting. The whisky had a good hold of him, making his head feel too light, making it feel like he was listing to one side. He flexed his shoulders, an ache settling in his muscles as he kept his hands behind his head.

Ishmael pulled the heavy Imburleigh pistol out first, his hands clumsy from all the whisky they'd shared, making him fumble when it caught on Tashué's coat. The gun that had killed Edgar Hale, smashed a bullet through his skull and left him nothing but bleeding, oozing meat in his own apartment—how had life spun so hard and so fast out of control? That death had come too easily, like Tashué had spent the last nineteen years lying to himself about the kind of man he was. The army had made him a killer, and he'd tried to shave those sharp edges off himself, but they hadn't gone away like he'd thought—they were just covered until he needed to unsheathe them again. Those edges had killed Hale and almost killed Rainer.

"I know I said it already," Ishmael said, snapping Tashué out of the wild twist of his thoughts. "But I really, *really* mean it. Don't do anything stupid. Don't get yourself killed. You're not allowed to die today, you hear me?"

"Yeah, Ishmael, sure," Tashué said. "I'll try my best."

"Tashué!" Ishmael pulled the cavalry knife out next, tossing it away. The blade hit the loose shale of the riverbank, sinking deep, the hilt standing up, pointing at the slate grey sky like a gravestone for Keoh's last resting place. "That's not fucking good enough!"

Tashué started to reach for Ishmael—he wanted to wrap his arms around Ishmael's body and crush him in close and tell him that everything was going to be fine. Nothing felt fucking fine, but he wanted to say it anyway, wanted to make it true. He'd be fine in the Rift with Jason, but the words didn't come soon enough.

"Keep your fucking hands behind your head!" the Patroller snapped.

"Yeah, alright," Tashué said, lacing his fingers together tighter. He must have moved more than he realized. "Of course."

"You too," another Patroller grunted.

"What?" Ishmael scoffed. "I'm fucking helping you—"

"Ishmael Saeati?"

"No," Ishmael said, the word coming so fast it must have been a drunken reflex. "Ishmael Kol Khara."

"Put your *fucking* hands behind your head!"

"I told you, I'm not Ishmael Saeati." Ishmael put his hands behind his head anyway, lacing his fingers together and leaning forward, away from the guns, bowing low between his knees. "Isn't that the drunken idiot who makes watches? I've never met him. Just had the unfortunate coincidence of the same first name."

Some small, sober part of Tashué's brain tried to tell him this wasn't the time to fight, not with so many guns pointed at their backs. "He didn't do anything!" he said anyway, the words burning hot through his last shred of good sense.

"What am I under arrest for?" Ishmael asked. "Dominion legal code states that the arrested party has the right to know the nature of the charges against them at the time of the arrest."

"You're under arrest for being fucking mouthy," the Patroller grunted.

Ishmael laughed, the sound too liquid and wild. "That's never been a crime in this country."

The Patroller put a foot on Ishmael's back and shoved him down, face first into the rocky scree of the riverbank. Another Patroller grabbed Tashué by the wrist, pulling it down behind his back to clamp the first manacle into place. Someone dropped down to grab Ishmael's wrists, earning a shout of pain from Ishmael that rattled straight through Tashué's skull. The rage snapped to life so fast, Tashué couldn't think. The tension in his body forced him up, to his feet, a step toward Ishmael

—hands grabbed him, but he thrashed away from them, his elbow catching *someone.*

"Stop!" Ishmael shouted, turning his head in the gravel so he could look at Tashué in the eye. "Don't fight it, Tashué, stop—we'll deal with this at the jail, we'll get word to Wolfe and get this settled—just fucking stop or they'll kill you and I can't help you if you're dead! Tashué! You can't help Jason if you're dead!"

Jason—

Too late.

They came in a rush, bodies and hands and a truncheon. Something hit his side and it punched the air out of him so completely it cut the legs out from under him. His knees hit the rocky scree of the riverbank, and then more people were on him. A hit on his shoulder—a hit on his back—

White behind his eyes.

Jason, I'm sorry.

White pain that swallowed him whole.

And then nothing.

13

ILLEA
DAY 33

W hat a day, what a messy, incredible, chaotic, exciting day. Everything felt ripe with opportunity, filled to bursting with possibility.

Illea's body buzzed with all the energy, all the surprise. It wasn't often that the political field of this city caught her off guard, but today—she hadn't seen the scale of Tashué Blackwood's explosion coming. Something had been simmering in him since he met Rainer but this was better than anything she could have planned.

"Illea." Eirdis Redbone caught up to her through the crowd, hooking their arms together. She had a particular knack for presenting the entire history of her career in her appearance. Everything in every suit or gown she wore was deliberately chosen—a ragged kerchief here, a modest hairstyle there—to remind people that she came up from Brickheart, but clothes of the highest quality so that no one ever questioned if she belonged in Highfield for political functions. She wore a trouser suit for this event, because the half-drunk working class crowd was her most secure voter and they liked the homespun charm of a woman in a suit. "What happened? Someone attacked Rainer?"

"Rainer's very own face of the National Tainted Registration Authority attacked him," Illea laughed. There was no point trying to hide her delight, not now. "He's taken Rainer away to talk to him. 'Talk' being a glorious understatement. Nathaniel's gone to smooth it all over, and Ishmael and Blackwood have walked away, but North Star bless us all, this will be an incredible boon for your candidacy."

"Nathaniel didn't want to go after Rainer and the Authority this election cycle," Eirdis said. She had an excellent orator's voice, that delivered powerful speeches when she was on her chosen stage, but she also knew how to keep her voice pitched quiet so they could talk while they moved through the crowd. "He thought it would turn too many of the wealthy voters against me this time, since the Authority's been growing more powerful lately."

"We didn't orchestrate this," Illea said. She hefted up her skirts and headed back up the big steps to the front of the hospital. "It's one of those random and wild gifts that the universe bestows now and then. And since it's a gift of chance, we'd be fools to squander the chance, wouldn't we?"

Eirdis nodded. "I think we would. Where are we going?"

Illea paused at the top of the steps, breathing slow to avoid looking too winded. Her gown was too heavy for this much walking, and the hunger was starting to eat through her composure, making her stomach feel too tight. "I'm going to find General Clannaugh. I'd like to arrange a meeting for the pair of you, hopefully soon. I suspect you'll have a lot to talk about, given all this with Blackwood."

"I haven't met Blackwood yet—tell me about him, so I can give a good speech."

"He's the one who held the Ridge," Illea said. "He was given the White Shield for it."

Eirdis nodded, her fingers flexing and clenching like she was snatching ideas out of the air. "He was at the Market fire, wasn't he? Myron gave him another medal for it."

"That's him," Illea said. "Served ten years in the military, nineteen in the Authority."

"Which quarter is he from?" Eirdis asked. Her eyes were bright with eagerness, with politics. "The Market?"

"No, he's from Brickheart."

Eirdis nodded, and then she was off. That was all the information she needed to make a hero out of the man.

Bothain met Illea on the inside of the door, laying a hand on her back and leading her away from the larger crowd. "I hear there's been a commotion, Miss Winter."

"There has been, General Clannaugh. Where's Mallory?"

"She went chasing after Saeati when she heard things were happening. I wouldn't have expected someone as pragmatic as her to be drawn in by Ishmael Saeati of all people, but I suppose I shouldn't be surprised that he's able to manipulate a good heart like Mallory Imburleigh."

Illea retreated into an alcove, sidestepping the chaos. She met Bothain's eyes, bracing herself. "What's an energy unit, Bothain? That's what Captain Blackwood was so incensed about—energy units."

Bothain didn't look away. He didn't flinch or shrink. He gave the tiniest of shrugs, but his thin mouth was also pulling into a smile. Had he known, somehow, that this would happen? It couldn't be possible. He had no connection to Tashué Blackwood that Illea knew about. But then, Illea didn't believe in coincidences. There was something more, drawing it all together. There had to be.

He reached for his timepiece and studied the face of it for a long moment. "Where's Rainer now?"

"I'm not sure. He walked away with Nathaniel."

Bothain's eyebrows quirked up as he tucked the timepiece away. "I didn't get the chance to explore. Is there a place we can speak privately but preferably with a window so we can keep an eye on the crowd?"

"If I know Rainer, he'll come slinking through the rear courtyard if he decides to come back here at all. He definitely won't try to make his way through the crowd out front. He might not even come back. He might have gone to ground somewhere else to lick his wounds."

Bothain nodded. "Lead the way, if you don't mind, Miss Winter. If he doesn't come back, we'll go hunting for him."

Illea stepped out of the alcove and across the crowd. She plucked a pastry off a tray as it passed in front of her, eating it slowly to try to stave off the rising discomfort. Bothain didn't comment on her eating as they walked, and she took a small cake next, the sponge soaked with a whisky and honey glaze, spiced with merry tasting cinnamon and nutmeg. It wasn't enough. She'd need to eat a proper meal soon, or else the tremble would set itself in her hands, and the nausea would be incurable until she had the chance to sleep.

Up to the second floor and down the long hall, she walked through the freshly-built ward, past new beds and starched linens. It seemed there had been people up here today; some crumbs on one windowsill, an empty glass on a tray table, but everyone had flooded downstairs to catch the gossip of what had happened. Bothain walked to the big window, looking down at the courtyard. There wasn't any less chaos down there;

carriages jostled for position, and people from Highview and Drystone edged in around them to get in to be close to the source of this newest city upheaval, making it harder for the horse-drawn carriages to maneuver.

"What's your hand in this, Bothain?"

"My hand?" Bothain asked, turning to Illea. "Would that I could claim credit for all this, but alas—I'm only here to try to help get the police force through legislation. By any means necessary, I've been told."

"Told by whom? Maes?"

Bothain nodded. He was so still, standing there by the window, the light of the sun turning his hair to spun gold. Illea's heart took up a double-time beat, rattling her ribcage, making her lungs ache. She couldn't help but edge closer to Bothain, drawn by the stillness of him, by the secrets he was holding.

"Why should the General of the diplomatic division care about a provincial police force in Yaelsmuir?"

Bothain shrugged and spread his hands, turning so he leaned on the window frame. He crossed his arms over his chest as he looked at Illea a while, his head cocked in that way that signalled he was considering his words carefully. "Surely you know that the Yael police force is the proto-type for the rest of the country. If this program succeeds, the Crowne will roll it from one province to the next until it's a national program. What better way to keep an eye on the expanding network of Crowne abolitionists than a coordinated police force? We can stop the spread of sedition before it takes root, and Maes gains another branch of power."

"I wasn't aware you felt so strongly about protecting the monarchy," Illea said. "I was under the impression that you northern types were rather more stubbornly independent."

Bothain grinned. He slid the back of one finger across Illea's exposed collarbone, his knuckle trailing all the way down until it was stopped by the lacy edge of Illea's bodice. "One doesn't refuse the opportunity to be closer to the centre of power in this country just because one's ancestors believed in independence. You were right when you said I was wasting my time under Rainer. Maes presented me with an opportunity, and I took it. Tell me about Blackwood. Who is he? What's his angle?"

"He's a tinman from Brickheart," Illea said as Bothain came closer still. He thought he was being very smooth and surreptitious, but there was nothing subtle about the way his presence loomed over Illea, no space left between their bodies. His hand roamed around to the back of her neck, drifting along her hairline. "I don't know what his angle is because I don't know what he's talking about. What are energy units, Bothain?"

"Energy units are Rainer's undoing," Bothain whispered. The words and the weight of his voice sent a shiver down Illea's spine, sent frissons across her scalp that made her ears burn. "Who is Blackwood? Is he Red Dawn?"

"Rainer Elsworth says the Army of the Red Dawn has no coordinated presence in Yaelsmuir."

Bothain laughed. "Sure, and bears shit bars of gold up in the mountains. No one actually believes that, do they?"

Footsteps in the hall before Illea could answer—she turned to the sound, cursing the intruder. Perhaps Bothain would be more forthcoming with answers if they were somewhere more fully private. Men had a way of telling her what she wanted to know when they were in her sitting room, when the awareness of her bed pulled at their simple minds and they would do anything to gain themselves access to her body.

"General Clannaugh?" the runner asked. Out of breath and covered in sweat, the boy had earned his title, apparently.

"Yes," Bothain grunted.

"Rainer Elsworth sent this for you, General."

Bothain held out a hand, and the runner closed the distance between them, giving the note over. "Where is he?"

The youth pulled a kerchief from his pocket, mopping sweat off his face. "At House One, General."

Bothain unfolded the note and scowled at it. "It seems I'm in need of a carriage, young man. There will be a healthy tip in it for you if you can hail one by the time I get downstairs."

"Yes, General."

The boy was off again, leaving the smell of his sweaty wool uniform in the ward.

"I told you he wouldn't come slinking back here," Illea said.

Bothain swept his arm around Illea's waist, drawing her closer and sucking in a slow, deep breath like he was filling himself with her scent, or perhaps the scent of the whole city. Or perhaps he was just breathing in the moment, the possibility, the impending chaos that would shift the balance of power in the province forever. If they played everything right, the power shift would be most beneficial for both of them. And Maes, by extension, but he felt rather like an unknown element and that made

Illea uneasy. The man mostly kept to himself, only raising to national gossip recently during his famous fight with his co-General, Deri, who pioneered the provincial diplomat program. Maes destroyed it before it could really grow roots, earning an unending hatred from Nathaniel, who fought for the provincial program almost as fiercely as Deri had. A shame, too, since it gave the provinces a way to work together. Which was probably why Maes wanted to get rid of it. The biggest threat to the tired old monument of the Crowne was not an external force but the slow internal march of progress to a more enlightened world, embodied by provincial autonomy.

"Would that we had time to catch up properly, but it seems our evening is quite suddenly spoken for," Bothain said. "Will you come with me to talk to Rainer?"

Illea gave the smallest roll of her eyes, turning her face away from Bothain to look out the window at the courtyard below them. "I'd rather not spend my evening helping Myron get elected. I think my energy would be better spent here, with Eirdis. She'll be whipping up the crowd to a delicious froth by now."

Bothain's restraint finally crumbled, and he kissed Illea's temple, her jaw, wandering closer to her mouth like he hoped she would turn into him. "What if I promise you the best view of Rainer's fall?"

Illea tilted her head toward him, meeting his cold, bright eyes. "Only if you promise to find a way to get your police force without having Myron elected. I'm finished with him, Bothain. I want him out of my house. I want him driven out of this city in shame. I want the whole country to know about the collapse of his power, and I want them all to know I outlasted him."

Bothain grinned. "Illea Winter, you have a deal."

Illea smiled and leaned forward, letting Bothain kiss her. Just once, a brief brush of their lips, but she could feel the tension rolling through him, the excitement. "I want you to tell me about the energy units on the way. So I know what I'm dealing with."

The very first National Tainted Registration Authority station house stood in Drystone, and it was a long ride as Bothain explained the energy units. For the first time since she learnt of her pregnancy, a keen awareness of the life growing in her body had taken root in Illea's every thought. She'd kept her hopes guarded and restrained so far. Her struggles with her own fertility had been complicated at best. Of course this wasn't exactly the way she imagined things would go once the problems were solved, and there was still a risk of early miscarriage. So she didn't want to let her hopes sink too deeply into this moment, this almost-child. But this day seemed built to bring her attention to all the ways her mind and body and future were changing.

It had only been a few weeks. If it weren't for the way her healer monitored her health with near obsessive attention, she wouldn't have even known something was so different. She would have chalked the fatigue and the nausea up to some seasonal illness and the ample dose of stress from the cursed election.

Only a few weeks shouldn't have changed her at all.

And yet, as Bothain explained the energy units, it took all of Illea's restraint not to lay her hands across her navel. It was a ridiculous impulse. Her hands wouldn't do anything to protect her child, not from internal threats and not from the external weight of Bothain's words.

She'd encountered the term energy units before. The phrase appeared a few times in the negotiations Mallory conducted with Rainer while they were planning the Uhl factory, but she hadn't known what the words really meant. *The legal term for the tainted who fire the foundries and such* was Rainer's explanation. Illea and Mallory lost interest quickly— Mallory wanted craftspeople and artisans and access to the directed work program. So, no energy units for the Uhl factory.

They hadn't realized what they were saying no to. No children produced by the Breeding Program, designed to be more powerful than the average tainted, bred and crossbred like livestock. For efficiency, like Rainer said. Right before Tashué Blackwood held a gun to his skull.

She'd never imagined Tashué Blackwood would bring *this* when Nathaniel asked her to bring the cavalry captain to Rainer's attention. But she couldn't have asked for a better election cycle if her only goal was to block Myron's reelection. Blackwood had delivered everything she needed and more.

A shame he probably wouldn't survive the night. There was no way Rainer would take him quietly and allow him to stand in a courtroom and repeat his accusations through his defence counsel.

But then, maybe that was a good thing. If her healer's timeline for the pregnancy was correct, he was the father of Illea's child. She had no interest in tying her life to his for the foreseeable future. In this, her reputation was especially valuable. She wasn't anywhere near as promiscuous as the gossip alleged—if she was, she'd scarcely have time to do anything else—but the rumours of her voracious appetite would cast uncertainty to her child's parentage once the news broke. Her child was Winter and that was all that mattered.

Although, her Winter child was busy making her terribly ill. She needed to eat something, to sit a moment and catch her breath. She needed to say something, but she was loathe to give any hint of weakness. She wasn't ready to explain her condition, wasn't ready for the men around her to start making loaded comments about her delicate constitution or how she needed to slow down and take it easy.

But Bothain noticed. He paused as they stepped through the big doors, before they entered the foyer and met the small crowd of people milling around. The inside was lit by tainted-powered brights, casting light into every corner to chase the late autumn gloom out of the building.

"Are you well, Miss Winter?" At least he whispered it. "You're looking rather pale."

"Fine." Leave it to Bothain not to realize or care how impolite it was to so bluntly comment on her complexion. It was one of the things she liked about him—he used his energy more efficiently than trying to keep up with the standard of manners set by White Crown, but at times like this, it rankled more than a little. "It's been rather a more eventful day than I was expecting, is all."

Bothain nodded, putting a hand on Illea's back, just above her bustle. "We'll send for some coffee and something to eat. Something more substantial than honey cakes and pastries."

"Thank you."

Up the another set of stairs, where Rainer had commandeered a brightly lit office overlooking the public park. Illea vaguely recognized the man hovering at Rainer's elbow. He'd been at the station house in Brickheart when they recruited Tashué, the man who nearly fainted whenever Tashué made a joke as though he thought he would be held responsible for Tashué's lack of reverence toward the city's most powerful people. Illea couldn't remember the man's name.

Rainer's hands shook. He had all the pallor of a man who might vomit at any time. She took no small amount of joy from the fact he looked significantly worse than she did, but North Star preserve her, she prayed he wouldn't actually lose control. That would set her off for certain.

"Did you see what happened?" Rainer asked, as Bothain led Illea into the office. "Did you see?"

"I didn't, Rainer," Bothain said. He had the soothing tone of a man talking to a spooked horse, but somehow his voice didn't adapt well to that sound and he seemed tense and annoyed. "I was inside. I heard the gossip, though."

"The man's a wild animal. A wild fucking animal—I told Wolfe to arrest him, but the bastard tried to talk me out of it—who does he think he is?" Rainer poured brandy with shaking hands, splashing some of it across the borrowed desk, but then he whirled on Illea with his glass in his hand and his eyes unnaturally wide. "You—you brought him into this. You're the one who told me to trust him—did you set me up, you snake-tongued whore?"

In spite of the surge of fury that roared through Illea's body, she laughed. "You never minded my snake tongue when I used it on you, Rainer Elsworth. It's only once I stopped letting you wave your prick at me that you started calling me a whore."

The little man gave a high-pitched cough, looking at the door like he wanted nothing more than to retreat from the room, but Bothain was standing in the way.

Rainer scowled, shaking his head. "You didn't answer my question—what secrets did you whisper in his ear?"

Illea lifted her chin, breathing slow to keep her stomach under control. "What secrets indeed, Rainer? I certainly didn't tell him any. We were entirely too busy enjoying each other's bodies to spare a single thought for *you*. If Blackwood has your secrets, someone else gave them to him."

Rainer shook his head, draining the brandy. "What do I do? Bothain—this is your mess, too, don't stand there looking so bloody smug—what do I do?"

Bothain and all his division medals and the weight of his scorn took up so much space in the little office. He watched Rainer with a steady gaze, and an angry curl to his lip that he didn't even bother trying to hide. And Rainer paled even more under that look, shifting his weight from one foot to the other, licking his lips a few times. Regretting his harsh words, no doubt.

Bothain let Rainer squirm a while longer, turning to the little man by the door. "What's your name, sir?"

"Khosran, General. Commander Khosran."

Bothain reached into his pocket, pulling out some coins and counting a few into Khosran's hand. "It's going to be a long night, Commander Khosran. We appreciate the use of your office, and we'll need some coffee. The best coffee in Drystone, if you please, and something to eat for Miss Winter. As fast as possible."

"Something sweet," Illea said. "And not too heavy."

"Yes, General," the little man said, looking down at the coins in his hand. "If I may, before I go?"

"Quickly," Bothain said.

"There've been rumours about Davik Kaine surfacing in Cattle Bone Bay. I know everyone says that Powell Iwan holds the Bay, but I don't know—I've heard Kaine's name a lot the last little while. I wonder if he's involved, is all."

Bothain swung toward Rainer, and Illea could feel the next hot surge of his rage like heat waves from a wood stove burning out of control. "Davik Kaine?" He threw the words at Rainer like a sharp accusation. "You left that part out when you asked for my help, Rainer."

Rainer laughed, the sound nervous and brittle, filling Illea with savage joy. The panic in his eyes was delicious. She wished she could drink it, intoxicate herself with it. He shook his head, draining the glass of brandy, shooting a glare at the little man. "The Red Dawn has no organized presence in Yaelsmuir, and there are rumours of Davik Kaine in every city in the Dominion. It doesn't mean anything."

Bothain growled low in his throat, rubbing the bridge of his nose with stiff fingers. "The coffee please, Commander Khosran."

"Yes, General."

Khosran slipped out the door, moving fast. Illea eyed the desk chair, wishing she could sit in it. But it was too close to where Rainer was hovering.

"Sweep the Bay," Bothain said. "Round up as many people as you can. Fill the jail to bursting."

"Why?" Rainer scoffed. "What's the Bay got to do with anything?"

"Aside from the fact that Davik Kaine might be there? Nothing. But a man held a gun to your head this morning, and you're on the eve of an election. You need to remind this city who is in charge before they descend into chaos. You cannot allow a man to wave a gun in your face with no consequences."

"I can't do that, Bothain—you don't understand—this city—I can't just walk into the Bay and start arresting people. It will start riots."

"So what?" Bothain snapped.

"He's afraid of Powell Iwan," Illea supplied. "And rightly so. The old man is a canny enemy, and Rainer can't afford to anger him now, so close to the election. The last time Iwan got involved in an election, the Governor elect was so destroyed that he had to leave Yaelsmuir when Iwan was done with him."

"How did he get so much control over this city?" Bothain scoffed. "And you're perfectly happy to let him keep it, are you?"

"Powell Iwan had a strangle hold on shipping through the Bay long before we ever came to the political field," Rainer bristled. "But we're stuck with him, and we have to move carefully, or he'll bathe the city in blood like he did in the early days when he was gaining control."

"So you're telling me that you can't arrest feral tainted in the Bay?" Bothain asked. "The Authority is a national program, born right here in Yaelsmuir, and an old man on the docks has closed off an entire quarter of the city to you?"

"It's not closed off," Rainer stammered. "We've agreements in place —there's an understanding, between Iwan and the Mayor's office and the Governor—it's a peace accord, to keep things running smoothly."

"And because of that peace accord, your city is harbouring a dangerous fugitive, and it's the Authority's policy to deny the powerful and radical presence of the Army of the Red Dawn," Bothain said dryly. "Have I got that about right?"

Rainer shook his head. "There's no proof that Davik Kaine is really here, Bothain. You're so obsessed with the man, but there's no reason to believe the rumours are true. I can arrest people in Brickheart, maybe. That's where Blackwood is from, isn't it? I'll send tinmen through the Row, scooping up anyone who even spoke to him."

"That won't help you," Illea said. Best give half-decent advice so Rainer thought she was still interested in helping him. "Brickheart won't stand for it, and their outrage will cost you votes. A raid on the Bay would work because there aren't any voters for Myron in the Bay, so it costs you nothing. Brickheart is different—they lean Redbone, but plenty of them are employed by Winter voters, and they'll want to show their loyalty. A raid will drive them away. They won't stand for their neighbours being arrested because of the actions of one man they may or may not know."

Bothain bared his teeth again, shaking his head. "You'll need a show of force. Show this city you can't be bullied or intimidated. I'm telling you, you need to sweep the Bay. That's what the fraternization laws are *for*, so that we can act decisively when we need to, and arrest them for congregating."

"I can't!" Rainer snapped, his face flushing with his panic. "Listen to me—it's not an option. There aren't enough tinmen in this city to organize an action like that. We're dangerously short staffed, and if we ignite the powder keg that is Cattle Bone Bay, we haven't enough tinmen to control the carnage."

The silence in the office was so thick, Illea thought she could hear the mechanical workings of Bothain's mind grinding along. It was a sobering thought, stripping some of the glee out of Illea's mood. If an uprising happened as a result of all of this, Rainer didn't have enough bodies to put it down. Which was good for Eirdis's campaign, perhaps, but at what cost?

No cost is too high, her business mind told her. And it was an easy stance to take when one imagined violence in the Bay. There was always violence in the Bay. But what was to stop it from crossing the river to Highfield if Rainer didn't get it under control?

"What about Patrollers?" Bothain asked. "The Authority holds legal jurisdiction over all civilian bodies. Could you enlist them under Authority control?"

"I could—with the Mayor's signature. But I shan't be counting on that. I'm not letting them get away with this." Rainer took a long drink of his brandy. "I've sent good people after him."

"Enquiry?" Bothain asked.

Rainer's eyes bulged again, and he darted a nervous glance at Illea, his tongue sliding across his lips, a little pink worm under his overly waxed moustache. "I wouldn't…"

Bothain huffed. "We've no time to dance around secrets. Did you send Enquiry after him or not?"

Rainer nodded. "Five. They'll take over from the arresting Patrollers. They'll find out about where he learned all these things, him and Saeati both, curse them, the smug, meddling bastards."

"Wait," Illea gasped. "You sent Patrollers after Ishmael? Why ever for? He wasn't involved. He dragged Blackwood off you—he saved your foul life, Rainer. And you had him arrested, too?"

"There's no way he wasn't involved. I know you're fond of him, Illea —though I can't for the life of me imagine why—but the man is a snake. Tell her what you told me, Bothain. He pretends to be a useless drunk, but he's hiding things—"

Bothain held up a hand, the simple motion silencing Rainer. "You fucking idiot. You told Patrollers to arrest Ishmael Saeati? Are you fucking mad? You don't know what that man is capable of."

Rainer shook his head. "He can't escape five Enquiry Officers. They'll find out what he knows and have him dealt with once and for all."

The sickness ate through every last shred of Illea's composure. She put her hand on the wall to steady herself—it wasn't only the nausea, it was a cold feeling over her skin and sweat on the back of her neck and ringing in her ears that made it hard to know for sure if she was standing or if she was falling.

"What are Enquiry Officers?" she asked, and even her own voice seemed terribly small and far away.

"Dead by now, I'm sure," Bothain laughed. "You've really fucked yourself this time, Rainer. I would gloat but I'm supposed to be helping you. Ishmael Saeati is not a man you want as an enemy."

Rainer shook his head. "He'll be dead before midnight, Bothain— the Officers will take care of everything."

"Rainer!" Illea snapped. "What are Enquiry Officers?"

"They're bounty hunters," Bothain said, only glancing at Illea. "They hunt down feral tainted and neutralize the threat."

"They kill tainted," Illea said. "Don't waste my time with pretty euphemisms—you're talking about people who track and murder tainted."

Bothain shrugged. "According to Article 38 subsection J of Crowne law, the NTRA is a full autonomous body of the law, in charge of all tainted in the Dominion. Any unregistered tainted is outlaw and thus outside the protection of Crowne governance, leaving the Authority to deal with non-compliance as they see fit."

"You don't have to quote law to me," Illea snapped. "I just want to know what we're dealing with. Neither Ishmael nor Blackwood are Talented, so how will you justify murdering them? Nathaniel will be campaigning for your head, Rainer. And I've half a mind to help him get it! Blackwood can burn for all I care, but Ishmael?"

Rainer shook his head, grabbing the bottle of brandy again, his grip so tight on the bottle it turned his knuckles bone white. "He brought this on himself, getting involved."

"Remember those words when I've burned your career to the ground," Illea hissed. "When people wonder why I've turned on you, I'll tell them that much. He brought this on himself with what he did to Ishmael Saeati."

"Illea—" Rainer scoffed, stepping closer.

Illea slapped the bottle out of Rainer's hand. The glass shattered on the wood floor, spraying shards and brandy everywhere, up the walls, up the sides of the desk, all across Rainer's trousers and his shiny leather shoes. "Save it for the Queen. I'm sure she'll want to know why you murdered one of her favourite citizens. I hope I get to watch you try to justify this to her."

Rainer's eyes bulged. Finally a threat made some impact, and it only served to make Illea all the more furious. He wasn't intimidated by the prospect of her wrath.

More the fool him.

14

TASHUÉ

DAY 33

The swaying of the cart made him sick—or maybe that was the whisky—or the shot to the head. The rattling made his head hurt so fucking much, every divot in the cobblestone road jostling him, shaking the headache deeper into his skull.

Fuck everything. He'd made a real mess of it this time.

Ishmael talked incessantly—Tashué could barely make out half of the things Ishmael said over the buzzing in his own head. Something about the law and the criminal code. The steady stream of words helped Tashué grasp onto something long enough to stay on the right side of consciousness. Maybe none of the words were for the Patrollers, who weren't responding to any the things Ishmael said anyway.

It was taking too long to get to the jail.

Or maybe it wasn't. Maybe the whisky made him spin off to something adjacent to time, making every moment stretch immeasurably so that he had no idea how many minutes were passing.

Stella's voice lived in his memory—*in Cruinnich, they would call you a man who moves mountains*. He could almost see her, skin kissed by the distant light of the brights outside his window when she stretched herself out on top of him, her scars and her freckles and the curve of her breasts borne to him, the curly mass of her hair all about her shoulders. He could see her so clearly that he could almost touch her, except of course he couldn't. Because he couldn't move mountains. He was drunk and beaten in the back of a prisoner transport wagon, headed to jail for his stupidity.

It was definitely taking too long. From the bank of the Brightwash to the Yaelsmuir city jail shouldn't have been much of a ride—it was only halfway through Brickheart, maybe a dozen blocks. Bad traffic could make the distance stretch for hours, but their wagon had been moving at a steady clip the entire time Tashué was awake.

"Where are you taking us?" Ishmael asked. "We're on the fucking bridge—why are we crossing the river?"

No one answered.

Tashué forced his eyes open even though it made his skull ache. The space around him was crowded with so many people—so many legs and pairs of city-issue boots making a jail cell around him already, and all of them with guns.

And Ishmael's bare feet looking incongruous, as they oozed blood onto the wooden wagon floor.

"Why are there so many riders following the wagon?" Ishmael asked. He shifted, just a little, his foot resting on Tashué's shoulder. Anchoring them together through touch, maybe. Or silently asking Tashué to stay down for now. "There's what, four of them? Five? And six of you in here—seems a little fucking much, doesn't it? A whole escort for a pair of drunks you pulled off the riverbank?"

The answer felt entirely too obvious.

Rainer had taken the morning—maybe part of the afternoon, what time was it?—to find Patrollers he trusted, and they would take Tashué out to the forest and put him down like a rabid dog. Tashué knew too much and Rainer wouldn't allow him to survive long enough to hit the jail cell. Someone had probably already turned up to the city jail to report the death, and now it had to be done.

And Tashué deserved it.

He'd been stupid, getting drunk and going to Rainer and spilling the things he knew. So incredibly stupid, and they were going to kill him for it. And now Ishmael was caught up in Tashué's mess. That felt even worse. Ishmael hadn't been part of any of Tashué's idiotic decisions. He'd walked at Tashué's side and drank with him because that's what Ishmael did—whatever the people of Highview thought of him, he was loyal once someone got under the prickly exterior of the way he behaved. That loyalty was going to be the end of him. Because Tashué got too drunk and

too angry instead of doing something intelligent about the energy
units.

"Where do you take your prisoners to murder them quietly these
days?" Ishmael asked, his voice rising, louder, angry, like he hoped people
outside the wagon would hear his outrage. Not that it would help either
of them. "The city is so fucking crowded, hey? Can't account for how
many people are going to see. What explanation do you have for driving
the prisoner transport wagon right out of the city, instead of stopping at
the city jail?"

"We are transporting you for questioning," one Patroller said stiffly,
the first time Tashué had heard any of them talk since the riverbank. "If
you cooperate, you'll be fine."

"Sure," Tashué grunted. The weight of the wagon shifted, tilting
Tashué forward—they must have crossed the river and the wagon was
making its way down the ramp to get off the bridge. He closed his eyes
again, rolling toward Ishmael, but the chain keeping him on the floor of
the wagon pulled taut, and he couldn't roll all the way. He was stuck on
his back, staring up past the guns as the wagon rattled along the road,
the jostling making it hard for his eyes to focus on any particular thing.
"If I cooperate, you'll cart us right back to the city jail and hand us over
to the warden, right? I believe you."

The Patroller shook her head but didn't say anything else.

"Rainer wants us alive, you said," Ishmael pressed. "So he must want
something. But he knows our answers are going to be bad for him politi-
cally, and he doesn't want anyone to hear what we have to say otherwise
he would have us questioned at the jail." He pushed on Tashué with his
foot, which was probably the most movement he could get away with
since the wagon was so damned crowded. "Makes me wonder what
questions Rainer has for our Captain Blackwood here. Something to do
with those energy units, maybe. What do you think, Captain? What have
you got to say that's got Rainer sweating so fucking much?"

Tashué turned to the woman who seemed to be in charge—the one
who Ishmael threw all his bitter questions toward, the one who spoke to
them. Late twenties, Tashué thought, maybe early thirties—she sat stiff
backed in the wagon and she held her rifle like someone who was
comfortable using it. Relaxed, but ready to fire it in an instant, finger on
the trigger guard but not the trigger.

"Did you serve, Patroller?" Tashué asked. "Foreign deployment? Or
domestic guard, maybe?"

The Patroller said nothing, her mouth a hard, tight line as she kept her eye on Ishmael.

"I gave the cavalry ten years," Tashué said. "And you know what they gave me? Fifty lashes and a White Shield. How's that for military justice? Flogged me for winning and then gave me a medal for it. They hand out medals and floggings for the wildest shit, I swear. They teach officers to think and then get angry if we use our education. Is the City Civilian Patrol like that? Do they want you to think, or do they want you to follow orders?"

The Patroller gave a little shake of her head—Tashué was failing to impress her. "If you cooperate, there's no reason for anyone to get hurt."

"That's not true, is it?" Tashué asked. "Ishmael's right, isn't he? Rainer doesn't want me talking where people can hear me. Did you hear about the children? Energy units, that's what Rainer called them. Energy units that aren't human—energy units that need to be refined to be more efficient. Fucking *children*. I found the body of one of his energy units, did you know that? None of the papers were willing to run the news. I think the girl I found was about ten or eleven when she died—her name was Lizanne Gian Ly. I don't think she was a hundred pounds when she died. It had to be less since she didn't have any arms and legs. Rainer said it makes them lighter and easier to transport. Did you know any of that, Patroller?"

Another shake of the Patroller's head—not a disagreement, exactly, but maybe a denial. No, she didn't know. Maybe she didn't believe it.

The wagon's wheels hit a different texture of road—the cobblestones were bumpy, but they were consistent in their rattle, a constant punctuation that shook Tashué's teeth as the wagon rolled over every gap between the stone. But the road leading out of Yaelsmuir wasn't cobbled; it was packed earth, and it gave the jostling of the wagon a completely different rhythm.

"Do you have any children, Patroller?" Tashué asked. He swung to the next Patroller—a man, older than the woman in charge. "How about you, do you have any children? I have one—I guess he isn't a child anymore. But I remember when he was small enough that I could hold him in one hand, and I remember when he was about the same age as Lizanne. He was so fucking clumsy at that age—always bumping into shit around the apartment and dropping things, and catching his head on door frames. Like he didn't ever know where his limbs were. But at least he had limbs, I guess. At least the Authority didn't cut them off to make him *easier to transport*. That's what Rainer said. I'll never forget those words. If I get through this day alive, I'll repeat those fucking words every chance I get. He was talking about children, for fuck's sake. He said they're assets to run our economy, who needed to be refined into something more powerful and more efficient. He said they weren't human, those children from the Breeding Program. Remember that the next time you take a tram across town. It's powered by a child with Talent and no arms or legs—a child Rainer Elsworth doesn't consider human."

The wagon stopped.

The doors swung open.

The sun was low on the horizon already, the long beams spilling light into the wagon to cut sky-spun gold across Tashué's body. His dress greens had new blood stains on them. Whose blood was that, his or Ishmael's? He couldn't tell.

The man who opened the back of the wagon wasn't a Patroller. He wasn't wearing the uniform or the hat, but just a regular suit. A heavy winter coat. He didn't have a badge pinned to his jacket or his coat. He watched Tashué with cold blue eyes, his head slowly cocking to one side. He had Talent in him, swirling like a poisonous knot. It was jarring how clearly Tashué could feel it. He'd always been able to sense Talent, like a scent that hung in the air, a pheromone his own Talent recognized. That sense was sharper since... when? Since Stella, maybe. Like she'd opened him up to his own capabilities, spreading them wide so they permeated every fibre of his being. Could he use his Talent to save himself? To save Ishmael?

"If you'll step down, gentlemen," the man said. "There's no need for a big production."

"Fuck you," Ishmael said. "The wagon is nice. If you just want to ask us some questions, why don't you come in here where the Patrollers can hear the answers?"

The man sighed. "Mr. Saeati, is it?"

"Eat shit," Ishmael said.

"Children," Tashué said again. "They're cutting up children. They're going to kill us in the fucking woods because they don't want this city to know about the children. They're going to murder us to shut us up because our whole economy collapses without *energy units*, but those energy units are fucking *children* and if you don't do anything now that you know, you're as guilty as the people who cut their arms and legs away. You hear me? Now you know, and now you carry the burden of letting it happen. I hope you're brave enough to do something about it."

Silence. Did they believe him, or did they think he was a raving drunk?

"I'm not in the mood for the melodrama, gentlemen," the man said. He stared at Tashué with cold, hard eyes, his face a mask of... something. Tashué couldn't tell if it was anger or some kind of primal, violent joy, like he was truly looking forward to the parts that came next. "The pair of you can come calmly, or we can hog tie you and drag you behind our horses. The road is rough around here—it'll beat the fight right out of you."

"What if he can't walk?" Ishmael asked.

The man gave a lazy shrug. "Then we drag him."

Ishmael took his foot off Tashué's shoulder, leaving behind a dark bloodstain on Tashué's uniform. "Go easy, Captain."

"You can unlock the big one now, Patroller," the man said. "We'll take it from here, one way or another."

The Patroller nodded, and someone else leaned down to unlock the hinge that kept Tashué shackled to the floor of the wagon, but he struggled with it—the lock was old and it seemed to resist being opened. The Patroller in charge met Tashué's eyes for a moment as she waited—just a moment, one spasm of doubt crossing her features.

"If I'm not telling the truth, why has Rainer and this shit-eating asshole gone through all this trouble to cart us out here?" Tashué asked, one last attempt to get through to her. If Tashué and Ishmael were going to die out in the Dunnenbrahl because they were too drunk to get themselves out of this mess, maybe he could plant a seed of doubt in someone's head so they would go back to the city and do... something. Fucking anything. "If I was lying, Rainer wouldn't be so scared of what I have to say. He'd just throw me in a jail cell and let me rot."

The hinge finally sprang open, giving an angry squeal as it moved and released the end of the chain attached to Tashué's manacles. The man grabbed Tashué by the ankle, dragging him to the door, then grabbed him by the front of the coat and hauled him up into a sitting position. Tashué looked down at his feet, hanging out the back of the cart. Bare and bleeding still, water dripping from the hem of his trousers.

The sun hung low over the Dunnenbrahl, trying to sink down past the horizon and leaving long shadows through the skeletal trees. They had stopped in a clearing with enough space for the riders to congregate around the wagon, the thin hunter's track uneven and muddy from all the recent rain. Being out here made him ache for Stella. She'd gone east, into the bitter cold and the wilderness, toward the distant mountains. He should have gone with her. He was supposed to stay to help Jason, but instead he'd gotten drunk and Jason was still in the Rift and nothing was better. Everything was worse, and he was going to die if he didn't think of something.

Tashué moved his body slowly, testing the limits of his limbs. Things ached, pulled, burned—the beating left its echoes of pain in his muscles, his joints, and he took the weight carefully to see if the lingering dizziness would get worse. It was trying to be a nice day out here, the sun decently strong even though it was setting. But here he was, standing on the old hunter's road. Making eye contact with the man who was going to kill him.

Five in all—two women and three men, each of them in regular suits without badges, bundled against the cold. They all had horses and guns—the leader of the group and one of the women standing close to the wagon, the other three riders still on horseback with their hands on their rifles. The leader had left his rifle hanging from his saddle, but the woman on foot had hers slung casually over her shoulder like she didn't expect to need it. All of their saddles had the full horn like cattle drivers and a wide-backed saddle for long rides.

Tashué flexed his hands, returning movement to his half-numb fingers. The leader gestured for Tashué to come closer, just once, giving Tashué one last chance to obey. Something crackled in the air, something wild and animal and violent. Tashué took one step, another, closing the distance between them only slowly, flexing his fingers more. The manacles dug into his wrists and hot blood trickled down from where the iron cut him open, but he still had strength in his big hands. How fast could he close the gap between them, how fast could he get his hands around this fucker's throat?

How fast would everyone else react?

But his bare feet scraped awkwardly along the road, catching on a divot in the mud. Too clumsy and too sore. His blood sat red on the surface of the dark road, dancing in his footprints.

"You too, Saeati," the leader said. "Let's go."

Ishmael grunted as he stood, his feet shuffling along the bottom of the wagon. Tashué glanced back in time to see Ishmael sit on the edge, just like Tashué had, except Ishmael moved faster, his limbs sharp and precise. He sat for a moment, hands behind his back, looking down at the ground, watching the steady drip drip drip of water that leaked from his trouser leg and then mixed with the blood coming from one of the wounds. The man in charge whistled through his teeth and jerked his head toward Ishmael, and the woman on foot grabbed Ishmael by the front of the coat.

Ishmael let himself fall. It was the only way to describe it. It almost looked like he was too drunk to land on his feet as he came out of the back of the wagon, but his movements before had been too fluid, too easy. He *let* himself fall and made a show of landing hard and gave a grunt for good measure, but it was all wrong.

Two of the riders still on horseback maneuvered their mounts through the clearing, coming to the broad side of the wagon.

"This track should be wide enough for you to keep on it a mile or so," one of the riders said. "Is it a mile, Matt, or two miles?"

"Two miles," the second rider said. He spat onto the trail and shifted in his saddle. The youngest of them, Tashué thought, his face round and friendly. "Or thereabouts. And then the track'll fork, and you wanna hang a left. It'll loop you back to the city in no time."

"I thought it was right," the first man said, brushing moss off his knee.

"No, stupid, it was right when we were headed down to the city. It's left if you're trying to turn around."

The woman on foot swung the back door of the wagon closed, throwing the exterior latch shut. Another squeaky hinge howled louder than the two riders bickering. Dread clawed up Tashué's throat—the Patrollers couldn't open the door from the inside with the latch closed like that, and the riders were still babbling, failing to give any useful directions back to the city, the pair of them angling their horses to block the track. The wrongness of it all sat in the clearing like a poisonous fog. Tashué flexed his hands again, taking a half-step.

The man in charge nodded.

The riders blocking the wagon dragged their rifles to bear and fired —the shots roared in Tashué's ears, leaving his vision blank-white from the bright muzzle flash. The driver of the cart hit the road with a scream, and the horse team pulling the wagon whinnied, one of them half-darting forward. The door rattled—the Patrollers inside, trying to get out.

Tashué lunged for the leader—but something dropped over Tashué's head. A rope. It pulled taut in an instant, the coarse jute ripping against his skin, yanking him off balance. He fell hard, landing flat on his back, the impact punching the air out of his lungs. The rope wasn't tight enough to prevent him from breathing completely, but each breath was an ugly struggle, panic and fury warring for dominance. He rolled halfway onto his side, trying to get back up.

Ishmael moved so fast Tashué's dazed eyes couldn't track it as the evening light lost ground to night's long shadows—one moment Ishmael was on the ground with his hands shackled behind his back, and the next he had his hands in front of him and he was on his feet. He looped the chain around the woman's neck, hauling her in close. The woman twisted, thrashed, but Ishmael had her, dragging the woman with him like a hostage, the chain digging hard, lines into the woman's throat.

Something twitched in the centre of Tashué's chest, something half-alive and separate from him. His Talent. It battered against the beating of his own heart and made his ligament scream in protest at the pressure.

In Cruinnich, they would call you a man who moves mountains, Stella told him.

If there was any moment to use his Talent, it was fucking *now*, except it had hooks in him. He could feel it, but he couldn't make it do anything. He squeezed his eyes shut and tried to imagine it, the force Stella described to him, the slumbering beast he'd been half aware of all his life, but it wouldn't fucking move. It was just there, pressure he couldn't release.

More shots, flashing in the clearing as the shadows grew longer and deeper, ripping apart the side of the wagon, throwing splinters everywhere, and the Patrollers inside screamed, shot back.

Tension on the rope—dragging Tashué like the leader had promised, pulling him down the road, away from the wagon.

Tashué tried to push his fingers into the rope, kicked against the road. No decisions, only instinct and thrashing, trying to get slack in the rope, trying to get a breath. His bare heel caught on a stone and pain ripped through him, hot and angry.

The rope went slack, and Tashué stopped sliding through the mud, and he could breathe again. Tashué half-rolled, trying to get up. Get up. If he could just get up—but what could he do against those guns? Still roaring, each shot like thunder in a storm of lead and gunpowder and blood.

Ishmael lay flat on his back in front of the wagon, the woman on top of him, the chain of the manacles around the woman's neck, and the leader was watching—standing back with his hands on his hips, watching, because to get closer to the wagon was to step in the line of fire.

Up, to his knees—Tashué twisted to face the woman who had the rope but it was already too late to do anything. She'd tossed it over the branch of a tree and tied it to her saddle horn. As Tashué surged to his feet to try to get closer to her, she sprang back up into the saddle. Kicked her horse forward to pull away the slack and then he couldn't move anymore. The rope scraped over the tree bark until it started to lift him. His bare toes scraped the mud, unable to find enough traction to move him, his whole spine stretching miserably with his own weight. He felt the horse's every movement through the rope, every time it shifted its weight impatiently, like it wanted to get going. Tashué grabbed the rope, trying to force his fingers into it, his nails clawing his own skin in the process.

The guns went quiet, and Tashué watched Ishmael kick the dead body away from him. He grabbed the dead woman's rifle and rolled under the wagon. The two riders reloaded their rifles with slow, methodical movements, like the pair of them weren't in any hurry to get Ishmael cornered. Those big .45s had obliterated one wall of the wagon, turning the six Patrollers inside and their driver into nothing but heaps and chunks of bone and meat and stinking innards, all that blood leaking from the wagon in a red bath that soaked into the mud.

Tashué grabbed the rope over his head instead of trying to get his fingers into it. All he needed was an inch of slack and then he could breathe properly. If he could get his feet planted on the ground, he could charge at the rider who had him roped, but there wasn't enough room. He turned a useless pirouette on the tips of his bloodied toes, gasping, the rope burning, scraping, ripping the skin below the line of his beard. He could breathe just enough to keep himself conscious. For all the good it did him.

Out of the corner of his eye, he spotted Ishmael, clothes soaked with mud and blood—he rolled out from under the wagon and sprang to his feet, hefting that stolen rifle, pointing at the woman who had roped Tashué up. Pulled the trigger. The hammer clicked uselessly on an empty chamber. Flash of white as he bared his teeth in an angry snarl—with his hands manacled together he couldn't hold the rifle to his shoulder and rack the action to load another round, so he grabbed the lever action in one filthy fist and let the rifle drop, the weight of it carrying the lever action open—he snapped his arm back up and the rifle popped back up, the action completing its movement—

But it had taken too long.

Matt, the man on horseback with the young face, lifted his rifle and fired through the wagon. Ishmael dropped.

For a horrible, sickening moment, Tashué thought Ishmael was shot. A canyon of despair ripped itself open through him. But then Ishmael was on his feet again and running. Full tilt, ignoring the bloody mess that his feet must have been, body turning into a black-clad wraith in the shadow-soaked trees, the rifle still in his hands.

The leader threw up his hands like it was all a minor inconvenience. Matt gave a wild, playful whoop, using his reins to slap his horse's flanks. The big bay was off like a shot, heading for a gap between the trees, and the other man followed. The leader kicked the dead body that Ishmael had left behind, just once like he was checking if the woman would wake up. Tashué couldn't do anything but watch as the leader of the group reached into the newly destroyed side wall of the wagon, sliding his hand along the floorboards and scooping up a handful of blood. He came down the road slowly, so much blood in his hand that it was dripping, dripping, the patter of it on the road like a nail through Tashué's temple with every drip drip drip drip drip. The leader of the group grinned and reached up, spreading the blood across Tashué's face.

"There you go, Blackwood," he said, still smiling. "I hope you enjoy it. You earned it. You killed all those people, after all."

"Fuck you," Tashué huffed, his voice half-caught by the rope that made it so hard to breathe. The blood cooled fast against his skin, thickening, clotting, itching. "I didn't—"

The leader shrugged, wiping his hand down the front of Tashué's jacket and leaving a long, dark smear. "But you did. Couldn't keep your fucking mouth shut, could you? Set him down, Tracy, so he can catch his breath and answer a few questions."

The rope loosened, and Tashué dropped to his knees, sucking in as many deep breaths as he could, the air leaving a horrible rasp along the inside of his throat. His Talent twisted, battling against the inside of him like he'd swallowed an angry polecat.

Breathe—and think.

But he couldn't think. He was so fucking tired. The whisky left him with a headache and a sour stomach and the desire to sleep forever. Fuck these people. Fuck Rainer for sending them. Where the hell had he found them? Mercenary killers, willing to shoot down Patrollers? Were they Enquiry Officers like Siras, stationed in fucking Yaelsmuir?

How had Tashué served the Authority for nineteen years and not *known?*

"I'm going to ask you some questions, Blackwood," the leader said. "If you answer them, this'll be over nice and quick. If you give us a hard time, we're going to hurt you. It's that simple. We'll skip the part where you and I argue about it all, and I won't bother threatening you, because I think you believe me when I say Tracy will happily hang you from this big old spruce tree while we wait for Matt and Del to come back with Mr. Eat Shit out there. Yes?"

Tashué forced his eyes open, looking up at the man. His features were reduced to vague shapes, dusk shadows swallowing the details. But Tashué would remember those bright blue eyes for the rest of his life— however short that might be. "Yeah," he grunted, his throat aching. "Sure. Can I have a smoke first? It's been a long fucking day."

The leader cocked his head to one side, looking down at Tashué a while. Maybe he'd expected more arguing or Tashué making a big show about not cooperating. He finally shrugged, searching Tashué's pockets. Tashué's only weapons—his pistol and his knife—were gone. On the bank of the Brightwash last he saw them.

He found Tashué's sketchbook and flipped through it briefly, but it was getting too dark for him to see any details, the trees obscuring the last light of the setting sun. He stashed it in his own pocket instead. Thank fuck Tashué had given the photos of Lizanne to Allie, maybe she was doing something useful with them by now.

The man found Tashué's cigarillo case, flicking it open—it was battered from the violence of the last few weeks, the silver stained with blood. The hinges creaked, only opening halfway. Fuck, how had his life changed so completely? A few weeks. The man took a cigarillo from the case, sparking a match from his own box. The sulphur popped and flared, lighting the man's features again, making his eyes shine, light leaving a shadow in the scar across the bridge of his nose. He took a big mouthful of smoke and breathed it into Tashué's face.

"Fuck you," Tashué muttered. Sweet North Star, he wanted a smoke. His whole body itched with the craving. Of all the stupid things to think about after his own almost-hanging, it was the craving for tobacco that was driving him out of his own skin.

The leader laughed, tossing Tashué's cigarillo case on the path.

"You're smoking the real cheap shit, Blackwood. I know the Authority pays enough for you to buy better tobacco than this. And you, living alone, with no one to support but yourself. Where does your money go?" He took another drag from the cigarillo, blowing into Tashué's face again. "Are you affiliated with the Army of the Red Dawn? Do you wander down to the Bay and spend your wages on Red Dawn whores? I hear Davik's got the best in town. Is that how you got involved in this shit?"

Tashué shook his head. "The Chief Administrator of the National Tainted Registration Authority says there is no organized presence of the Red Dawn in Yaelsmuir."

"Then how did you get yourself into this mess, hey?" the woman asked, shifting in her saddle. The rope tugged every time her big horse fidgeted.

"I found a body of a child on the riverbank, and I just wanted to know how she died." Tashué reached up, grabbing the rope again with both hands. The rope stuttered as it dragged along the rough surface of the branch it was draped over. There was enough give in it that Tashué could stop the rope from pulling at his neck every time the fucking horse moved. "A child. How can you live with yourself knowing what the Authority does to children?"

"Save your righteous indignation for someone who cares," the woman muttered. "It's boring."

"Fuck you," Tashué snapped. "Fuck all of you. Just fucking kill me, then. I don't know anything about the Red Dawn. All I wanted was to know what happened to the girl I found. I wanted to know who she was and how she died. Her name was Lizanne Gian Ly. A fucking child. She deserved to be seen."

"How did you find out, then?" the leader asked. "Someone must have told you. Who was it?"

"Edgar Hale," Tashué said.

"Where is he now?"

Tashué looked the man in the eye, which shone in the gathering darkness, lit by the cherry red end of the cigarillo when he took a drag and the big face of the mostly full moon. "I fucking killed him. He killed Lizanne Gian Ly, so I dislocated both his arms and put a bullet through his head. Made me feel better."

The leader chuckled. "Well, Mr. Blackwood, that's very kind of you. I appreciate the help. How did you find Hale? Was he Red Dawn?"

"I don't know," Tashué said. "I don't know anything about the Red Dawn. I found Hale while trying to figure out what happened to the girl, and he told me what he knew."

"And who did you tell?" the woman asked. "After you killed Hale, who did you run your big mouth to?"

"No one," Tashué said, shaking his head. "I didn't get the chance."

"Except Saeati and all them Patrollers?" the woman asked. "That's it?"

"Yeah, that's it," Tashué grunted, spiteful joy tearing through him. "And everyone in hearing distance in Brickheart. Everyone who came to General Wolfe's hospital opening and everyone who started to gather because they heard the shouting. So you can kill me if you want, but are you going to slaughter half of Brickheart? Elsworth's fucked, and so is everyone working for him."

The leader sighed at Tashué's defiance. "Where is Allie Tei?"

Fuck—Allie. What had Wolfe said the night Tashué brought Allie to Highfield? Tashué didn't remember exactly—but Wolfe had believed Rainer wouldn't come for Allie now that Wolfe was protecting her. Tashué prayed Wolfe was right.

Tashué shook his head again. "I don't know. What do you want with Allie Tei? Isn't she just a reporter for the gossip rags?"

"Mr. Blackwood, don't play dumb with me. Where is Allie Tei? We know you were seen with her the night she disappeared. The night the two of you killed one of ours."

"I killed her, too," Tashué said. "I took her to an alley and killed her, and that's why no one's seen her alive since. Did your job for you, didn't I? That's why you're asking about her, right? You want to shut her up too? I did it already."

The leader tilted his head to one side. "Whyever would you do that, Mr. Blackwood?"

"Because I wanted her, and she said no," Tashué said, even though the words made him want to peel his own tongue. "I thought we had something. I thought she wanted me, but then she tried to push me away—it all happened so fast."

The leader leaned closer. He loomed over Tashué, blowing smoke out his nose. Fuck these people. Tashué had to stop them, somehow. If he let go of the rope and got his hands around the leader's throat—or better yet, the chain between his manacles, just like Ishmael had—it wouldn't matter if the woman hauled Tashué up into the air, at least the leader would die up there, too. Ishmael was out there in the forest, he'd deal with the rest of them, surely. Whatever it took, so long as these fuckers couldn't go chasing after Allie Tei.

"Did you fuck her before she died, or after?"

Tashué shook his head. "I don't remember."

The woman on horseback snorted. "Don't remember? You're lying."

"Fuck you," Tashué said. "I was drunk. I didn't mean to——"

"Tell me about it," the leader insisted. "Tell me how you killed her. Did you take all her clothes off before you fucked her, or did she still have her clothes on? Did you strangle her—you've got such big hands, it would be easy for you. Did you look her in the eyes and watch the life fade? Tell me how you did it. I want to hear it. Every beautiful detail."

Tashué shook his head again. The moonlight danced on the edges of his features, but Tashué's tired eyes couldn't tell exactly how close he was. Was he still out of reach?

"I don't remember. Just fucking kill me," he croaked, keeping his voice quiet. Maybe it would lure the fucker a little closer. Tashué shifted his weight forward, just enough that he could stand in a hurry. "I don't remember."

The woman horked phlegm from the back of her throat and spat into the forest. "I'm bored, Sarge. He's just going to keep saying he doesn't know anything, and we'll be here all fucking night."

Gunshots clapped through the forest. Not as distant as Tashué would have expected. Ishmael mustn't have gotten far, or he'd circled around to start coming back.

"We killin' him, then?" the woman asked. "I'm hungry."

"Fine." The leader flicked the cigarillo at Tashué's face. Tashué flinched back, but the lit end hit his cheek, kissing him with pain before it fell to the damp ground, sizzling when the ember hit the puddle Tashué's knee was sunk into. "Hoist him up."

Tashué lunged, shooting up to his feet even though they were half-numb from kneeling. His hands caught something. Cloth. A lapel. The rope pulled tight, but his hands *had* the bastard and dragged him closer. Another shift got the manacle chain around the leader's neck, just like Tashué hoped—but the rope pulled so hard, his feet left the ground and the leader twisted, dropping out of Tashué's grasp and laughing. Fucking laughing.

The rope kept pulling, hauling Tashué straight up, up, until the entirety of his weight was suspended by the noose. Tashué reached over his head to grab the rope again, trying to drag himself up to get a bit of slack—he couldn't breathe.

He couldn't breathe.

"You alright, boss?" the woman asked.

"Big fucker's faster than he looks," the leader laughed.

White spots danced in his vision and the rope dug so hard into his throat that he could feel himself bleeding and the bones of his spine screamed their protest at the weight and the pressure and the pulling.

And he couldn't breathe.

Somewhere in the forest, more gunshots. Was it closer or farther away? He couldn't tell. A horse screamed with pain, a horrible, piercing sound that rattled over Tashué's senses.

In Cruinnich, they would call you a man who moves mountains.

He didn't want to move mountains; he wanted to breathe.

His Talent swirled so hard it made his senses scream incoherent pain, like rocks rolling through his bones, like ice shards ripping him from the inside out. He couldn't control it, couldn't make it stop. It kept building in him—pushing at the edges of him like he was a kettle coming to the boil, and the steam was looking for a place to escape—

"Bring him down—let's see if he's changed his story about Tei. I don't want to be chasing her all fucking winter in this shit city."

Down, he was falling down, down—his feet hit the forest floor but his knees buckled. He twisted at least, landing on his shoulder instead of flat on his back, sucking air into his greedy lungs. The pain from his Talent lingered, grinding against him. It was going to kill him faster than the fucking rope would kill him, because these people wanted to toy with him, but his own Talent was going to tear him apart and save them the trouble.

He'd never see Jason again. He'd never hold his son in his arms and he'd never get to apologize properly for all the ways he'd failed to understand what Jason had been trying to tell him all these years. He'd thought Jason was being stubborn, but Jason was being wise and brave and Tashué had been too blind, too emotionally stagnant, to *hear* what Jason was trying to tell him.

And Stella—how many days since she left? How long had she been out in this weather, this bitter cold and wind and rain? How far was she from the city now? He could almost see her, sitting in a camp not far from here, her bedroll ready for her and a fire cooking for her, her copper hair stuck with branches and leaves, her face smeared with dirt.

He should have gone with her. He shouldn't have let her and Ceridwen go without him. He'd wanted to stay for Jason, but he fucked everything.

"What's he thinking about, Tracy?" the leader asked. "Is he thinking about Tei? Where is she?"

"No, not Tei—pretty little redhead," the woman said. "Must be someone nearby—he seems to think she's camped out in the forest."

Panic raced through Tashué's body, hot and fast—she could see his thoughts? Why hadn't he felt it, the invasion of her Talent into his mind? How much else did she see? He tried to push all thoughts from his head, everything, trying to picture a big black nothingness—

"Redhead, is it?" the leader asked.

"Do you know the name Ffyanwy Rhydderch?" the woman asked. "Is that your redhead? Duncreek found her down this way, said she was fucking some big tinman."

Don't think—

He rolled to his feet, pushing himself up even though his joints were screaming from the Talent built up in them, boiling the very cartilage that sat between the bones. Fighting through the panic, pushing away any thoughts of Stella.

Talent was the only way out of this, but he couldn't control it, couldn't direct it, couldn't push it out—it was just lurking, waiting, pressure in his body and his mind. It was going to fucking kill him. But if he could release it, maybe it would kill them, too.

"I take that panic of yours to mean you've heard the name once or twice," the leader laughed. "Where is she? Did you kill her, too?"

Tashué took a deep breath. The Talent surged the hardest when he was up in the air, when he was hanging from the rope, when his whole body screamed with the instinct to live—maybe that was the key to releasing the Talent now, maybe it would panic again and it would rip through him, and maybe he would kill these people. Fuck them. They couldn't find Allie or Stella if he obliterated them all.

He stretched himself up, standing as straight as he could—at least when they hoisted him up again, he could tell the Keeper of the Keys he'd died on his feet.

The leader was standing too far away for Tashué to reach him with any part of his body, so Tashué spat at him. It was so dark that Tashué couldn't see if the spit hit the man at all, but he did hear the way the man sucked in a breath—maybe Tashué had hit him right in the face. Good. Fuck him.

Something moved up the track—little more than a shadow, kissed by moonlight, but Tashué still recognized the shape of a horse. Was it Ishmael returning victorious, or was it the men who'd chased him, dragging his body back?

"I'm going to enjoy killing you," Tashué said.

The blue-eyed man laughed. "Oh, Blackwood, I have to give you credit. You're much more fun than I thought you'd be."

15

ISHMAEL
DAY 33

Running in the forest was real *shit* barefoot.

Leaf litter made a carpet but it also hid the things that hurt the most—rocks and roots and uneven ground, turned into an undulating ocean of red and orange and brown, the details fading fast as the sun went down. But he didn't have time for pain or fear or a better plan. It was time to fucking run, no matter how much blood he left on the trail behind him.

Hook hard left, jump over a big fucking rock—the landing wasn't good, his ankle twisted a little too much, but instead of trying to catch himself he just let himself go down. Drop, twist, roll, spring back to his feet. Pain.

Doesn't matter. Go.

Behind him, the pair of riders were whooping and howling like a pair of kids off on an adventure—a pair of hunting dogs baying at their prey. The sound cut through the forest, marking their position every time they broke the quiet, so Ishmael knew to keep left. Always left. It kept him away from the thinner parts of the forest where they could maneuver their horses, and eventually it would lead him back to the hunter's track so he could circle back and shoot the cunt on the horse, the one trying her best to hang Tashué from a tree. Hopefully Tashué could keep his captors talking long enough for Ishmael to get back. Hopefully the idiot wasn't already dead.

His ankle hurt.

He pushed hard, but his foundation was falling apart. Feet, ankle. Every step was becoming agony, burning hot and vicious up his legs, the steady impact bringing more and more pain.

The younger rider—Matt—was getting closer. His baying cut through the forest and it was definitely getting louder. The crashing of branches and sticks—the horse was fighting through the brush, maybe, but Ishmael couldn't see the shape of him anywhere. Not that visibility was very good. Even though most of the trees had lost their leaves to the autumn winds and cold, there were still evergreens that stood tall and fat, blocking out the last light of dusk to turn the world into murky shadows. Copses of cedar made a dark green line at the edge of Ishmael's vision, and a wild tangle of white-barked aspen stood together so thick that even though they were just trunks, they might as well have been a wall of long white bone.

He needed fucking boots, and he needed time. A moment to catch his breath, to staunch the bleeding in his feet. But he didn't have time and neither did Tashué.

Think! Fucking think! Stop panicking and think—you know this stretch of forest —you've been out here a million times with Amias, with the stupid boring hunting parties—

That copse of cedar, he recognized it. He'd camped there with Amias a few times. It was a living hell in the summer because mosquitoes loved the cedar, but this time of year it was a great shelter from the weather.

He tightened his grip on the rifle and headed for the cedar. Tracks cut through this forest like a rabbit's warren, meeting each other half a hundred times, twisting this way and that. If the riders were on the tracks and following Ishmael, they would pass around the cedar copse, and he could fucking shoot them.

Into the copse. He dropped to his stomach. He wasn't a great shot, and his body was so shaky from the running that he'd miss for sure if he was standing up. Prone position was best, Deri taught him, sighing at Ishmael's general incompetence when it came to pointing a gun at things and pulling a trigger. He said a lot of shit about how Ishmael was left eye dominant but right-handed, so Ishmael explained that he was ambidextrous for almost everything. Deri started teaching him to shoot left-handed, but none of that made him any better. Ishmael figured it was all the stillness it required. Deri could do it. All the hunters he'd ever known could do it, especially Amias. When a rifle was in their hands and their quarry was in their sights, they became a statue, a monument to death, but Ishmael had never once in his life mastered that much patience.

He rested the butt of the rifle against his shoulder, but pain flared there, too. *Don't touch it, don't think about it, don't have time—*

He'd felt some kind of impact when he was standing on the far side of the wagon, trying to line up his shot at the woman on horseback. For a moment he'd thought it was a bullet, but a .45 slug from that close would have ripped his shoulder right off, so it must have been shrapnel thrown off the wagon, a chunk of wood turned airborne. He shifted the rifle to the other side. He'd shoot right-handed, then.

"I told you to shut the hell up," one of the riders said. They were coming along the road, like Ishmael hoped, but it was too fucking dark here in this thick tangle of forest. "He probably heard you from a mile away and he's long fucking gone."

"Del, relax," the second rider laughed. "No way he got far. He's barefoot and bleeding—he's gone to ground somewhere like a little frightened rabbit." The rider howled like a hunting dog, the sound eerily accurate, so loud and echoing that it made Ishmael's spine go too tight with tension. "Where'd you go, little rabbit?"

"Matt, shut the fuck up!"

Matt laughed. "Unclench your asshole, would you? We're just having fun."

"You're acting like he's gonna be easy," Del hissed, the words a harsh almost-whisper, but Ishmael still heard each word clearly—it went to show how close they were, that their words were coming to him so easily. "Like you think he doesn't know what he's doing. He killed the new kid when we thought he was still fucking drunk, so quit telling him exactly where we are."

"The new kid was stupid, got too close and let her guard down."

"Well, you're being stupid, too!"

Ishmael shifted as slowly as he could. Judging by the direction their bickering was coming from, they must have been coming down the track that was behind him, so he had to turn around. Moonlight made a glow on the serpentine path. If they stayed on it, the track would lead them all the way to General Wolfe's backyard. It was tempting to run all the way there, to wake the dog handlers and the hunting staff. They would tear this forest apart and find these two assholes, as well as the two left back on the road—but Ishmael didn't think his feet would carry him that far, and he knew for certain Tashué didn't have that much time.

What was the advice Deri gave him about shooting? He couldn't remember. Something about breathing while he lined up his shot—not holding his breath but shooting when his lungs were... were what? Full or empty?

Fucking hell, fuck this shit. Fuck this forest and fuck this stupid gun and fuck these idiots especially.

Something crawled through the air, lazy and heavy, like the taste of ozone before a big storm. Talent—one of them was using Talent.

They went quiet. The sound of their horses had stopped—they weren't coming down the trail anymore.

Bastards must have used their Talent to find him, and now they were making a plan.

Ishmael dragged himself forward on his stomach through the cedars and the gnarled roots, keeping the gun pointed out at the road. Didn't matter if they knew where he was, if he could shoot them, it would be over. But the shadows were thicker than when he'd first entered the copse and the details were falling away—everything was vague shapes and he couldn't tell which long line was a tree or a shrub and which might have been a horse's leg. If he started shooting, maybe they'd give their positions away by moving—but that would give his position away, too, and he didn't know how much running he had left in him or how many shots were in the stolen rifle.

A twig snapped.

Ishmael squeezed his eyes shut, forcing himself to breathe slow and quiet. To listen. Was the twig behind him or in front of him? Horses made a lot of noise in the forest, but he couldn't tell which sounds were wind in the trees and which his hunters. Fuck this forest, everyone in the city said it was haunted, probably because forests were so loud, and the trees made human shapes in the darkness, taunting people. Ghosts, people said, creeping through the undergrowth, looking for people to devour, except Ishmael didn't have time to worry about fucking ghosts because there were two *people* trying to hunt him down.

Something rustled—breathing. Someone was close, behind him, so close Ishmael could hear them breathing.

He rolled onto his back, pulling the rifle up, squeeze the trigger. The roar of gunpowder made his ears ring. The muzzle flash lit a figure, the older of the two riders, Del, in the cedar copse with

Ishmael. Del dropped. But he wasn't dead, he was still breathing, cursing, crawling through the copse, scrambling like it was a race now. Ishmael tried to rack a new round, but he couldn't do it with his hands still in fucking manacles. He rolled to his knees and tried to stand, but his ankle gave a hot bolt of pain that sucked the air out of his lungs, and he fell back down. He dropped the rifle so he could grab it by the barrel. A gunshot behind him, cutting through the copse, spraying his back with bark and wood, turning the smell of cedar extra oily and half burnt. He threw himself down, rolling left just in time—another gunshot in front of him, lighting Del's silhouette, the bullet punching into the ground where Ishmael had been a second ago, throwing up clods of dirt and chunks of root. Ishmael surged up, fuck the pain, ignore the pain, on his feet, and the sound of Del racking his lever action gave Ishmael something to aim for. He swung the rifle like a club. The wooden stock hit bone. A crack and a human howl of pain, and Ishmael's momentum carried him forward so his body hit Del, and they fell hard together. Habit made him reach for the knife he kept in his boot, but he wasn't fucking *wearing* his boots. Another shot, Matt shooting blindly into the copse like he didn't care if he hit Ishmael or Del so long as he hit something—but that thick-air-Talent feeling hadn't left so maybe the fucker knew exactly where Ishmael was.

Del thrashed, twisting, swinging. The darkness was so thick that all Ishmael saw was the outline of him, but that was enough. Ishmael let himself roll to the side but dragged Del with him, pushing the chain between his manacles up so it pressed against Del's throat even though it made his shoulder scream with agony. He reached both hands around Del's neck, lacing his fingers together so they locked at the base of Del's skull. Del gave a choking, wet gurgle, blood and spit leaking onto Ishmael's face. Ishmael lifted his legs to drape them around Del's waist, locking his ankles together to hold their bodies close and minimize Del's desperate thrashing. Del hit Ishmael in the torso, punches raining down against Ishmael's ribs and the soft bits below them, but Ishmael grit his teeth and hung on. Choking, spluttering, gurgling, thrashing, desperation making Del useless. His punches lost their strength quickly and he started to slump, but Ishmael hung on.

More footsteps—the other rider was coming into the copse.

Ishmael kicked Del away, wriggling out from under him, rolling, but he knew already Del wasn't dead—he hadn't held on long enough. He had to move anyway. Up, up even though it hurt, up and away, grab a gun, the lever still halfway open, fucking *run.*

"Del, fuck, are you alright? Get up!"

Del made a few horribly animal sounds that were half-choked with blood. Ishmael stopped running long enough to get his hand around the lever action, jerking the stupid rifle back and forth to get the chamber loaded with another round. Out of the cedar, there was just enough moonlight that he could see the forest.

He stopped, just a moment. Watching the cedar copse. But if they were coming out, they weren't following him directly. If he was lucky, Matt was dragging Del out of the copse the opposite way that Ishmael had gone, which would buy him time to get back to the big road where the wagon had stopped. If he was *really* lucky, Del was out of commission for fighting.

Fucking whisky and fucking Tashué—this should have been easier, but Ishmael's whole body was a mess from the drinking, never mind everything that came after. Barefoot in the forest like some kind of amateur. If Deri could see him now, the bastard would probably laugh at him. And then later, when they were safe, he would rip Ishmael apart for fucking this up so bad.

I put twenty fucking years into your career, teaching you how to be a weapon, Ishmael imagined Deri rumbling, *and* this *is how you get yourself killed?*

To the track—Del had left his horse on the road, and the big beast was standing mostly still, waiting for a rider to tell it what to do. Cropping half-dead grass from the side of the trail.

Everything hurt but Ishmael forced himself to move slow. "Hey, big guy," he said, his voice trembling with exhaustion, his chest heaving with the need to catch his breath. "How about you and me go for a bit of a ride, hey? I got a friend who needs my help but my fucking feet hurt." So long as he kept his voice calm, it didn't matter what he said to the damned horse. He remembered that much. Stay calm and move slow. The horse seemed unimpressed with him, which was probably good. It flicked its ears toward him but then went back to cropping grass. Ishmael edged around to the side of it, reaching out. He hated the way his hand trembled when it closed around the reins. The pain was eating through his training, through his battle-fury rush. The pain and the exhaustion. He'd woken up half-drunk and hung over and then went back to drinking and now this. Thank the gods for traffic—it had taken the wagon so long to get across the river and out of the city, it had given his body some time to sober up some. "Let's go back to the party, hey? See if we can help the big idiot that got me into this mess."

The horse let him get even closer. He draped the rifle over his shoulder so he could use both hands. One hand on the saddle horn and the other on the high back, a foot in the stirrup. Except that was his bad ankle, and the pressure it took to get himself off the ground sucked the air out of his lungs again, dragged a strangled gasp from his throat. The horse startled at that, like it wasn't sure about the sound, taking a few steps. Ishmael hopped along beside the stupid thing, half-dragged with one foot in the stirrup and his hands on the saddle, and it hurt so bad he couldn't see. Couldn't think. Couldn't breathe. Up, fucking get *up*.

He used the strength of his arms to drag himself up, and then he was finally high enough to swing his weight over the saddle and get his foot down the other side. He was a better rider than he was a shot, at least. Back straight, heels down, that's what Amias taught him. But Ishmael's ankle hurt way too much for him to push his heel down that far. It felt fitting, almost, that he should die in the same forest that took Amias—the most gifted horseman Ishmael had ever met, but he'd still fallen from his horse in this fucking forest and bled to death, so maybe shit like that was why people said the place was haunted.

He pulled the rifle off his shoulder, bracing it against his body so he could shoot at least once if he needed to, then kicked the horse with his good foot. The big animal gave a snort, head coming up. But it didn't go. Ishmael kicked its flanks again and the horse only danced in place, like it could feel his urgency to get moving, but maybe the darkness made it nervous. The fucking thing was supposed to make this easier, but instead it was going to get him killed. He whipped the reins back, the leather hitting his leg and the flank of the stolen horse, and finally it started down the trail. The horse's hooves sucked and squelched in the mud, which at least was a sign they were still on the track, but it made it impossible to hear for sure if anyone was close. Impossible to stay quiet. He closed his eyes, trying to focus on his breathing. Deep breath in, filling his lungs completely until they ached, slow breath out. If he did that enough, it would reduce the feeling that he was out of breath, and it would help his heart rate slow again so it didn't roar as insistently in his ears. Trying to listen for his pursuers only seemed to make him hyper aware of how much noise this stupid horse was making.

Fuck the horse and fuck the mud. He slid down out of the saddle, biting back a grunt of pain as his ankle took his weight, fighting against the stinging, burning heat that seared through his feet as the mud invaded all the open wounds. He slapped the horse's flank as hard as he could, sending it surging down the path, and staggered away, back to the tangle of the trees.

A gunshot lit the path. For one perfect moment, Ishmael could see another horse, behind his, the rider in the saddle and holding his rifle. His face was bleeding, his jaw hanging slack—Del. Maybe his jaw was broken, but he was riding and fighting anyway.

Ishmael hefted his rifle and aimed for the spot that had been lit by that muzzle flash and fired.

Del's horse screamed, the sound a horrible, ripping, tearing sound that drilled into Ishmael's eardrums.

"Got you now, little rabbit."

The cold, hard barrel of another rifle pressed against the back of Ishmael's neck.

Fuck.

"Easy now. Play nice, and I'll bring you back to the road alive so you can kiss your big dumb friend goodbye. How's that sound?"

Ishmael dropped his rifle and spun. His hands closed around the barrel of the rifle instead and pushed it up toward the sky—just in time. Matt pulled the trigger and lit the forest again, the bullet tearing up through branches, raining debris over Ishmael's head, shoulders. Don't think about the pain. He hauled the gun hard, dragging Matt closer. Snapped his head forward. His forehead hit nose, and Matt gave an angry yelp. Ishmael snapped a leg out, hooking his foot against Matt's ankle, and it threw Matt off balance, but he caught himself, his shoulder scraping audibly against the trunk of a tree, and then he twisted his rifle out of Ishmael's grasp.

Matt swung his rifle, and Ishmael tried to move. Not fast enough.

Pain. Burning through his chest, punching all the air out of his lungs.

Knees hit the forest floor before he even knew he was falling. He tilted forward and caught himself with his hands, pressing into the leaf litter. Matt kicked Ishmael in the ribs, making his chest seize. Ishmael collapsed, gasping, choking on his own desperate need to breathe.

"Fucking hell, you really made me work for it."

Matt grabbed the chain between Ishmael's manacles and started pulling him, dragging him through the forest, back to the thin track. The road was dappled here and there with the bright light of the moon, piercing the winter-bare canopy. The clouds must have cleared.

The horse Ishmael shot was still screaming. It was on the trail, thrashing, kicking, trying to get back up, like it didn't know part of its head was blown open and it was as good as dead. And Del was blown open, too, his neck mostly gone, torn away by the impact of the .45 round.

"Fucking sonofabitch, you killed Del. You piece of shit. I'm going to hurt you so much. I'm going to make you squeal, little fucking rabbit, I'm going to peel the skin off you while you're still alive and make you pay for this shit."

16

TASHUÉ

DAY 33

Moonlight kissed the silhouette of the rider coming down the road—it wasn't Ishmael. It was Matt, the rider with the young face. Ishmael staggered behind the horse, limping, barely able to keep up—his manacles were roped to the saddle. When he fell, Matt kicked his horse into a trot so Ishmael was dragged through the mud. He twisted so at least he was on his back.

Everything in Tashué turned to white-hot rage. There was something about fury like that, something that burned up all the pain. All the fear, all the uncertainty, all the exhaustion. His Talent twisted. He pushed at it again, trying to drag all that force out of his chest, but it was still anchored somewhere in him so that pushing on it felt an awful lot like trying to turn himself inside out.

"Where's Del?" the woman called.

"Motherfucker killed him," Matt said, drawing his horse to a stop beside the woman. "Thought we could rough him up a bit before we kill him back."

"Perfect timing," the leader said. "Get him up on his feet."

"Fuck you," Ishmael huffed. "If you want to kill me, you can kill me while I'm lying down. I'm fucking tired."

"Ishmael." Tashué couldn't think of anything to follow that up with. He couldn't make any promises, couldn't ask if Ishmael was alright. He was so clearly not alright.

204 | LEGACY OF BRICK & BONE

"Tashué, don't give them anything," Ishmael said. "Doesn't matter what they do to me, don't say fucking anything."

Tashué clenched his fists, even though flexing inside his manacles hurt. "I've been questioned before, Ishmael."

"They're playing tough, Matt," the leader said. "Why don't you hurt yours a bit, see if it makes Blackwood feel a bit more talkative."

"My pleasure," Matt said brightly.

Fuck this kid especially. Tashué tried again to push his Talent out, and it dragged at his heart so hard the beat stuttered. He sucked in a strangled half-breath, pushing his hands into his chest. His Talent was going to kill him, and there was a strange sort of peace that came with that awareness. Fitting after hiding from it so long. So long as it saved Ishmael, worth it.

Matt tossed his reins to the woman and dropped down from the saddle. He followed the rope back to Ishmael, who twisted away, rolling to his feet even though it made him shout when he brought weight down on his left leg. Matt didn't even try to catch Ishmael—he swung his rifle like a club and hit Ishmael in the knee as he shifted his weight.

Ishmael howled and dropped back down. Instinct made Tashué move, trying to go toward Ishmael, fuck that sound was so horrible, but the rope dragged him back.

"Where's Tei, Blackwood?" the leader roared.

"Fuck you!" Tashué snapped.

"Hoist him up again, see if Saeati knows anything."

Ishmael screamed louder, like the pain was mixing with outrage, with defiance. The big mare walked forward again and the rope dragged across the branch above Tashué's head, scraping, dropping bark on his shoulders. Tashué tried not to struggle against it. Don't waste the energy. Not yet. He took as deep a breath as he could before the shifting force lifted him off his feet. His lungs were full as he left the ground, at least.

"Where's Allie Tei?" the woman shouted.

"Who?" Ishmael howled. "I don't fucking know! I was drinking with the big asshole, and this is the trouble he gets me into, fuck!"

Tashué's Talent boiled. It seethed—

—it ripped through the hard walls he'd built around it with his fear. Stella said his Talent was immense, and now he understood—he'd never quickened because he'd never *allowed* it to quicken. He had used it against itself, forging the strength it had into a cage that kept it small and contained because he was terrified of it. Because his mother had told him, all his life, *follow the law and you'll stay safe* and the law said Talent was dangerous and it must be contained—

But now, Rhodrishi and Stella had woken it, had left fault lines in the cage by touching it with their Talent, and it ripped out of him like an avalanche. Into the forest, into the bodies around him, into the night sky, making him aware of everything and nothing because he couldn't focus on any thought at all because his brain was screaming, begging for blood flow. The rope that was killing him, and the rough texture of its fibres. The tree that was holding him up, going dormant as winter came on. The horse that pulled the rope, a big mare, her heart beating slow and steady, the sound a distant, comforting thrum except he was going to die. And these fucking people. Three of them left, standing in the forest like pinpoints of rot, their Talents ugly and twisted with their cruelty. When his Talent touched theirs, their awareness snapped into him. The fear that bloomed in them was delicious.

"I thought you said he didn't have any Talent!" the leader shouted.

"I thought he didn't!" the woman said. "I didn't fucking *feel* anything!"

"Useless fucking cow!"

Tashué's fury hit the whole forest like a percussion blast.

The tree beside him exploded, throwing wooden shrapnel everywhere. Pain bloomed in Tashué's side, hot and red and vicious. Falling, falling so fast, but at least he could breathe. He hit the ground harder than before. The rope pulled taut again before he could stand—the horse bolted through the forest, back to the hunter's track, dragging Tashué across the ground behind it, and he couldn't breathe again. The forest floor pummelled his whole body, root and fallen branch and jutting rock beating against him as he slid past.

He tried to reach out to the rope to break it, seeing the long strands of jute with his Talent. All he had to do was break the fibres, and he'd be free, but his Talent was a wild and vicious thing. It broke everything around him, tearing deep runnels through the ground as he slid. Ripping brush from the earth, snapping trees, throwing broken shards of rock into the sky. The horse screamed, bellowed, and Tashué's slide lost momentum, and he finally fell still.

Deep breaths of air, gulping, his whole body buzzing. His Talent and the shock insulated him from the pain that ate at the edge of his awareness—pain didn't matter, pain was a blessing, because he was breathing again, air sliding down his raw throat and into his lungs.

Tashué rolled to his knees and then to his feet. Everything hurt, but it was distant. The mare thrashed on the trail, lit by the glow of the moon. It gave an angry, fearful bellow and rolled back to its feet.

Movement on the ground where the horse used to be—the moonlight saved him, glinting on gunmetal as the woman lifted her rifle. She rolled to her knees, a strangled gasp of pain escaping her throat as she moved. She fired, but the shot didn't come anywhere close—the hot lead of the bullet tearing through the air above his head left a weal of awareness through his Talent like a brand, burning the skin on the back of his neck, right behind his ears. That anger-fuelled force snapped out of him too easily, too eagerly, ripped through the woman with all the savage violence that woke it. Her body buckled under the pressure—she didn't even have the chance to scream before he burst her beating heart, and the life bled into her crumpled chest cavity. Fuck her.

He turned back the way he'd come, forcing himself to move even though his joints hurt so much that it felt like his Talent had popped all of his cartilage. His whole body trembled, muscles exhausted like he'd run a gruelling marathon. He couldn't tell if it was the hanging or the explosion of his Talent, or maybe it was both, leaving him feeling empty and hollow. But he couldn't rest, not yet. Ishmael was still on the road, somewhere. Hopefully alive, fuck.

Another step, back down the track. He wasn't sure how far the horse had dragged him. That same, steady moonlight danced around him, showing the destruction he'd wrought. Burst trees and ripped runnels in the earth.

His Talent was still sliding around him, a nebulous web, an extension of his mind and his will. Through it, he saw and felt the places his own skin was torn—a chunk of wood had ripped through his uniform and scored a deep, ugly wound over his rib cage, and his whole side was bathed in blood and clotted with dirt he'd thrown everywhere. Cuts on his face and his hands and his arms—it was mystifying that he hadn't killed himself with all that force. He'd expected to die. Maybe he was dying, maybe the hollow feeling was his Talent bleeding life out of him.

The forest had its own slumbering force, a great hibernating beast that swirled beneath the earth like boiling groundwater. It came aware of him like an eldritch being, casting its awareness over him and then receding. Deciding he was uninteresting in the grand scheme of the whole forest, maybe. Or casting mercy on him because his Talent earned tolerance.

The track was chaos, blocked by trees and branches and clods of earth, all turned up like a mortar had landed. Ishmael—where was Ishmael?

Someone made a sound like gurgling, choking—the leader was on the ground. A piece of wood in his throat, ripping open his windpipe and his jugular. Hands grasped for the chunk of wood, but when it moved, he bled faster. His meagre Talent swirled in an effort to stem the blood flow and save himself, but he couldn't quite close the wound enough. Just like Gianna, who fought for her life after Duskan shot her, but the leader didn't have half her strength. And Tashué felt no guilt this time.

Tashué dropped to his knees beside the man, meeting his unfocused gaze as moonlight kissed his face. "I told you I would enjoy this."

Tashué grabbed the piece of wood, his hand closing around splinters and hot, slick blood. It took a moment to get a good grip. He wrenched it out of the wound, tearing more skin, more muscle. Without the wood to keep pressure, the jugular bled fast, red and hot as it poured out of the man's body with the rhythm of his heartbeat. The bastard choked, splattering Tashué's face. The sound echoed in Tashué's ears, and he could hear the man's heart stuttering, struggling, and then it went silent. The pleasure was vicious and savage, killer instinct that had been honed and nurtured by the military and had never really faded, no matter how hard he'd tried to convince himself he wasn't *this* man anymore. What a load of shit that was. He'd never been gentle because the world was savage and brutal and gentle things didn't survive. They were burned away and reduced to dust and ash and blood.

Silver shone in the rubble—his cigarillo case. Habit made him grab it without thinking, and the craving for tobacco redoubled in strength, but this wasn't the time.

Ishmael—he'd dragged himself to the wagon and now he sat propped against one of the wheels, both his hands resting on his knee. Relief flooded Tashué's chest. He sank down beside Ishmael, Talent swirling around them both.

"Holy fuck, Tashué," Ishmael breathed.

"I know," Tashué grunted. What else could he say? He knew. It was awful and horrifying and shocking. But he didn't have time to think about it because not all of his enemies were confirmed dead yet. "Where's the last one?"

Ishmael gave a wild, angry laugh. "My good friend Matt?" He spat the name like a curse. "I don't know. He fucked off somewhere when the tree exploded. I tried to go after him, but my knee is fucked."

Tashué slid his hands down either side of Ishmael's knee, but he didn't need to touch it to be aware of the damage. He could see it in his mind's eye as surely as if Ishmael's trousers and skin were peeled back— the distended muscle, the displaced kneecap.

"Your knee is dislocated," Tashué said.

Ishmael hissed through his teeth. "I know."

"I have to push it back—the longer it's out, the worse the damage."

"I know! Just do it already! I fixed it once but the fucking thing popped back out while I was—"

Tashué grabbed Ishmael's leg while he was still talking, pulling it straight as he put weight on the kneecap with the other hand. The feeling of the kneecap shifting under his hand was horrible, but it jumped back into place like it was pleased to return to where it belonged. Ishmael gave a sound that was half-scream, half-laughter, his body shuddering with the relief.

"Fuck you," Ishmael laughed. "Holy shit. This is what I get for drinking with you, hey?"

Tashué squeezed Ishmael's arm. He didn't like the wild, desperate edge to Ishmael's voice. "Can you get up?"

"I don't know. Give me a minute."

"Sure, Ishmael. Take your time. There's nothing else going on or anything."

A gunshot clapped through the forest—Tashué grabbed Ishmael and pushed him down, covering Ishmael's body with his own. Ishmael gave a shout of pain, curling in on himself under the shield of Tashué's bulk. Tashué's Talent rose, a ripple of his own vicious anger leaking out into the world. Matt—standing among the trees, cloaked in the darkness. He racked his rifle again and fired, showered Tashué's shoulders with wood debris when the slug hit the wagon. Racked again, shot, the bullet punching into the wheel they were lying in front of—he was using his Talent to try to target them in the shadow of the wagon, and he was getting closer.

But his Talent gave Tashué a line to follow, straight through the forest to where Matt was half hidden behind a tree trunk. Tashué felt the rifle as if it were in his own hands, felt the steel barrel and the grains of gunpowder and the lead bullet and the wooden stock and the flesh and bone of hands. He felt the flex of Matt's fingers as the young man squeezed the trigger. Tashué pushed against the barrel of the gun, collapsing the gunmetal. The gunpowder ignited but with the barrel collapsed, the force of the gun made the whole barrel explode. Matt screamed, dropping his rifle, pushing his hands against his face—Tashué saw it all like photographs flipping through his mind's eye. Tashué rolled his Talent through the fucker's whole body, and the sound of collapsing bone ground against the inside of Tashué's skull. Matt screamed, and Tashué's Talent kept pushing and he couldn't make it stop, even if he wanted to. Tashué crushed *everything* until the man was nothing but skin and pulverized muscle and grit that used to be bone.

"Is the fucker dead?" Ishmael asked into the silence that was left once Matt stopped screaming.

"Yeah," Tashué grunted, pushing himself up. Something heavy landed in his chest, like a mortar that would explode once he had the chance to think about what he'd done. The last time he felt like this, it was after his first enemy engagement. Instinct and training took over in battle, but in the quiet moments after, you had to come to terms with what you'd done, had to face the lies you told yourself about the kind of person you were. That was almost thirty years ago. And now he was evolving again. Once he was still long enough, once he was safe, it would blow him open and he'd really fucking feel it. But for now, he grabbed his cigarillo case from the mud where he'd dropped it to tend to Ishmael and flicked it open. "Smoke?"

"Yeah," Ishmael said. He took a cigarillo from the case as Tashué searched his pockets for his matches. "Fuck yeah."

The sulphur pop was comforting and he watched Ishmael's face as the other man leaned in to light his cigarillo. It was impossible to tell the mud from the blood from the developing bruises. The first breath of smoke when Tashué lit his own cigarillo was a moment of peace.

"I'm going to see if I can catch a horse," Tashué said, exhaling the smoke over their heads. He'd survived enough enemy contact to know he couldn't rest long. He had to get his wounded soldiers to a safe place. "We'll get you up into the saddle and I'll walk. We should go to General Wolfe, I think. Make sure Allie Tei is safe."

"Yeah," Ishmael said. He had to force the word past his teeth, like his mouth was stiff and uncooperative. "That's what I was thinking. You should get some boots if we're walking."

Tashué shook his head, looking down at his hands. They were on the shadow side of the wagon, and he couldn't see anything with the way the moonlight was blocked, but he knew his hands were steady. His Talent buzzed in his head, in his joints. Alive, awake, twisting around him like a heat halo. "There's no way any of their boots fit me."

"Yours are in the wagon. The Patrollers picked them up before we left the river bank, when you were out cold. I told you not to fight, you fucking asshole."

"They were arresting you," Tashué grunted. "I wasn't thinking."

"Sure. So listen. From now on, we're going to do a whole lot more thinking, alright? Because all your 'not thinking' is getting my ass kicked and I don't like it."

"Yeah," Tashué said. He rose slowly, feeling all the aches in his muscles, in his bones, in his feet. "Sorry."

He held himself on the splintered remains of the wagon, making his way around to the back door. Every step hurt. The ground was too cold and too hard, and his feet were too exposed, too bloody. Didn't matter. He had to get them both moving.

He dragged the rear door open, bracing himself against the carnage. The ripped open side of the wagon let in enough light to shine in all the blood, the stench of meat and shit sitting in the wagon like a cloud. He almost said fuck it. Forget it.

"Tashué," Ishmael said. He shook the chain between his manacles, the iron rattle sliding too cold down Tashué's spine. "You should try to find the keys."

"Fuck off."

"Can you break the metal with your Talent?" Ishmael asked.

"I don't fucking know." Could he? If he tried to break the manacles, would he accidentally crush Ishmael's bones? His awareness swirled, but it was pulled toward the blood, the gore, shifting through all the human remains with too much eagerness, and he had to drag it back again. Fuck, it felt like a sentiment creature living in his mind, a bloodhound hungry for a hunt.

"Then we need the keys," Ishmael said.

Metal gleamed in all that blood. Guns and the bolt that held him to the floor. Crowns, copper and a few silvers. His boots were under the bench, beside Ishmael's. He couldn't reach them from where he stood and he had to climb up, had to press his hands into all that blood. He couldn't stand; the ceiling of the wagon was too low and he didn't trust his bare feet to hold his weight on the slippery, gore-soaked wood floor. So he crawled. Pushed his hands through the chunks and the sharp bits and grabbed his boots. He threw them out the back, his teeth clamped around the cigarillo, wishing with everything he had that the tobacco was strong enough to drown out the smell of so much death. He tossed Ishmael's boots out, too, gritting his teeth against the bile that rose in his throat.

Bodies, clothes, bone. Metal. He tried to tell himself that none of it was as bad as his worst postings. Tried to tell himself that he'd lived through worse. But that felt like a pile of shit while he crawled through the gore that used to be Patrollers. It was worse than the Market fire; the ash scorched away a lot of the smells, and the rescue efforts let him face one body at a time.

The keys were in what was left of someone's pocket, beside a chunk of meat that used to be thigh.

He shoved himself backward, sliding through the viscera until his legs went out of the wagon first. He dropped, his feet screaming at the catch of his weight. His knees buckled, and he was already gagging, but he fought hard against it, clenched his fists and his teeth until the feeling passed. Maybe he'd waded through worse shit in his career as a soldier, but that career ended fucking twenty years ago because he was tired of wading through the remains of good people, and whisky-fuelled nausea had been eating at the corners of his awareness all fucking day.

But he had boots. And keys.

He pushed his hands through the mud just to get the horrible sticky blood feeling off his palms, but it didn't help. It stuck between his fingers, under his nails, in all the creases, and mud covered it all, like a coat of plaster. The bastards, the vicious, horrible bastards who shot the wagon all to shit—maybe they were dead, but if there was even the slightest chance Rainer was responsible, Tashué would make him pay for every ounce of blood, every shard of bone.

Tashué settled beside Ishmael again once the gagging passed, pushing the sticky keys into Ishmael's hand. Ishmael sucked in a deep breath, and it trembled. He was shivering. Fighting it, that's why his voice sounded so stiff. Ishmael spat on the keys, wiping the blood away with filthy fingers and fumbling to find the keyhole in the side of the manacles. His hands were trembling so much, the key scraped against everything.

"Hey," Tashué said. "You alright?"

Ishmael tried to breathe slow, but the sound was ragged and trembling. "Just fucking cold."

The key finally found the keyhole and the first manacle sprang open, releasing Tashué's wrist. Tashué pulled the key out of his manacle and unlocked Ishmael's, freeing both his hands before unlocking the second manacle from his own wrist. Tashué pressed his hands against Ishmael's face, against his neck. His skin was cold but also damp—sweat from the exertion of running, and now it was cooling him down too fast and all the trauma was setting in his body. Tashué's Talent twisted, swirled, touching all of the damage in Ishmael's body—his knee, his ankle, the tattered mess of his feet, the pools of blood forming under his skin that would make ghastly bruises. Tashué looked for wounds that might have sent Ishmael into true shock—bleeding in his organs or damage to his spine, but those places at least looked fine. Tashué's Talent twitched through each wound it did find, but Tashué held back the force of it. He didn't know if it was a safe thing, to push healing without any training. Would his Talent break things instead? He held his cigarillo between his teeth so he could fight with his boots. They were stiff and sticky with blood, and the insides were still wet from the river, but it was better than trying to walk in the forest barefoot any more. All the ripped places in the soles of his feet screamed their protest, hot and stinging, more blood sinking into the insides of his boots. He didn't bother tying them. He shrugged out of his coat, tattered and muddy though it was.

"No, don't—you're just as cold as I am," Ishmael said, but the words were mangled by his chattering teeth. He tried to push the coat away as Tashué laid it over him, but Tashué didn't let him. "Let's get moving."

"I'm fine for a minute. You've always been miserable when it gets cold, but you never dress warm enough."

Ishmael laughed at that, pulling the army issue coat up to his face. "Sorry, Captain. Wasn't expecting tactical wilderness survival drills tonight."

"I'll take my coat back once we get you in better shape," Tashué said, pushing himself up again. His feet hurt so fucking much, throbbing in his boots, every step trying to steal air out of his lungs, but the urgency of getting Ishmael safe drove him through the pain. "I'll be back."

"Sure."

The leader wasn't far away, his boots shining in the moonlight, his blood making a dark stain across the front of his coat. Tashué searched his pockets, looking for something sharp. Bullets for his rifle, a purse of copper and silver crowns, Tashué stuffed it all into his own pockets. A badge. Even in the moonlight, Tashué couldn't make out what was written on it, but he recognized the outline. He'd carried a tin badge that was the same shape for nineteen years. The metal felt different, caught the light in a dim gold hue. Maybe brass or bronze instead of tin. He shoved it into his pocket. Proof the Authority had done this. Not that he really thought anyone would believe him, fuck. Did all five of the bastards have badges? He wanted to search them all, but he didn't have time. He found his notebook in another pocket, and the relief that hit his chest at the weight of it made him tremble. He wasn't usually so deeply attached to his sketchbooks—he'd long since given up on finding any use for the skill other than keeping his hands busy when he was still for too long, or helping him with his case work. But this notebook had Lizanne's face, how he imagined her alive, and somehow the return of it to his hand felt like a fire was landing in his spine. Fucking Rainer.

His searching hands found a hunting knife.

Tashué drew it from its sheath at the man's belt. He grabbed the bastard's sleeves and dragged the heavy leather coat off him. He pulled the boots off him, too, the thick wool socks. The hunting knife made easy work of the man's trousers, the sleeves of his jacket, his shirt, turning them into strips of bandage. He would have taken the man's rifle, but the bastard had left it with his horse and that horse was long gone.

Back to Ishmael, he dropped to his knees in the mud. He stabilized Ishmael's knee first, winding the makeshift bandages around either side to keep the kneecap in place. Ishmael grunted at all the movement, his whole body taken with shivering. Tashué pulled the socks up over Ishmael's feet, then used more of the bandage strips to bind his ankle.

"I grabbed his boots for you. They're bigger so I can fit them over the bandages, and they're dry. Then I'm going to get you up, and we'll head down the road to where I last saw a horse. We're going to pray a bit that it's still there."

"Sure," Ishmael said, his teeth chattering around the word. He pushed his good foot into the stolen boot, and Tashué pulled the laces tight. "You know it's a good plan when it's dependant on a few prayers."

"You're better at praying than I am, so you better get it right," Tashué said. He flicked the cigarillo away, the ember sizzling in the mud. "Let's go, soldier. Up on your feet."

"Take your coat back first, Captain," Ishmael said. "You can't be in much better shape than I am."

Tashué grabbed his coat, shoving his arms into it just to get Ishmael to cooperate. He took Ishmael's hand and hauled him up and he helped

Ishmael into the second coat, pulling the collar up around his face. It was good and heavy, and it would help him keep his body heat. Hopefully. But he was so damned cold already. If it was even remotely safe to stay here, he'd light a fire instead, turn the wagon into a bonfire, strip Ishmael out of his clothes to warm the surface of his skin, but he had no idea if there would be other people looking for them. How long before the Patrollers were noticed missing? How long before the forest was crawling with a search party? They had to go.

"Are you praying yet?"

"We don't need to pray," Ishmael said, shaking his head. "It's not that bad. Praying is for when things are real desperate. I've survived worse shit than this—we're going on a little jaunt through the forest, aren't we?"

Tashué forced a laugh for Ishmael's sake, holding Ishmael steady. He wasn't sure he ever wanted to come back to this forest after he felt the slumbering power that lived in earth and mulch and root. Did the whole world feel like this when you had Talent? Or was *this* forest especially powerful somehow?

"Yeah, sure," Tashué said instead of thinking about that force. "It's practically romantic."

Ishmael laughed, too, wild and brittle. "If this is how you do romance these days, it's no wonder that whisperer of yours is spooked. I'll have to teach you how to have a softer hand. Not everyone likes a rough ride like I do."

When Tashué laughed again, it wasn't a happy sound. The rush of this horrible fight was still in him, the swirling Talent, the weight of the last few weeks. Stella, and everything. "About that."

"Oh fuck, that sounds bad. What now? What did you do?"

Tashué got under Ishmael's arm to help take his weight, grabbing the back of the double layered coats to keep him stable. They hobbled down the road, the mud squelching beneath Tashué's boots, holding on to him and making every step so much harder. Ice formed over the surface of the mud, cracking when his weight came down. He steered Ishmael toward the edge of the path where it was mostly dry. They went wide around a massive chunk of broken wood, half a branch almost blocking the path completely. His Talent had done that, burst the tree he was hanging from, and the awareness was eating at the corners of him. He didn't talk to his parents about Talent, back when they were still alive— they were both so strong, stonesmith and healer. He never realized that it lived in you like a separate being, an extra sense, a thing that drew in sensory input so fast it was like he saw the whole forest. What other surprises did it have for him?

"She told me about the children," he said, trying to keep his focus on Ishmael, on walking. One step and then another. "The energy units. It's all shit. She said she knew Davik Kaine in Cruinnich, and it was his idea to murder these children because they were energy units, and he wanted people to know what the Authority was doing. As far as she knows, he never went through with it in Cruinnich, but now he's here, and one of his people killed Lizanne and the others Allie found."

"Ah fuck," Ishmael breathed. "Fucking Davik."

"You know him?"

Ishmael sneered, his teeth glinting in the moonlight. There was blood on them. "I've had the extreme displeasure of working with him recently. Fucking cockhead. Thinks he's big shit in the Bay, runs his brothel down by the tracks and the new pugilist club for Iwan. He's involved in all this shit?"

"Seems like it. Iwan pointed me to the man who killed the children, Hale. He said it was all Kaine's idea."

"Hale," Ishmael repeated. "Edgar Hale?"

"That's the fucker. You know him, too?"

"No, I didn't get the pleasure of meeting him. I thought Iwan was going to ask me to kill him, but he said someone else was going to take care of it." He took a last drag from his cigarillo and tossed it away, shaking his head. "Did you take care of it, Tashué?"

Maybe he was supposed to deny it or get defensive about it. If he was talking to anyone else, maybe he would have said something evasive. Something about how Powell Iwan demanded it, how he didn't have any other choice. But Ishmael... Though they'd never really talked about what Ishmael did as a diplomat for the Dominion, Tashué knew the shape of it. The truth lay in the cracks and crevices between words, in the lost and distant look he caught in Ishmael's eyes sometimes when they were drinking together. Ishmael knew what it meant to kill because it was necessary. *I thought Iwan was going to ask me to kill him* said plenty.

"It was easier than I expected it would be," Tashué admitted. "But it didn't feel like it helped anything."

"It never does," Ishmael said.

Around the bend, and the big mare was standing in the road where he left her. The dead woman was still in the road, kissed by the moonlight that gleamed on her rifle. The mare shivered, her reins trailing. Her head came up when Tashué and Ishmael rounded into view, but she didn't look like she was going to bolt. Ishmael grabbed a low hanging tree branch, clinging to it so he didn't have to put any weight on his twice-battered leg. Tashué approached the horse slowly, forcing patience even as the impatience and the urgency tried to make him move faster. He didn't know how far they had to go to get to Wolfe's house, but he knew Ishmael wouldn't be able to walk much longer. He didn't dare leave Ishmael behind. They might have been close to the city, but the forest and the cold were still deadly, and Tashué had no idea which direction to go. Maybe if he used his Talent, if he stretched himself out—even as he thought of it, his Talent twisted down the track, bleeding into trees, into earth, into stone. The current of Talent lived beneath the earth, grasping at him like a hungry river, tearing into him and snatching at the very beating of his heart. And that force still, groaning against Tashué's senses.

Tashué recoiled so fast, the whole world seemed to tilt from beneath him. He staggered, his head spinning, his knee striking a stone in the path.

Fuck Talent. The horse was their best shot.

"Whoa there, friend," Tashué said in a low, soothing voice, pushing himself back up to his feet. A groan ripped out of his throat—every joint seized for a moment when he was halfway up and he had to force himself through the pain. He edged closer, catching the trailing reins so she couldn't bolt. "I'm sorry for all that. Didn't mean to hurt you."

The big grey kicked nervously at the ground. Tashué made soothing noises at her, low and mellow, stroking her neck and her face. She was trembling, pain or fear or the cold leaving her as rattled as he was. He searched her legs for injury or any sign of lameness. She was holding her weight well on all four hooves—a good sign. Her belly was fine, the saddle still strapped on. There—her flank—her flesh was torn and ragged, blood seeping from the wound. Her mottled fur almost hid it, but the blood gleamed softly in the light when he turned her toward the moon. Tashué winced, fingers probing the ragged edge. The horse flinched and snorted and tried to dance away, but Tashué held the reins tight. If he trusted his Talent at all, maybe he could heal the wound, but he had no idea what he was doing and he didn't know if he even *could* heal, or if he'd make it worse. Make himself worse, too, for that matter —healing was painful for the patient and the healer alike, and he had no idea how much more his could take before… before what? If this was his quickening, was it over now? If this was what a powerful quickening felt like, it was no wonder Rhodrishi worried about the mortality rate of the Breeding Program children.

"Come with me, big girl," Tashué said, tugging the reins only gently to get her to follow. One hesitant step after another. "If you carry Ishmael back to the city for me, I'll make sure someone has a good look at you to fix the damage I did. How's that sound?"

The horse snorted again. He rubbed her forehead with his knuckles. All the energy was fading out of him, settling on his shoulders, making him wish he could lie down somewhere and sleep for a week. All the pain was starting to grind against his senses, making it harder and harder to think. But he didn't have time to hurt. However bad his wounds were, Ishmael was worse. He led the mare down the trail as slowly as he could bear it. The mare followed, thank the North Star. He paused long enough to scoop up the woman's rifle without looking at her face.

Ishmael had lowered himself down to the ground, propping himself against the tree. Shivering still. "Fuck horses," he said, teeth chattering even louder. "Last time I got on a horse, the fucking thing almost got me killed because it wouldn't move."

"All you have to do is get up and hang on," Tashué said, grabbing Ishmael's arm and helping him lever his way back up to one foot. "You tell me how to get through the forest and I'll lead her. And if it looks like someone's coming after us, you shoot them."

"I'm a shit shot, Tashué."

"I thought you were a deadly weapon of the Dominion and all that," Tashué said. He slung the rifle over his shoulder so he could use both hands to hold Ishmael steady. Tashué had minimized how hard it was going to be to get up with one bad leg and he knew it, but he didn't think he needed to tell Ishmael how bad the whole thing was going to hurt. "What kind of deadly weapon can't shoot?"

"I'm more of a short-range weapon," Ishmael grunted. "Better with my hands."

"Well, you better not shoot me, then. Are you ready?"

Ishmael groaned. "No."

"Too bad, it's time anyway. Lift yourself with your arms, and I'll help you swing over. It's better than walking."

"Yeah, sure, just that one small thing."

Tashué held on to Ishmael long enough for him to get ahold of the saddle horn and the cantle, but Ishmael gave another groan of pain.

"Fuck, my shoulder!"

"Oh, your shoulder's fucked, too?" Tashué asked. "Really milking this for all it's worth, aren't you? Needed to be the centre of attention and so you took all the best wounds, is that it?"

Ishmael gave another of his wild, brittle laughs, glancing over his shoulder. "Well if you're going to waste a good beating by being all stoic and heroic and shit, I might as well bask in all the glory of being the tragically wounded one. Too bad there isn't anyone beautiful around to feel sorry for me."

"What am I, then? Not good enough for you anymore?"

Ishmael gave another tired, ragged cackle. "You're the cause of all my fucking problems. I don't want *your* pity."

"Not even if I promise to kiss it better?"

Ishmael's hand tightened on the saddle horn, the moonlight shining on his knuckles as they went pale with the exertion. "Lost your chance, Captain. I only get desperate once, and you turned me down cold." He sucked in a deep breath as the mare shifted, half-impatient, half-stressed. "I don't know how to get up without putting weight on my bad leg."

"When you're ready, you're going to jump," Tashué said, grabbing Ishmael around the waist. "You'll go up and lean forward and get your torso across the saddle. Once you're up there, you can swing your bad leg over the back of the saddle and sit up. Don't worry about getting your foot in the stirrup—I'll lead her down the track with the reins. Just hang on to the saddle horn and tell me where to go."

Ishmael nodded, taking a few deep breaths. "Sure. Fine. That sounds like shit, but let's do it. I hate this fucking forest. Nothing good ever happens out here. I'm always either bored out of my skull or everything is falling to shit. I'm ready."

"On the count of three."

Ishmael nodded again.

"One. Two. Three!"

Ishmael jumped and pulled himself up with his arms, and Tashué lifted him high out of the jump. Ishmael howled with more pain—his shoulder must have been bad. The horse startled, trying to dance away, but Tashué shoved Ishmael's body toward the saddle, and he landed with his chest on the seat, punching the air out of his lungs with a breathy grunt. Tashué grabbed Ishmael's thighs, helping him slide up a little higher, helping him swing around, all while Ishmael grunted and hissed through his clenched teeth like the pain was driving him half out of his mind.

"Fuck." He pushed himself upright and grimaced, resting a hand on his knee. "Bastard. Why are you fine? They hung you from a fucking tree. Your Talent—I don't know much about Talent, but I can feel it and that was *strong*. You should be having an existential breakdown, shouldn't you?"

"I'll probably feel it later, once you're safe," Tashué said. He swung the rifle off his shoulder, passing it up to Ishmael. "Helps, having you to focus on."

Ishmael took the rifle in both hands, squeezing it for a moment like it was a life raft dragging him out of the wild current. "Well, you're welcome. I'm glad I could be so helpful in keeping the dark demons of your inner turmoil at bay. Truly, I'm a hero."

"Exactly," Tashué said. "Now, which way do I go?"

Ishmael swayed in the saddle as he looked around, like he couldn't quite master balancing himself in the saddle and moving. "Ah—fuck. Just head that way a while, away from the carnage. There'll be a landmark eventually—the hunting houses mark these trails so people always have a way to get back to somewhere civilized."

"Hang on, then. And don't shoot me in the back. You only put your finger on the trigger when you're ready to kill something."

"Sir, yessir."

Walk. Just walk. Don't think about Talent and don't think about the bodies they were leaving behind and definitely don't think about Stella and Ceridwen, out in the wilderness *somewhere*. If he started thinking, that existential load of how massively his life had shifted would hit him. This wasn't the time for thinking, only walking. Watching their back trail on the off chance someone found the carnage and came after them.

"Watch the trees, or if there are any big rocks beside the trail," Ishmael said. "There'll be mile markers that will tell us exactly where we are, and then I'll know which way to turn on the next fork."

Don't think about the way his feet hurt with every step, don't think about the way the cold had moved into his chest, don't think about the way he was starting to shiver now, too. They couldn't be *that* far. The rich side of the river wasn't especially populated, and they couldn't have been too far from the Boardwalk Market.

Ishmael groaned. "Fuck, I'm going to be sick."

Tashué glanced back in time to see Ishmael fold over himself, his head dipping down too low. He caught Ishmael's shoulder so the bastard didn't fall head first. Ishmael's whole body tensed as he fought against the gagging, but there was no resisting it. He choked and whimpered, and finally his heaving brought up a thin stream of bile. Ishmael only groaned again, grabbing the shoulder of Tashué's coat and making a fist in the fabric. He seemed to be listing like a boat taking on water, sinking lower and lower over the mare's neck.

"Hey, don't pass out," Tashué said, pushing Ishmael upright. He put his hand on Ishmael's forehead. Had Tashué missed something? Shock, or a concussion—or maybe it was the whisky, finally purging out of him. "I'm too heavy to ride double, and this poor horse has suffered enough tonight. Sit up."

Ishmael shook his head. "I'm fine." He sat up some, but not as straight as he was before. Still had the rifle in his hand, at least. "Just keep going. I'm fine."

But he wasn't fine. And Tashué didn't know how to help him. So they had to move. It was probably time for him to start praying.

17

STELLA

DAY 33

"Tomorrow's the most dangerous leg," Ozra said, as they set up another camp. He spoke gently, mindful of how tired Stella was. Four days of their winding path north and west, getting closer to the Brightwash while always avoiding the busy road and the fields stretched around it. "We haven't any choice but to go out in the open to get to the river. I figure about noon or so, we'll be at the open stretch. After that, we won't be stopping until we get to the mill town. We probably won't reach it 'til after nightfall, but it'll be worth pushing. We can sleep in town, have a good breakfast, and then take the barge across."

"What kind of breakfast?" Ceridwen asked. Apparently they hadn't been speaking quietly enough, and she'd snuck closer to hear. "Something other than soup?"

"Aye, girl, I'll get you the miller's breakfast." He loosened the saddle girth around Caraid's body and started the slow process of lifting his bags and his saddle off the painted gelding's back. "Potatoes and onions and baked ham, fried up real nice, and then mixed with eggs 'til they're all scrambled and golden. Toast dripping with butter and maybe a big pot of coffee."

Ceridwen's nose wrinkled, but her eyes sparkled at the sound of all that food. "I don't drink coffee."

"Maybe I'll share the coffee with Lieutenant Mahalouwan, then. I'll bet she drinks it black, all bitter and too strong, just like her."

Kazrani laughed. "I won't stand for you insulting the only good way to make coffee, Mr. Sgèin. That may be a transgression too far."

"That's how Mr. Blackwood takes his coffee," Ceridwen said. "So it must be the best way to drink it."

"I'm betrayed and outnumbered," Ozra scoffed, holding his hand over his heart. "I expected it from our Lieutenant, but not from you, sweet girl."

Stella left them to their playful bickering, unpacking her bedroll and finding a good spot for her and Ceridwen. Perhaps it was a sign of her growing resilience that Ozra had mentioned the danger, but Ceridwen was drawn in by the prospect of a good breakfast.

The first snowflake kissed Stella's cheek with cold, melting in an instant but sending a shiver up her spine. Winter's march was unstoppable. It didn't care that they were desperate, that they were running. It had arrived.

"Come, Ceridwen," Stella said, brushing the spot of moisture off her cheek. "You can get our fire going for our soup, and we'll dream of the logger's breakfast waiting for us."

Ceridwen knelt by the space Rhodrishi had cleared, shredding the bark that Ozra had taught her to use as kindling. She popped one of the long matches, trying to get the bark caught, but a gust of wind that sent little thick flecks of snow swirling through their camp defeated her. She sighed and sparked another match. And a third when the second burned all the way to the end and the bark failed to catch.

"Um," Ceridwen said, her voice wavering like it did when she was uncertain. "I can't get it started. I'm sorry. It's harder to do it out here than it is at home in a wood stove."

Stella crouched down beside Ceridwen, beside the would-be fire. "Here, Ceridwen, watch this. We'll get things going a little faster."

Stella gathered up the bark they used as kindling, building it into a pile in her palms. Making fire was one of the easiest things—simply a gathering and application of heat, like Ozra said yesterday. It was harder in the winter; with the air so cold, it was a challenge to find enough heat to get flames started. But her life as Ffyanwy Rhydderch of Rhydderch Stone had taught her where to look for heat no matter what time of year it was—deep in the earth. So few people thought to look into the earth, because to touch loam and clay and bedrock was to find something cold. But deeper than that, the world was a hot and volatile thing, burning and churning. All she had to do was take some of that intensity, borrowing the tiniest bit of it, dragging it up through the ground. That heat passed through her body, as it usually did. But this time, everything burned a little too acutely, and panic roared through her senses. It felt too much like Siras's assault, when he couldn't quite focus on any specific part of her but wanted to burn and crush every cell of her.

But she closed her eyes. Fought against the panic. It wasn't Siras; it didn't hurt that much. The stream she'd created was a gentle and familiar thing, flowing through her and into the tinder she held.

She felt Rhodrishi's Talent, too, billowing like hot summer breeze across an open field.

"Are you sure you should be using your Talent?" Rhodrishi asked softly.

"I can do this," Stella said, opening her eyes again. "Just this one little thing. I need to—" Her voice quavered and tried to crack. It seemed such a silly thing to be upset over, but it was more than lighting a fire. "I need to do this one small thing and feel like myself again."

Rhodrishi nodded—perhaps he understood her fear of losing herself piece by piece. Or perhaps he felt her desperation in the air between them.

Stella focused on the shredded bark in her hands, turning the heat she'd pulled from the ground into a tiny, intense pinpoint in the kindling. She took a deep breath, blowing on it, sending a little column of smoke twirling through her fingers. Then flames jumped and juddered, young and precious—Stella blew again, encouraging it to grow until it caught to the twigs, and she held a bundle of fire in her hands. She set it down in the centre of the fire pit, adding twigs and more chunks of bark. One more long blow and the bigger things had caught, flames crackling, climbing, hungry and eager.

"There," Stella said, adding a few more sticks, bigger ones this time —the fire was well caught, its light dancing off the rock beside them to give their camp a warm, comfortable glow. "That should do it."

Ceridwen clapped her hands together, her face beaming with her big smile. "How'd you do that, Mam? Can you teach me?"

"A dear old friend taught me that trick," Stella said. "It's simple, really. All you do is find heat somewhere and start the fire—blowing on it just makes it look like I've done something special, doesn't it? But that's Davik for you—always one for a big show."

It felt strange to say that name out loud again. For so long, the people of her past were trapped inside her, bundled up with her pain, packed away with the woman she *used* to be. But speaking the names to Allie and Tashué and Rhodrishi had unlocked them, breaking the bonds that kept them hidden. She wasn't *only* Stella. She wasn't contained by the story she'd created for that forged paperwork anymore. People knew she wasn't a widow with her stevedore-husband gone to the Keeper of the Keys.

"Do you mean Davik Kaine?" Ozra asked, spreading his bedroll by the fire. "You knew him?"

"Surely there's more than one man named Davik in the Dominion," Kazrani scoffed.

"I know, but—"

"Yes, Davik Kaine," Stella said. "I knew him a long time ago."

"My condolences," Ozra muttered.

"What's that supposed to mean?" Stella asked.

"Ah—just that Davik Kaine is the sort of man who, well—" He glanced at Ceridwen, shifting uncomfortably, a blush creeping up his neck. "Who knows a lot of women. But doesn't exactly respect them."

"Who's Davik Kaine?" Ceridwen asked.

"A criminal," Kazrani muttered.

Stella huffed at Ozra and Kazrani, shaking her head. "He wasn't always…" *He wasn't always what?* Any of the words she tried to grasp seemed insufficient. To call him a child murderer seemed unnecessarily traumatizing with Ceridwen sitting and listening, but that had almost been the truth back in Cruinnich. And there was a very real chance he was responsible for the children Tashué and Allie found. When Tashué said Davik's name, Stella's whole body had filled with fury. But now she was just… heartbroken. She'd loved Davik, once. "There was a time when he was young, and he wasn't so angry about everything. A time when he was just a sweet young man with a lot of big dreams. Back before the Authority took everything he cared about and left him holding nothing but dust."

"Do you mean back in his manor days, when his family was still rich?" Ozra asked.

"Yes," Stella said. "When Kaine Brick was still alive."

Ozra looked uncomfortable, like he'd been caught in something he didn't know how to handle, shifting from one foot to the other. He cleared his throat, pushing his fingers through his hair to shake out the road dust. "Was his family as rich as he likes to pretend they were?" Almost, but not quite, changing the subject.

Stella shrugged. "Kaine Brick was an unstable business. His father took too many gambles, forced it to grow too fast. He also had a habit of taking too much out of the business to make sure his wife was in the best fashion, and his house was always filled to bursting with guests and fancy parties. It's hard to say how wealthy the business and the family actually were, but Gerald Kaine certainly spent money like he was royalty."

"Sounds like you knew the family well," Ozra said softly. He was watching her now, perhaps watching her a little too closely. "Did you work for them?"

"No," Stella said. Perhaps that was the wrong thing to say—perhaps she should have lied to keep her identity secret. Perhaps she should stop talking all together. But she couldn't bring herself to lie anymore. Now that she'd started telling some people parts of the truth, it was harder to keep the lie going. "I didn't work for them."

"Was he your friend, Mam?" Ceridwen asked. She fed sticks into the fire, watching the flames dance. "When you were little?"

"He was," Stella said. "I've known him since I was younger than you, Ceridwen. He and I both learnt to use our Talents together. I haven't seen him since we were both in our twenties."

"You didn't encounter him in Yaelsmuir?" Ozra asked. "He settled down there after Aelwyd Rhydderch and her folk chased him out of Cruinnich."

Another name that made her ache—Aelwyd. Of course Aelwyd and Davik would come to conflict. Aelwyd was perhaps the strongest, bravest person Stella had known in her entire life, a hurricane in miniature form.

"How come he was chased out of Cruinnich?" Ceridwen asked before Stella could decide what to say. "How do you get chased out of a whole city?"

Stella sighed, putting an arm around Ceridwen's shoulders, tugging her closer. *By being so brutal that the whole city was bathed in blood because of him.* "He made terrible choices, Pigeon. Because he was angry. Angry at the Authority, perhaps angry at the whole world. A lot of people died."

"Still sounds like he's a criminal," Kazrani muttered. "Whether you were fond of him or not doesn't wash the blood off his hands. All of the Dominion heard about the violence in the streets of Cruinnich."

"The Authority is responsible for plenty of that violence," Ozra scoffed. "Bothain Clannaugh didn't get named the Fist of the North because of his measured, reasonable response to civil unrest."

"Civil unrest is a funny way to refer to a rebel organization setting off bombs," Kazrani said.

"What's a bomb, Mam?" Ceridwen asked.

"Ah—it's a thing that explodes on purpose," Stella said softly. "They can really hurt a lot of people."

Ceridwen's lip quivered, just a little. "Like the Market fire hurt a lot of people?"

"Yes, Pigeon," Stella said. She took the tail of Ceridwen's braid, letting it slide through her hands. Kazrani's tight plait had held admirably, far better than any plait Stella had ever accomplished. "But they also use things like that for mining and breaking rock. Davik set them off in empty mines to protest how the Authority used Talented labour up in the mountains. He collapsed a lot of good mines, drove the mine owners half mad."

Ceridwen's brow knitted together and she turned to look at the fire. The flash of grief had smoothed itself away, and now she had that thinking expression, her mouth pulled into a sour pucker, her eyes following the flames as they grew in their fire pit. "What's protest mean?"

"It's a way for people to come together to make their voices heard when they don't agree with how things are done," Rhodrishi said. "There's a lot to disagree with in this country."

"Who set the bombs in the city streets, then?" Kazrani asked, bristling.

"I don't know, Lieutenant Mahalouwan," Stella huffed. "I wasn't there to see it. But since you seem so sure whose fault it was, perhaps you were there."

"I fail to be swayed by 'he used to be a good person,' Miss White-rock," Kazrani said, her hands clenching at her sides. "That may have been true once, but there was a time when he became so radically violent that his own rebel army chased him out of his city. So, you'll forgive me for being a little distressed to hear he's apparently loose in Yaelsmuir, where there are people I care very deeply about, instead of being brought to account for the things he did up north."

"How does one account for the mistakes they made?" Rhodrishi asked. "Where does the balancing happen for you, Lieutenant? Is it only in the court of law, or can a person atone for their mistakes some other way? Davik Kaine established a smugglers' road that is helping to feed people that might be starving without him. The drought four years ago would have killed scores of people—and then the winter after was so early and so cold, it would have killed scores more. But the supplies we got from Davik Kaine through Ozra and the other brave souls who run that road saved lives in communities that are barely hanging on. Communities no one else in the Dominion seems to care about."

Kazrani sighed, looking up at the sky. "I don't know, Colonel. I don't know if any of it balances. But I do know what he's responsible for in Cruinnich. Say what you want about empty mines and what have you, but the reality is he started something that ended in incredible bloodshed. And before you argue with me about who holds culpability between the Red Dawn and the Authority, I also know what Edgar Hale said about those children. The ones Tashué and Miss Tei found. And I remember what you said about what he wanted to do in Cruinnich." She pushed herself to her feet while Stella reeled, shooting a pointed look at Ceridwen before tapping the girl on the shoulder. "Why don't you fetch some of those nice squash from your mam's saddle bags? Roast squash would fill us up, I think."

"Yes, Miss Mahalouwan," Ceridwen said, pushing herself to her feet.

The three of them sat around the fire, staring into the silence that was left in the wake of another almost-argument. Stella stared into the flames she'd made and tried not to think about the version of Davik she saw last. Come home from Kona's funeral in the mountains, every thought clouded by an ugly mixture of grief and rage. A funeral that Stella—Ffyanwy—couldn't attend because Bothain forbade it. And Davik, boiling with righteous anger—talking about energy units. Forgetting that they were children, and not some inanimate *thing*. Forgetting that they were fighting a war over humanity, which couldn't be won by indiscriminate violence because violence like that stripped people's souls bare and reduced them to blood and meat and bone.

Kazrani was right. Whatever Ffyanwy felt for Davik *once*, at some point he'd become a man willing to kill children. And half the reason she'd become Stella.

"How did you know Davik Kaine back then, Miss Whiterock?" Ozra asked softly. He pushed a few burning pieces of wood close to the soup pot and the kettle. "I seem to recall he only had eyes for Ffyanwy Rhydderch in those days. He left a string of unhappy lovers in his wake because they all knew he wanted to marry her. At least—that's the stories people tell of him. He still talks about her if you sit and drink with him. To hear him tell it, she owns all the goodness in him."

Stella grit her teeth together rather than answer. She could feel what he was really asking, what he was dancing around but not quite saying.

He suspected the truth because she had said too much. Because just like everyone always seemed to know that Davik was hopelessly in love with Ffyanwy, they also knew that Ffyanwy couldn't help but love Davik, even when their lives drove them apart. Even when Bothain stood between them. Right up until it all went so terribly wrong. Right up until Ceridwen.

"They say that's what drove him right mad in those last years," Ozra went on. "The way her husband was treating her, and he couldn't do nothing. The fact that she disappeared—lots of folks say she was killed by Clannaugh."

"Ozra—" Rhodrishi said, but then he fell silent, like he couldn't decide what to say beyond that.

Perhaps neither Rhodrishi nor Ozra knew about the children. To them, Davik was a flawed, philandering hero, and those were all too easy to come by. Stella couldn't find the words to explain that she didn't want to talk about Davik anymore, though she was the one who brought him up. She couldn't do it, couldn't talk about the children Davik was willing to kill when Ceridwen would come back to the fire at any moment.

"He still talks about her is all I'm trying to say," Ozra said. "He's down in Yaelsmuir, fighting for her because he thinks Clannaugh killed her. For all his flaws, I know he'd do anything to protect her if he knew she was alive."

Stella took a deep breath, the words striking her deep. Cold, empty, freezing shock—like falling into a river. And then heat. Anger and pain, frustration. The fierceness of the emotion took her by surprise. Nine years, she'd been running. And yet those men, the three of them—Bothain, Siras, Davik—still had so much power over her. It felt stupid and juvenile to think it wasn't fair. Life wasn't fair—but there were no other words to so effectively sum up the powerlessness she felt. The injustice of it.

Ceridwen came back with a squash tucked under each arm, and Stella turned her face away, into the shadows so Ceridwen didn't have to see her crying anymore.

"How's that kettle going, wee girl?" Ozra asked. "Can you see it from where you are?"

"I think there's a bit of steam coming out of the spout," Ceridwen said, handing the squash to Rhodrishi, who settled them beside the flames to begin cooking. "Just a bit, though. Could you tell me a happy story, Mam? About your friend, Davik, before he got so angry?"

Stella sighed, clenching her hands in her lap. It had been a mistake to say Davik's name out loud. It felt wrong to tell Ceridwen happy stories about the man who might have killed her. *We have to do something, to make people see—we have to expose what they're doing with those fucking energy units.* "I don't know, Ceridwen. It was all so long ago."

The silence stretched again, and Stella stared into the darkness, listening to the flames crackle and pop as moisture escaped the wood. She wished someone would say something, longed for words to fill the void of discomfort that hung in the air, but even Ceridwen stayed quiet. She didn't know that name—Stella had made *sure* of it—but she must have sensed the weight sitting in the camp. Kazrani and Ceridwen peeled the skin off nobs of garlic, and Kazrani cut little holes into the flesh of the winter squash, forcing the cloves in before rolling the squash into the fire to cook.

Sweet North Star save her, she was going to start crying again. She'd cried so damned much since the day Tashué saw Ceridwen's tattoo—perhaps she should start cutting her emotions away again so she could be empty and numb.

She pushed herself slowly to her feet. She needed a moment without so many people watching her—if she was going to listen to silence, she'd rather be alone.

"Mam, where are you going?"

"Just a little walk for a moment, Ceridwen," Stella breathed, forcing the words past the lump in her throat. "I won't go far. You stay and help Miss Mahalouwan with dinner."

She walked down to the bank of the creek, listening to the water babble over rock and root—it was too dark to see how wide it was or get a sense for how deep it might be, but the water sounded like it was moving fast. She followed the bank away from the camp.

"Miss Whiterock." Ozra's voice carried easily through the darkness, and Stella could hear his boots crushing the shale of the creek bank. "May I walk with you a stretch, Miss Whiterock?"

Stella gulped a deep breath, trying to force the emotion back down. "Certainly, Mr. Sgèin."

He was quiet for a while, walking along the water, his boots splashing into puddles as they made their way along the bank. "I lived near Cruinnich… for a time. Because of the way I could find things, sometimes Bothain Clannaugh called on me. He wanted me to use my Talent to help fucking Duncreek track folks down when they disappeared. He usually sent Siras after members of the Red Dawn who had cut and run. I lied, every time. Sent Siras the wrong way. A little rebellion, you know? Once he came up to the mountain where the Authority was keeping me. Threatened to shoot me for sending him chasing this own tail round and round in useless circles. I told him it wasn't my fault that the person he was looking for wasn't where I saw them by the time he got there. I told him he could go ahead and shoot me." He shrugged. "He didn't. It would have been too much trouble, even for him. So, I was still alive when, ah—when Miss Rhydderch disappeared. Bothain called me down to Cruinnich, as he did in those days, and asked me to figure out which way she went. I said she went south, heading for the Dunnenbrahl. I half hoped Siras would get himself killed by wild Talent down that way—it has a way of eating up vile men like him. Or maybe he'd run afoul of Winter's loggers. They ain't got much patience for folks carrying the bronze, like I said. But I suppose he stayed away from them. Anyway, I hoped it would give Miss Rhydderch time to get away, as far as possible, since she wasn't heading south at all when I saw her running with her wee baby. She was running west. I take it... I take it eventually he figured out I'd lied again, got himself pointing the right way."

Her face felt pinched and too tight, her head aching. She chewed hard on her grief, on the ugly twist of emotions, clenching her teeth until her jaw ached, trying to get it back under control.

"He did," she whispered. "The folks on the west coast were very kind and they warned..." She stumbled on the next part, the part where she was supposed to continue the farce and refer to herself in the third person like she wasn't Ffyanwy Rhydderch, but she couldn't do it. Ozra had obviously guessed, and Stella was tired of hiding Ffyanwy's existence. Near a decade of being Stella was crumbling apart. The first cracks had splintered through the foundation of the lie when she told Tashué the truth, and then they spread further when she talked to Allie Tei. Every person who knew the truth was a rebellion against Bothain. That's what the Authority had done to all of them—turned the very act of existing into a resistance. And Bothain hadn't silenced Ffyanwy. He'd tried for years, and she'd run to save Ceridwen, but she still had a *voice*. "The folks in the nearby village warned me that someone was looking for me. So I took Ceridwen and I ran again. I stayed in Obisza for a time, but not very long. I worked my way down to Yaelsmuir. But while I was there, I think I was so tired that I forgot to be afraid of him. I stayed too long, and he caught up to me."

The heat, the pain. Her body remembered it too well. She had to fight to breathe, hissing air through her clenched teeth. The swallowed emotion was curdling in her stomach—she was going to be sick if she didn't get herself under control. Was it because she was hungry? Had she eaten something that wasn't sitting well? She stopped walking, edging closer to the creek until she heard her boots splashing in the water. She leaned down cupped water between her hands, splashing it on her face, hoping it would wash the emotions away, giving her relief from the intensity. But it wasn't enough. She couldn't catch her breath at all—she was gasping, choking.

Ozra reached out to her, touching her arm at first. Just a little touch. She barely felt it through her clothes. She plunged her hands into the water again, splashing more on her face. It was so cold it made her breath hitch. Ozra shifted a little, coming closer. Closer. He slid his big hand down her back, then back up again, resting on her shoulder. He didn't pull her or force her to come closer. He stood beside her, the one hand on her as if he wanted her to know that she wasn't alone.

"I'm sorry," Stella breathed, using her sleeves to wipe her face. "You must think me half mad."

"Not at all, Miss Whiterock," Ozra said. He said her chosen name so carefully, so gently, speaking each syllable deliberately. "I know what it's like to run from the past. It's not easy to bear a weight like that. I know how exhausting it is."

Stella took a deep breath, rubbing her eyes again. "What are you running from, Ozra Sgèin?"

He sighed, shifting. "From the Authority. From my mistakes. From all the ways I could've been better." He slid his hand across her back again and she couldn't help but lean into him. He had such strong, comforting hands. "You did a good thing, running when you did. I take it you ran to protect your girl? They say Miss Rhydderch was devoted to her hospital —say that's why she couldn't be alive anywhere. 'Cause she wouldn't leave her hospital for nothing. But for a child—that makes sense."

Stella nodded again, glancing back toward the camp. The night had swallowed any sign of it, the flames well hidden by Rhodrishi's careful positioning of the camp fire.

"Can I ask who her father is?" Ozra whispered. "Is it Bothain?"

Stella shook her head. "No, not him. Not Davik, either."

"Good for you," Ozra said, and he didn't press it any further. "You did the right thing, protecting her. Our children are so precious."

"Do you have any children?" Stella asked. Better to think about him and his life than wallow in her own suffering anymore.

His breath hitched. Perhaps it wasn't better, not for him. Stella turned to look at him, but she couldn't see the details of his face. She regretted the question, though, the regretted the heaviness in the air between them.

"Well... None that've survived."

Stella winced. It was her turn to reach out to him, cupping her hand against his cheek, feeling the rough tangle of his dark beard beneath her palm. He leaned into her hand, taking a slow, deep breath. "I'm sorry, Ozra. I know what that pain is like, too."

"You mean your son?"

Stella sighed, nodding. "Perhaps Rhion was part of Bothain, too, but I loved that boy more than I ever thought possible. He would be fourteen now. Nearly a man. I can't help but wonder who he would have become, if only he'd had the chance."

Ozra nodded, turning his face toward the half-hidden moon. "Aye, my oldest would be about the same. If he were still alive. But they're all gone, all the lives I made. I found 'em each with my Talent, so I could know where they were. It meant I felt each of them die. I just about went out of my mind, feeling them all slip away."

Stella reached out, grasping through the darkness. She found his hand, all rough calluses and deep lines. All her favourite memories belonged to people with calluses on their hands—Tashué, Davik, Kona. The Jitabvi horse farmer she'd met out west—what was her name? Stella couldn't remember. She hadn't spent long out there, and so much of her time was spent alone in the little rented cottage, watching Ceridwen grow. Watching her learn to walk, watching her curls grow long enough to cover the tattoo on the back of her neck.

Something passed through her Talent. Something wild and a little ugly—Ozra, and his incredible storm? No. It was something else—something coming from far away. A dull roar, echoing through all of Talent like the rumbling an avalanche made.

Ozra groaned, both his hands coming up and clamping on his skull. A word tried to escape his mouth, but Stella couldn't guess the shape of it. And then he dropped.

His body hit the creek bank before Stella could even think to catch him, a splash of water signalling that he'd gone down. Stella reached for him, but the rumbling through her turned to pain, a snap of it across her whole body, setting her nerves on fire. And then gone. Leaving her trembling in the memory of agony that didn't belong to her. Ozra's Talent had spilled out again, that storm she saw the first night, except it spread wide so it was only a thin film of energy that stretched as far as Stella could feel, like a coating of ice across the whole world after a night of freezing rain.

And the woman.

She stood in the moonlight, as clear as a real body, silk nightgown hanging still around her figure even though wind whipped over the surface of the creek. Blood on the white silk turned to a dark, angry stain. Standing between Ozra and the camp.

A wild sound broke out of Stella's throat, a call for help that wasn't fully formed. She reached for Ozra, grabbing his arm, the leather of his duster stiff beneath her hands as she gripped it and tried to drag him out of the water. But he was heavier than he looked, skinny as he was. Stella's boots slipped and slithered in the rocky scree of the bank. She fell, her backside landing in the water, the brutal chill of it passing through her whole body and constricting her lungs, making it hard to breathe.

Kissed by the moonlight, the woman's mouth was moving. But Stella couldn't hear any words.

"Ozra!" Stella called. He was face up, at least. She grabbed his arm and shook, digging her heels into the creek bank and hauling him as hard as she could. Toward the dry forest floor, away from the woman. "Ozra!"

He stirred a little, only a little, muscles twitching like he was trying to move but couldn't master the coordination. Made a sound like a wounded animal. Stella shifted so she could pull him onto her lap so that his head, at least, was out of the shallow water in case he woke and tried to roll over.

"Rhodrishi!" Stella cried, louder, as loud as her voice would carry, to hell with who else heard. She pulled harder and Ozra slid a little, coat scratching on the rocks beneath him, water sloshing. Another groan. Sweet North Star, at least he was alive, but there were a million questions swirling through Stella's head so fast she couldn't grasp any of them long enough to consider them. What happened? Why had it affected Ozra so badly? Who was the woman, watching them, trying to speak? "Rhodrishi!"

But there was no sound of approach. How far from camp were they —had Rhodrishi reacted badly to whatever happened in the Talent, too?

Was he lying at their camp right now, half-conscious like Ozra—all the horrible ways he could have fallen flitted through Stella's anxiety, blooming new, terrible questions—what if he'd fainted while he was tending to the fire?

She dragged Ozra again, moving backward in slow increments—moving her body back an inch, maybe two, and then pulling him up onto her lap again. Again. Again. Until they were both out of the horribly frigid water, on the forest floor. The woman didn't follow. She stood with her bare feet in the water, looking toward the camp. Shifting—one moment she looked like she was pregnant and the next Stella could swear she was holding an infant, a little squirming child who didn't want to be restrained by her mother's arms. And then she was alone again. Covered in blood.

"Ozra," Stella said again. The cold water had her, soaking into her clothes. She shivered so hard it made her teeth clatter, made her hands tremble. Made it hard to speak. "Ozra, damnit!"

Ozra gave another groan, louder than the others before, his whole body moving this time. He reached for something above his face, fingers flexing and then clenching. And his Talent gathered strength in the air, sharpening and condensing until it was pressure in the air again instead of the thin, brittle coating. Footsteps beside them, running through the water—Stella looked up, half expecting to see the ghost-woman approaching. But it was Kazrani. She was following the sinuous curve of the creek, boots kicking up great sprays of water that glimmered like jewels in the moonlight. She passed right through the ghost-woman.

"What happened?" Kazrani asked. She grabbed Ozra's arm and hauled him even farther from the bank, off Stella's lap. She was shorter than both Ozra and Stella, but so incredibly strong, moving Ozra's body like it was nothing. "Is he wounded?"

"I don't know," Stella gasped. She stood, the water from the creek sloughing off her trousers, pooling in her boots. "Something happened to our Talent, and then he collapsed. I don't know!"

"Something happened to Rhodrishi, too," Kazrani muttered.

There were no words for the terror that passed through Stella. Not Rhodrishi, not now. They were so close to safety. "Is he alright?"

"He's fine. Dizzy for a moment, but fine. He said someone quickened."

Stella shook her head, struggling to grasp the meaning. Surely Kazrani was mistaken—how could a quickening cause *this*?

"Up you get now, Mr. Sgèin," Kazrani said, hauling Ozra up into a sitting position and crouching behind him to keep him upright. "You've given our Miss Whiterock a terrible scare, and you're soaking wet, which is a bad way to be this time of year."

"I'm fine," Ozra grunted, and the sound of his voice flooded Stella with relief. "It's fine. I just need a moment—bleedin' hell, that was something."

"What happened?" Stella asked, her chattering teeth mangling the words. "What was it?"

"Someone's Talent—blew right through the fabric. Knocked me out of myself for a moment."

Stella looked toward the creek. Toward the ghost-woman. She'd turned her back on Ozra, and she was holding that child again, and the babe was crying. Screaming. Face red, body rigid with distress, but Stella couldn't hear it at all even though she knew children well enough to know that a cry like that would be bone-rattling to everyone nearby.

"Ozra, who is she?" Stella asked, the cold and the uncertainty making her voice tremble.

He looked directly at the woman and the babe she carried. He didn't question who Stella was talking about—he knew immediately. "Ah—you see her?"

The babe disappeared, and ghost-woman took a step toward the camp, her silk dripping blood that disappeared before it hit the surface of the water.

"I can see her," Stella said, scarcely believing it herself even as she spoke the words, "but I can't hear her. She was trying to say something to you while you were down."

Ozra's fingers twitched like he was fighting the urge to reach toward the woman. "No one's ever seen her before."

"Seen who?" Kazrani huffed.

"Eilidh," Ozra said simply, the name carrying the weight of his whole heart, so heavy and filled with longing that it made Stella's heart skip a beat even though she didn't know the name. It gave her substance, gave her identity, gave her a facet of reality that hadn't existed before.

"A ghost," Stella said.

Kazrani grunted. "Never mind all that," she said, even though the suspicion in her voice seemed to say she minded it very much. "We need to get you back to camp and dried off before you catch hypothermia. We can't be dragging around a half-dead trail guide."

18

LORNE

DAY 33

The box came while Lorne was training.

His whole life was training. Hitting the heaviest punching bag with his fists wrapped in cotton, drilling through the combinations Davik wanted him to memorize. László held it steady so he could move faster, so it didn't jostle so much every time he hit it. Everything they did was designed to change the routing of Lorne's instincts, to get him to stop using his feet and his knees and his elbows to hit people so he would follow the rules of the National Pugilism League. No kicking, no elbows, no head butting, no biting. Fists only.

If he wasn't hitting things or lifting weights or using the cursed jumprope, he was eating. Delicious things he'd never had before because he couldn't possibly afford them, things Davik had delivered from the pub he owned across the street or things László made upstairs in the apartment above the club—where Lorne apparently lived now. But with all the training, he was only ever up there to collapse into the big, comfortable bed in his big, comfortable room. And it was a good thing exhaustion snatched him so fast because Davik brought a woman or two up to his own room every night, but Lorne was usually asleep before they got loud. Then the next thing he knew it was morning again and time to train some more. His muscles were so tired that getting out of bed *hurt* and then he went back to more training and his muscles hurt more and more until suddenly the pain just... disappeared. Moving became the most natural state of being. He was being rebuilt, one fibre at a time.

If he wasn't eating or training or sleeping, he was watching other boxers spar while Davik and László explained… everything. This footwork and that reach and watch this wiry fucker's left hook, he's knocked more than his fair share of teeth out with that hook. Things that Lorne did with instinct and experience had names in the pugilist club, and László rattled them off like they were a prayer to some ancient god of violence.

"If you know so much about boxing and you love it so much, how come you aren't going to be the Bay's first pugilist?" Lorne asked.

László laughed. He laughed so damned much, like the whole world was a joke to entertain him. "I would make a terrible boxer. I don't like getting punched in the face."

"Why not?"

"Because it fucking hurts."

"I mean, sure, but… you like the sport so much."

"It's not unusual to not want to be punched in the face, Lorne," László said, hooking his arm around Lorne's shoulders and dragging their bodies together. That was another habit of his—like he couldn't bear to be alone in the world, so he pulled people closer and closer to have skin against his. "In fact, of the two of us, you're the strange one since you seem to be fine with it. Like it's just a normal part of your life. Eat, sleep, fuck, shit, get punched in the face."

"That's what I'm here to do, isn't it? I don't like getting punched in the face either. That's why I prefer to win."

"Even if you win, you still get hit a few times. But it looks good on you. The scars and the cuts. You make it work. You make bleeding sexy. But my face is too pretty for any of that."

That made Lorne blush because it felt too damn good when László said shit like that, but he also felt guilty. Every moment of every day, he felt guilty because his life—painful though it was with all the muscle aches and the exhaustion—was good. He wasn't hungry anymore, and he wasn't cold, and he always knew exactly where he was going to sleep, and László massaged all the aches and pains out of his body, and life was good. Easy.

László spotted the courier first, and he peeled away from the punching bag. He was fastest to meet the man halfway through the club. He signed for the box and bounded back to Lorne.

"Are you excited?" László asked, pushing the box into Lorne's hands. Like a hat box, but square, wrapped in paper like a gift, closed with twine. A shipping label was pasted to the top.

Lorne Coswyn
c/o Davik Kaine
18 Border Street E
Cattle Bone Bay

"Excited for what?" Lorne asked. The box was heavier than he expected when he saw László carrying it, or Lorne's arms were fucking tired. His hands trembled these days when he wasn't moving, like his muscles had forgotten how to be still. Sometimes it felt like every fibre of the meat that made him was being teased apart and then fused back together in a different shape than before. Except he didn't know what exactly was different.

"Ah, they're here!" Davik said.

"What are they?" Lorne asked, staring down at the label. He couldn't quite take his eyes off it. Lorne Coswyn, care of Davik Kaine. The words struck him hard. Maybe because it had been so long since he was in the care of anyone, and being in the care of Davik Kaine meant his own room in the apartment upstairs, with a bed so big that it could fit three, and that warm comfortable radiator. It meant there were clothes coming for him soon—Davik and László had a tailor come by to take Lorne's measurements.

But all he wanted was Jason.

Davik said this club was for Jason, but Lorne still wasn't really clear how any of this was supposed to help Jason.

"Your gloves, laddie," Davik said. "Your very own boxing gloves, like a proper pugilist finally."

"Sure," Lorne said. "Ecstatic. All my dreams are coming true."

Davik snorted. "We'll have to work on your enthusiasm."

He took the box from Lorne's hands, heading to the stage and resting it on the edge. People were watching, frozen in whatever they were doing to keep an eye on the box. Lorne followed Davik to the stage, trying not to notice how much people were staring. Were gloves *really* that exciting? Half the people here had their own boxing gloves. Mostly he could ignore the way people watched him—all the training kept him too exhausted to finish most of his thoughts—but the times when he stood still made him uncomfortably aware of how he always seemed to be in the centre of the room. Like the Bay was a hurricane and Davik was the eye of the storm. So he watched Davik's hands instead. Davik had old scars on his knuckles, faded with time. Powder burns on his hands. His fingers were thick and strong, careful with the way he unfolded the paper from around the box. He had a list of numbers tattooed on the back of his left hand, but a burn scar had almost obliterated the 2 near the knuckle of his middle finger. Lorne wondered what the numbers were for.

"Relax," Davik laughed. "They're just gloves. Come try 'em on, see how they feel."

László gave Lorne a little shove toward the stage. Davik finally pulled the top off the box. The gloves were white leather, fat and shiny. Lorne couldn't imagine the point of processing leather that much, to strip away the colour until it looked like a summer cloud. Seemed like a waste. He was supposed to hit people with these fucking things. Weren't they going to get dirty?

They sat in the box on a bed of shredded paper, as if the leather needed to be protected while they were being shipped across the city. Such a strange and exact analogy for this whole place—people came and wore expensive gloves and gave their violence pretty names and rigid rules like that made it all more civilized, but it was still just violence. Blood and sweat and the feeling of making your opponent smaller by defeating them. The feeling of being defeated, the way it sliced a way a little piece of who you thought you were.

László came close, leaning over Lorne's shoulder, his sweaty chest pressing against Lorne's back as he leaned in to get as close to the gloves as he could. "They look real fucking good, Dav." The reverence in his voice made it sound like he was praying to that god of violence again. He slid a single finger across the curve of one glove, leaving a thin line of sweat and his fingerprint across all that shiny white. "They look *real* sharp."

They did look sharp. Expensive. Wasteful. But the white leather gleamed indulgently. Lorne wanted to wipe László's smudge off the curve.

"Nothing but the best for Mr. Lightning," Davik said, picking up the gloves and knocking them together once. The sound they made sent a shiver down Lorne's spine. What would they sound like when they hit a person's body? "They *do* look flash, don't they?"

"Why white?" Lorne asked. "I thought boxing gloves were red or brown."

"Because no one else has white gloves," Davik said winking at Lorne. "And Mr. Lightning from the Bay should have something no one else has, shouldn't he? Since Mr. Lightning from the Bay is making history and all. You like 'em? The white was László's idea. They'll match your coat."

"Sure," Lorne said. "They look good. I'm getting a white coat?"

"Well, shit," László laughed. "Was that positivity from Lorne Coswyn? I might die of shock!"

Davik loosened the ties on one glove with quick fingers, holding the cuff open. Lorne had to lean hard into it to get his hand all the way into the glove. The leather was stiff and restrictive. It was supposed to reduce injury. Supposed to be easier on his hands and easier on his opponent's face. But he didn't understand why anyone would add cushioning when they were hitting people on purpose.

"How come I'm getting so much white shit? Won't it all get dirty?"

"Absolutely," Davik said with a grin. "That's the point."

László caught Lorne's shoulder, pulling them close again. "Regular gloves are blood coloured so no one can see the stains, but that's shit. Everyone should see what you've done. Every fight will leave new stains and the whole city will know how much blood you've spilt."

A shiver darted down Lorne's spine, and he didn't know if it was dread or excitement. The whole damn club had that effect on him, all the time.

"How does that feel?" Davik asked.

"Fucking strange," Lorne muttered.

"Aye, laddie, we get it. It's all new, and you're proper tired, and you don't handle change well. But are they too tight?"

Lorne tried to flex his fingers in the gloves, and the leather gave a reluctant creak. "How the fuck am I supposed to know if they're too tight? You asked me how they felt. I said they felt strange. It all feels too tight, even the cotton."

"There's the fighter we know and love," László laughed, wrapping both his arms around Lorne's chest and resting his chin on Lorne's shoulder. "Dav's trying to ask if it's so tight that it hurts."

Lorne flexed his fingers again. Thinking about the gloves instead of thinking about how László was so comfortable inside Lorne's personal space, or how Lorne didn't mind it. László and Davik both kept hemming Lorne in, making a cage out of their bodies, except Lorne didn't hate it like he normally would. Maybe it was one of the things being rebuilt with his muscles. Maybe he was too tired to care.

"No. I guess it doesn't hurt."

"Good then," Davik said, patting Lorne's shoulder. "Let's get the other one on, see if you burst into flames."

"I don't have a choice, do I?" Lorne pushed his hand into the other glove, watching Davik's scarred, nimble fingers work the laces. "Match is soon, isn't it?"

"Aye, it is. You'll give them a try on the bag, get a feel for them. And then we'll get you up in the ring, and you can use them on some poor volunteer, hey? The league bookie's coming tonight to take your stats, so we'll let you show off a wee bit."

Lorne didn't bother asking what 'taking his stats' meant. If Davik wanted Lorne to know, Davik would tell him. Lorne flexed his hands a few more times, looking down at all the white leather instead of letting himself notice everyone watching him, like they were waiting to see what the gloves could do.

"You'll get used to them, laddie," Davik said, patting Lorne's shoulders. "I know it's not easy, what you're trying to learn to do, in the middle of all this ripe shite, but you're doing good. I'm proud of you."

Lorne focused on his breathing, slow and steady, rather than dwelling on the way his stomach fluttered at those words. *I'm proud of you.*

When was the last time someone told him that?

He was supposed to hate this man. Supposed to keep an eye on him for Vasska.

So why'd he like Davik Kaine so much?

F ists high, body loose. Back to the punching bag to work on the combinations Davik had taught him. Right, left, left, right, right, left, fists up. The gloves were fucking heavy and he was certain they slowed his fists down. Felt like the weight of them would pull his arms right out of their sockets if he swung and missed. Davik made him go until he was so frustrated he couldn't think anymore, and then Davik pointed him at the high ring in the centre, the one everyone avoided like it was a sacred place they weren't allowed to go.

"Time to get on up there, laddie," Davik said. "I built it for you, after all. That's your throne. The first ever Bay pugilist. From up there you'll base your reign of terror on this city. Heaven help anyone who steps into your realm."

Lorne's whole body burned. He hated how much he liked it. He walked away from the Army because he didn't want to be this person. He left the division because he didn't like how they wanted to turn human beings into weapons and meat.

But that ring, that canvas throne, called to him. It hooked something in his ribcage and dragged him closer. Made him feel whole and complete.

He climbed up onto the canvas. It was different than the stage at the Hive. Higher, more isolated, with the ropes around the edge to keep him inside. The canvas made a different sound than bare wood did. The whole club vibrated up through the canvas and into his legs, into his heart, investing him with their energy and all their aspirations and all the pride they felt for being Bay. Like he was built to stand there, like the ring was designed to vibrate at the same frequency of his heartbeat.

László and Rowan climbed up after him. Rowan had pads that looked like a hat.

"What the hell is that for?" Lorne asked.

"To protect that ugly face of yours," László said with a wink, grabbing the pads from Rowan's hands. He pulled them down over Lorne's head and tied the horrible, uncomfortable thing under Lorne's chin. "Can't send you into the exhibition match with fresh wounds, can we?"

"I don't know," Lorne said. "I don't care."

"The bookie will care, so shut up."

The pads covered Lorne's ears, his forehead, most of his cheeks, hemming in around his eyes, cutting off his peripheral vision. He hated the way the pads chafed and rubbed and the string cut into his chin, but with the boxing gloves on he couldn't do anything about them. No matter how much he wanted to rip the damned thing off, his hands were useless for anything but punching. Which felt apt, he had to admit. László turned him around to face the opponent who had climbed into the ring while he wasn't paying attention. The man had red-brown gloves and the same pads on his head, obscuring his features so much that Lorne couldn't tell if he knew the guy or not.

"Bookie arrived," László said, patting Lorne's shoulders. "Don't forget—fists only."

"Sure."

Lorne stepped into the centre of the ring to meet the new opponent. He threw the first few punches, just to feel the weight of the gloves and the man dodged each one with an effortless bob of his head and sway of his shoulders—László called it slipping, and Lorne's opponent was excellent at it. But then, Lorne knew his punches were shit. Telegraphed and too slow because the gloves felt fucking weird. Too heavy.

But even as he took the swings, his could *feel* his body learning, knowledge swelling between the muscle and the ligaments like fluid, to be absorbed through his bones and into his marrow to flow through his veins. Swing, hook, jab, his chest and his shoulders and started to adjust for the weight of the gloves. Already. Part of him knew he was learning too fast—even he couldn't possibly be picking it up this quickly. But the rest of him, his mind and his body and everything that made him, loved every moment of this evolution.

Lorne's left was starting to get mean and fast like it was meant to be, but his opponent kept slipping it. Swung at Lorne as he came up. It caught Lorne below the ribs, emptying his lungs. The impact of the gloves slapped, stinging, lighting Lorne's whole body on fire. Lighting his temper on fire.

He stepped through the pain and swung again. Faster. His opponent slipped and jabbed and tried to get out of the way but Lorne didn't let him keep any space, stepping in, crowding him. Lorne caught his opponent's chest, his shoulders, spraying sweat everywhere, at one point spraying blood and spit because Lorne busted his opponent's lip, and then the man went down, and Lorne was on top of him, hitting, hitting, hitting, the leather weird and heavy on his hands, making a barrier between knuckles and skin that turned him half-numb and vibrated up his arms and let him keep swinging. The wet slap sound rang in Lorne's ears. His shoulders strained, and his chest pulled, and his whole body shifted with the incredible weight of each swing because the gloves were so damned heavy, but his hands didn't hurt.

He didn't stop swinging until someone grabbed him by whatever limbs they could catch ahold of and dragged him back along the canvas. Dragged him so hard and so fast he could feel the canvas ripping the skin off his hip where his trousers hung too low. He let himself go limp, let himself slide, his world hemmed in by the fucking pads that made it hard to hear. Made it so he couldn't see anything but the corners of his pads and the ceiling. Floor joists and metal pipes for all the indoor plumbing, and not a speck of dust or stray cobweb to be seen. And his heart, hammering so hard it made his vision vibrate with every beat, like the force of it shook

"Holy shit," László laughed, kneeling beside Lorne so his face entered Lorne's vision. He pulled the tie beneath Lorne's chin that kept the pads in place. "It's working. I can't believe it's really working. I didn't think I could—"

"What's working?" Lorne asked. "What do you mean?"

László pushed the pads off Lorne's head, tossing them aside. Without the pads covering his ears, the inarticulate roar that lived in the club hit Lorne like a sledgehammer to the skull, so many layers of shouting that he couldn't identify any particular voice, any particular words. It was just a wall of noise.

"You really let *loose*, don't you?" László laughed.

"I've never seen anyone move like that," Rowan said. The first time Lorne had ever heard Rowan say anything that wasn't petulant and unimpressed. "I shouldn't be surprised but holy *shit*."

Lorne blinked, trying to shake the buzzing out of his ears. An ache settled in his shoulders, so deep it felt like the muscles were wrapped too tightly around the bone. "What did you mean when you said it's working?"

László twisted away from Lorne and shouted across the ring. "Walk it off, sweetheart!"

"Fuck you, László! The mad bastard almost killed him!"

And László laughed again.

Lorne rolled onto his side, but the pain flared through his hip, reminding him the skin was all ripped to shit. He tried to touch the wound to see how extensive it was, but the glove. He couldn't feel anything but the inside of the glove. Red blood smeared on the white leather, blood from the man he'd taken down, blood from his hip. The first stains already.

He spat on the canvas. There was blood in his mouth—he must have caught a hit that busted up the inside of his cheek even with the pads.

Davik whistled, the sound high and shrill, catching Lorne's attention. "Come say hi, Mr. Lightning."

Rowan pushed Lorne's shoulder, guiding him toward Davik and the woman standing with him. Lorne rolled under the bottom rope, dropping down to his feet. He shook the sweat out of his hair, the buzzing out of his head. He spat again, trying to get the taste of blood out of his mouth, but it was no use. The woman with Davik pulled her spectacles off the bridge of her nose, tucking them away into her breast pocket as Lorne approached.

"Mr. Coswyn," she said, smiling wide and bright like watching Lorne almost kill a man was the highlight of her day. "It's a pleasure to meet you, finally. I've heard some wild stories about you, and now I'm starting to wonder if they're true after all."

Lorne looked down at his gloves again, at the blood on them, at the sweat dancing on his forearms and over his hair. Back at the ring, Rowan and László helped to drag Lorne's opponent to his feet. Guilt hit Lorne hard. It was supposed to be sparring. He was supposed to pull his punches but he hadn't at all and now the guy was down so hard they were struggling to wake him up.

"I don't know." Felt weird, chatting after that fight. It got mean and wild real fast. Lorne's body still felt like it needed to keep swinging. "Depends on what you heard, I guess."

"Pugilist matches used to be duels to the death," the woman said.

Lorne snapped back around to her, turning so fast it made him dizzy. The acid settled in his chest, the thing that made him want to peel his skin off, but he couldn't walk away from the feeling and he couldn't drink it away, either, because he was supposed to stand here and talk to the league bookie. She folded both her hands over the notebook she held, standing straight and tall and almost demure, except her eyes slid over his bare chest and lingered on the canvas burn on his hip, the blood soaking slowly into his trousers at the waistband.

"Pugilist matches," she said again, "used to be duels to the death. It hasn't been in practice for about a hundred years now, and certainly there were plenty of bareknuckle fight rings that didn't expect their fighters to kill each other, but true pugilism started as death matches. Over in some of the Commonwealth countries, although I can never remember which. The gloves, I believe, were introduced as a way to prolong the matches. The rules evolved to turn it into a sport of endurance, and at some point we stopped expecting our pugilists to kill each other. And now here we are, with the National Pugilism League in the Dominion, and you, a warrior from another time, who doesn't quite seem to know that pugilism isn't to the death anymore."

"I'm sorry," Lorne said, a reflex, tumbling out of him—shit, had he gotten the club in trouble?

"Don't be sorry, laddie," Davik said. "You gave Miss Brady a good showing of your potential, didn't you? She's been working for the league a proper long time, and I'm sure she appreciates a good fight."

Miss Brady from the League smiled, the skin around her eyes crinkling into the soft crow's feet of a face that smiled a lot, her chin tilting toward the ring like she wanted to watch them walk Lorne's opponent off, but she was too busy studying Lorne. "You absolutely did. Like I said, it's a pleasure to meet you. The Bay's very first pugilist."

"Uh—thank you," Lorne said. "I don't know if I'm a real pugilist yet."

"You're certainly making leaps and bounds in the right direction. I'm impressed with the speed at which you're adjusting. We'll have to leave a note in your file—make sure the referee knows to stop you when the round's over." She shrugged. "The scale should be just about ready by now—shall we go, Mr. Kaine? I'll show you how it works and Mr. Coswyn's healer can take a look at his hip."

"What do you need to weigh me for?" Lorne asked.

"It's for the league, son." Davik whistled, catching Rowan's attention and waving him over. "Let's go."

L orne didn't like the look of the scale. It looked entirely too much like the livestock scales that they walked the pigs and cows over up in the Market, where merchants dickered about price and quality. Sometimes the breeding stock went back up into the farmlands, but mostly they came down to the Bay to be turned into dead weight. They set it up in Davik's office against one of the bare walls, and a man was fiddling with its moving parts, the metal clanking together ominously.

"Why do you need to know how much I weigh?" Lorne asked again, stalled in the doorway to Davik's office. There were two change rooms in this back hallway, one for Lorne and the other for whatever opponents the club hosted, but for whatever reason they'd installed the scale across from Davik's big walnut desk, making the office feel even smaller than before. "What does that matter?"

Miss Brady stood beside the scale with the notebook in her hand, smiling at Lorne. "The league likes to track the details of their fighters and their matches. For posterity."

Lorne shook his head. "What does posterity mean?"

"It's for gambling," Davik said, shoving Lorne past the door's threshold and into the office proper. "They use it to calculate odds on a match. They'll list your height, weight, arm length, and glove size. Same with your opponent. They use all those numbers to set the odds on your match."

Lorne wanted to wipe sweat off his face, but he still had the damn gloves on. He wiped his face with his arms instead, looking around the office for a towel. His change room had towels for him, but Davik's office had paper everywhere and the stupid scale and Davik's big desk—and wardrobe bags, hanging on the back of Davik's chair, the kind that protected very expensive clothes.

"Wouldn't wins and loses be a better indication of odds?"

"Aye, they would do, but you haven't any of those yet, have you?" Davik said. He grabbed Lorne's gloves, unlacing them so Lorne could finally pull his hands out. Lorne flexed his hands. They felt strange after being released from that much weight, and some ghostly memory of the impacts of his gloves on that opponent's face lived in his knuckles, like the gloves had only delayed the nerve's reception of that much force, made it last longer. "And even when you do, they'll keep track of how you do against men that're bigger than you, and men that're taller. I don't think there's anyone smaller than you fighting right now."

"We'll see," Miss Brady said. "There're some fresh faces coming up in Brickheart."

"Won't matter much, will it?" Rowan said, closing the door behind him. "Ari Odegaard will thrash them all."

"That's entirely likely, yes," Miss Brady said. "But once the tourney season starts, Mr. Coswyn will have to fight his way up through the list like everyone else."

"He'll do great, won't he?" Davik said. He rested his hands on Lorne's shoulders. "Why don't you get your trousers off so Row can take a look at your hip before you get up on the scale. And you can relax, yeah? I promise we won't be selling you to the slaughter houses. Ain't nothin' to you but soup bones anyway. You're worth more to me with gloves on than hanging in a butcher's cold house."

Lorne sighed as he pulled the cotton wraps off his hands. Then his suspenders, kicking off his boots until he was down to his drawers and his ragged socks. This club had gotten him used to stripping down to his drawers no matter how many people were hovering around. Rowan winced, watching the blood track down Lorne's leg, making dancing red lines through the hair on Lorne's thigh.

"Ripped yourself up real good, Mr. Lightning."

Lorne touched the edge of the wound, the pain eating through the post-fight tremble, getting ahold of his nerves. It wasn't that bad. A large patch of ripped, canvas burnt skin—but it was shallow.

"A bandage should do it for now, I think," Rowan said. "I don't think it needs much more than that."

Davik nodded, and Rowan found what he needed on one of the shelves, cutting a large pad of cotton gauze and wrapping a long bandage around Lorne's waist to keep the gauze in place over the wound. The man working on the scale pushed himself to his feet, and then Miss Brady stepped forward to fiddle with a few things. She stood on the scale herself, adjusting the slide until it balanced.

"We're all set for you, Mr. Coswyn," she said brightly, stepping down. She pulled her spectacles from her pocket again, perching them on her nose and coaxing them out of the awkward tilt that made them skew a little too much to the left. "Let's see how much your soup bones weigh."

Lorne pressed his hand into the bandage, the pain of it cutting through indecision and fear. He could walk up to the scale. All he had to do was put one foot after another. He tried to tell himself that the dread didn't make any sense. It was just a scale. Just his weight. The whole thing clanked when he stepped onto it. Miss Brady fiddled with the slide. Davik hovered close to her, watching everything she did, and Lorne could swear she was leaning in closer to Davik. It would feel strange to stand in between the bookie and Davik while they were busy flirting, except Davik flirted with everyone.

The slide finally balanced, settling on Lorne's weight. 132. She nodded, tilting her head so she could look through her spectacles at her notebook to write it down.

"Up against the wall, if you please," she said. "Back straight, head high."

Lorne moved to the wall, getting his heels against the plaster, getting his head as straight as he could. Miss Brady stood on her tiptoes to make a pencil mark on the wall at the top of Lorne's head, and then Lorne stepped away and the man measured the space between the floor and the mark. Five foot nine.

"I'll take your measurements now, Mr. Coswyn. No need to get nervous—I'll measure a bunch of things like your arms and your chest." She met Lorne's eyes, pulling the measuring tape from around her neck and offering Lorne a wink. "Hold out your arms, darling. I'll try to make this as painless as possible."

"Sure," Lorne said.

She measured his chest, his shoulders, his biceps, his waist, the length of his arms. Each number she took down felt insufficient. He'd never been reduced to numbers before, and they made him achingly aware of how lean he was. He wondered what numbers the other boxers would have, if all of their numbers would be bigger.

Doesn't matter, he tried to tell himself. *You're smaller than Ijaz, and you won that fight. So it doesn't matter.*

"Has the league set a day for the opening bouts yet?" Davik asked, crossing his arms over his chest again and flexing a bit like he wanted to show off the lines of his forearms even though Miss Brady was only measuring Lorne. The brickwork tattoos always shifted when he did that, the flexing of his muscles making them dance.

"Not yet, Mr. Kaine. Those dates are generally announced after the solstice. In the new year."

"Is that it, Da?" Rowan interrupted. "Can we go?"

Miss Brady waved a hand at him. "Yes, of course. Please, don't let me impose on your schedule, Mr. Coswyn."

"Don't mind the boy, Deirdre," Davik said. "It's never an imposition. If you've time this evening, I'd love to meet you for a few pints across the street at the *Dripping Bucket,* and we can discuss the history of the Dominion Pugilism League."

"The *Dripping Bucket* is *your* whorehouse, isn't it?" Miss Brady asked.

Davik grinned. "Only from the second floor up. The pub on the ground floor is the best in the Bay if I do say so myself, and since it's mine, we can have as many pints as you want."

"That sounds wonderful." Miss Brady tucked her notebook away into her pocket. "Does your pugilist have his paperwork yet? He needs it forty-eight hours ahead of the first match."

"What paperwork?" Lorne asked.

Miss Brady adjusted her spectacles again. "The league requires proof that you aren't tainted. We don't run a division with tainted, since it gives fighters an unfair advantage. Only registered healers should be using Talent. A station house can assess you and sign off on your league paperwork, proving that you aren't tainted. Same as the paperwork you attained so you could officially be a coach, Davik. And you'll need paperwork for your son, too, if he's going to act as a healer's assistant. Will you be helping Miss Dargis at the match, young Mr. Kaine?"

"Ah—no—she won't be back from White Crown in time," Rowan said, his voice catching on each word like he'd been caught at something he wasn't supposed to be doing. "Her brother László will be taking the lead and I'll be filling the gaps."

Miss Brady's mouth twisted to one side and she tapped her pencil on her notebook. "The league has Miss Dargis on record, so we'll need you to file for whoever's taken her place. We'll need to see his registration paperwork at headquarters—and Rowan will need to be assessed to prove he isn't tainted—or if he is, he'll need registration. You filed your paperwork, haven't you, Mr. Kaine? To prove to the league you're clean so you can coach?"

Lorne fought to keep his face neutral and uninterested instead of wincing. What a shit word—clean. The opposite of tainted was clean, according to the league. It took all of Lorne's self control to keep his mouth shut. If he was just a dumb fighter at a club that didn't have anything to do with the Talented, he had no reason to argue with the league bookie about whether or not *clean* was a reasonable word, even though it filled him with fury and no small measure of shame. Technically, he was fucking *clean*, but the word sank into his skin like a dagger.

Davik's smile never wavered, but Lorne could sense the shift in him. The charm had lost a bit of its shine, his motions gone sharper. Lorne wondered if Miss Brady noticed, or if Lorne was especially attuned to Davik's moods already. How long had he been staying here? Less than a week, surely. But he already had an eye for the shifting winds of Hurricane Davik.

"Rowan inherited his Talent from his mam," Davik said, his voice excessively smooth and mellow like he was working hard to stay charming.

"Is she a healer as well?" Miss Brady asked.

"No, she wasn't," Rowan cut in, putting special emphasis on *wasn't* as if to highlight the implication that his mother was dead. If he couldn't make Miss Brady feel bad about the word clean, he'd apparently decided to make her feel bad about his mother. "She learned to use her Talent the old way, spreading it across different skills so that it was well-rounded and useful. And then she died anyway, in the Cruinnich riots when the Authority was killing anyone without paperwork."

"Rowan," Davik said.

"What?" Rowan snapped. "She asked if Mam was a healer—and I'm answering."

Miss Brady's head tilted to one side as curiosity drew her in. "Did she know the other Davik Kaine? The one who started the riots?"

Rowan gave a stiff shrug, shooting a glare at his father. "Sure, she knew him. Didn't mean she deserved to die, though. Not at the hands of

Clannaugh and his death squads. Just because she wasn't *clean* didn't mean she was a criminal."

"Rowan," Davik said again, turning the two syllables of his son's name into a fierce admonition. "Walk it off."

"Sure," Rowan said, turning on his heel without looking at Miss Brady again, slamming the door behind him on his way out.

Miss Brady shifted, watching Davik like she was waiting for some signal from him as to whether she should feel bad or not. Lorne didn't know what he was supposed to do—leave, stay, chase after Rowan? He scooped up his gloves, knocking the leather together so he could move, wiping the drying blood off the white. The stains had sunk into the grain.

"You'll have to excuse him, Deidre," Davik said. "He's at that age where it feels like he's always spoiling for a fight."

Miss Brady nodded, pulling her spectacles off her nose and tucking them into her pocket. "It's not easy for a boy to lose his mother. How old was he when she died?"

"Young," Davik said. "So young I'm not sure if he actually remembers her, or if he's just made memories out of the stories people tell about her."

"I'm sorry she was swept up in the trouble up north." Miss Brady looked genuinely sad, but in a distant way, like when rich people talked about how terrible it was that poor children were hungry, but then spread their hands and said there was nothing they could do. That was what being clean meant to her. It let her know that the tainted were suffering but gave her space to absolve herself from needing to do anything. "You have a rather infamous namesake, Davik. The other Davik Kaine has a lot to answer for if he's still alive."

Davik shrugged, painting on an easy smile. How did he do it? How did one man have so much guile that he convinced a whole city he wasn't *that* Davik Kaine? "I hear he went back to Teshii. He spent a few years out that way when he was young. They say that's where he learned to talk to crowds."

"Hopefully he's finished talking to crowds. The Dominion has seen enough of his trouble." She shrugged the topic off, tucking her pencil behind her ear and slipping her notebook away into a pocket. "You've left all the paperwork rather late, but if you go to the Brickheart station house, they should be able to help you quickly. They'll have stacks of all the right forms for Mr. Odegaard and his team. His pugilist club puts up a lot of fighters every tourney season. Tell them I sent you and they'll have you seen today."

"Thank you, Deirdre," Davik said, offering a hand. "I'll see you tonight at the *Bucket*."

Miss Brady shook Davik's hand and saw herself out, leaving static tension in the air behind her. Davik's smile disappeared as soon as Miss Brady and her assistant left. He grabbed a towel from the pile he kept in the corner, wiping his face in sharp movements like he was trying to scrub the anger away. The scale stood as a monument to the league and the word clean, all that metal catching the fury that Davik had been hiding all through the conversation and radiating it out at Lorne. It hurt to breathe. Lorne's chest was so tense from swallowing all the things he wanted to say that he couldn't quite take a full breath in. He wasn't used to swallowing a fight like that. He didn't know where to put all the tension.

"Are you alright?" Lorne asked.

"Fine, laddie," Davik said, although he clearly wasn't *fine*. He seethed below the surface. "Just fine."

Lorne tied his gloves together and hung them around his neck. They didn't go in here—he hung them in the change room that was designated for him, where he left all his clothes, all his towels. "You don't have to come with me to the station house. Tell me what to ask for, I can go myself. They'll sense your Talent if you go, won't they? So it's fine, I can go. I can read well enough to know what I'm signing."

Davik's head cocked to one side, his smile returning. Not the wide, showy thing he used to impress people. Something smaller and so sharp, he could use it to slice someone if he had a mind to. "You're smarter than you want people to think, aren't you?"

Lorne shrugged, sliding his finger over one of the bloodstains. Dry already, soaked into the leather. "I don't know. I don't care what people think."

"Sure you don't. Everyone cares what people think about them. We feel the eyes on us, all the time, trying to gauge how we're getting through the world. Maybe you don't care if people like you or not, but I'm damned sure you care if a Patroller is watching you with a suspicious eye, or if someone with something to prove thinks you're a threat."

"Is that why you're so charming? So that people don't think you're a threat?"

"Aye," Davik said, his voice low, like he was telling a heavy secret.

"When you're born tainted, you learn real quick that people who think you're a threat might well shoot you in the streets. So you smile. And you make them feel safe. And you hope you've convinced them so they don't shoot you in the back when you walk away."

Sounded about right. And it was the thing Jason struggled with the most. *I shouldn't have to smile for them,* he'd say, if he were here. "Is Rowan going to be alright?" Lorne asked instead of thinking about Jason and his beautiful scowl.

Davik shrugged, heading over to the desk where the wardrobe bags hung from the back of his chair. "He'll go find some of his friends, and they'll tell him how brave and impressive he was for getting mouthy with the league bookie. When he turns up tonight or tomorrow morning, I'll give him shit for it when so much is riding on the club, but he knows me well enough to know I'm proper proud of him for standing like that. You did good, though. There's room for Rowan to be mouthy and I can blame it on his age, but if you start popping off about the word clean, the league will wonder why the fuck you care."

Lorne nodded. "That's what I figured."

Davik lifted the wardrobe bags from his chair, and set them side by side on his desk. "Aye, I could see it in your eye. Ain't easy for you to keep your mouth shut, is it? You're fitting in better than I expected. Come try your coat on, hey? It came in while you were fighting. We'll put you in a shirt without holes and pit stains, make you look like a proper celebrity."

Lorne pushed his hand through his hair, wringing the sweat out. "But I'm still sweaty and gross."

A knock on the door, and then it swung open. László, wearing that big smile of his, which lay in the room like a balm on both of their tempers. "Vasska Czarny is over at the *Bucket,* asking for you."

Davik sighed, opening the ties that kept the wardrobe bag closed. He looked surprisingly tired, worn so thin for a moment that Lorne could see right through his eyes and into all the shit he carried but hid under his charm. "Did Mr. Czarny say what he wanted?"

"Don't think so. Can I come? I'm hungry."

"Don't I have to go to Brickheart for paperwork?" Lorne asked.

Davik snorted. "Fuck no. If anything, Mr. Czarny has kindly saved us a trip to the Hive. I'll let him know that we need the forms and he'll get good forgeries faster than you can sneeze. Clean yourself up, Mr. Lightning, and we'll meet him for pints."

László grabbed a towel off the shelf and threw it at Lorne's head.

Lorne caught it before it hit his face, rubbing all the sweat out of his hair. He used to think all the heat this place generated was wasteful, but all the time he spent standing around in not enough clothes made him appreciate it. Davik pulled the new clothes out of their bags, laying trousers and jackets and freshly starched shirts out. And then the coat. The leather was the colour of fresh cream, the inner lining pure white lambs' fleece, the wool still raw and curling, looking deliciously warm and entirely too indulgent. Lorne couldn't even fathom how much it must have cost.

"Dav, this is too much," Lorne said. "I can't keep a white coat clean."

"Don't worry about that," Davik laughed. "It's leather—it won't get dirty, it'll get *character*. It's perfect for you. Matches your gloves, doesn't it? Everywhere you go, people will know who you are. There he goes, Lorne the Lledewydd Lightning, the Bay fighter with the white gloves and the white coat. You're a celebrity now, remember? Let the people of this city love you, I promise it won't hurt. Don't look at me like that—get some clothes on and then try the coat."

Lorne sighed and grabbed clothes from the pile. It all smelled too clean, but it was the only fault he could find with any of it. The wool was thick and buttery soft, and the linen shirt was sturdy, the jacket lined with black silk. Davik pushed the coat into Lorne's hands, and he pulled it on. It was heavier than he expected, the leather supple and soft, the hem almost down to his knees. The collar was high and structured, so that it stood straight up when Davik turned it up around his face, the fleece promising to keep him warm through the cruelest of Yaelsmuir's winter wind.

"I look ridiculous," Lorne muttered, pushing the collar back down.

"You look amazing," László said, turning the collar up again. "It's perfect for you."

"Give me my old coat," Lorne muttered, pushing the collar down again.

"You're not wearing that ratty old rag with your new suit and that's final," Davik said.

"Everything fits him real well, Dav," László said, sliding his hand down the front of Lorne's coat, smoothing everything out. "Looks real good. But I still say the trousers should have been tighter. So everyone can see how big his cock is."

Breathing suddenly became too taxing a task and Lorne just about choked on his own tongue.

"I thought maybe you'd burn all the clothes if I tried that," Davik said with a grin. He turned the collar up again, pushing his hands through Lorne's hair to try to arrange it into some orderly style. "You'll get used to the coat. And when it's a million degrees below freezing, you'll thank me for it. Now let's go, show you off to Mr. Czarny."

19

STELLA

DAY 33

"I drift sometimes," Ozra said. Rhodrishi helped him out of his clothes, peeling off a layer at a time. His teeth chattered, just like Stella's. The ghost of Eilidh was gone. She disappeared as they walked back to camp, fading like fog under the hot morning sun. "I've the Wrath, like I said. I haven't used my Talent in a long time, but that quickening, shite. It was so sudden, it pulled me right out of myself."

Wind howled up from the south, wet with the threat of a storm. Rhodrishi hung a rope from the branches of the willow, stretching it as close to the fire as he could. He handed Ozra's sweater to Ceridwen, who crushed all the water out of it with her little hands. This, at least, was something she was utterly prepared for, having done laundry for the neighbours for so long.

Stella's shirt was dry, at least. She had to take off the bottom half of her clothes—boots, socks, trousers, drawers—and once she did, Kazrani wrapped a fire-warmed blanket around Stella's legs to coax the warmth back into her skin. Stella held the blanket in place, her bare feet sinking into the carpet of willow leaves beneath her.

"How could someone's quickening be so strong that we all felt it?" Stella asked.

"I suspect people around him felt it, too," Rhodrishi said softly. "But the only reason it reached so far to us is because we're connected to him already."

A shiver passed up and down Stella's spine, stronger than the cold. Making her scalp tight, making her heart stutter. "No." It was all she could manage to say. *No*, as if she could make it untrue.

"What?" Kazrani asked. She pushed Stella's boots closer to the fire. "What's wrong?"

"Rhodrishi, no," Stella said again. "That can't be right."

"Blackwood, is it?" Ozra asked. "The man you all left behind?"

No one spoke.

Ceridwen sniffled softly as she hung Ozra's sweater from the line. She took up his shirt next, squeezing the water into a growing puddle between her feet and the fire pit. She was shaking.

"Come here, Pigeon," Stella said. "It's fine."

Except it didn't feel fine. She'd never felt a quickening like that. The only thing that came close was the day her son's Talent woke. With all the traumas life had thrown her way, that was still the worst day of her entire life.

Ceridwen shook her head, wiping her eyes with a corner of Ozra's shirt. "I have to finish. Mr. Sgèin needs his clothes dry before he freezes half to death."

"You're kind to help me, wee girl," Ozra said. "Thank you."

"What's happened to him?" Kazrani pressed. The thin hold she had on her own composure sounded like it was starting to crack. "What's he done now?"

"His Talent has finally woken," Rhodrishi said. "That great beast I've been dreading since the day I met him. The force of it sent a blast through the connection we have."

"Then how did it effect Mr. Sgèin?" Kazrani huffed.

"Proximity, I think," Ozra said, rubbing his hands together. He wrapped his blanket around his body to hide himself before taking off his drawers, kicking the ragged old things toward the fire. "I was standing with Miss Whiterock, and my Talent has always hooked onto the strength of other people as a way to see them."

"Did you see him?" Ceridwen asked. "Did you see Mr. Blackwood when it happened?"

Ozra's eyes lingered on Ceridwen a moment too long, giving away his lie. "No, sweet girl. I didn't."

"I felt him," Ceridwen said, wiping her eyes. "He was angry and scared and in pain. Is he hurt? Is it his Talent that made him feel that way?"

"I don't know, Pigeon."

The answer was so terribly insufficient.

Ceridwen whimpered. Her shoulders hitched, and she pressed a hand to her mouth. The fire lit her face enough for Stella to see the horrible details of her expression, the squeezed shut eyes, the twisted brow, the trembling. Stella went to her, ducking under the rope line. And Ceridwen crumbled. Stella caught her, hugging her close, leaning over to kiss her hair, her face, the tear tracks on her cheeks. And the comfort only seemed to redouble the grief, and Ceridwen pressed her face into Stella's arms. Sobbing. So loud that no one could speak over the sound. Not that there was anything worth saying.

Stella looked to Ozra, who stood shivering in his blankets, watching them. His mouth twisted with something like pain. She had so many questions for him, questions that swamped even the thought of his ghost.

What had he seen, that drove him to lie to Ceridwen?

She didn't dare wonder at the possible answers. If Tashué were dead, something would break in her. Something deep and without hope.

So, she held Ceridwen as the girl wept, and when Ceridwen finally cried herself out, she helped the girl to her bedroll and lay with her until Ceridwen fell into her restless, exhausted sleep while the fire crackled, drying their clothes on their makeshift rope line so that hopefully they could keep travelling in the morning. Away from Yaelsmuir, into the Dunnenbrahl, leaving Tashué behind.

Kazrani foraged more wood than they usually used overnight, so they could keep the fire banked high. Ozra didn't have any spare clothes at all, so he sat beside the flames, wrapped in his blanket, bare toes resting on a rock that caught the warmth of the blaze.

"What did you see?" Stella asked, her voice a harsh, painful whisper, but she didn't dare wake Ceridwen, not now.

"Violence," Ozra whispered back. "It was ugly, Miss Whiterock."

"His quickening was violent, or there was violence happening that prompted it?"

"Both."

Stella huffed, shaking her head. "Can you tell me what you saw, instead of dancing around it? I'm not going to wither away just because you tell me something that's hard to hear." Except that wasn't true. She wanted it to be true, but wanting strength wasn't the same as having it. If trauma made someone into glass, she was delicate and untempered, with fissures in the surface of her. Tashué dying would shatter her. It didn't matter how insistently she told herself she barely knew him. In his arms, she learnt to hope again. If that was gone?

"I don't mean any offence by it," Ozra said finally. Was he lying again? She couldn't tell. "It's just that I don't *know* what I saw. It happened so fast, and when I drift like that I see so much. All the wilderness between here and the city, and the city proper, too. All the streets in it, and the river. It's so much to take in all at once, so I can't parse it all out. All I know is that he was in the Dunnenbrahl, and there was violence. Blood. He's alive, or at least he was when I woke. But more than that, I don't know."

Stella pressed her hands against her face, her fingers cold and painful. "Why the Dunnenbrahl?" she asked, even though she knew already Ozra didn't have an answer.

Ozra shook his head. "Don't know. Not far from the city limits, I don't think."

Stella dropped her hands to her blanket-wrapped lap, the wool scratchy and uncomfortable against her bare skin, but it was better than sitting half naked. "How far are we from the city?"

"Are you thinking about going back?" Kazrani asked.

"Shouldn't we at least consider it?" Stella countered. "If he's in danger, perhaps we could make it back in time to help."

"Help how?" Kazrani asked, though her voice strained with the words. "He knew what he was staying to fight for. For Jason. For that little girl he found. And we left for a reason. For *your* girl. We've done all this to protect her. Nothing's changed since we left. She'll be in danger if we go back."

"What girl?" Ozra asked. "That's the second time you've mentioned it—the girl he found."

Stella looked toward Ceridwen's sleeping form, straining her ears to pick up the sound of Ceridwen's snoring. It wasn't so loud, but it was definitely there, in the background, beneath the sound of the fire. "Do you know what I mean when I say the words *energy units*?"

Ozra's face spasmed as viscerally as if Stella or Kazrani had balled up a fist and punched him in the gut. "Of course I do. The wee ones from the cursed Breeding Program, made for their Talent and their strength."

"He found one," Stella said softly. "He didn't know. People in Yaelsmuir, they don't know. You forget, sometimes, that the Authority keeps these secrets, and people don't know how their trams take them around the city so efficiently. But now that he does know, he won't stop until everyone in Yaelsmuir sees the truth and he brings the Authority to account for what they did." The building energy sent a fresh shiver down her spine. It was so tempting to think Tashué could do it. If anyone could bring the Authority to its knees, it was him, the man who could move mountains. But that seemed too hopeful a possibility for the cruel world Stella had come to know. Davik had tried to fight the Authority, and all he gained was pain. "Or until they kill him."

The possibility suddenly seemed entirely too imminent.

"Stella," Kazrani said, as if she knew already the way Stella's thoughts were twisting and sought to head them off before she could speak the words bubbling up in her.

"We should go back," Stella interrupted. "We should go back and help—or clean up his mess."

"We're out here for a reason," Rhodrishi said. She hadn't heard him approach, but he was standing over them now, half lit by the fire.

"What would you do?" Stella asked. "You talked about revolution. If your son is right, and it's finally here—would you keep running away? Or would you stand and fight for everything you've been wanting to see since the day you first heard the Authority's name?"

"I would choose my child," Rhodrishi said. "What good is revolution if our children aren't here to see it? Sometimes the revolutionary act is simply keeping them safe in a world where they're anything *but* safe."

"I tried to choose the idea of revolution once," Ozra said, pushing his feet even closer to the fire, so close it had to hurt, but maybe the physical pain was easier to bear than the emotion of the moment. "It cost me everything."

"What about Duncreek?" Kazrani asked. "If you can see between here and Yaelsmuir, can you find him with your Talent?"

Ozra shook his head. "I told you, I can't see details. It's too much, seeing all that at once."

"But could you try?" Kazrani pressed. "If you knew who you were looking for, could you?"

"I can't control it anymore," Ozra said. "That's what I'm trying to tell you—I'm just as likely to wander all the way to the Commonwealth as I am to stay here to search for Duncreek. If I could, I swear to you, I would. But I'm sorry, I can't."

Kazrani scowled but turned to Stella. Perhaps she didn't consider the argument over. "You should try to get some sleep. I know it doesn't seem possible, but you should lay with your Ceridwen and try. We've a long day tomorrow and a lot of ground to cover."

Ceridwen's whole body radiated warmth like a coal plucked from the fire when Stella settled down beside her. Wishing again, no doubt, her Talent the most gentle of strengths, like the summer breeze that could become something terrible but for now was sweet and innocent, something Stella could barely feel but for the warmth it made.

It was only as she lay awake, her mind spinning in every direction at once, that she realized she should have asked Ozra about his ghost. Eilidh, and the child she sometimes carried.

But perhaps she already knew the answer. *It cost me everything*, he said. When she asked about his children, his answer was *none that survived*.

20

LORNE

DAY 33

Lorne hadn't been to the *Dripping Bucket* before, but he had been to other pubs like it. There were plenty of them standing on the outer edges of the Bay, closest to Highview and Drystone. A wide array of alcohol that wasn't typically available in the poor quarters —single malt whiskies, aged brandies, vodkas, gins, sparkling wine from the southern provinces—drew in rich clientele that wanted to spend the evening with Bay company because they got a thrill out of being around people reputed to be hard-worn and a little dangerous and, on the whole, horny.

And Bay folks filled these pubs to bursting because it was the best way to get alcohol they couldn't afford, more food than they probably saw all week, and a roof and a bed for the night. The risk of meeting someone that liked things too rough was far outweighed by the potential rewards. They just had to compete with the whores who were practically residents of these places. The *Dripping Bucket* wasn't technically a whorehouse despite what Miss Brady said, but there were plenty of professionals here since it was miles safer than being out on the streets.

There wasn't enough sawdust in the city to make the floor seem clean or the air seem fresh, but at least the kitchen churned out food that smelled like salt and garlic and grease and sugar. Bodies jostled, tables were packed, the bar was lined with customers waiting for their drinks.

Vasska sat at the bar with a pint, looking just as relaxed and comfortable as he ever did at the Hive.

"Mr. Czarny," Davik said brightly, offering Vasska a hand. "It's good to see you. It's been a while."

"It has, hasn't it?" Vasska said, turning in his stool to accept the handshake. "I was curious to see how our pugilist is progressing. We miss him at the Hive, but people are excited to have the Bay represented in the league, finally."

"If you wanted to see him progressing, you should have come on over to the club," Davik said. "You're welcome any time, Mr. Czarny."

Vasska shrugged a little. "I wasn't sure if I was intruding."

László hooked his arm in Vasska's, dragging Lorne with him so they all stood together. "It's never an intrusion, Mr. Czarny. You helped us build that club—it's as much yours as it is ours."

Vasska shrugged again. "We only gave you the funds and the building to get started. It's Mr. Kaine's vision and determination that made it happen." He looked past László to Lorne. "Your face is healing well, Mr. Coswyn. Nice coat."

Lorne shrugged. The leather and the fleece sat heavy on his shoulders. It was cooler in the pub than in the club, but the coat was still too warm. Sweat trickled down Lorne's back. More fucking guilt—he was supposed to try to help Vasska, but he hadn't had time to think about anyone or anything but boxing. "League says I need a healer, so I guess I have a healer now. I don't feel important enough to have a healer."

Vasska smiled, shifting in his seat so he leaned against the bar. Like he was right at home here among these people who might be his enemies. "You certainly look important enough, dressed like that."

"He looks real good, doesn't he?" László said, flipping up Lorne's collar again. "It's loose still, so he's got room to put a bit of weight on before the tourney season."

"Just leave it down," Lorne muttered, pushing László's hands away.

László huffed. "You're no fun."

"He does take himself very seriously, doesn't he?" Vasska said, leaning against László, the pair of them studying Lorne like a curious specimen. "Mr. Coswyn is where fun goes to die a slow, agonizing death."

Lorne squirmed, pushing the coat open to try to cool himself down. Was he blushing? Fuck's sake, he was blushing like an idiot. "Fuck off."

"Mr. Czarny," Davik cut in. "If you don't mind, we need Authority papers for him, to prove he ain't tainted. Need 'em forty-eight hours before the first match."

Vasska nodded, looking down at his timepiece as if to remind himself of the date. "Left it rather close to the deadline, didn't you?"

Davik shrugged. "This being my first league match, there've been a few details that slipped away from me. We'll also need papers saying László is our healer and another set for Rowan so he can help."

Vasska glanced at László, an amused smile dancing over his features. "Not all that long ago, you said you'd rather die than carry paperwork. Even if they were forgeries."

László shrugged. "I meant it when I said it, but it's worth it for the club. If we don't have a healer, we can't put up a fighter, and Rowan ain't ready to do it on his own. And Irén couldn't heal a paper cut. So I guess it's me. You should come by the club and see his gloves—they came in today. Are you here long enough to have something to eat? We could get a table, and we can tell you all about our plans for the club."

Vasska glanced at Davik and Lorne. "I think that's a good idea. We should talk."

That didn't sound good.

László led Vasska into the crowd. Lorne tried to follow, but Davik caught him by the thick coat sleeve and held him at the bar. He flicked his fingers at the publican to catch the man's attention. The publican dropped everything to come, leaning close to hear Davik over the chaos of the crowd.

"Drinks for all of us, Cyril, and the boys are hungry."

"Yes sir, Mr. Kaine," Cyril said, peeling away.

"How are things between you and Czarny?" Davik asked.

"Things between us?" Lorne echoed, hoping he sounded mystified and frustrated in the right way, instead of like an idiot who washed out of the diplomatic division because he hated spying, who had been asked to spy and was failing at it. It was one thing to run his network of people who sold gossip for him to give to Powell Iwan or General Wolfe, but this part was shit. "I don't fucking know, Davik. I don't know anything. I asked him questions about *you* when I was looking for answers about the girl Tashué found. He told me to leave it alone. And then I got the shit kicked out of me at the Hive. So I expected things between you and me to be really fucking bad, but here we are, aren't we? Shows I don't know anything. Last time I saw him, he asked me to look for information for him. He heard a rumour someone had started that tenement fire on purpose, and he wanted to know if I could find anyone who saw it."

"And? Did you?"

"When did I have time for that?" Lorne scoffed, spreading his hands. "In between the skip rope and protein breaks? And then he said some shit about remembering who was loyal to him. Felt an awful lot like he was saying he'd remember who gave him a hard time, too."

"He threatened you?" Davik asked.

"I thought so," Lorne muttered. One of the things he remembered from the division was that lying always worked best when you were mostly telling the truth. "He insists it wasn't like that, but I don't know."

Davik shrugged, turning away from the bar. "Let's find out, shall we?"

Shit. Had Lorne sold the act too well? Was Vasska going to catch hell from Davik now? Shit.

Davik headed for the table, cleaving through the crowd like an icebreaker. People moved out of his way before he even reached them, giving him a clear path. Lorne tried to follow—somehow he'd have to balance things so Vasska knew Lorne hadn't sold him out without signalling to Davik that he was playing both sides. Fuck—this was exactly why he hated this.

Lorne slid into the bench across from Vasska and László. Davik settled beside Lorne, blocking Lorne against the wall, opposite Vasska. Lorne couldn't get out unless Davik let him out. Once, it would have bothered him. Would have sent him crawling up the walls with anxiety. But he didn't eat or drink or even breathe without instruction from Davik. This was his life now. The awareness of his own change felt... strange. Or maybe the strange feeling came from seeing Vasska—the collision of Lorne's old life at the Hive and his new life at the pugilist club. It had only been a few days, but the trajectory of everything had changed. His life got knocked off the course it was on when Orix didn't let him off the stage after Ijaz finally went down. Or maybe 'knocked off course' was wrong because at that moment, he'd been on course to fucking nowhere. Waiting for Jason, sending money to Alys, accomplishing nothing. A becalm, stranding him far away from everything he wanted. But Hurricane Davik had been frothing up back then and all that furious wind had caught Lorne's sails and now he was riding the storm waves and praying it would bring him closer to Jason.

"How's business, Mr. Kaine?" Vasska asked.

"Business?" Davik echoed with a shrug. "It runs. People like to drink and fuck and fight, don't they? So there's always plenty of business. All the plumbing is working nicely—in the club and at the Qasani temple. We'll try to get it started here at the *Bucket*, too, but this old building... well. We'll have to run things up through the walls and treat the place real gentle since she's a little worn and tired. She's worth it though, isn't she? We've a lot of memories in this place."

"It's served you very well since you arrived in Yaelsmuir," Vasska agreed.

Davik nodded. "Aye, exactly. We'll hold off 'til spring for now, I think. Did your grandad decide where else in the Bay he wants plumbing?"

"Not yet," Vasska said. "But I'm hoping you'd be willing to send your people to come take a look at that tenement building that burned down. It's mine now. It's empty and needs extensive repairs after the fire, so maybe we could run plumbing through it while we're fixing everything up?"

The tenement building. That fire wasn't as bad as the fire that devoured so much of the Market, but the tenement fire lived in Lorne's nightmares. His days were a blur of László and Davik and boxing, but at night, he saw the woman with the haunted eyes. The one who escaped the Breeding Program and told Tashué about her children. He saw the flames that ate it all up. He saw the ash and the bodies that were left after the Yaelsmuir autumn rain put the fire out.

"Plumbing in a tenement building, hey?" Davik asked. "How about that. I'll send my well finders, see what they say. I don't imagine there'll be a problem."

The bartender arrived with pints of stout, the head cream-coloured and indulgently thick. "Be a few minutes for the meal, Mr. Kaine."

"Thank you."

"Just in time," Irén said, sliding into the bench beside Vasska. Lorne hadn't seen much of Irén. If László hadn't said they were twins, Lorne never would have guessed—close inspection revealed the familiar resemblance of their faces, but that's where the similarities ended. László towered above his sister. Irén had black hair instead of László's sandy blond, which she didn't bother plaiting or styling at all—she had tied it back at some point in the day, but curls were escaping, framing her face. She wasn't involved in the pugilist club much; she ate her breakfast with everyone and then disappeared. She leaned across Vasska and stole the pint right out of László's hand. "Nice to see you, Mr. Czarny."

"Bitch," László scoffed.

"Grandad will be pleased to hear about all the progress," Vasska said, ignoring the twins. "But Mr. Coswyn isn't the only young man Grandad has been asking about."

"Aha—there it is," Davik said, his voice gone extra buttery and his smile gone predatory. Each of them had a weaponized smile, except Lorne. "The reason you're here. This is the part where you ask me why Jason Blackwood is still in the Rift, yeah?"

Jason. It was the first time his name had been uttered since Lorne turned up at the club, and the realization made the days since feel like they'd stretched immeasurably.

Vasska nodded. "It is, Mr. Kaine. Grandad gave you that task some weeks ago, and there doesn't seem to be any progress. He's growing impatient. Especially with the news out of Brickheart today."

"What news out of Brickheart?" Lorne blurted. "What happened?"

"What's some tinman trying to kill Elsworth got to do with the Blackwood kid and getting him out of the Rift?" Irén asked.

"When that tinman is Jason Blackwood's father?" Vasska asked. "Everything."

Ringing in Lorne's ears like he'd been punched in the back of the head. Drowning out thought and emotion and reason. A moment of nothing. And then everything, all at once. Panic. Jason. Grief.

"Tashué?" Lorne finally asked, pushing the words past his panic. "What happened to Tashué? What did he do?"

"I'm not a miracle worker, Mr. Czarny," Davik said, ignoring Lorne's question. "I can't snap my fingers and have the Blackwood boy appear for you, no matter what kind of trouble his father got himself into."

"What kind of trouble?" Lorne pressed, desperation making him loud. Demanding their attention. "Dav, what happened in Brickheart?"

"You haven't heard?" Vasska asked.

Lorne slapped both his hands on the table, making the beers jump and slosh across the tabletop. It didn't help to let the tension out—it only wound him tighter, setting springs in his muscles that needed to go off. "I've been fucking boxing, like you told me to! Heard *what?*"

"He held a gun to Rainer Elsworth's head and threatened to pull the trigger," Vasska said, the words delivered gently, regretfully, like an apology. "General Wolfe went down to the city jail to make sure he wasn't murdered in his cell, but the arresting Patrollers never turned up. He's missing—him and Ishmael both."

"Saeati was arrested, too?" Davik asked, his eyebrows climbing up with his surprise. "Shit."

"So... what?" Lorne breathed. But even as he tried to put all the questions flitting through his head to words, he already knew the horrible answer. "They're dead. That's what you're saying, right? They never turned up to the prison because they're dead. They did something stupid and the Patrollers shot them for it and they're not at the city jail because they're fucking *dead*."

Davik reached for his pint and took a slow sip. "Of all the ways I thought Saeati would catch a bullet, I have to admit, I didn't expect it to be over Rainer Elsworth. How'd he get pulled into Blackwood's mess?"

"Didn't you say him and Blackwood had history, Dav?" Irén asked. "That's why Iwan asked us to get the Blackwood boy out—Saeati asked for it."

Davik shrugged. "Saeati said it was for Wolfe. Guess that wasn't the whole story, like I thought." He turned his dark eyes on Lorne, fingers playing slowly through his beard. "What say you, laddie? You must know —the Blackwoods are like family to you, aren't they?"

Lorne shook his head, but it didn't help anything. He was going to be sick. He took a long pull of his beer, but it didn't cool him. It put more fluid in his stomach for him to lose if the nausea won. "Sure, but I don't know anything about Ishmael Saeati. Tashué doesn't tell me about his personal life. I didn't even know him and Tashué had history at all until a few days ago. A few weeks ago? I don't even know anymore. Doesn't matter now, does it? If they're both dead, nothing matters at all."

"What's the delay with Jason?" Vasska asked, catching control of the conversation again. "Maybe if I could tell Grandad what exactly is going on, he'd be more comfortable with the wait."

"Now, Mr. Czarny, you know I ain't going to say," Davik said. "You're putting me in a position to say no to you, and I don't like that— but I need to guard my secrets, don't I? We're working with the people and the resources we have, and we got hurdles to get around, but we're making progress. I promise."

Lorne looked down at his beer, watching the head slide down the inside of the glass. Reeling, tilting, dizzy. Everything Davik said sounded good and bad—there were plans to get Jason out, but they weren't progressing. And Tashué was gone.

It didn't seem possible. If someone as big and *present* as Tashué had died, shouldn't it leave a big hole in reality that Lorne could feel? It couldn't be right that he was gone and Lorne hadn't known until now. It felt like a thing he should have been able to sense, except he'd been so fucking busy learning how to be a boxer that most of the world had stopped existing.

"Mr. Kaine," Vasska said, his voice gone sharp. But also pleading. He wanted them to work together, that's what he told Lorne.

"It ain't personal, Mr. Czarny," Irén cut in. "It's delicate, is all. It's a big ask. If it were anyone else, we'd slip him out with a bribe or two, no problem. Would've gone like that if we started this before people knew his name. But now? After everyone knows he broke suppression? When he goes missing, people are going to have questions, and we gotta make sure the right answers are all lined up. The Breeding Program wants him and we had to slow that process down a bit to give us time to think. I'm going to make sure it all happens right as we sort it out."

Holy fuck—

Had Irén really implied that they had interfered with the Breeding Program to keep Jason out of there? They'd somehow slowed his transfer —how? And she was going in? It was the best news he'd heard since Jason was arrested, but he still felt sick. Jason was coming out, but Tashué was dead.

The sound of a fight rose up above the usual chaos of the pub, setting Lorne's teeth on edge. Everything in him wanted to get up and wade into the violence, release the pain and hope and confusion into his arms so he could batter someone senseless and so he didn't have to think at all.

Irén huffed, putting her beer back down. "Excuse me, Mr. Czarny."

She pushed herself to her feet and stomped off. Lorne watched her disappear into the crowd, his whole body itching. Whatever it was, he should wade into the chaos with her. But he couldn't. Davik was blocking him in.

"Hey," László said softly, his voice barely above a whisper. Just for him and Lorne. He reached across the table, laying his fingers on the back of Lorne's hand. Even the feeling of his fingers was so complicated it made Lorne want to crawl out of his own skin. László felt good, but Jason— "You alright?"

"Do you visit him?" Vasska asked before Lorne could even think of an answer for László.

"Of course I visit him," Lorne snapped. Except Lorne hadn't visited, not since he started here. The last time he visited Jason was the day he delivered the news that Keoh had died.

"He should hear it from you," Vasska said. "The news about his father—he should hear it from you."

"Why do you care, Vasska?" Lorne asked. The words came out so fast he didn't even feel them build in his chest first. His mouth started moving. He needed to swing or run or fight or *something* but instead he was sitting here with Davik and László and Vasska, fucking talking. As if talking had ever helped anything. "Why does your dear old grandad care, hey? Why does Powell Iwan want him? What are you going to ask him to do once he's out?"

"Lorne, it's not like that—"

"Bullshit it's not like that," Lorne snapped. "Everyone has a purpose for Powell Iwan, don't they? Everyone is a tool. So what does Powell Iwan want with Jason? What's all this for?"

"Is this still about your fight?" Vasska scoffed. "I thought I made things very clear for you, Lorne. You could have been killed and left in an alley to rot because that's what Edgar Hale wanted, but instead Grandad protected you. Do you realize how lucky you are? How much this quarter *loves* you? Fucking look at you, sitting in on meetings with the very organization you were sticking your nose into. A month ago, the Red Dawn wanted you dead, and now you're rising right up to the top, aren't you? Did you ask Davik if he knew what Hale wanted us to do to you, or did you just accept that Davik was your new boss?"

"László said they didn't know—"

"Oh László said that, did he?" Vasska interrupted. "It must be nice for him that you just take his word instead of holding a grudge against him for the actions of other people that he had no control over. What do I have to do to get that kind of forgiveness from you? Maybe if I throw some money at you to help pay for that expensive coat and a new wardrobe, would that be enough?" He thrust his hand into his pocket and tossed a fistful of coins on the table between them. Copper and silver clattered over the wood, clinking against the glasses, some of them tumbling into Lorne's lap. Davik slapped a hand down on a half-silver, catching it before it spun off to the floor. "Is that enough to buy your forgiveness, Lorne?"

Davik slid the half-silver in front of Lorne, lifting his hand to leave it resting in the spilt beer from Lorne's pint glass, crown side up. "I think it's safe to say he ain't threatening you, laddie."

Lorne blinked at the coins, the anger crumbling away fast. Things were moving in too many different directions, making it impossible to have the right emotions in any given moment. Davik had said *let's find out,* and somewhere along the way, Vasska had let down his high guard enough that the pair of them had argued like they did when they were alone. Had Davik done that somehow? Or maybe it was stupid to assume that Lorne's fury came from anywhere but himself, and it was waiting for an excuse to unfold.

"Not bad for a night's work, Mr. Lightning," László said, sweeping a hand across the table, lifting pints out of the way so he could gather all the crowns in a pile. And he laughed, slicing the tension wide open, letting it bleed empty. "We'll make a proper whore out of you in no time."

Vasska slid a few of the stray coins in front of László, into the pile that László was making. "Go ahead and put that toward the cost of his fancy coat. Maybe then he'll remember I told him the Bay takes care of him."

"Yes sir, Mr. Czarny." László beamed, sliding the coins across the table one at a time from one pile to the next—counting the silver and copper, his mouth moving as he kept track of the sum.

"We're working on the Blackwood boy, Mr. Czarny," Davik said, pushing the last of the coins toward László. "It's been a fucking mess, but I'm not going to lie down and give up, am I? Like Irén said, she'll head in. Make sure the rest of the steps run smooth."

"Irén's going to the Rift on purpose?" Vasska asked.

"Yeah," László said, softly, the joy draining out of his features in an instant. "I offered, but Dav said I wasn't allowed because I needed to stay and be a healer. She's the only other person with the stones to do it."

"Why didn't you tell me you were asking for volunteers?" Lorne breathed. "I would have gone in a heartbeat."

"You're missing the only qualification that matters, son," Davik muttered into his beer, pausing long enough to take a sip. Long enough to let Lorne's heart stop beating while he waited for the rest of the answer. If Davik was about to say that Lorne didn't have the stones, he would put Davik's teeth into the back of his damn throat. "The Rift'll notice you ain't got Talent."

"But I could help—"

"You're helping by fighting," Davik interrupted. "By being the Bay's first pugilist, which'll draw crowd from the whole city."

"I don't see how any of it helps Jason," Lorne pressed. "I'm trying to figure out how it all connects. Why boxing? All the paperwork you have to get for the league, and the thing Miss Brady said about the Talented. Why go through so much? If it's to launder money, why not just open another public house, or another brothel?"

Davik's eyebrow quirked. "You know a few things about laundering money, laddie?"

Lorne shrugged, cursing himself. Stupid to talk about money with someone as smart as Davik Kaine.

"Said too much, did you?" Davik asked with a grin. "Aye, I know about your businesses and about the big fat bank account in Drystone you use to shuffle your finances from here to Teshii. For your wee sister."

"How did you know that?" Lorne asked.

"Iwan and I were looking into you when we were figuring everything out. Needed to see if you were the sort of man we could work with. The banker wouldn't say if you were holding the money there or using it to send across the wire, but they confirmed you were a regular client."

Lorne shook his head, looking between Davik, László, Vasska. They all knew. He'd kept this secret for years, but now they knew. That's why Powell had asked him, that day in the Hive, when it felt like a threat. It wasn't a threat, it was Powell trying to decide if he could send Lorne down to work with Davik.

"I don't see what that has to do with Jason," Lorne scoffed, his last line of desperate, empty defence. "I'm doing everything you tell me, aren't I? I'm learning to fight and I'm eating what you say I have to eat and I'm doing any stupid thing you tell me for exercise, so can you tell me how I'm helping Jason?"

"Listen, would you?" László huffed. "The match is a political fundraiser, and the one time Powell Iwan lets Patrollers in the Bay is when the politicians are prancing around. If the club is so full that people are climbing up the walls, the Redbone campaign will need dozens of Patrollers for crowd control. If the Mayor thinks there's a chance the crowd could riot? Half the Patrollers in the city will be down here to try to keep the peace. Which means fewer Patrollers on hand for special duty to help the Authority. It's a long walk, the Rift to the Breeding Program."

"Are you saying—"

"Yes," Davik interrupted, turning the word into a sibilant hiss that silenced Lorne immediately. "That's exactly what he means. Now shut up before you announce it to the whole fucking pub."

Lorne sank back into his seat, watching the condensation slide down the side of his pint glass. Davik needed him to fight in the boxing match because the match was a distraction for whatever Davik had planned for getting Jason.

Davik huffed, drumming his fingers on the table. "Well, hopefully that eases your mind some, Mr. Czarny. We're working on it. Listen, since you're here to talk business, we've got a shipment coming down from the north soon, and I would appreciate it if the shipment wasn't held in the Hive too long."

Vasska sipped his beer like he needed the time to pivot back to business. Or maybe the minute was just to show he was thinking about everything. "What kind of shipment?"

Davik shrugged. "The sort that needs careful handling, Mr. Czarny. The sort that rebel armies need to keep themselves going."

"I won't have another fire in my quarter, Mr. Kaine," Vasska said, his voice gone stiff.

"No, it's nothing like that," Davik said, waving a hand. "That thermite that fucked the Market wasn't mine."

"Sure, but what kind of delicate things am I expecting? Are you building bombs again?"

What a question. What a *fucking* question. It sat on the table between them, the words piled like Vasska's coins, and Davik waited a moment before answering, like he wanted to let Vasska sweat a bit. And Lorne sweat plenty, because he wanted more answers than anyone was apparently willing or able to give him. Tashué, Ishmael, Jason—but then Vasska said *are you building bombs again* and the whole world screeched to a halt.

"No, Mr. Czarny." Davik drained his pint, setting it near the edge of the table. "I haven't touched explosives in a good long while. They're too unpredictable, aren't they? Too volatile. It's plain old guns, coming down from Obisza. It's been a bit of a journey, getting my hands on them. I'd appreciate it if they came to me quickly."

"How many guns?"

"A significant number of guns."

Holy fuck. Lorne knew Davik's people were rebels, but the knowledge was a distant thing, hard to grasp. He'd only ever seen the surface of it because he'd only been around a few days, and Davik kept him plenty busy learning to box. But now suddenly Lorne was sitting in the middle of it all, in the crowded pub. Guns coming down the river, building bombs. Tashué dead. Rescuing Jason from the Breeding Program.

"When's the last time you built bombs, Dav?" Lorne asked, his thoughts sparking so fast he couldn't keep them separated. Davik had said the club was important for getting Jason out, so Lorne boxed for the club. For Jason. For guns and bombs, apparently.

Davik waved a hand like bombs weren't such a big deal to him. How'd he get all those burn scars on his hands? Was it from building bombs? "Not since Cruinnich, laddie."

"I'll keep an eye out for a significant number of guns," Vasska said. "And I'll make sure they make it through to you. Dare I ask what you're stockpiling guns for?"

Davik shrugged, draining the last of his beer. "These are uncertain times, Mr. Czarny. It's prudent for my people to make sure they can defend themselves in case things get ugly around here. Seems like they'll be coming just in time. They're from the Uhl factory. You'll know 'em when you see them, I'm sure. Everyone says the new Uhl guns are something special."

"You're going to let me have one, right Dav?" László asked. "I been dying to get my hands on those Uhls."

Davik grinned and winked at László. "Of course. Who else would get the first one but you?"

Vasska sipped his beer in the silence that stretched around the mention of guns and bombs. He was the only one at the table with more than half his pint left. "Grandad wants me to ask you about Mr. Blackwood since we're being honest with each other. He wonders if you had anything to do with what happened—if you've got anything to do with his disappearance. Did you put him up to it? Did you rescue him from the arrest, and that's why he's missing now?"

Hope bloomed. Maybe Tashué wasn't dead. Lorne looked to Davik, praying that Davik would say yes. Tashué was alive and Davik was hiding him and all the guns and the bombs and the plans for the Rift were to save the two people in Yaelsmuir Lorne loved most. The Blackwoods, the family he'd been craving since... since forever. The family he almost had with Alys's father.

But Davik shook his head and Lorne couldn't read anything at all in Davik's dark eyes.

"Why would I get myself involved with some tinman?" Davik asked, and it sounded like the truth. And Lorne's world felt smaller.

"He's Jason's father," Vasska said slowly. "And he's the one who sent Lorne looking for Hale. It's not unreasonable of me to think you went looking for him, is it? Or maybe he was looking for you, and you let him find you. I don't much care about how it happened. If Mr. Blackwood is alive somewhere in the Bay, I would like to help. The Bay stands its best chance if you and I are united in our handling of things from here on."

"I appreciate that, Mr. Czarny," Davik said. "And I agree. We've got to stand strong against whatever the Authority tries to throw at us, especially now. I can see how you might think I was involved, but I wasn't. We didn't have anything to do with Blackwood, but we'll catch the blame for it, won't we? Elsworth will use it as an excuse to stir up trouble in the Bay, so I say fuck Blackwood. If I see him, I'll send him your way. You have my word. Maybe you and your grandad will know what the hell to do with him, because I sure as fuck wouldn't have a clue."

Lorne slid his finger through the pile of coins, leaving a trail through the centre of them. He didn't think Davik was lying. And maybe he shouldn't be surprised. It hadn't felt true when Alys's father died, either. Lorne went on living his life, waiting for Rhion Coswyn to come back from one last fishing trip, but he didn't come back. His ship docked at Gaffryn without him because the sea just took without rhyme or reason. The sea took everything eventually.

"Lorne," Vasska said softly. "Have you seen him?"

Fucking Tashué. Everything always came back to him. He'd fucked around with things bigger than he'd understood—and dragged Lorne into the fucking mess with him, catching him that beating in the Hive—and now Tashué was in the middle of shit. Or dead, left his pile of shit left behind for Lorne and Jason to deal with.

"No." The word ripped a hole through Lorne's chest. He wished he was lying. He wished it were all an elaborate act to keep Tashué safe. "If he's alive somewhere and you see him before I do, you mind giving him a message for me?"

"Sure," Vasska said.

Lorne pushed both his hands through his hair as if he could pull the anxiety and the grief right out by the roots. "Tell him to go fuck himself."

Irén dragged a man over to the table, holding him by the neck even though he was near a foot taller than her, forcing him along in an awkward bent over shuffle. She slammed the man's face on the tabletop, making the empty pint glasses shiver, making the coins dance. The man gave a howl of pain, trying to struggle, but Irén squeezed his neck harder, leaning over him.

"You owe Mr. Kaine an apology, you dog-faced goat fucker."

Davik only glanced at the man. "What's he apologizing for, Irén?"

"He's been warned a few times about getting grabby when girls tell him no, and he ain't listening. So he's banned from the *Bucket* now, but I told him he had to apologize to you for disrespecting your rules and your girls when you've done so much for this quarter."

"Yes, sir, Mr. Kaine," the man gasped. Blood was oozing onto the table—Lorne couldn't see if it was coming from the man's mouth or his nose. It was a spread of red, crawling over the varnished wood. It only made Lorne angrier, more restless. He should have gotten up with Irén and waded into the fight with her so he could make someone bleed. "I'm sorry, Mr. Kaine. I didn't mean no harm—"

"That's a wet pile of shit and you know it," Irén interrupted. "You were told no. You didn't listen. Now get the fuck out of here before I get really angry."

Irén shoved the man off the table, and he fell hard, scrambling to get back to his feet. The blood came from his nose, dripping on the floor and down the front of his shirt as he lurched toward the door. Davik looked down at the mess on the table. Irén huffed at it, stomping away to the bar.

Lorne turned in the bench, elbowing Davik in the side. "Let me out, Dav."

"Let you out where?" Davik asked.

"I need to go for a walk. I need to go—" *Hit something. See Jason. Find Tashué.* None of the options would do him any good. "Just let me out."

Davik slid out of the booth. Lorne all but leapt to his feet, knocking past more than a few people on the way to the bar. It took all the self control he had to walk instead of running. It wasn't that hard to catch up to Irén. She moved fast, but Lorne was faster, had longer legs. He caught her arm, and she spun on him with her fist cocked like she was perfectly ready to knock his teeth out. She paused when her gaze landed on his face. Lowered her fist. The crowd hemmed them in, a wall of bodies and noise that made Lorne feel more alone.

"Thank you," Lorne said. The words hurt on the way out, like glass catching in his throat. "I would trade places with you in a heartbeat, if I could."

Irén shrugged. Maybe she didn't know Lorne well enough to let down her guard. She glanced over Lorne's shoulder, through the crowd. "Take care of him, yeah? Don't let him do anything too stupid."

Lorne followed her eyes—László moved through the crowd next, weaving through people, smiling at the people that stopped him to flirt or kiss him on the cheek. That smile of his was beaming, glowing, a force of nature.

"He gets melodramatic when he's upset," Irén said, catching Lorne's arm to get his attention back. "Gets in the habit of feeling sorry for himself, and then things get real ugly. Just keep an eye on him for me, yeah? Make sure he's alright until I get out. I shouldn't be in long. It's when he starts saying he ain't hungry that you gotta worry about him."

Lorne nodded. "Sure, Irén. I'll make sure he's eating as much as I am."

She nodded, shrugged, turned away, the moment awkward and too heavy. The pair of them knowing that more needed to be said but neither with the emotional depth to know what. Irén went to the bar, and Lorne followed because he didn't want to go back to the table to hear any more fucking business about guns and bombs. He was here to box.

Irén leaned over and sent the bartender back to the table to clean up the blood. László caught up, sliding his hand up Lorne's back, but the leather coat was so thick and heavy he barely felt it. László pushed into the empty space between Irén and Lorne, so that Lorne was leaning on him and he was leaning on the bar and Irén stood like a sentry at László's other shoulder.

"Why Jason?" Lorne asked. "Why does he matter so much that Davik's sending you in? Davik doesn't know him. Doesn't know me. He's just the Blackwood kid."

Irén glanced at Lorne with an eyebrow cocked. "Does it matter why? Isn't it enough that we want the same thing you want?"

Lorne shook his head, trying to grasp the words to explain the unease. As nice as it was to imagine that Davik wanted to save Jason because Jason deserved it, he knew the world didn't work that way. No matter how bad he wanted to believe that Davik was saving people because he was *good* or some naive bullshit like that, he knew there had to be more. "I don't know," he said, instead of saying any of that. "I just... He's been in there so long, and no one cared before."

278 | LEGACY OF BRICK & BONE

"It's because Jason broke the suppression," László whispered, pushing in close, the words just for them. The noise of the crowd almost drowned the words out, but Lorne still felt them echoing through his bones. "He's hoping Jason can do it again. Or at least tell people how he did it. We've been trying to figure it out so we can get into the Breeding Program, but we can't. Maybe he can teach us how."

Lorne nodded. It was comforting, knowing there was a reason. Davik had a purpose for Jason. He'd get Jason out.

"I want a boat," Irén said, her voice ringing over the din.

"You have a boat," László grunted. "You want me to get another barge?"

"No, I mean—on the island. I want a skiff or something, hidden somewhere—so I can get my ass off that fucking rock in a hurry if I have to. In case Dav's plans fall apart again, yeah?"

László nodded. "Right. Of course. I'll get it done."

"Hey," Vasska said. He put both his arms on the bar, glancing up at Lorne. "You hanging in there, Mr. Lightning?"

Lorne sighed, emptying his lungs so completely, he felt hollow. Half of himself, incomplete until he got Jason back. For all that the good news of Jason getting out gave him something to hope for, there was other news looming in the corners of his mind that he couldn't get away from.

"What happened in Brickheart?" Lorne asked. He was so damned hot in his coat, with so many bodies pressed against him, but he had to admit that it was comfortable to be crammed between Vasska and László. A reminder that Vasska was right, that he wasn't alone anymore. "How did Tashué get arrested?"

"Trying to kill Rainer Elsworth, I heard," László said, nodding to the publican who delivered another round of pints even though Lorne couldn't remember anyone asking for them. László pressed one of the pints into Lorne's hand, and the glass was deliciously cold, the beer chilled by the frigid weather. "I didn't realize it was him, though. We heard some big tinman."

"But *why*?" Lorne pressed.

"He wanted to know about the energy units," Vasska said. "He was asking Elsworth about the energy units."

Lorne sucked back too much beer in one long swallow, trying to get his head around all these meaningless words. "What the fuck is an energy unit?"

Vasska glanced at László, then at Lorne. He looked down at his own pint, watching the head settle like it was helping him arrange his thoughts into words. He looked at László again. "You didn't tell him? I thought it was in the Red Dawn prep material."

László shrugged. "He's here to box. We didn't know if we could trust him."

"What are energy units?" Lorne snapped, his temper wearing too thin again. "I want to know—if Tashué got himself fucking *killed* over it, I want to know."

Vasska scooped up his pint. "Maybe we should go sit back down and order another round."

"We just *got* another round. Could you just tell me?"

Vasska huffed. "It's a long story and one I don't like telling sober."

Back to the table. Davik was up, standing in the mill of people while the bartender scrubbed the blood away. The man Irén had beaten was long gone.

"Dav," László said, hooking his arm around Lorne's waist. "He wants to know about the energy units."

Davik sighed, long and exhausted and sad, and something cold invaded Lorne's whole body. "Right. Let's grab something a little stronger than a beer, hey? And we'll tell you about Valen Gian Ly, too."

"Gian Ly," Lorne echoed. "That's Keoh's last name."

"Aye, laddie. Come sit down. You'll need the drink."

It was fucking raining. Again. The air was thick and wet and cold and the rain pelted Lorne when he stepped into it, running through his hair, down his face, soaking his clothes, washing the sweat away from his skin. Not just rain—sleet, frozen and stinging, covering the edges of windowsills and the steps outside of buildings with a thin sheen of ice.

He'd never felt more useless, more helpless in his entire life. At least problems had been easy to solve when Rhion Coswyn didn't come back from the ocean. His mother may have been hiding in the opium smoke, and Lorne couldn't do anything to draw her back, but he could take care of Alys. He could carry his baby sister out of the house and keep her busy. He could walk to town and beg for food or steal it. He could climb down the cliff to the water and hunt for edible creatures that clung to the rocks. He could make Alys happy. She was so cute when she laughed.

None of the problems he had now felt solvable. Everything was falling apart, and he needed to *do* something, but all he could do was wear the stupid boxing gloves and learn to fight. He needed to see Jason, but it was too late at night. It would have to wait until morning—maybe there would be more news about Tashué by then, so that when Lorne told Jason his father was dead, too, Lorne would be able to give Jason more answers than when he'd told Jason his mother died. What happened, how he died, where his body was now. He had all the whys now, at least. Why had Tashué snapped? Because energy fucking units.

Both of Jason's parents in a week. Lorne wouldn't wish this pain on anyone, and here it was, coming for the person he loved the most in the whole world. And he was still there, in that fucking place. Lorne wouldn't be able to hug him or comfort him. He'd have to sit on the wrong side of the grate *again*. Irén was going in, at least. Maybe he'd tell Jason about Valen, give him something to hope for, and keep the bad news until Jason was out. Until the day of the boxing match wasn't too long of a wait.

He stepped out from under the awning that covered the *Dripping Bucket*'s door, his boots soaking into the ice-water slush that gathered between the cobbles. Letting the rain and the sleet pummel his whole body. Water beaded on the surface of the new leather. Even though it was brutally cold, it didn't take the heat out of the panic in his chest. Ice clung to his hair, his clothes, freezing him up on the outside, turning him to a statue, a monument to uselessness. Energy units, fuck.

The door to the *Dripping Bucket* swung open behind him, releasing the sound of the pub in a wave. Voices, glasses, chairs scraping, a fiddler had started playing—Vasska came out into the cold.

Lorne turned away from him, trying to head down the road. Away. Anywhere away. He didn't want to see anyone. He needed some time to be numb and shocked and lost so that he could go back to whatever Davik needed him to do. The fight was for Jason, so that was something. At least he wasn't as useless as he felt.

Vasska caught him by the arm, dragged him back. Lorne turned to him to say something, but no words came.

"I just wanted to make sure you were alright," Vasska said, half shouting over the ugly rain. "It's a lot to process all at once."

Lorne shook his head and tried to say something, but he couldn't force himself to make any sounds, no matter how hard he tried. It was just dark, and raining, and cold. The city was quiet. There weren't any brights here—the nearest ones were on the tram tracks that cut these streets off from the rest of the Bay—but the city still had a bit of a sheen as everyone did their best to keep their lives rolling through the night with candles and oil lamps and great crackling fires in big hearths. He couldn't see the details of Vasska's face. Just his hair, drooping in the rain, and the glint of his eyes.

"It looks like you're fitting in with them," Vasska said. "It's good. I was worried about you, but it looks like you're going to be fine. Just be careful, yeah? László can be a bit of a loose screw."

Resentment crawled across Lorne's shoulders. After everything László had done for Lorne, here Vasska was dismissing him, calling him a loose screw. "László is fine."

"Yeah, sure," Vasska said. "He's great. It's good that you're getting along. But he can be a wild and a bit dangerous is all I'm saying."

Lorne shrugged Vasska's hands off his arms. "How long have you known?"

"About László?" Vasska scoffed. "The Dargis family has been chaos since they got to Yaelsmuir. But the Bay swallows up chaos, doesn't it? Make it feel at home."

"I mean the energy units," Lorne said. "How long have you *known*?"

Vasska shook his head. "Why does it matter?"

"I asked you." Lorne grabbed Vasska's sleeve, the wool soggy in his hand. "I asked you how much you knew. About the Red Dawn and everything they were doing. I asked you if it had anything to do with the girl. Remember? We sat on top of the Hive, and I asked you what you knew, and you said *too much*. So now I'm wondering if you knew all this shit back then, when you told me to leave it alone."

"Lorne, I didn't want you to get killed."

The fury hit Lorne's chest so hard all he could do was scream to let it out. He pressed his hands to his own chest and he roared at the sky, at the rain, at the hopelessness of it all. Vasska tried to grab Lorne again, but Lorne shoved him back, shoved him so hard that Vasska staggered, and his back hit a wall, his profile lit by the glow coming from the nearby window.

"I could have done something!" Lorne howled, stepping after Vasska, fists clenched. "I could have done something sooner!"

"What?" Vasska snapped back, pushing himself off the wall. "What could you have done, hey? You going to wave your boxing gloves and make the Authority disappear? Fuck you, Lorne, none of this is on me!"

"Tashué is on you! He found out and something snapped and now he's dead and it's your fucking fault, you hear me? That's on you! I could have done something—we were looking for answers, and if you'd told me then, I could have helped him, but you took that chance away from me! And now he's dead because you told me to leave it alone!"

"What would you have done?" Vasska said, half-laughing, half-yelling, entirely desperate and wild, leaning in even though he had to know full well that if Lorne decided to start swinging, it would be ugly and over fast. "What could you have possibly done differently? You aren't a politician, Lorne. You aren't a soldier, and you aren't a revolutionary. You're just a guy who hits things for a living, isn't that right? So what the fuck do you think you could have done to save Tashué from himself?"

Lorne's hands shot out, grabbing Vasska's coat, dragging him closer, so close that their noses pressed together in the rain, so that the water sluiced off Vasska's face and onto Lorne's shoulders. "You don't get to call me a useless idiot, not when you sent me here! Not when you watched me fight for five fucking years, not when the Hive makes you so much money. Maybe I'm a guy who hits things for a living, but at least I'm not a coward who doesn't speak up to protect *children*, for fuck's sake!"

Vasska grabbed Lorne's hands, but he didn't lean away. He blinked the water out of his face and he took a deep breath. "Are you calling me a coward, Lorne?"

"I'm just a dumb fighter, aren't I?" Lorne asked. "So I say what I see and let smart guys like you figure it out from there."

Footsteps in the rain—László. He caught Lorne's shoulder, dragging Lorne away from Vasska. "Hey, what the fuck are you doing? Let him go. Hey, Lorne, look at me. Let him go!"

Lorne released his fists, the bones grinding against themselves, the fury unsatisfied.

"I'm sorry about this, Mr. Czarny," László said, pushing Lorne back, stepping in front of Vasska and smoothing out the front of Vasska's coat. "I'm sure he didn't mean nothing by it. We wind up pugilists so tight that they're always about to go off, aren't they?"

"It's fine, László," Vasska said, pushing László's fussing hands away. "It's fine. I've known Lorne a long time, and I know when he's so angry that he has to take it out on someone. It's not personal."

Somehow, that stung worse than anything else Vasska could have said. It drained all the fury out of Lorne, filled him with shame instead. He was just a dumb fighter, wound too tight. Hurting people he cared about because he didn't know how to exist without anger to protect him.

László threw his arm around Lorne's shoulders again, steering him back toward the pugilist club. "Let's get you out of the rain, Mr. Lightning. You'll have to get to work early tomorrow if we're going to make time to visit the Rift."

"Yeah," Lorne said, letting László guide him across the street. "I need to see him."

Lorne looked back over his shoulder to Vasska—he should apologize at least—but Vasska had already turned away. Headed back into the *Bucket*, holding the door open the door for Miss Brady, who paused on the stoop long enough to shake the water off her umbrella before heading in.

"Come out of the rain, you idiot," László said.

"Wait—would you come with me? If I went to Brickheart?"

László shrugged. He stood in the doorway to the pugilist club, lit by the bright interior behind him. "What's in Brickheart?"

"Tashué's apartment—if he's been arrested, they'll search his things, won't they? I'd like to get what I can. For Jason, you know? For when he gets out. It would be nice to give him some of his father's things."

"Yeah," László said, stepping out of the doorway and letting the door swing shut behind him. "Sure. Let's go to Brickheart."

21

TASHUÉ

DAY 34

It was a long walk through the forest. As the rush from all the violence faded away, all the pains of his body came to him layer by layer. Just when he thought it was really bad, it got worse, like his nerves were turning on bit by bit. He was so tired, bone-weary and sore, his whole body aching with every line of his muscles, every ligament and piece of cartilage. His neck and shoulders felt yanked out of alignment. Pain flared everywhere, places that had been battered by the Patrollers when they came to arrest him and by the horse dragging him down the path.

Didn't matter how much he hurt, didn't matter how it felt like he couldn't catch his breath—he had to keep walking. All of it would be dealt with, so long as they made it to Wolfe's house. Ishmael would be tended to, and Tashué would strip out of his clothes to see what wounds were hidden under layers of wool and dried, crusted mud. Washing and tending to their wounds would help him return to some vestiges of who he was before the Enquiry Officers hanged him from the fucking tree. Before his Talent woke and he slaughtered three people with too much righteous glee.

Except some part of him knew there was no going backward. His Talent was awake, and he couldn't make it stop. It was bleeding into the whole world around him and wrapping around every tree he passed and feeling the moisture in the autumn-wet air. He felt the ice that formed in the mud and the creatures that hid from them as he and the horse plodded on and on. The memory of his brutality lived in his eardrums, in his nerves. He could *feel* it, the way the bone disintegrated. The way that woman's heart popped like an overfull waterskin. It all made the walk exhausting to a level he'd never felt in his entire life.

Night's long, looming shadows made it harder to tell how much time was passing. The mile markers kept him company at least—but it only made it feel like each mile was taking forever. He'd plod on and on and on for what felt like half the fucking night, and he'd convince himself that he hadn't seen a mile marker yet because he'd missed one or two since it was so dark and he was so tired, and he'd made more progress than he dared hope—only for another marker to appear in the moonlight, announcing his exhausting lack of progress.

And then the rain came. The clouds opened up and dumped on them, a wall of almost frozen water soaking them to the bone. Shivering wracked Tashué's body. All the stiff and bruised muscles resented the tension.

He tried to keep Ishmael talking, but it was getting hard to think in sentences, never mind saying them out loud—shouting them over the roar of the rain took so much energy. And Ishmael took longer and longer to answer, his words losing their grim humour and turning monosyllabic. Tashué tried to keep an eye on him. His head bowed beneath the water, his dark hair turning limp around his face. At some point, Ishmael had dropped the rifle. But taking his eyes off the track that long only made Tashué stub his boots on the rocks and the uneven trail. He hit a root, and it took him down. He rolled with the fall so he hit his shoulder and not his face, and when he lay in the dirt, all that exhaustion caught him. He couldn't get up. He couldn't walk another step.

The rain soaked his whole body, bouncing off the muddy hunter's track. Maybe it was easier to close his eyes and let the cold have him. He didn't want to destroy this city. Ten years soldiering taught him the shape of conflict, and this one was going to be bad. If they could get people to listen, to hear them, it would upend everything. A rebellion, a revolution —that was the outcome they were *hoping* for.

But if they failed, the pair of them would die like Rainer wanted, and Rainer would go back to making fucking energy units out of children.

That's what made him get back up.

Children.

Lizanne and all of Keoh's children.

The woman who escaped the Breeding Program, only to die in the Bay.

Stella, running with Ceridwen, hiding that horrible tattoo with every last shred of strength she had.

Jason.

Up. For Stella and Ceridwen and Jason and Lizanne. He owed it to them to make some sense out of all of this. Walk, even though it hurt. Even though he shivered so bad, it was a struggle to coordinate each step. Even though his mind splintered in a million directions to make room for all the information that hit his mind through his Talent. Sometimes he caught himself holding his breath—forgetting to fucking *breathe* because the sensory input of it was too much.

This had to be what going insane felt like.

Too many thoughts, all at once, another step, another—he was holding his breath again.

The road twisted. The forest came to an abrupt end.

Tashué stopped dead, jarred by the sudden sprawling space in front of him after spending so much time surrounded by the forest. It had only been a few hours, but so much had changed, and he'd never been so viscerally aware of the world before, and it felt for a while like the forest was all there was. And then it ended. He could make out the open space of the lawn and a massive, stately house, the whitewashed wood exterior looking like bone in the haze of the downpour. A few windows were lit from within, but not many. It took him a moment to even remember where he was and why he was here; Amias's gravestone, standing in the lawn like a white scar in the darkness, jolted him back to reality.

Wolfe's house.

Stepping out into the open sent fresh tension through his body. The grass felt different beneath his boots after so long on the track. Wet and slick and soft. Even the mare shied before following, but a little insistence from him had her trailing along behind him like she had all night.

The lawn felt... different. There was still a current of energy that tugged at his awareness, but that massive power that felt sentient ended at the tree line. It *was* the Dunnenbrahl, the forest turned into a beast that lay in wait for... what?

Didn't matter. They were out now.

He glanced back at Ishmael, trying to summon enough coherence to say something about how they made it. But Ishmael was sagging.

Holding the saddle horn like Tashué had told him, but listing. His whole body dropping like he was melting right off the horse's back, into the darkness.

Tashué staggered back to Ishmael's side, forcing his body to move faster than it had in hours. He got his arms around Ishmael's chest as Ishmael fell, all of his weight hitting Tashué's arms. Tashué's exhausted legs gave out under the sudden burden and he dropped to his knees, but at least he'd caught Ishmael from falling face-first in the grass.

Light flickering at the edge of his vision—his Talent snapped to life, a cornered animal, vicious and furious, hyperaware of each footstep that he shouldn't be able to hear over the roar of all the ugly rain, but his Talent heard it somehow, like the sound reverberated off the inside of his skull. He could feel the bones that made the feet and the heartbeats that fuelled them. The temptation to crush everything was tempered only by his exhaustion, his own horror at his own capabilities.

"Sir!" A frantic voice behind him, a man coming to stand with him, shouting over the rain. The lantern battled the darkness, rain tinging and hissing as it hit the hot glass cover that protected the flame. "Mr. Saeati —what happened?"

"Help me get him inside," Tashué gasped. Could they even hear him over the rain? "Help me lift him, but easy on his leg."

"What happened?" Another voice. "Fetch the General, quickly!"

Ishmael stirred—the fainting spell was temporary, at least, and he was moving again. Hands lifted Ishmael, but Tashué couldn't bring himself to let Ishmael go. Up, to his feet, even though it hurt everything. He held Ishmael by the shoulders, and someone supported Ishmael's legs, and they walked him across the lawn. Someone took the reins of the big mare, guiding her toward the stable.

They carried Ishmael to the same back door that Ishmael had led Tashué through. How long ago was that? The morning after Illea's banquet—so much had changed since then. They stepped into the kitchen again, the ovens crackling happily like they were still in use. What time was it?

"I think he's hypothermic," Tashué said, his voice rasping through his exhaustion.

"Put him down by the fire." The house cook, dressed in only his trousers and his thin undershirt, like he'd jumped from bed to see what was happening. "Get his clothes off him, let's see the damage."

The warmth from the kitchen circled Tashué's body like a blanket, a kiss. He sank down to his knees with Ishmael because he couldn't bear to stand another moment, but he couldn't let go, either. He'd done this. He'd waded into the Brightwash, and Ishmael had followed. His stupidity, his fury, his impulsiveness had hit Ishmael harder, and if Ishmael died before they could warm him up, it would be Tashué's fault. Ishmael opened his eyes and made fists in Tashué's coat again, his jaw trembling, teeth chattering. Water from both of them spread on the floor around him.

A dog came through the crowd of legs, all shaggy fur and a wet pink tongue, tail wagging frantically as she sniffed at the blood and licked Ishmael's face. Her fur was brown and cream, but around her mouth and her eyes, it had all gone grey and white.

"Hey, soldier," Tashué said. "You've got even more attention now. I hope you're happy."

A weak laugh from Ishmael washed Tashué with relief. "I'm great. This is what I planned all along. Hey there, old girl." He reached up, wrapping his arm around the dog's neck. "I'm alright, I promise."

"Leave it to you to die of the cold before it's even properly winter," the cook grunted, pulling the boot off Ishmael's foot. "Here lies that idiot Saeati. Couldn't dress for the weather to save his life, because scarves aren't in fashion this year."

Someone opened the wood stove and banked the fire up high, nursing more heat and more light into the kitchen. They banked up the fire in the brickwork stew stove, too, so that heat assailed them from all sides. Someone else used a taper to light the oil lamps, filling the room with a peaceful, dancing glow.

The tapping of General Wolfe's cane was so familiar that it broke through the numbness in Tashué's chest, making his limbs tremble. They were safe.

"What happened?" Wolfe asked.

Tashué dragged his head up, shifting so he could lean against the wall beside the massive cast iron cookstove, the hard tile bearing his weight when he couldn't anymore. The heat of it hurt his rain-numb skin, his body prickly and itchy with the return of warmth, but he couldn't summon the energy to move. "It's a long fucking story, General."

Wolfe looked exhausted, too. He sank down on a stool, his hand gripping his bad leg, fingers digging into his trousers. "I've time, Captain. I've been looking for the pair of you all day."

"Don't mind me, General," the cook said. "We need to get him undressed." The cook snapped his fingers at the dog, shooing her out of the way. "Move, you pest. Go."

The dog gave a thin whine, shifting her weight to rest her head on Ishmael's leg, her tail wagging against Tashué's arm.

Ishmael rested a hand on her head, sinking his fingers into the shaggy fur. "Brats stick together, don't they, Iffa?"

"Let's go, get your clothes off," the cook insisted. "You wanted to be the centre of attention, now you have to follow instructions. You'll never warm up in those wet clothes and I'm too damned busy to deal with your dead body on my floor."

Ishmael sat up to struggle out of the pair of coats he wore, and Tashué helped with clumsy, exhausted hands. The coat that Tashué had taken off the leader was easy to strip away, but Ishmael's coat was stuck on something that made Ishmael groan and tense again, which made the dog pin her ears back and try to lick Ishmael's face. They peeled his jacket off more slowly—his shirt and his waistcoat underneath were turned red-brown with blood. The cook thrust a pair of scissors into Tashué's hand, and he cut the clothes open, a straight line up Ishmael's back that revealed new bruises and more blood—he pushed the tattered shirt forward, off Ishmael's shoulder. The left side, the shoulder that had the swirling mosaic of line tattoos, was ripped by wooden shards.

As he worked, Tashué told the story of everything that had happened in slow, halting words. He started at the arrest—the part of the story he could admit he deserved. Drunk on the bank of the river after threatening to blow Rainer's skull open. Wolfe listened to that part impassively. Maybe he thought Tashué deserved it, too. Tashué slid his hand across the tattoos, across the blood, feeling the places were wood jutted out from Ishmael's skin like he was being reclaimed by the forest. And he was so much thinner than the last time Tashué had seen Ishmael's body. Guilt ripped through him anew. He hadn't noticed. He'd noticed the tan and the distant look in Ishmael's eye, but he hadn't noticed how thin he was under his layers, how much weight had fallen out of his face. If he was a better friend, he would have noticed. Whatever had gone wrong between them as lovers, Tashué still *cared*, but he'd been so wrapped up in his own self-pity that he hadn't seen how much Ishmael had been struggling.

They helped Ishmael out of his trousers next, revealing the wounds that hid beneath the sock and the swollen mess of his ankle. He hissed and groaned as someone helped him out of his trousers, and the cook put his hands on Ishmael's knee like he was testing the stability of the kneecap. The cook lay warm towels across Ishmael's body, paying careful care around his knee.

Tashué's Talent twitched to life as he watched and tried to talk, swirling through Ishmael's torn skin. He hadn't noticed these wounds when they were in the forest—or maybe there had been so many wounds that he hadn't been able to tell the difference between the bruises and these cuts. His awareness rolled through it now, every place the skin was broken and the places where the wood went down to muscle, the wooden invaders like hot coals in Tashué's mind. He swirled further, Ishmael's heartbeat in Tashué's ears. Ishmael's cool body temperature hit Tashué's senses, but so too did the hot towels that seeped warmth back into Ishmael's skin. All the sources of pain got so tangled in Tashué's awareness that he couldn't tell which wounds were his and which were Ishmael's. The stream of his words came to an abrupt end. He couldn't talk and feel this, couldn't untangle himself. He could *feel* Ishmael's voice, except Ishmael wasn't speaking. Chittering through him like the rattle of dry autumn leaves in the wind, and the flash of a face Tashué didn't know—dark, laughing eyes and cigar smoke and grey hair dancing in the pure black.

"Captain," the cook said, dragging Tashué back to the surface. "Your turn. Get out of those clothes."

Someone grabbed Ishmael by the good arm, helping him sit up enough to get out of Tashué's way. The cavalry dress greens were ruined by blood and mud and ragged tears. He eased out of the heavy coat first and then the uniform jacket. There was blood on his medals, on the lines of ribbons that told the story of his career. He reached for them, but his hands were trembling too much with the cold to undo the pins. And the wound on the side of his hand—the one that he'd gotten while he was digging survivors out of the wreckage of the market fire, the one that Stella stitched back together—it was bleeding again. Some of it was healed, and he'd taken the stitches out a few days ago, but the parts that were still scabbed over had been ripped open in the chaos.

"Pass them here, Captain," Wolfe said. "I'll get them off. The uniform isn't fit to be rags, I'm afraid. We'll have to order you another."

Nervous, exhausted laughter bubbled up from Tashué's throat. "Do they issue dress uniforms to fugitives?"

"Why don't you tell me the rest of what happened, and we'll figure out how to fix it."

Ishmael took up the job of storytelling as the cook pulled the splinters out of his shoulder one by one, like talking shielded Ishmael from the pain. The murdered Patrollers, the riders whose bodies decorated the Dunnenbrahl. He wasn't shivering anymore, at least.

"They were asking about Allie," Tashué said, jolting out of his half-stupor. "Where is she? Is she safe?"

"I'm right here," Allie said, her voice ringing clear over the chaos in the kitchen. "You had us very worried."

Tashué lifted his head to look through the crowd. Allie stood at the edge of the chaos, still dressed for the day. Just like Wolfe. What time was it? How long had they been out there in that forest? It couldn't have been more than a few hours, and yet it felt like his whole life had bounced onto a new path from the moment he was loaded into that prisoner transport wagon. Weeks had been devoured by the biggest mile markers he'd seen in a long time. Finding Lizanne on the riverbank was the first cold shock since Jason was arrested. Seeing the tattoo on Ceridwen's neck was the second. And now this. Enquiry Officers, the Dunnenbrahl, the blood of Patrollers who were killed simply for hearing the truth.

He reached into his pocket for the badge. His hands shook when he pulled it out. Every muscle was so damned tired, but he lifted that badge even though it felt like the heaviest thing in the world. The bronze shone like polished gold in the kitchen, lit by oil lamps and the roaring fire in the stove. The National Tainted Registration Authority shape was unmistakable, and the name was etched into the face like any other badge he'd ever seen, but this one didn't have a badge number or a name like the tin and the brass he'd carried. His hands left a smear of Ishmael's blood on the leather and the metal.

"That was on one of them," Tashué said.

Allie came first, like she was the only one who wasn't afraid to touch the damn thing. She sank down beside Tashué and Ishmael, enduring the dog's frantic, anxious attention so she could take the badge. "I've one of these, too. It was on the man who tried to kill me. My colleague— remember him? You took the gun from him?"

Tashué nodded. "He tried his best to help."

Allie gave a dry, tight smile. "He did better than we could have hoped. He searched the body after we left and found a badge like this. Apparently the Authority came before the Patrollers, and they directed the investigation. He thought that was a little strange, but then we understand why, don't we?"

"Of course," Tashué said. "Can't have Patrollers finding badges for a branch of the Authority that's supposed to be a secret."

"You're supposed to be undressing," Allie said softly. "We can't have you freezing to death before we figure out how to deal with this mess."

Tashué started on his waistcoat buttons, but his hands were even less useful than usual.

"We need people out in the woods," Wolfe said. "To find the bodies before Rainer comes to clean it all up."

"You can't say we were here," Ishmael said. The cook poured warm water over Ishmael's shoulder, washing the mess of blood away, and it rolled down Ishmael's back to soak into Tashué's clothes. "You'll be arrested for harbouring fugitives. We can't stay. Say your hunters were out late, and they stumbled on the bodies—say you don't know where we are."

"Any decent tracker will see the path you left to get here," the cook said. His big, scarred hands pressed a cloth against the wound, mopping up the new ooze of fresh blood. Where had all that wood come from? Was it splinters of the tree Tashué had exploded with his Talent? Or when Matt shot through the wagon to try to get Ishmael? "With all the rain, the mud is perfect for leaving tracks."

Ishmael shook his head. "Send the hunters over the path we left, make sure they churn it up as they go. Send dogs and everything. Riders on horses. Come back over the same path, and then our tracks will blend into everything else."

"How did you get away?" Allie asked.

"We killed them," Tashué said, and the trembling redoubled. His chest spasmed, and he couldn't breathe again. Couldn't breathe and couldn't think. He was the echo of what he'd done—and Stella asked him if he was afraid of the notion he had Talent, sweet North Star, of course he was afraid—he'd known all his fucking life that he was danger-ous. The army had honed his natural inclination to violence and stoked the fires of his temper, but he'd known, he'd always known that he couldn't be trusted with power such as this—fuck. He wasn't good and soft and nurturing like his mother, wasn't steady and quiet like his father. Somewhere along the way, some red hot rage had been smelted into his personality and maybe he'd known his Talent would only be an exten-sion of that anger, even back then. Maybe his mother knew, too—maybe that's why she was so insistent that he follow the laws to keep himself safe. Bones, dissolving like chalk. Muscle popping under the force of his temper. "Ishmael killed two himself, and I killed the other three."

"How?" Allie pressed. "How did you—"

"It doesn't matter how," Ishmael cut in. "They tried to kill us. We killed them. It doesn't matter how." He pushed his hands into the bucket of hot water, rubbing the mud off his fingers before splashing warm water onto his face. "Your hand is getting worse."

"No, it's fine," Tashué said, even though fucking nothing was fine. "I'm so fucking cold, I can't—"

"Let me help," Allie said, pushing Tashué's hands out of the way. "I've undressed you once before. This is turning into an odd habit for the pair of us."

In spite of all the exhaustion and the fear, Tashué laughed again. Allie helped him unbutton everything, stripping the layers away. His shirt caught the wound over his ribs, tugging at skin, stealing the air out of him.

"I'm sorry," Allie gasped. "The fabric is caught in the wound."

Allie eased the shirt away, revealing a long, ugly gash, where a chunk of wood from the tree had hit him in the ribs and torn a bloody swathe across his flesh. He'd gotten through this in better shape than he thought —maybe his Talent had shielded him somehow when he was being dragged, maybe that was why those runnels were left in the ground. Everyone helped him up to his feet and he stood right in a bucket of water, wincing at the heat as it swirled through the raw open wounds, at the way the water swirled dark with mud and blood.

"I killed them with Talent," Tashué said, turning to look Wolfe in the eye. It was better to tell him so he knew what he was dealing with. "It quickened when they were trying to hang me. I killed the three left standing. So as well as being a fugitive from the City Civilian Patrollers for uttering threats against Rainer Elsworth, I suppose I'm now also a feral non-compliant and a fugitive from the National Tainted Registration Authority."

Silence.

It seemed impossible for a room so filled with people who had such a sense of urgency to be silent, but for a long, stretching moment, the kitchen was frozen in time. Wolfe's face remained a mask that was impossible to read. Tashué waited, something buzzing in his ears. Tinnitus, filling the silence. Making his head hurt.

"Tashué," Allie said. But then there wasn't anything else from her— maybe she didn't know what else to say.

"I know," Tashué said. "I'm as surprised as you are. I had no idea—"

Except that wasn't *really* true. Stella told him. Rhodrishi told him. Heredity told him. He'd been hiding from it, but that wasn't the same as not knowing.

Allie reached out and grabbed Tashué's hand, squeezing it hard with both of hers. "I'm glad you've survived this. That scar I gave you is looking well healed."

Tashué put his hand to the scar, little more than a scab now, the new skin peeking out from the edges. It was hard to believe she'd shot him a few days ago, and Rhodrishi had healed him once again. And now, just when Tashué had the most questions, the most hunger for understanding who he was and how he fit into the world, Rhodrishi was gone with Stella and Ceridwen.

"Someone's gone to round up the hunters?" Wolfe asked, pushing himself to his feet.

"Yes, General," the cook said.

Even as he said it, the sound of hunting dogs baying rattled through the kitchen even over the patter of the rain on the glass panes of the windows. The dog in Ishmael's lap lifted her head, ears tilting toward the sound. The tiny kitchen window showed one of the outbuildings—the kennels, apparently, shaggy little hunting dogs bouncing out of the doors and into the darkness beyond like they couldn't imagine a better way to spend the night in a rain storm. The kitchen door creaked open, letting more of the chaotic sound in. Oskar, the Wolfe house carriage driver—he'd driven Tashué home from Highfield that morning after the banquet.

"Your horse is in fine shape, Captain," Oskar said. "I threw some stitches into the big wound, but she'll be well enough in no time. She's a beautiful creature. But she's got a brand on her. Says NTRA. I understand there's some discretion needed tonight, so I was wondering what you'd like to do with her, since having her here with that brand might lead to some questions as to how we came in possession of her."

"I'll take her," Tashué said. "Ishmael said we can't stay. We'll leave in the morning and he can ride her out of here again, since he won't be in any shape to walk anywhere for a while."

"I'm told you have a story to tell me, Miss Tei," Ishmael said. "Our Captain Blackwood filled me in on the broad strokes, but he says you have photographs. I'd like to see them before we go."

Allie nodded. And sighed. She sounded as tired as Tashué felt. "Yes. I'll go get them."

22

ISHMAEL

DAY 34

They hefted Ishmael up off the floor once all the mud and blood and cold was scrubbed away, but Cook brought another bucket of warm water for Ishmael to soak his feet in. It was going to fucking hurt, getting all the mud and forest debris out of those wounds, but it would be better than letting his feet rot and fall off. Cook bandaged Ishmael's knee and his ankle, moving as slowly and carefully as he could, but the jostling still fucking hurt. Fuck that forest and fuck Rainer and fucking his stupid badge-carrying lackeys who would slaughter people within reach of the city like they weren't even afraid they'd get caught.

Cook brought out a needle and twine next, but Ishmael waved him off. "Captain Blackwood needs that more than I do."

Tashué lifted his arm, though the movement had to be agonizing, and Cook started the slow work of drawing the ragged skin together over his ribcage. Tashué watched, his features drawn and exhausted but his eyes shining with something Ishmael had never seen in him before. Maybe that was his soldier's eyes, the hard edge that came to people who fought and killed for a living, and maybe Ishmael hadn't seen it before because Tashué had retired long before they met. Or maybe it was the battle that had to be happening inside him—nineteen years serving the Authority, and the Authority had tried to hang him from a fucking tree in the Dunnenbrahl. And that Talent—Ishmael hadn't seen what happened, but he sure as fuck felt it, the moment of its incredible force hitting the whole clearing so hard it knocked the air out of Ishmael's lungs. He counted himself lucky he wasn't crushed by the chunks of spruce that rained down everywhere.

"You're very good at that," Tashué said, like he couldn't bear the silence. He watched Cook's hands turn elegant in the way they hooked flesh together and tied twine to close the gashes.

"Served my five in the healer's corps," Cook said. "I ain't Talented—but they still need hands to do the mundane work, don't they? Thought about going to one of the fancy schools to be a proper surgeon, but a five-year pension wasn't enough to pay for a fancy school, so I took the job here. And then, I don't know. The General pays a fair wage for his house staff, and tying up the spring roast doesn't give me nightmares the way tying up a soldier's insides does."

"You're still having nightmares?" Ishmael asked.

"Not often," Cook said with a shrug. "Here and there. War leaves it mark, don't it?"

"It does that," Tashué said.

Hattie came down with fresh clothes, her face blank and trying to maintain control, but her lip trembled. Just a little. "I'm sorry, Mr. Blackwood, I think the best clothes for you belong to our Cook, and everything he has smells like garlic no matter how many times I wash them. Your shoulders are too wide to borrow anything from the General."

"That's fine, Hattie," Ishmael said when Tashué looked completely out of his depth. "There's nothing wrong with smelling like garlic, and I promise Captain Blackwood isn't going to be offended."

She lay the clothes on the counter, fussing with them like she didn't know what to do with her hands. When the clothes failed to offer her any solutions, she turned to the pile of rags that were once Tashué's and Ishmael's clothes and started gathering them up.

Panic spasmed through Ishmael's chest so fast he started to stand before he remembered his knee wouldn't take his weight at all. "Wait—don't—pass my things here."

Hattie brought it all to the table instead of pitching it in the roaring fire like Ishmael feared she would, and Ishmael grabbed the scraps and rifled through the pockets. He kept so much shit in his pockets all the time—a bag of dates, crusted with his blood, his pocket watch, so soaked that there was water beading under the glass. Deri's letter, where was it? He couldn't remember which pocket he'd stashed it away into. He hadn't had the chance to think about it at all because fucking Tashué had eaten up all of Ishmael's attention.

He found it in his jacket pocket. Soaked, just like everything else. A small whine escaped his throat before he could stop it. He eased the envelope open. The paper was dry only in small patches, the ink spreading in abstract shapes like dye, the words ruined. Illegible. Here and there, he could discern a word or two—*romantic*, down at the bottom. *But sometimes I* and the next line *let Maes have.*

His hands shook as he laid the ruined letter on the table in front of him. There was no saving it. Even if he left it to dry, most of Deri's words had been washed away. He pressed his palm into the disintegrating wax seal, trying to assemble himself in some kind of order, but nothing was in order at all. He was mostly naked and battered in Wolfe's kitchen after the Authority tried to kill him simply for hearing things that were true, and his survival was not thanks to any of his skills but because a person he'd known for years had Talent he never knew about. And Deri had sent him a letter at some point before he died, but Maes had gotten ahold of it and was taunting him with it. And now Ishmael couldn't know what Deri had written. Maes had probably read it so many times he'd memorized the words.

It was all, somewhat predictably, shit. The exact shape of the shit was a complete surprise, but the presence of the giant mounds of it seemed perfectly normal as far as Ishmael was concerned. Everything was always shit.

Hattie took over emptying pockets, and she set things out on the table in an orderly line, no doubt making a plan to clean whatever needed cleaning. And even though Cook was stitching the wound over Tashué's ribcage, even though it had to hurt more than Ishmael dared consider, Tashué reached out and put his hand on Ishmael's shoulder, giving it a squeeze that made Ishmael's bruises ache. He must have seen Ishmael's wild panic. He always did, somehow, no matter how hard Ishmael tried to hide it.

"Deri wrote to me before he died," Ishmael said, by way of flimsy explanation. "I didn't get the chance to read it."

"Ishmael," Tashué said, his voice cracking open with so much pain, it made Ishmael's throat too tight. "I'm sorry."

Wolfe's cane announced his return, and Allie trailed in behind him. She carried a big crate with both hands and set it on the table. She pulled a smaller box out of it, moving reverently and slowly, like it held all the weight of the world.

"I don't know how much Tashué told you," she said, resting the box on the table in front of Ishmael. "I know it's been a long night, but I'm going to start at the beginning, to make sure you have everything. I'm sure a diplomat would want the whole story."

Ishmael nodded, but didn't say anything. There wasn't room in the air for him to add his words.

It was hard to look at the photographs of the children, but he forced himself to look anyway. The shock of a dead child never wore off, no matter how many conflicts he'd been a part of, no matter how much death he bore witness to. Even Deri, with all his gruff exterior and his jaded world view, needed moments to deeply and viscerally mourn dead children when their work brought them in such uncomfortable proximity to the hard realities of war.

If ever there comes a time when we aren't horribly shocked by child casualties, then we need to retire.

Ishmael couldn't help but wonder what Deri would think of these children. The photographs felt like a tribute to cruelty and greed—all the photographs showed the hard lines where their shoulders ended because the arms had been removed, and the work had been done expertly. He'd seen enough amputations to know a good one, and they'd pulled the shoulder right out of joint instead of sawing at the bone, then sewed the skin shut to make a neat line.

"That ain't right," Cook whispered. He recognized the skill too, no doubt, since it was his job for five years. And like he said, war—no matter how long gone in a person's past—left its mark. "What's the point of it?"

"To make them lighter," Tashué said. "And easier to transport."

Ugly fucking words. It was shocking when Tashué said it in Brick-heart, but now that the proof was spread out in front of them, it was the most vile thing Ishmael had ever seen in his life. He'd always known Rainer was a shitstain of a man, but this was worse than he could have imagined.

Allie explained it all, the boy she found, the girl Tashué found. The things that Hale said, the man that came to kill her in her office, and the badge her colleague found. The same as the badge Tashué found on the people who tried to kill them tonight.

"We were going to find some way to prove it," Allie said, laying her badge trophy on the counter beside Tashué's. Hers had blood on it, too. "Something we can publish to start tearing it all down." Her eyes cut across to Tashué, and for a moment she looked so incredibly sad that something trembled in Ishmael's chest. "What happened?"

Tashué shook his head. He couldn't look at her. He put his hand on the photo of the girl he found—Lizanne—and didn't look at anyone. "I was drunk, and I was angry. I wasn't thinking."

"We really should be going. We can't be here when they start searching."

"Ishmael, you can't be serious," Wolfe rumbled. "The state of both of you—"

"I'm absolutely serious, General," Ishmael interrupted. "Eventually Bothain and Rainer will get word that their Patrollers and the officers are missing, and they'll start searching. We cannot be here when that happens, or they'll arrest you for harbouring us."

"I'll come with you," Allie said, gathering up her photographs and her sparse newspaper articles and the long list of notes. "I'll wager they'll try to search the property since Mr. Saeati lives here, and I don't expect they'll be impressed to find me, since I killed one of theirs."

"You're probably right about that, Miss Tei," Ishmael said. Saying her name set off a new wave of shame. Tashué had asked him to help this woman, and he'd forgotten because he was drinking. Feeling sorry for himself after the carnage of the Market fire. After killing Losek for Powell Iwan.

He needed to stand and get dressed and start moving, but he was so tired. He could rest his head on this table and sleep here for a day or two. He'd done it before—staggered home drunk and lain between the wood stove and the wall so he could sleep in the heat that tried to half-cook him while the kitchen came to life around him. But there wasn't time.

"Where will you go?" Wolfe asked.

"Maybe it's best that I don't tell you," Ishmael said. "Plausible deniability."

Wolfe shook his head, his face flashing with the first cracks of his composure. "I'll see Rainer swing, North Star help me. I've always thought the man was a slug, but this is unconscionable. I should have listened to you sooner. I should have let you rip him apart when we had the chance."

Ishmael grimaced, shaking his head. "I didn't have enough, not then.

And we didn't know all of this. Even this won't be enough, but it's a start."

"How could it not be enough?" Hattie gasped, wiping her face. "The poor wee children—"

"I know, Hattie, the photographs are ghastly," Ishmael said. "But there's not yet any proof that shows Rainer and the Authority are responsible. So that's our job now, isn't it? That's why we can't stay. We have to keep moving, stay ahead of Rainer, keep him on the defensive."

"How are you going to do that when you can't walk?" Wolfe huffed.

Ishmael shrugged. "I don't need to walk to tell Captain Blackwood what to do."

Tashué didn't seem to be listening. He grabbed his timepiece from the table, closing his hand around it. Ishmael watched Tashué's face, trying to read his expression, but it was distressingly blank. He was silent in a way that didn't suit him. Tashué tried to open the cover of his timepiece, but the hinges were bent out of shape, and the cover only opened a little. It was enough to let the broken glass fall out, and Ishmael winced at the glittering shards. He knew the weight of a broken watch when it held so much more than the ability to tell time.

"I can fix it," Ishmael said softly. "It's just a matter of pressing the case back into shape and replacing whatever's broken inside. We'll leave it here, and I'll fix it later." It felt like a lie to imply things would ever be settled enough for him to sit and fix a watch, but some sympathetic panic crawled through his chest. His father had built that watch, and it was the last gift Tashué's father had given him.

"Ah, no," Tashué said. He tipped the watch to one side, sending the rest of the glass tumbling out across the surface of the table. "I'll keep this with me. It seems a decent reminder of how fucking stupid I get when I drink angry. I knew I shouldn't, but I did it anyway because I felt so..." He sighed, pressing the cover closed. "If I'm going to die, I'd like to have it on me."

Silence again. Ishmael fumbled for words, trying to come up with something comforting and honest, something that might help, but nothing seemed right. The pair of them fell too easily into a bottle when the world was too much to face, but this time was worse than ever before.

The kitchen door swung open. One of the hunters came in, tracking mud over the footprints Tashué and Ishmael left.

"General—there are other people in the forest now. The Authority and the Patrollers—they want us to leave so they can take over the investigation, they said, but the others stayed behind to argue with them some, to give me time to get back here. The one Authority fucker said he wanted you to come out to talk to them, I said I'd come get you. Said it would take a while since you were probably in bed and all that, and it wouldn't do to drag you out into this rain. I think I bought you all some time, but it won't be much. Rain's letting off now."

"That's it, then," Ishmael said. "We have to go."

"Back in the saddle?" Tashué asked.

Ishmael grimaced. "I guess that's what I have to do, isn't it?"

23

TASHUÉ

DAY 34

As soon as they crossed the footbridge into the Bay, Allie kicked her horse into a canter, sending it bolting through the streets to get ahead of them, whipping her reins back against the horse's flanks to drive it faster. Tashué wanted to follow. The big grey mare would eat up the distance in no time. But he couldn't leave Ishmael to ride on his own—Ishmael couldn't put his feet in the stirrups to balance himself with his ankle and his knee so fucked. Tashué held the reins and Ishmael's old gelding followed along at a slow, uninterested lope. Allie would let Powell know they were coming.

There was something familiar about returning to the saddle that stripped the intensity out of Tashué's pain. Drained the lingering horror at what he'd done. Gruelling forced marches and moving battle lines and ambushing enemy soldiers had taught him how to settle on horseback and ignore everything. Didn't matter how tired he was, didn't matter how little he'd slept, didn't matter what wounds he was carrying, didn't matter what brutality he'd left behind, orders were orders, and sometimes you had to move out.

Tashué's Talent never stopped. It wasn't bad before they crossed the footbridge; travelling along the riverbank was quiet, and the only sounds his Talent latched on to were made my Ishmael and Allie, their horses, and the river. The steady roar of the Brightwash made it easier to ignore things he wasn't used to being aware of. But across the bridge, there was so much more to *hear*. Too many heartbeats, too many arguments, too many chair legs scraping on floors he couldn't even see, and when they passed a brothel, he could hear people fucking. He couldn't make it stop, couldn't drown it out, couldn't keep his awareness inside his own head. It made the city heavier, more imposing.

He focused on Ishmael. On the steady, tired heartbeat and the sound of his breathing. On their horses—their hearts were even slower, their massive lungs like the roaring of the ocean. If he listened to Ishmael's heart—to the unrelenting rhythm of it, thump-thump, thump-thump, thump-thump, he didn't sink into Ishmael's memories and the way they flashed through his mind's eye. Thump-thump, he didn't get lost in the chaos of the city. Thump-thump, he could remember who he was.

How did anyone with Talent keep their fucking sanity? Were they all so uncomfortably aware of the whole world, all the time?

The mare's hoof caught a cobblestone, and she stumbled, sending her heart lurching. Tashué reached down and patted her neck, his hand sinking into the thick grey coat.

"I know you're tired," he told her. "We're almost done."

Allie came thundering back, her springy gelding dodging the sparse, late-night traffic with excited energy, like he couldn't imagine any better life than weaving through the city as fast as Allie would let him. She had to fight him hard to get him to slow down, and her own face was lit with the excitement of the speed, her breath coming in short gasps.

"Vasska was up already—he said the whole city has been waiting to hear what happened to you. He said to bring you to the office I've been using. Vasska and Mr. Iwan will meet us there."

Allie led them to the dry-docks. The workers all froze when the three of them rode into the chaos, like they'd been reduced to tintype photographs of a warehouse instead of real living people.

"Miss Tei," someone said.

"Good morning, gentlemen," Allie said, sliding down from her horse, springing on her feet when she landed. "Don't mind us. Mr. Iwan will be by shortly to meet us."

"Of course, Miss Tei."

"You've come a long way, Allie," Tashué said. "I seem to remember a time when you said you'd never been to the Bay before."

Allie gave a tight smile, taking the reins of Ishmael's gelding. "Life has been interesting since I met you."

"Captain Blackwood has that effect on people," Ishmael grunted.

Tashué shifted his weight and dropped down from the saddle—the pain that roared up through his feet took him off guard, made his knees weak. A strangled, animal sound escaped his throat, and he caught the mare's mane to keep himself upright. Fuck, he'd forgotten how bad his feet were, and the moment he took his weight on them, they were more than happy to remind him.

"You have a stable somewhere nearby?" Allie asked.

"Ah, no, Miss Tei. Just the stockyards. Ain't no stables in the Bay since there ain't no horse-drawn cabs."

"Just keep them out of the way for now," Ishmael said. "We'll figure it out in the morning."

Tashué took a step toward Ishmael. Just one, to prove to his body that he could. He could walk, and it wasn't the end of him. It hurt so fucking much, but he didn't have a choice. He couldn't stop now. Another step. He reached up and braced Ishmael's side, and the way Ishmael shifted his weight to lean on Tashué made Tashué's feet scream even more, but Ishmael was worse off than Tashué, and he couldn't get down out of the saddle alone. He had to half-fall into Tashué's arms. It took every ounce of strength Tashué had left not to drop Ishmael right to the warehouse floor.

"I'm sorry to tell you both we have to make it up two flights of stairs," Allie said. "But then there's a surprisingly large bed and the pair of you can rest a bit while we wait for Mr. Iwan."

"Been a while since I shared a bed with you, Captain," Ishmael said.

Tashué laughed. He had to. And it was probably why Ishmael said it —to draw the last shred of strength out of both of them by making light of the whole problem. Two flights of stairs, fuck. "We'll take it easy this time. Nothing too acrobatic."

Ishmael nodded "Just this one time, it's a deal."

Every step was a struggle and a victory. Tashué clung to Ishmael to keep him going, and Ishmael braced himself on the wall to go up one step at a time. Allie followed along behind, like she thought she could catch them if they fell backward, except she was so much smaller than both of them. Surely they would crush her if they fell. Up and up and up until Tashué felt sick again, all the pain turning to sour nausea in his stomach. But finally, the door. Allie pushed a key into Tashué's hand, and they almost fell through the threshold and onto the floor before Tashué caught them both on the doorframe. Ishmael sank down slowly, lying flat on his back on the hardwood, panting and gasping, holding his knee like he was trying to crush the pain right back out of the joint. Tashué sat on the floor beside Ishmael so Allie had to climb over them to get in.

Most of the Bay didn't have brights, but the dry-docks did so they could be worked around the clock. The glow of them through the windows turned the office into vague shapes instead of complete darkness. A desk, a wood stove. A pile of logs to feed it. Cookware and a kettle, hanging from the ceiling.

Tashué put his hands on Ishmael's knee, the pain making him dizzy. Whose pain was it? He couldn't tell anymore. It lived in his nerves, all over his body, like his Talent was covetous of it, torturing him with it. At least with the pain, there wasn't room in his mind for anything else. He didn't hear the heartbeats from the people below.

Allie came forward with an old cloth, the cold of it radiating around her hand. Ice, probably from an ice box somewhere in the room. "Here, ice it a while," she said. "It will help. I think I hear someone downstairs already."

"Help me up," Ishmael said, lifting a hand. "I have to be up off the floor at least."

Ishmael didn't have to hobble far to get to the desk. There were only two chairs at it—one tucked under the centre, another on the other side, resting against the wall until it was needed. Ishmael took the extra chair, leaving the big one for Powell. Allie lay the rag-wrapped ice across Ishmael's knee. Footsteps on the stairs—the door swung open as Tashué hovered at Ishmael's shoulder. All he wanted to do was collapse onto the bed that hid behind a partition in the far corner, but it wasn't time yet. Allie stepped to the door, meeting Vasska as he stepped inside first, brushing snow off his shoulders. It made the ache of it all keener. Stella was out there somewhere, and now it was snowing. Tashué didn't know what came next for him and Ishmael, and now it was fucking *snowing*. It seemed to underscore the desperate corner they'd backed themselves into. Winter revolution, blood and snow, ice and unrest. It was all going to be shit.

"Mr. Blackwood," Vasska said. "I have to admit, I'm pleasantly surprised to see you're still alive."

"So am I," Tashué grunted.

Vasska laughed at that, pushing his hand through his messy blond hair. There were dark shadows under his eyes, the only hint of what must have been incredible fatigue. Tashué's broken timepiece couldn't tell him what time it was. But maybe he didn't want to know. Allie and Vasska turned to the wood stove, working together to get a fire going. The glow of it built and spilled into the office so they could see each other. Allie used a taper to light oil lamps, filling the room with smoke and light. The overwhelming chattering feeling came back, invading his senses—Vasska's heart and the sound of footsteps on the stairs, Powell Iwan and Adley and the weight of Adley's Talent coming up the stairs like a pillar of stone.

Vasska returned to the stairs in time to offer Powell his arm. The climb up had taxed the old man, sending his breath wheezing and rattling through his chest as he fought against the coughing that had plagued him last time Tashué saw him. Talent swirled, Tashué's new reality. Powell's heart was unsteady and weak, the lungs weighed down with fluid, the joints old and worn. Adley trailed behind him, his dark eyes sweeping over Ishmael and Tashué both, taking stock. His Talent flared in response to Tashué, and a wall slipped between Tashué's Talent and Powell's body, keeping him out like shutters that had been pulled closed. Vasska, too, was shut off from Tashué's awareness. A relief—if only someone would do that to the whole city. Maybe he could do that, too. Maybe he could draw a curtain around himself to shut the world out.

"That's some Talent you've found yourself with, Mr. Blackwood," Adley grunted, voice like tired gravel. "It becomes you."

"It saved me," Tashué said. "But I think it's going to drive me out of my mind."

Adley nodded. "It takes a while to get used to it. Imagine it like stemming the blood flow from a wound. If you're bleeding, you don't scoop your blood up off the floor and try to stuff it back in, yeah? You put a tourniquet above the wound, tie it real tight."

"Where?" Tashué asked.

"You been to the Rift to visit your boy, haven't you?"

Tashué nodded.

Adley tapped the back of his head. "The place where your head hurts when the suppression gets ahold of you—that's where."

Powell shuffled across the room to the desk, sinking into the big leather chair like it was his throne. He took a breath like he meant to say something, but it set off an ugly round of coughing. Hacking, chunky, rattling his whole frame. He folded over himself and braced his chest and covered his mouth with a handkerchief, coughing and coughing until his whole face was red, and the veins in his neck were bulging, and he looked like he was going to faint. The unfolding of Adley's Talent was immense, taking up so much space in the room that it was harder to draw breath. What could Adley do to help Powell? Surely not much, even if he was a proper healer. Death came for everyone eventually, and the rattle of that cough sounded terrible.

Powell's coughing subsided, and he sagged back against his chair. Adley handed him a fresh kerchief. Powell wiped tears out of his eyes, his hands shaking with the exertion. Ishmael shifted even though it made his pain flare—there was no barrier between Tashué and Ishmael, so Tashué was stuck feeling Ishmael's pain. Powell offered a hand, and Ishmael reached across to take it, folding both his hands around Powell's. The sound of Powell struggling to catch his breath battled the silence as everyone waited for him to recover enough to speak.

Tashué took the moment of stillness to turn his Talent inward, like Adley said. It all bled out of his mind, this force that made him too aware. He'd kept it chained all these years, preventing his own quickening until he was up in that tree. He could do it again. But focusing on the power of it dragged that sound back to the surface of his memory— grinding bone, the horrible gush of blood when the heart exploded.

"I don't know why I didn't go farther south when I had the chance," Powell muttered, his voice thin and trembling. "Somewhere hot and dry."

"I'll take you somewhere, maybe," Ishmael said softly. Their voices came to Tashué only distantly as he kept his eyes closed, trying to feel the extent of his own Talent so he could know it well enough to contain it. Those two deaths weren't any worse than any of the other people he killed. Dead was dead. "After the election, when things are quiet. We'll book passage to the Salt Isles."

"Hotter than that," Powell grunted. "Take me to the Derccian empire. Somewhere with sand dunes."

"I'll take you to Ibashah then," Ishmael said. "The capitol, Beishrim, is gorgeous. Black granite mountains as far as the eye can see, and Beishrim is in the valley between the Black Mountains and the Qasan. It's all stunning. And hot."

"That's close to where our Captain Blackwood made himself infamous, isn't it?" Powell asked. "Near the Black Ridge, wasn't it? What were our soldiers doing there?"

Tashué's eyes flared open, the words hitting him like bricks.

"They were defending the pass for the Azeeraji, who were holding out on the other side," Adley said before Tashué could summon the mental energy to say something about the Ridge. Sweet North Star, he was so fucking tired of people talking about the Ridge. This wasn't the conversation he was expecting at all. "The Derccian Empire was protecting the Azeeraji borders, since they're a part of the empire. The Dominion Army has a trade agreement with the Derccian Emperor."

"The deal is soldiers for opium," Ishmael said. "But it's shit Derccian opium that the empire wants to get rid of. The people of the Dominion are being ripped off."

"Isn't the common story that the 12th was the division that saved the Ridge?" Vasska asked, looking up at Tashué. There was more than a little panic there, grief bubbling and waiting for its chance to overflow. And maybe talking about anything distracted him from the pain of facing the loss of his family, but why'd it have to be the Ridge? "Why do they get the credit when your service was so valorous it earned you the White Shield?"

"We don't have to do this," Tashué said. They were all looking at him but not talking to him. "It doesn't matter. It happened twenty years ago —more than that."

"It matters because I say it matters," Powell grunted, his voice trembling with the remembered exertion of all that coughing. "Bothain Clannaugh is in my city with his new designation as General of the 12th, and here you are, sitting in my office, asking for my help."

"Bothain Clannaugh?" Tashué echoed. "As in the Fist of the North? I thought he was Provincial Administrator of Fuar—"

Ishmael scowled. "I'd like to tell him where he can shove his great northern fist. He used to be the Provincial Administrator, but now he's the General of the 12th, like Mr. Iwan said."

Powell nodded, his eyes fixed on Tashué's face. Fury lurked behind them, but it was under control. For now. "You've stepped in a ripe pile of dogshit this time, *Captain*. And you're tracking your stench down into my quarter, no doubt hoping that I'll protect you now that you're a fugitive from both bodies of law in this country. So, I'd like to know the bigger politics of it all before I decide how hard I'm willing to work to try to save you from the pile of shit. Especially if the Dominion military is involved. Ain't danced with them too much. They play real dirty, don't they? In theory the laws keep them out of homeland politics, but we all know laws are pieces of pretty paper that rich people use to hide their crimes. Who better than to advise me on military politics than our favourite diplomat, hey? What's the matter boy? You don't look like you're enjoying yourself as much as you usually do when we're talking about politics."

"My knee, Mr. Iwan," Ishmael said. He dragged the ice up his leg to give the knee a break from the cold. "It's sore from our little adventure through the Dunnenbrahl."

Adley's Talent crawled over the space between them like a questing hand. Ishmael flinched, hand spasming like he would push the feeling away. Could he sense Talent?

"It's been dislocated," Adley said.

"Would you like Adley to help?" Powell asked.

"Thank you, Mr. Iwan, but no."

"I can make it a bit better, at least——"

Tashué tried to imagine the same curtain that Adley used, his Talent like a billowing fabric that wrapped around Ishmael—and it worked. The sound of the city had fallen away. In keeping away from Ishmael, Tashué had also hemmed his awareness in. He couldn't hear Allie's heart anymore, or the constant movement in the warehouse below them. The emptiness made his ears ring louder, made his head throb like it did at the Ridge. Adley hit the Talent-fabric, his eyes flicking to Tashué like he was surprised to find a boundary in front of him.

"He said no," Tashué said.

"You're a fast learner, Captain Blackwood."

Powell waved a hand at Tashué and Adley. "I'm waiting for my answer, Saeati."

Ishmael settled the ice on his knee again. "Maddox is dead now, and Clannaugh wasn't there. The politics of the Ridge don't matter except for the fact that it's the reason General Wolfe chose Captain Blackwood for the business with the Authority. And all those medals the 12th has will be the reason Maes wanted to control it. He sent Clannaugh through the Academy to get his stars so the 12th's General would be loyal to him. The real problem is Winter's police force. Clannaugh said as much. If Myron Winter wins this election, Clannaugh and his 12th will be our police force. Your hold on the Bay has lasted through a lot, Mr. Iwan, but I'll wager Clannaugh won't stand for it. He'll want it all. That's why Maes chose him for all this. The Fist of the North is poised to close around Yaelsmuir to make an example out of us, and unfortunately we gave him an excuse to do it sooner rather than later."

Powell sighed slowly, his fingers drumming on the arm of his big chair. "And now you're both here for protection, since you've gone and got yourself rather infamous, is that it?"

"That's exactly it, Mr. Iwan," Ishmael said quickly. Something had changed in Ishmael's demeanour, something subtle. Trying to define exactly what felt somewhat like trying to catch sight of a white tracer in Tashué's vision. The edges had been sanded down, maybe—he was more differential than Tashué had ever seen him before. He was more direct. He spoke as if there was a stopwatch timing him, without a single wasted syllable or pause. Was it the pain that sucked the performance out of him, or was this simply what he sounded like when he was *working*? "I thought you would extend a bit of grace to us, seeing as we've been loyal all this time, and Rainer's been such a pain in your ass. We thought if anyone would want to shelter us while we finally undo his career, it would be you."

Powell's lips pulled back into something between a snarl and a smile, bearing aged teeth and anemic gums, his chin tilting up. "You thought all that, did you boy? It's not that there's nowhere else to go for a fugitive of the law but the Bay, and it's not that you wanted my help talking to Davik Kaine seeing as you're suddenly allies to his cause and your best shot at surviving all this is with his help?"

"Davik—" Tashué breathed, revulsion crawling under his skin.

"Davik Kaine is a means to an end, Mr. Iwan," Ishmael interrupted. "We know who holds the Bay, and we know where to go for protection and permission."

Powell sat quietly for a while, studying Allie and Ishmael and Tashué in turn, like a butcher examining a carcass to identify what kind of meat it was and where the best cuts were. The silence and the stillness ate at Tashué's nerves, making him so tense his teeth ached. Davik Kaine? He hadn't agreed to that. Ishmael hadn't mentioned it when they were at Wolfe's. How serious was he?

"What about you, girl?" Powell asked, his eyes settling on Allie. "How do you fit into all this? Whose side are you on?"

Allie stiffened, looking at Powell, her face carefully neutral. "Whose side?"

Powell grunted, nodded. "You heard me."

Tashué shifted his weight so he stood in front of Allie, blocking Powell's line of sight. "Miss Tei is with me, Mr. Iwan."

"Tashué," Ishmael said, the sound like a wince.

"You're new around these streets, Mr. Blackwood," Powell said slowly, but he leaned forward as he said it. Just a little. "And you've come down here under extraordinary circumstances. So, I'll forgive you your impertinence. But this is how things are done in my quarter. This old man spends a lot of time talking while he makes decisions, and you'll indulge me the time or you'll find some other quarter to hide in while you lick your wounds. Are we clear?"

"You'll excuse him, Mr. Iwan," Ishmael cut in again. "Someone tried to hang him from a tree this evening. It tends to make a man restless."

Powell flicked his fingers at Ishmael, like he wasn't interested in the details of Tashué's almost-hanging. "So, young lady, what's your answer? You come around with your little stack of papers you want to make copies of and make eyes at my grandson and let him chase you around, but what's your end goal? Are you here for the thrill of it? For the story you'll get to publish? Or do you just enjoy flirting with the future of this city?"

Allie and Vasska blushed at each other like they'd been caught at something. It made them both look so young. The pair of them were in their twenties, and facing the biggest societal upheaval the Dominion had seen since the rise against the Godking. It made Tashué feel so incredibly tired. How did either of them even have the energy to blush?

"Grandad," Vasska huffed.

Powell waved a hand, dismissing Vasska's outrage before his grandson could say anything else. "I ain't complaining. I'm fucking delighted, aren't I? It's about damned time. And if you're about to be in the middle of all my business, I'd like to know exactly where you stand."

"We haven't—" Allie stammered. "Mr. Czarny and I aren't—"

"Stay focused, girl," Powell said, tapping the desk. "I'm not talking about sex. I'm talking about politics. I'm sure Mr. Saeati will try to say you can't separate them, but I think it's safe to say we're in a terrible mess whether you're fucking my grandson or not, what with all that dogshit our Mr. Blackwood is tracking through the Bay. So—what are you here for?"

Allie stood up straighter, her chin lifted, defiant. "I'm on the children's side, Mr. Iwan."

Powell grunted at her. "And what does that mean?"

"It means I intend to use the space you loaned to me to copy every document I can get my hands on, Mr. Iwan. I plan to distribute them through the city as swiftly and aggressively as possible. It means I'll follow Mr. Blackwood anywhere and do anything to bring it all to light. I hope that Mayor Wolfe is as outraged as he seemed when we spoke to him. I hope he doesn't do the thing that politicians are wont to do and change his mind when things get bad in the interest of keeping peace. But he's ordered a printing press for me to use, so I hope that means he agrees that peaceful measures are unethical against an administration that uses the bodies of children as energy units. Peaceful measures sound too much like letting Rainer Elsworth get away with what he's done for the sake of civility."

"I don't expect a young woman born and bred in Highview to be so scornful of civility," Powell said slowly, cocking one eyebrow. The light from all the oil lamps danced in the deep lines that the expression folded into his face. "Folks over there tend to cloak themselves in their precious civility to try to convince the other side of the river they deserve respect."

"I can't say I much care what the people of Highfield think of me, considering the people of Highfield are making energy units out of children and murdering anyone who thinks that's a terrible thing." All of Allie's blushing and squirming was gone. And Tashué's heart burned with pride. He'd never imagined, when she found him in the *Pint Under* with her oversized satchel and all that curiosity in her dark eyes, that their paths would lead them to this. "If that's what civility looks like, I want no part in it. I'm hoping you deem Mr. Blackwood worthy of your protection so that he can stand for the revolution. For the children."

"Revolution is a big word, young lady."

"Yes sir, Mr. Iwan," Allie said. "Whose side are *you* on?"

Fucking hell. The balls on her.

Powell laughed at that, which set him coughing again. He held his kerchief to his mouth, the sound rumbling from his chest as he fought against it. It passed quickly this time, and he took a slow breath, his eyes shifting to Tashué. "You'll be happy, Mr. Blackwood. I've made a decision."

"Thank you, Mr. Iwan."

Powell waved to Adley. The big man came forward, resting something on the desk—the metallic tap on the wood sounded coldly familiar, and then Adley's hand moved away, revealing the empty bullet casing. Such a little thing, a spent bullet casing. If Tashué had shot and powder, he could reload it and make it useful again. "Last time I saw you, you promised me something."

"Yes sir, Mr. Iwan." Tashué hoped he sounded half as steady as Allie, even though he was exhausted, even though the swirl of his Talent dragged him through the whole building if he didn't focus on the curtain that kept him firmly planted in this room. Even though he was reasonably sure his feet were bleeding again from all the standing. That shell casing had a gravity all of its own, dragging Tashué closer to it even though he wasn't moving. Just a bit of brass, gleaming softly in the harsh light of the lamps, but suddenly it was the centre of the room. The bullet that killed Hale, the casing that Tashué had given to Iwan as a promise. "I remember."

"Good, so I don't have to waste any time threatening you or reminding you," Powell said. "Because if I had to do any of that, I would be worried you're stupider than I thought, and you don't want me thinking I've overestimated your potential, do you?"

Tashué stifled a sigh, forcing himself to stay straight instead of sagging under the weight of his exhaustion. Powell wanted to play his little game, fine. "Of course not, Mr. Iwan."

Powell nodded, his eyes drifting down to the casing. His fingers drummed on the desk, nails clacking on wood, the silence stretching and thinning like a great length of elastic, building pressure at the base of Tashué's skull.

"There's no quiet way forward, Grandad," Vasska interrupted. "I know you're trying to imagine a future that keeps the Bay safe and out of trouble, but this isn't the moment for quiet, like Miss Tei said. Rainer will rip the city apart for Captain Blackwood and Mr. Saeati no matter what we do, but if we move right and decisively now, we'll get the better of Elsworth, Clannaugh, and Governor Winter all at once. It's what we need to keep the police force out of the Bay and crush the Authority once and for all."

Powell shook his head, clearing his throat a few times. His hand tightened around his kerchief, but some force of will kept him from coughing this time. "I've been keeping these people safe for forty years. There are grown men in this quarter who don't know how bad it was before because they were born in peace. You don't know how precious that is, Vasska. You're all aglow with the idea of changing the world, but you don't know what it's like to watch people bleed all over the cobbles because the city thinks we're no better than fat sows for the slaughter. That's what you're asking me for—you want to rip apart the Authority because you're all alight with dreams of valour and revolution, but they won't go easy. Our people in this quarter will be the ones who pay with the most blood. And you, young and hungry as you are, don't know what it's like to wonder if we could have protected them from their own government. Ask our Captain Blackwood what that feels like. He lived it on that dusty old ridge of his. I imagine he'll tell you how there isn't a single shred of his soul that he wouldn't give to bring back the lives that were thrown away. Even now, twenty years later, I bet he still sometimes catches the smell of a funeral pyre or a bad wound, and he makes a wish that his memory wasn't real. Isn't that right, Captain?"

"The blood's coming one way or another, Mr. Iwan," Ishmael said before Tashué could answer. Because Tashué would agree—he would give anything to save the people who were so casually thrown away on that cursed mountain pass. But he would also explain that this was different. The Authority needed to be stopped at any cost. "Clannaugh will want to make a mess of things to get Myron elected and have his police force ratified. They'll probably try to have it done by emergency order before the election, which means they'll be down here getting people agitated to see if they can get us to riot."

"So then the answer is to keep our people calm," Powell said.

Ishmael shook his head, resting his hand on the ice and shifting it. The only hint of his pain. "The answer is to move carefully so we get ahead of Clannaugh without him realizing. He'll be hungry for Kaine."

"So we give him Kaine," Powell said. "We string him along a while, let him wag his cock all over the Bay long enough to make him feel like a man, and then we hand him Kaine's head to broker a peace."

Ishmael nodded, sliding the ice up his leg again, shaking water off his hands. "We'll send Vasska across the river to make it happen."

"Me?" Vasska asked.

"You're perfect for this," Ishmael said. "Young, pretty, polite. You'll blend right into Highfield and never once look out of place. You can walk up to Wolfe's estate without anyone questioning why you're there— you dress well enough to fit in. Wolfe can introduce you to Illea, and then Illea can sit you down with Clannaugh. You'll tell a good story about how your dear old grandad is feeling embarrassed and a little guilty for all that's been going on under his nose—he wants the Bay to run smoothly and fuck these Red Dawn idiots, they're messing with everything. As a gesture of peace and cooperation, Powell Iwan has sent him a gift. You'll hand over Kaine's literal fucking head."

"When I said we'd give Clannaugh a head, it was a figure of speech," Powell said.

"I know," Ishmael said, his mouth hooking into a smile so sharp, it sent a shiver down Tashué's spine. "But it's good. You can say Kaine is the one responsible for all the chaos. Say that Mr. Iwan is tired of Kaine's shit and arranged to have him taken care of. Hand him the box with the head in it, and he'll know you mean fucking business. We'll get a cake box, the kind where the sides fall away when you take the top off."

"Boy, I love your mind," Powell chuckled. "It's beautiful. A head in a cake box. Shall we dust it with icing sugar?"

Ishmael shrugged and grinned, pushing some stray waves of hair out of his face, gone unruly now that his hair had the chance to dry. "Maybe some of those little roses, the ones made of royal icing, hard as candy."

"It won't be enough, will it?" Tashué asked. Even as some part of his mind—the part that tried to hang on to the idea of his own civility—screamed a protest at the brutality of a severed head with icing sugar and hard candy, the rest of him knew it was worth it. Whatever it took to rip it all apart. Fuck Kaine and fuck the Authority. But it wouldn't be that easy, surely. "Rainer will want me, too. It won't stop them."

Ishmael shrugged. "It gets rid of Kaine and brings Clannaugh to the negotiation table with Powell. We'll have to figure out where to hide you. Maybe we'll make you dead. Or get you out of Yaelsmuir."

"Make me dead?" It all sounded too simple, too optimistic.

Ishmael spread his hands. "A good, dramatic hero's death and then we smuggle you out of the city. With you gone and Davik's head in his hands, Clannaugh runs out of excuses."

"But what about Rainer?" Tashué asked. "What about the children?"

Ishmael waved a hand. "I'll figure it out later."

"Ishmael, you can't be serious—"

"Captain," Ishmael interrupted, sliding the ice down to his knee again. "I'll figure it out *later*."

Tashué grit his teeth together, biting back the anger, the stream of words. He had to trust that Ishmael knew what he was doing, or he'd crumble.

Powell nodded. "I like it. We'll let him get that son of yours out of the Rift, and then we'll deliver his head across the river."

"My son?" Tashué echoed. The words emptied him completely. He was hollow, a vessel that didn't yet hold any hope, but it was welling in his seams and threatening to wash him away. The exhaustion meant nothing in the face of Powell Iwan talked about Jason. "He's getting Jason out?"

"Allegedly," Ishmael said. "Although it's taking a while so I'm starting to wonder if he's fucking you around, Mr. Iwan. And if that's the case, he won't be inclined to cooperate any faster now."

Powell nodded, eyes flicking to Tashué. "See if you can't invest him with a sense of urgency. I promised the Mayor I'd get it done for you, and I don't like to offer powerful men like Mayor Wolfe empty promises."

"Me?" Tashué asked.

"Yes, you," Powell snapped. "You came to me all in a lather with that cute little bullet of yours, asking for your son and making promises." He leaned forward, flicking the casing and sending it spinning over the desk. Ishmael's hand snapped out. He caught it as it fell from the ledge, but the sudden movement made Ishmael wince. Powell ignored the show of pain. He looked up at Tashué again, pressing his lips together and breathing slowly like he was fighting against a round of coughing. "You'll go down to that pugilist club and make yourself available to Kaine. Put some pressure on him to get your boy out of the Rift. Time's running out. One way or another, Kaine's head is going to buy me peace with Clannaugh and Elsworth."

Ishmael held up the bullet casing, and Tashué plucked it out of Ishmael's palm. It had such weight suddenly. It was nothing but hollow brass, but somehow it held Jason's whole life.

"And then you'll stand in the gap," Powell said. "That's what you promised me. Kaine's death will make a great gaping hole down there, and you'll stand in the centre of it and pull it closed for me. None of this fucking off down the river. Understood?"

"Yes sir, Mr. Iwan," Tashué said, closing his hand around the casing. "Whatever it takes to protect my son."

He almost said *and get justice for the children*, but Ishmael shifted in his seat enough to press his good knee against Tashué's leg. So he left it at that. For Jason. It wasn't a lie.

Powell made his way back to his feet and started the shuffle toward the door. He moved slower than when Tashué had last seen him. Only a few days ago—a week?—but so much had changed. He hadn't seen Jason since. Hadn't seen Lorne either for that matter.

Vasska lingered after his grandfather left, eyes flicked between

Ishmael, Tashué, Allie. "I'm glad you're alive, Mr. Blackwood. Something tells me you're the very man to change all the things my grandfather has allowed to fester in the interest of keeping the Bay peaceful—or near enough to it. What should I do with the horses? We don't host horses down here very often unless they're meat."

"The two smaller ones should go back to Wolfe's stables," Allie said. "I don't know about the big grey."

"I'll need her in the morning," Tashué said. "I'll bring her with me to Davik's club."

Vasska let himself out.

Ishmael exhaled, tossing the rag and the ice onto the desk. "The pair of you are going to be the death of me. Ishmael muttered. "Help me up, you fucking idiot."

"Why am I a fucking idiot?" Tashué scoffed.

"If you make me list the reasons, we'll be here until next year."

Tashué took Ishmael's hand and hauled him up, but Ishmael let out a strangled gasp, both hands catching Tashué's coat and turning into angry fists. Whatever they were about to argue about melted away. Everything hurt. The exhaustion couldn't be ignored anymore. They retreated to the bed, which was indulgently wide, the down-stuffed mattress clothed in linens that could rival any bed in Highfield. Ishmael sank into it first, breathing a long sigh of relief. Tashué helped him ease his boots off, tugged off his coat.

"I should go," Tashué said. "Find Kaine myself, get things moving."

"This is why you're a fucking idiot," Ishmael said, easing himself back. He hooked his hands under the bad leg to lift it up into the bed. "Just give me a few hours to sleep, and I'll come with you."

"But Jason—"

"Tashué, shut *up!*" Ishmael snapped, but there was no anger in the words. Just exhaustion. "You're not going down to find Kaine alone, or you'll fuck this up more. Remember the part where I said we weren't doing it your way anymore? Your way involves not thinking and getting us in the deepest shit imaginable when it could have been avoided. So now we're doing it my way, because I know what I'm doing. My way is a few hours' sleep and then we stick together. Got it?"

Relief. It drained all of the tension out of him. There was something comforting in the knowledge that someone was taking over. Ishmael's career was built for this. He knew how to swim in the fast river of politics without drowning. Tashué didn't have to do anything but follow orders.

His hands were so tired, they shook as he tried to unbutton his coat. He couldn't summon the coordination, not even in his good hand. "I'll sleep on the floor. The pair of you can fit in the bed."

"Don't be ridiculous," Allie said. She unbuttoned Tashué's coat quickly, tugging the sleeves off his arms as every muscle of his body screamed with battered fatigue. "There's room enough for all of us."

"He snores," Ishmael said.

"At least my snoring doesn't cause physical injury," Tashué muttered. "He kicks and thrashes."

"So you can put your big snoring body between us," Allie said. "Protect me from him."

Tashué laughed. It was easier to laugh than to admit how relieved he was that he didn't have to take the floor. Everything hurt so damned much already. There was a time in his career he could sleep anywhere. On the open ground, his body twisted between rocks. On the narrow path alongside a cliff's edge. In the saddle. And then he'd spring back up to his feet in the morning, ready to face the new day of marching or fighting or whatever miserable reality the military had in store for him. But it had been too many decades since then.

Ishmael crawled up to the pillow and collapsed. Allie walked around the bed, dragging the covers over Ishmael's shoulders.

"After you, Tashué," Allie said. She blew out the lanterns one by one. "I supposed crawling into bed with you is the next natural progression of our relationship after I put my finger in your body."

Ishmael laughed, the sound distant and exhausted. "Now there's a story I need to hear."

"Maybe later, when this is all over," Allie said. "We'll have a few drinks and I'll tell you about the time Tashué Blackwood made me put my finger in his abdomen. I'm still not convinced it was necessary."

"Might not have been," Ishmael said. "That's soldier's humour for you."

"What does Kol Khara mean?" Tashué asked, kicking off his boots. They were still wet, and the borrowed socks were soaked and bloody from the wounds on his feet. "When the Patrollers asked for your name, you said Kol Khara, but I swear I've heard you say that before. Is it someone you know?"

Ishmael laughed, his voice fading. Tired. So tired he was half asleep already. "It means *eat shit*. It's the name I always gave whenever I was in trouble down in the Bay because I didn't want anyone to tell my father I was causing trouble again. Just a habit, I guess."

"Eat shit, hey?"

The mattress was inviting, and the sheets were soft and it sent a pang of guilt through him. Somewhere out there in the wilderness, Stella was sleeping on rocks and open ground, wearing her boots and sheltering in a bedroll. Horses hobbled nearby. Maybe praying for the weather to hold. Was it snowing on her, too?

He wrapped an arm around Ishmael's shoulders out of habit, pulling himself close to Ishmael to leave as much room as he could for Allie on the other side of the bed. Ishmael leaned into him, a sigh unwinding the tension. Allie slipped into the blankets once all the lanterns were out. She stretched out against Tashué's back, their clothes rumpling between them. She pressed her face against his shoulder and breathed out, long and slow, like she'd only been breathing halfway all this time and this was the first time she'd truly exhaled. And it made him ache for Stella even more.

"I'm glad you didn't die, Tashué," she said into the darkness. "I've grown rather fond of you. I think Miss Whiterock would be disappointed with us both if you didn't survive all this."

Tashué wanted to say something, but the trembling set itself in his hands. The stillness and the darkness left too much room to be aware of what had happened. New wounds lay across the old ones, new bruises setting beneath his skin.

And his Talent, this beast he'd been hiding from all his life—those people in the forest—it didn't matter how many times he told himself that it was them or him, that he was defending himself and Ishmael from their would-be murderers, his Talent twisted over the sound of those bones collapsing, again and again until it took up permanent residence in his the core of him. He could almost feel it, the cartilage in his joints trembling, the fibre of his own bones shivering sympathetic dread.

Ishmael shifted slowly, turning toward Tashué. He caught Tashué's hands and squeezed them, avoiding all the places that were still trying to heal. He didn't say anything. He held Tashué's trembling hands in both of his, bearing witness to the shift happening, lacing their fingers together so Tashué knew he wasn't alone. Allie was asleep already—he could hear the pattern of her breathing behind his back, low and heavy, her fingers twitching against his side in response to whatever dream had her.

"They were going to kill you," Tashué said.

"Yeah, they were," Ishmael whispered. "You, too. You saved us when I couldn't."

"From the mess *I* made."

"Yeah, well, that's why you're going to listen to me from now on. Maybe we can get through this with fewer messes like that."

Tashué nodded, squeezing his eyes shut, surrendering the whole world.

"Been a while for you, hey?" Ishmael asked. "Since your last big mess."

"It's not that. I never…"

"Never thought you'd make trees explode?"

"Yeah."

Ishmael nodded—Tashué heard it and felt it, the shift of his head against the pillow, the scrap of his hair on the linen. "What's it like?"

"It feels like…" The ache in Tashué's skull rang insistently, like his Talent was pushing against the self-imposed vise he made to keep it under control. "It feels like too much. Too much awareness, too much memory. I can feel the people I killed like they're trapped inside me. If I let go, I can feel the whole fucking city, grinding against me."

"We'll find someone who can teach you how to use it. After some sleep."

"Sure."

It was a relief, an exhale. The words had unwound the tension in him, and it didn't sit so acidic in his veins anymore. Saying it out loud took the power out of his fear. It was a new part of his life, and he'd figure it out if they lived long enough.

He dreamt of Stella.

24

TASHUÉ
DAY 34

He dreamt of the house in Cruinnich. Of soft rugs and long hallways and double-paned windows that let the sunlight stream in. Of wooden bannisters and white-painted crown molding, of paintings and photographs hanging from every spare space, turning each wall into a scattered collage of art and life captured in still moments.

Stella sat on the floor, on the soft pile of the rug, toys scattered all around her, wooden things in the shapes of animals and trains, so much like all the toys Tashué had in his childhood, all the toys he'd bought for Jason before Jason even existed, and now they sat in Jason's empty room. Toys that were well made and well loved. For a time.

"Tashué," she said, her voice such a cascade of emotion that it made Tashué crumble at the edges. She reached for him, trembling fingers touching his cheek, running through his beard. "Are you really here?"

He caught her hand and pressed a kiss into her palm. Her clothes were so beautiful. White lace sat delicately on her neck, on her shoulders, her hair braided and curled and piled atop her head with combs, jewels, pins. Copper curls, shining in the sunlight that came in the windows.

His hands were filthy. Blood from his wounds, mud from the forest. Stella's stitches still held the wound on the side of his hand together. He wore his ruined dress greens, the wool ragged. He half expected to see smears of mud on the rug beneath him, but he didn't seem to be leaving a trace of himself in her clean house.

"Where is 'here?'" he asked. "Isn't this a dream?"

"It is." She looked down at the rug, at the toys. "I have this dream often. No matter how long I called myself Stella, Ffyanwy's life follows me everywhere. As it should. I wouldn't ever want to forget, but..." She picked up one of the toys, a lion, its mane carved in loving detail. She passed it back and forth between her hands like she was testing the weight of it in her dream. Her movements were slow and strained, like maybe it weighed too much. She looked up at him again, studying like she didn't believe he was really here with her. "What happened? We felt you quicken. We wondered if it had killed you."

"The Authority came for me. They had these." He offered her the badge he'd taken from the leader of the group. The dream of it carried the same amount of weight it had in real life. It reflected the light of General Wolfe's fire, like that image of it was the only way he could conjure it.

"Enquiry," Stella said, leaning away from it, her nose wrinkling in distaste. "They found you?"

"I made myself too easy to find by being stupid." He closed his fist around the badge. "My Talent saved me. And now... I don't know."

A small noise like an interrupted sob jumped from her throat. She caught the front of his waistcoat with both hands and dragged him against her. She kissed him hard, with urgency and desperation, her lips hungry and her body trembling. He wrapped his arms around her, kissing her back. Having her in his arms again felt like the healing of a wound—he'd been bleeding since she left and holding her again stemmed the flow. It had only been a few days. It had been an eternity.

She broke the kiss, craning her head back to look him in the eye. "You aren't allowed to die, Tashué Blackwood. I can't do this without you. Please. You don't get to leave me in the wreckage of all this, not after the promises you made."

He kissed her again. It was the only thing he could do. He wanted to offer her some sliver of comfort, but he didn't know how to promise he'd be fine when he held the bronze badge from the man who tried to kill him. Fuck Rainer. Tashué wouldn't stop until the bastard was dead—but what room did that leave for him to make any promises to her?

The innocent, beautiful sound of a toddler babbling to his toys interrupted before Tashué could find any words. A boy sat amongst the toys.

If Tashué had to guess, he'd say the boy was about two, or near enough to it. The boy played with a set of wooden keys on a ring—one of the keys wet with drool and dented with tiny teeth marks. His hair was growing into bright red corkscrew curls that bounced when he shook the keys. He'd seen this child in Stella's thoughts once before—when Rhodrishi was healing her and the three of them bled into each other through their Talents.

"Is this your son?"

She nodded. Her fingers slid over his curls, but not through them. She knew better than to try, clearly. The corkscrew curls were inviting, but a trap.

"He's beautiful, Stella."

She forced a tired, pained smile. Her face was younger than Tashué ever saw it, but there was an old bruise all along the left side of her jaw. Fading into her complexion but still just visible. He hadn't noticed it before—had it materialized into the dream in the same way as her son, the same as the badge?

"I'm not Stella yet," she said. "In this dream, my name is still Ffyanwy."

"Ffyanwy," he echoed. He'd only said that name a few times, back when she was still in Yaelsmuir. Back when she told him everything.

The smile again, a little stronger than before, but still tired. "I like hearing you say my name. I didn't realize before how much I missed *being* Ffyanwy. Even though everything had become so painful."

Her son started babbling before he could say, knocking the wooden keys against the floor. She turned the wooden lion over in her hands a few times, watching her son play. "He liked the rattles best. And the animals. He liked it when we made animal sounds. It was the one and only thing Bothain was good at. Getting down on the floor and playing with him. We didn't have keys like those, though. They exist only in my dreams, as if my mind won't let me forget that he went to the Keeper of the Keys so young."

"What's his name?" Tashué asked, catching one of her stray hairs and wrapping it around his finger. His hands didn't leave a single grain of dirt on her, as if his dream knew that this mess was his alone.

"Rhion," she said, the name escaping like a held breath. "Bothain wanted a Fuar name, but I fought for Rhion. My grandfather's name—it's such a common name out west, but it meant so much. That was the last battle I won, I think. Giving my son the name that he deserved. And this day that we're seeing, it's the last good memory before Rhion died. I put him to bed after this, not knowing that it would be the last time he played with his toys. And Siras—he ruined this gown with his filthy hands." She touched the lace over her chest, fingers running across the delicate pattern of flowers and filigree. "I can't remember if those memories were both the same night, or if my dreams push these things together. I don't think I would wear white lace to sit on the floor and play with my son. His hands were always so sticky. The staff were always giving him snacks—it was the only thing that distracted him from his own temper. I wore this to a formal event for the hospital. I only got to wear it once before Siras... But maybe the event was the same day... I don't remember. It was all so long ago. A different life." She turned to Tashué, eyes searching his face. "Where are you? Are you safe? Ozra said you were in the Dunnenbrahl."

"Ozra?"

She waved her hand. "It's a long story. Are you safe? Please, can you tell me you're safe?"

"I was in the Dunnenbrahl when I quickened—that's where they took us, me and Ishmael. I don't know if I can say I'm safe with everything... We're in the Bay. I'm going to go find Davik."

"Davik?" she echoed.

Tashué nodded. "I don't have a choice but to stand with him a while. And then... I don't know. Powell and Ishmael will take care of it."

She bit her lip, tears gathering in her eyes again. She kissed him, more slowly than before, like she was savouring the moment. When she broke away, he cupped her face with both his hands, kissing the tear tracks on her cheeks. The salt on his lips tasted so real. Her son shook his keys harder, drawing both of their attention. Rhion put his fingers in his mouth, chewing on them with his back gums. He must have new teeth coming in.

"Davik's always been good at that," she said, wiping her cheeks. "At placing himself in the middle of things, at making himself seem indispensable. He can manipulate emotions to make you feel safe with him."

Something that felt an awful lot like shame twisted in his chest. She'd missed what he meant when he said *Powell and Ishmael will take care of it*, and he couldn't bring himself to clarify. She'd sounded so angry the last time they'd talked about Davik, but this time something had changed.

"Is that what he did to you?" he asked, even though he wasn't sure he wanted to know the answer. He was planning to be at least complicit in this man's murder. How well did Stella—Ffyanwy?—know him? When Tashué told her he'd killed Edgar Hale, she'd simply said 'good.' Would she react the same way when he told her about Davik Kaine?

"In the beginning?" she said, her eyes turning up to the nearest window like she could see through it to the past. "No. At first we were just young and attracted to each other. We grew up together, the three of us. My mother struggled with her health since she was young, so she had a healer live with us permanently. Her daughter, Kona..." She shrugged. "Life was almost innocent in those days. It didn't start until he came back from Teshii. He went off to business school to try to save Kaine Brick, but there was no saving it. So much changed while he was gone. For all of us."

Little Rhion pushed himself up. It was a slow thing, watching the toddler put his hands into the rug first, and then get his feet under him, and then up, up. He came across the room, shaking his keys, his fingers in his mouth. Chewing on them with those sore gums, drool dripping from his chin.

"I missed this age with Jason," Tashué said softly. He slid his hand across the beautiful red curls, softer than threads of silk. The years he'd missed ached like a festering wound that refused to heal. How old was Jason when he cut his first teeth? Did they come in slowly, or a bunch at once? He'd never know. Jason couldn't possibly answer, and Keoh was gone. And he'd held a grudge so long that he hadn't asked her while she was alive. "This was about the age Tevir was when I met him. Kaz's son. He was smaller, I think. But wound up like a spring, all the time. So much energy it spilt out of him, all over the place."

"That's my Rhion," she said. Rhion walked between him and Stella. No, Ffyanwy. Rhion clambered into Ffyanwy's lap. She wiped the drool off his chin with a practiced swipe and wrapped her arms around him. She kissed his face, his hair. "He was always so surly. I think his Talent was hurting him, from the very beginning. I wish I'd known."

"I don't understand any of this," Tashué said, shaking his head. "I've never shared dreams with people before."

"It's our Talent, drawing us together. Kona called it walking the dreampath. Now that your Talent is quickened fully, we can see each other and feel each other."

She reached for him again, dragging him closer. They squished Rhion between them in spite of his squirming, and she kissed Tashué again. Every time her lips touched him, the ugly things inside of him healed just a little more. But even the healing hurt—he was responsible for so much pain. Maybe he deserved all these wounds. All this shame.

"I need to help Ishmael. His knee—the Enquiry Officer dislocated it. We need to get moving, but I have no idea what I'm doing. I don't want to make it worse."

Rhion squirmed, fussing, his voice thin and impatient. She kissed the top of his head, her brow furrowing with her pensiveness.

"It's not as complicated as the Authority makes it out to be. Some things are dangerous, yes—disease, infection, these things are precarious to draw out, and that part does require training to know how to do it carefully. There's a risk of pulling the infection into the healer. Bones can't be rushed much, or they never heal properly, and the patient will be in pain for the rest of their life. The brain is the most complicated. But tissue problems are the easiest—open wounds or pulled ligaments. It's a matter of speeding the natural process. The trick is not to force it or try to impose your will on the wound. The body knows what to do."

"How?"

Stella sighed, taking Tashué's hand and pulling it into her lap. Her finger traced the edge of the wound, the same one she stitched shut after the Market fire. "First you know the body. And then you understand the damage. Sink your Talent into the shape of it, and understand every fibre of it. It's going to hurt. Your body is going to try to tell you that all that pain is yours."

Tashué nodded. "I've done that. My Talent did that without me even trying."

She nodded. "Good. It knows already—your mother was a healer?"

"She was. Does it matter? Is the shape of Talent hereditary?"

"No... but also yes. Talent is hereditary, and the inherent strength of it. In theory it's a blank slate, and we can use it however we want, but at the same time, it seems to... remember. No one I've ever spoken to knew for certain if we're predisposed to things because they were in the lines of our family or if these things come up in us because we're exposed to it as we grow. Your mother was a healer, so it's possible your Talent knows already how it's done. Kona seemed to think our Talent is shaped by those that come before us because we're connected to them and our Talents remember them." She let go of his hand, leaning low over Rhion and planting a kiss in his downy soft curls. He shook his keys at her, the sound like a rattle of old bone instead of wood. "You feel it, and you see it, and you know the edges of it. But you don't try to change it. Trying to fuse the bone or knit the flesh yourself with Talent is how you make bones that never feel like they've healed, or wounds that burst open because the scar tissue is too fragile. It's more like… you wash energy through it. Imagine your willpower is a river that flows through every tissue that isn't as it should be, and that energy becomes fuel for the body to do what comes naturally. The body heals itself. You only help."

Rhion squirmed against her, cutting her off with his twisting, fussing, his free hand tugging at his ear, his other hand clutching the key ring so tightly that his fat little knuckles were turning white.

"Don't go yet, my sweet boy," Ffyanwy whispered. "I still have the whole day with you."

He calmed in Ffyanwy's lap, putting the keys in his mouth again. But the sound of him crying hadn't gone away. It was echoing through the house, his terrible screaming, distant and quiet but so painful. It made Tashué's chest tight, that sound. It reminded him so much of Jason as an infant, before Tashué left Jason and Keoh behind for one last deployment. What could Jason and Rhion have in common that it made them both scream like that? He hadn't heard pain so intense in most of the other children he'd known. Colic didn't sound this bad. Teething didn't reach such a shattering, desperate pitch.

Was it their Talent, like she said? Was Jason's Talent hurting him back then, when he screamed until Tashué could swear the window panes were rattling, and Keoh sobbed as Tashué tried to comfort them both?

Tashué reached out, taking Rhion's little feet in his hands, pressing his thumb into the soft sole. Warm and pliant, skin that hadn't had time to make calluses yet. He wished there was something more he could do. Could he change the dream for her? If he exerted enough willpower, could he make the memory of the crying stop, so that she could enjoy a moment in the afternoon sun with her son?

Rhion's cries got louder. Stronger. It didn't seem possible, but the sound of it became a nail directly into Tashué's skull. Wailing, screeching. Ffyanwy's face was streaked with tears. She held Rhion against her shoulder, cradling his head, fingers in his hair, kissing his face.

And Bothain's panicked voice came from somewhere in the house. Tashué had never heard it before, and yet he knew. "Do something—Ffyanwy, do something!"

She shook her head, meeting Tashué's eye. She looked so tired, the grief stripping her back to bare bones and raw nerves. "I tried everything

—there's nothing I could have done. You can't stop a quickening once it begins. I'm sure you know, after what you went through. Imagine trying to bring that to a stop. It doesn't usually start so young, and his body couldn't handle it. If I'd known it was going to come so soon, and so terribly, I could have knotted his Talent until he was old enough and strong enough to survive it. Kona taught me how—we did it together, to help people hide from the Authority. That's how I knew to do it for Ceridwen when I took her."

Darkness crawled through the room, erasing the toys on the floor and the sun-kissed windows of the sitting room; they were in the nursery instead, Rhion's crib in a corner, but Ffyanwy was still clutching him. And Rhion's Talent swirled in the room like a maelstrom, a vicious hurricane—Tashué couldn't feel it, but he could see it, twisting and writhing in the darkness. Bothain was in the room, naked to the waist, clammy with sweat, wild with panic—

"Ffyanwy, what's happening to him? Do something! Why aren't you doing anything!"

Ffyanwy held Tashué's gaze, tears dripping from her chin into Rhion's hair. "I tried. I tried everything. If only Kona was there, maybe she would have known what to do, but Bothain hated Kona. He was always so furious when she came into our house, so she stopped coming to try to keep the peace. But there would never be peace, not in this house. Not with him."

Tashué caught her face. He couldn't bear it, watching her cry, her words slipping toward blaming herself. He kissed her tears, her cheeks, her lips, kissing the top of Rhion's head—he could smell Rhion's hair, that specific scent that young children always had, and the salt of Ffyanwy's tears, and the panic-sweat that coated her body.

"You can't leave me," she said, catching Tashué's coat with one hand. "I can't lose you, too. You have to survive."

"I'll try."

She leaned away from him, shaking her head, baring her teeth in a snarl, temper rising. "That's not good enough, Tashué!"

"What do you want me to do?" Tashué asked. "Make promises I can't keep? Tell you a lie? I don't know what's going to happen here. Davik and Powell and Bothain and Rainer—they're going to rip apart the city. I'm going to do everything in my power to rip it apart, too. Ishmael thinks it'll come to civil war. I have to fight. I have to see this through. For the children."

She looked over her shoulder at Bothain, at his looming figure, a shadow in the dark room, blond hair glinting. "Bothain is in Yaelsmuir?"

"He is," Tashué said. "I'm sorry—you were right to run." Even as he said it, the words felt like a lie. He never should have let her go.

She clutched Rhion closer, squeezing him hard as the maelstrom of Rhion's Talent and Bothain's panic twisted around them. "Tashué—don't trust Davik."

"I *don't*," Tashué said, but he didn't know what else to say. To tell her that Davik was as good as dead seemed too cruel in the midst of this dream of loss.

"But you will." She looked him dead in the eye, desperation making her lean even closer. "One day soon, you just *will*, and you won't know what's changed. You won't question it, either. That's what he does. No matter what's happening, no matter what deals he makes with you—try to remember that I told you not to trust Davik Kaine."

The house disintegrated. Rhion went silent—disappeared. They were sitting in the darkness, the quiet. The clean plaster walls were replaced by the trailing boughs of a willow tree, the art replaced by a clothes line, strung between the branches, the floor replaced by the hard ground and the form of people sleeping in bedrolls. She was Stella again, or at least the woman he knew. Older, with dark circles beneath her eyes. It was that look of exhaustion that drew him to her when he met Ceridwen. The way Stella sat on the steps of her building, watching Ceridwen play in the street, looking like she could just as soon sleep on the stairs. But Ceridwen's joy made her smile, and he knew what it was like to be so tired but so completely enraptured by a child. He felt drawn to that exhaustion and that joy.

She was hovering somewhere between dream and wakefulness, but Tashué could feel her holding on to him, clinging to the moment. She reached out to him again and kissed him, but the feeling of her was like the mist that clung to the ground on a cold autumn morning.

And then—fear. He could taste it in the air, bitter as smoke. Her fear. He looked into the crumbling dream and saw a figure of a man—a tangle of red hair and a dirty blue bowler. A scar across his lip and another on his eyebrow.

"Siras," Stella said.

The dream dissolved completely—she'd woken up, leaving him drifting in his own sleep. The figure of Siras lingered in the corner of his vision, never close enough for him to see clearly, but always a little bit there.

Ishmael moved restlessly in his sleep, groaning with pain, waking Tashué completely. He lay in the big bed in Cattle Bone Bay, Ishmael and Allie on either side of him. Panic made his heart hammer but he couldn't move without disturbing Ishmael and Allie. Had he really seen Stella? And Siras, for that matter?

His Talent swirled around him like a tired, twisting stream, dragging too many details to his awareness. Downstairs, the warehouse was bustling. Outside the walls, the city was awake and trying to get things done. It seemed less insistent than yesterday, like sleeping had taken the sharpness out of his senses, but the onslaught of it all still made his ears buzz. Adley told him the source of his Talent was somewhere in his mind —if he put pressure on it, he could stop it from bleeding everywhere. He tried to summon the feeling of the suppression headache, the one that brought such stillness to his head, it made his ears ring. The layers of awareness fell away slowly. The warehouse, the nearby river became more distant. Until finally he couldn't hear them at all. His awareness shrank to this room—three heartbeats and the conflicting rhythms of their breathing. The half-healed bruise around Allie's neck from the night Enquiry came for her. All of Ishmael's wounds, ugly and swollen. Tashué's body, battered by everything. His feet ached and his ribs hurt where the stitches pulled, but Ishmael was plenty reminder that it could have been much worse. It seemed horribly unfair that Ishmael was worse off than Tashué. He was only involved by accident, because of his loyalty.

Tashué moved slowly to try not to disturb either of them, but the only way to get out of bed was to climb over one of them. At least he'd been intimate with Ishmael before, so climbing over him didn't feel so much like an invasion. Ishmael groaned again, half waking, shifting, pushing Tashué away. Then rolling into the big empty space Tashué left in the bed.

Tashué rested his weight slowly on his feet, and the pain wasn't as confronting as he expected it would be. Still, he padded slowly to the wood stove, the floor cold against his wounds. The fire had died while they were sleeping, leaving the office-apartment brutally cold. The process of getting a new fire going gave him something to do with his hands as he waited for the last of the tremble to leave, while as he worked on cutting more layers away, until he was alone in his head. He was still too aware of his own body, of the feeling of his blood pumping, of the edges of his own wounds. But at least was only his pain, now. His heartbeat. If he had cigarillos, a smoke would make him feel more like himself, but his case was ruined and the cigarillos inside had been soaked by the rain, so he left them behind at Wolfe's house.

Tashué—don't trust Davik.

Tashué sighed, feeding kindling into the small flames in the firebox. Was it a dream, or had he really seen her? When she kissed him, did she feel it, too? There was so much about Talent he didn't understand. But that advice, *don't trust Davik*, seemed to go without saying. He wondered why she was so insistent.

Ishmael groaned again in his sleep, shifting under the blankets, searching for a comfortable position. His knee probably wouldn't let him find one—he probably hadn't fallen into a deep, restful sleep. Tashué closed the wood stove door, the hinges giving the angry squeal of iron that wasn't used enough. He dragged the chair through the apartment, positioning it at the edge of the bed so he could sit. Ishmael and Allie had shifted closer to each other, and Ishmael had draped an arm around Allie in some instinct that always drove him to pull people against him, like only when his skin touched someone else did he truly know peace. Allie's hair made a great black curtain over her pillow, trailing close to Ishmael's face. He wanted to let them sleep forever, the pair of them, swallowed by the big bed and the thick blankets, beautiful and safe. But it wasn't his decision to make, and neither of them wanted to be safe.

He pushed the blanket back slowly, a small increment at a time, until Ishmael's leg was uncovered. Ishmael had kicked off his trousers at some point, although Tashué couldn't remember if he'd done that before they climbed into the bed or some time later. The bandages that Cook had wrapped around the knee were tied so expertly that they looked like they'd hold into the next century. Awareness of the wounds on Ishmael's body pulsed across Tashué's sense. He probably didn't need to touch Ishmael to heal him, not with the way his Talent spread so far, but he did anyway. Now that he had it under control, he didn't want to let go of it again. He slid his hands carefully up Ishmael's leg, coming to the knee as gently as he could. It only took the slightest consideration to turn the full attention of his Talent to the wound, like it had only been waiting for permission—thinking about it like a separate and sentient being that shared his consciousness only resurrected the feeling of panic, but he pushed it away with all the stubbornness that saw him through everything else he'd been afraid of in his life.

The swelling in the ligaments and muscles was vicious and angry, radiating hot pain. Images flashed through his mind that didn't belong to him—Ishmael's dreams. An apartment in a desert city, sandstone walls and big windows that were shaded by a bright blue awning. The heat so thick he could see it dancing off the street below. A man by the window, desert wind in his salt and pepper hair, sweat beading down the muscles of his bare back, dancing in old scars like little clear jewels. Drinking coffee from delicate bone porcelain.

Tashué tried to ignore those images, those private thoughts. Maybe he should have asked Ishmael before starting this. He should have known he would see things that weren't for him, but in his eagerness to help fix the damage he'd caused, he'd forgotten.

Ishmael rolled toward him, eyes cracking open, his face passing through slow stages of pain and waking up. Tashué pulled his hands away, trying to pull his Talent out of Ishmael's body, too, but it hung on like it was resentful of being interrupted.

"Sorry," Tashué said. "I thought I'd try…"

"You think you can heal it?" Ishmael asked.

Tashué nodded. "A little bit, at least. To get the process started."

Ishmael pushed himself up on his elbows, watching Tashué for a long time. "You've always been the sort that tries to run before you even learn how to walk."

Tashué shrugged, leaning farther back on his chair and crossing his arms over his chest. Images of the man standing by the window lingered in the air between them, like they had become an impression on Tashué's Talent. Who was he? There was so much about Ishmael's life that Tashué didn't know.

"Seems like a stupid time to be afraid of the tools we have," Tashué said finally. *Afraid* was too small a word for the terror, for the vicious and ugly shame that lived beside the memory of turning two people to dust and pulp. But maybe if he used this incredible force to heal bodies instead of destroying them, it would take the last layers of guilt out of him. "If we're going to do this, it's ridiculous to keep hiding from my own Talent. Right?"

"Sure," Ishmael said. "Yeah. Deri's healer—he taught me how to feel Talent—he said anyone can learn to use Talent if they try hard enough.

Not strong enough to become healers, but little things. You ever hear that?"

Tashué shook his head.

"Makes a kind of sense, I guess. It's willpower, right? I had to learn how to feel it. Deri insisted. But I never took it further than that. It all seemed like too much concentrating, too much internal shit. Maybe I should have done it. But then, Deri didn't learn, either. There's something a little bit terrifying about knowing what we can do. Especially when you don't *want* to be the kind of person who's good at destroying things. That always fucked me up. I wanted to believe we were building toward a better future in the division, but the reality was that we were destroying the present in the hopes that something better would build itself."

Tashué pulled the bandages into place, smoothing them out so they lay flat again. "Who's Deri?"

"My General," Ishmael said. "My handler. He trained me. That was before he was promoted to General, but I think his favourite pastime was being smug about being better than me, so he kept it up even after he was promoted."

Tashué glanced over at Allie—she was still sleeping, the blankets pulled all the way up to her eyes, almost completely swallowing her. But Ishmael was watching him like he was waiting for a reaction. "I thought Wolfe managed your career?"

Ishmael smiled, thin and hollow. "Everyone in Yaelsmuir seems to think that. But no—he doesn't have any say over diplomatic division. I live there with him. He pulled me out of a gutter after my parents died. I think he needed someone to frown paternally at after his son died and his daughter left. And I needed someone to keep me halfway sane when I was home from deployment."

"I've never heard you say anything so… specific about the division," Tashué said softly.

Ishmael shrugged, sinking back down and resting his head on his pillow. "It's treason. For me to say it, and for you to hear it. But we're insurrectionists now anyway, so what are they going to do? Kill us twice?"

Tashué slid his hands up Ishmael's leg again. The lines of the mountain tattoo crawled down to his mangled knee. He remembered when Ishmael came back with the tattoo still healing, black scabs coming off in crusty lines. That was the first time they really hurt each other, because

Ishmael was angry and desperate, but he couldn't talk about any of the things that were eating him alive. So instead, he took a swing at Tashué when they were both drinking, and Tashué had never mastered the art of walking away from a fight. Like an idiot, he tried to restrain Ishmael, and that's when he learned how *skilled* Ishmael was at causing pain.

They still fucked after, though. Because sometimes, Tashué gloried in his own anger as much as Ishmael did.

"Do you want me to try?" Tashué asked. Allie would wake up soon. They had to get ready to move. "See if I can make it a bit better?"

Ishmael nodded. "Better you than Adley."

Tashué only had time to blink before his Talent moved like it knew his intention, acting in the way Stella instructed. His willpower was a river that flooded every fibre of Ishmael's muscle, every band of tendon and ligament, every angry nerve. Even the ink, black lines buried shallow in the skin. He could see Ishmael's body doing all the things it took to repair damage. Redistributing fluid, rebuilding tissue—faster and faster until Ishmael jerked, gasping, his body going tense, the pain rattling the air around them, building its intensity until it felt like the muscles were tearing all over again. Ishmael whimpered, his voice trembling, pushing himself up onto one elbow, reaching for his knee, grabbing Tashué's wrist and squeezing so hard Tashué could swear he felt his bones grind together. Or maybe that was the memory of him grinding his enemy's bones. It must have woken Allie—she reached out and put a hand on Ishmael's shoulder. He grabbed her hand, his loose sleeve falling down far enough to show the watch tattoo on his forearm. And Ishmael's thoughts clung to the image of the man Tashué had seen in Ishmael's dream, using it like a photograph to focus on, a life raft to keep himself from drowning in the pain. Both of them on the roof in a desert city, watching the sun set into the Black Mountains, the wind cooling the sweat on their bodies. Deri, maybe.

And Tashué hung on to Stella. The memory of her lying on top of him in his bedroom. Her skin turned to ivory as the darkness washed all the colour out of the world.

Do you feel their pain, when you take it from them? he'd asked.

All of it. Every broken bone, every wasting disease. There are days when I feel my body could buckle beneath it all, as if it would crush me and I would cease to exist. I would only be a storm of pain, like a hurricane drifting across the ocean.

The flow of his own Talent thickened to a reluctant sludge—or maybe that was Ishmael's body, resisting the stream of it. He'd pushed the healing as far as it would go, maybe. He let go of all that energy, hands trembling with the exertion and pain. But it was better. A few days' worth of healing, crammed into the space between seconds.

"Fuck," Ishmael breathed, sagging back against the bed. "Was it as good for you as it was for me?"

Tashué laughed again. "Fucking terrible. Every second of it."

"Thank fuck for that."

"Healing on your first day after your Talent quickened?" Allie said. "I'm starting to think you're an overachiever, Tashué."

"Does it even count as over-achieving if I didn't quicken until my forties?"

Footsteps on the stairs. Tashué's Talent billowed out, toward the sound—Vasska. He'd come back alone. Tashué didn't want to hear Vasska's heartbeat and the gurgle of his stomach and the rush of air into his lungs. He pulled that curtain closed again, the one that kept his Talent under control, the headache settling into place. Was this his whole life now? Willingly setting a vise into his own skull to keep himself contained?

Vasska let himself in, standing awkwardly near the stove and blushing furiously at Allie as she rolled out of bed, running her fingers through her hair to comb the tangles out. She'd slept in her trousers and her shirt, but still the sight of her looking so disheveled apparently turned Vasska into half a mess.

"I thought you would appreciate a bit of help getting down to the pugilist club," Vasska said. "Since I don't think Mr. Saeati can walk all that way, and I'm reasonably sure you won't be interested in taking the tram. I also brought crutches and a cane, depending on how he's feeling. And breakfast. I didn't think there was any food left in this old office."

"Thank you, Vasska," Ishmael said, rolling slowly from the bed. "We're ready to go, then?"

25

JASON
DAY 34

"Is it true?" Jason asked. He stood in the visitation room, watching Lorne. Maybe he should have greeted the love of his life with something a little bit less aggressive, but the rumours that had been bouncing around the Rift about Tashué were driving Jason out of his mind. "About my father—is it true?"

Lorne sighed, his shoulders sagging. Only belatedly did Jason notice Lorne had a new coat. It looked incredible on him. Creamy white leather and perfectly lush fleece at the collar and cuff—and a decent suit underneath it for the first time since... ever. And maybe it was worth mentioning. The coat, his new clothes. But all Jason could think about was the rumours.

Lorne fiddled with the buttons down the front of the coat. "I've been trying to figure out how to break it to you gently..."

Jason shook his head. Sweet North Star, he'd prayed it wasn't true, but Lorne's response squeezed the last bit of hope out of him. "A tinman getting himself arrested is popular gossip in a place like this." His voice trembled more than he would like to admit, but more than a few people had been speculating gleefully about whether or not Tashué Blackwood was dead. "It's true? That's why you wanted to break it to me gently?"

"Jason," Lorne said. "Sit down."

The whole world tilted to one side, throwing him off balance. Words failed. Jason stared through the grate at Lorne, frozen by his disbelief, numb. For now. Somewhere in his mind there was an awareness that he would *feel* this later and it would fucking hurt worse than anything he'd ever faced, but for now it was a dull buzzing through his senses. His mind trying, and failing, to grasp words.

"Jason," Lorne said again. How long had Jason been standing there, frozen in the moment before the pain landed? "Hey, look at me. Please? Just look at me and take a breath."

Jason pushed his hands into his hair, pulling hard at the roots so he could focus on something less all-consuming than the buzz of almost-rooted panic. The sharpness of it was simpler. Hot and immediate making it easier to deal with than the yawning pit of terror he'd been dodging since the moment he'd heard the first rumour. Sometime yesterday, just before evening. And then the rumours got worse at morning shift change. Nothing had managed to make him feel the crushing weight of being incarcerated like facing the fact that both of his parents were gone, and there was nothing he could do. There would be no funeral for him to attend, no community that would close around him. He was *here*, and they were gone.

"I'm going to die here." The words leapt out of him so fast he didn't even feel them coming. "I can't—I won't—I'm going to die here and nothing can save me."

Lorne dragged his chair out with a clatter so loud it made Jason flinch. Lorne stepped onto the seat, using it as a stool to climb right up onto the table. He pressed his hands against the grate. "Come here. Come up here and put your hands on mine and breathe. Please?"

Jason took a slow breath, forcing movement from his body. If he couldn't think or feel, at least he could touch Lorne. He climbed up onto the table. Their heads almost scraped the stone ceiling and all the heat from the oil lamps gathered up here with the smoke, making Jason's eyes itchy and watery. But he pressed his hands against Lorne's palms. He wanted to curl his fingers against Lorne's so they were holding hands, but the grate stopped him. Still, Lorne's warmth and solidness through the metal grate made breathing easier. He wondered why no one had thought of it sooner. Except someone *had* thought of it. His father pressed his hand against the grate like he wished he could reach right through. That was the last time they saw each other, the day his father got banned for smashing the chair against the grate and punching a guard. Maybe his father had wished that Jason would press his hand against the other side. Jason should have done it back when he had the chance. Sweet North Star, that might have been his last chance to touch his father, and he'd missed it because he was angry. Furious, hopeless, alone—taking it all out on his father. How alike they were after all.

"You're not going to die in here," Lorne said with perfect confidence. "Listen—"

"Is he dead?" Jason interrupted. "Everyone's saying he's dead. Those are just rumours, right? He's just been arrested. Tell me he's been arrested, and he's fine."

A vicious, ugly, selfish hope burned through him. He wouldn't wish the Rift on anyone, and yet... If his father had been arrested by the Authority and he had Talent, that should mean his father would come *here*. They could hug again. Jason could lose himself in those giant arms, in that crushing hug. North Star save him, he'd give anything to hug his father again.

"He's missing," Lorne said slowly, speaking so carefully Jason knew it meant more, but Lorne couldn't commit to the words. "He never turned up at the jail. The Patrollers who arrested him and Ishmael were found dead in the Dunnenbrahl. No one has any idea what happened. Not yet."

Jason took a slow breath, resting his forehead against the grate. "The bastard."

Lorne rested his forehead against Jason's, and that felt even better than pressing their hands together. "I know."

"Ishmael too?"

"Yeah," Lorne said softly. "Ishmael too. I didn't know they were... close."

Jason shrugged. "They were... messy. Mostly I remember them fighting. Probably because my father doesn't listen to people. He hears what he wants to hear and then makes decisions from there. They were arrested together?"

Lorne nodded.

"Why? Why did they...?"

Lorne sighed—and then started talking. The whole horrible story unfolded in the thick smoke-smelling air around their heads, each word slicing Jason open like a fresh wound. The girl from the river—the one his father had asked Jason about, the one with the tattoo on her neck—was mutilated by the Authority. An energy unit. At some point, Jason had to stop thinking about it. He had to stop absorbing the words and look at Lorne. He hadn't shaved since the fight that fucked up his face, and his facial hair grew in on his cheeks, on his chin. Watching Lorne put his body through such punishment made being in here worse. If Jason hadn't been arrested and sent here, would he know how to heal by now? What was his Talent even capable of? Except the cuts were well sealed and not much more than vivid pink weals, and the blood in the white of his eye had dissipated. It was more healing than the ten days since the fight should have allowed. Someone had been helping the process along.

"Your face looks better," Jason said, just to talk about something other than energy units. What horrible, ugly words for describing children.

Lorne touched his lip, where the scab was peeling away to reveal freshly healed skin.

"Yeah. Iwan sent me to be the Bay's first real pugilist. So now I have my own healer and shit. I live in the club with Davik Kaine and his family. It's… weird. But it's good. Which makes it even stranger. Considering everything."

"You're living with Davik Kaine? Is it true he's the leader of the Red Dawn?"

"The official answer is no," Lorne whispered. Not that anyone could hear him from outside. "He's convinced everyone who asks that he's some other Davik Kaine. I don't know how he does it. He can convince people just about anything. He smiles, and he talks with that charming northern accent, and you believe him. But the real answer is yes. He's got the Bay in the palm of his hand, and most of the city doesn't even know it."

Jason nodded, wiping his eyes to try to clear the gritty smoke feeling. It was good for Lorne to finally have a roof to live under, a steady home, and yet it was one more reminder of the life they almost had but lost. Five years, they'd known each other. But now they had known each other longer separated by the grate than they had spent together outside in the full world.

And energy units. That thought rolled through everything, an ugly echo that was trying to shift Jason's relationship with his own emotions. What did his tiny, petty loneliness mean in a world with energy units?

Jason closed his eyes and listened to the sound of Lorne's breathing for a while. It was the sound of comfort. A sound like home felt—making him more complete. But thinking of Lorne only made him think about his father, about the little apartment in the Row with all of his grandparent's things, scattered about like his father was forever holding his breath, waiting for things to go back to the way they used to be. Any day now they'd step through the door beneath the nibu and the apartment would be full to bursting with people.

Had Tashué kept Jason's bedroom in the same state of breath-holding? If he walked out of the Rift and went back to the Row, would he find his room exactly as he left it three years ago? All those wooden toys he loved as a child because the animals fascinated him. When he was older, he loved them still because the art of it inspired him. The ones he played with the most had been worn smooth, but some of them still had the occasional tool mark where the wood had been carved away too deeply, leading Jason to imagine what the process of turning a chunk of wood into a fish looked like. His grandfather made some of them. Were the toys still there?

If his father was dead because the words energy units rightfully drove him out of his mind, Jason would inherit that apartment next. If he ever got out of here, would he hold it as a generational tribute to all the Blackwoods that had lived there before him, or would he want to scrub it clean and start fresh?

It would mean throwing out the bottle of Ladovaugh that sat above the kitchen—Jason's first dram of whisky, which knocked him on his ass and convinced him he wasn't a whisky drinker. And the wardrobe, the one where his father kept his notepads, and all those drawings he did. His father never did anything with them, never framed them or displayed them or sold them. He drew until his sketchbooks were full to bursting with the most incredible art but then he stashed them away. But thinking about getting rid of those things—in this hypothetical situation where Jason was out of the Rift so he could take over the apartment next—felt too much like trying to erase his father from that place, and if he'd really died because he wanted to stand for those children, he deserved someone to remember him.

But maybe none of it would matter, because he was still in here. Maybe everything in that apartment was already gone—how long would the landlady keep Tashué's things once the news broke that Tashué was dead and no one was going to pay rent?

Lorne sighed, shifting, pulling his head back to look Jason in the eye. "Jason—there's something else. Something you should know. Davik wanted me to tell you, but..." He pushed his hands harder against the grate like he could shove right through it. "I can wait if you want. Dav said he's going to get you out, so I can wait 'til you're out."

Jason furrowed his brow, turning to Lorne, searching his face. He had that hard set to his mouth, the one that used to make Jason kiss him to make him relax, except it had been three years since they kissed. "What do you mean? What else has happened? Are you sick—"

"No, it's not me," Lorne said. "It's... are you sure you want to know?"

"You can't do that," Jason gasped. "You can't lay something like that at my feet and then back out because you're too scared to tell me! You can't leave this for me to decide. Just tell me!"

Lorne sighed and sank down, kneeling on the table and unscrewing the bolts that kept the grate in place. "Sure. Fine. But please, don't lose it, alright? I know everything is shit for you but when you lose it, I want to hold you and I can't and it just... I can't breathe when you aren't breathing. So don't stop breathing this time. Please?"

Jason sank down to his knees because he didn't think he could stand another moment, not with all these loaded words that meant nothing. All this dread.

"I have something for you," Lorne went on. "I can't... I can't leave it with you, just in case. We shouldn't have it at all. But Dav wanted me to show you so you understand that he knows how big it all is, and he's serious about getting you out. He's sending someone in, one of his people. You're not going to die here. Dav won't let it happen. He thought you should know about Valen."

"Lorne, would you tell me! What about Valen?"

"I'm trying!" Lorne huffed, pulling the last screw loose and dragging up the grate. "It's easier to show you."

Lorne pulled a piece of paper from his pocket, and Jason's heart skipped a beat. The last time Lorne gave him a paper, it was because his mother had died. So now what? What new, terrible news was coming at him this time? Lorne slid the paper under the grate. Jason hated it for existing. He didn't want it. He didn't have the strength to withstand whatever was coming next. But curiosity made him grab it anyway. He unfolded it, but instead of being hit in the chest, he was mystified. He didn't understand what the code was.

Jason shook his head, looking up at Lorne. "What is this? It's just numbers and dates, I don't—what do the numbers mean?"

"It's a list of all the children living in creche from the year Valen was born," Lorne said slowly. "They'll graduate in the spring. Dav said he doesn't know where they go after that parade so he wants to get them soon."

"Lorne," Jason gasped.

"He's number 27," Lorne continued. "Halfway down the page. 1693-0239-8983—Valen Gian Ly. He's alive, Jason. He's right there. One of Dav's people got the list when they found out you and me were going to be involved with everything Dav is doing. He wanted me to show you so that you *understand* what he's fighting for—your brother is alive. And Dav's hoping that once the Red Dawn gets you out of here, you'll stay here in Yaelsmuir and help him fight. He wants to get into the Breeding Program, get everyone out. He's hoping you'll be able to help."

Jason took a slow breath, but his whole body was trembling. Somehow the thought of his brother hit him harder than the death of his mother. Because the death of his mother was the end of something— she was gone and it was no longer possible to make his peace with her— but news that his brother was *alive* was a precious beginning, a pinprick of hope. But the problem with hope was it made him look at the future and wonder again if he'd ever get out of this fucking place.

"Why me?"

Lorne spread his hands, giving a helpless shrug. "You broke suppression."

Jason touched the numbers on the page, trying to imagine the child they represented. Would Valen look like their mother? Who was his father? How much had he grown since their mother pushed his footprint onto that page? He hadn't seen any children in three years. "He's alive."

"Yes, Jason. He's alive."

"But if he graduates creche in the spring, they'll take him some-where. They'll make him an *energy unit*."

"Yeah," Lorne said.

"So it's true?" Jason's knees ached from kneeling on the table, and his back ached from being so hunched. But he didn't want to climb down because sitting in his chair meant putting more space between his body's and Lorne's, and being so close made it all easier to deal with. "One of Davik's people, she came to me. After. She asked me hypothetically if I would take the chance to get out of here. But it's not hypothetical, is it? There's something…"

Lorne nodded. "Something, yeah. Something real. He's sent Irén Dargis in, and I know he wouldn't toss her in here for a bluff. I don't know what they're going to do, but it's happening soon. That's what you were telling me about, right? The last time I was here, you said there was a way out."

Jason nodded, but even that made him feel small and alone. It was true that someone had approached him, and when he told Lorne about it, he'd said he could tear the Authority apart. But nothing had happened since then, leaving Jason drifting through this place, half connected to reality.

Everything was shit. His father was dead, just like his mother. He'd never get the chance to tell his mother he forgave her, and he'd never get the chance to tell his father he was sorry.

But his brother was still alive. Valen Gian Ly, born in the spring like Jason.

Something to fight for.

26

ILLEA

DAY 34

Eirdis Redbone based her campaign office in Brickheart, even though she lived in Highview now. Even though she could have married Wolfe and moved into his house in Highfield. It was a deliberate part of her image, since the majority of her passionate votes were from the poorer quarters: Brickheart, the Bay, In the Tracks. To set her office in a rich quarter would be seen as abandoning the very people that supported her career, and she would never be the wealthy quarter's candidate. She needed the middle class and poor votes.

The campaign office was pure chaos—a whole block of apartments above a public house turned into work space by cramming writing desks into each room instead of tables and beds and wardrobes. One water closet for the whole floor, and dozens of people flitting back and forth to see to Eirdis's every need and whim.

Illea waded through them all. They had a particular way of moving through the apartments and up and down the hall like there were traffic lanes painted on the floor that only they could see. But Illea's presence created a disruption in the flow, and they jostled each other in their attempt to keep working whilst also getting out of Illea's way. Mallory was with Eirdis already, looking perfectly at home in the chaos. And her worthless brother, Langston, why did *he* come? He didn't usually care for talking about politics. He must have been drawn in by the hope of more scandal. He was probably kicking himself for missing the banquet *and* the hospital opening, and now he would tag along to everything. He flirted rather ineffectually with some of Eirdis's staff, the poor girls dodging his advances with admirable restraint.

"Things are going well now that Miss Rhydderch has gotten involved with the foundation," Mallory said as they closed the distance. Talking about the Uhl factory to pass the time, then. She stood with her back ramrod straight, excessively restrained, even by her standards. Langston wasn't to be trusted, and it must have been strange for her to talk business in front of him. And of course there was the matter of everything that had happened yesterday, which they were supposed to be discussing, but Langston was hovering like a vulture, waiting to snap up scraps of gossip. "Our surveyor missed some signs of high bedrock when we were planning the building site, so Miss Rhydderch has come back down to build the foundation herself. She has such incredible Talent."

"Aelwyd Rhydderch is a force of nature," Eirdis agreed. She looked the same as she always did—primed and ready to talk politics. Illea had only ever seen her let down her guard in private settings with Wolfe, when there was no one else to bear witness to her softer edges. "Will you be using her services for the rail line from Yaelsmuir to Obisza if you get the contract?"

Mallory nodded, catching Illea's hand and kissing her on the cheek by way of greeting. "Our proposition to the Queen's Voting Council included a quote for crushed stone supplied by Rhydderch. I can think of no one better to pair with."

One of Eirdis's aides interrupted, tugging on Eirdis's sleeve. "Forgive me, Miss Redbone, but we should leave for the Market soon while the weather is good."

"What's happening in the Market?" Langston asked.

"Speeches, Langston," Mallory huffed. "This is a political campaign."

"I don't suppose there's been any word about Blackwood?" Eirdis cut in.

Illea nodded. "No concrete news. He's still missing."

"So we're presuming he's still alive somewhere," Mallory said.

Illea sighed. "No, Mallory. We aren't presuming that at all."

"So we carry on, then," Eirdis said, before Illea could elaborate. "I'm not sure how I'll successfully continue opposing the police force when Captain Blackwood is busy demonstrating how valuable unified law enforcement might be."

"One sympathizes with the man, though," Langston said. "How many of us can really say we've never thought about blowing a hole in Rainer's skull at one time or another?"

"Langston," Mallory huffed. "Honestly."

"As objectionable as Langston generally is, this time he's actually right," Illea said.

"Of course I'm right," Langston scoffed.

Illea looked around the office, scanning all the milling faces. "Has the General not yet arrived?"

Eirdis looked up from whatever paper she was signing. "Not yet. I'd thought he would come with you. I've been at the office since last night, haven't seen him since yesterday at the hospital."

Illea shook her head, something cold prickling its way across her scalp. "I saw him last night—he was headed to the jail to see if he could track down Ishmael and Mr. Blackwood. He said he'd come here early—said I should take my leisure arriving. Shall we wait for him, Eirdis?"

Eirdis sighed, going still for a moment. She closed her eyes like she'd blinked but then forgot to open them again. "Would that I could, but I haven't the time to spare."

Illea nodded. "You'll want to try to reduce Blackwood's culpability, in that case. As much as I'm loath to give Langston credit for anything, he's right in this. Blackwood will be somewhat of a folk hero for people in your voting base. How are we expecting the Market to vote?"

"They generally split," Eirdis said.

Illea let her eyes drift over the crowd. There was something comforting about the facelessness of them, the sheer number of them becoming like background noise that had ceased to have any identifiable meaning. "Blackwood will play well for you in the Market, since he was there for so long, fighting the fire. Make sure to mention him as often as possible while you're there today. He's still the man that won the Blackwood Medal for Exceptional Bravery, after all. Brickheart, too—he was from here. I'll expect people will feel kinship to him. For the rest of the city, we can play on what sort of grief and anger must have driven a man —with such an impeccable career!—to be so alienated from the very organization he used to represent. Rainer will try to make him into a villainous thug, but we'll focus on the reasons Blackwood snapped. Make him into a doomed, tragic hero who stood against the incredible injustice Rainer has been committing against the people of this nation and all that."

Someone jostled into the group, carrying a sheaf of papers. Eirdis took them, signed them, and shoved them back into the aide's hands. "A hero who got drunk and threatened to blow open a man's skull in a public space, Illea."

"Eirdis," Illea sighed, "people in Highfield and Highview still indulge in duels. Men waving guns at each other isn't as scandalous as all that."

"Most people in Highfield use proxies now for their duels," Mallory said. "They pay people to wave guns at each other on their behalf."

Illea shook her head. "A distinction without a difference."

"I know you haven't much experience with guns, but I can assure you, there is a *large* difference between waving a gun at another person yourself and paying someone to wave guns for you." Mallory shot a sly glance at her brother. "Isn't that right, Langston?"

Langston rolled his eyes. "I haven't seen you fight any duels lately, Mallory."

"I haven't seen you fight any either," Mallory countered. "In fact, no one's been waving a gun on your behalf since your favourite proxy turned you down. Seems your honour is rather less fragile now that Mr. Dargis refuses to shoot for you."

Langston snorted. "It sounds like you have been keeping a close eye on me."

"Someone needs to supervise you since you insist on carrying on like a spoilt child."

"I think this illustrates my point perfectly," Illea cut in. She plucked a thin pastry off Eirdis's desk. Everything Eirdis had on offer was perfect to snack on while talking and working—tiny morsels, easily eaten in a bite or two, nothing sticky or gummy or especially dry. "Guns are waved for Langston's honour and no one has arrested him yet. Blackwood's image is still salvageable so long as we remind people that it was about honour. And Rainer killed him for it."

"Is that what we think has happened?" Mallory asked, her voice gone small and breathy, like it was a fight to even get the words out. "They've both been murdered—Captain Blackwood and Ishmael?"

"It doesn't matter," Illea said. "So long as they're missing, our story will be that they're dead because of him. But we can hope. Perhaps he escaped and fled."

Mallory opened her mouth to speak again, but words seemed to fail her. She tilted her head back, eyes pointing up at the ceiling. The room went still and quiet as the staff went about their work without speaking anymore. Making room for the grief and the shock, waiting for more conversation. Even Langston seemed to soften at the sight of his sister's distress, reaching out to her and putting a hand on her shoulder.

"I thought you didn't like our irreverent Mr. Saeati," Langston said.

"Langston," Mallory gasped. "Shut *up*."

Langston snarled, snatching his hand back as if Mallory had burned him. "Is it true, then? The things Blackwood said?"

"That doesn't matter, either," Illea said. "The rumours themselves might be enough to finally unravel Rainer's grip on Yaelsmuir, and when we chase him out of the city in disgrace, Myron's career collapses."

"Illea, you know I love you dearly," Mallory said slowly, her voice brittle with scarcely contained emotion. "You were a sister to me through a difficult time in my life, and I'll be forever grateful. But I vehemently disagree. Of course it matters if those vile things are true. We're talking about children. They aren't commodities to be traded on the market as fuel to run an empire."

"Of course they are," Illea said. "We all are. This entire world is built on consumption, Mallory. Consumption of food, of drink. We consume each other and call it sex. We consume the wealth of someone else's family and call it marriage. We burn across the world, fighting with other countries for the rights to consume—we call that trade agreements and diplomatic relations and war."

Running footsteps halted conversation. Illea turned in time to see a youth struggling through the crowd, her brow slick with sweat even though it was bitterly cold outside—one of Wolfe's servants, wearing his livery and a massive wool coat that didn't fit her, like she'd grabbed someone else's coat in her rush to get out of Wolfe's house. Heavens, had she run all the way here? It seemed impossible, and yet the way she was panting, it seemed entirely likely.

"Miss Redbone," she gasped, without propriety or deference. "Miss Winter—General Wolfe sent for you."

"What's happened?" Eirdis asked. "What's wrong?"

The girl shook her head, pushing both her hands into her hair, her eyes wild. "The Authority says he was complicit—I don't know. I don't understand any of it! They're all over the manor, searching—he sent me to come get you both. I've the carriage downstairs."

Nathaniel's house was chaos.

Illea expected it of Eirdis's office, but Nathaniel's house always maintained a sense of calm. His staff were all experts at handling anything, whether they had planned for it or not. Keeping his house orderly seemed to be the way Nathaniel coped with all the things he couldn't quite get ahold of. The death of his wife, the death of his son, the abrupt departure of his daughter. His military career, leaving ghosts behind his eyes that only the people who knew him best could see. His house was always perfect.

Except today, under the invasion of the Authority.

Officers were everywhere—on the grounds, in each room. Rummaging through furniture and opening every door, every drawer, pulling up rugs like they thought a man could hide under the tight Derccian weave. Nathaniel stood at the foot of his stairs, leaning heavily on his cane. He was still in his dress blues from the event yesterday, his eyes dark-ringed and tired, but lit with a fury the likes of which Illea hadn't seen in a long time. Cook sat in one hallway with manacles clamped to his wrists and blood oozing from a split lip.

"What's the meaning of this?" Eirdis snapped, stomping through the chaos like she thought she could calm the storm. "You've no right to tear through the Mayor's house!"

"When the Mayor is suspected of harbouring fugitives of the Authority who murdered Patrollers and Authority Officers in cold blood?" someone said. "We've every right, madam. You'll stand aside without interfering, or I'll see you arrested and held for questioning."

"For *what?*" Eirdis scoffed.

"For anything I want!" the man snapped. Sweet North Star, the audacity of the man, talking to Eirdis like that. It was proof that Rainer was too confident, making the people under him entirely too comfortable.

"Eirdis," Nathaniel said. "Just stay out of the way for now. Let them search. They won't find anything. Neither Captain Blackwood nor Ishmael have been here."

"General," Mallory said, cleaving through the chaos to catch Nathaniel's arm. "What's happened? What is this about?"

"Something's happened in the Dunnenbrahl, so Rainer thinks the pair of them have come here and he's sent his people to search," Nathaniel said. He prodded Cook's boot with his cane. "And this idiot got in a fist fight with a tinman, as if my morning hasn't been trying enough."

"He pushed Hattie," Cook grunted. "So I pushed him back."

"What does the Dunnenbrahl have to do with Ishmael and Captain Blackwood?" Mallory cut in.

"Sounds like Rainer had them carted out there to have them questioned and murdered," Illea said brightly. "That's what he said he intended to do, after all. And apparently, Tashué Blackwood isn't silenced so easily. Sounds less like murder and more like self-defence, doesn't it?"

"It's murder until proven otherwise," the Authority man bristled.

"Let's go see, shall we?" Langston said. "Go find out ourselves if it looks like murder or self-defence."

"My, Langston, for once I think you're rather brilliant," Illea said brightly. "Have Oskar saddle some horses, and we'll go help, won't we? I trust you still have side saddles in the stable, General?"

"Illea, the best thing is to be patient—"

"Patient?" Mallory scoffed. "Ishmael is missing, and Rainer is apparently framing him for murder. I think the time for patience is well past."

"Illea," Nathaniel said again, catching Illea's arm. Something grim crossed over his face, something that pulled at the lines of his features and made him look even more exhausted. "There's nothing for you out there. Let General Imburleigh go if she thinks it's right, but... Just stay. Stay here with me until they're finished. We can talk about Eirdis's strategy going forward, and General Imburleigh can report back—"

Illea wrenched her arm out of Nathaniel's grasp. "I'm not going to take some fainting spell over a bit of blood." Somehow the warning made her even more curious. If Ishmael was alive out there somewhere, she wanted to know. If Tashué Blackwood was alive—it wasn't what she expected, but she wanted to see it all for herself. "I trust Rainer is out there, panicking over the mess of it all. I'll look him in the eye and watch him fall into his ruin. He deserves it, for dragging Ishmael into everything."

And Bothain would be out there, too. Illea couldn't help but wonder what he would make of it all—his words echoed anew through her head. Only a day ago. A long day, but she remembered each syllable with perfect clarity.

What if I promised you the best view of Rainer's fall?

What a view, indeed.

27

ISHMAEL

DAY 34

"He's going to get me killed," Vasska said.

He fought hard to keep his face looking impassive and calm, but Ishmael knew him well enough to see the cracks in his composure. The tightness around his eyes, the stiffness in his motions. There was no hiding from each other with the four of them crammed into the carriage. Allie sat with Tashué since he took up so much room on his bench, giving Ishmael more room to protect his knee by sitting with Vasska. At least Ishmael's knee didn't hurt as much as before. Vasska had brought him crutches and that helped him keep his weight off his fucked leg, but gods, his shoulder hurt. It had started to bleed again by the time he made his way down, and the blood was crusted under his shirt. The pain was still insistent, and the rattling of the cart on the rough streets didn't help, but Tashué had eased the swelling. With that Talent he'd been hiding. That Talent burst trees like mortar fire, Talent that they didn't have time to talk about but for the moment before he fell asleep.

"He's doing all this to protect me," Vasska continued, "but he's going to get me fucking killed. I think he doesn't fully grasp the scale of it all. I don't know... I can't tell if it's his mind slipping or if he's got in his head that this is a good old-fashioned scrap like he used to have when he was younger or what. But he doesn't..." He bit off whatever he was going to say, watching the city roll past them outside the small carriage window.

"He seemed to grasp it fine last night," Allie said. "Talking about revolution and settling things with Kaine."

"You're the one who mentioned revolution, Miss Tei," Vasska said. "That's not what he wants. He wants to protect the Bay from carnage, and I understand—I do. Davik Kaine said the same thing, which shows how similar they are. But Grandad, he doesn't care about the children. He'll use this whole mess to get rid of Davik, and nothing will change. He doesn't care about the children at all, and he's hoping this storm will blow over."

Fucking hell. Ishmael *knew* it.

"Does he know about the energy units?" Allie pressed. "About what it all means?"

Vasska sighed. The carriage rattled Vasska and Ishmael together, their shoulders colliding. "The last time we talked about it, he said someone has to burn to feed the fire. He's had us keep it quiet, but I just…"

"Children," Allie said.

Vasska nodded, smoothing out the legs of his trousers so they sat flat and neat over his knees. Whatever flirting existed between them wasn't surviving the weight of this particular conversation. "And I was a coward. I didn't say anything because I couldn't begin to imagine what to do. But now more and more people know, so I'm not going to stay silent anymore."

"How long have *you* known?" Ishmael asked.

Anger spasmed across Vasska's face, and he turned to Ishmael, both his fists clenched in his lap. "If you're working yourself up to get angry that I didn't tell you, I tried. I asked you to come back and talk to me, remember? The day you were visiting with Kaine—the last time you were in the Bay." He paused a while, meeting Ishmael's eyes leaving the rest unsaid, waiting for Ishmael to remember the moment. He was talking about the day Powell told Ishmael to kill Losek. For Davik, for Jason. Still guarding Ishmael's secrets, even though everything was unravelling. "Lorne Coswyn was sniffing around, looking for information about the Red Dawn for him," he shot a meaningful look toward Tashué, "and I knew it was going to implode if they turned anything up. I wanted to tell you everything I knew so you could help me get ahead of it. I asked you to come see me, remember? But you *never* came back."

Anxiety and shame and guilt through Ishmael's chest. Gods, he could have gotten ahead of this. He'd missed it all. Tashué had asked him about the Red Dawn, too. Control of it all had been in his grasp weeks ago, and he'd let it slip away because he had no idea what was in his hands, and it had nearly gotten both him and Tashué killed.

You really fucked this one up, Saeati, came Deri's voice, rumbling through Ishmael's memory. Gods, how long ago was that? Fifteen years? More. The last time he worked under Deri's supervision, Ishmael's last test before being set loose.

Ishmael could still taste his own rage, fuelled by embarrassment and frustration and the way he hated how much he liked the shape of Deri's smile. That was before they started sleeping together. When Deri was still trying to be distant.

Maybe you could quit grinning at me and tell me how to fucking fix it!

When Ishmael closed his eyes, he could still *see* the way Deri leaned against the window frame, sunlight streaming all around him, making him seem ethereal and otherworldly. Smoke twisted in the beams of sun —Ishmael couldn't remember if Deri was smoking tobacco or hashish or something else, but he did remember the way the wind from the window tickled Deri's hair and made all that wavy black sway. Sunlight caught the greys. Already greying in his early thirties. The image was imprinted into the backs of his eyelids, and he carried it with him everywhere. Forever. Deri had always seemed the embodiment of what Dominion diplomats were supposed to be: aloof, fierce, fearless. That was the fantasy that Deri sold to him when Deri recruited him from the Academy prison. The reality was more complicated than that, of course. But in moments like that, Ishmael believed in the vicious capability of his mentor.

He pulled Deri's seal out of his pocket, the soggy envelope and the broken wax. The paper had dried wavy and distorted, and there were ink stains from Deri's words, run off the letter.

"Mr. Czarny." Allie's voice dropped and her eyes bore into Vasska. "How long *have* you known?"

Vasska sighed. He'd noticed the strength in her gaze, maybe, and he couldn't look her in the eye. He watched Tashué instead, which only made Ishmael realize how quiet Tashué had been since they left the borrowed office. The last thing he said was something encouraging as Ishmael made his slow, painful way down the stairs, and then he went silent.

"He told me about it all last winter," Vasska said finally. "The last time he thought he was dying, and he was trying to plan how I'd survive in the mess that he'll inevitably leave behind. He does this every winter now. Every winter I have to listen to him and Adley plan who they'll kill to protect me. If Davik catches wind of the things Grandad has been saying, he'll kill Grandad, and then he'll come for me because he'll think I was complicit in it. And every time I try to tell Grandad that I can work with Davik, he doesn't believe me. He says he knows Davik will come for me because it's what *he* would do if the situation were reversed. I can't make him stop."

"He isn't wrong," Ishmael said. "Your Grandad, I mean. Kaine needs to go before he takes everything. He's going to try. He doesn't want to be second and he'll use the violence as an excuse to make a grab for the rest of the Bay."

"I understand that, Mr. Saeati," Vasska said slowly. "But now? Under normal circumstances, maybe we would fight it out. But I can't hold the Bay *and* fight Clannaugh on my own."

Tashué sighed, shifting in his seat to swing to Vasska. "Do you have any cigarillos? Mine were ruined by the rain."

"Are you bored, Captain?" Ishmael snapped as Vasska shuffled through his pockets. "Maybe you could summon enough energy to follow the conversation and contribute a little, pretend some of this shit matters to you."

"What do you want me to say, exactly?" Tashué grunted. He leaned forward to accept a cigarillo case and a box of matches from Vasska's hand. "There's nothing I can say because I'm completely out of my depth. It's even more of a mess than I knew, and I made it worse. So I'm going to let you take over like you said. I'm waiting for my orders."

"You don't have to be a fucking ass about it," Ishmael scoffed. "This isn't the time for some kind of crisis—"

"I'm not having a crisis," Tashué interrupted, popping a match on the wall of the carriage and lit his cigarillo with infuriatingly slow, calm breaths. "I'm not throwing a tantrum and I'm not trying to be an ass. If anything, I have perfect clarity." His attention drifted out the window as he drew in the first long, slow drag of smoke, his chest filling so completely he took up more space on the bench and then he exhaled, emptying himself completely. "Davik Kaine said he's getting Jason out. Three and a half years I haven't been able to do *anything* to save my son, and now Kaine is doing it. You said this is the way forward, and I trust you. No matter how much I hate Kaine on principal, it's worth it for Jason."

"Alright then," Ishmael said. The weight of that reality—that he was the man in charge of giving Tashué Blackwood of the Black Ridge orders—settled on his shoulders.

"Wait—what principal?" Vasska asked. "What have you got against him? This fight, this is what Davik Kaine has been working toward for half his life. Exposing the Authority for who they are, what they've built. He's been in Yaelsmuir building this for a decade. More. So, even if Grandad gives you the order to kill him tonight, his people are well funded, well established, and angry. It won't be like Cruinnich, where his own people chased him off. He's been smarter this time. And now that Clannaugh is here, he'll be twice as vicious, looking for vengeance for Ffyanwy Rhydderch. All the more reason to make him an ally. He has the resources we'll need."

The name caught in Ishmael's throat, sent a shiver of tension through his body. Allie guarded her reaction perfectly, not showing any hint that she knew that name. Tashué's only reaction was a slow clench of his fist as he shifted his attention back out the window, blowing more smoke through the narrow opening, out into the swirling snow. Ffyanwy Rhydderch, the healer—Stella Whiterock the whisperer. She'd left the city, Allie said as Ishmael stared down at all those terrible photographs. Fled with Ceridwen. Ishmael remembered that girl, though he'd only met her the once at the volunteer effort to clean up the wreckage of the Market fire. The delightful little girl at the baker table, who sold him a loaf of bread in exchange for a bag of candy. Compassionate, intelligent, and so brave. And it didn't even matter that she was delightful and charming—she could have been a perfect little shit, no *child* deserved to be mutilated so that they had no arms and legs, to be killed and dumped in a river for someone else to find.

"He loved her," Ishmael said. He pushed away thoughts of Stella and Ceridwen. Think about Davik instead, think about Ffyanwy, erase Stella from his own mind for now. If she didn't exist, he couldn't give away her secret and she could keep running in anonymity, hiding herself and the child she saved behind the name Whiterock. "Didn't he? That's the story I heard, anyway—they loved each other but she chose Clannaugh for her hospital. And then Clannaugh killed her."

"That's the rumour, but there's never been proof. At least, not enough proof to arrest Bothain for it, but I imagine it's hard to find Patrollers with the spine it would take to arrest Clannaugh even if there were proof." Vasska shrugged. "To hear Davik tell it, Ffyanwy forged the stars in the sky. I like him, Ishmael. He hasn't gotten on well with Grandad lately because he's been so... animated. Stubborn. But I think he actually wants change. Good change. The same change that we're fighting for. It seems foolish to throw away an ally so easily."

The thought of anyone liking Davik made Ishmael's skin crawl. The vicious, manipulative asshole mustn't have cornered Vasska in a carriage and held him by the throat. Davik must have put on his best charm for Vasska, because it was in his best interest for Vasska to like him, as this conversation so clearly demonstrated. To trust him. To believe that they were on the same side when Powell was probably right about Davik planning to get rid of Vasska in the interest of seizing control of the Hive.

"You're talking about making peace with the man who ordered the deaths of those children," Allie said into the stretching silence. The anger in her voice took up physical space in the carriage. "He wants change so desperately, he's willing to get it by murdering children. Children who didn't ask to be born and mutilated by the Authority in the first place. Davik Kaine decided they were disposable anyway. Anything for his resistance, right?"

Vasska spread his hands. "What proof do you have that Kaine had anything to do with that, other than it's what Hale said?"

"Why would he lie?" Allie countered.

"Aside from the fact that a man was threatening to kill him?" Another pointed glance at Tashué, which Tashué ignored, focusing on his cigarillo. "Because he was Edgar Hale. You never had the misfortune of meeting him, but lying came as naturally to him as breathing. If he thought it would have saved his life, he would have said anything to Mr. Blackwood."

Allie scoffed, shaking her head. "Are you saying Davik Kaine had nothing to do with the deaths of the children we found?"

Vasska frowned, picking lint off his trousers. Sitting up against him, Ishmael could feel the tension coiled in the younger man, resting on his shoulders and down his spine. "I'm saying that I don't know for certain one way or another, Miss Tei."

Allie shook her head, dissatisfied with the answer. She rested a hand on Tashué's knee, catching his attention. "Was he lying, Tashué? You were the one in the room with him."

Tashué shrugged, forcing his hand out of its fist and laying it on top of Allie's hand. Something passed between them through a twitch in both of their fingers, that sort of shared understanding that came to people who had been through the shit together. "I told you what he said, Allie. I believed him when he said it. Where'd he get the children? How could he have found so many of them without help? Seems like a load of shit that he could have pulled all that off alone. If he was as much of a braggart as people say, then wouldn't he have run his mouth about it? Why do it and then keep it a secret? He was doing it to impress Kaine, with or without Kaine's help. Kaine knew."

Silence again. Or near enough to it, with the steady clop of the horse's hooves and the creak of the carriage and the thrum of the city outside.

"I expected the streets to be more chaotic by now," Allie said, her eyes drifting to the window beside Tashué. "After everything yesterday, and Tashué going *missing* according to the Patrollers and the Authority. I thought they'd be crawling around the city by now, searching for him. What is he waiting for, do you think?"

"Who," Ishmael asked, glancing across at Allie. "Elsworth?"

Allie nodded. "All of them, I suppose. Elsworth, Clannaugh. Even Kaine—he must know the storm's coming. Do you think he'll act first?"

Ishmael sighed, giving a shrug. "I expect Clannaugh and Elsworth are waiting for an excuse. Some act of violence or otherwise threatening behaviour that can be used as proof that the Bay is responsible for Captain Blackwood's actions or are harbouring him there after the fact. It'll be a fine line that he's treading, especially in the election cycle. He won't want to wait too long or people will think Winter and Elsworth are too weak. But if he moves too aggressively without enough support, the middle-class swing votes will fall to Redbone, who is anti-police force. And if Winter loses this election, no police force for Clannaugh and Maes. I'm not sure what Kaine is waiting for. Maybe he's waiting to see what Clannaugh will do."

"So the plan is to move fast before Elsworth buckles and starts raiding the Bay," Tashué said.

Ishmael leaned forward, carefully so as not to hurt his knee any more. He snatched the cigarillo from Tashué's fingers. Vasska's tobacco was good, and the smoke was also comforting. Smelled a little like Deri. "The plan is to make nice with Davik Kaine and let him lead a while." To present himself and Tashué as bait, but he wasn't sure if Tashué would be so calm and cooperative if he knew that, so he kept that part silent. There was no way Davik would believe Ishmael was around to help, but if he was smart, he'd keep Ishmael and Tashué close to use as bargaining chips once shit got ugly. The trick would be to act and sell Kaine out before Kaine had the chance to do it to them. "And then we'll see."

28

ILLEA
DAY 34

S now drifted gently through the forest, piercing the bare canopy to rest like dust on branch and stone. The strange, invasive quiet always made Illea feel small and alone. Perhaps she wouldn't have hated the Dunnenbrahl so much if it weren't for the memory of Amias, bleeding all over the forest floor, all over her clothes, filling her dreams with red. Perhaps once she even liked it out here, if only because he loved it so much. Ever since he died, it was the place that took him from her. Now it was the reason she lived her life with a steady, aching anxiety under the surface of her every thought, every action. It used to be pure terror—paralyzing her, making it impossible to do anything, because everything she did opened her to imagining how it might kill her even if it was a thing she'd done a hundred times before—but now it was simply a dull throb. Life went on, until it didn't. And the Dunnenbrahl was her family's fortune. Her family's property. So she made an uneasy peace with it, no matter what her loggers said about it being haunted.

Langston, for all that his company was annoying at best, was a good horseman and a decent tracker. Not that it took much skill to follow the tracks out to where the carnage happened. The path was churned mud by all the traffic that had crossed over it, snow gathering in hoof prints and wagon tracks alike, guiding them as sure as if the road was paved for them.

Illea had never seen a battlefield. She'd travelled, but her father only took her to safe places, far away from all the many conflicts of the world. But Amias had seen plenty. He'd served his five with his General's stars, and he'd told Illea the stories of it. His official stance was that it was terrible, that he hated it. That's what all civilized people said about war. That it was a noble pursuit if fought for the right reasons, but the savagery and brutality of it was a terrible human cost. Such a shame. Such a waste.

The truth was evident not in what he said but in the way his eyes danced when he explained how awful it all was. The rush of it obviously had him entranced. He described the destruction wrought by mortar fire with careful detail that showed how fascinated he was by it. When she challenged his assertion that he thought it was terrible and he sounded rather fascinated by it all, he shrugged it off.

A lot of people died, Illea.

As if that made it untrue that he was thrilled by the fact that his division won whatever battle he was describing.

As she rode into the wreckage, she imagined it Amias might have gleefully described it. Like one of his battlefields, where mortars hit trees and turned them into shrapnel. *Like so much kindling,* he said, as he built the fire in the hearth of his bedroom, where they were hiding from both of their parents.

That was the first thing she noticed as they rode. Burst trees, like they'd been hit by those terrible mortars, littering the ground with shreds of wood. Whatever had fallen on the path had been churned into the mud by all the people who had passed over it, but that still left plenty of debris on either side of the track.

"Who brought mortars to an arrest?" Langston asked.

It was comforting, somehow, that he imagined the same thing. What else could reduce full growth trees to nothing but kindling, save a team of loggers?

Mallory only shook her head. "I don't smell gunpowder."

"So?" Langston asked.

"Usually when someone fires mortars, you can smell it for a while."

"But Mallory, what else could it *be*?"

"I don't know," Mallory admitted. "Perhaps it was mortar fire—and they were far away from the arrest. But that begs the question, why would they fire mortars from so far away unless they didn't care if Captain Blackwood and Ishmael lived or died? It doesn't make sense."

Ditches had been torn into the path and around it on either side. As if something incredibly heavy had been dragged, leaving runnels of torn earth like trenches.

Voices came softly through the trees and the snow, muffled by the forest. Out of the stillness, chaos bloomed. Patrollers and Authority officers. Some of Nathaniel's hunters, still in their Wolfe livery, had been arrested. Manacles clamped their hands together and they sat in the mud, their horses tied to trees out of their reach. Bothain, in the centre of it all.

More trees destroyed.

And the bodies.

One lay in the centre of the road, a woman. She was dead, although Illea couldn't tell why. She hadn't bled to death. Snow gathered on her face, on her still open eyes, piling there like two tiny white shrouds. Further up, a dozen tinmen or so, milling around.

Illea clenched her teeth against the rising nausea. She should have eaten more at Nathaniel's house while the staff saddled the horses. She'd tried to tell herself that this pregnancy wouldn't change her life except in ways that she allowed change, but that was already proving to be incredibly naive. Every moment, she needed to mind whether or not she was hungry, or the nausea would come. And now, dead bodies.

She swallowed the bile and sat up straighter, wishing it away. Damn it all, she wouldn't let these people see her composure anything but perfect. Rainer stood in the road, looking pale, pacing through the half-frozen mud. And Bothain, standing in the swirling snow flecks of white on his shoulders and in his hair. The only person standing still like the chaos around him brought him peace.

The second body was more gruesome. His throat had been ripped open by some weapon or debris, and the snow on him had soaked up the blood, turning into an icy red crust when it froze again.

The Patroller's wagon—blown apart. Illea couldn't tell what force had ripped the sides open like that. More mortar fire? The back doors were open, and Illea thought she could see shapes—bodies. More bodies. Ripped apart just like the wooden walls, shards of bone sticking up from the gore, protected from the snow so it was all a sea of red.

"Miss Winter," Bothain said. "General Imburleigh. What are you doing here?"

"We wanted to see for ourselves," Mallory said stiffly. If she was moved by all the death, it only showed in her face as anger. Fury. "What have you done, Mr. Elsworth?"

"What have *I* done?" Rainer squealed. He stood near the wagon with eyes as wide and goggling as some caricature, his moustache gathering snowflakes. He watched as another body was dragged into the chaos. The man's head had been blown half off, his jaw and only some parts of his face left behind. "This was Blackwood and Saeati. They're wild fucking animals!"

"I find it impossible to believe that two men were capable of all this," Mallory said. "They didn't have any weapons with them when they were arrested. And why in the name of every level of hell were they on this side of the river, when they should have been transported to the jail?"

"We believe the wagon was hijacked by the Red Dawn," Bothain said smoothly, delivering a practiced line. "Shotgun fire killed every Patroller in the wagon, and it's likely that Talent killed the Enquiry Officers."

"What's an Enquiry Officer?" Langston asked.

Bothain glanced up at Langston as if he was an unexpected pest. Which he was, generally speaking. "They were accompanying the wagon to the jail cell, to question the arrestees. They must have followed the wagon out, only to be slain by Blackwood and his Red Dawn allies."

A man approached the wagon slowly, face drained of all colour. He reached in tentatively, grabbing a piece of cloth—except the cloth was apparently someone's trouser, and the shredded bit of leg came with it. The man gagged, dropping the piece of leg to the ground.

Illea squeezed her eyes shut, tightening her grip on the reins and focusing on the shift of the horse beneath her. They were going to empty out that wagon. She couldn't watch. She couldn't witness every piece of human body being sifted through. This was a mistake. A terrible mistake. She'd thought Nathaniel was being needlessly paternal when he said she didn't need to come out here, since she had no real love for the forest, but she hadn't imagined the potential for carnage. He must have heard people talking about what they'd seen, must have known how terrible it was.

"That's a bloody lie," Mallory said. "How could the Red Dawn have hijacked the wagon while you had Officers following it? Someone in the city would have noticed. And why would the Red Dawn care a wit for Captain Blackwood and Ishmael Saeati?"

"General Imburleigh, I understand that it's all very shocking," Bothain said smoothly. "But we've been here all morning sifting through carnage, and this seems to be the most plausible explanation."

"That doesn't answer my question, General Clannaugh. Why would the Red Dawn do all of this for Tashué Blackwood?"

"Because of his Talent, I expect," Bothain said blandly, as if the conversation was beginning to bore him.

"That doesn't make any sense," Langston pressed, but he had a brittle, half-panicked edge to his voice. "The man was a tinman. Doesn't that mean he doesn't have any Talent? They don't let the tainted carry badges, do they?"

"Talent is hereditary," Bothain said. "The son has enormous Talent, and I looked at Blackwood's file before we came out here—his parents were a healer and a stonesmith. It's impossible to believe the man has no Talent at all. It may have been lying dormant at the time of his assessment, thus it was missed by the Authority, but Tashué Blackwood absolutely has Talent. It's possible he was in league with the Red Dawn for some time, and they engineered this whole thing."

Someone gagged again. Illea opened her eyes before she could stop herself and immediately regretted it. They were dragging all those body parts out the wagon and trying to lay the remains out on the road, as if they were counting the arms and legs present. And one of the men trying to do the job had staggered away to the edge of the forest, where he bent over double to vomit in the underbrush.

The nausea hit Illea so hard, it made her whole body too light. She eased herself out of the borrowed saddle, her boots sinking deep into the mud. If she was going to faint, best not be in the saddle.

"Miss Winter," Bothain said. "Are you alright?"

Illea shook her head, but she didn't dare speak. She pressed her fingers to her lips, taking a step down the road. Away. She didn't know where, just away. Away from people watching her, away from the corpses, away from the sound of the man in the brush, vomiting.

Talent was hereditary.

Of all the things in the clearing, that bothered her the most. Talent was hereditary, and her child was Winter, but Tashué Blackwood was the father. And even if no one knew but her, it still meant that her child... would her child be tainted, too?

What life could her child expect in the Dominion?

If the Authority survived the implosion of Rainer's career, she could do whatever it took to dodge the registration and keep her child safe from the grasping control. She'd have to talk to Aelwyd, perhaps—it was a good thing Aelwyd was coming down for the train proposal. It would give Illea time to talk to someone who was used to side-stepping Authority rule. Aelwyd didn't have children, but surely she had a plan for how to keep her family safe.

Sweet North Star, the nausea.

"Illea," Mallory called, but she didn't say anything else. Perhaps there was nothing to say.

She stopped walking, pressing her fingers to her lips even harder. She cursed the nausea with every shred of anger she could muster as if that would beat it back, but it hung on. She resented it for making her look weak in front of so many people. In front of Rainer after she'd promised to destroy him.

Bothain was lying to protect Rainer, and Illea couldn't say anything to counter it or question it because the nausea wouldn't let her speak.

"Miss Winter," Bothain said again. He was closer, right over her shoulder. He put a hand on her arm. "Are you alright?"

Illea shook her head. Nothing was alright. Nothing at all.

"I don't think Saeati or Blackwood were in here, General Clannaugh," one of the men next to the wagon. "There are enough remains to suggest the six Patrollers were all in there when they were shot at, but not Blackwood and Saeati."

"Sweet North Star have mercy," Langston whispered. "They'll get a hero's funeral, Rainer. Every single one of the poor sods."

"Illea," Bothain said. "Come sit down. You don't look well."

Illea opened her eyes to tell Bothain to leave her be—

A terrible mistake.

She was standing a few horrible feet away from another dead body. All clues as to who he was were obliterated—he looked like a soft clay figure that had once been a person but had been crushed by a child's temper tantrum, his skin barely holding the insides of him anymore because they were stretched to their limit, jutting at strange angles as the broken bone underneath pressed at the surface of him.

The tenuous control Illea had over her stomach snapped, and she vomited at the corpse's feet.

29

OZRA
DAY 34

The ghost of Eilidh Rae hovered at the edge of Ozra's vision as he led the travellers away from Greene's Creek, swinging hard west. If they followed the creek long enough, it would wind its way up to the Brightwash, but that way was too slow. It would take near a week still to get across the river, over too much open ground. Snow danced in the air around them, gathering on stones and melting into the puddles that dotted the soft underbrush where the rotting leaf litter made a bit of heat. White webs of frost ate the edges of everything. Their breath made billowing white plumes that drifted through the weak, early winter sun. It was time to get settled somewhere. The mill town would offer them refuge, and if the weather got worse, they could at least shelter there a while. Let Siras show his face at a Winter-owned mill town, with Winter-employed loggers and millwrights. They didn't have much patience for the Authority so close to the Dunnenbrahl. Anyone who sought to regulate a thing as unknowable and natural as Talent wasn't to be trusted.

They only travelled a couple hours before the forest started to thin. Ozra stopped them in a clearing that was screened in by a thick tangle of red dogwood and trailing five-leaf ivy. Even though both plants had lost leaves to winter's oncoming chill, both made a wall of twig and vine that made the clearing hard to see if you were passing through. They dismounted to eat, to let the horses rest before their last push, but

Rhodrishi was anxious—Ozra could feel it in the air between them. They were only stopped a moment or two before Rhodrishi pulled Ozra aside.

"It's possible that Siras Duncreek is closer than we hoped. She saw him in her dream last night. It could be nothing—could be a nightmare, brought on by understandable anxiety. But it's possible he's found her dreampath. She was connected to Tashué at the time, sharing a dream with him."

"He's alive then?" Ozra asked. "Blackwood?"

Rhodrishi spread his hands, looking up toward the twirling snow. It settled in his hair, blending in with the grey. "I very much hope so."

Ozra sucked his teeth. Habit made him try to rest his hands on the butts of his revolvers, but Mahalouwan still had them. "What do you want me to do, Rhodrishi? Is she wanting to go back?"

"No, I don't think so—it's just that we should be careful. We've been moving with the assumption that Duncreek can't use his Talent to find us, but if he's found her dreampath…"

"It's possible he knows exactly where she is."

Rhodrishi pressed his lips together, glancing at Stella and Ceridwen. And he nodded.

"Right," Ozra said, climbing back into Caraid's saddle. "Wait here. With your gun out, just in case. There's a ridge over that way, I'm going to go see if there's any sign of travel out in the open."

"I'll go with you," Mahalouwan said. "I'd like to see our route."

"Go easy on him, Lieutenant," Rhodrishi said. "I'd like him back in one piece."

"He looks good and sturdy, Colonel," Mahalouwan said, her mouth turning in that crooked smile of hers and her eyes flashing with mischief. "He can take some rough handling."

Sweet North Star, the woman was trying to drive him mad.

Caraid shifted impatiently beneath him. For all that he was getting to be an old horse, he was still happiest when they were on the move. Stillness had never suited either of them. But something held Ozra in place, even though his own body itched to go, too. The ghost of Eilidh had been so restless for so long. Angry and half vengeful, like she wanted him to remember how he'd failed her in life. Pulling him, forcing him to travel. Until he met up with these people. Rhodrishi and Lieutenant Mahalouwan, and their charges. Wee Ceridwen and Stella Whiterock—Ffyanwy Rhydderch. He tried to tell himself it didn't matter. No one person was more important than anyone else, especially when it came to protecting them from the Authority.

But it did matter.

Ffyanwy Rhydderch was like the spirit of the entire north, bundled into the form of one woman. Born free and proud and mountain, both noble and wild. And then the Authority stripped her essence away, layer by layer, punishment for her vibrancy. And maybe Bothain Clannaugh was northern-born too, but he was Authority to the core—self-serving and ruthless, believing Talent was truly a curse, believing in the purity of people with no discernible abilities. Those ideas were born in the south when the Godking scoured his hatred across the continent to force it into one nation under his rule.

But she'd survived. She'd escaped Bothain and she remade herself to protect her child, and she held on against incredible odds—and Ozra couldn't think of anything more northern than that. It reminded him of everything he'd hoped to be, once. Before the Authority started stripping layers off him, too.

Eilidh was calmer around Stella. Maybe she'd led him this way because she wanted him to make it right. He'd failed to save her from the Authority, but maybe Stella was a second chance to give some purpose to his worthless, cursed existence.

"Mr. Sgèin," Mahalouwan said, her voice gone flinty again. "If you're going to help me find Siras, you're pointed the wrong way."

Ozra sighed, turning Caraid around, and the gelding gave a toss of his head and a snort—his desires to move apparently snuffed out when he realized that meant leaving the other horses behind. He rather liked being around Rhodrishi's big mare. "That's enough of your attitude, old man. Now's not the time for flirting, it's the time for hunting bronze."

Mahalouwan turned in her saddle, looking over her shoulder at Ozra as her pony headed away from the clearing. "What's that supposed to mean?"

Ozra kicked Caraid after her, and the gelding caught up early, his gangly long legs eating up the distance. "Enquiry Officers like Siras carry bronze badges. They're worth a few coins up north, them bronze badges. I know plenty of people who got their warrior tattoos by bringing an Enquiry badge home."

Mahalouwan's whole body went stiff again, and she turned away from Ozra, silent as she let him pull into the lead. The sudden silence buzzed between them, her anger louder than the sounds of the forest, which only gave his mind space to twist through his own winding thoughts.

How had she found herself in this moment, travelling through the wilderness with Stella Whiterock?

Ffyanwy Rhydderch, shite. He hadn't recognized her, even though he'd seen her a few times back when she lived in Cruinnich. He'd stood in her house when Bothain sent for him. He'd been to her hospital to meet Davik Kaine. He'd looked her in the eye and she shook his hand even though they were caked with road dust. But if he remembered correctly, hers were caked with blood. He remembered thinking how much her untameable copper hair reminded him of his sister Asha, who had the same colour. Like their mother. He remembered the pang of longing for his whole family when he looked into her sharp green eyes. He'd used his Talent to find her when Bothain asked him to, watched her head west along the smugglers' road to get away from Cruinnich as fast as she could with her wee infant tied to her back.

But he hadn't placed her face at all when he rode into their camp at the crofter's cottage. Time had stripped away the details of her features away from his memory, and he'd forgotten the subtle cleft in her chin and the particular turn of her nose, the way her eyes always looked a little bit sad, even when she smiled. Even when they started talking about Siras and Bothain, it hadn't occurred to him to wonder who she was. It didn't connect in his mind until she said that thing about Davik Kaine. Who else but Ffyanwy Rhydderch would speak so lovingly of Davik Kaine?

Did her lover, Tashué Blackwood, know who she really was? Did Mahalouwan?

"How'd you find yourself out here, Lieutenant Mahalouwan?" Ozra called. "I understand why Rhodrishi is doing this—but why are you doing it? Seems like this whole endeavour is somewhat against your comfort."

"What's *that* supposed to mean?" Mahalouwan snorted, shooting a glower over her shoulder. "What about me makes you think I wouldn't protect a woman and a child?"

"It's not so much who you're protecting," Ozra said, looking at her. Except it was. But maybe she didn't know, and it wasn't Ozra's place to say. "It's what you're protecting them from. You balked when you heard I was a smuggler, you're angry about us using Talent. You talk about the law like it's some good and wholesome thing, and just now you were mighty offended to learn that folks up north kill Enquiry Officers. Not usually the type we see out here on the road."

She shook her head, resting her hand on the butt of her rifle like she had half a mind to give him the bullet she'd been promising. "This isn't how I expected to find myself, no."

"How'd you get out here, then? Why leave Yaelsmuir? For a fugitive from the precious law."

"My Captain needed me to do this," Mahalouwan said. "He would have come himself, but he had to stay in the city for his son."

"Is that Blackwood? Your Captain."

"Yes."

"So he ordered you out here, did he?"

She huffed again, and when Ozra glanced over his shoulder at her, she was glaring daggers at him. He took no small amount of satisfaction from seeing her so uncomfortable, and with her words *people like you* still ringing in his head days after she said it, he didn't feel as bad about it as he probably ought to.

"It's not like that," she said. "He didn't order me—he didn't even ask me, because he thought I wouldn't understand. And he's right—I don't understand. I don't understand how we spent the last nineteen years in that fucking city, and now everything we believed in is built on…" She hissed a long breath from between clenched teeth, like she was trying to force the tension out of her chest. "Energy units, breeding programs, Enquiry Officers. It's all fucking vile. But…" He glanced back at her again, and he thought she looked terribly sad this time, but she tried to arrange her features into something more neutral when she noticed him looking. The forest thinned even more, giving her space to ride beside him, her pony keeping pace with Caraid. "I spent my whole life knowing certain things. Knowing them in the very marrow of my bones. Talent is dangerous. The Wrath can kill."

The threads of her memory trailed around her, angry and painful and frayed. The beautiful rolling grasslands, verdant hills and valleys—stained with blood. Two men arguing, fighting, and then the younger fell, his chest staved in by some unseen force—

"And now I have to trust you, apparently, when my entire life's experience says you're the enemy. How do I know you aren't leading us into a trap? How do I know you won't sell us to the Authority the first chance you get for a few gold coins to rub together?"

He'd never been accused of selling folks to the Authority. The notion was so absurd that it didn't even make him angry like when she said *people like you* that first day. How little she understood the very people she declared her enemy. "Lieutenant Mahalouwan, I hate the Authority with every fibre of my being. Every drop of my blood, every shard of my bones every strand of my hair was made to hate the Authority. I wouldn't sell anyone to them, not even my greatest enemies. Not even Siras Duncreek. And before you ask, I won't sell you to anyone else, for that matter. What's a man like me going to do with gold, anyway? Can't eat it. Can't feed it to Caraid. If I toss it in the fire, it won't keep me warm. I'm done saying yes to the Authority. They stripped everything human out of me, turned me into something uglier than I thought possible. And I let them do it, because I told myself that doing what it took to survive was a rebellion of its own. Now, after everything, I don't know if surviving was enough. Maybe I should've fought harder, even if it meant giving them an excuse to kill me like so many others before me." Ozra shrugged. "But I didn't, so here I am. Maybe if I fight for the White-rocks, at least I can salvage some shred of who I used to be. That's worth far more than all the gold in the Dominion."

"You're a real bushman, aren't you, Ozra?" Mahalouwan said, a bit of a smile pulling at one side of her mouth, her head tilting back again. Sweet North Star, she had a stunning smile, and he cursed her for it, this woman who called him her enemy but who he was tempted to like. "Can't imagine anything more than meat on your campfire and bullets in your gun and a blanket around your shoulders."

Ozra glanced back toward the clearing they'd left behind. He couldn't see it, which was good. And Eilidh hadn't followed, but he could still feel her tugging at his senses. Like she was an anchor resting with the Whiterocks, letting out enough rope for him to travel, but not too far before she started dragging him back. "Maybe a roof over my head, one day. But just a small roof, one that I don't have to work too hard to upkeep, so I don't have to feel like I'm tied underneath it."

"Someone to tend the hearth fire when you're gone?"

"No. Someone to come wandering with me. Someone who knows what it means to be Kishoan—or someone who wants to learn."

"And what's it mean, then?"

Ozra sighed, looking at Mahalouwan again. She had a pleading look on her face, like she was begging him to make it all make sense. "It ain't in my habit to explain myself to the people who declare themselves my enemy."

Mahalouwan shrugged. "What about people who declare themselves your reluctant and confused ally?"

"Is that what we are? Because if it is, then I'll start asking for my guns back."

Mahalouwan's scowl returned in an instant, so fast it was like it had never gone anywhere. Apparently the thought of putting weapons into his hands was still too much of a leap.

"It means resistance, Lieutenant Mahalouwan," Ozra said. Maybe if he put some effort into trusting her, she'd return in kind. "It means rejecting the idea that there's any sanctity in the laws of the Authority and fighting against them with every living breath. There ain't no law, whether it's written by man or the Crowne or the Godking himself, that would make me trust a system that turns anyone's children into energy units. And I won't be ashamed of the things I do to resist that. I know you understand what those words mean. I saw the look on your face when Miss Whiterock asked me about them."

Her face made that hard, brittle mask again, the one she wore so often when she wasn't joking about shooting him. "I'm out here, aren't I?" she asked, her voice surprisingly soft. "Protecting the Whiterocks, even though that means I'm an outlaw."

"Sure," Ozra said. "And I'll give you credit for that."

Ozra could feel the cliff nearby, even if he couldn't see it yet—its looming presence changed the way the wind flowed, the way sound moved. And then the trail came beside it, the stone emerging from the forest like some slumbering giant. Five-leaf ivy clung in ropey vines to the rock face, but winter had stripped the leaves away. The trail rose along the cliff face—creeping juniper spilled over the ledges to catch the sun's rays, a curtain of prickly green. On, on, higher—and then the rising hillside met the level of the cliff, and the trail twisted north, following the rise. Under different circumstances, Ozra would have stopped to forage from the medicine field they rode around. Wild rose bushes still had dry, shrivelled leaves and plump red-orange rose hips. Farther away in the clearing, a little spread of wintergreen, merry red berries low to the ground. Highbush cranberries, hanging from their tall branches. But they didn't have time. They had to reach the mill town tonight. There was nowhere safe for them to stop between the forest edge and the town.

Ozra tugged Caraid to a stop, dropping down out of the saddle and tying the reins to a trailing branch. "The forest thins at the top of the ridge, and we'll be able to see the road to Yaelsmuir, and all the open space around it. We won't be able to see if there's anyone behind us, but at least we can check to see if there's active patrols ahead of us."

Mahalouwan nodded. That thin and brittle look she always wore disappeared. She looked flushed with life, like the prospect of a fight filled her with excitement and purpose. "If we're to be allies, I need to know the truth. And if you lie to me again, I'm going to shoot you and tell Colonel Kheir we were ambushed."

Ozra sighed, his shoulders sagging. "We've an awful lot of ground to cover before we get to town."

"So you'd best not fuck around, hey?" She put her hand on her rifle, drawing it halfway out of the leather scabbard hanging from her saddle. He knew from the look in her eye—calm and sure and at peace—she'd pull it out and put a chunk of lead through his chest, like she kept promising to, and she'd never once doubt herself for it after he was dead. And maybe he could use his Talent to stop her somehow, but maybe he couldn't. Depended on how fast she was. Depended on whether or not he could even focus his Talent at all anymore, or if he'd go drifting the moment he tried anything. The way he'd been knocked all the way to Yaelsmuir simply because Stella felt some man he didn't know quicken didn't fill Ozra with confidence in his ability to control it. "Why did you follow us here? What are you after?"

"What do you want me to say?" Ozra asked, spreading his hands. "You don't trust Talent, you don't trust me, you don't like the way I survive. You won't like my answer."

"I'll like it if it sounds like the truth."

"Do you believe in ghosts, Lieutenant Mahalouwan?" Ozra asked. "They say people with Talent are more likely to see them—some think the apparition isn't the person's spirit so much as it's their Talent, lingering in the world, after the body's died and the soul's gone on to the next life. Kishoan threadwalkers say that Talent is a force that connects us all—the fabric, it's called—and the ghosts we see are the Talent's memory recalling someone, like an echo that lingers long after someone's left the canyon. But that doesn't explain haunted places that hurt folks whether they've got Talent or not. So maybe all three things are true."

Mahalouwan interrupted with a huff, shifting in her saddle. "I thought you didn't want to waste any time."

"I don't," Ozra said, bristling again. "That's why I'm trying to explain myself in a hurry. You sneer at Talent, so I wonder what you think about ghosts. That crofter's hut you stayed in—folks say it's haunted. Would you believe me, if I told you the stories I've heard about it? Or would you say it's all superstition and fear-mongering? And since we don't want to waste any time, why don't you come down, and we can head up the ridge? You can even bring that great big gun of yours so you can shoot me in the back if you see fit to."

She smirked at him, dragging her rifle out and resting the barrel on her shoulder. "Spirituality is not fear-mongering, no." She slid down from the saddle, landing easily and tying her pony to the same tree as Caraid, where they could reach some withered greens. "Spirituality is not a thing to take lightly; the dead do not simply cease to exist because their bodies have returned to the earth."

"Right," Ozra said. He headed up the last of the incline, leaning into the aggressive slope. He followed the thickest spots of the trees to hide their silhouettes. Mahalouwan followed, trailing a little behind him so she could shoot him in the back like he said she could. Sweet North Star, he was so tired. "I don't know if she's truly a ghost or her Talent, wandering loose since her body died—or maybe the fabric of Talent is holding her memory, and it's following me around."

"You mean Eilidh?" Mahalouwan asked. "The ghost that Stella saw?"

"Aye, Eilidh. No one else has ever seen her before."

"Who is she?"

Ozra looked down at his feet, watching them plod along the incline instead of looking at Mahalouwan. He couldn't bear to watch that cold calculation of his worth, not when he was talking about Eilidh. "Someone who I—ah, I loved her. But I failed her. I tried to protect her from the Authority. I tried to take her away from where they had us. But I failed—and she's the one that paid the price for my failure. I've been seeing her lately. She's been telling me to come this way, dragging me along. She's calmed since I found you folks. I don't know if she sent me this way because she wanted me to find you, or if she wanted us to go east and finding you was an accident—or maybe I ain't seeing her at all, and it's the hand of the North Star, guiding me to innocent people who need help. Doesn't matter to me how I came to be here, I don't think. Now that I *know* who I'm travelling with. Helping seems like a good way for me to spend my time. And if I die to protect them, so be it. Better than me rotting in the Dunnenbrahl on my own, year over year."

"A ghost led you this way," Mahalouwan repeated.

"Yes, ma'am."

"How'd she die, your ghost?" Mahalouwan asked.

Ozra sighed. The slope strained his whole body, his legs, his lungs, his heart, and the plumes his breath made got thicker and heavier as every inhale gulped at the air. He was used to letting Caraid do all the work. "Authority. How else?"

"How long ago?"

"Is this a test, Lieutenant?" He stopped short of the crest of the ridge, putting his hands on his hips. The wind was stronger up here, so high with the trees so thin, and it leached all the heat out of his skin. Snow swirled all around their heads, some down out of the slate grey sky. It was going to be a cold, hard day, and the night would come even faster if the storm was going to last. "You gonna shoot me if I get any of these answers wrong?"

That grin of hers again. How'd she manage to make him like her, even with the ripe shite she said about laws? "Maybe I will."

"How do you know if I'm lying or not?"

Mahalouwan shrugged, turning her face into the wind. "I've a good ear for it."

"Authority killed her seven years ago now." Ozra's chest pulled, and he reached up, grabbing the front of his shirt and clenching a fist in the threadbare linen. Pulling, tugging, trying to catch his breath. He blinked through the tears that stung his eyes, that made it hard to see. He turned his gaze up at the sky, watching the snow. "Ah—shite. Took the air out of me, a little, saying that out loud. Don't think I've ever said it before."

He couldn't look at Mahalouwan while he tried to pull himself back together. He couldn't bear it if she was staring at him with those flat eyes, her hand on her gun. Or maybe she was scowling again, and he couldn't handle that, either. He thought maybe if he met her eye and saw her judgement, he'd ask her to go ahead and shoot him. Be easier, dying. Easier than dealing with this pain any more. Be easier than taking any more judgement from someone who believed in the fucking law.

But she didn't shoot him—she sighed. "Right, then. Let's go take a look."

Ozra nodded, dropping down to his knees to crawl the rest of the way. Focus on the earth and the rock beneath his hands, instead of grief squeezing his chest. He didn't have time to feel sorry for himself, no matter how much he was inclined to. He was looking for Siras fucking Duncreek.

Mahalouwan dropped down beside him, moving forward on knees and elbows, her rifle cradled across her forearms and pointing away from Ozra's face. Mud and brush made a mess of their clothes, but his old leather duster had been through plenty worse. He was pretty sure it was still stained with Eilidh's blood, but those stains were mottled in with the rest of the dirt and blood he'd encountered over the years. Ozra's knees grumbled at the unaccustomed use, his hands ached with the cold coming up from the rock and the earth and the frost that melted under his palm. The drop yawned in front of him. The wind cut hard over the ridge and the valley below, billowing in his fleece collar, in his hair. He should have a hat. But he'd lost the last one he'd made sometime in the spring, and he'd been travelling so hard to follow Eilidh east that he hadn't had time to knit another.

Mahalouwan crawled right up to the edge without hesitating. Completely unintimidated by the drop, it seemed. The rolling hills stretched out beneath them, and the road snaked wide across the open stretch of land. Figures moved in a cluster, headed south. Mahalouwan pulled out her binoculars, tracking the travellers for a while.

"The Authority patrols, they wear badges out here?"

"Sometimes," Ozra said. His ears ached with the cold. "The bronze or the tin."

Mahalouwan turned away from the travellers on the road. There was a wagon or two, trundling along—probably not Authority. She scanned the far hills, north and south. "Where's the mill town from here?"

Ozra moved closer to her, pointing so his arm hung right off the big open space, wind dragging at his arm as he pointed. "The rise there, there's a roadhouse on it. You can see the smoke comin' out of the chimney. It's a straight shot north-west as the crow flies from there. But to get there, we gotta go north-west through the hills and then turn due north once we hit the river."

"I don't see anything," Mahalouwan huffed. "That drifting you do, can you spread yourself out, see if you can find patrols?"

"If I could, I would. But I can't control it, and I doubt I'd be able to come back this time."

She huffed again, rolling onto her side ever so slightly so she could look him in the eye. "And this is the best route? There isn't anything safer?"

"We could follow the creek up to the Brightwash, but that takes about four days or so, and then there's another three before there's another crossing. It's a few days out in the open instead of one. Or we could swing south, through the forest. But there ain't any crossings between here and the city. Cross at the Market on a barge, or walk right through the streets and use the bridge."

She sighed. "This is the best option."

"Aye," Ozra said. "This is the best option."

Mahalouwan rolled back to her stomach, watching through her binoculars a while. "Right. If it's the best, then we should get going. Even if it's all shit."

30

TASHUÉ
DAY 34

Vasska had the carriage drop them around the corner from the front door, letting the whole group approach on foot. Ishmael only took one of the crutches Vasska brought, using it to hobble down the street without putting as much weight on his bad leg. Snow clung to the corners of the world, frozen dust like a promise of the brutal winter to come. Had it snowed on Stella and Ceridwen? Was it colder where they were if they were heading toward the mountains?

"It would have been better if you used both crutches," Tashué said.

"I can't," Ishmael grunted. "It hurts my shoulder too much. Besides, it's good like this. Kaine doesn't like me, so he'll enjoy watching me struggle."

The door to the pugilist club was marked by a hanging wooden sign carved with a pair of boxing gloves, and the stairs were a challenge for Ishmael with his single crutch, but Allie helped him up every step. The inside of the club was warmer than he expected. High ceilings made the room feel impossibly big, even as the crowd milled across the space. People were packed in knots where they could, leaving big empty rings around those exercising or sparring or training. There must have been a few kegs somewhere; at least half of the people had pint glasses in their hands. And the Talent. Tashué could feel it everywhere, like the glow from a wood stove—so many people had Talent that Tashué couldn't even pinpoint each source like the collective heat of dozens of bricks of coal. He fought to pull his Talent in again. He must have let it slip—apparently he had to concentrate on keeping it contained.

As Tashué's eyes scanned the crowd, he realized he'd never actually seen Davik Kaine. He'd been thinking about the man for days—surely not yet weeks?—but he had no idea what Kaine looked like, or how to pick him out of the crowd. But Vasska and Ishmael obviously did, so Tashué let Vasska lead. Tashué spotted someone he actually recognized —Lorne, stripped to the waist, body bathed in sweat, fists sporting white boxing gloves, head dipped. He was doing the same combination of punches over and over, gloves hitting the punching bag with obsessive precision.

"What's Coswyn doing here?" Ishmael asked.

"You didn't hear?" Vasska asked, glancing over his shoulder. "Mr. Coswyn is the Bay's first real pugilist. He'll be representing the Bay in Eirdis Redbone's exhibition match."

"Why him?" Ishmael asked.

"Because he survived against Ijaz the Hammer," Allie said. "Right? That's what the sports pages have been saying."

"Sure," Vasska said. "And Grandad was impressed with how he took that beating after. How he got back up."

Anxiety prickled across Tashué's skin like old sweat. How much did Davik and his Red Dawn thugs know about that beating *after*? Was Hale really working alone? Was Lorne even safe here?

He looked plenty safe. The wounds he'd taken in that fight were well healed, even though that was… what? Only a few days ago. He wore new trousers, without any darns or holes in them, and brand new boots, laced tight, the soles squeaking on the waxed floor as he moved. Three men stood with him; one shirtless like Lorne, tall and lanky with a scar that looked like a bullet wound in his abdomen. One young and awkward, probably still a teenager. And then a looming man, all breadth and charisma even as he stood still, watching Lorne assault the punching bag. Dressed in good quality trousers and a clean shirt and worn leather boots, he stood with his hands on his hips and his sleeves rolled up to his elbows to show off his tattoos. Salt-and-pepper hair was combed back from his face, his beard thick and well-groomed.

Lorne didn't see them coming; he was too absorbed in what he was doing. The combination was fast and vicious, exactly the sort of latent speed that Lorne had gotten his nickname for. Once they were closer, Tashué could hear his measured, disciplined breathing, hissing in and out as his fists flew. Right, left, left, right, right, left, fists up to his face. Right, left, left, right, right, left, fists up.

"Again. Faster."

Right, left, left, right, right, left, fists up.

"Faster, like you want to win. Do you know who you're up against? Again! Faster!"

Tashué winced in sympathy at the fatigue that must be burning through Lorne's muscles. His fists were a little lower, his arms a little slower, his face dripping with sweat.

Lorne's coach spotted Vasska first, and then his eyes slid over everyone else as they jostled their way to the edge of the open space around Lorne. He reached out and slapped Lorne on the back of the neck, the sound like a thunderclap.

"Look alive, laddie, you've got an audience. Again, show Mr. Czarny you're making the Bay proud. Faster."

Lorne let out an animal growl but started swinging again, pushing through some barrier of exhaustion and somehow going faster. The two younger men—Tashué thought he felt their Talents swirling right through Lorne's body, but maybe not. It disappeared as soon as he noticed it.

"Nice of you to join us, Mr. Czarny," the man said, turning away from Lorne and offering Vasska a handshake. "And you've brought company. I'd hoped you were dead somewhere, Saeati. Would have made my day, going to your funeral."

"You can't get rid of me that easily, Davik," Ishmael grunted.

"What happened to your knee?"

Ishmael shrugged, making a big show of adjusting his balance with the crutch. "Authority happened."

Davik Kaine laughed. The sound was big and joyful and almost infectious, except that it was also sharp-edged with scorn. "Couldn't have happened to a more deserving asshole. And you, Miss...?"

"Allie Tei," Allie said, offering a hand by some habit, even though she stood stiffly and leaned away from Davik.

"Allie Tei," Davik echoed, taking the handshake, his head cocked to one side as he considered Allie. "I've heard your name before, Miss Tei. Powell Iwan asked me if I had anything to do with what happened to you at your office at the Highview Times. I asked him why the fuck I would give two shits about a reporter from the Highview Times. That's when he told me that this particular reporter was looking into the shit

Edgar Hale was doing before someone killed him. I said I'd like to meet that reporter one day, shake her hand. Must have had a lot of sand, that reporter. To chase around after Hale and survive an Enquiry Officer."

Allie shrugged. Between staring down Powell Iwan and now Davik Kaine, she had a hell of a lot of sand, indeed. "Hale alleged that he was killing children for you, Mr. Kaine."

"Hale was a runny turd," the youngest boy said. "He wanted to be big, and Da didn't trust him. He started talking about doing something that proved to Da that he meant business, something that would make Da proud."

"Why would Edgar Hale think killing children would make you proud, Davik?" Ishmael asked. "What about you gave him that impression?"

Davik scowled, looking between Allie and Ishmael and Vasska. "He heard what I tried to do in Cruinnich. I was a different man, back then. I was so angry about everything the Authority took from me, and I lost sight of what it meant to fight against them."

"So what are you now?" Ishmael asked. "Not angry anymore?"

"Oh, I'm still mighty angry," Davik said, his voice rumbling from somewhere deep in his chest, rolling like distant thunder. "So angry I can feel my bones boiling. But I'm older now, and I understand a few things about the world and how to get things done, don't I?"

Lorne finally quit hitting the bag, turning to face Tashué. His bright blue eyes were as hot with anger as Tashué had ever seen them, cracking open the distance between them so it seemed an impossible gulf even though Lorne was almost within reach. He swiped the sweat out of his face with his bare arm, and that only seemed to make him angrier.

"I told Jason you were missing, you fucking asshole," Lorne said. "I went in there this morning and told him you're probably dead, and it was the worst thing I've done in my entire life. Second worst was telling him his mother was dead—something you should have done, but you couldn't, could you? And now you wander in here like you belong here? Fuck you."

Davik's eyes snapped to Tashué, his head cocking to one side as he realized exactly who he was looking at. As if he hadn't even noticed Tashué before, not with Ishmael and Allie and Vasska standing in between them.

"You're not going to introduce yourself, big man?" Davik asked.

Tashué shrugged. "Doesn't sound like I need to."

"Could Mr. Coswyn spare you a while?" Vasska asked. "I really think we should sit and have a conversation."

"I'm coming," Lorne said before Davik could answer for him. "I want to hear whatever bullshit excuses he has for this whole fucking mess."

"You don't want to go see Jason, tell him about his father?" the shirtless boy asked.

"I can't," Lorne said with an angry shake of his head. "I can't visit twice in one day."

Davik shrugged a few times, like something was chafing him and he was trying to shake it off. "Fine. C'mere, let me unlace you. Rowan, go tell whoever's working the *Bucket* to deliver enough lunch for everyone."

Rowan, the youngest boy, rolled his eyes and peeled away, but the shirtless one hovered close to Lorne like he thought he was protecting Lorne from something. Lorne shoved his hands toward Davik. Something cold slid up Tashué's spine, like hatred but too detached and too distant. He expected himself to be angrier, more filled with trembling, unreasoning hatred. His emotions were usually so *hot*, so furious. But somehow seeing Lorne here already took the fire out of Tashué's chest, replaced it with guilt instead. Because he was right about Jason. Tashué should have been there to tell Jason about his mother.

"You think you can hobble yourself up my stairs, Saeati?" Davik asked. "Or do you need me to drag you up by your hair to spare your knee?"

"Try it," Tashué said before he could think better of opening his mouth at all. So much for making nice with Davik Kaine. "See what happens."

Davik flashed Tashué his too-friendly, artificial smile, holding up his hands. But his eyes looked bright, entertained. Maybe this was the best way to make nice with Davik. Maybe he loved all the posturing. "Take it easy, big man. Saeati and I have a way, is all."

"Don't mind my bodyguard, Davik," Ishmael said, nudging Tashué in the chest with one elbow. "He's a little wound up after everything. Lead the way up the stairs, and we'll tell you all about it."

The second floor was a well-furnished apartment, the rooms tight and cozy, lit with gaslights. There couldn't have been many gas lines through the Bay, but Davik also had plumbing so apparently he had spared no expense in his renovation of the place, making it more modern than at least half the city. Radiators rattled beneath each window, generating all that warmth that made the place feel too hot and too dry. Lorne paused in the kitchen to grab a towel and a whole jug of water, mopping the sweat off his face and out of his hair.

"I thought the plan for Blackwood was that you'd be the one taking care of him, Mr. Czarny," Davik said, leading everyone down the long hallway.

Vasska shrugged, walking in step with Davik. "Are you saying no to more experienced soldiers for your army, Mr. Kaine?"

Davik snorted. He opened the door to a study, a desk and chairs giving the place the feeling of an office. Sofas and chairs clustered around a big, empty hearth. The radiator gave the room more than enough warmth. "I'm saying no to harbouring a wanted fugitive. I'm saying no to drawing more ire from the Authority and the Patrollers."

"You're the one who guessed the Authority would come looking for trouble no matter what," Vasska said. "Why not be as prepared as possible?"

"I'm trying to be," Davik said. "And I'm preparing by telling you to take your big tinman and fuck off."

"I'm surprised at you, Davik," Ishmael said. He hobbled slowly to a chair and sank down with a satisfied groan. Allie hovered next to the chair, not yet ready to let her guard down enough to sit. "I never would have thought of you as a coward."

"Ishmael," Vasska huffed.

"Don't *Ishmael* me," Ishmael huffed back. "You're not my mother or my priest."

"You have a priest?" the lanky boy laughed, sinking down into a sofa and spreading himself into a luxurious slouch. Like a cat, taking up as much room as possible. "That's rich."

"I do have a priest, dear László," Ishmael said. "But Qasani priests aren't all pinched and stuffy and judgemental like Sisters of the North Star. Best opium in the city is at a Qasani temple."

"Well, shit," the lanky boy said. László. He caught Lorne's hand and dragged him down onto the sofa. Lorne half-fell and half-sat, perching on the edge of the seat like he wasn't sure if he was ready to relax. "Does your priest take conversions?"

Tashué turned away from them all, toward the sideboard where the bottles of whisky were lined up like soldiers at muster. Davik had opted to leave all his whisky in their original bottles instead of using decanters, the labels declaring the wide variety. A few bottles of Ladovaugh—including the same 18-year Tashué had from his father, although Davik's was mostly full—and a few bottles of Rhydderch whisky. He'd never made the connection before. Was the same Rhydderch as Stella's true name? The stonesmiths from up north. Had his father's family ever worked for Rhydderch Stone? Was his father the first stonesmith in the Guinne line, or was he carrying a family skill? And if his line came from up north... how long had Rhydderch Stone been up there, mining the mountains?

He grabbed one of the Rhydderch bottles, feeling the familiar, comforting weight of it. He didn't drink Rhydderch usually—it was good, which meant it could get expensive—but whisky bottles all felt the same in the hand. Clear glass showed off the deep and rich reddish colour, catching the light from the sconce on the wall. He slid his thumb over the label, searching the details of it for clues about Stella's family, and his too for that matter. But of course it didn't have any answers. It was just a bottle of whisky, aged in brandy barrels from the Commonwealth.

"Get a grip, Davik," Ishmael said. Tashué had missed whatever they were arguing about. Him, probably. "And admit that you're scared. Captain Blackwood would be invaluable to your cause given everything he's been through over the last twelve hours. But he's wanted, and your balls are sweating over it, so you're pretending to be too tough for help."

"How could a disgraced tinman possibly help me?" Davik scoffed. He'd settled in a plush leather armchair while Tashué wasn't looking, facing Ishmael so they could glare at each other. "What *exactly* do you think he can say that I can't possibly get from anyone else in the Bay—people who haven't been my enemy for two decades, people who haven't carried the tin and put my own people into the Rift and into early graves. He waves his big impressive gun around once, and you think that's enough to make up for nineteen years? Fuck off."

Tashué gave his best, most exhausted sigh. His feet hurt so damned much. He wanted to sit, but he knew when he did, he'd want to pull his boots off. They were still wet from the river. "I'm not here to measure cocks with you, Mr. Kaine. Yes, I carried the tin. But I didn't know what it represented. We could argue that I should have known. You're right. We can argue that not knowing doesn't make my complicity any less vile. You'll be right again. But the fact is that now I know about the children they call energy units, and I know about Enquiry Officers hunting people down and murdering them, and now I want to help fight it."

"You want to help, do you?" Davik asked. "Help do what, exactly? Get your boy off and fuck off?"

"No." Tashué slid his thumb over the Rhydderch name, imagining it let him reach out to Stella and touch her, too. It was a good thing she left, with Davik and Bothain here, fighting over the city. "I want to rip it all apart like you do."

Davik sighed, running his fingers through his beard a few times before smoothing the hairs back down. He crossed his arms over his chest, tapped his heels on the floor a few times. "Is this a threat, Mr. Czarny? Get the Blackwood boy out or the big father will hang me out one of my windows like Hale?"

"Not at all, Mr. Kaine," Vasska said smoothly. "It's a peace offering. You and me and Captain Blackwood are all standing for the same thing."

"And you've brought your bullet-proof reporter here for what, exactly?" Davik asked. "To document your heroics for the big papers? You're Wolfe's lackey, aren't you, tinman? You going to run for Mayor once it's all over?"

Tashué couldn't help but laugh. "I think I've become too infamous, even for Yaelsmuir politics."

"Captain Blackwood and I met when we were looking for answers about what happened to those children," Allie said. "I've collected as much evidence I could find about them, including the photographs the mortuaries took of their bodies. I'll blanket this city with evidence of the Authority's crimes, whether you want my help or not. I think it will be swifter and more effective if we work together, even though I find your assertions that you don't know what Hale was doing dubious at best, and I find you personally deplorable for having a hand in it. Or even suspecting it might be happening and not stopping it. Whatever excuse you keep handy for your plausible deniability, I don't believe it. However, I'm of the opinion that the Authority is so big a foe, so terrible a monument to brutality, that I'm willing to set aside my hatred of you and your organization in the interest of getting justice for the children. Hale is gone, at least. But the larger, more pressing reality is they wouldn't have been vulnerable to him if they hadn't been turned into energy units in the first place."

"My, Miss Tei," Davik said slowly. "Speak your mind loud and clear, don't you?"

Allie shrugged. "I'm very tired, Mr. Kaine. I'm tired of wasting time and bickering over territory while the Authority hunts us down to protect their secrets. I want to do something."

"What about you, Saeati?" Davik asked, stretching out a leg and prodding Ishmael's good foot with the toe of his boot. "Are you here to stand on your good leg, or are you going to run back to Mayor Wolfe and report everything I'm doing?"

"General Wolfe knows we're down here," Ishmael said. "Miss Tei and Mr. Blackwood told him everything they know. He spent the morning lying to the Authority to give us time to get away."

Davik laughed. "A politician spent the morning lying? Fancy that. Isn't that just a regular day at the office for our Mayor?"

"Davik," Ishmael said, drawing the name out in slow enunciation. "You're not listening. General Wolfe *knows* why we're here. He knows what we're fighting against, and he knows what we're willing to do. Whatever happens down here, he condones it. Anything to topple Elsworth and the Governor, and stop the police force from existing."

Davik cocked his head at that, eyes flicking between Vasska, Ishmael, and Tashué. One by one, taking their measure as the silence stretched.

"What do we need permission from the Mayor for?" László snorted. "We do what we want down here, Ishmael. I thought you would know that by now."

"László," Davik said.

"Yeah, Dav?"

"Shut the fuck up a second."

László scoffed, sitting up straighter. "Excuse me?"

"László, darling," Ishmael said. "I know it's hard to grasp things like this because that beautiful head of yours wasn't made for thinking, so I'll walk it out for you. General Wolfe—the Mayor—has the power over the City Civilian Patrol. They can't get involved in civil unrest without his permission. And if he condones your actions in the pursuit of justice against the Authority, he won't issue arrest warrants for anyone involved in the aforementioned civil unrest."

The words landed heavy in the room—Tashué watched the doubt

cross Allie's face. Lorne's too. Tashué felt it in his own chest, even though it helped their case. It didn't sound right, that they could tear the city apart and get away with it.

László didn't have any such doubt. The joy that crossed his face in that moment was savage and predatory. He looked to Davik, then Vasska. And simmered in the possibility a moment, another, time stretching so quietly that Tashué could swear he heard a clock somewhere in the apartment, ticking every second away.

"How come our big Blackwood was arrested in the first place?" László asked finally. "If the Mayor ain't going to send Patrollers after us, why'd he send them after him?"

"He didn't send them," Ishmael said. "He tried to talk Elsworth out of them, but apparently Elsworth went to a Patroller station and filed formal charges."

"What's to stop him from filing charges all of us when shit down here gets fun?" László asked.

Ishmael sighed, spreading his hands. "As a victim of an assault, Elsworth had the grounds to file against his assaulter. But he can't order the Patrollers on a city-wide level without the Mayor's signature. He can probably pull some of them in for riot patrol, but otherwise? He'll have to use tinmen."

"And the Authority is short-staffed," Tashué said. "Our house was struggling under our caseload and Elsworth admitted there wasn't anyone spare to replenish our ranks. I asked around, before everything." 'Before everything' sounded so dishonest, a coward's way of saying 'before I went out of my mind with self-pity and whisky so I thought it would be a good idea to bring Keoh's urn to Elsworth.' But mentioning the self-pity slid dangerously close to talking about Stella. So 'before everything' would have to do. "Every house is under the necessary officer count to manage their cases."

"Still had enough tinmen to go shoot Gianna Tarbrook, though, didn't you?" László said.

"I think that's *why* Elsworth sent us after Glaen and Gianna," Tashué said. "The face of the Authority shit was for the election, sure, but it was also supposed to be a recruitment tool for the Authority. That's why he sent us with guns and a photographer. Their service numbers are low and they need more troops—they had us do the same thing in the military."

Davik nodded a few times, pushing himself to his feet. He

wandered slowly to the sideboard, pulling a pair of glasses from the shelf. "What if I tell the lot of you that I don't need help getting the younger Blackwood out of the Rift. What if I said everything is ready, and we're waiting for pieces to fall into place. If I don't let you help with your boy, are you still all afire to take down the Authority?" He set the glasses side by side, pointing at the bottle of Rhydderch Tashué was still holding.

"Yessir, Mr. Kaine," Tashué said, handing the bottle over. "I didn't think you'd trust me enough to let me get involved with Jason. So my offer to help extends to anything. Whatever it takes to earn your trust. I'm offering my military background and an education in leadership from the Officer's Academy. This is the time to mobilize and get serious about the Red Dawn being a real threat to civility. We need something more, an overwhelming avalanche of proof like Allie said, so people can't turn away anymore."

"What do you suggest, then?" Davik passed the bottle back and forth between his hands a few times, the whisky sloshing in the glass. "What proof?"

"Proof is all over the city," Tashué said, spreading his hands. "All we need to do is find it and take it."

Davik bared his teeth, shaking his head. "I'll need something a touch more specific than that. Like Miss Tei said, the Authority's a'huntin'."

"The station houses," Tashué said. Even though saying it made him think of Beckett and his new baby, of Lian guarding the desk, of Celia at the typewriters. So many people who didn't know what they were participating in. "House One will have the most—that's where we file deaths like Gianna Tarbrook. We can prove she was killed for nothing. And then the Breeding Program. I stood in that hallway with all that fucking paperwork—we can take every page."

The front door creaked open on hinges so loud and stiff, they could hear it from the study. Footsteps down the hall, and the smell of garlic and onions and fat. Rowan led a man carrying a pot that gave off a rich, savoury scent that made Tashué's mouth water.

"I hope yesterday's pork and beans are alright, Mr. Kaine," the publican said. "That's what we had ready in a hurry, in any case. If you need anything else, we'll have it over as soon as we can."

"Thank you, Cyril," Davik said. "That'll do for now. Just set it down on the sideboard."

Cyril nodded, hustling across the study to set the pot among the bottles of whisky. László was on his feet immediately, coming to stand beside Tashué so he could get to the pot first.

"Go get some plates, Row," László said, pulling the lid off the pot and releasing a hot curl of steam that smelled of fat and molasses and garlic. "And a big spoon."

"You go get them," Rowan muttered. "I went and got the damned food."

"Row, just go," Davik said.

Rowan huffed and stomped out of the room as László reached right into the pot, picking a piece of fat off the top. He groaned as he ate it, licking molasses gravy off his fingers. "C'mere, Mr. Lightning. I know you've been working up an appetite."

Lorne came without question but also without speaking. Holding onto his surly silence like it was a shield to protect him. He stood with László, on the other side like he was trying to keep Tashué at a distance, avoiding Tashué's gaze completely. László scooped up another piece of pork and put it in Lorne's mouth.

"Whose pork do you buy?" Ishmael asked before the publican could follow Rowan out. "Wolfe's?"

"Not exclusively, sir," the publican said. "Whoever's got the best price at the market."

Ishmael wrinkled his nose. "What else have you got cooking?"

"Soup'll be ready in an hour or two."

"Pork or beef broth?"

"Beef, sir."

Ishmael nodded, resting his hand on his knee. The pain must have been flaring, but Tashué hadn't felt it. Relief, and then fresh guilt echoing after it. He had to fight against the urge to reach out, to try to ease some of the pain. He didn't know what would happen—what Davik could do —if Tashué let his guard down.

"I'll take the soup when it's ready," Ishmael said.

"Yes, sir."

"Nothing but Wolfe pork for our high and mighty Mr. Saeati, is it?" Davik asked as the publican hustled himself out.

"It's a myth that Powell Iwan feeds his enemies to the pigs," László said with a snort. "Just a fun story that other people like to tell when they don't understand how killing a man works. Who needs pigs when you've got the Brightwash for hiding bodies?"

"How sure are you?" Ishmael countered. "Will you be having the unknown pork, Vasska?"

Vasska shrugged. "I prefer Wolfe pork, too. Better quality, they say."

"Fuck's sake," Lorne muttered, stopping his chewing like he was thinking about spitting it out.

László laughed, picking another piece off the top. "The first gator I killed, this one here?" He scooped up his necklace with the other hand, holding up a massive tooth that hung from it like a lucky charm. "He was a man eater, too. That's the reason we were hunting it. Anyway, we ate him after I shot him. Made him taste better, I figure." He put the piece in his mouth and winked at Tashué as he licked molasses off his fingertips. He probably thought he was being clever or flirty, but all Tashué could see was how young he was. Sure, maybe in his early twenties, but early twenties seemed so damned far away these days. Jason was in his early twenties, too, and Tashué remembered holding Jason in one hand when he was born. "You ever eat a creature powerful enough to eat a man, Captain Blackwood? They taste real fine."

"I'm not hungry," Tashué said. The thought of pig teeth cracking open human bone to get to the marrow took the appetite out of him.

"Shame, that. Big man like you, I thought you'd have a huge appetite."

Lorne huffed. "Fucking hell, László. You can't flirt with *him*. He's Jason's father."

László scoffed, elbowing Lorne. "A man being a father makes him off limits? Fuck off. I don't answer to you, no matter how cute you are when you blush."

Davik pulled the cork from the bottle of Rhydderch finally, the familiar squeal of cork on glass setting an echo of longing in Tashué's blood. If only life was simple enough for him to sit with Davik and ask questions about the Rhydderch whisky and whether it was connected to Stella's family. But life wasn't simple. Life was complicated and ugly, and time was ticking.

"It seems I'm taking in a lot of Powell Iwan's strays these days."

Lorne bristled, one fist clenching. "What's that supposed to mean? Are you calling me a stray?"

Davik shrugged, pouring whisky into both glasses. "If the gloves fit, Mr. Lightning."

"Fuck you, Dav." Lorne walked away, slumping back down onto the sofa near Vasska. "How about I see if my glove fits right in your mouth, hey?"

Davik grinned and met Tashué's eye. "He always been such a merry ray of sunshine?"

"Always," Tashué said. "At least the five years I've known him."

"You should have a drink, Captain," Davik said, knocking his glass off the second one, filling the room with a bright note that rang for a surprisingly long time. "The Rhydderch Red is plenty nice. Tastes like a summer night up north, when the girls have been eating wild grapes so their lips are sweet and sour when you kiss them, and the air always tastes like bonfire because no one wants to get to sleep when the days are so long." He grinned and sipped it, like he was sharing a profound secret. "You'll want a bit of fire in your veins when I tell you what I want to do."

Tashué shook his head. "I shouldn't."

Davik shrugged. "Suit yourself."

Rowan came back with a stack of bowls and spoons. He set the whole armful down on one of the tables, and László grabbed two bowls to serve himself and Lorne.

"I don't give a shit about your station houses, tinman," Davik said slowly, his voice gone sharp and low. "I don't care about your stacks of paperwork or how your healer Tarbrook died. I don't need proof that it was your fault. Everything I want is bigger than that. You follow?"

Allie bristled, leaning forward in her seat. "But the proof—"

Davik held up a hand a hand to her. "Excuse me, Miss Tei, but I was very patient through all your big speeches about proof and how much you hate me. So now it's my turn."

Allie clamped her mouth shut, folding her hands in her lap like it was some default posture when she was in a tense moment. "If you say so, Mr. Kaine."

"I'm not interested in proving a damn thing," Davik said. "We're past that. The tainted have been screaming at the tops of our lungs for decades, trying to prove how vile it all is, but it's never enough. We bleed in the streets every day, begging for mercy, and people say we're getting what we deserve. Instead of wasting my breath another day, I'm going to go ahead and help myself to the things I want. You're right I want to go into the Breeding Program, but not for fucking paper. Burn the paper, I don't give a shit. I'm going for wee ones. For the children, and for the women who made them. I'm going to walk them out of that place in a grand old freedom parade, and the Authority will know they can't stop us. Aye?"

"Dav," László said, his mouth half full with pork, mangling his words. "Are you sure? Can we trust these people?"

"What say you, Mr. Lightning? Can we trust your big mountain of a father in law?"

"What do you expect me to say?" Lorne scoffed. "Of course I *want* you to trust him. Because if you don't, what happens? You'll kill him, right?"

The room went quiet and a little bit cold. Everything went slow. Davik's eyes never left Tashué's face. He sipped his whisky, and he smiled a little. His Talent swirled, lazy and slow, a heartbeat that Tashué could hear because his own Talent was ever aware, ever vigilant. There was nothing to say to break the tension, nothing to do but wait.

"I asked you a question, Mr. Lightning," Davik said. "Can I trust that Tashué Blackwood is here to fight *for* me and *with* me?"

"For you?" Lorne asked. "No. But for Jason? Yes. Absolutely yes. He'll do anything for Jason."

"Right then." Davik drained the rest of his whisky and rested the glass on the sideboard, scooping up the bottle like he was thinking about pouring himself some more. "Before I can get into the Breeding Program, I need your boy. And to get your boy out, I need these streets to be quiet. If we give the Authority reason to suspect problems from us, they'll lock down the Rift so tight, no one will get in or out. And I need money. Crowns, bank notes, the whole lot of it. I need mountains upon mountains of it—because once we're into the Breeding Program, it'll be war, won't it? And fighting a war is expensive. So that beautiful idiot boy of mine right there," he pointed over Tashué's shoulder at László, who was spooning pork and beans into his mouth, "is going to rob a bank for me. And if you're serious about helping me, then I'm going to send you along with him. Since you're all aflame to save your boy, this is my price. You help him take the crowns, or you fuck off back to Powell Iwan or General Wolfe—whichever one sent you—and say I turned you away. How's that?"

"Fuck off," Tashué said. He scooped up the glass, watching the red-gold whisky swirl, catching the light from the lamps to make the whole glass glow. "You aren't serious."

Davik laughed. "What did you expect? That we'd be down here writing letters of discontent. *Dear Mr. Elsworth. On behalf of the hoard of tainted whom you've been oppressing for your entire career, we hereby request that you cease and desist all violent action against us, or else we'll be extremely unhappy from here out. Sincerely, Davik Kaine and the Army of the Red Dawn."*

"Has a nice ring to it, though," László said. "Maybe we should print out a million letters like that, paste them on every brightpost in the city. See if it helps things."

"Maybe we can nail one right to Elsworth's skull," Rowan said.

Ishmael laughed. "I like it, Row, but I don't think anyone's getting within ten feet of Rainer Elsworth from here on. I'll wager my life's savings that he's got bodyguards by now."

"You're the one who said you had military experience, Captain," Davik pressed, leaning closer to Tashué, his eyes glittering with excitement. "How many times has a revolution happened by asking nicely? Knocking on doors and saying *please sir, we don't want trouble, we just want to be treated like human beings."*

"I wouldn't know, Davik," Tashué said. Talent buzzed in his ears, an angry animal rattling at the cage that kept it still. "By the time I was deployed, all the polite asking was over."

"Let's ask Saeati, then," Davik said, swinging to Ishmael. "What say you, Mr. Diplomat? You bounce across the world and make backroom deals for peace and war, don't you? You think we can beg our way to something better?"

"Do you want the long answer or the short answer?" Ishmael said.

"Which answer will I like the most?" Davik asked.

Ishmael shrugged, sighed. "It's more complicated than you're trying to imply, Davik."

"Before the lot of you argue anymore about banks and laws, I feel I should clarify," Allie cut in. "My intention to write articles about the Authority is not negotiable. Mayor Wolfe purchased a printing press and all the required pieces, and they'll be delivering to the Bay any day now. I'll be running my paper as an underground publication. If you've the nerve for it, I could set up somewhere nearby. I would appreciate the help—there's a lot of work to be done. If you haven't, Mr. Iwan has offered some warehouse space near the dry-docks. I'll be further away, and I'm sure Mr. Iwan and Mr. Czarny can offer me the helping hands I need."

Davik laughed, resting his empty glass on the sideboard. "If I have the nerve? Shite, I have to say I underestimated you, Miss Tei."

"Can you really say you're surprised?" Vasska asked.

"I suppose I can't. Very well, then, Miss Tei. What sort of material will you be printing?"

"Oh, you know, the usual things that make the average editor sweat a little. Criticism of the Crowne and the Authority. Inflammatory press and product of sedition."

"I thought smear campaigns were a staple of every newspaper," Rowan said. "It's the purpose of half our papers."

"Of provincial and local level politicians, yes," Allie said. "But criticizing the Crowne or any of the Crowne-endorsed national programs is a dangerous game at best. You have to step carefully or you could be charged with inciting rebellion. It's why General Wolfe wanted us to wait for proof when we went to him the first time—with concrete proof, legitimate papers have a bit more legal protection. But now? Our Mr. Blackwood went and made himself a tragic hero, and then Rainer Elsworth killed him for it. And he killed the much beloved, if a little infamous, Ishmael Saeati. I'll publish whatever I have to in order to make the population of this city furious. I want every citizen to wonder what secrets Rainer Elsworth is trying to protect. And if I'm here, with you, we can work on this underground project together."

"Are you offering me a say in what articles get printed?" Davik asked.

"To an extent, yes," Allie said. "But I'm rather hoping Mr. Saeati will help in that regard, as well. His career in diplomacy makes him an excellent asset in the terms of writing radicalizing propaganda."

Davik tilted his head to one side, turning to look at Tashué. "So, what about you tinman? Your reporter is choosing her side. Are you with me, or not?"

Tashué sighed. He threw back the whole serving, feeling it burn all the way down, the sweetness and the smoke of it lingering on his tongue, battling for supremacy. He turned the glass over, resting it rim-side down on the sideboard to deny himself any more, no matter how much he wanted it.

Robbing a fucking bank, shit.

31

JASON
DAY 34

R ezji had small, elegant hands, but they were always stained with blood. Her chore was slaughtering chickens for the kitchen, and the constant need for meat to feed so many people meant she could never clean all the blood from beneath her nails or from the creases of her knuckles before it was time for her to make more carcasses from living things. Jason didn't know her last name or where she was from, or where she got the scar on her face that blinded her in one eye, but he knew the only important thing about her: she was Red Dawn, and she was the one who said the Army of the Red Dawn wanted him out of the Rift.

Hunger stripped so many people of any spare weight, turning them all to lean pieces of gristle and shards of bone, and she was no exception. But in spite of that huger that gnawed at them all, she ate slowly. Maybe she liked to sit in the mess hall and enjoy the absence of death. Maybe it was hard to eat when she'd spent the day killing for tomorrow's meal. Or maybe she wasn't afraid of anyone stealing her food because she was secure in her knowledge that she was untouchable.

It must have been a nice feeling.

"I need to know when," Jason said. He stared down at his bowl. Thin broth with onions and scraps of chicken. It was good only in that way that all food was good when you were ravenous all the time. "I need to know how much longer."

Rezji only shrugged. She had to tilt her head to look at Jason with her one good eye. He'd wondered more than once if a proper registered healer could have helped her or if it was too late now. "Soon."

"I know, soon," Jason whispered. The only place in the Rift that had any privacy was the visitation rooms. Everywhere else, Jason had to be careful with what he said and who he said it to since people were always watching. Guards, proxies, fellow inmates—everyone kept half an eye on him since he broke the suppression. "I need more than that. Please, Rezji. They're going to ship me to the Breeding Program whether I register or not, aren't they? I don't know why they've waited so long already. And then what happens to me once they finally decide to transfer me? Can your people get me out of there?"

He bit off any more words before he really started babbling. He couldn't say anything about his father, and he couldn't say anything about his brother Valen and how desperately he wanted to meet his mother's last child, or he'd really fall apart. He'd learned fast that he had to hide his cracks and his fault lines before someone exploited them. Some people liked to hit him in the cracked places and watch him splinter for the fun of it.

Rezji was staring at him. She wore her hair down, not bothering to plait it or tie it. Curls and tangles curtained her face. Her head tilted slowly to one side, her mouth pulling. Not as blank as her expression usually was when she looked at him, but not exactly an outpouring of emotion.

"I heard he was arrested," she said. "Your father. For threatening to shoot Rainer Elsworth."

"That's what Lorne said," Jason gasped, fighting to breathe, fighting to keep himself held together. Fighting to keep himself blank and empty like Rezji was. But Lorne's words filled him and rattled around his chest and he couldn't get rid of them. "It's probably true. He's been losing his grip lately."

"I heard he's still missing."

Jason nodded, wiping his eyes quickly. "Yeah. Probably dead."

"I liked him."

Jason looked up at Rezji, searching her face. "You—what?"

"He was my Officer for a time." She rubbed the scars around her eye, like it was all vaguely itchy. "Years ago. Not for long. But I liked him. A fool for taking the tin, but kind when he didn't need to be."

"I didn't know he was your tinman." How many people in here hated

Jason because his father wore that stupid badge? He'd never heard anyone say something nice about his father before. "How long ago?"

"Five years?" Rezji's gaze drifted upward to the ceiling, her fingers twitching like she was counting something. "Six. Only temporary, before the Authority placed me at a job. Moved to Drystone after. That's where all the stonesmiths live. Next tinman was cruel. Kept grabbing my ass like it was his due. Made me like your father more."

"I'm sorry," Jason said softly.

He only had more questions—how did she wind up here? How did she know Davik Kaine? But those questions were too loaded. Rift etiquette was that you didn't ask how people got here. The answer all boiled down to the same thing anyway—they were all tainted meat and the Authority got to do what they wanted. And good sense meant he wasn't about to say Kaine's name out loud while he sat in the mess hall. Davik Kaine and the Army of the Red Dawn were words you whispered at night when people's snoring drowned out your voice, and there wasn't enough light for anyone to read your lips.

Rezji shrugged and went back to eating, her movements slow and too leisurely. Resentment flared to life. He imagined himself taking her bowl and spoon and hurling them across the room. Standing on the table and demanding answers. Jason had gone looking for Davik Kaine, once. Somewhere around his fifteenth birthday, he'd realized he couldn't hide his Talent forever. It had been quickening slowly for years. So, he went down to the Bay and chased the rumours of Davik Kaine and his army of tainted meat, but he hadn't found anything.

Well, he found Lorne down there in the Bay. Or maybe Lorne found him. Either way, he'd left the Bay convinced that Davik Kaine was a myth. A lie. A stupid dream.

But now Davik Kaine was looking for him, and no one would—or could—answer any of Jason's questions. His foot was still sore from the broken toe he earned the day he helped Glaen Forsooth—one of his father's arrestees, of course. His body was still sore from the beating he caught. Or maybe he was always sore, his whole body aching all the time forever now, because he was hungry and because he slept on a wooden slab. But the fury, it burned in him, fuelled by grief and fear. Fuck the Authority. They'd taken his mother from him. They'd given her opium until she smoked herself to death. And the rest of his siblings—were any of them alive other than Valen? And now they'd taken his father, too. They'd probably killed him somewhere so he couldn't spread the horrible things he knew. That's why there were bodies in the Dunnenbrahl. They'd taken him out there to silence him, but he and Ishmael fought like the stubborn men they were, and they'd taken all those Patrollers to the Keeper's Gate with them.

"Rezji," he whispered instead of climbing up on the table and raging at her to let the pressure out. "Please. I need to know when."

She dropped her spoon into the bowl, pushing it away as she rose to her feet. "Be patient. Soon."

Jason's hands twitched with the urge to catch her hand and drag her back down. He wanted to grab her and shake her. He wanted to scream at her and demand answers. He wanted to make her do whatever it was she was planning *now* so they could break the whole fucking place down and walk away. He needed to get out of here. He'd bust down the Rift and the Breeding Program, and then he'd go out to the Dunnenbrahl to see the place where his father died, so he wouldn't ever forget what the Authority took.

But he didn't grab her. He took a deep breath and tried to force all that emotion back down.

She pushed her hands into her pockets as she walked away, motioning for Glaen Forsooth to follow. Back down to wherever they went to kill all those chickens. Glaen stood a while, watching Jason a little too intently. Like he wanted to say something too. Maybe he wanted to shake Jason for answers like Jason wanted to shake Rezji.

Glaen Forsooth's steady attention since he arrived at the Rift and found out who Jason was—Tashué Blackwood's son—was like an itch on the back of Jason's neck, ever present. Burning with its intensity. Grating on his nerves. He probably wanted his cock polished like everyone else in this cursed place. Rezji said he was mooning over a dead woman, so maybe he was looking for a distraction and decided that Jason was just non-threatening enough. Or maybe he liked the idea of stuffing it to the son of the man who arrested him.

Fuck this place.

Jason pushed himself to his feet, grabbing his bowl and Rezji's, tossing them together. He stomped away from the table—he should have known better than to stomp. Stomping brought too much attention.

A hand caught his arm. He twisted to get away. But the resistance set him off balance. He staggered, elbow knocking someone who was standing too close, crowding in. Whoever he knocked shoved back against him. The same person grabbed him again. Verrit. Dragging Jason in close.

"Where are you going, Jason? All in a mood and everything?"

Jason wrenched his arm away from Verrit, trying to shove the bastard off him, but the way Verrit grabbed his arm knocked both bowls from his hands. They shattered on the stone floor, the sound high and splintering, as sharp as the shards the bowls made, both spoons clattering and ringing as they bounced away.

And then there was silence.

Everyone was watching.

Guards were coming closer.

"I'm sorry," Jason said, lifting his hands. Regret and fear ripped through him so fast he felt sick. "I didn't mean to break anything."

"Of course you didn't," Verrit said, too loud. His voice rang in the quiet hall, a performer on his favourite stage. "It was an accident, right?"

"Right," Jason breathed.

"You're having a hard month, Blackwood," Verrit said. "Every time you have a visitor, you're especially riled up. I wonder if you need to take a break from having visitors for a while?"

Jason's heart seized in his chest. Verrit wasn't a guard, but there weren't enough guards in the Rift so some of the inmates were given proxy privileges. Verrit's word was as good as one of the guards, and if he recommended that Jason's visitations be revoked, there was nothing Jason could say.

"No, I'm fine," Jason said, too quickly. The thought of never seeing anyone he loved was too terrible. Lorne was the only visitor he had left and every moment with him in that room was precious. "It's nothing. I'm fine. I hate it here. Don't we all hate it here?"

Verrit shrugged. "I think you should apologize again, Jason. Good and loud this time, so the guards can hear you. So they can relax and know you don't mean any harm. They're so nervous around you these days."

"You're right," Jason breathed, and he hated himself for how much his body trembled. "I'm sorry. I didn't mean to break anything. It was an accident."

"Show me how sorry you are, Jason." Verrit smiled, and it made bile rise in Jason's throat. "Down on your knees. Ask me for forgiveness."

Jason squeezed his eyes shut again. Everything trembled. All his muscles, all his bones. Quivered and shook beneath his skin. His meagre serving of precious food was going to come back up, and he was going to vomit at Verrit's feet and it would make everything worse. He kept his hands up so Verrit had no excuse to hit him, so the guards had no reason to call him threatening. He went down slowly. One knee, and then the other. Pain flared, taking him by surprise. His knee must have hit some shards of the bowls. Porcelain scraped against the stone beneath his weight but Jason didn't move. Best not to move. Best not to give Verrit an invitation to make things worse.

"I'm sorry," Jason said again. Loud as he could, even though his traitorous voice was trembling. The humiliation battled with the pain. "Please forgive me, Verrit. I didn't meant to break anything. You took me by surprise—"

"Oh, it's my fault?" Verrit asked.

"No—that's not what I meant," Jason said, looking up at Verrit. Meeting those cruel eyes, looking at the way his mouth twisted with his foul grin. He couldn't take another beating. "It was my fault. Please forgive me. I'm sorry."

Verrit reached down. His hand slid under Jason's jaw, cupping Jason's chin. "That's better. You're so much easier to get along with these days. Like you've finally learned your place here. It only took three years, hey? You think your daddy would be proud of you, down there on your knees? Maybe he's watching over you now that the Authority gave him the bullet he deserved."

Jason squeezed his eyes shut again. And a calm came over him. There was something comforting in knowing what Verrit wanted. He'd lost interest in the beatings, and he'd focused on some other way to exert his power over Jason, and this horrible dance was familiar. He hated it, hated how he was always surrounded by people who assumed they were entitled to his body, and he hated how filthy he felt after, but at least it didn't hurt as much. At least it didn't leave him with broken bones. "You're right. I'm sorry."

Verrit's hand drifted up, pushing into Jason's hair. All he needed to do was survive the Rift long enough to get out. Soon, Rezji said. And Davik Kaine had sent Lorne in here with that paper with Valen's number, because he wanted Jason to fight for the Red Dawn and the promise that someone was coming in to help. That *had* to mean he was serious about getting Jason out. All Jason had to do was survive, and he'd been doing *this* to survive for years.

"Up you get," Verrit said. "On your feet, now."

Jason rose carefully, keeping his hands up. One knee felt too hot. He knew that feeling. He was bleeding, and the nerves hadn't caught up to the pain yet. Verrit grabbed him by the arm, turning him toward the staircase. And Verrit leaned closer, his chest brushing against Jason's back, his breath hot in Jason's ear.

"You're going to show me how sorry you are."

Breathe, Lorne's voice told him, echoing through his head. *Take a deep breath. Don't let them see you cry.*

Verrit rested his hand on Jason's back, like he was ready to push Jason right down the stairs if Jason got too mouthy. And he would get away with it because the guards would be happy for Jason to be down for a while.

Down to the cellars, where they stored the dry goods. Potatoes, onions, braids of garlic. The chalky scent of rolled oats. Dust motes swirled in the sunbeams from the tiny windows. One of the bags must have contained rotten onions, the smell was thick and sour, coating Jason's mouth with every breath he took.

Jason hated Verrit for bringing him *here*. He liked it down here, rotten onion smell aside. He came down here sometimes to enjoy the quiet, to be alone. To feel his Talent. But now he was here with Verrit, and all he'd ever be able to think about was how this was one more place where he gave his dignity away in exchange for survival.

There was one spot in the Rift where he could pretend his life wasn't a waking nightmare. One spot where he could sit and feel his Talent. The headache eased its grip and his own willpower flooded in his veins, his blood feeling like it shimmered as it flowed through him. If he concentrated especially hard, he could heal himself, just a little. It was difficult, since the space wasn't big enough to fit his whole body, and he didn't know much about healing. But it was something. Better than nothing.

He could cry now, if he wanted to. He could sob and scream and make all the noises he'd refused to make when Verrit was using him. He could trash this place, throw bags of oats, kick over piles of onions. Waste weeks' worth of food out of spite. He wanted to. He *needed* to—he could feel the tension building in his muscles like acid, vicious emotion eating him from the inside out. But he couldn't. He'd swallowed it while he was refusing to make sounds for Verrit, and now he couldn't access it anymore. He was numb, distant. Floating away from himself. Retreating to some safe place—only there were no safe places for him. He was empty and dirty. And small.

He cursed himself for wishing he could learn to be smaller. He didn't like this version of himself at all. But he still couldn't grasp the emotion, couldn't feel it fully and properly. He was an imitation of himself, a poorly forged copy.

And he couldn't help but think about what Verrit said—*you think your daddy would be proud of you, down there on your knees*—and he remembered the time his father saw him sucking cock in the courtyard behind their building, except the cock belonged to one of the bullies who loved to make Jason miserable. And when Jason went upstairs to the little apartment, his father made some stupid joke about Jason and the bully settling their differences the old-fashioned way—and it should have been funny except Jason burst into tears. Because nothing had been settled. Nothing would get better. Even then, he knew it would only get worse.

Why do you do something like that if you don't like it? You don't have to do anything you want to. You can say no. You don't owe anyone anything.

Jason remembered thinking how much easier it must be to feel you didn't owe anyone anything when you were six-foot-four. He remembered wondering if he'd ever grow as tall and broad as his father, remembered cursing him for his confidence.

If I don't do something, they don't leave me alone. They're relentless, picking away at me, layer by layer, like they're trying to make me disappear. If I do things like that, then they leave me alone for a while.

He remembered the whole conversation too clearly. Remembered his father sitting on the sofa beside him. Remembered his father pulling him into one of his crushing, smothering hugs. His father was so good at hugging. And he remembered wanting to lean into it, wanting to bask in it, but instead he'd squirmed and sulked and pushed his father away. He couldn't remember why he pushed his father away so much, when all Jason ever wanted was a million giant, crushing hugs. That was the last earnest conversation they'd had, because Jason had gone down to the Bay a few weeks later. His Talent made him desperate.

Now he was here, and he hadn't hugged his father in three years. And there was a very real chance he'd never hug his father ever again because it was entirely likely that his father had died in the Dunnenbrahl, like everyone said.

He sat in the corner where the layer of suppression failed to meet so it didn't make a perfect seal, and he wondered if children were the ones making the shield that stood between every inmate and their Talent. Energy units, like Lorne said. He'd heard the guards use those words a time or two.

He closed his eyes, and he could feel the shape of the suppression with his Talent. Like a fog that wouldn't move, thick and impenetrable. In a circle, with an outer edge that he could almost trace all the way around the Rift. He could see the grounds beyond the circle, could find the river rushing around the island. If he could somehow pierce the fog, maybe he could see the person in the centre of it? He could see if it was a child, like Lorne said? But if they didn't have arms and legs, did he really want to see that?

Footsteps whispered on the steps. Jason didn't move. The guards and the proxies didn't walk softly. *They* didn't need to.

Glaen.

He came slowly, his small, elegant hands stained with old blood beneath his nails like always, his sad eyes fixed on Jason.

Jason sighed. Fucking Glaen. Ever since the little man was processed into the Rift—ever since he first found Jason down here, the day Jason broke his toe on a step—Glaen had been hovering in the periphery of Jason's vision like he had something to say but couldn't quite work up the courage.

"Why are you still following me?" Jason asked. He was surprised by how small his voice sounded. He'd expected this, but it was still frustrating. Disappointing. Exhausting.

"I thought... I thought I should..." Glaen fumbled into silence, wringing his hands together. "I wondered if you were alright, is all. If you needed help."

"Alright," Jason scoffed. Emotion bubbled to life, threatening to spill up into his chest, and it was almost a relief to feel it coming. But then it stalled. Caught on something. Died. "Sure. I'm alright. Just fine. I'm having a little vacation down here."

"Can I..." Glaen took a half a step closer. Chicken feathers flecked his trousers, permanently ingrained into the wool. Would he smell like chicken carcasses when he got close? "Can I look at your knee?"

Jason's body went ugly tense. Two in one day. Fantastic. "Why?"

"It's just that I know a healer—*knew* a healer. She showed me how to make sure wounds don't get infected. It's like you said—you don't want an infection in this place. Do they even have healers in here, if we need them?"

"If we beg enough," Jason said, closing his eyes. He remembered the day Glaen was talking about—Glaen had slipped climbing out of his bunk the first time and gotten splinters in his hands so thick and deep that it made his hands bleed. "There's a room on the main floor where healers can work. But they don't usually waste resources on us. We're just prisoners, after all."

"May I look?" Glaen asked. "I'd like to make sure… It seems like it's the least I can do."

Jason sighed, leaning forward. His trousers were so big and loose that he could drag the wool trouser leg all the way up to his thigh. He was surprised how bad his knee looked. Blood still oozed from the wound. There was still pottery imbedded in his skin and blood clotted in the hair all the way down to his ragged sock. Glaen reached out slowly, trying to pick the pottery shard out of the wound. Even the pain was distant, like something in him had broken, severed. Maybe he'd feel it later.

"Did he hurt you anywhere else?" Glaen asked. He didn't look Jason in the eye when he asked it, like he didn't dare bear witness to the answer.

"Hurt me?" Jason echoed. What a stupid thing to ask. "No, not really. Just humiliated and degraded me. At least he doesn't beat me anymore. Small victories, I guess."

Glaen winced. He watched Jason a while longer, his hands hovering over Jason's knee. Jason looked down at the wound, at the blood. And he couldn't help but think about Lorne and his healer and his club. Jason was *happy* that Lorne was finally being taken care of, finally had a roof over his head, but sweet North Star, what Jason wouldn't give to have someone heal him and turn his wounds to distant scars. His Talent swirled in his body, but it was impotent, useless. The space was too small for him to do anything more than feel it. He could send a bit of that energy down to his knee, at least, help the healing along.

"Is that why you were down here that night?" Glaen whispered. "Because you can…"

Fear—finally, an emotion, but fuck, the fear burned so hot that Jason couldn't breathe. He caught Glaen's hand and squeezed it as hard as he could, making fucking sure Glaen was paying attention. "I'm not doing anything. Just looking for peace and quiet. You hear me?"

"I won't tell anyone," Glaen whispered, leaning closer. "I'm not a fool."

Jason squeezed his eyes shut. His Talent flowed through him like a sandstorm, scrubbing everything away. "There are spots down here. The energy units—" Fuck, those words were *awful* now that he knew what they meant. "They can only cover a limited area. There's supposed to be enough of them to cover everything, but there are gaps down here where they don't overlap anymore. I think one of them is dying." *A child, a fucking child.* "Or else they're losing strength. The gaps are getting bigger."

"Why don't you break down the wall?" Glaen breathed. "Walk right out of here."

Jason shook his head, looking toward the nearest wall. It was a few feet away, the stone cold and hard and unforgiving. "My Talent won't reach the wall because the suppression is there. I can do whatever I want in this small space, but I can't send energy out of it."

Glaen held his hand into the space, and Jason watched the older man's fingers shake. Probably trying to use his Talent. Jason wondered what he used to do. His tattoo said 2, non-compliant, which meant he'd at least registered at some point. Jason shifted on the sack of oats, making room.

"You need your head in the gap," Jason said softly. "The ability to use Talent comes from the mind. That's why we all live with the fucking headache all the time."

Glaen rested his weight on the bag of oats, shifting close to Jason. His face broke into something halfway between a sob and a smile, and Jason could feel Glaen's Talent swirling beside him. It wasn't especially strong. Gentle, like the kind of summer rain that fell so finely that it was barely a step above a mist. It was surprisingly intimate to sit beside someone else's Talent for the first time since... since before the Rift.

But Jason felt so vulnerable, too. All these years here, he'd kept the secret of this spot. He supposed there were likely other people who knew it was here, but no one talked about it. Sharing secrets was opening yourself up to danger.

"You can't tell anyone," Jason said. "You'll get us both killed, if you tell. You know that, right?"

Glaen opened his eyes, looking at Jason with the expression of a startled rabbit. "Killed?"

Jason nodded. "They wouldn't let us live, if they knew. Tainted in the

Rift, using their Talents? They'd kill us both if they even suspected it was possible. And don't even think about trying to bargain for your life by telling them that I've done it. Knowing is enough for them to convict you —they'd kill you to keep the secret, to buy themselves time to fix the problem."

"You don't have to threaten me," Glaen breathed. His mouth turned into a petulant frown—the man had no ability to guard his expression. "I wouldn't—you don't know me very well, but I wouldn't betray you like that. I—" Glaen shook his head, wringing his hands together some more. "I should have said something. I should have stood up, instead of watching. I'm sorry."

Emotion again, trying to come to life—guilt, fear, revulsion. Jason shook his head, looking down at his knee. The bleeding had stopped, at least. His Talent had done that, turning it into a hard scab. "It wouldn't have helped anything. Verrit would have beaten us both and then beaten me some more to make a point. He's been beating me for years because I used to be too stubborn to know to keep my mouth shut. If I'd been quiet like you, instead of an idiot, he wouldn't hate me so much now—" Those vicious emotions were building, making his hands shake, making it hard to breathe. His fault, this was all his fault. If he were smarter, if he didn't have so much of a temper, if he'd learnt to listen sooner—on and on, in the useless circles that always haunted him. He tried to tell himself he'd be out of this soon, but the reality of being here seemed so permanent and immovable that anything else seemed impossible. Like the world outside these walls had ceased to exist.

"I don't think you're an idiot," Glaen whispered, interrupting Jason's spiralling thoughts. "And I don't think it's a good thing to be quiet, and to stand by while terrible things happen. I think you're very brave, Jason Blackwood. Older than your years, and braver than you should have to be."

Emotion finally burst to life at full force. Tears cut hot tracks down his cheeks. "I'm tired of being brave. It's gotten me nothing but misery."

Glaen put a hand on Jason's arm, his touch so whisper soft. His clothes smelled chalky from the chicken feathers, but Jason didn't care. When Jason didn't shrug him off, Glaen shifted, sliding his arms around Jason's shoulders and pulling them together in a tentative hug. It was too much, too much kindness, too much comfort. Jason covered his face with his hands, trying to hold the sobs in, but it was no use. Such a simple thing, a hug, but it had been so long since anyone hugged him. The only

406 | LEGACY OF BRICK & BONE

reason he was touched these days was people trying to possess him and dominate him. Glaen's arms were small, and he was too timid to hug especially hard, and it felt so good to be touched with compassion instead of anger or lust.

But it still wasn't his father's hug. The one thing he wanted most in the whole fucking world—the one thing he'd probably never get to experience again because his father was probably dead.

"I hate him," Jason gasped, the words tumbling out of his mouth before he could stop them.

"Who?" Glaen asked. "The proxy?"

"My father. The bastard. The absolute bastard." Jason's voice trembled with anger and grief. He clenched his fists, pushing them into his own ribcage so he could focus on the physical pain. "All my life, he's carried that stupid fucking badge—all my life he's been telling me to follow the laws, to obey, to sit down, to be quiet. My mother went to the Breeding Program because of him. She died there because he couldn't let go of the image of his own superiority. The Authority killed her because he can't bear to be wrong. And I'm here, and he's fucking arrested because—what? Because he drank too fucking much and needed to find a better thing to be right about. I hate him. I hate him so much—"

Terrible, ugly, horrible thing to say. He regretted it as soon as the words were out of his mouth. It wasn't true. All the individual statements could have been the truth, except he didn't hate his father at all. The last time they were together, Jason had said *you can't help me anymore, you never could fucking help me* and a spasm of pain crossed Tashué Blackwood's face so deep and visceral that it looked like Jason had torn his father's beating heart out. Jason could imagine the things his father might have said if only Jason hadn't stormed out of the room—*all I ever wanted was to protect you*, maybe. *I'm scared for you, Jason. I love you. Please let me help you.*

But none of these things had been said, and now his father was gone. Jason couldn't fix the terrible wound he'd inflicted and now he was doomed to rot with it.

"I'm sorry your father let you down," Glaen said, pushing his hand through Jason's hair. He sounded so calm. "In a perfect world, family would see eye to eye. We'd all get along and support each other. But the world is far from perfect, isn't it?"

Glaen's gentle compassion sent waves of shame rolling through Jason. The weight of them wore the sharp edges off his anger and his pain. Of all the people in the world who should have hated Tashué Blackwood, Glaen had every right to be at the top of the list. Jason had heard the stories of the arrest. Glaen cried out for Gianna in his sleep every night. But instead of hating the man who arrested him and caused the death of his lover, Glaen had such gentle words, and it made Jason's anger taste sour and petty.

For a moment, he swore he could hear children whispering. The sound like distant, delicate bells, drifting through his mind. But then it was gone, so maybe it was just his imagination. Maybe he invented the sound because he was thinking so hard about the children and who they might be. Thinking about his brother. Valen Gian Ly. He wished he'd memorized his brother's number before he gave the paper back to Lorne.

32

OZRA

DAY 34

The coyote that had followed Ozra for nearly a year loped along the ridge of the nearest hill, half-hidden in the scrub, its mottled brown and grey and black fur blending in with the winter grass. It was comforting to know the coyote was up there, at the edge of Ozra's vision—if it was walking out in the open like that, it must have been reasonably secure in the surroundings.

The sun tracked behind their backs, and wind pushed the clouds open so that the snow eased to swirling drifts, and Ozra's whole body ached for his guns. He was acutely and viciously aware of the missing weight in his gun belt, of the empty scabbard hanging from his saddle, left-over sunchokes settled at the bottom. Maybe he could bludgeon someone to death with it if he swung real hard.

He glanced back at his charges as they rode, watching Rhodrishi first and then Stella. She was so wound up, trembling with her anxiety. He wished there was a better trail, some way to get her across the river that didn't fill her with terror.

The coyote stopped dead in its tracks, its body going tense. Ozra drew hard on Caraid's reins, holding up a hand for everyone to stop behind him. His Talent writhed in his mind, trying to bleed out into the landscape, the temptation to see across the distance making it act without his consent—but he didn't need his Talent, when that coyote was standing at the top of the hill, its ears pricked toward something. Its tail twitched a few times, and then it turned, hunching low to slink away into the shrub to hide.

"Shite," Ozra breathed. "Bring 'em back to the forest."

"How do you know it's not some farmer out in his field?" Mahalouwan asked. She had the sense to whisper, at least, pitching her voice so low that Ozra barely heard her.

"Ain't no fucking farmer's fields along this stretch," Ozra whispered back. "Just the road and the Authority patrolling. We're going back to the forest."

Mahalouwan huffed, shaking her head. "We should keep going. You said yourself, this is the best way to get across the river. We have to cross eventually."

Ozra grit his teeth so hard together he thought they would crack. She was right, but going forward now when there was someone out there was a mistake. He wheeled Caraid around to point the gelding back the way they'd come. Caraid snorted, stamped an impatient foot. "We'll hunker down somewhere for the rest of the daylight hours and then make our way in the dark. We'll hit the town by daybreak, eat, and then camp on the forest side of the river."

"If that was an option, why didn't you say so sooner?" Mahalouwan pressed. "If it's a better choice—"

"It isn't a better choice. It's a shite choice! We'll be travelling *all night* with the wee one, and we'll need to pray that there aren't any clouds to block the starlight or we're in right trouble, but it's better than going forward into a bloody Authority patrol right now."

"Mam," Ceridwen said, a little too loud, carrying a little too far—she had that impatient, urgent sound, like she'd asked a few times and hadn't gotten an answer. "Why are we stopped?"

"Pigeon," Stella breathed, "sssh—"

Ozra winced. He kicked Caraid toward Rhodrishi and Ceridwen. "Rhodrishi will lead the way back, and I'll watch our rear, and we'll go calmly and quietly—"

The sound of horses rolled over the hills, a long, high whinny of a long-distance greeting. Caraid's ears pricked up immediately, and he whinnied back, the sound like a screech on Ozra's raw nerves, echoing over the hills.

"Ah, you fucking *bastard*," Ozra growled. "Rhodrishi, go—bring them back to cover!"

Rhodrishi nodded, didn't question. "This way, Ceridwen girl. Back into the forest with us. Remember how to post to the trot?"

"Yes, Rhodrishi," Ceridwen said, gripping the pommel with both hands like Ozra told her.

"Good, sweet girl. Here we go."

Rhodrishi kicked his horse on, and Stella followed, all the colour drained out of her face. The little Hitjurgavit ponies made a game effort of keeping up, but their short legs made it a mighty challenge. Rhodrishi had to tug his reins to keep his mare from taking off at full tilt, the big roan no doubt sensing all the stress.

"Give me my gun," Ozra said. "Go with them."

"You're going to fight?" Mahalouwan asked, her voice surprisingly brittle—he didn't understand why she'd lost her colour, too—she was a soldier, wasn't she? She was used to spilling blood. She looked so fucking calm before, when he'd brought her up the edge. Why was shooting him so easy to contemplate but fighting the Authority wasn't?

"Only if it's necessary," Ozra lied, trying not to hate her for her sudden hesitation. He didn't have time. "Only if they're coming after us. Maybe it's nothing."

Mahalouwan grimaced, shaking her head, but she dragged Ozra's rifle out of her saddle bag and tossed it to him. He caught it out of the air, and the weight in his hand was perfect comfort, familiarity and violence and safety and a history of fighting for his life that she clearly didn't fully understand. Mahalouwan kicked her pony after the others. Caraid tried to follow, but Ozra wheeled him around, directing him up straight up the face of the hill. He pulled Caraid to a stop shy of the crest. He dropped the reins and fished in his pocket for the bullets, pushing them past the side gate and filling the rifle with the potential for death. He slid down out of the saddle, dropping to his stomach to creep up the last of the rise until he could see the next hill without showing himself. Fat load of good the sneaking would do if Caraid was going to announce their presence again. North Star save him from a friendly fucking horse.

There were six of them, the whole lot wearing bronze badges that shone in the emerging winter sun. They were moving fast, trotting along their ridge, straight toward the forest. Must have been a road or at least a dependable track up there, for them to feel safe to move so quick. And one of them had Talent—Ozra could feel it, spilling out of him like a net, a web, hooked on to Ceridwen, nearly dragging Ozra out of his own head—shite. The leader had sensed Ceridwen's incredible power, and they were hunting her down. How far had they come? Had they only sensed her as they were passing, or had they come a long way, pulled toward that wee girl and the web she made around herself with her wishing?

Ozra brought his rifle up in front of him, fiddling with the sight until he had the distance. It was a long shot, even for an Imburleigh, and he only had the one shot before they knew he was hunting them back. One shot and then they'd make a decision—either scatter or head faster for the forest or turn and charge at him.

He set his finger on the cold metal of the trigger, smoothed by use and time. His finger fit so perfectly against it. This gun that had seen him through so much. The massive gelding that the leader was riding made a steady, predictable rhythm. Ozra could feel the stride of that horse like feeling the thump of his own heart, *one two, one two, one two, one two,* the Enquiry Officer posting to the trot with perfect grace. The massive horses ate the distance with their long, powerful legs.

One two, one two—the horses were coming closer, along their ridge— *one two, one*—Ozra fired.

Gunpowder roared, and the Imburleigh gave its familiar, mighty kick. The bullet took the first rider straight through the chest as he came to the top of his post, perfectly timed. The Officer sagged backward over the horse's flanks as blood rushed from the bullet wound, and the big gelding broke into a gallop, startled by the sound and the sudden shift of weight. The Officers passed Ozra's resting point, driving their horses faster along the road. Ozra racked another round but leapt to his feet, whistling for Caraid. He fired again at their backs, but it was a shit shot, and it hit the hill where it rose behind them, throwing up a clod of dirt and rock and snow.

Caraid came up the hill, and Ozra vaulted up into the saddle, kicking Caraid's sides without even picking up the reins. Caraid charged along the crest of the hill, following the Officers—though they were yards away, on the next ridge, and they were all scrabbling for their guns, twisting in their saddles to see their attacker.

Caraid's familiar rhythm sent Ozra up and down as he brought his rifle up again. Wind and snow roared around Ozra's head, pulling at his clothes, ugly cold and screaming for his attention, and the air tasted damp and heavy with all the snow—it all affected the trajectory of a bullet.

One Officer got a pistol out and fired, but far too soon—the bullet didn't come anywhere close. Ozra took a deep breath and fired back, rifle bucking in his hands and a puff of cordite blowing into Ozra's face. On the other ridge, an Officer gave a barking shout, but it wasn't a killing wound—the Officer clutched his shoulder and swayed but stayed upright, kicking his horse harder, faster.

Ozra grabbed Caraid's reins, turning the gelding back down the hill and into the valley charging north still. He dragged Caraid down to a trot, then swung him around, racking a fresh round and hefting the rifle up to point at the top of the hill, waiting for a face to appear so he could blow it the fuck apart.

But no one came.

Shite, they weren't taking his bait. They were still after Ceridwen.

Back up the hill, then.

Caraid surged forward, always eager. The man Ozra had killed was lying where he fell, the riderless horse running ahead of its peers, and the five survivors were making their way down from the ridge. Four kept south, toward the forest. Only one peeled away, charging toward Ozra. Ozra fired again, but the man had a good fucking horse. It swerved wide. The Enquiry Officer fired back, a puff of stone dust rising from the hill ahead of Caraid; it was still swirling in the air when Caraid thundered through it, leaving its chalky taste in Ozra's mouth. The Enquiry Officer had a revolver, and he fired again, again.

Ozra hauled on the reins, turning Caraid back down the hill, then hauled the gelding to a dead stop. He leapt out of the saddle, slapping Caraid's rump, sending the paint cantering up the opposite hill out of the way.

Ozra racked another round into his rifle and dropped to a knee. Breathe deep, nice and slow. How many bullets did he have left? Damn it all. He couldn't remember how many rounds he'd managed to get into it as he rode up the hill. The Imburleigh repeater held ten rounds, but he hadn't counted how many he'd put in the damned gun.

The Officer came charging over the crest of the hill, directly at Ozra, and shit the big horse moved faster than Ozra expected. Ozra fired, but the lead didn't find flesh, another shite shot. Ozra dove out of the way, rolling over his shoulder and springing up to his feet. The horse veered to one side, and the rider lurched with the sudden shift. Ozra racked, fired, his whole body buzzing with the percussion of his gunshot. And the rider went down, falling hard, rolling, leaving a smear of blood on the ground.

Ozra must have hit him after all. The horse kept running down the hill. The Enquiry Officer surged to his feet, lunging. Ozra swung his rifle, catching the Officer in the face with the wooden stock—the man shouted with pain, blood spraying from his mouth, but momentum carried him on. He hit Ozra in the chest, dragging him to the ground, pinning the rifle between them.

The Enquiry Officer reared up, cocking his right fist—left hand still pinning the rifle to Ozra's chest. Ozra held the rifle with both hands and yanked it upward, dragging it over his head, and the Officer fell forward again before he could land that punch. Ozra twisted, swung, aiming for the blood that soaked the side of the Officer's jacket. Hot blood beneath Ozra's fist, spraying with each impact, the crunch-shift of broken bone, and the Officer screamed, biting the air, desperate animal eyes bulging. He folded, tilting to one side. Ozra followed, punching again, again, spraying himself with the other man's blood, knuckles aching and wet, and the man fell to the ground, screaming, screaming, clutching his side. Ozra reared up to his knees, racking another round into the chamber. Pulled the trigger and the rifle bucked, eager for blood, the close range turning the man's head into a jumble of blood and bone and brain sprayed across the hill and melting the snow like hot paint.

Ozra's chest heaved as he fought to catch his breath.

Shite. He was getting rusty. Been a while since a fight like that. Was a time when it wouldn't have lasted so damn long, and he wouldn't have missed so many fucking shots.

Habit made him grab the bronze fucking badge, ripping it off the Officer's coat and stashing it in his pocket. Maybe he'd post it to the Hand so his family knew he was still alive. Still fighting.

He whistled for Caraid, the sound shrill and carrying well over the hills. No time to recover, even though his lungs burned, and his heart galloped faster than any of the horses. He reloaded as he jogged down the hill, slotting rounds into the side gate in motions as familiar to him as breathing until the rifle was full again. Ten rounds. He pushed himself into a loping run, heading south to the forest. Caraid came trotting from the other side of the hill, slowing as he headed down the slope toward Ozra. They met in the valley between the two hills, Ozra's boots splashing through a half-hearted stream, Caraid's hooves throwing up clods of mud. Ozra sprang up into the saddle, kicking Caraid on again. Faster, as fast as the paint would go, rising in the saddle and leaning over Caraid's neck.

Caraid was lathered in sweat by the time they reached the edge of the forest and Ozra hauled him down to a walk, making his way slowly over uneven ground. Caraid's hard breathing drowned out the sounds of the forest. Ozra searched everywhere, vigilant for any track the Officers had left behind. There ahead—blood on some leaves, from the man he'd shot in the shoulder. How far ahead were they? He couldn't hear their horses, not with Caraid huffing and puffing and snorting in his exhausted excitement.

Ozra slid down from the saddle, his feet hitting the solid ground. His legs were tired already, but he didn't have *time* for tired. He cradled his rifle across his chest and pushed himself on, into a run. He could go faster through the brush himself, without Caraid trying to pick his way through trees and over roots. His body could fit through smaller spaces than Caraid could, and moving fast on horseback through the forest without a good trail was to invite a snapped leg and a dead horse. He leapt over a fallen log, cut west, following the sight of more blood.

It was taking too long to find tracks. There was so much forest spilling out around him, so many directions for the Enquiry Officers to go—

He reached for his Talent, casting it out like a fisherman's net, a web tumbling into the forest in every direction. He should have done this sooner. He should have tried, and then they wouldn't be in this fucking mess. The whole forest bloomed in his mind, every root and rock and branch, every hunter's trail and tributary stream. There—on one of the tracks cutting through the brush, so narrow and twisting that they were forced to keep their horses at a walk. Only two of them. Ozra pushed more Talent through his muscles, fuel to drive him past the natural exhaustion and the building ache—to hell with whether he survived it or not, so long as he caught up with Rhodrishi and Stella, it was worth it.

Ozra veered off the track as he started to close the gap, plunging back into the brush, squeezing between a pair of trees and feeling the bark tear at his clothes. Something thorny caught his leg, roots and rocks threatened to turn his ankle. Run, keep running, faster, ignore the pain, he was catching up—

The Officer at the rear swung toward the sound of Ozra approaching. Ozra threw himself into the brush. A rifle boomed, and splinters sprayed Ozra's face as he fell, hot and cutting. He hit the forest floor and knocked the air out of his own lungs but rolled back up, to his knees. Brought his rifle to his shoulder. He didn't need to see where they were to shoot them, not when his Talent let him see the whole forest, and he could find the intense rhythm of their beating hearts. They were too far, even for an Imburleigh, the gap between them widening again when he'd gone down. Took a shot anyway, because if they were busy shooting at him at least they weren't after Ceridwen and Stella, and maybe if he shot at them enough, the sound would help Mahalouwan and Rhodrishi knew where their pursuers were. Bullets cut around him, missing badly since they were out of range, but they kept shooting. Peppering the forest with bullets, making it harder for him to follow. They were moving away from him, following Ceridwen still.

His Talent spilled out further and further out of control, oil seeping from a busted gasket, until he could see Rhodrishi's big roan and two of the ponies, trotting down the trail where it widened. Their saddles were empty. The Officers followed the tracks the horses were leaving on the trail, probably oblivious to the fact that Rhodrishi and Ceridwen and Stella weren't in the saddle anymore.

Where was Mahalouwan?

And where were the other two Officers?

Run. Deal with the two Officers he could see, figure out the rest after. Run, keep running, but his Talent was already stretching too far, he couldn't focus anymore. He should have been in pain from running so long but he didn't feel it. He saw too much of the forest, too many details that didn't matter. Badger in its den. Fox, farther away. Deer running, away from all the noise. Black bear on the flanks of the mountains, four cubs from last winter—four! Good for her; a mother who could birth and rear four cubs at once was doing very well indeed.

Focus!

Running.

Blood coming at him.

Round a bend and the Officer he shot in the shoulder was charging back toward him. Ozra dropped to one knee. Shot-in-the-shoulder lifted his pistol. Fired over his horse's head. Ozra closed his eyes because it was better to shoot with his Talent, to know with the perfection of that sense where the man's body was, when the eye was just a little too slow and a little too imperfect.

Trigger—gun powder—rifle kicked—bullet hit the bronze badge first and punched right through to flesh and bone to shred open the Officer's beating heart.

Dive out of the way. Horse thundered past. The second Officer, coming. A shot—an impact hit Ozra like a brick. Pain. Distant. Demanding attention. He tried to heft his rifle but his chest was burning, hot, angry. Didn't matter—move anyway, move or die, shoot again or die, rack another round and brace for the .45 mule kick, pull the trigger —Ozra could feel it, the pain, the fear, the swallowing blackness of death. Not his death—just the Enquiry Officer and Ozra's Talent feeling the end of another soul, the fabric swallowing another broken thread.

Tried to take a step but he didn't know if his feet were on the forest floor or in the creek or in the Guard river or in the mountains. Tried to breathe but he didn't know who he was. Was he Ozra, was he the bear, was he the badger, was he the dying Officers. He *was* the forest, all of it, every leaf and root and branch, every stone and ounce of soil, every living thing. Every dead thing, too.

He had the badge in his hand. He didn't remember picking it up. Torn copper and dripping blood and ripped leather.

Falling.

Falling to the ground, falling into the fabric, spreading too far, way too far—

33

STELLA
DAY 34

Ceridwen was brave right up until the first gunshot echoed through the forest, and then she started to cry.

She clung to the pommel of her saddle like Ozra told her and cried as she bounced along the track, posting to the trot with perfect rhythm even though she was falling apart.

The thunderous clap did the opposite to Stella. It stripped away her panic and bathed her in the cold, hard, ugly reality. They were in the forest and foes were coming and there was no more time for doubt or fear or regret. There was only the inevitability of violence.

Kazrani cursed and whirled her pony around, charging back toward the tree line. Rhodrishi led the ponies off the track they'd followed, onto a smaller hunters' trail that wound thin and hazardous beside one of the low streams that fed Greene's Creek. He veered right into the brush, crashing through shrubs and weaving around trees before dragging his mare to a stop. He dropped down from the saddle, wincing when he hit the ground a little too hard.

"Time to get down, Ceridwen," he said. "We'll go the rest of the way on foot."

"But the horses are faster—I can't run like a horse—"

"We're not going to run, my darling, we're going to hide," Rhodrishi said. "We'll send Grippni and the others back to the road to make tracks for us, and then we'll find a safe place in the forest."

Stella dragged Tashué's rifle out of the scabbard and slid down. "Time to go, Pigeon. Kazrani and Ozra know how to fight, and we'll find a safe place in the forest."

Ceridwen's lip trembled, and she shook her head, her cheeks gleaming bright with all her spent tears. "But Mam, Grippni will get lost all by herself!"

"She won't, Pigeon," Stella said, holding out a hand to Ceridwen, resisting the urge to grab Ceridwen and haul her out of the saddle. "She'll be with Rhodrishi's horse and my pony, and they'll all take care of each other, won't they?"

"They will," Rhodrishi said. "My girl comes when I call her. When this is all over, we'll call them back to us. But this is our chance to get away, and we need to go *now*."

Ceridwen's face crumpled into wrenching, whole-body sobs, but she kicked her feet out of the stirrups and dropped clumsily to the ground. Stella slung Tashué's rifle over one shoulder, holding the strap in place, and grabbed Ceridwen's hand, hauling her through the forest. And Rhodrishi led the way, loping at a jog but he was limping. He pressed his hand into his hip as he ran.

She followed Rhodrishi as he cut between trees and around jutting rocks, letting the slope of the forest floor guide them down, down, into a valley. Branches ripped at their clothes, at their hair—one hand on the rifle and one hand holding Ceridwen, Stella couldn't clear branches out of her way—they ripped shallow divots across her cheeks until her whole face was stinging, hot and bleeding, but there was no time to stop.

Ceridwen staggered. Fell. A loud wail leapt from her. Stella skidded to a clumsy, exhausted stop. Ceridwen had fallen over a rock, and her hands were ripped by the impact of catching herself, ice and snow melting against her bloody palms, and her whole body trembled. Stella swung the rifle off her shoulder, tossing it to Rhodrishi. She grabbed Ceridwen by both arms and hauled her up, to her feet, and then lifted her right off the ground—she was too big, too heavy, nearly ten, not a wee baby anymore like the infant she carried on her back while she travelled west, but there was no *time*. No time for weakness or fatigue or doubt. Ceridwen pressed her face into Stella's shoulder, wrapping her arms around Stella's neck and her legs around Stella's waist, and Stella held on to her with every shred of strength she had and more still, strength she didn't know she had left. She nodded at Rhodrishi, and he started again, slower than before. Stella's whole body burned with the fatigue, her legs screaming, but it didn't matter. She plodded on and on, and Rhodrishi slowed again when she fell behind. She could feel his Talent, swirling like warm water through her muscles, washing the exhaustion away in a gentle cleanse.

"Just a little farther," he said. "And then we can slow down."

Gunshots reached the forest, clapping through the trees, and a horse screamed a terrible, screeching roar of a sound. Ceridwen buried her face harder into Stella's shoulder, so hard it made Stella's collarbone ache. More gunshots.

Rhodrishi turned, heading straight for a rising cliff face that loomed in the forest. He followed the line of granite a while and then ducked inside. The cavern he found swallowed them, and the darkness left Stella almost blind as her eyes struggled to adjust to the shadows. It was terribly quiet in there, silence so pressing that it made the sound of her own breathing louder, the sound of her heart roaring blood through her ears and Ceridwen's crying making a nightmare song. She snuffled and whimpered, her little body trembling in Stella's arms.

Rhodrishi cursed softly. "It's the next one," he said. "The next cave will lead us right through to high ground a few miles from here. They won't think to look for us up there. Can you go a little farther?"

Stella nodded but she couldn't catch her breath enough to speak. Rhodrishi put a hand on her other shoulder, squeezing hard, meeting her eye. Perhaps he wanted to ask if she was sure, or offer to carry Ceridwen, but of course he couldn't make that offer because he was already in pain. Already at the very limit of his endurance. Stella sucked in long, slow breaths, fighting to satisfy her aching lungs.

"I'm ready."

Rhodrishi nodded and led Stella back out again. He moved more slowly this time, his head swivelling every which way to watch for pursuers. He froze. A whispered curse from his lips sent fresh panic burning through Stella's whole soul. He turned, grabbing Stella's arm and turning her around again, and then Stella saw it—a horse, moving through the brush, a flash of gold coming toward them. That wasn't any of their horses.

Stella turned and ran back toward the cave, moving as carefully as she could, praying the rider didn't see them. Praying they were quiet enough to blend into the sounds of the forest. *North Star, if there's any grace for us, please—*

Into the darkness again. Her breathing seemed even louder now that she knew there was someone out there, looking for them.

"I'm sorry, Mam," Ceridwen whimpered. "I'm sorry. This is all my fault—I'm sorry!"

"Hush, Ceridwen," Stella whispered, rubbing Ceridwen's back. "It's not your fault. We're going to stay here a moment and catch our breath."

"I was wishing—I'm sorry I was wishing—I couldn't help it. I'm tired of being out here, Mam, I wanted to go home—I was wishing that we'd all go home so we could see Mr. Blackwood again—I'm sorry! I shouldn't have been wishing, and now they found us like you said, and I'm sorry—"

"It's alright, Pigeon," Stella whispered. "Hush. We need to be quiet or they'll find us—"

Rhodrishi took Ceridwen's hand, tugging her out of Stella's arms. Stella put Ceridwen down, and Rhodrishi thrust the rifle back into Stella's hands, taking his own rifle off his shoulder so they both had guns ready.

"It's time to wish again," Rhodrishi whispered, pulling Ceridwen to the very back of the cave. The light of the forest became like a lantern, one solitary glow, and all around them was dark, cold granite walls. There was a curve to it, but it narrowed to a sliver they couldn't squeeze into. He pressed his back against stone, pushing Ceridwen behind him so she slipped easily into the crevice and he guarded her with his body. "Wish they don't find us. Wish that we're hidden very well in our little cave so that no one finds us here. Wish, Ceridwen. Wish with everything you have."

"I can't—" Ceridwen sobbed. "I don't know—I'm scared. Mam, I'm scared!"

"I know, Pigeon," Stella said. "Take a deep breath—"

A shadow passed in front of the mouth of the cave, and Stella spun around to face it, hefting the gun up. Ceridwen screamed, burying her face into Rhodrishi's back, covering her ears, shrinking to take up as little space as possible.

"Come on out now, and no one else needs to get hurt."

It sounded like a boy, his voice trembling a little, lacking the gravity of a warrior in command like Ozra or Tashué or Kazrani. Stella took a deep breath, taking a step forward—the sun backlit his silhouette turning him into a dark, featureless figure.

"We're not going anywhere," Stella said. "We're staying right here, and you're going to walk away like you never saw us. I'm trying to protect my daughter. Do you hear her crying? She's a child. Tell your people you couldn't find us, and we'll go on minding our own business."

The boy scoffed. "Minding your own—"

Stella stepped closer, into the light, so that he could see the rifle pointing at his chest. And he did see it, his eyes going wide, his hand going to the revolver on his hip. A sign of his inexperience that he didn't have it out already. The youth of him opened a yawning pit of despair in Stella's chest. He couldn't be finished growing yet. No more than fourteen, fifteen at most. Hardly any older than her son would be if he'd survived. A child himself and yet wearing that horrible bronze badge anyway.

"I don't want to kill you, son," she said, as strong and firm as she could muster, "but I will. So help me, I will. To protect my daughter, I'll do it. But I don't have to. Walk away. Pretend you never saw us and go."

The boy swallowed, and he pulled the pistol halfway out of the holster. "You're a fugitive from the law," he said, his voice trembling even more. "You're both tainted," he said. "I can feel it."

"Aye, we are. You're right. But we don't mean to hurt anyone—we're looking for a quiet place to live our lives in peace. I'm sick of this world. Sick to death of being a piece of meat for the Authority to carve and sell however they want. I just want to take my child somewhere quiet, so she doesn't have to live the life I lived. Is that so wrong?"

"You say you don't want to hurt anyone, but one of you killed two officers and there's plenty wrong with *that*." His voice was getting firmer, braver, and his hand was moving in incremental inches, drawing his revolver. He licked his lips like he was weighing the odds of whether he could get his revolver the rest of the way out of its holster in time to shoot Stella before she shot him. Something bled into the air between them, some memory that didn't belong to her, like her Talent had linked them together by accident—he'd been practicing his draw, trying to get as fast as his brother was. "You lot oughta face justice for what you done."

"There's no justice here, son." Stella thumbed back the hammer of Tashué's big rifle, the click of it echoing ominously in the cave. So loud. What would happen when she fired? Would she only draw more Officers to their hiding place? She wished her voice was as hard and flinty as

Kazrani's. Perhaps if it was, he would walk away, and she wouldn't have to shoot another *child* to protect Ceridwen. She lay her finger on the cold, hard trigger. And tried to find something hard enough and bleak enough in her soul that would let her put lead through this boy's chest, come what may. "Just a woman with a gun, willing to do whatever it takes to protect her child. But I don't want to. You hear me? I don't want to kill anyone. I'm a healer. I've spent all my life helping people. A forty-five is a big, ugly round. Have you ever seen what it does to a person from close range? I have. I've tried to save people from guns like this, but I never could because it rips the body all to shreds when you're standing so close. Better hope I hit you in the chest or the head, so it kills you quick."

"I wish he would leave," Ceridwen said, her voice rising in a trembling whisper that echoed through the cave toward the mouth, toward the boy. And Stella could feel her Talent spilling around with the words, a massive thing that unfolded faster than ever. How had she never felt it before? "I wish he would leave. I wish he would leave. I wish he would *leave!*"

The boy took a step back. He took another, and then a third. He was at the mouth of the cave again, his clothes whipping in the wind that slid along the cliff face. His hand trembled so hard that she could hear the chamber of his gun shaking, metal clattering against itself, but he pushed the revolver back into the holster.

"I wish he would leave," Ceridwen said again. Louder. "I wish he would leave, I wish he would leave!"

Another step back and his body was completely out of the cave. Snow swirled around him like glitter, beautiful and sparkling in the sunlight.

His mouth gaped open and then snapped shut so hard Stella could hear his teeth clack together. He was fighting Ceridwen's influence. His hand came up, pistol clearing the holster.

A gunshot ripped through Stella's thoughts before she could act. The flash of it beside her sent white sparks through her vision. The boy's head exploded, throwing blood everywhere. His body spasmed, and it was enough to pull the trigger of his pistol—the pop of it wasn't as loud as Rhodrishi's .45, but it was still plenty mean. The bullet hit the cave floor, throwing shards of stone everywhere. The boy's body crumpled like a marionette with snapped strings, landing in a heap. Ceridwen screamed, sobbing, the sound cutting through Stella's every nerve and bringing tears to her eyes—she wanted to go to Ceridwen and hold her, but she didn't dare turn away in case there were more Officers out there, waiting to come toward the sound of a gunshot.

Blood ran down into the cave in a vivid red line, snaking and sinuous, heading straight for Stella's boots. Rhodrishi exhaled slowly, the puff of his breath dancing with the line of smoke that came from the barrel of his gun. He racked the lever of his rifle, the spent shell leaping out of the chamber and landing in the blood. The silence in the cave was met only with the ringing in Stella's ears. It was exactly as terrible as she imagined it would be, but the threat didn't feel over. Would any more officers come toward the sound?

Another shadow and Ceridwen screamed, the sound of her terror making Stella's breath catch in her throat. She hefted the gun up—

Kazrani. She stood over the boy's body a moment like she was checking to see if he was dead. Her clothes were torn, covered in dirt and twigs and blood—so much blood, running down her leg.

Kazrani turned to Stella, wavering on her feet. "Good shot, Colonel."

Rhodrishi pointed his rifle at the cave floor. "Easy, at this range."

Stella nodded. Her whole body trembled as she lowered the rifle, pointing it at the bloody puddle in front of her feet. With her thumb on the hammer, she squeezed the trigger gently, guiding the hammer back into place as carefully as she could so it wouldn't set off the round.

Kazrani pressed her hand into her thigh below her hip, and Stella could see the blood seeping through her fingers. "I hesitated," she breathed. She shook her head, her braids tumbling all about her shoulders. "I've never hesitated before. But I've never shot anyone with a badge before, either."

Stella turned to Ceridwen, fighting the urge to throw Tashué's gun aside to put some distance between herself and the terrible reality they found themselves in. She slung it over her shoulder instead. "It's alright, Pigeon," she breathed, pulling Ceridwen into a tight, smothering hug. "You did so well with your wishing. You did so well." She kissed Ceridwen's face and pushed her stray hairs back and wiped the tears from the girl's face. "We're safe."

"He was leaving," Ceridwen whimpered, squeezing her eyes shut. "He was leaving!"

"I know," Stella said. "You did so well. But he fought against it, and Rhodrishi did what he had to for us, and now we're safe."

"Are there any more?" Rhodrishi asked.

Kazrani shook her head, looking out toward the forest. "Don't know. I haven't heard anymore gunshots, though. So either Ozra killed the others, or they killed him—I don't know."

"You're wounded, Lieutenant," Rhodrishi said.

Kazrani laughed, the sound brittle and wild. "Shot in the ass, how do you like that? I saw this one's partner but that badge—I hesitated, and he didn't. Bastard killed my horse, and then one of the other ones shot Ozra. But I couldn't stay with him, I had to come find you—"

Ozra— "Where is he?"

Kazrani turned and started running. Limping, bleeding, but running. Faster than she looked. Leaving blood splattering on the snow-kissed forest. Stella ran with her, pushing through the pain in her muscles.

Ceridwen had wished they would go back—Stella should have gone back, and now Ozra—sweet North Star, she prayed that Ozra was still alive.

"I hesitated," Kazrani said again. And again and again, like she was punishing herself with each repetition. Her voice was thin and strained—pain, anger, frustration, fear. Fear for Ozra. "I've never hesitated in my fucking life, but I saw that badge—that fucking badge—and for a second, I thought—*my brother*. I could have shot him in the back and put an end to it, but the badge—and now Ozra—"

"I hesitated, too." Stella's voice wasn't any stronger. "He was so young. I couldn't—he would have killed us if it weren't for Rhodrishi. I'm out here to protect my daughter, but I hesitated anyway because he was just a boy."

"Brothers, I think," Kazrani said. "Yours and mine. They'll go to the Keeper of the Keys together, at least."

Flashes of white and brown and black in the forest. Ozra's horse—lathered in sweat, reins trailing, the leggy paint stood over Ozra's prone form as he lay in the brush. They wouldn't have found him otherwise. His big coat blended into the grey-brown tones of leaf litter and winter-bare branches. He could have been part of the fallen log he was resting against.

Stella reached him first, dropping to her knees in the tangle of brush, branches tearing at her clothes, at her hands. Didn't matter. She didn't have time for her own pain. Blood—she couldn't see how bad it was with all the undergrowth around him, half-hiding him, the forest floor soaking up the evidence. But his side was soaked with it, leaving her hands sticky and stained when she touched him. He was breathing. At least he was breathing.

Stella looked around for Rhodrishi, but he'd stayed behind in the cave with Ceridwen.

"Ozra!" Stella reached for her Talent even as she called his name. "Ozra Sgèin, can you hear me?"

Her awareness sank into Ozra's body in an instant, like it was waiting to be called on. The wound was mean and angry through his shoulder but it wasn't bad enough to render him unconscious like this.

But his Talent was swirling, too. That's why he wasn't responding to her. He couldn't. He was the whole forest, every tree, every leaf, every beating heart of every living creature. She fought hard against the current of it, but it was pulling her down, down. She was losing the shape of her identity, losing the edges of who she was, melting into Ozra's incredible strength.

The wound, she told herself. She didn't know if she was speaking out loud or thinking. *Focus on the wound!*

The hole in his muscle—the bullet had hit arm below the shoulder, and there was a tiny hairline fracture in the bone below the ball of the joint. And the bleeding. He was luckier than the boy—the bullet had found him from a long range, giving it time to lose velocity before it hit him instead of blowing the joint right off him.

"Help me," Stella said. "Help me get him up. We'll bring him to the cave at least—I can't close his wound until I get the bullet out."

"How bad is it?" Kazrani asked.

"Survivable, so long as we can clean it well enough. And we can drag him back from wherever he's gone."

"His Talent again?"

Stella nodded. "His Talent has him."

Kazrani scowled and hooked her arms under Ozra's shoulders, hefting him up. Stella grabbed him by the ankles, but she didn't know if she was helping at all or shuffling along as Kazrani bore most of his weight, even though the other woman limped and bled as she went. And Ozra's Talent swirled, like a current Stella couldn't quite resist, his strength dragging her into his thoughts, into the things he saw and heard and felt. The pain from the shoulder wound roared through Stella's nerves. And a voice—

Damn you, Ozra, why did you have to tell me what they did, why did you have to look?

I'm sorry, Eilidh, I had to know.

"Ozra," Stella gasped to hear her own voice so she wouldn't drown in Ozra's Talent. "Ozra, please come back. Please."

They were Ozra and Stella together—no, not only Stella, Ffyanwy too. Their memories came together, blending, flickering between them until the borders between who they were became indistinct and formless.

They saw his ghost. Eilidh Rae. Strawberry blond hair and freckles on her nose. The labour for their second babe was long and miserable, and Eilidh was at the end of her strength, but Ozra sat with her in her bed and kissed her face and spoke with his beautiful burr in her ear.

It's a girl this time, Eilidh. I saw it. A girl. Just a little longer and you'll hold our baby girl. Don't give up yet.

Keep walking. One foot after the other, push through the pain that didn't belong to her and the exhaustion that tried to turn her into nothing.

The midwife gave the babe to Ozra first because once she was in the world, Eilidh was so exhausted that she couldn't hold up her head let alone her child. Ozra lay beside Eilidh on the bed as Eilidh delivered the after birth, holding the babe between them so that the child could smell her mother and feel her skin, and he kissed the girl's wispy red hair— such beautiful hair, red and curly already.

Keep walking!

Aelwyd was with Ffyanwy when the labour pains came. Just as Ozra held Eilidh's hand, Aelwyd let Ffyanwy cling to her and borrow her strength. Of course the one good thing that Ffyanwy and Bothain had done together would result in this much pain. Of course bringing life into the world would hurt so much worse than anything Bothain had done to her in his cruelty and anger. But holding her son, ah, that was beautiful. When that boy came into her arms, a human that had come into existence in her body, a boy that was both of them and neither of them because he was his own person, that was the purest and simplest thing in the whole world. No matter what she felt for Bothain Clannaugh, she would always love their son.

"Mam!"

Ceridwen.

"Mam! Mam! What's wrong with Ozra?"

Stella fought hard against the current of Ozra's consciousness, hanging on to the sound of Ceridwen's voice. There wasn't any pain anymore. For a moment, she wondered if this was death—if Ozra had dragged her under and there was nothing left for her to feel because they'd both ceased to be.

34

ILLEA
DAY 34

Tilde's hands were cold. They were always cold, no matter the season. Perhaps it was because she had such long limbs, making her taller than even most men. Or perhaps it was because she used her energy so diligently on Illea, ever vigilant, ready to intervene if something terrible happened. It used to be that Tilde followed Illea everywhere, but lately Illea had been heading out into the world without her healer. Perhaps it was time for Illea to have Tilde as a constant companion again. Just in case something happened with the pregnancy.

"Things are going well," Tilde said, nodding. Her voice was husky and low, a soothing pitch that Illea had liked from the moment they met. Over a decade ago, now. Both her cold hands clasped over one of Illea's, her eyes distant and staring out the window. "You're feeling ill every day now?"

"Only if I let myself get too hungry," Illea said. "Or eat too much. Or breathe too deeply. Or move too swiftly."

Tilde's steady gaze fixed on Illea's face, one eyebrow arching. "Or, apparently, ride out into the Dunnenbrahl to see the wreckage of men being violent."

Illea stifled a sigh, looking out the window. From here, she could see the tops of the tallest trees, winter-bare and reaching for the moody evening sky, which still danced with snow. She didn't know what to say.

The carnage was terrible, yes, but it wasn't the fallen bodies that haunted her thoughts.

Tilde shrugged, accepting that she wasn't getting a response on that matter. "If the nausea ever gets so bad you can't eat at all, let me know immediately."

Illea nodded. "Can you tell me anything about it?"

"I can tell you it's the size of a dried lentil." Tilde squeezed Illea's hand and smiled, her wide mouth making every facial expression stunningly animated. "Smaller than my smallest fingernail. Just a little speck."

A speck. She used to try to imagine what her children would look like when she thought they would be Amias's children, too. Illea was the spitting image of her mother, a precise copy. She didn't remember her mother at all, but there were enough portraits in her manor to prove it. Amias had carried features from both his parents—his father's beautiful olive skin, his mother's stunning gold hair, eyes that couldn't seem to decide what colour they were, always shifting depending on what he wore and whether or not the sun was shining. Which features would carry through to a Wolfe Winter child?

But those things weren't to be. Amias was gone. She'd never know.

Which of his parents did Tashué Blackwood take after? Would her child look like him—would it inherit those startling amber eyes of his? And how much of his Talent would her child carry?

Illea closed her eyes. So many conflicting emotions vied for supremacy that she didn't know what she felt anymore. At least Myron wasn't around much, giving her time and space to process everything without having to see him in her house. He'd been hiding out at his favourite prostitute's house since the banquet, turning up only occasionally when he had no choice.

The secret was starting to spread, though. Today, she told Mallory, out there in the forest, on the way back down the trail. Mallory was so worried about her since she wasn't usually the type to have such a delicate constitution, and she'd nearly fainted after all that vomiting. It was a bit of a relief, to tell another mother. Mallory understood better than anyone what it was like to face this coming child while also being so central to the gossip of the whole Dominion. She promised to go back to Nathaniel's house and assure him that Illea was fine—and stand with him as the Authority tore his house apart.

Eventually the news of her pregnancy would leak into the gossip cycle, and then the stories would start. Illea knew from her friendship with Mallory a wealthy woman's pregnancy was invitation for everyone to speculate about her sex life, especially if there was any room for questions. Most people didn't know Mallory was already with child when she left to marry Alistair, but the abruptness of her departure led to wild speculation. And since everyone in Yaelsmuir had been speaking about Illea's sexual partners before she was old enough to even have any, she was used to it. Or, she told herself she was used to it. But thinking about the intrusiveness that would come when people started whispering about her child, too, made her loathe this city.

"Mistress," Beatrice said, interrupting Illea's wandering thoughts. "General Clannaugh has asked if you'll see him. He knows it's late, and he sends his apologies, but he says he's concerned."

Illea opened her eyes to glance at the mantle clock. Its steady ticking was a comfort, the Saeati logo proudly gold-leafed on the face. She couldn't help but wonder if Ishmael had survived all that bloodshed, out in the forest. If she counted her friends, people who she cared about no matter what came of her life, she had to admit that Ishmael was high on the list. He had a good head for business, even if he tried to convince people he didn't by pretending to be a lecherous fool, and an even better head for politics. Life with him in it was always *interesting*. But, most importantly, he was once Amias's closest friend, making him a connection to when things were simpler. Happier. From the time Ishmael moved to the Boardwalk Market, it seemed like he was always around the Wolfe house, turning him and Amias into a matched set. Langston and Mallory, too, for a time, but then Langston wandered off, drawn to people who thought he was interesting, and Mallory got pregnant and went off to Cruinnich to marry a man that didn't mind she was carrying someone's child already. Ishmael went to the Officer's Academy, and it gave Amias the ammunition he needed to convince his father that he was ready to go, too.

"Tell the General I'm fine," Illea said, dragging herself out of the past. "Tell him I send my thanks for his attention, and tell him my healer is tending to me, but happily she is unconcerned about my overall health. If he leaves, then see him out. If he insists, set him in the library to wait."

"Yes, Mistress."

Tilde's mouth pressed together in that way it did when she was being judgemental, her eyes swinging up to the ceiling as she waited for Beatrice to head back out again.

"What?" Illea asked. It wasn't exactly typical for the house staff to question their Mistress, but Tilde wasn't exactly typical, either. She'd been with Illea since the week after Amias died. Her father had hired Tilde as an offering to soothe Illea's panic, at a time when grief disguised itself with fear—fear of leaving the house lest something happen, fear of taking a bath lest she slip and fall, fear of eating lest she choke and die—fear of everything, because it seemed so impossible that Amias Wolfe could have died by falling from a horse, of all things. "Why are you making *that* face?"

"You're testing him," Tilde said.

Illea shrugged. "If he leaves, he isn't as invested in all of this as I thought he was, and he isn't worth my attention."

Tilde made a little grunt in the back of her throat, pushing herself to her feet and moving to the window, where there was a tray of food. Beatrice made sure there was something to eat in every room in the house since Illea never could predict when her stomach would decide it was too hungry and start threatening her with more nausea. "A missing wife casts a long and ugly shadow, Mistress. Are you sure he's worth your attention, whether he's invested or not?"

"You of all people know how a reputation can outpace the truth," Illea said. "And I'm not marrying the man. I'm only using him for his connections and his ambition. He said he was here to engineer Rainer's demise, and that could make him an invaluable ally."

"I'm sure the using is mutual."

"And what if it is?" Illea asked. "Am I only supposed to use people who are innocent of the world, who don't have their own goals and dreams? Is that better or worse?"

"I'm allowed to worry about you, Illea. It's my job, and I've been doing it for more than a decade now." Tilde swept up the tray and carried it over to Illea. "You should eat something before you go down. So that you can have your full strength if there's to be any using. It would rather sully your chances of being well used if you vomit in front of General Clannaugh twice in one day. The pears look nice, and we've that nice bread that Savvas makes, the one with the walnuts. Some of those ginger cookies that Beatrice is so fond of."

"Dates and cookies, then," Illea said.

Tilde gave an exaggerated *tsk* and rested the tray on the table beside Illea. "Nothing but sweets, Illea Winter, shame on you."

Illea smiled, looking over her shoulder at Tilde. She looked handsome, standing in the weak winter sunlight that came in from the window, her hair a mix of red-gold and white, the lines on her face well earned. "I believe I've earned the right to have as many cookies as I see fit, thank you very much."

"Alright then," Tilde said, assembling a plate of dates and ginger cookies. "I won't tell anyone who likes gossip, so we won't have rumours about your terrible indulgences." She rested the plate on the table beside Illea's chair, taking a cookie off the pile. "My daughter loved these when she was little. You remind me of her, sometimes. You have the same stubborn set to your jaw that she always did."

Illea smiled. "Is it really a surprise that you raised a stubborn daughter?"

Tilde laughed. "No, I suppose it isn't. And I was right to do it. The world needs more stubborn women."

Illea picked up a date, breaking it in half. It had already been pitted by someone in the kitchen. "Can you tell yet if it has Talent?" Illea asked. "Bothain said it's hereditary."

"It is," Tilde said slowly, her head cocking to one side. "And you haven't any yourself, so unless the father is Talented…"

"He may well be," Illea supplied. "I didn't know when I had him, but his parents had Talent, as does his son."

Tilde didn't speak right away, and in the stretching silence, Illea knew the answer. "The one from the banquet? The same man arrested yesterday?"

Illea nodded.

Tilde shrugged, waving the thought away. "It's too soon to tell anything like that. None of that matters. What matters is that you carry it to term, and it survives infancy. What matters is that it's *yours*, and it will grow up in this house and fill these halls with all the chaos you can imagine and then some. The rest, we'll deal with when the child is born."

"It's that easy, is it?"

"Nothing about parenting is easy, Illea. It's simple, but it's never easy." She rested a hand on Illea's again, her fingers even colder than before. "But I'll be here, every step of the way, to remind you that it's normal to be frustrated about everything, and it's normal to feel like you're doing everything wrong, and it's normal to feel overwhelmed all the time. And I'll remind you to cherish every infuriating moment of it."

Illea laughed, pulling a cookie off the pile, the crystallized ginger on top shimmering with sugar. "You make parenting sound so inviting."

"You know I've never been one to sugarcoat things," Tilde said with a shrug. "I'd rather you know what mess you've gotten yourself into."

Beatrice eased back into the room. "General Clannaugh has taken up residence in the library, Mistress. He said he won't be shaken off so easily, and he wants to see you for himself, to make sure you're well."

What mess indeed. Illea smiled at Tilde, even as Tilde frowned. "I suppose he's ready to be used."

35

TASHUÉ

DAY 34

"Which bank?" Tashué asked.

The raised voices in the pugilist club became a steady, inarticulate roar as Lorne squared up against his sparring partner. Money changed hands as dozens of people bet on the outcome, and someone started a chant. *Lightning! Lightning! Lightning!*

Tashué stood on the edge of the ring to watch, leaning both his arms on the top rope. László, beside him, leaned on the post. Smoking a cigarillo with hashish in it—Tashué knew that smell anywhere, knew the soft glaze that came over László's eyes with every lungful he took in. Tashué almost asked László to share because the energy of the crowd was making his heart beat too fucking fast, and the noise came up through the canvas floor like a big drum, rattling through Tashué's feet, his femurs, his hips. But it was better to stay sharp. Keep his mind under control, keep his eye on everything. His Talent was hard enough to rein in as it was; he wasn't ready to find out what it would be like to wrestle it with half his faculties smothered by hashish.

"Now, Mr. Guinne, you don't *really* expect me to tell you that the first day I met you, do you?" László asked slowly. He blew a line of smoke up toward the ceiling and grinned. "You gotta romance me slow before I go spilling all my secrets to you."

Guinne. It had been a long time since he'd gone by his father's name. Hearing Guinne spoken by the people around him made all the years since he'd signed *Blackwood* on his military paperwork feel heavier. Nearly thirty years, he'd been calling himself Blackwood, but the first thirteen years of his life, he was Tashué Guinne. And now he was Guinne again because he couldn't well let the people here call him Blackwood since Blackwood was a wanted fugitive. It felt like he'd discarded years of his own history but also reclaimed things he'd lost when he made the switch. But it didn't really fit his new reality, either. His fine Bellmore suit down in the Bay, his body battered from the almost-arrest, his father's broken watch sitting in the pocket of his waistcoat that surely cost as much as rent on his apartment in the Row. How the fuck did he get here?

He knew he stood out, but the clothes he borrowed from Wolfe's house fit so badly that it was a relief to take them off when Lorne revealed he'd rescued things from Tashué's apartment. His piles and piles of sketchpads, his cavalry sabre, the clothes that Illea sent him sometime in the haze of time after Stella left. The suit was too nice, the deep mahogany hue that couldn't seem to decide if it was red or brown, the white chalk stripe in the fabric making him look even taller. The silk on the back of the waistcoat and the lining of the jacket—it all fit perfectly. And no one seemed to ask any questions. László introduced him as Dav's old friend Mr. Guinne and everyone shook his hand and accepted it as truth and moved on with getting the club ready.

Davik put his fingers between his lips, and he whistled loud, the sound ringing. "Get on him, damnit! Quit dancing like you wanna give him a wee kiss!"

"When, then?" Tashué asked. "When is it happening?"

László glanced at Tashué again. "Does that mean you're coming?"

Tashué pressed his fingers harder into the cover of his notepad. The relief that swamped him at seeing them again took him by surprise. They were just *paper*, but they were also memories. He didn't have any photographs of his father, but he had sketches. And he did have a few photographs of his mother, and each of them was stashed in one of these notebooks between pages and cover because he'd brought them with him when he was deployed after she died, and he'd never put them back into their frames. One photograph of his mother and his grandmother, if he remembered correctly. One photograph of Keoh, but it was blurry because she moved. He slid his fingers over the spines as they towered on the desk, counting—Lorne had brought every single one of them. Tashué kept them all over the years. He couldn't throw them away when they were filled. It didn't matter how beat up, how stained, how wet and warped they were, he couldn't let them go.

He'd taken one out of the pile, carried it with him downstairs as if having this old sketches in his hand again would pull him and Jason closer together. He'd made these drawings with his back a mess of scars and with his mother dead and in the ground. He'd missed her funeral. He'd made these drawings on the ship down to the Spice Isles, leaving Jason behind as an infant with Keoh to serve the military that sent him home to die from the flogging they'd given him for the crime of wanting to survive. He'd made these drawings on the Spice Isles, in General Wolfe's study while they talked about fatherhood, and Wolfe tried to warn him that it would be harder than he could ever imagine. He'd made these drawings half in shock, half in love with every day of the future because every day of the future had his son in it. He'd made these drawings, incredulous of how small his boy was, how his tiny body fit into Tashué's hands.

He drew it over and over, the image of it seared into his mind. His infant son, so recently born that his wispy black hair was still wet, fitting in his two hands. He drew it over and over and over, until it was nearly perfect. His artist's eye saw all the mistakes he'd made, all the imperfections. The knuckle joints that were off, the perspective of Jason's foot that made it look not quite right, the numerous times he'd gotten the shape of Jason's mouth wrong. And the middle of the book, stained with beer, because someone—Amias, maybe?—had leaned across the table and knocked over a pint and sent a wave of red ale spreading across the table. Skip a few pages, which were too soaked and warped by the beer, and then the sketches got better and better after that, like he'd gotten all the mistakes out of the way in the first pages, and his skill at hands and feet and the very particular assembly of Jason's face became muscle memory in his fingers.

He was here for Jason.

Whatever had happened in twenty ugly years between the moment when he held Jason in his hands and now, he was here for Jason. He would have left with Stella, but he stayed for Jason. Because he'd left, once. He'd left his infant son in Yaelsmuir when all he wanted to do was stay, he left to serve a military he didn't believe in anymore. He'd cursed himself for leaving back then—but by then it was already too late. By then, Keoh had left him and kept Jason away for four years.

Jason had come back, but then Tashué lost him again to the Rift. If he wished for Jason hard enough, could his Talent draw them together?

Lorne's sparring partner swung for Lorne's head, the sudden action pulling Tashué back into the moment. Lorne slipped the punch easily, swung back. The pair of them entered something so smooth and perfect, it looked like they were dancing. But dancing with violence. Lorne's form was brilliant, which seemed to defy reason—he wasn't a boxer. He'd been fighting in the Hive in his whole-body style for five years. It wasn't possible to retrain his instincts and his form that quickly. How long had he been here? A week? Two?

And yet the proof was there, in his arms, in his shoulders, in the way his boots danced over the canvas, in the way his hips rolled delicately. He looked like he'd been training for this all his life.

The first punch landed—the sparring partner's glove caught Lorne's shoulder in a glancing blow. Another slid in under Lorne's guard and caught him in the gut, but he twisted with it, his movement robbing the punch of its power. He swung back once, twice, a third time—the fourth caught the sparring partner in the pads covering his ears and the side of his face, spinning him so hard he almost fell. And then Lorne was on him, vicious, unrelenting, hitting him again, again, again.

László's Talent slid into the air.

At first Tashué thought he was imagining it—or maybe Tashué was losing his grip on his own Talent and felt everything again. But no. Talent twisted between them like the smoke from László's cigarillo, winding through Lorne's body, filling the space between the muscle fibre with energy that moved Lorne faster, pushing him through the very limits of his body's capability and beyond, until he was nothing but flying fists. His boxing gloves were a storm, unleashed on the hapless sparring partner. The sparring partner twisted, caught Lorne in the sternum with a vicious right, and they broke apart. Went back to dancing around each other, recovering strength and focus.

"What are you doing to his muscles?" Tashué asked.

László turned to Tashué only slowly, like he'd been caught at something and he didn't want to startle too much so he didn't look so guilty. He smiled, leaning a little closer. Trusting Tashué with a secret. "You felt that, did you?"

"What exactly am I feeling?" Tashué asked. He didn't like it—did Lorne know László was doing something? But he was here to make nice. Here to make these people trust him. "All this Talent shit, it's new to me. I didn't quicken until out there in the forest. It's all so fucking loud, and I don't know what's normal and what's too much—I'm trying to get a grip on it."

László's mouth twisted with something sympathetic. "The violent quickenings are like that, I hear. You learn to guard yourself, with time. It's like…" His fingers swirled in the air like he was fishing for the right word.

"Like stemming the flow of blood," Tashué said. "That's what someone told me. I have to keep pressure on it or else I bleed everywhere."

"Sure, if you like. There's a way to do it that takes less concentration. I'll teach you how, if you want."

"After you tell me what you were doing to his muscles."

László shrugged, offering the cigarillo to Tashué. Tashué waved it off. "He wouldn't be ready otherwise. Sending him up into the ring with Ari Odegaard unprepared? We might as well send him up for execution."

"Ari is back to fighting?" Tashué asked. "I thought he was off after he fucked his ankle."

László's eyebrow arched, and he glanced at Tashué, blowing smoke over Tashué's head. "You follow pugilism, hey?"

"I used to fight at Ari's club, in the sabre duels. They sponsored my fees to run in the sword tourney because I had a reputation of not losing."

"A reputation of not losing." László laughed. "Sure, Mr. Guinne. Is that your way of saying you always won?"

Tashué shrugged. "Ari's ankle is better?"

László nodded. "He's coming back out of retirement for Redbone's exhibition match. If our Mr. Lightning went up there with his whole-body habit and his inability to guard himself, he would have been slaughtered. I seen a few men get killed in the ring, biting off a bigger fight than they could chew. Didn't seem right to let him eat it by himself because Powell Iwan was dragging his wrinkly old heels to get us a fighter in time. I don't know if Iwan wants us to lose the match and be humiliated or if he doesn't understand the difference between a Hive fight and a boxing match, but it felt an awful lot like he was sending our Mr. Lightning down to us to die." László shrugged, taking in a breath of smoke and then blowing it up at the ceiling. He kept his head craned back like he was watching it swirl. "Maybe Iwan was tossing him down here as a peace offering so Dav could get retribution for Hale."

"But you're protecting him instead?" Tashué asked. "Feeding knowledge into his body so he's a pugilist over night. Why?"

"Dav said to make him ready, so I'm making him ready."

"Isn't it dangerous, changing the body that much with Talent?" Tashué asked. "That's how the Ash Child got turned to stone. He pushed too hard until one day his Talent started to calcify his muscles."

"Sure, it's dangerous." László glanced at Tashué and gave a lazy shrug. "I'll stop once I think he's got a half a chance of surviving that exhibition match, and then if the club is still running after, we'll keep up with his training the old-fashioned way. And it's illegal as far as the league is concerned, but I'm hoping they won't notice. It's all still better than letting the poor fucker step into the ring with Ari Odegaard unprepared."

"But *why*?"

László laughed, looking at Tashué again. "I thought he was your son's lover. Shouldn't you be happy that I'm helping him so he doesn't get his stupid thick head punched in?"

"I am happy," Tashué said. "But why is Davik helping him when some might say it's his fault Hale got killed?"

"Got killed," László laughed. "When it's his fault Powell Iwan asked *you* to put a bullet in Hale, you mean? When it's *your* fault, too? It ain't about boxing, is it? You're asking me if you and Mr. Lightning are even safe here after what the pair of you did?"

"Sure," Tashué said. "Since we're being honest with each other, getting to know one another. Why doesn't Davik kill me and Lorne and dump us both in the river as one final fuck you to Iwan?"

"Since we're being honest with each other," László echoed. He took one last drag of his cigarillo, blowing the smoke over the ring. He licked his thumb and his forefinger, pinching out the ember of the cigarillo and tucking it behind his ear. "I don't know for sure. Dav doesn't tell me everything. He keeps things close to the vest, you know? Just in case. But I have a guess. You want to hear it?"

Lorne burst into action again, a cascade of punches that hit his opponent from every angle. Davik whistled and clapped, and the whole room seemed to explode with cheering. The energy of it felt different, more immediate than ever before—like Tashué felt it twice. Once with all the usual senses, and once again with Talent, like it sucked in all that excitement and poured it in to his veins. It made his heart beat too fast, hammering against his ribcage like he was the one fighting.

This time, László didn't reach his Talent toward Lorne. And Lorne moved brilliantly without it, a flurry of arms and those white gloves flashing.

"Do I want to hear your guess?" Tashué asked, forcing himself to breathe slow, to hang on to some shred of calm. "Sure. Hit me."

László grinned, wide and liquid. He hooked a finger at Tashué, motioning for Tashué to come closer. Leaning away as he did it so his back was against the corner post. Tashué stifled a sigh and leaned in. László caught him by the front of the waistcoat, hooking a finger in the wool and pulling him closer still. Warm brown eyes were wild and bright, the smell of tobacco and hashish lingering around him, the smell of garlic and molasses on his breath. He seemed so young, like a boy playing make-believe. Pretending he was the sort of man who could execute a bank robbery. But Tashué knew that look in his eye. The look that a killer got after a while, even if he had soft cheeks that he was only just growing into. The look that said he knew how to hunt and how to take a life and how to explode into unimaginable violence even though his face was painted with a dopey hashish grin at this moment.

"My guess is that's exactly what Powell Iwan wants," László said. "First he sent our Lightning down here to us, his face all smashed up from the beating Hale asked for. And the Lightning, a fucking idiot with no ability to watch his own mouth, all wound up and cruising for a fight because as far as he was concerned, he wasn't finished yet. Iwan wanted us to know exactly who he was. But Lorne said he'd do anything for Jason, and Dav believed him. Dav's always been good at that. Looking someone right in the soul and knowing if he can use them or not. So, we didn't kill him and set on training him, and we sent word to Iwan that Mr. Lightning here is going to be incredible. Great news. And what does canny old Iwan do next? Sends Dav an even bigger hunk of bait. Two of them—you and Saeati, imagine Dav's luck. He hates Saeati, and you? A tinman? Wanted by the Authority, no less. There's no fucking *way* Iwan thinks we'll all make peace. He wants you and Saeati and Dav to rip each other apart, and then when Dav wins and puts you and Mr. Lightning and Saeati in the river for retribution for Hale, suddenly Iwan has the last excuse he needs to send his people down here and clean Dav out. Take the club as his, since he paid for so much of it, maybe prop Mr. Czarny up in Dav's place. And then he's got his Bay back to run it how he wants. And that's exactly why Dav won't do it. He's not going to kill Lorne Coswyn, and he's not going to kill Ishmael Saeati, and he's not going to kill the very mysterious Mr. Guinne because he's been around

Powell Iwan a while and he knows poisonous bait when he catches a whiff of it."

Something hot slid down Tashué's spine, like he was bleeding on his own bones. And then it went cold. Across his chest, in his gut, settling in his joints.

"Besides," László said, "Hale was runny shit. Dav was trying to figure out how to get rid of him and pin it on Iwan, but you took care of it for us, didn't you? And now Dav knows what you're willing to do. For Jason, right? You killed Hale for Jason."

Tashué nodded. It was close enough to the truth. For Jason, and those children. And maybe for himself because it felt good to solve a problem that easy.

László grinned, reaching up and patting Tashué's cheek, his hand warm against skin and facial hair. "How close am I? About the shape of it, you think?"

"I didn't fucking well know I was bait when I came down here." Tashué wasn't sure exactly if he was playing along with László for effect or if he thought László was right. He didn't know Powell Iwan at all, except by reputation. Canny, ruthless, holding the Bay against *any* foe.

"You didn't, hey?" László asked. "You're either stupid, or you thought you were making a good deal."

"I guess I'm stupider than I thought," Tashué muttered.

"Oh, Mr. Guinne, I doubt that very much," László said, his voice dropping to a bedroom purr. His finger slid down Tashué's chest, to the Bellmore trousers, brushing over the buttons one by one on his way further down. "What deal did you make?"

Tashué caught László's hand and squeezed it, pulling it away from his trousers. "I didn't make any deal. I got the impression Powell wanted me out of the Hive as fast as possible. Like maybe he didn't want to risk his neck protecting me, but didn't want to turn me away, either. It was Vasska's idea to come down here." The lie was so flimsy, but it was close enough to the truth that hopefully László wouldn't challenge it.

"Mr. Czarny?" László asked, his head tilting so he could look toward the bar, over Tashué's shoulder. "I can't ever get a read on him. Sometimes it seems like he's working a little too hard to get friendly with Davik."

Tashué followed László's gaze, where Vasska and Allie and Ishmael were hunched over Allie's notepad, a mess of pints and food cluttering the bar around their elbows. Ishmael had that disinterested affect he always had when he was paying the most attention to things, and Vasska and Allie were blushing at each other as Allie wrote something down, in her fast and illegible shorthand. She had ink on her fingers already, the black spreading across one knuckle. Had Tashué underestimated Vasska's cunning because he was young and he blushed at Allie? If Tashué was bait, did Vasska know? Or was he honestly hoping to make peace with Davik, like he said?

"Why does Davik hate Ishmael?" Tashué asked.

László shrugged. "Don't know. Why don't you ask Saeati? He must be hurting real bad, limping his sorry ass down here to ask Davik for protection. That or he's in on the deal. Do you want me to teach you how to heal him? I can show you how to have him walking normally again by fight night."

"I think I've got a handle on it."

László shrugged. "Suit yourself."

Lorne's opponent hit the canvas. People rushed in, leaping over the ropes to get on top of Lorne and drag him away before he hit the man after he was unconscious. László laughed, like he was the happiest kid in the world, slithering like a cat through the ropes and walking across the canvas. He threw both his arms around Lorne's chest, pulling Lorne into a fierce hug and kissing Lorne's cheek. And Lorne melted into László for a moment, pressing his face into the hallow beneath László's jaw like he was basking in the smell of László's skin. Right up until he noticed Tashué watching, and then he pushed László away. Gloves glistening with his opponent's sweat and blood, his body drenched from the fight, his chest heaving. Davik was on him next, laughing, lifting him right up off the canvas and slapping his back.

"You're doing damn fine, laddie! Damn fine. I'm proud of you, shit. You're doing better than I dared hope!"

Lorne blushed and squirmed. And he didn't look at Tashué while he glowed with all the attention. He was ashamed of it, maybe. Embarrassed that Tashué saw it.

Because he was comfortable here. He liked it. The club, the roof, the rattling radiators that kept him warm, the big bedroom where he had things waiting for Jason. The hugs from László, the pride from Davik. He loved every moment of it.

Would Lorne ever forgive Tashué and Ishmael when Davik died? Tashué wasn't sure. And it wasn't a good feeling. It settled in his gut like a cannon ball. Like mortar fire, waiting to explode.

36

ILLEA
DAY 34

Bothain had changed before he came to Illea's home, and she appreciated the thought. Clean boots and clean hands, he'd scrubbed any evidence of his grim morning away. The images of death flashed through her head again. Had Bothain touched any of those bodies, or had he left that work to everyone else?

He'd made himself at home in her library, lounging by the hearth and helping himself to some whisky. He stood when Illea stepped in, and his eyes ran over her whole body. She wasn't dressed as she should be for receiving guests—Beatrice had let her hair down into a single loose braid, and Illea hadn't bothered dressing completely after bathing when she got back from the forest. She had a corset and a petticoat, but only a dressing gown over them instead of proper clothes. Bothain let out his breath slowly, like he knew this was a test, and he wanted to react properly. He was smart enough to know that everything was a test as far as Illea was concerned, but every now and then—like right now—she caught him off guard and had the immense pleasure of watching him panic a little. He wanted to say something, wanted to touch her because the thin silk invited the touch and the attention, but the last time he'd seen her, she was half-fainted and vomiting in the snow.

"Miss Winter," he said, recovering himself quickly. "Your servant said you were feeling better, but I wanted to see for myself."

"I am," Illea said. "Thank you for checking on me, General Clannaugh. I appreciate it, given everything you're juggling at the moment. What with protecting Rainer from his own downfall."

Bothain rolled his eyes, turning away from Illea and returning to her sideboard to refill his whisky glass. "I'm not protecting Rainer from anything. I'd hoped to talk to you sooner, to explain it all. I thought you would come down to White Crown over the summer, at least to be there when I received my General's stars."

"I was busy," Illea said. She wrapped the end of her braid through her fingers, which drew Bothain's attention back to her. His eyes tracked along her hair, lingering for a moment at her throat before finally settling on her face. "I have businesses to run, Bothain. I can't flit down the river on a whim, no matter how impressive the star ceremony is."

"I know," Bothain said, the first smile touching his mouth. "That's part of your charm. You make me ache for you until I can't bear to wait a moment longer, and then you waltz into the room wearing nothing but a dressing gown so I can't think anymore."

Illea smiled. "I'm wearing a bit more than a dressing gown, Bothain. These old floors are cold."

He laughed as he swept up his glass. "Will you come sit with me in your library, Miss Winter? You, your dressing gown, and whatever you're hiding beneath it. We should talk about Rainer."

"That's probably the least attractive thing you've ever said to me."

Bothain's nose wrinkled with distaste. "I know. I think I vomited in my mouth when I said it, and yet needs must. I would hate for all of this mess to become a wedge between us when we're both working toward the same thing."

Illea entered the library, but she didn't sit, not yet. Let him sweat a little and earn it. The library was deliciously warm, and her staff kept the books free of dust, the whole room smelling of the citrus oil they used to polish the wood furniture. Beatrice had arranged for a small tray of fruit to sit on one of the tables, but her stomach was content for now.

"You're looking refreshed," Bothain said, following her to the hearth. "I'm glad to see it."

"Things have been busier than usual this election cycle," Illea said with a shrug. "The exhaustion crept up on me."

Bothain stood close enough to touch her, taking a chance and sliding the back of one finger across her exposed collarbone. Illea crossed her arms over her chest, pulling her dressing gown closed. Bothain took the hint, and his hand retreated. He rested his shoulder against the mantle so that the hearth and the fire stood between them. The light of the flames danced on his silhouette, shining in his golden hair, laying shadows in the lines starting to appear around his mouth and on his forehead.

"I suppose you're here to implore me to ask General Wolfe where Ishmael Saeati is," Illea said, her chin lifting as she looked Bothain in the eye. "You'll make a grand speech about how Rainer's collapse is nigh and you're here to run the police force for Maes, and to that end you *must* find Ishmael and Captain Blackwood so that you can prove your competence. And since you promised to get the police force without Myron's re-election, you'll insist that you need results so that General Maes will pat you on the pretty blond head and let you run the police force on his behalf."

"Actually," Bothain said, swirling his glass and watching the whisky dance. He looked almost humble with his head bowed like that, his broad shoulders slumped a little to show a hint of his fatigue. "No."

Illea didn't even bother hiding her surprise, letting her eyebrows arch up. "No?"

"You're right that I think General Wolfe knows where Blackwood and Saeati are—or at least he had a hand in the escape." He paused long enough to sip his whisky, meeting Illea's eye. His eye contact was always so intrusive and steady, like he was catching Illea and pinning her in place. Illea looked back at him, standing tall. "I don't believe his hunters happened upon the carnage by accident in a rainstorm. But honestly? It doesn't matter if I find Blackwood and Saeati or not. I mean, General Maes would be very pleased if I produced Saeati's body." He winced when he said it, his gaze softening. His fingers twitched like he wanted to touch her, but her arms were still crossed over her chest. "I know you're fond of him. If it's any comfort, Saeati probably took this chance to leave. If the man is half as smart as Maes thinks he is, he's on his way out of the Dominion by now."

Illea met Bothain's gaze, letting her expression go flat. It wouldn't serve her—or Ishmael for that matter—for her to argue with Bothain about whether or not he'd flee the city.

"Why is Maes so concerned with Ishmael?" Illea asked.

Bothain shrugged, hiding his discomfort behind a sip of whisky. "I'm sure you can imagine why, Illea. I know how brilliant you are."

Illea sighed, playing with her braid again, letting it twist over her hand. "Maes is quite jealous of power, isn't he? Guards it like an ancient dragon on a hoard of gold."

"I won't tell him you said that," Bothain said, his mouth pulling into that restrained smile of his. "But yes."

"I won't tell him you agreed with me," Illea countered. "Ishmael is a threat to Maes because of his connection to the late General Deri, or at least that's what Maes is telling himself. That's what the little performance with the letter was about—Maes was letting Ishmael know that he was still being watched, even though Deri is gone."

Bothain tilted his head to one side, like he was weighing the exact words individually for their worth. "In a manner, yes."

Sometimes Illea hated how good Bothain was at piquing her interest. But then if he wasn't so adept at keeping her attention, he wouldn't be so valuable an ally. "Which part is wrong?"

"Maes wanted me to let Saeati know that he was being watched, but he also hoped that Saeati would run. Lead him to... well. Let's say, the rest of Deri's allies, who have scattered since his death."

"Why are we *saying* the rest of Deri's allies?" Illea asked. "Who else is Maes looking for?"

Bothain looked away for a moment, his eyes flicking up to the ceiling. "At times, Maes's vigilance makes him sound paranoid."

"And?" Illea pressed.

"Best not, Illea darling," Bothain said. "Not this time. Suffice it to say Maes is suspicious of anyone who showed the slightest affinity for General Deri, and talking about him with too much interest is a dangerous habit, even though he seems to be dead."

"Seems to be dead?" Illea echoed. "That only makes me more curious, Bothain."

"I know," Bothain said with a smile. He leaned a little closer, like he was sharing a secret. "Later, when there's more time. I promise."

Illea huffed, unfolding her arms. All her clothes had caught the heat of the fire and sweat danced on her thighs. She sank down into the biggest, most inviting chair she had in the library, the one with the soft arms, upholstered in lush green velvet. She propped her feet up on the nearby leather footstool, stretching her toes toward the fire. She had to be careful with Bothain—if she pried too insistently at his secrets, he got annoyed and defensive. Bothain rested his back against the mantle so he could keep watching her, his eyes tracking her up and down again like he was trying to guess if she was still feeling ill and what she might do if he joined her in the chair. In many ways, he was challenging to read, but his appetites always appeared so clearly in his eyes.

"You said Maes was the one who wrote you and convinced you to retire from the Authority and go to the Academy," she said instead of pushing the matter. "And Maes guided you through the testing—that's what you meant when you told Mallory he was your tutor."

"I didn't cheat, if that's what you're asking," Bothain said. "But yes, Maes helped to make sure I was prepared. We both knew that the 12th wouldn't go to anyone but the best."

"So you became the best."

Bothain grinned again, sipping at his whisky in a poor attempt to look humble. "You could say that."

"Spare me your false modesty, Bothain. My interest is also in making alliances with the best."

Bothain's eyes flashed with his predatory, hungry smile. "How fortunate for me."

"What does it have to do with Rainer, Myron, and Yael's police force?"

"Your mind is a delight, Illea," Bothain said. "I love watching you spin it all out. You get a glow behind your eyes that only ever appears when you're honing in on other people's schemes."

"Is this your way of saying you don't intend to tell me, and you'd rather I keep guessing?"

Bothain sipped his whisky slowly. "It would be my immense pleasure if you so indulged me."

Illea rolled her eyes at him. "Fine. The police force would be immensely powerful, given the time and funding to roll out on a national level. A provincial police force was never the end goal—it was always to be a national program, like the Authority. And if Maes is jealous of power, then he would loathe Rainer for having control of such a force. Rainer can't be challenged for the Authority because it's a thing that he's inherited by climbing up through the ranks of an organization older than Maes's entire career. But the police force, that's new. And there's room to maneuver it away from Rainer before he even starts it. Like you said, a national organization that tracks criminals and keeps files on federal crimes would be an invaluable tool for the Crowne and all of her allies."

"Or a tool for her enemies, who might seek to bring the Crowne to its natural and inevitable end."

Illea cocked her head to one side, watching Bothain's face. "You're always teasing me, Bothain. Which is Maes? An ally, or an enemy?"

Bothain drained the last of his whisky, leaving the glass on the mantle. "He's not a supporter of the current Crowne, but he's a loyalist in theory."

Illea wrinkled her nose. "That answer is terribly unsatisfying."

Bothain shrugged. "It's the truth."

Illea shifted, letting her dressing gown fall open, inviting Bothain's eyes back to her skin. She loved how immediate the reaction was from him, how completely she captured his attention. The rest of the night stretched out in her imagination, making her heart beat faster. Bothain was an enthusiastic and aggressive partner, and she hadn't been with him for a while. The last time was in Cruinnich, maybe. Before he left the Authority.

"So, Maes sent you up here to somehow juggle the contradictory goals of ruining Rainer whilst also getting the police force ratified," she said, letting her voice go slow and lazy. "You would have thrown your weight behind Myron's campaign until he was elected, and then you would have crushed Rainer. With the very same secrets that Captain Blackwood has thrown into the public eye. The things about the energy units."

Bothain grinned, resting his glass on the mantle and abandoning it, half full. He came slowly toward Illea, giving her time to give some signal that she didn't want his attention, but she wanted it so badly that she had to restrain herself from asking for it. She needed to let Bothain distract her a while and stop thinking about Tashué Blackwood and his piercing amber eyes and his Talent. She hated him, just a little. She didn't expect to have any passion to spare for him; he was a man who served a need. But here she was with his child, and him with his Talent, making everything so horribly complicated. Thank the North Star that Bothain had a plan to destroy the man, one way or another.

Bothain settled on the edge of her footstool, sliding his finger over her ankle, her wool stocking standing as a barrier between them for now, but if she knew him, that wouldn't last long.

"If it weren't for the fact we are both married, I would ask you to be my wife. Your brilliance is a breath of fresh air."

"Don't do that," Illea said. "Once I finally rid myself of Myron, I won't be marrying again."

"I am devastated," Bothain said, but he tugged at Illea's stockings, testing how well they were secured. They didn't budge.

"You said yourself that you're still married, anyway," Illea said.

"She'll be missing ten years soon." Bothain's fingers drifted up Illea's stockings, following the line of the cable knit up her thighs. "I could declare her legally dead, but I expect Aelwyd will fight it, and it won't be worth the effort. But I can declare our marriage bonds null and void, freeing me to marry again if I wanted."

"You'd lose your stake in her estate," Illea said. But even as she said it, her heart leapt with joy on Aelwyd's behalf. However Illea decided to use Bothain, he'd been a scourge on Aelwyd's family at a time when they were trying to find any sign of Ffyanwy and grieve what looked like a permanent and unexplainable loss.

Bothain shrugged, oblivious to Illea's conflicting interests. "The Rhydderch estate is pennies in comparison to all I can accomplish with Maes's support and the police force. My ties to Ffyanwy are dead weight at this point."

"Does Maes have some distant Crowne cousin to marry you off to, then?"

Another shrug, but his fingers found the top of her stockings, and that took most of his attention. His fingers teased the hem like he couldn't decide if he wanted to drag them down or let his hand wander up higher. The warm brush of his fingertips on her skin made her whole body burn for him.

"I'm sure he's trying," Bothain said. "I don't want a Crowne cousin. Ties to the Crowne will also be dead weight, and I don't want someone with an inclination toward loyalty to Maes."

"What do you want, then?" Illea asked. "What do you think will be the perfect match for Bothain Clannaugh and his brand new police force and all the power he's stolen from Maes's grasp?"

Bothain gave a wolfish grin. His other hand caught Illea by the ankle and lifted her leg up so he could sit between them. He dug his heels into the floor and dragged the footstool closer to Illea's chair, pushing the petticoats up to her knees. "Ah, well, I have played my hand too early, and you've already turned me down, so I won't try again just yet. Maybe after my marriage bonds are void. Hopefully yours will be too, by then."

"I told you, I don't want to marry again," Illea muttered.

"What a coincidence. Neither do I."

Illea put her foot on Bothain's chest, pushing a little to remind him she could shove him right off the footstool if she wanted. "You're too bold, Bothain Clannaugh."

His hand wandered farther, his fingers finding the wetness of her. His grin widened. "Illea Winter, you aren't wearing any drawers."

"Am I not?" Illea asked airily, fighting hard against the urge to lean into his fingers. "What a terrible oversight. Whatever shall I do to defend my modesty?"

Bothain laughed, sliding the footstool closer still. "What indeed?"

"How does Maes plan to convince the Queen to turn the 12th into a police force?"

Bothain groaned. "Illea, heaven help me, won't you let me enjoy you?"

"Keep up, Bothain," Illea laughed. She slid closer to him, pushing herself up straighter so she could shrug the dressing gown off completely. "I thought it was illegal to deploy military divisions on the mainland— that's the whole reason Maes gave for cancelling the provincial diplomat program after Deri died."

Bothain leaned in, wrapping an arm around Illea's waist and crushing her against his chest. And she let him, heaven help *her*, she leaned hard into him and breathed in the musky scent of him.

"There will be some frustrating legal maneuvering to accomplish," he muttered, his words half muddled as he pressed his lips against the side of her neck. She held his shoulders, letting him pull her weight onto his lap, her petticoats splayed around both their legs and bunched up against his chest. "Maes intends to have the 12th reclassified as a peace-time force, to skirt the laws."

Illea closed her eyes, tilting her head back. Sweet North Star, he felt so good, his body and his mouth, and the way his hands grabbed her thighs. The way she felt like herself, her body buzzing with energy, her mind alight with all the schemes of men and how she could twist their ambitions to serve her best. She'd only been feeling ill a few days, but it felt an eternity when she thought of the coming months of how her body would change. But this, this was still entirely hers.

"Maes strikes me as the type who bleats most loudly about the law when it suits his desires, and then undercuts it whenever he needs to in order to get what he wants."

Bothain laughed, his fingers sliding between her legs when her weight was properly balanced on his lap. "I won't tell him you said that, either."

"I won't tell him you agree with me again."

Bothain kissed her neck, her jaw, his teeth scraping against her skin like he wanted to bite her. "I was planning on prostrating myself at Eirdis Redbone's feet and begging her to consider the force, but it seems that your tinman toy gave us the perfect way around the election."

Illea leaned back, pushing his face away. "My tinman toy?"

Bothain froze at the dangerous edge in Illea's voice, and his hesitation gave her a fresh thrill. "Everyone heard about the banquet, Illea. One of your more delicious scandals, I should say. With the Queen here, no less."

Illea pushed her hand through all the blond hair, making a fist in it and pulling, earning a wince-groan, Bothain's expression turning to a delicious mix of fear and lust. Eyes wider, mouth open, head tilted up to her like he hoped she would bite him back. "One of the things I've always liked about you thus far is that you don't get jealous and possessive when my other lovers are mentioned," Illea said slowly, letting him sweat each word. "I hope that isn't about to change."

"Of course not," Bothain said quickly. "It's only that this particular lover of yours is suddenly rather important, isn't he? Are you hoping to protect him from the fallout of all this?"

Illea shrugged. She kissed him, savouring the whisky on his lips and the panic that oozed from him. "Why should I? He's just a tinman, as you said."

Bothain exhaled slowly, his relief bleeding into the air between them. He dared move again, kissing Illea's chin once, gently, like he was testing her reaction. When she leaned into him again, his hands started their wandering. He found the ties of her petticoat and worked slowly on the knot. "For a moment you seemed defensive of him. Saeati I understand —there's history."

History indeed. At some point in this conversation, Illea would have to find the space to tell Bothain that she was carrying a child. The details of whose it was would be left unsaid, but if he was to be an ally, she needed to at least appear to be confiding in him. If he found out later, from someone else, he would be annoyed she hadn't told him.

"You aren't going to look for Ishmael and Captain Blackwood at all," Illea said, the thought clicking in her head so suddenly she couldn't hold it in. She leaned back again to watch his face in case he tried to evade the answer. This time, she wouldn't let her deter him so easily. "That's what you said no about—you aren't going to search for them because they're worth more to you missing than found. That's why you said the Army of the Red Dawn hijacked the wagon—that's what you plan on telling the press, and that's the news you'll send down to White Crown. Rainer said the Authority is too short staffed for decisive action against the rebels, so you'll have the Queen to declare a national emergency. Maes can deploy the 12th as peacekeepers, and then you'll allow Powell Iwan and his Cattle Bone Bay thugs wreak so much havoc that the Queen ratifies the police force herself. If you're lucky, before the election even runs."

Bothain grinned, beaming and hungry. He kissed Illea on the mouth, crushing them together again. She leaned into the kiss, rocking against the hardness of him, pushing so insistently against her even through his trousers. His hands lost the thin veneer of restraint, his teeth closing on her lip for one deliciously painful moment.

"It would take an incredible wave of violence to drive the Queen to ratify the police force so quickly," Illea said. She needed to say it, to lay the words between them to see his reaction. "She would be wary of shifting the balance of power that much. And if Maes is as scheming as you say, I doubt she trusts him enough to give him that much control over the Dominion."

"Yes," Bothain breathed, his eyes fixed on her face like he wanted to measure her reaction, too. "An incredible amount of violence indeed. The Army of the Red Dawn is notorious for the amount of violence they're able to unleash upon a city, and unfortunately for Yaelsmuir, it seems to have become the newest home for Davik Kaine."

Illea slid her hand down Bothain's chest until she found his erection. He groaned, leaning back, giving her enough space to start unbuttoning the front of his trousers. "Is that true, or is that what you're going to tell the Queen?"

"Does it matter?" Bothain asked, his voice gone breathy and unfocused. "What difference does it make if the end goal is the same?"

Voices outside the library. The sound stilled Illea's heart and then set it beating again with fury. Stomping. Slamming doors. Only one person would dare slam doors in her house. Myron, curse him, he'd turned up.

"Myron, this isn't the time," Rainer's voice, echoing in the hallways, squealing a little with his fear. "We should go. There's too much to do— you need to practice your speech for tomorrow—"

"I want to set eyes on her," Myron said. "If the bitch is ill, I want to see it for myself. Perhaps I'll finally be free of her."

A growl rumbled in Bothain's chest, his fingers squeezing Illea's thighs. "Do you want me to get rid of him?"

"If you do, won't Rainer know that you aren't interrupted in helping him?"

"It doesn't matter if he knows, not now. With everything Blackwood has started, I don't need Rainer to get the force."

Illea nodded—and then their time was up. She'd left the door open because she hadn't expected to need privacy in her house, and the light of the crackling fire must have drawn Myron's attention straight to them. She wouldn't look over her shoulder. She made herself that promise, that vow, so that she wouldn't even give him the satisfaction of attention. She watched Bothain's face instead, as his eyes tracked away from her and toward the doorway.

"Well," Myron said. His voice rattled around the library and made the hair on the back of Illea's neck stand on end, but she didn't look at him. "It seems she's feeling fine indeed. Her usual whorish self, I think. You lied to me, Rainer. You said she was ill."

Rainer spluttered behind Illea's back, perhaps remembering exactly why he and Myron were talking about Illea's health. With glee, in all likelihood. With hope that something terrible had stricken Illea to her bed for a while, so she wouldn't interfere with the election. Perhaps even something bad enough to kill her, so Myron would inherit everything he didn't deserve.

The thought of it tried to make her hot and furious, but she didn't let it. Refused to give the fury room to bloom in her chest, refused to allow Myron and Rainer such control over her mood.

"Myron," Rainer said. "We should go. This isn't the time to stir up trouble, not with General Clannaugh coming all this way to support your campaign."

"I beg your pardon, General Clannaugh," Myron said, but his drunken tongue mangled the pronunciation of Bothain's name, or maybe he'd over exaggerated it on purpose to be especially obnoxious. "I assume the Winter house be hosting you for the entire night? My wife is a voracious whore in all her appetites, and I'll wager you're almost man enough to keep up with her!"

"Myron!" Rainer snapped.

Bothain chuckled, the sound low and dangerous. He pulled Illea closer, planting his feet flat on the floor like he'd get up at a moment's notice, like he could lift Illea in his arms and start walking. "That's alright, Mr. Elsworth. There's no shame in a man like Myron admitting that he routinely fails to please women. Happens to the best of us now and then. Happens to the rest of us on a regular basis."

Myron snorted. "Which one are you?"

"The best," Illea said. She tilted her head toward Myron only slightly, enough that she could see his figure in the doorway. "And in case you need the whole joke explained, you are the rest, Myron. The very lowest standard."

Myron laughed. "And I suppose you've collected the largest sample size of anyone in this city."

"I'm bored, Bothain," Illea said. "I want to get on with the night before I lose interest."

"My apologies, Miss Winter," Bothain said. And he did it—he braced himself, his whole body flexing, arms supporting her as he pushed himself to his feet. He lifted her right up off the footstool, and she couldn't help but laugh, hooking her ankles together behind his back and hugging both arms around his shoulders. "I'll see you up to a more private room immediately."

"I trust you to see yourself out, Rainer," Illea said as icily as she could manage while Bothain bulled his way right through the door, past the both of them. "And if you ever set foot in my house again, I'll see you charged for trespassing."

Myron and Rainer spluttered, and Bothain left them behind, heading for the stairs.

"Where shall we go first, Miss Winter?" Bothain asked, his voice rising to make sure Rainer and Myron could hear. "This is such a big, beautiful manor. There are so many rooms I'd love to explore, lots of furniture I'd like to test. I've never fucked you in your own house before."

Illea laughed again, pushing her hands into Bothain's hair, kissing him slowly. "You're a filthy degenerate, Bothain Clannaugh."

He grinned, nipping her bottom lip. "I know. It's why you like me. Maybe I'll have you right here on the stairs to get us started."

The next thing she knew, Bothain had set her down on the steps, and he dragged off her petticoat, tossing it over the bannister so it fluttered down to the floor. He knelt a few steps below her, hands sliding over bare thighs, pushing them farther apart. The air here was so cold, sitting sharp on her skin, the wool rug of the stairs rough beneath her, but Bothain's hands were warm and delicious and when his tongue slid across the inside of her thigh, she melted.

She could see Myron and Rainer at the bottom of the stairs, arguing, but they didn't matter at all.

Her staff gathered at the commotion. Savvas used his bulk and the wild look behind his eye to herd Rainer and Myron right back out of the house.

Bothain's tongue found the cleft of her, and he groaned with pleasure, the rumble of it shaking all the way up her body. She pushed her hands into Bothain's hair and pushed against his mouth and the pressure hurt perfectly, stripping away the last of her restraint. She groaned, closing her eyes and letting her head tilt back to rest on the step as the front door slammed shut. Bothain didn't stop just because they were gone; his hunger only seemed to grow in the face of his victory, and he slid his finger into her with the same feverish pace as his mouth, and the world ceased to matter.

When the intensity became too much, when her whole body trembled with the pleasure, Bothain pushed himself to his feet again and pulled her up with him. Up, up, to her bedroom, shedding his clothes as he went, leaving a trail of cloth in the hallway. He pushed her down onto her bed and knelt between her legs and fucked her hard, holding her thighs so tight it was sure to leave bruises. And she let him, because it was the only time she felt weightless. The exquisite pain that came with pleasure, the rough handling, the way her body trembled, it stripped away everything. She was living in one moment at a time, and the man didn't matter at all so long as he was strong and wild and rough with her, because the primal anger of it all made it easier to accept that it wasn't Amias.

It wasn't until after they were both spent that it occurred to Bothain to help her out of her corset and strip off her stockings and cast aside her chemise. He kissed her everywhere, mouth trailing along bone and flesh, teeth nipping the underside of her breasts until she was almost ready to go again, but then he slumped down beside her, wrapping his big arms around her.

"I suppose you'll be off to see Redbone and Wolfe tomorrow to strategize," he murmured into her hair, bringing her back to reality with such abruptness that it was as if her bones gained weight. "See if you can convince her to run a smear campaign against Rainer, and once the police force is in hand, I'll have him arrested."

"Arrested," Illea echoed. She had to admit, she liked the sound of it. "Maes wants to take over the Authority, too? Get rid of Rainer, and install one of his puppets."

Bothain shrugged against Illea, kissing her shoulder, sliding a finger up her sternum where sweat glistened between her breasts. "It wasn't part of the plan, no. But with everything, we'll need to bring the matter to a satisfying end. Once Rainer is arrested, the Red Dawn won't have much left to fight for, will they? We can make a round of arrests from the Bay and Brickheart and call the issue settled."

"Will it actually be settled, or will we be calling it settled?" Illea asked.

"What difference does it make? Cattle Bone Bay doesn't have a reputation of being a safe and peaceful quarter. We'll arrest as many people as we need to send the message, and then if they keep agitating, we have a police force to crush them with."

Illea rolled onto her side, draping her leg over Bothain's hip and looking past him to the window. From this angle, she couldn't see the forest. Just the snow, swirling above it. "You should meet with Powell Iwan."

"Why?" Bothain scoffed. "What could the old man possibly offer me that I couldn't take for myself?"

Illea tsked, tapping Bothain's chest. "Ever the brute, General Clannaugh. Not everything needs to be taken. Powell Iwan could give you information. The old man isn't fond of interruptions to Bay business, and he'll be interested in striking a bargain to keep his Hive running smoothly."

"I'm not interested in bargains."

"I know that," Illea huffed. "But Powell Iwan doesn't. What information might he have that would help you? Nothing happens in Cattle Bone Bay without his permission. If there's really a Red Dawn presence, it'll be because he allowed it and made bargains with someone else. If it's really Kaine, it would be worth knowing who you're up against."

"It doesn't matter if it's really Kaine or not," Bothain muttered, sliding his hand along Illea's leg.

"Not on the surface, no—you can spin whatever lies you want to the Queen. No one can prove Kaine *isn't* here. But if it is him, if gives you an advantage. You've faced him as an enemy before. You know how he responds, what he's willing to do. You can use that against him, force him to give you what you want. If you need violence, what path can you lay in front of his feet that will lead him there so he looks like the aggressor?"

Bothain snarled. "Kaine's always been rather more of a weasel than a lion. Ferocious when backed into a corner, perhaps, but he'd rather hide more often than not."

"Exactly. So, if it's really him, what corners might you create around him? Make it so he has no choice. Drive a wedge between him and Iwan.

One might already exist. Make it worse. Force him to react instead of waiting for him to show himself."

Bothain nodded, turning his face toward Illea and laying a kiss on her collarbone. "Iwan will meet with me?"

"I can arrange it. I've done business with him before."

Bothain rolled toward Illea completely, pulling her against his chest. "Whatever would I do without you?"

"Don't start," Illea muttered, but she kissed him to soften the rejection.

"Illea, listen—I know you'll be inclined to protect General Wolfe," Bothain said softly. "He's been like a father to you for a long time, and I don't begrudge you the relationship or the instinct to protect your own. I've no qualm with Wolfe. You should know that. He's a canny old soldier and he has an impressive career."

Illea pushed Bothain back so she could look him in the eye, something cold sliding down her spine and peeling off the heady pleasure. "Are you about to threaten me, Bothain?"

"Not at all, my darling." He kissed her again to soften his words. Her throat, her jaw, her hair. "Maes has no love for Wolfe and no trust for him either. Wolfe and Deri were close. Perhaps not friends, but they stood together on too many votes for Maes's taste. He'll be watching Wolfe's actions closely through all this. I don't want him involved, for your sake—if Maes thinks he's a threat... He is ruthless when he identifies his enemies. I've arranged for Authority Officers to guard Wolfe's manor, to keep him under house arrest."

Illea put her hand on Bothain's chest, pushing him back so she could look him in the eye. "House arrest? How dare you—"

"Illea," Bothain said, catching her hand and squeezing it. "It's for his own good. If he goes down to the Bay to look for Saeati or is otherwise seen to interfere, I don't know what end Maes will plan for him. It's better for him to stay on this side of the river. It's better for *you*. I'm trying to protect him from his own foolish impulses."

If it weren't so late, if she weren't so determined to make her alliance with Bothain work, if she didn't want so desperately to let Bothain destroy Rainer and Myron both in one fell swoop, Illea would have rolled from her bed and dressed and gone to Nathaniel's house immediately. She hadn't seen him since this morning, when the Authority Officers were tearing everything apart. Did he know where Ishmael was, like

Bothain suspected? What foolish things would he do to protect Ishmael from Rainer?

She rolled away from Bothain, kicking her way out of the blankets and rising from the edge of the bed. Beatrice was there already, handing her a fresh dressing gown.

"Illea," Bothain said again, an edge of anger in his voice, a note of frustration and danger. "Don't be angry with me. I'm doing my best to clean up this spectacular mess—"

"I'm not angry at you," Illea interrupted. It was half a lie, but she couldn't afford to fight with him, not now. "I need something to drink and something to eat."

"Yes, Mistress," Beatrice whispered.

She faded back in an instant, pouring tea from the pot she had nearby; she must have prepared it and brought it up while Illea and Bothain were still in their throes of vigorous passion, knowing Illea would need it. She pressed the teacup into Illea's hand, the brew smelling of ginger and honey and whatever herbs Tilde had prescribed to help settle Illea's stomach.

"Savvas sent up some pudding, Mistress," Beatrice whispered. "He said he thought you'd need something indulgent after working up such an appetite."

Illea couldn't help but laugh. Bless Savvas and Beatrice too for knowing her so well. For anticipating the cruel whims of her stomach already. "Tell him he's an incorrigible scoundrel who should mind his own business."

Beatrice smiled, her eyes glittering with a touch of mischief. "Yes Mistress."

Illea settled beside the hearth with the tea as Beatrice served the pudding from the tray she'd brought up—a steamed pudding studded with ginger and cranberries and cinnamon, served with a syrupy, thick toffee sauce and fresh sweet cream.

"A heavy dessert for so late at night," Bothain said, watching from the bed. He'd propped his head up on one hand, his blue eyes fixed on her like he was hunting her. Although perhaps it wasn't her body that he was so fixated on now; perhaps it was her mind and the secrets he knew she was keeping. They didn't share everything, the pair of them. They traded scraps of the truth when it was convenient, and they both knew it.

"I need to eat constantly or the nausea comes back," Illea said.

Savvas had heated the pudding before sending it up, and the toffee sauce was deliciously sticky.

Bothain didn't say anything for a long time, watching Illea eat. "What's the source of it?" he asked finally. "The nausea, I mean. I never asked before. You looked better, so I assumed it was over. But it'll come back?"

The tension in the air was thick as humidity—he knew. He'd guessed.

"I'm with child, Bothain," Illea said, letting her voice go as soft and vulnerable as she could manage. "It's incredibly early still. The only reason I know for certain is because of my healer."

"I thought you couldn't conceive," Bothain said slowly, testing the idea still, testing the words.

"I couldn't for a long time," Illea said. "Obviously. And now, clearly, I can. Thanks to her attention."

"That's why you're suddenly anxious to be rid of Myron," he said. "You were content to wait him out before, but now you want him gone before he learns of the child. It couldn't possibly be his, but you're still his wife, and he could lay legal claim."

Illea smiled. All the tension was gone. He looked terribly pleased with himself that she'd trusted him with this secret. "You're very astute, General Clannaugh."

He rolled from the bed, padding naked across the room. Sweat still clung to his face, lighting the lines of his shoulders and his arms, dancing in the soft blond hair on his body. "Well, Miss Winter, I suppose we'd best be rid of that husband of yours. Do you think our little performance tonight will work to drive him out of the city in shame?"

Illea laughed. "If only it were that easy."

He knelt on the floor in front of her feet, pushing her dressing gown open so he could kiss her knee and her calf. "We'll have to keep trying. I do so love a challenge."

37

OZRA

DAY 34

He wandered.

He wasn't only the forest anymore; he was the past, too. Walking along the threads that haunted his dreams for years.

He saw Eilidh and the beautiful babes they made together, small and strong, each of them coming into the world with an indignant scream because any child born of Ozra Sgèin and Eilidh Rae inherited a mighty temper. He saw Ailig, the last of them, golden curls and beautiful hazel eyes and that heart-rending cry of his, the sound all his children made because the force of their Talent hurt them terribly. Ozra knew how to sooth pain like that—he learnt how with his youngest siblings—but the Authority was especially strict about how he could use his Talent. Especially since he had the Wrath by the time he was making children for them.

Eilidh, the day she died. Snow swirling in the high mountain peaks, and her blood, horribly bright and pumping faster than he could stop it, turning everything from clean white to vivid, awful red. Freezing on the stone. The smell of gunpowder and ice in the air.

He saw threads that didn't belong to him. Stella's threads, spread out around him because she was trying to help him, but his Wrath had swallowed her, too.

He saw her copper hair and elegant limbs. In Fuar, before the name

Stella Whiterock existed for her. When she was still Ffyanwy Rhydderch. In the summer, with the sun baking down, long yellow grass swaying in the dry breeze. A road, cutting through the plain, toward the mountains in the distance. Young women, a dozen, maybe two dozen, stripped out of their crinolettes and petticoats, down to their drawers—some taking off their corsets so they wore only their thin chemises—some letting their hair down, too. A race. Feet bare or in stockings, running along the unpaved stretch of road beyond the city, kicking up the red-gold Fuar dust. The fastest girl tore ahead of all of them in a heartbeat, but this was a race of distance instead of a sprint, and Ffyanwy outpaced each racer with a steady run that never faltered or faded. Until Ffyanwy was at the lead, running so far ahead that she might as well be running alone. Running with such strength that maybe she could run right up into the mountains and never stop until she was running up among the clouds. He could hear her breath, steady, steady, disciplined, measured, in, out, in, out, with the rhythm of her footsteps. He could hear her heart pounding, blood rushing, so young and strong. Not yet betrayed by the whole world.

He saw her in the long grass after the race, dust sticking to her sweat. Hands trailing through the blades, pulling seeds off the stalks. Ffyanwy loved this land, this wild place beside the road, where the grass rolled through the foothills beneath the benevolent gaze of the mountains. A young man following her, trying to catch her, but she was fast, dodging him when he got close but never moving too far away. She didn't *really* want to get away. He had dark hair and warm brown eyes and hands with scars on them, but when she let him catch her, his hands were gentle. Davik Kaine. By the time Ozra knew him, he had tattoos on his hands and malevolent scorn half-hidden behind his dark eyes. But at this point in his thread, the world hadn't betrayed him yet, either. He still had things to hope for.

Davik pulled Ffyanwy down into the grass, the pair of them casting away their clothes until they were both naked. Davik's touch was tender, his scarred hand sliding between Ffyanwy's strong legs, making her gasp. Ozra could smell the grass and the dust and Ffyanwy's breath, Ffyanwy's hair, Ffyanwy's sweat—somehow he knew this memory wasn't Stella's but rather Davik's, hooked to Stella like a tow-line that kept their Talents together no matter how far apart they drifted.

Did Davik know their threads were tied together? Did he sense that she was still alive, or did he believe the rumours that Ffyanwy Rhydderch was dead?

The sound of Ceridwen's voice dragged him back to the forest. Her words tangled all around him, guiding him out of all the threads that were trying to smother him.

"I wish he would wake up!"

He saw Ceridwen's thread, just for a moment. Learning to walk in a stone cottage on the coast, her curls swishing with every step, covering some mark on the back of her neck that flashed harsh black now and then as the curls bounced. She clutched a blanket in her hands, kept tripping on it, but didn't know enough to put it down.

He knew that blanket. He knew that plaid, and he knew that bighorn sheep skin sewn to the back of it.

No, couldn't be—Ceridwen was Stella's child—his dreams were smashing threads together, hooking his memories onto Ceridwen's life because all his children had luscious curls like that and the reddish hair reminded him of the only girl that Eilidh had, the one she named Lioslaith and the first one to die. The girl who broke a part of his soul because feeling her Talent snuff out after the Authority took her was the worst moment of his life. Ceridwen's thread didn't have *that* blanket and the mark on her neck, below her curls, was something else—it wasn't a tattoo.

"Good job, Pigeon," Stella said, her voice echoing strangely around Ozra's head. "He's finally waking up."

Fire. Stone walls. Smoke from the fire, steam from the kettle and the pot as they both simmered, twisting up, pooling on the cave roof and then sliding out a crack through the cliff. Rhodrishi by the fire, moving the pot and kettle out of the flames. Ceridwen, against the far wall, weeping softly. Stella sitting with her, holding her close and stroking her hair, speaking in low tones that reminded Ozra of home. Stella with copper red curls falling out of her plait and blood smeared on her cheeks —was she wounded?

Ozra certainly was.

The pain ripped through him, hot and furious, tingling down his arms and through his chest. Bones and nerves and muscle, all damaged. It made his fingers tremble, made his hand numb. Blood coating his skin, sticky beneath his clothes, hot and cold at once.

"I'm going to undress you, Mr. Sgèin," Mahalouwan said, her face hovering in front of Ozra as she leaned over him. Blood and dirt on her face, twigs and moss in her hair, caught on the silk. Stripped out of her heavy layers, down to her shirt and her thick suspenders and her trousers, caked in blood. "But don't think that means you're off the hook. If you make any moves I don't like, I'll still shoot you."

Ozra flexed his fingers. They moved. It hurt, but they moved. "I think someone's beat you to it."

Mahalouwan laughed, the sound brittle and wild. "Someone sure did, but Miss Whiterock assures us you're going to survive it so long as Colonel Kheir can get it clean."

Ozra looked toward Stella, her face pale beneath all that blood, her eyes distant as she stroked Ceridwen's hair. "Her first—you should check on her first."

Stella shook her head, her eyes finally focusing on something. On Ozra's face, and then sweeping over the blood on the ground beneath him. "I'm not wounded, Ozra." Her voice drifted too easily, like it didn't have any weight anymore. "The blood's yours."

Mahalouwan's hands worked the buttons of Ozra's coat. She grabbed him by the shoulder that wasn't shot, hauling him up, but it made her face twist with pain. She pressed her hand into her thigh, into the blood that stained her trousers, turning crusty and dark. How long had he been unconscious?

"What happened to you?" Ozra asked.

"Shot in the ass, how do you like that?" Mahalouwan laughed. "I hope it's got the chance to heal before I see Tashué again, or else I'll never hear the end of it."

Rhodrishi knelt behind Ozra, pulling the heavy leather duster down off Ozra's shoulders. The fleece was caked in blood. "All I have to do is get the bullet out, and then we can clean the wound. I'd like to try to close it, but I don't know if either of us can use our Talents. My heart, and Miss Whiterock's Wrath—I don't know. We'll flush it out, at least."

"We should get moving," Ozra said. "We're too close to the road here—the sound of the gunshots will have carried, and we don't know how many more bronze fuckers are out there."

"You know better than that, Ozra," Stella said. "The longer we leave your wounds unattended and filthy, the higher the chances you'll get gangrene."

"We'll let them clean us up, and then we'll go," Mahalouwan said.

"Travel through the night like you said. We'll stop at the mill town, feel sorry for ourselves for a day or so, then make for the logging camp."

"I don't want to go to the logging camp!" Ceridwen cried. "I want to go home. I want to go back to Yaelsmuir, where we belong!"

"I know, Pigeon. I'm sorry—" Stella's voice caught, hitched, went thin and brittle. "We can't—not yet."

Rhodrishi dragged Ozra's sweater up, and he tried to lift both his arms, but the bullet wound reminded him of its existence with a miserable flare of pain that sucked the air right out of his chest. He made a strangled, whimpering sound before he could bite it back. Rhodrishi guided the sweater off Ozra's body one limb at a time to reveal all the blood that drenched the off-white shirt underneath. Rhodrishi pulled Ozra's suspenders off his shoulders, and Mahalouwan started on the buttons of the shirt. Her hands trembled.

"I can take care of it, Lieutenant," Rhodrishi said, but he sounded so tired. "Lie down by the fire, and I'll see to your wound after."

Mahalouwan shook her head, baring her teeth in a pain-drawn snarl. Sweat beaded on her upper lip, down her temples. "It's better to keep busy."

Ozra pulled his good arm out of the sleeve, and Rhodrishi peeled the linen off, the blood dry and clinging to the fabric so that it pulled at the hair on Ozra's chest, on his arms. The fire danced on all his tattoos, the thread lines that tracked the history of his education up one arm and dancing over his heart. The present threads, the past threads. He didn't have the tattoos for the future threads yet. The Authority caught him before he could learn. His warrior tattoos on the other arm, cataloguing the bronze badges he'd taken off of corpses. And one Duncreek, the first man he'd killed when the bastard came to the Hand looking for trouble —Ozra's *first* tattoo, which he earned when he was only a year or two older than Ceridwen.

"Bring me that pot, Ceridwen. I need the tweezers."

Ceridwen snuffled and gulped, but rose to her feet and lifted the pot where it had been cooling, twisting steam into the air, the firelight dancing on the soot-stained metal. Rhodrishi plunged his hand into the pot of water, plucking out a pair of long-handled tweezers and then using the recently-boiled water to wash the accumulated travel stains from his fingers.

"Lie down, Ozra," he said. "Arm out, facing the fire, so I can see. The bullet's lodged in the underside of your arm, up near the joint. I'm going to try with tweezers first, but if I can't get it, I'll have to cut your arm. It's going to hurt, either way. I'm sorry."

"Why do you have to take it out?" Ceridwen asked. Her voice still trembled, but that prodigious curiosity of hers drove the question out. "Why not leave it so you don't have to hurt him anymore?"

"Bullets are dirty, Pigeon." Stella said, a bit of peace returned to her voice now that they were talking about wounds. "They hold onto little pieces of whatever they pass through and push all that debris into the wound. And where the bullet is—up near Mr. Sgèin's shoulder—there's a chance it will drift up into the joint and cause far more harm as it lodges itself against the bones. Sometimes these things are necessary. It's scary to invite so much more pain, but if we do nothing, there's a very real chance Mr. Sgèin could die from this wound. So we hurt him a little more to undo the damage and to prevent it from getting worse."

Ceridwen squeezed her eyes shut, shaking her head.

"He'll be fine now, Ceridwen," Mahalouwan said, helping Ozra shift closer to the fire. "We were most worried about him not waking up because of that foul Wrath of his, but here he is. The wound itself isn't so bad. I'm sure our Mr. Sgèin has lived through much worse than whatever Colonel Kheir is about to do to him. Isn't that right, Mr. Sgèin?"

"Aye," Ozra said, stretching out his arm. He couldn't help but look at the wound, at the ragged hole it ripped through his arm. Not in the underside, but straight on the front, below the shoulder—the bullet must have bounced off the bone to end up on the underside. "Much worse indeed."

"That's an impressive scar," Mahalouwan said. Her fingers brushed over the mottled tissue across his chest, so thick that no hair grew there anymore. "Looks like a burn, but small—did something fall on you?"

Ozra shook his head. "It was a tattoo that I didn't want to have anymore."

Mahalouwan's eyebrows climbed right up her face. "You did that to yourself?"

Ozra nodded. "With a hot knife."

"That sounds like it would hurt a lot!" Ceridwen gasped, her eyes flaring open.

"Aye, it did, wee girl," Ozra said. "But it's like your man said, sometimes you need the pain to undo a thing that's worse."

Rhodrishi shook water off his hands, kneeling beside Ozra's chest, angling himself so his body didn't block any of the precious light the fire made. "Dump that out for me, Ceridwen, and then add fresh water from that stream and more salt."

"Yes, Rhodrishi." Ceridwen swept up the pot and brought it to a spring that ran from one wall of the cave.

Rhodrishi looked down at Ozra again, and his features arranged into a tired smile. "Here I apologized for how much pain I'm about to subject you to, but I'm starting to think you like the pain almost as much as you like flirting with Lieutenant Mahalouwan while she threatens to shoot you."

Ozra forced a laugh. "Some pains are easier to bear than others."

"Come help me hold him down, Stella, in case he squirms as much when I hurt him as he does when Lieutenant Mahalouwan flirts back."

Stella knelt beside Rhodrishi, staying out of the way of the light. She rested both her hands on Ozra's shoulders. "I'd whisper the pain away, but I don't know—"

Ozra nodded. "The Wrath. I dragged you under, didn't I? I'm sorry."

Tears fell from her eyes when she nodded. He hadn't seen them before the movement of her head shook them loose, and they landed on his shoulder to make little pale spots among his dried blood. "I don't know if I'll come back if I go drifting like that again."

"I'm sorry," Ozra said again, because he didn't know what else to say. How much of his life had she seen? How much of hers?

Mahalouwan put her hands on his chest, fingers trailing over the scar tissue like she needed to feel it for herself to prove to herself that it was real. Rhodrishi angled himself to lay a knee on Ozra's elbow, wincing as he moved like his joints were admonishing him for kneeling on the stone.

"Come hold his hand, Ceridwen," Stella said. "Maybe you can wish it doesn't hurt him too much."

Ceridwen dropped to her knees, wiping her eyes with her sleeves. It left smears of dirt across her cheeks, and her lip still trembled with half-suppressed grief, but she took Ozra's good hand and squeezed it with all her might. "You'll be good strong glass when you're done."

"Glass?" Ozra echoed.

Ceridwen nodded. "That's what Mr. Blackwood told me. They take sand and put it into the fire, and all that heat turns the sand into glass. That's how marbles are made. He said when things hurt us, they're like the fire. And then when we cool, we get to see what kind of glass we are."

"He sounds like a wise man, your Mr. Blackwood."

Ceridwen nodded again, but Rhodrishi moved, and there was no more space left in his mind for words. The tweezers were still hot from being sterilized in the boiling water and the wild, angry nerves screamed their protest. Ozra's whole body jerked with the ferocity of it, which only made it hurt more—he could *feel* the tweezers dragging through the vicious, open wound. He squeezed Ceridwen's hand before he could think, but she gasped like he was hurting her, and he forced himself to let go.

"Most people have a new tattoo cover the one they don't like," Stella said.

Distracting him, maybe. Except the scar, the memory of it hurt almost worse than the fucking tweezers. Ozra shook her head, trying to force a nonchalance he didn't feel. He watched the shadows and light dance together on the roof of the cave, the smoke swirling up there like a painted scene that shifted from one moment to the next.

"I wanted it off. Gone completely." He usually lied about his scar when people asked, something about being drunk and stupid and ending up with an idiot tattoo so he got drunk again one night and got rid of it with a hot knife and a handful of snow to soothe the pain after it was done. But Eilidh—her ghost was somewhere, following him. And here he was with Stella-Ffyanwy, who understood what the Authority did. "This one was from the Authority."

"I've never known the Authority to tattoo people, except for the Rift," Mahalouwan said. Her mouth twisted, and her eyes flicked at Ceridwen. "And the... the girl, and others like her. The energy units."

"Breeding Program gave it to me," he said. Even though it hurt. The words distracted him from the tweezers. Such a little point, his wound no larger than the width of his smallest finger, but by all that was holy, the pain of it seared him. "They like to keep track of us, to measure the success of the breeding lines. I burnt it off when I ran. I thought I was going to die out in the wilderness, and I didn't want their ink on my body when I returned to the earth."

"Oh, Ozra," Stella said softly. "When you see Eilidh's ghost, sometimes she's holding a child—"

"Aye." Ozra cast his eyes through the cave. He couldn't see Eilidh anywhere. He wondered what that meant. "One of the wee ones we made for the Authority. I didn't know what they did after they took the wee ones from us—and then, when I saw it, I told her and we made a plan to run. She'd wanted to run, since the first day I met her. Can't say I blame her. Must be even worse for the women. I tried to be kind—I tried to wait until she was ready for me. I didn't care what my guards said about me or what they did to me, but I wouldn't force myself on any of the women. Maybe that's not good enough, because we were all there against our will. Prisoners. But I didn't put a hand on them until they said yes. But I thought that…"

Rhodrishi's hand moved slowly, and Ozra could feel the slide of the bullet, too. Through the hole it made, putting pressure on the wound, scraping against bone. It stole the breath from him, cutting off the flow of words.

"You thought what?" Mahalouwan pressed, dragging him out of the shock of it.

Ozra squeezed his eyes shut, forcing himself to breathe, forcing himself to catch each word and push it out past his gritted teeth. "I thought surviving was something noble. I thought if I survived, even in that foul place, it would be a victory. And one day when someone stood and ripped it all to shreds, I'd be there to help. And my children, their existence would be my gift to the future, and then when the revolution came, I'd find them and teach them who we are and what we stand for. A future with more Kishoan children sounded like it was worth fighting for. I know it sounds stupid, saying it out loud now that I know how bad it all is and what they do to the children. But I was young, and I didn't *know*. I thought they were simply teaching them to use their Talent, but instead…"

"Energy units," Stella whispered.

"Aye," Ozra said, glancing at Ceridwen. The poor wee girl was crying again, and he cursed himself for talking about it. But now that he'd started, he couldn't stop. He'd never told this story before, never said these words out loud, and it was liberating to be able to share with someone who wanted to hear, who understood what it all meant. Mahalouwan was watching him, and her hostility had fallen away. Fighting for them had earned some shred of trust, maybe. Or maybe it was the bullet hole and the blood that earned her tolerance. "When they were born, I used my Talent to hook on theirs. I couldn't see them, but I could feel them even when the Authority took them. No matter how far they went, I could feel their Talent. But then the girl we made, she died right after they took her, and I walked the threads of the rest of them to see where they were. To see if I could reach them. And I saw the truth. You know, don't you?"

"Yes, Ozra," Mahalouwan said, and there was a strange kind of relief in it. He'd been alone so long, running from this truth and hiding who he was. Even in the forest when he was surrounded by loggers, he was alone because the words *energy units* lived in his heart, and none of them shared the weight of what those words meant. "We know. There's no peaceful way to change that vile organization."

Ceridwen snuffled again. She hadn't even tried to fight her tears. She held his hands with both of hers and wept, turning her face splotchy red and wet. "I'm sorry, Ceridwen. You shouldn't have to hear all this."

"We're running from Siras Duncreek," she said. Her voice thick with all that grief. "But also from the Authority."

"You're lucky your mam has been able to take such good care of you, wee girl," Ozra said. "I tried—ah. I tried to take her and my youngest, my Ailig, but none of it... You and your mam, you've been blessed."

"What was the girl's name?" Ceridwen asked. "The one who died."

Ozra tried to smile to offer her some comfort, but he didn't have any comfort to give. He was just a raw open wound, festering for all these years, turned into an abscess instead of a man. "Lioslaith. The fattest of them—her cheeks were so plump and so round, she was like a wee pudding, wasn't she? And so beautiful, like her mam."

"What was your number?" Stella asked. "That's what you burned off your chest, isn't it? Your Breeding Program number."

Ozra nodded. "Aye, that cursed thing. 0579."

The bullet finally came free. Relief washed through Ozra's whole body, but the pain didn't stop, of course. Even though the bullet was gone, the flesh was still ripped open, the bone still cracked. Rhodrishi held the bullet in the light for a moment, showing the mangled mess of it, the blood and the chunk of muscle that stuck to one especially sharp corner. He dropped the bullet onto Ozra's chest, leaving a smear of blood on the burn scar. The way the shadows played on the deep lines of his face, he looked angry.

"Fetch me the kettle, Ceridwen." Maybe it was a trick of his mind, but Ozra thought Rhodrishi's voice had gone hard and sharp, matching the expression. "We have to flush the wound out."

Ceridwen pushed herself to her feet, wiping her eyes as she moved away. Rhodrishi moved so he was over Ozra's face, putting his hands on Ozra's cheeks and hovering there until Ozra looked the older man in the eye. Those dark eyes *were* angry, like a storm gathering at night, his mouth twisting into a ferocious snarl Ozra had never seen from him before.

"It's easy to hate yourself for the man you became to survive," Rhodrishi said, his voice clipped and offering no quarter. "And maybe those things are complicated, bordering on detestable, and they'll haunt you for the rest of your life. And you may never be able to forgive yourself for the evils you participated in. But now you have the chance to fight against the very system that tried to take your humanity from you. Your survival *is* a victory."

Ozra's chest spasmed. Rhodrishi's words were so sharp and so true, they tore open the skin over his infected soul and Ozra's whole being bled all over Rhodrishi's hands. He fought the urge to look away from the intensity in Rhodrishi's eyes, the way they seared him like the older man was cauterizing Ozra's wounds so they didn't get infected again. Ozra grabbed the bullet instead, closing his hand around the sticky, misshapen lead. "Yes, sir."

Ceridwen approached with the kettle, tears dripping from her chin. "I'm sorry your daughter died, Mr. Sgèin."

"Aye, girl," Ozra said. "Me too."

Rhodrishi poured the hot saltwater over the bullet wound. It burned, but it was a healing kind of pain, one he was familiar with. It washed the blood and the dirt off his arm, sending a pink trail of water along the cave floor to pool against the far wall. Stella helped him sit up and poured more water, letting it run over his shoulder, over the wound, and her Talent swirled like a habit she couldn't break. She sank into his wound so gently he barely felt her, but he could see pieces of her again —her hospital, beautiful old stone in the heart of Cruinnich, crisp white linens on empty beds, the sunlight swirling in the open windows. A temple to the Godking, once. And now a place of healing and hope. And death, because even with the most skilled healers in all the world tending to you, death still found you eventually. The healing came slowly, rolling as gently through the wound as healing could, enough to make the bleeding stop, enough to form a scab over the surface of it to keep it clean. It hurt, but in a familiar way. A pain that felt like friendship.

"I'm sorry, Ozra," Mahalouwan said, and the depth of grief in her voice took him by surprise. "I never had to face the pain of losing my own child, but I've known plenty of parents who have. In the Hadia, there's a long ritual for the death of a child. It's the only death that becomes a braid."

"I'd have a lot of braids, then."

Mahalouwan sighed, wiping her bloody hands on her trousers. It didn't help. It ingrained the dirt and the blood more deeply into the creases of her knuckles. "How many?"

Ozra shook his head. He couldn't do it, he couldn't lay the number at her feet. "Too many."

"Your turn, Lieutenant," Rhodrishi said. "Fill the kettle with fresh water, Ceridwen, and more salt. We'll get it boiling so we can wash the Lieutenant's ass."

A laugh bubbled through Mahalouwan's throat, and it cut through all the horrible grief. "I thought I'd be a bit older than this before I needed help cleaning my own ass."

She shrugged out of her suspenders, pushing her trousers down and turning to point her backside at the fire. The blood had dried on her leg, all that dark making her skin look paler than it was. The wound was rent open and ugly—right around the spot the leg and the arse met, right through the muscle.

"Well, the bullet went clean through, so I don't have to go fishing around for lead," Rhodrishi said. "I think the most we can do is wash it. You'll be limping for a while."

Mahalouwan shook her head. "If I limp, it means I'm alive, and I'll take it. Make it quick so we can go."

"We're still going to the logging camp?" Ceridwen asked. "I don't want to go."

"Ceridwen," Mahalouwan said, with that tone that allowed no room for argument. "I know you're scared, and I know today seemed impossible to you. It isn't easy, watching a man die, even when he's your enemy. I'm sorry you've got to carry it. But we can't stop now. We can't stop and we can't stay here and we can't go back, either. The only way is forward."

Ceridwen turned her eyes up to the ceiling and let the tears flow out of her. Stella went to her, crouching beside her and pulling her into a hug. Those low words again, barely above a whisper and so filled with love. And Eilidh, beside them both. Standing barefoot in the pool of blood laced water, the heavy hang of all that indulgent silk glowing in the crackle of the fire.

Something smelled strange down in the cave. Like smoke, but thicker, so sludgy in the air that it coated the inside of Ozra's mouth. It reminded Ozra of smoking hashish, the way that smoke stole all your attention, the way the oils sat on your tongue; but it didn't smell like hashish at all.

When had that smell started? He didn't remember it when he woke up—maybe Rhodrishi had put something Ozra wasn't familiar with into the camp fire, and it was only catching now. Kishoan and Pashibé healers had different flora to work with, and therefore different herb lore. Whatever it was, it sent a spasm of agitation up his chest. They had to get moving soon, and they had to be ready to defend themselves.

"Where's your horse?" Ozra asked, rolling to his feet. "I'm taking my guns back."

"You shouldn't be going out there alone," Rhodrishi said. His voice echoed strangely in the cave, or maybe the echo was in Ozra's head.

"I'll be fast." He picked up his clothes, one layer at a time. He was so bloody tired. Moving felt like he was under water, fighting against the weight of the whole river. Putting his shirt on wasn't as difficult as he'd expected it would be, pain echoing through the joint but only from far away. The smoke, maybe—a painkiller. Blood made a hot, wet line down his shoulder. He hadn't moved carefully enough, and he'd already split open the scab Stella had set in the wound. "If we're making a run for it, I need my revolvers. I can shoot them one handed, at least. And I'll fetch her saddle bags while I'm out there."

"I'll show you the way," Stella said. Her voice was slow with her fatigue. It made Ozra's body ache in sympathy; they were all so damned tired, but they couldn't stay here. They had to ride through the night, had to get to the mill town. "We passed the poor beast on the way here."

"Mam, no!" Ceridwen squealed, grasping her mother's coat. "Don't leave me here!"

"Hush, Pigeon. It'll be just a moment. Stay here with Rhodrishi and Kazrani—we'll be right back."

Ceridwen whimpered, curling herself into a tight ball and hugging her blanket to her.

"It's alright, Ceridwen," Mahalouwan said. "Your mam will be right back. Ozra's right, we need our supplies and then we'll be on our way."

Ozra grabbed his rifle. Except he would be fucking useless with his rifle, with his shoulder so fucked. Could he brace it on his body and fire it one handed? Maybe. Maybe not. Maybe it would be an expensive club that he could swing to crack someone's skull. He needed his pistols.

Walking up the slope of the cave was like climbing an impossible obstacle. Every footstep stretched forever. His calves burned, and his chest felt too tight, like panic he wasn't aware of had him by the lungs. The smell of smoke was getting stronger, which didn't make any sense. Rhodrishi had the fire expertly placed beneath a fissure in the cave wall, letting the smoke vent up through the crack. But the thick smell, the oily one that felt like a dream, rolled down over them as they hiked up, up.

The cave bent, and the light of the fire disappeared, the darkness swallowing them. Up, up, feet dragging, eyes useless.

Stella gave a high gasp, and she fell. Ozra felt it and heard it rather than being able to see any details of it; one moment she was beside him, walking in step with him, the next moment the air beside his shoulder was empty of her presence, and her rifle rattled against the stone when it hit the cave floor. Ozra reached for her, finding her shoulder in the darkness, making a fist in her coat.

"I tripped over something," she said. "What is this? It wasn't here when we came down."

She pushed something against him, like she was looking for his hands. His shoulder throbbed as he moved it without thinking, the pain eating deep, the bone crying its torment. Even flexing his fingers was agony. But he flexed them anyway to feel whatever it was that Stella was trying to give to him. Metal. Warm to the touch even though it was fucking cold outside.

He lurched up the last few steps, carrying whatever it was out of the cave and into the moonlight. A hole for a fuse, a vent. It smelled of the strange smoke that made the world feel too heavy and too slow. It wasn't smoking anymore, but the smell still lingered anyway, soot gathered on the vents where the smoke must have spilled out of the whole thing.

Ozra dropped it. It fell at his feet almost silently, except he felt the shock of it roll up his skeleton, into his skull. He looked around him, but the world was spinning. Not so fast that he felt dizzy. An aimless drift. Like the forest was dancing and it wanted him to dance, too. And it was mighty tempting, to sink his feet into the forest floor, to swathe himself in loam, to let his Talent loose in the fabric of it all so that he wasn't simply Ozra anymore. He could be the whole forest again and dance away from the pain in his shoulder and the pain in his soul.

But Stella stood beside him, the moonlight glinting on her copper red hair, her mouth like a shadow across her features. And he thought he could hear Ceridwen weeping. It wasn't possible to still hear her, not with how deep that cave was, twisting and turning to hide them down there.

But the sound lived in his ears like tinnitus, a steady pressure that kept him in his body.

"We have to go," he said, and he could almost see the way the words rolled through the air, like stones making a ripple on the surface of still water. "We have to get out of here now."

38

OZRA

DAY 35

The horses were still saddled, including a few mounts Mahalouwan had gathered up from the fallen Officers. Desperation clawed at Ozra's throat, sitting bunched in his shoulders. The forest crawled with some unnatural life, trees making shadows that looked like men. The clouds in the night-dark sky, fat and lit by the winter moon, became a writhing carcass infested with maggots. Some distant part of his mind knew it was the smoke. The smoke—whatever it was—was making him hallucinate, turning his anxiety into things that weren't real, but knowing that didn't make it easier to witness.

Someone had put that canister of smoke in the cave. Someone had come close, and none of them noticed because they were busy tending to Ozra. Someone was out in the forest, waiting for the smoke to incapacitate them.

They had to *go*.

Ceridwen cried. Whimpered. So small, so young, she couldn't possibly have any experience with smoke that changed the way her mind worked. What did she see? The same things as Ozra, or some other things her mind invented?

Ozra caught her hand, squeezing it hard as he led her to Caraid. "You're alright, Ceridwen. It's the smoke, making us see things that ain't there. None of the scary things you're seeing are real, I promise. I'll put you on Caraid's back, how's that sound? That way, you can just close your eyes. Caraid and I will take good care of you, and you can wait for this to pass."

"But Grippni!" Ceridwen's poor wee voice trembled with her panic. "What about Grippni? I don't want to leave her behind!"

"Don't you worry," Ozra said, catching Caraid's reins. Don't look at Caraid's face, don't look at the hellish beast with teeth too big for a horse and eyes that burned with malevolent fire—that wasn't Caraid, it was his mind conjuring nightmares. "Good luck and friends are good to have on the road, ain't they? Grippni will follow us along, see? She'll follow you anywhere, won't she?"

"What is it?" Mahalouwan asked. And she couldn't seem to articulate what *it* was, but she didn't need to. Everyone knew. *It* was the smoke that ate into their minds.

"I don't know," Rhodrishi said. His hands still had blood on them. It dripped from his fingers and burned the underbrush, lighting clotted red fires around his feet. "I've never encountered anything quite like this."

"If someone's done this to us, doesn't that mean they're close?" Mahalouwan pressed. "Doesn't it mean they're out there, waiting for us to move?"

"Or they were hoping we'd stay in the cave so they could corner us down there where there's no way out," Ozra said. Don't look at the snow that gathered on her shoulders because it looked too much like skin flaking away from her face in too big chunks, falling bloody on her coat. Snow wasn't bloody.

"Why not shoot us as we walked out?" Mahalouwan pressed. "Why not storm the cave when we weren't keeping guard?"

Ceridwen cried louder. Her Talent swirled, a vicious gale of energy, swathing her. Trying to protect her, but it didn't know what to protect her from.

"Lieutenant Mahalouwan!" Ozra snapped, fighting against his own disorientation, fighting against the massive pull of Ceridwen's Talent. "We ain't shot. Whoever it is, they didn't think they could take us in a fair fight. We have to go before they get their courage up. Close your eyes, sweet girl. Just close your eyes and hang on, and we'll wait for it to pass. By morning, we'll be in town and having breakfast and a great big pot of coffee. How's that sound, hey?"

He hooked his hands beneath Ceridwen's arms, lifting her up into Caraid's saddle. Pain screamed through his shoulder, tearing a gasp from his chest. He stalled with Ceridwen halfway up, but she was high enough to hook her foot in his stirrup and pull herself up into the saddle.

Eilidh stood beside Caraid's shoulder, reaching up to touch Ceridwen's hair as the girl passed the ghost. If Ceridwen noticed, she didn't show it; her eyes were screwed shut like Ozra told her, and she clung to the horn of his saddle with all the strength she had, her face soaked with tears. Snow danced in her hair, tumbling sharp and angry down her back. And Eilidh stood, her face turned up toward Ceridwen, the moon lighting her features with an ethereal glow. Even with all the fear, all the urgency, everything in Ozra's body wanted to reached out to Eilidh and pull her to him. To kiss her hair and her cheeks, even if she was covered in blood. It was all over her, soaked into her silk, running in fat rivulets down her face that didn't seem to have any source at all—it was the hallucination, trying to make her ugly and fearful, but he still thought she was the most beautiful soul he'd ever met.

"Where are you taking her?" Stella caught Ozra's good arm, tugging him away from Eilidh, away from Ceridwen. Her Talent was wild and feral, like a cornered animal. A healer's Talent was a powerful thing if she chose to wield it as a weapon. "You can't take her from me, Ozra—you can't!"

"I'm not taking her," Ozra said. Flexing his fingers hurt. Moving his arm hurt. But he reached for her anyway, ignoring the way the snow turned to hovering insects that bit her cheeks. "I'm going to ride with her so she doesn't have to look. We'll make our way to the mill town and come morning it'll all be over, and we'll be safe. But we haven't time to argue, Stella. We need to *go*."

"He's right," Mahalouwan said, catching Stella's hand and pushing the reins of one of the horses into her hand. "Take the palomino. She's faster than your pony, and she's got plenty of wind in her hooves. You follow Ozra, and Colonel Kheir will ride with you, and I'll watch behind."

"Can I have her guide rope?" Ceridwen asked. "So she doesn't get left behind?"

"Your mam doesn't need a guide rope, sweet girl," Rhodrishi said.

"Not Mam," Ceridwen said, shaking her head. She opened her eyes and fixed them on Ozra, staring at his face with such intensity that he knew she was ignoring all the terrible things that her mind thought she saw. "Grippni! Can I hold her guide rope like you used to? Please?"

Rhodrishi scooped up the rope in an instant, pushing it into Ceridwen's hand. "That's a good idea, Ceridwen. That way you can stick together."

Ozra slid his rifle into its scabbard. If he needed to shoot it, he'd find a damn way. His Talent was trying to bleed out of him, into the forest again. Like all the power of Ceridwen's and Stella's Talents was coaxing his to life again, or maybe it was the smoke, breaking through the tiny bit of control he had left. He closed his eyes and focused on his body, on the pain. If he went drifting again so soon, he might never come back. He pushed his hand into the wound on his shoulder, letting it roar through his senses, letting it be an anchor that kept him here. Blood, hot beneath his fingers, his heartbeat, too fast in his chest—he wasn't the forest and he wasn't drifting, he was Ozra Sgèin and he had to ride.

"Slide forward now, Ceridwen, that's a good girl. Far as you can go, and hang on to the saddle horn."

She wiggled her way forward on the saddle, clinging to Grippni's rope. Ozra's shoulder screamed at him, viciously angry, but he hefted himself up anyway. Something tore, ripped, and he was bleeding again, bleeding bad. He could feel the hot sluice of it down his arm, crawling beneath his clothes. His mind tried to make it some slithering beast, teeth gnashing at his shoulder, ripping away more flesh than the bullet had. He slapped the wound hard—the pain struck his whole chest. Stupid. Stupid. It wasn't real, none of it was real—sweet North Star what *was* the vile smoke?

Didn't matter. They had to go.

The forest on this side of the river didn't have the same kind of eldritch power as the Dunnenbrahl. But the forest was still a thing to be respected, especially at night. There was life in places like this that went beyond human understanding, life that lived between the trees and in the deep crevices of the earth, life that lurked around the corner at the edge of vision. Someone with Talent came to know this on an instinctual level; you didn't question the eddies of energy you felt swirling between the rocks or the way you could sometimes feel things moving even though you couldn't see anything. It simply was the way of the forest.

The smoke made terror of the forest that Ozra had never felt before. The trees swayed, threatening, leaning in, branches that turned to hands and tried to grip the back of his neck as he passed. Rocks shimmered with malevolent energy, unfolding into great beasts that stalked the horses. Merry little Grippni, with the grey mane that fell over her eyes like an overdue haircut, chomped at the air with slathering teeth, her hooves digging into the ground as they rode and leaving blood behind. The carcass of a dead horse in the road writhed like it was trying to come back to life, its limbs twitching. Something grew from its flank, some terrible new creature with grasping hands—no. That was Lieutenant Mahalouwan. She'd ridden ahead and climbed down from her saddle to drag her old saddle bags open. That was her dead pony. Something had been eating it already, its belly ripped open by predators.

"What happened to your pony?" Ceridwen wailed.

"Don't look, Ceridwen," Mahalouwan said. "The poor beast was shot by the Officers. He didn't feel any pain, I promise. He died a hero, carrying me in battle. Just don't look—you don't need to see."

The bullet hole in the pony's head made the lie obvious, at least to Ozra. The pony had taken a shot to the back, the same shot that passed through Mahalouwan's arse. She'd probably shot it through the skull after, to end its suffering.

Mahalouwan pushed herself to her feet, her hands dripping with the pony's viscera—no. That didn't make any sense, because she'd only been rifling through the saddle bags. Her belongings spilled across the forest floor, glinting in the steady moonlight. She limped right over to Caraid, holding up Ozra's pistols.

"You might need them, Mr. Sgèin."

"Ceridwen," Ozra said. "Grab my guns for me. Lieutenant Mahalouwan is handing them up to me, but I can't reach with my bad arm. Don't look at her pony, you don't need to see that."

Ceridwen whimpered, her hand trembling as she reached for the gun. She passed it to Ozra's good hand and he shifted to slide it home into the holster at his side, under his coat, the fleece interior turned stiff and crusty with all his blood. He didn't bother trying to put away the second one. He held it, his finger on the trigger guard. If he saw a single real person out here, he'd put a chunk of lead in them and think about the consequences later.

"Take Caraid's reins for me, Ceridwen," Ozra said. "One hand is enough. Just enough that if Caraid tries to wander off the track, you'll haul on him for me. Ready?"

Ceridwen whimpered again. "Ready."

———

Forest gave way to the great rolling foothills where they were attacked the first time. Moon and snow turned the hills bone white. Turned them to animal carcasses too big to be any recognizable creature, a monument to death and rot. He tried to tell himself that it couldn't be real; if he was surrounded by so much moldering flesh, he would be able to smell it. And the air only smelled like winter. Crisp, clean. Fresh snow. Dormant earth.

His coyote friend followed. Distantly, so Ozra could only see the vague shape of him as he walked under the moon.

And Eilidh never left Ozra's side.

Pain thudded in his shoulder with every step Caraid took, and he clung to it, trying to keep himself grounded. But his Talent wandered. Threads became physical things that caught him and pulled him. He'd lived this before, and he knew from experience that there was no fighting it when the fabric of Talent had him like this. All he could do was surrender and let himself tumble through the things he saw.

Ceridwen's thread dragged itself straight through his heart, playing her whole, short life through his Talent in reverse. Running across the wilderness, away from her home. Living in Yaelsmuir—a teacup with a broken handle, wrapped and packed into the saddle bags because it reminded her of the neighbour boy she liked. Tashué Blackwood, the mountain of a man who lived next door and who shared his sweets with Ceridwen. Before Yaelsmuir—living in Obisza, picking buffalo grass out in those endless plains. Smaller out on the west coast, learning to walk in an old stone cottage. Drooling because she was teething, chewing on her fat wee fingers to soothe the pain. Carrying a blanket, tripping on it—

That blanket again. It couldn't be right, him seeing it with her. She was Stella's child, so she couldn't possibly have *that* blanket. His own thread showed him Eilidh making that blanket as their girl grew in her belly. With a length of plaid from a wool skirt that she didn't wear anymore, and a square of fleece. He'd hunted that bighorn sheep, taken it down in the high passes above the mountain fortress, and he'd cleaned the hide himself in the lonely hallways to keep his days busy a while. Eilidh cried as she sewed the hems, because the thread she stitched with didn't match the colour of the plaid, but it was all she had. Cried because her life hadn't gone the way she imagined at all, and every time their girl moved in her belly, she was reminded of the boy they'd made before, reminded that the Authority would take this one too. But she made the blanket anyway, because she thought it would be nice for their girl to have something from them after she left, so she could grow knowing her parents loved her even though she was gone.

That was before they knew what they did. He made twenty-three children for the Authority, and they took every single one of them. And the girl was the first to die, the one who made him wonder what happened to them after the Authority took them.

His sweet Lioslaith with the red-gold curls. His imagination put Lioslaith's blanket in Ceridwen's thread because Ceridwen had those same corkscrew curls, maybe. It happened when you didn't pay attention to the threads, when you didn't make sure you were only following the one.

The world felt too light and too far away. The plodding of Caraid's hooves were a rhythm he only barely felt. But the pain in his shoulder, that was enough to remind him he had a body. He wasn't a formless Talent, wandering the fabric and the threads. Not yet, anyway. He was still alive for now.

And Ceridwen needed him to hang on because if he fell out of the saddle, he'd surely drag her with him. He pressed his feet into his stirrups to know they were there beneath his boots, and he tightened his grip on his revolver and he let the threads pass around him without fighting them. It was better than watching the countryside turn to shadowy nightmares.

The bleeding from his shoulder had stopped, at least. The blood dried on his skin, making his shirt stick to him. He'd need to clean it out again once they were in town. And North Star preserve him, he'd want to sleep half a week to recover from all this.

Caraid staggered, giving Ozra a miserable lurch that just about sent his heart leaping up through his mouth. Ceridwen cried out and then started weeping again, softly, sounding so bone tired that Ozra almost wept with her. She didn't deserve any of this. But the sun was rising, slowly at first, the light only starting to spill through the hills, lending more detail to the sky and the rock around them. It had snowed softly all night, and everything was glimmering white, their horses leaving a track that anyone could follow. But it didn't seem to matter because they were still alone out here on the land.

"It's alright, Ceridwen," Ozra said. "Caraid's tired is all. He didn't mean to give you a fright. He ain't as young and spry as he used to be, and he's done a lot of running today. Lean forward for me, give him a pat on the neck. Tell him he's doing fine."

"I'm tired," she said.

"That's alright, girl, of course you are. We're almost there."

She snuffled and leaned forward, brushing snow off of Caraid's mane and patting his neck even as she clutched the rope that kept Grippni plodding along beside them. "You hear that, Caraid?" she whimpered. "We're almost there."

Caraid's ears flicked back at the sound of his name and gave a tired snort.

"Pull on the reins now," Ozra said. "Just a gentle tug. Surely he'll stop at the slightest pressure, being as tired as he is."

Sure enough, Caraid stopped walking before Ceridwen even pulled the reins, his head hanging low. He mouthed at the snow, probably thirsty. And hungry too.

"I'll get down, walk a while to give him a rest," Ozra said. "And you can ride Grippni. I'll lead both horses, how's that sound? Another hour, maybe two, and then we'll be on the bank of the river. After that, it ain't long to the mill town."

Ceridwen nodded, dropping the reins. Ozra shifted his weight slowly, dropping down. Weakness crawled up his legs, to his head. He caught hold of his stirrup, leaning on Caraid's side until his feet would hold him. At least Caraid's face looked like a horse again.

Mahalouwan rode up closer to Ozra. Her face was grey and tight with pain, her trousers and her saddle and even the flank of her stolen Authority horse glittered with her blood. Ozra couldn't imagine the agony of being in the saddle, shot in the arse like that. Sitting would be torture, but the alternative was standing, which would also fucking hurt. Or walking, which she did with her limp.

"Why have we stopped?" she asked, her voice so thin it sounded like a piece of glass breaking on stone.

"Just giving Caraid a break," Ozra said. "I'll walk, and Ceridwen can go back to riding her pony. We're almost there."

Ceridwen dropped down.

Behind them, Rhodrishi's mare was nosing at the snow, too, pushing it aside to try to find something to eat beneath it. Rhodrishi didn't look good, sitting slumped in his saddle like he was barely hanging on, a hand on his chest.

And behind him… nothing.

The place where Stella should be, there was only hills and snow and their tracks, snaking back the way they'd come.

"Where's Mam?" Ceridwen asked.

The question was so innocuous at first, but then the horror of the words gripped them all. Mahalouwan spun her horse around. Rhodrishi fought to sit up straighter. Ceridwen started crying again, a keening wail that built in strength.

"Where's Mam?" she howled. She darted through the snow, through the tracks. "Mam! Mam!"

Mahalouwan hissed a curse and kicked her horse hard. The stolen Authority mount wasn't as tired as the other horses, and it sprang forward with all the glee of a war mount, tearing up clods of snow and mud with its big hooves. She steered the horse wide around Ceridwen, passing her in an instant and following their tracks back.

Ozra forced his body to move, to run, the snow wet and cold, slowing him down. Slowing Ceridwen down, too. She tripped and fell. Ozra caught up to her as she sobbed into the snow. He hooked his good arm around her, dragging her up. She surged back to life, twisting, flailing, screaming, nothing but the same word over and over, *mam, mam, mam!*

"Ceridwen, go with Rhodrishi," Ozra said. And he cursed himself with every shred of strength he had, working himself up into the self-loathing fury he'd need to fuel him on to go back the way they came. It didn't matter how tired he was—he'd failed Stella. The smoke and his Wrath had taken him so completely he'd lost awareness of her somewhere along the road. He'd find her. "Go on now, get on Grippni. Your pony will carry you the rest of the way to the mill town, and you'll get a room for us. And we'll go get your mam and bring her back."

"We can't leave her!" Ceridwen screamed. "Mam!"

Rhodrishi came, leading his horse and Grippni through the snow. He sank to his knees, taking Ceridwen in his arms. "We aren't leaving her. Come with me now, let Ozra go after Lieutenant Mahalouwan. They'll find her. We'll go to town and tell them they're coming and we'll get a room ready."

"No! I'm not leaving her. I'm not going! Please don't make me go—we have to find her!"

Rhodrishi sighed, his shoulders sagging. So tired, Ozra could feel it radiating off him like a cold draft. "Alright," he said. "But you need to help us, Ceridwen. Lieutenant Mahalouwan and Ozra, they're both bleeding badly—I know I told you not to use your Talent yet, but it's time now. You need to wish them strong. And the horses, too—poor Caraid is going to die if we push him too much harder, but if you wish for him to be healthy, he can keep going. I'll help, with my Talent. We'll wrap the lot of us in the strength of our Talent, and we'll go find your mam together."

Ceridwen nodded, wiping her eyes, her whole body shaking. "I'm ready."

"Good girl, go get in your saddle now. We'll have to ride hard to catch up to Lieutenant Mahalouwan."

Ceridwen staggered through the snow to get to her pony. Their Talent unfolded immediately, the pair of them—Ceridwen wishing and Rhodrishi guiding her power. Pain redoubled in Ozra's wound as healing force flowed through. And with Talent everywhere, Ozra could hear Rhodrishi's heartbeat. Struggling. Stuttering.

Ozra caught Rhodrishi's arm, squeezing it hard to keep himself in the moment. The threads, the Wrath, they'd take him again. "Your heart—"

"I should have done it sooner," Rhodrishi said. "I should have done something sooner, something to clear the intoxicant from us, or something to pull our senses back. She's gone. I didn't do it because I was afraid to die, and now I fear I've doomed her."

Ozra nodded. That, at least, he understood.

"If I hold on to you, can you find her?" Rhodrishi asked. "I'll try to anchor you here so you can come back. Find her so we know which way to go."

Ceridwen kicked Grippni on, following the tracks Mahalouwan had left. The little pony trotted through the snow. Ozra tried to stand to climb onto Caraid's back again, but he couldn't. Something lived in his Talent, something ugly—the smoke. Somehow it had cleared from his senses, but the hallucinations came back the moment he touched his Talent. Dark and filled with fear, tearing across his senses—didn't matter. Find Stella.

He spilled fast across the foothills, watching the line of tracks they'd left, no matter what horrors tried to distract him. Snow that writhed with unnatural life, crawling up his legs, eating at his blood. Didn't matter.

None of it was real. The tracks led all the way back to the forest, sweet North Star, they'd ridden all fucking night without her.

There. The road. Horses and a wagon and the golden palomino. Headed south on the real road, back toward Yaelsmuir.

"Heaven help her," Ozra breathed, and he didn't know if the words came from his mouth or rolled through his Talent, but he did know that Rhodrishi heard them anyway. "Siras has her."

39

STELLA

DAY 35

He came out of the nightmare forest.

The whole world turned into a horrible enemy, trees becoming leering men who reached for her, snatching at her hair, her clothes. The ground became a chasm that tried to swallow her, no matter what direction she pointed her horse. The palomino rode differently than the little Hitjurgavit pony that had carried her so far. It was faster, flightier, its body bunched and ready to bolt in any direction at the slightest provocation like it wanted to race. Stella leaned away from a tree that looked too much like Bothain and the palomino left the trail, lunging into the trees that were chasing her.

Someone followed her. She was sure of it. Another rider, in the forest with her. She turned the palomino away from the figure, trying to find her way back to the path, but it didn't seem to matter which direction she rode, the trail was gone. Swallowed by darkness and snow. She couldn't see Ceridwen anymore, couldn't see Kazrani or Ozra's horse, the paint that was always so easy to spot. That was worse than any terror the forest could offer. Ceridwen—she needed to find Ceridwen.

The palomino lunged, and Stella fought it back, wrestling with the reins. She couldn't go racing through the forest, no matter how badly she wanted to—she had to find the right direction. She tried to find her own tracks, maybe that would lead her back the way she came, but she couldn't tell the difference between hoof prints and the carrion-eaters stalking her. A swarm of beetles, following her horse's every step, crawling up its golden legs, come to devour her even though she wasn't dead yet—buzzards hopping through the brush, their malevolent eyes watching her. She tried to tell herself that it wasn't real, couldn't possibly be real—that's not how buzzards found their meals, and beetles like that wouldn't even be awake this time of year, but the fear was bone-deep instinct. Heart hammering, a scream caught in her throat, choking her, making it hard to breathe.

That's when she spotted Tashué.

He wore his cavalry greens, his medals glinting white in the moonlight. He looked as haggard and worn as when he came to her dream; blood on his uniform and a terrible bruise around his neck, mostly hidden by his growing beard but still dark enough to draw her eye past the tangle of hair. He walked toward her, and the palomino startled at the sight of him, rearing up. Stella clung to the reins and the saddle with all the strength she had left. The palomino's front hooves hit the ground again, and its body bunched like it was going to bolt, but she dragged the reins, turning it around in a tight circle instead so it had something to do with all that energy.

"Tashué," she said. "Help me find Ceridwen. I've lost her—and the others. I need to go back—"

"I know where she is," Tashué said. His voice sounded strange. Buzzing in her ears, the wrong pitch. He reached up and hooked his fingers in the palomino's bridle, holding it still. "Let me show you."

"How did you find me? How did you get here so fast?"

"I never should have let you go alone," Tashué said. The relief was so total it made her weep. Tears like acid, spilling down her cheeks. Dripping on her hands as they fought with the palomino's reins, washing Ozra's blood off her skin. "It's dangerous out here—come with me, and we'll find Ceridwen together."

She let go of the reins, squeezing her eyes shut. Tashué would lead her to Ceridwen, and she didn't have to watch the forest try to attack her anymore. The palomino followed him, like it was relieved, too. Relieved to have someone lead who wasn't in the midst of panic.

"How did you find me?" Stella asked. Just to hear his voice again. "How did you know to come this way?"

"I could feel you," Tashué said. Why did his voice sound so much different? It didn't sound like him. It sounded like a poorly-minted copy, buzzing like the way a gramophone disc popped and scratched, the music it carried sounding tinny and too far away compared to the real thing. "I'd follow you anywhere. You should know that."

Stella forced her eyes open, watching his back. There was something strange about the way he moved, a shuffling limp that favoured his left side. One hand held the palomino's reins, but the other cradled his chest.

"What happened to you?" Stella asked. "You're hurt—"

"It's nothing," he said, shaking his head. "We'll find Ceridwen, and everything will be fine."

It didn't feel fine. Nothing felt fine. Stella wiped her eyes with trembling hands, fighting against the building, bubbling dread. Nothing was fine at all. The forest was a terrible place, and Ceridwen was out there— and who had planted that smoke in their cave?

"We aren't alone out here," Stella said. "I think Siras found me... I don't know where he is."

"I know," Tashué said. "Don't worry about it. I've men with me, and they'll help protect you."

"Which men?" Stella asked. "Who?"

The narrow track lay like an open wound through the forest, beaten down by many feet and hooves before, worn down to the forest's bones. A wagon, a half dozen horses. They all loomed like living shadows, the moonlight glinting. Badges—they were wearing badges.

"Who are they?" Stella asked again.

"They're here to help," Tashué said again, but he sounded annoyed. Impatient. She couldn't remember a time he'd taken that tone with her. Even when they were fighting about the Authority, about Jason, his voice bled with his passion and his compassion. With love. *I'll do anything for you, don't you see? Just tell me what you want me to do, and I'll do it.* But now his voice was short and cold and a little bit mean. "Get down. The wagon will carry you, and you can relax. The hallucinations will pass, and we'll find Ceridwen for you."

Stella dropped down out of the saddle. Her muscles trembled with the relief. Riding all day, and then running from the Authority Officers, and then helping Ozra, and now the panic-grip her body had on the palomino to keep it under control. The exhaustion was so complete she almost fell. But Tashué caught her by the arm and kept her on her feet. His hand felt different. Not as big. And even though he *looked* like Tashué, somehow the presence of him was wrong, like his body wasn't taking up enough space.

"How did you know?" Stella asked.

"Know what?"

She shook her head. How much of the world could that smoke be changing? Nothing was right. These men, watching her, waiting like they were holding their breath. And Tashué didn't even smell right. Maybe it was the forest, stripping him of the scent he carried around the city—but she'd come to know the smell of his sweat and his skin and his hair so intimately that she'd know him anywhere, and this man beside her didn't *smell* right.

"How did you know about the hallucinations?" she asked.

Tashué's hand squeezed her arm too hard, so hard it hurt, made her cry out before she could bite back the noise. She dug her heels into the forest floor, leaning hard, away from him.

"Damnit, Ffyanwy, would you just—"

Siras.

That was Siras's voice.

The way he hissed her name, biting on it like he wanted to bite *her*, the way his temper snapped—it was Siras.

Stella wrenched her arm away, turning. If she could get back onto her horse, the palomino would carry her fast and true, away—but someone had taken it. One of the men with a badge pinned to his coat, he was standing between Stella and the horse's saddle, and when she staggered away from Siras, the man stepped into her way and pushed her back.

Siras's arms wrapped around her chest from behind. She kicked, twisted, but he had her. Threw an elbow backward, toward his left side, the side he was favouring. He grunted, folding, falling, but he still had her. Dragged her to the ground. She kicked again, trying to twist away, but Siras grabbed a fistful of her hair. She cried out, grabbing his wrist with both hands, trying to prise his fingers out of her hair, but his gloves protected him. Someone dropped to his knees in front of her, that horrible bronze badge like a fire that burned his humanity away. Hands reached for her face. Something in her mouth. She tried to spit it out, the horrible astringent taste of it making her gag. Powder, burning in her mouth, down her throat. But the man in front of her grabbed her whole face, forcing her jaw shut, making her bite her own tongue. The pair of them, holding her down, the forest opening a yawning chasm. Screaming, someone was screaming—it was her, screaming even though they'd forced her mouth closed. She was burning from the inside out even though the forest floor was ugly cold beneath her. Screaming and crying and fighting but the fighting was useless because Siras had her, and he had help this time, and her own mind turned the forest into a living beast that was eating pieces of her, gnawing on her like she was already dead, and all she had left to do was surrender and let herself return to the earth.

Her own screaming echoed in her skull, the powder flowing through her with every erratic beat of her terrified heart. Like the smoke, but so much worse. She could feel it turn her own Talent against her, ripping her apart. But then the Wrath had her and everything went quiet. Still. Numb. Like she had ceased to be. No, not quite that—she still *was*. She could still feel her skin and her heartbeat, she could still see the forest and those badges as they gathered around her, pinned to jackets and coats, men bundled against the winter chill. But it all mattered only distantly.

They lifted her up off the forest floor, and the roots of the forest chased her. Catching her clothes, tangling in her hair. Broken pieces of the forest in her mouth, in her eyes, eating her from the inside out. Reclaiming her body, one shred of her at a time.

They carried her to the wagon and dropped her inside like so much produce, like she was simply a harvest they'd haul back to the city.

"Bitch," Siras hissed. He didn't look like Tashué anymore. He was his usual self, except worse—his eyes were hollow shadows, and his fingers were embers that burned her when he touched her, and his chest was a black and rotten thing, dripping putrid flesh around her face. He grabbed her by the jaw and squeezed hard, forcing her to look at his too-bright green eyes. Summer that hated her, that's what she thought of them the last time she saw them. "Finally. I've got you now, Ffyanwy, and there's nowhere left for you to run."

"Let's go," one of the other men said. "Before the others notice they've lost her."

Siras grimaced, pulling his hand away from his side. Blood glittered on his palm, black and writhing. "Back to the road, then. Back to Yaelsmuir. Bothain should be there by now, and he'll be waiting."

The wagon rolled, rough and bouncing, through the forest. To the road. Stella shivered in the back of the wagon, too cold, too exposed, but she couldn't make herself move. There wasn't anything holding her down except her own Talent and whatever they had put in her mouth that made her feel so numb and distant. The horrors of the forest didn't cease, playing in front of her eyes like photographs she couldn't turn away from. The wagon swirled with maggots that crawled in her hair. The men dripped acid any time they came to look at her, like they were admiring a prize stag they'd hunted down. The bronze badges they wore became eyes that watched her, leering at her, catching the light of the rising sun to mock her.

She was so tired, but she couldn't sleep. Couldn't get up and run, even though the edge of the wagon was the only barrier in front of her. She reached for it, putting her hand over the edge, fingers grasping. The wood rotted beneath her touch, turning to sludge, making her gag again, but there was nothing in her stomach to bring up.

Siras came at some point after dawn, tying the reins of his horse to the side of the wagon so it clopped along behind. He sat on the edge, his feet dangling as he shrugged out of his coat, his jacket. He dragged up his shirt, bearing his chest and the spot he'd been nursing before. A bullet wound, through the meat between his ribs, the wound infected and oozing blood from when she'd hit him. He pressed on the wound and something popped, a gush of more blood and pus rushing out. For a stupid, disconnected moment, Stella's Talent twisted toward it, sinking into his skin, seeing the inflammation and the invasion of debris that made the wound so angry. She recoiled from it when she realized what her Talent was trying to do—no matter what oaths she took as a healer, she wouldn't help Siras Duncreek.

She closed her eyes and tried to turn away from him, clenching her fists, imagining herself holding her Talent in her hands, like reins of a runaway horse. She didn't want to see anything else. She wished for unconsciousness, for some yawning black nothingness that would save her from being awake. But she wasn't so lucky.

40

JASON
DAY 35

"I'm sorry," Lorne said. The words came out like a rush, like they had a time limit. Even though they just got in the room and Jason wasn't even sitting down yet. "I didn't know, yesterday. When I came and told you... I didn't know what had happened."

"Lorne," Jason said. He lifted his hands to try to catch Lorne's attention and saw his own fingers were trembling. He thought he knew what Lorne was talking about, and he didn't want to hear anymore. The nausea rolled through him. He didn't want to hear the details of his father's death. Those things would live forever in his mind, and he'd never get away from the pain. "Can you—can you slow down. Actually, stop. Please? I don't need to know any of it."

Lorne looked around the room, pushing his hands through his hair. He looked crazed, wound so tight part of him might explode. "Can they hear us in here?"

"I don't know," Jason said. "It's never been a problem before. So long as they don't walk in while we're talking. Why?"

Lorne walked closer to the desk, to the grate. He leaned over the table and pressed his hand into the metal, biting his lip for a moment. "Jason, come here."

Jason shook his head. "You can't tell me any more bad news while I'm in here. I can't take it. Just wait. If Davik really is as good as you say he is, I'll be out of here soon, right? And you can tell me after, when I'm out, so I don't have to listen to any more bad news in this fucking place—"

"Jason," Lorne interrupted. "Just come here. It's not bad news, I promise. Just come here so they can't hear."

The world stopped. Everything went quiet and far away. Jason had to force his body to move again, dragging his feet across the floor. He'd been here in this strange prison stasis for so long, living his hellish existence in the Rift while the people he was taken away from went on living their lives without him, but now Lorne kept visiting and saying things that changed Jason's reality. But it also changed nothing, because no matter what Lorne said, he was still fucking *here*. Twelve days. It had been twelve days since his father came in here and tried to touch Jason, twelve days since he'd seen his father one last time. Of course their last conversation was a fight.

He pressed his hand against Lorne's, the same way he wished he'd pressed his hand against his father's. He remembered his father's desperation, and he wished he could turn back time and feel his father's hand one last time. And maybe say something halfway decent. *I love you,* he should have said. *I know you're trying. I'm sorry nothing ever went right.*

"I can't, Lorne," Jason breathed. His mouth moved, and he didn't quite know if he was speaking out loud or not, but Lorne smiled his heart-wrenchingly sad smile. "Just wait."

"He's alive," Lorne whispered. "Jason, it's not bad news. He's alive."

Jason's mouth moved, but no sound came.

Lorne's face split into a grin. And it was beautiful. When was the last time he saw Lorne smile like that? "He came down to the club yesterday like he fucking owned the place. Asshole. Him and Dav, they're working together. He's alive."

"You're lying."

Lorne grinned even wider, his usually grim, sad eyes dancing with his joy. "I'm not. I want to punch him in the face every second of every day, but he's alive. He's helping Dav plan the shit they'll do once you get out of here. Dav said they can't get wild 'til after you're out—but once you're safe, they'll take all the proof they need to fuck it all."

"Oh—" Jason gasped. He was going to fall over. Collapse. Cease to exist. He'd been given a second chance. He'd get out of here and say all those things that had been burning in him. And tell his father to go fuck himself, too, for all the trouble he'd caused. "That bastard."

Lorne laughed. "I know."

Jason sank down into his chair. "What happened? Where was he? How…?"

Lorne shook his head, his eyes darting toward the door. "The Authority's looking for him, so maybe it's best that we don't…"

"Yeah," Jason said quickly. "Of course, yeah."

"Has she arrived yet?" Lorne asked.

"Has who arrived?"

"Irén Dargis. She went in, I don't know, yesterday morning maybe."

Jason shook his head, pressing his hands against the top of the table to make them stop trembling. "Not yet. When I was processed, it took a few days. They held me at the station house for a while, kept telling me I had one last chance to change my mind and register."

Thinking about those days filled him with new layers of old grief. He didn't let himself think about his arrest on purpose, because usually when he remembered what it was like to sit in the cellar beneath his father's station house, he would wish that he'd changed his mind back then. When he had the chance. He could have spared himself all this suffering if he'd given in and registered. Maybe he would be a healer by now, working in a hospital like his grandmother. And if he entertained thoughts like that, he would start to wonder if he should walk up to a guard and tell them he was ready to register. So he didn't let himself start that train of thought, because he knew it was a lie. He wouldn't register with a system that thought of him as bad meat, because no future in a system like that would be good. Whether he was in this place or out in the world, the Authority would find new and terrible ways to make him regret being alive, never mind if he was registered, so it wasn't worth thinking about.

He could indulge the thought now because he was forcing himself to believe he'd actually get out of this place on someone else's terms. Not the Authority's, but his own, and the Red Dawn's.

He remembered his tiny cell, under the station house, where he first became familiar with the headache of the suppression. Remembered the other people down there with him. Remembered hearing his father's voice through the floorboards, shouting and arguing with everyone up on the ground floor. Remembered the way his father came down into the cellar at night and brought Jason food and begged Jason to register. Slept on the floor in front of Jason's cell like he was guarding Jason from some-thing. His father's desperation had made Jason more convinced that refusal was the right and only choice. The fear in his father's voice made

Jason hate the Authority with every shred of his being. To think that Tashué Blackwood, who otherwise seemed so mountainous and immovable and unafraid, was terrified of the Authority made Jason resolute in his resistance.

They were both right. Right to fear, and right to resist. Tashué had survived, and Jason was getting out, and they'd tear it apart together. Jason would find Valen, and they would claw some vague shape of justice out of the world.

It was a beautiful thing, this feeling of hope. He'd forgotten what it was like.

He could hear the children whispering.

The one good thing about Verrit deciding that Jason belonged to him was that Jason could sit down in the cellar after dinner and before the curfew when everyone was expected in their bunks. He sat among the food and the cats, wrapped in the beautiful place where he could feel his Talent.

At first he thought he was going out of his mind. It seemed fitting that he should fall apart now, when people were finally getting him out of here. Lorne and Davik and his father would save him, but it wouldn't be any use because now he heard voices that didn't exist. There weren't any children in the Rift, like he told his father. How long ago was that? Right after his father found the girl.

Whether it made sense or not, the voices grew in form and substance until he could hear the words properly.

We didn't mean to hurt you.

We've never broken before. There were two different voices—this was more assertive than the first one. Still a child, but a bit louder, a bit more confident. *No one's ever broken through us like that. We aren't supposed to let anyone in. Or out. But we don't like hurting people.*

You're the strongest we've ever felt. As strong as us. And you know things.

"Who are you?" Jason asked. The words rolled through Jason's bones, through his mind—maybe his voice only existed in his mind, or maybe this was a dream? Or maybe he was speaking out loud in the empty cellar. He wasn't sure which.

We keep you in. The softer voice. *We're sorry. We don't want to hurt anyone, but when you broke through, Section Three got scared and didn't know how else to get you back in.*

"Section Three?" Jason echoed.

Section One guards the gate, the visitation rooms, and the place where the healer works, the stronger voice explained. *Section Two guards sleeping hall, the root cellar, and the transfer cells. I guard the kitchen and the garden—Section Three. Section Four is new. To make us stronger. Because we broke once, and we weren't supposed to. They said three sections weren't enough anymore, so they brought Section Four.*

The dawning horror shook Jason down to his core. These *were* energy units, the children in charge of the suppression. Children, but they didn't know their names. Section One, Section Two, Section Three, Section Four. Their understanding of their identities was limited to their purpose. He reached for the paper that Lorne had given when he told Jason his mother had died. The list she made with his siblings names and their footprints. Lizanne, Petrik, Gwinnith, Benjin, Dex, Valen.

Why didn't these children know the names their mothers gave them? No one cared enough to use their real names, maybe. Of course they didn't care. Why would anyone who thought of children as energy units care about something as humanizing as a child's name?

"I'm sorry," Jason said. "I didn't know that you were children when I broke through. I didn't mean to hurt you, either. Why can I hear you now? I've never heard you before."

We're not allowed to speak. But Section Two... We don't want Section Two to die.

You know about us. No one here knows about us except the Keeper.

"Who?" Jason asked. "The Keeper of the Keys?"

Who's that? the softer voice asked.

The Keeper—the one who comes for us.

Images flashed through Jason's mind—a man, with his badge pinned to his chest and catching the light whenever he moved. Carrying tubes and ghastly contraptions that Jason didn't understand.

Section Two is dying, and the Keeper won't help. But you—you can feel the gap. Section Two can't hold their perimeter anymore. Can you help? Can you make Section Two stronger?

"I don't know..." Jason whispered. "I'm not a healer."

Please?

The suppression unravelled, letting Jason's Talent leak through the barrier like water leaking through a crack in a dam.

Please, can you try? the softer voice asked. *We don't want Section Two to die.*

Jason reached out with his Talent. He had no idea what he was doing, but he had to try *something*. A child. A child used and abused by the Authority, and now the child was dying—did the Authority even care? Of course not. They would let the child die and replace them with a fresh energy unit.

His consciousness touched the child's Talent, and the child's pain and exhaustion splintered through Jason's anger. Her Talent was killing her. It was so strong that it strained her whole little body, and she was too young and too dedicated to her purpose—guarding the Rift—to even know how to stop.

"Anything I do will be temporary," Jason whispered. "Using your Talent is killing you."

I'm scared. A new voice, thin and weak and so tired. Section Two.

"I know," Jason whispered. "Me too. I'm scared all the time. Every minute of every day."

Can you try? the assertive voice asked. *Please? We just want more time. Anything you can do—please!*

Jason pulled on all the strength he could, letting it flow into the shape of the child's Talent. Like refilling a well that was in danger of going dry. It billowed and swirled, and Jason could see the child's world. The room, the tubes connected to her body. No windows, no sunlight. Only stone walls and pain.

But also more than that. Through their interconnected Talent, Jason could see the weak outline of the Rift, like a blueprint drawn out for him to see each room. And then the circumference of the child's section, the area of their purpose and responsibility. The sections overlapped enough that all the children were connected through their shared responsibilities. He could feel all four of them, like they were all holding a piece of him, and he was holding on to them in return. They made something warm together, something that combatted the cold, hard reality of where their bodies were kept. Something that chased the pain away. They weren't even in the same rooms together but rather in little closets around the Rift, in the centre of their sections. But the connection of them was beautiful and comforting. He could feel each of them, their personalities, their strength. He wondered if it was even possible for any of them to be his siblings. Valen was still in creche, but the others—where were they? Would he ever find them?

What a disgusting world. Fuck the Authority for everything. And they wanted Jason to *breed*, to make more of these children who didn't know their own names. If he could use his Talent, would he be able to get out of this place? Fuck waiting for Davik, he'd get himself out. He'd raze the walls, turning stone into dust until there was nothing left. He'd break apart this fucking island until the river swallowed it, so no one could ever be imprisoned here again—

Please don't! The assertive voice trembled with fresh panic. *If we fail, they'll kill us—*

"What if I could find you?" Jason asked. "What if I could find you and take you out of here?"

No! If we fail, they'll kill us, the assertive voice said again. *You can't!*

Pain seared in Jason's skull, like the suppression shield that kept him from his Talent, but worse. Vicious. Lighting the inside of his bones on fire, squeezing him so hard something was sure to collapse.

The pressure released. There for a moment and then gone. But the pain remained, echoing through the pulp of his bones. Jason pushed himself to his feet, stepping out of the safe little circle, the regular suppression headache clamping down. Dizziness, nausea—he staggered into the space between the bags and vomited.

Why did you do that? He was helping!

He was going to escape. We can't let him break the walls!

You wanted to ask for his help, and now you've hurt him worse than before!

Just breathe. That's what Lorne would tell him. Deep breath, in and out, breathe through it.

He wiped his face and crawled away from the pile of vomit he'd left behind, gulping a breath even though his mouth still tasted of sour bile, his throat burning with it.

I'm sorry, the child said. They sounded like they were weeping. *I thought you were going to try to go!*

"I won't," Jason gasped. He was awake for sure. None of this was a dream at all—he'd never felt pain that intense in his whole life. These children could kill him if they wanted to—they almost had. He put his hands to his head, touching his scalp, feeling the lines of his own skull beneath his fingertips. He half expected something to shift and collapse, but the bones held strong beneath his probing. They probably hadn't cracked his skull. Hopefully. Sweet North Star, how would he explain it if he went down to the infirmary and asked for help? He couldn't. He had to hope nothing was fractured. He'd know if his skull was *really* fractured, wouldn't he? "I'm sorry. I didn't mean to scare you. I promise I won't go anywhere. I'm going to go back upstairs and pretend none of this ever happened. It's almost curfew anyway."

They didn't answer.

They withdrew from his consciousness so completely, he felt dizzy in the absence of them. At least, he hoped the dizziness was caused by the absence of them and not some bleeding in his brain that was going to kill him the moment he stood up.

Fuck this place. Even on days he dared to hope for things, something else came and kicked him in the skull.

He pushed himself slowly to his feet, testing if his legs would hold him. He pressed a hand against the stack of onion bags to keep himself steady, the shift of their weight and the crackle of their dry skins offering some comfort.

Even his prodigious anger couldn't keep itself burning this time. No matter how terribly that pain had seared through him, they were just children. Frightened, abused children. One of them was dying, driving the rest to desperation. Of course they didn't trust him. Of course they were scared of what might happen to them if he tried anything.

"I'm sorry," he said again. "I didn't mean to scare you."

Nothing. Nothing but the headache.

"I'm going to try to find a way to help you," Jason said. He folded the list of his siblings carefully, replacing it in the small hidden pocket on the inside of his shirt. "I'll be back downstairs tomorrow night."

Either they ignored him, or they didn't hear him.

Didn't matter. They were children, and he'd help them anyway.

41

STELLA
DAY 35

The whole day stretched immeasurably, the ugly, scowling sun and the way the snow reflected its light and made the world too bright but still cold, the wagon rattling her around and making her body ache, the terrible powder burning its way through her senses.

At some point, she managed to close her eyes and keep them closed. Dreams crawled through her exhaustion, taunting her. Siras's face, Bothain's hands, the pair of them turning her house to a monument to her private humiliation, and Bothain in his office where he kept all his foul Authority paperwork because he imagined Ffyanwy to be afraid enough of him that she wouldn't tempt his temper by looking.

Leave it be, Ffyanwy. This is the way things are done.

Rhion, her sweet boy, screaming. Dying. And she couldn't stop it.

She saw things that didn't belong to her. Moments of Ozra's life that flashed through her mind when his Wrath dragged her down, his children and the women he made them with, the cold, lonely halls of the Breeding Program in the mountains above Cruinnich, the smothering blackness of the mines.

Hands on her clothes.

She tried to turn away, but when she opened her eyes, she saw Tashué's face beside her. She almost wept with relief. Was she still dreaming? Perhaps he'd found her. Or perhaps this whole horrible ordeal had been the nightmare—perhaps she had never left him—but no, they were under the open sky. The moon was approaching its complete fullness, and the light it spilled across the world danced on all that snow, making the wilderness glow like the city brights were watching over them.

"Tashué," Stella said. Her voice rasped miserably, so dry it almost hurt to speak. "How did you...?"

"I never should have left you," he said. He pulled her close. He smelled like blood, like a wound gone bad. He pushed her coat open, even though it was cold. "You've got blood on your hands. Are you wounded?"

"It's not mine," Stella said. She lifted her hands between her and Tashué, looking at them. They trembled. Blood was so ingrained into the creases that she'd never get it out again. This was what her hands used to look like back when she was Ffyanwy, working at the hospital, except without all the mud. "It's Ozra's—oh, Ozra—I need to go back—I need to find him. I need to tell him I'm sorry—all I ever wanted was to protect her—"

"Let me check. Just to be sure."

His hands opened the buttons of her trousers, one, and two, and three, but it was so cold out here in the open. In the wagon.

"I'm fine," Stella said, trying to catch his hands. "Tashué, stop—Siras is out here somewhere. Please, we need to find Ozra, and Ceridwen."

"They're fine," Tashué said. His voice sounded so strange. He pushed Stella down hard onto her back, kneeling between her legs. "They're fine, I've taken care of it—just let me—"

"Hey." Someone else. A voice she didn't know. "That's enough, fuck. Leave her be."

Tashué growled, a wild and ugly sound, his face twisting. It didn't look like him, didn't sound like him—something shifted around the edges of him, like layers of paint that were starting to wash away. Stella lifted her legs and shoved him back, and when her knee hit his chest, he gave a strangled, wild yelp that didn't sound like Tashué at all. And he swung. His knuckles hit her face and sent her reeling so hard she hit the side of the wagon and her skull roared with resentful pain, her cheek burning. A sob broke out of her, and she pressed her hands against her face even though it hurt, trembling taking root in the core of her that shook all the hope out of her. This was some continuation of her nightmares, it had to be, because surely Tashué would never hit her. He grabbed her and dragged her away from the edge of the wagon like he was going to hit her again, but then there was someone else in the wagon with them, pushing him away. The moonlight caught the glint of red hair—Siras. It wasn't Tashué, it was Siras.

Siras struggled with whoever was holding him until they were a twist of arms and legs and snapped curses. They fell right out of the wagon, and Siras gave another strangled, angry roar. Stella turned away, squeezing her eyes shut as tears burned hot—the slap had broken open her skin, and blood crawled down her cheek and over the bridge of her nose as she lay on her side, hot and vicious. She was so tired, so horribly tired, but this had to be a dream. Tashué wouldn't hurt her like that, and Siras wasn't real, it was all a miserable nightmare, and she'd wake up soon. At camp with Rhodrishi and Ozra and Kazrani, with Ceridwen tucked against her and so wonderfully warm because of all the wishing she did.

"It's a dream," she whispered to herself. "It's a dream, it's a dream, it's a dream."

The wagon shifted and someone was beside her. People were laughing, sharp and cruel.

"Miss Rhydderch," a voice said—the same voice that told Siras to leave her be. "Miss Rhydderch, are you alright? Can I see your face? I think you're bleeding."

If she didn't engage with the dream, it couldn't hurt her anymore. This was a terrible nightmare, and if she waited it out, she would wake.

"Miss Rhydderch, can you hear me?"

"It's a dream," she said. "It's a dream, it's a dream, it's just a dream."

A hand on her arm.

She twisted toward it, swinging with all the strength she had. Dream-Siras wouldn't fool her again—he'd never touch her again, curse him. Her hands hit skin and beard and cloth, everything. She saw a face, but it wasn't Siras. It wasn't anyone she recognized. He recoiled from her, sliding back to the opposite wall of the wagon that held her. And the laughing got louder, but she couldn't see the source of it.

"Alright, I'm sorry," the man in the wagon said. "I won't touch you again—I'm sorry."

She lay flat on her back, watching wisps of clouds slide over the face of the moon. The walls of the wagon blocked the edges of her vision, so it was her, and the wagon, and the man beside her. And the sad, distant moon. This horrible dream wouldn't let her go.

42

JASON
DAY 36

The new prisoner came in like a whirlwind, black curly hair and a chip on her shoulder and so much of energy. Jason wondered how long she'd last with energy like that. Surely this place would wear that chip down until it was so smooth that water would bead off it, until she was nothing but bones and despair like everyone else.

But maybe this place wouldn't wear her down. Maybe this was *her*, the one from the Red Dawn, the one who was supposed to get Jason out of this fucking place. Maybe she had all that energy and all those edges because she was untouchable.

She went straight to Rezji, and the pair of them threw their arms around each other and started whispering over their breakfasts, their foreheads pressed together like they couldn't bear to be in separate spaces. How long had Rezji been in here? He had no idea. He didn't really know her until she came to him and said *what if there was a way out of here?*

"Who do you think she is?" Jason whispered.

"They obviously know each other," Glaen said. They'd taken to eating their meals together, and Jason had to admit that the company was nice.

"Lovers, do you think?" Jason asked.

Glaen shrugged. "It would seem that way, wouldn't it?"

"It must be nice," Jason said. "To have someone you care about that much in here. Must make it feel like you're less alone. Less isolated from everything you thought your life would be."

Glaen glanced up at Rezji and the new prisoner, but then looked down again, looking ashamed or embarrassed, like it was too much intimacy and he was intruding. "Maybe you'll get out soon. And you'll get to see the people you love again, out there in the real world."

Jason sighed. The longing he felt for Lorne was easy and straightforward. Three and a half years away from the person he loved, and maybe the wait was almost over. But the longing he felt for his father was complicated and even a little ugly. The relief that Tashué was still alive was all-consuming. The rest of it was less clear. His father was still the man who let Jason down so many times, still the man who had completely failed to understand why Jason would resist the Authority until a child neither of them knew washed up on the riverbank. And what about the children here? If Jason broke out, who was going to help them?

"Maybe," he said. Because giving voice to any of those thoughts would make more trouble than he was ready to cope with.

Rezji and the new prisoner spent all of breakfast like that, locked together, eating slowly to make the moment stretch. When it was time for work, Rezji untangled herself from the new prisoner, speaking to the proxy in charge of assigning chores. Negotiations were swift and decisive, and then the proxy escorted the new prisoner away. Rezji turned, her gaze sweeping over the whole mess hall. She stood a while, watching Jason, her hands on her hips. She didn't seem especially happy, but maybe that was her expression. Generally unimpressed with everything. Although he was certain she looked more annoyed than usual. Jason watched her, waiting to see if she was going to say something to him. But she didn't say anything at all. Her gaze shifted to Glaen next, and she beckoned him to follow with a little tilt of her head. Glaen sighed, gathering up his bowl.

"That's my work whistle, I suppose," Glaen said. "Back to the mines."

Jason forced a laugh, trying to push away the dread, the exhaustion, the loneliness. The revulsion that lived under his skin, day and night, in this place. And his head still hurt from when the children panicked. Maybe the bone *was* fractured after all. Jason half-expected to wake up with his ears bleeding or something equally horrifying, but so far it was just pain. He hadn't had the chance to go back downstairs yet—hopefully they'd let him connect to them tonight, and he could apologize for scaring them.

"I didn't know chickens came from mines," Jason said, instead of thinking about the children or the pain.

"Oh, yes," Glaen said, patting Jason's hand. "You have to dig them out of stone very carefully. You don't want a chicken mine collapse. You can't *imagine* the carnage of a chicken-mine collapse."

"Be safe," Jason said, forcing a smile. "I wouldn't want to lose you to such a gruesome fate."

Once Glaen was gone, Jason felt miserably exposed and alone. Verrit wasn't in the mess hall, but surely it was only a matter of time before he turned up. Jason scraped the last of the gruel out of his bowl, pushing himself to his feet. Best if he got on with his day. Verrit didn't come out to the gardens. Gardeners stuck together, kept each other safe.

He still remembered the first time he stepped outside into the vicious heat of the summer, and the gardeners gave him water and wiped his tears and taught him how to pour his sorrow and his fear into the earth, so it could be hidden from view.

Of the gardeners that welcomed him that first day, three had died during his time here. Another two had been transferred to other jobs as a punishment for some infringement of the status quo. But the understanding remained, because newcomers carried on the tradition. The gardens were a safe place.

There wasn't much to do outside, not with winter coming. The snow was late this year, and though there were some winter crops, there wasn't much upkeep since bugs were dormant, and weeds were struggling. But that didn't stop the gardeners from going out every day until it was so snowy that there was no conceivable excuse to be out there. The key was to look busy enough to keep the proxies and the guards from questioning anything.

So Jason wasn't expecting to see anyone new out there. Not this time of year.

But the new prisoner *was* out there, bundled tight against the cold, that riot of black hair of hers covered by a scarf. She wasn't very tall, but somehow she took up a lot of space, standing in the middle of the gardens and scowling at the dirt like it was the reason she was cold. She looked up when Jason walked out. Smiled. Or something like a smile. Maybe it was a scowl. Hard to tell in the cold.

"Jason Blackwood?" she asked.

Jason froze. Panic swept through him. Why was she looking for him? What was *she* going to do? He clenched his fists, resisting the urge to run back into the building. "Irén?"

She pushed her hair out of her face, giving another scowl-smile. "How'd you know?"

"Lorne told me you were coming," Jason said, forcing himself to exhale. There wasn't any good reason to panic; this was hope. This was what it felt like to have options and a future. It had been so long since he had those things that he didn't know how to respond to them anymore, so that's why his hands shook, and his stomach twisted itself into knots. "This is how the Red Dawn takes care of people, is it? They toss you into the Rift so you can come chat with me?"

Irén glanced around at the other gardeners, hovering around the compost heap to look busy and stay out of the way. She jerked her head toward one of the farthest corners, the one closest to the spray of the river, which was full and running fast with all the rain and melted snow from the recent storms. Jason followed her over, ducking his head against the wind and the wet mist. She glanced back at the walls of the Rift, at the big door that let them out here like she half-expected someone to come looking for them.

"Just tossed me in is about right," Irén grunted. "Took me to the station house in the Bay and told them to send me up. Spent a few days at the fucking station house, freezing my ass off in their cellar, and now I'm here, code 1 for feral. Me and László were supposed to get our first tattoos together, but instead he gets to stay snug and warm in the fucking pugilist club with the cute new boxer, and I get inked up and tossed in here. Is it ever warm in here?"

The way she said *László and the cute new boxer* made Jason's heart flutter. Lorne, she meant Lorne. In here with his brand-new, white leather coat and his face all healed up from the last fight in the Hive, his eyes glowing with health and happiness. He'd mentioned László a time or two while they were talking around all the heavy things, but suddenly Jason found himself wondering what László Dargis was like. Did he look like his sister? Dark hair and wild eyes and that chip on her shoulder.

"Yeah," Jason said, fighting against any thoughts of László and the cute new boxer. His fear was so habitual now that it was looking for something to latch on to. "In the summer. When it's so hot that the wells can't keep up with our water consumption, and so we all have to choose between dehydration or getting the shits from drinking water from the river."

Irén Dargis rolled her eyes, pushing her hair out of her face again. "Fuck this place. Leave it to the Authority, hey?" She pulled her coat tighter around her, her shoulders bunching up to protect her cheeks from the wind and the water. "I hate the cold. I shoulda paid more attention to our sister when she was trying to teach us about healing shit, and maybe I coulda stayed at the club instead of László."

"It's not even that cold," Jason said. "Gets worse from here. Winter hasn't decided if it's staying yet."

"Fucking great." She kicked a stone so it skittered off between the bars of the fence that kept them in, then spun off into the water. "Good thing we're getting out in a couple days, hey?"

Jason gaped at her. Her confidence was stunning, beautiful, unbelievable. "Are you serious? You really think it'll happen that fast?"

"Yeah, I'm fucking serious," Irén scoffed. "I told Dav I wasn't gonna fuck around in here. I know it's taken a long time, and I know you're scared to hope—I know the waiting has been hard. If I'm honest, Davik hit more obstacles than he expected. We were going to smuggle you out like a load of laundry, but the people we were working with all fucked us. That's why I'm here. If things go well, we're out in two days, you and me. The day of the boxing match, we'll transfer to the Breeding Program."

"But I didn't register," Jason gasped.

Irén shrugged. "Long ride, here to the Breeding Program. Have to go right through the Bay, you know?"

"Yeah," Jason said. His whole heart lurched right up, like it was trying to fly away with the joy of it. "Right through the Bay."

Irén nodded, pulling up the collar of her coat. "Dangerous place, the Bay. And if Davik can't sort that in time, I've got a backup plan ready to carry us out of here. Just in case."

"A backup plan?" Jason echoed.

Irén shrugged. "A backup plan. The one thing you learn on the lake is that you always need a spare boat. Just in case."

Jason sighed, looking up at the high walls, the stone and the tiny windows. Miserable, hateful windows that never let enough light in to make the place feel habitable but always let too much cold in over the winter windows, that clotted with ice and rattled with the wind.

"You don't look happy," Irén said. "I expected you to look a little bit more... I don't know. Excited."

"I've been here a long time." Jason said. "This is as happy as I get until I see it."

Irén laughed. "The pair of you are perfect for each other."

"The pair of us?"

"You and Coswyn. He's all slow and reluctant and suspicious, too. Some people can't absorb good news. I guess I can understand it. I think we were like that, me and László. Back before Dav. When life kicks you in the teeth a few times, it's hard to trust the good things. But Dav takes care of his people, and you're everything that he would want around, so you can relax and feel it."

"Sure," Jason said, even as he refused to feel it. Even as he clawed his own soaring heart back into place, telling it to wait. Wait until he was out. "What about the children?"

"The children?"

Jason nodded, pulling his coat closed. "The children. The energy units. There's four of them in there, and one of them's dying. Will *Dav* take care of them?"

Irén followed his gaze toward the walls, her eyes tracking from one window to the next. "How do you know how many there are? Have you seen them?"

"Sort of. Will he help them?"

"I don't know," Irén admitted. "It wasn't part of the plan."

"Can we make it part of the plan?"

Irén shrugged. "Why don't we get out first. And then we'll figure it out."

Jason grimaced. He didn't like the idea of leaving them behind. But maybe Irén was right. What could they come up with in two days?

43

LORNE
DAY 36

"It's tradition," Davik explained.

They piled into an omnibus that passed close to the edge of the Bay. Davik and Rowan and László, and some others from the club. People who drifted at the edge of Lorne's life, making the club run. They cleaned things and fixed things and built things, and they rolled barrels of beer into the basement for the big night. No matter how busy Lorne was at any one moment, the club itself was always more chaotic, caught up in a mad race to get ready for the match. He was only one piece of many. He tried to learn everyone's names. Tom, the man with the kind eyes and the big smile, whose job it was to clean and stitch and maintain all the punching bags so they were in good condition. Charlee, with the flash of reddish hair and scars on her hands from all the work she did building the tap lines so the bar could keep the barrels of beer in the cellar. Others he couldn't remember, sitting together in a knot.

And Lorne, in his white leather coat in an omnibus packed to the brim with workers for the Industrial Quarter, work-stained and weary, but they smiled when they saw him. They whispered to each other until the whole omnibus was talking about pugilism.

"We're hosting Mr. Odegaard at our club," Davik continued. "So we go to his club, have a pint. The pair of you shake hands, and the sports reporters pop a photograph or two, and they run it in the papers to fire up publicity for the fight. And if any of you bawbags start any fucking trouble, I swear to everything holy, I'll start knocking your idiot heads together."

"Yeah, Dav," Tom chirped from halfway up the omnibus. There wasn't enough room for everyone to sit together. "We'll behave."

Ari Odegaard still fought for Brickheart even though he could go anywhere else in the city, people said. Apparently Highview had tried to poach him more than once, but he always turned them down flat. And there was reverence in their voices when they said it—allegiance to your quarter was respected in the Bay. Some people understood that money and a nice house didn't replace the feeling of knowing your whole quarter would fight and die for you if something bad happened. There was something about the people who knew what street you lived on, knew how hard your life was on that block. How hard you worked for whatever scrap of happiness and success you might have grabbed from the aether of a cruel, ugly world. And if you shared some of that happiness? Well, that made you a small god, didn't it?

The pugilist club in Brickheart was as busy as the one in the Bay. Busier. Bursting at the seams. So many bodies.

"Go see if you can clap eyes on Ari," Davik said. "With the fight coming, I'll wager he's working hard to get into condition. You remember what he looks like, László?"

"Course I do," László said. "You don't forget a beautiful man like Ari Odegaard."

Davik nodded and led Rowan to the bar. László caught Lorne's hand, dragging him through the crowd, Tom and Charlee trailing behind them. And they were small enough to navigate the gaps, to squeeze through the spaces that people left between themselves and people they didn't know, edging through the jostling bodies.

"There he is," László said, stopping at the edge of one crowd. "Look, there."

Lorne couldn't tell the difference between one fighter or another. They were all in excellent shape, all moving with perfect understanding of their bodies, all covered in sweat and not wearing much clothing. Gloves, so many pairs of gloves, all of them red-brown and in various states of wear and tear.

"Which one?" Lorne asked.

László stepped behind Lorne, guiding him to the very edge of an open space, where a number of fighters were sparring, and no one dared get close, or else they'd accidentally catch a fist. László wrapped one arm around Lorne's chest, turning him slightly, the other arm stretching over Lorne's shoulder to point through a gap in the bodies jostling all around them, directing Lorne's attention. "He's the one sparring with the big fucker. He's got blond hair and the tattoo on his back."

Lorne followed László's finger, searching through the confusion. Looking for ink, blond hair. So hard to tell one pair of boxing gloves from another, one pair of swinging arms.

"Beside the big red punching bag, to the left. The big fucker looks like he's trying hold in a shit because he knows if Ari forgets they're sparring and really hits him, he's going down. Because most people don't like to get punched in the face."

Blond hair tied back, drenched in sweat. The tattoo on his back—boxing gloves. His body wasn't as big as the man he was sparring, but his muscles were precise and even across his whole body. He swung with perfect control. His wind up looked like it was going to knock his opponent flat every time, but by the time it landed, his glove barely grazed the skin.

"Yeah," Lorne said, "I see him now."

Everything about Ari's movement was perfect, balanced, in total control, except maybe the shuffle of his feet as he took his steps. There was something slightly off, something almost unbalanced—Lorne wouldn't have even noticed if it weren't for the fact that everything else about Ari was utterly precise. Lorne wanted to see him let loose, wanted to see him take someone down. Wanted to see what those long arms were really capable of doing.

"Ari's the one who made pugilism popular in Yaelsmuir," Tom explained, shouting over the crowd. "Professional pugilism was a rich quarter's sport before because of all the training it takes. Anyone can fight in the amateur leagues, but no one can afford this much dedication except rich people. And then ten, fifteen years ago, this unknown fucker comes up through the ranks and thrashes everyone. Fucking *everyone*. It was incredible to watch. And everyone wondered how the fuck a guy from Brickheart could get so good. This club built him. They're the ones that started serving food and drink in the same building—it's how they could stay afloat and pay for Ari's healer and all the league fees and shit. And the thing that people love about him is the bastard is so damned friendly. He'll sit with his fans and have pints, and the club gives shit away if they think it'll help someone out."

"And now we've finally got our own club, like we're a proper part of this city," Charlee said. Her voice reverent, eyes shining with awe and pride. "You'll be the King of the Bay in no time, Mr. Lightning. You'll strike terror into the hearts of every fucking pugilist in this city. I ain't never seen anyone move like you. Won't be long before there'll be no stopping you."

Made Lorne's heart beat faster. Tension crawled across his body, delicious and ugly. He hated how much he liked it. Loved how it felt to watch Ari and imagine what it would be like to put gloves on and stand opposite him. With László's breath in his ear, László's chest pressed against his back, László's arms around him, it was easy to feel like the crowd was falling away. Like everyone else was just noise but not real people. A forest of flesh, its own thing Lorne was separate from. The other fighters didn't matter. The other people sparring, exercising, grappling—they didn't exist. It was just László and Lorne and his people from the Bay, watching Ari perform. László's heart beat so hard Lorne could feel it against his back, reverberating through both of them. Hard to tell which rhythm was László's heart and which was his own heart and which was the rhythm Ari was making with his sparring. Step, step, swing, step, swing, swing.

He understood, watching Ari, why László spoke of this violent sport like it was his religion. He understood why László rattled off the terms of pugilism like it was an incantation to an ancient and brutal god. The brutality was only half the truth; the other half was *beauty*. Ari's form and function and precision, the movement of his muscles and the way it made the tattoo of the gloves ripple, the sweat that beaded down his body.

Davik and Rowan came back with pints. László untangled himself from Lorne to take his pint, and it felt like a loss. The closeness was comforting in all the chaos. But the pint was comforting, too. The glass was cold in his hand and the beer was cool and crisp and light, refreshing against the heat and the chaos of the club.

"Where's mine?" Tom scoffed.

"What am I, your coin purse?" Davik said, shoving Tom with one elbow. "Fucking get your own."

"There's something funny about the way he's balanced," Lorne said, glancing at Davik. He looked right at home here, like he enjoyed the crush of a massive crowd. "He's... off. I can't tell what it is. But there's something wrong about the way he steps. I think."

"You've got a good eye, laddie," Davik said, grinning. He leaned close to Lorne to be heard over the crowd, dropping his arm around Lorne's shoulders. "He fucked up his ankle a while back. Broke it, I think, or at least sprained it something awful. He's been off… How long now?"

"Two years," Rowan supplied. "This'll be his first fight since."

László sipped his beer, leaning against Lorne ever so slightly. "Wonder if it's still sore or if he ain't used to putting all his weight on it."

Lorne drank back more beer. It sat cool in his stomach, but it made his body feel warmer. He was drinking too fast, but it was so hot in here, and he was still wearing his coat. Lorne tried to figure out how long they'd been standing here, watching. But he didn't know. All his heart-beats seemed to bleed together, all the moments. And Ari never slowed down.

And a cold weight settled in Lorne's stomach, a pit of ugly certainty that cut through the excitement and told him he couldn't beat Ari Odegaard at his own sport. It wasn't possible for him to win on skill or form. Not now. Maybe in a year after he had time to really learn form and forge new instincts, but he hadn't even been at the club for two whole weeks yet.

The crowd pressed in—getting closer, maybe more people were arriving. The fight shifted; Ari's opponent was getting tired. There was no more evading from Ari, no more dancing or springing, he was just hitting. Swing, swing, swing, swing, left or right, it didn't matter. Every swing hit exactly where it wanted to go and only just touched. Or maybe the hits were getting a bit heavier, maybe they were starting to sting a bit, because his opponent was trying harder to slip and guard instead of moving on any offence, but there was only so far he could go without getting hit by someone using a skip rope or swinging at a punching bag. And Ari didn't let him get away either, flanking him, using the shape of the crowd to hem him in, swing, swing, swing, swing, leaving red weals on his bare chest.

"There we go," Davik said, nudging Lorne with his elbow. "Hold real still now. Like a statue."

"What?" Lorne asked. "Why?"

Davik nodded to the other side of the fight. A photographer was setting up his camera, his flashbulb, pointing the lens right at Lorne and fiddling with it. "They're going to snap a shot of you watching, but it takes a second or two. Everyone moving will be blurry—which is fucking everyone. But you, you stand real still, and you'll be the only thing in focus. You and that coat of yours."

Standing still was easier said than done. László lifted his chin off Lorne's shoulder, but left his arm around Lorne's waist. Lorne drew in a slow breath and held it. Held it and focused on the feeling of cold condensation sliding down his pint glass under his fingers and counted the beats of his heart as Ari pounded his sparring partner into submission. Held it until Lorne felt like he was going to turn inside out.

The flashbulb popped and bathed the club with so much light that Lorne couldn't see anything for a long moment.

Ari's opponent dropped, and Lorne struggled to blink the white tracers out of his eyes so he could see what had happened. Had the man passed out? No—he was down to one knee, ending the sparring match. And Ari stepped back. Someone came forward to unlace Ari's gloves and pull them off, and then Ari unlaced his opponent's gloves. He laughed. Smiled. He had an incredible smile, shining and bright and warm, his blond beard doing nothing to hide it. Emphasizing it somehow. Towels for their sweat and the opponent was laughing, too, like the beating he took at the end was an expected part of it all. The photographer popped another flashbulb to capture the moment.

Ari tipped his head to the photographer as he towelled himself off. Only then did he seem to notice all the people looking at him. His eyes swept the crowd and he turned that flashbulb-bright smile on everyone. He spotted Lorne and his eyes tracked up and down Lorne's body like he was studying Lorne's coat—it must have been like a beacon, the white leather making him stand out among all the other bodies—and then he fixed his stare on Lorne's face. And he winked.

He understood now why Davik wanted him to see what was possible. How good he *could* be if he kept up his training. But he hated it, just a little. He hated how aware he was of his limitations and how much he wanted to win. How much he wanted to be good at boxing. It shouldn't have mattered to Lorne that he wasn't ready. The actual trajectory of his career didn't matter. The exhibition match was for Jason, to help get him out of the Rift.

But it mattered. It mattered so much it made his ligaments hurt. Like they were begging him to be better, to be good enough to face Ari Odegaard and win. In that moment, he'd give anything to be good enough to have a chance.

P ints lined up at the bar like golden sentries.

"Go easy," Davik said. "You'll have another with Ari, and we don't want you half in the keg by then."

People watched them. Some tried to hide it, glancing over now and then, but others didn't care if they were staring. A woman two stools down from Tom, taking notes in a pad like the one Allie always carried around. Tom leaned across the hapless patron between him and the reporter, but Lorne couldn't hear what they were saying. Talking about Lorne, though. That was the hardest part to wrap his head around. All these people, with an eye on him because his presence here excited them.

"We'll start you jogging in the morning," Davik said.

Lorne shook his head, snatching his beer off the bar. "Why?"

"To build your stamina, teach you to breathe," László said, leaning on the bar.

What the fuck were they talking about? "I know how to breathe, Dav."

"Aw, you're such a bright wee beam of sunshine," Davik said with a laugh, patting Lorne on the back. "I know that, laddie. But the running helps. This is what it takes. Just be glad I didn't start you with the stairs yet."

"What am I going to do with the stairs?"

"Walk up them," Davik said. "Over and over again. Until you'd rather die than walk up them one more time, and then do it again. It's good for your heart and your lungs and your thighs."

Lorne scowled. Davik was fucking joking, he had to be. "What do my thighs have to do with boxing?"

"Makes you springy," Rowan said brightly, scooping up his pint. "Springy legs are vital to moving quick."

"You're full of shit. The three of you are coming up with elaborate ways to torture me."

Davik laughed again, waving at another reporter. "While I'm going to enjoy watching you suffer, I promise all these things are part of the conditioning. My coach in Teshii laughed at all of my pain, and now we get to laugh at yours."

Lorne sucked back half the pint. That was definitely too fast, but he was so hot with his coat on and waiting for Ari felt strange. "How long were you in Teshii?"

"Lorne Coswyn, are you asking me personal details about my life? Like you want to get to know me?"

Lorne flushed more than the gentle teasing deserved. "I don't know. We're always talking about me and pugilism. Seems like the natural thing is to get to know you, right?"

Davik shrugged, a bit of his good humour dying. He spun his pint glass in one slow circle, watching the condensation slide down the side of the glass. "I was only in Teshii for the two years, and then I went back to Cruinnich."

"You don't talk about your time in Teshii much, Da," Rowan said.

Davik shrugged. "Teshii is like the parts of the Bay where the rich folk from Highview and Highfield come to chase tail, but worse. Folks with money are running around, searching for the next big sculptor or painter or dancer to patronize, and then the folks that hope to wind up in galleries and theatres chase money to get them there, and then there are the idiots going to school to try to learn to do something with their lives, chasing big ideas and spending family money."

"What were you in Teshii for?" László asked with a laugh. "Were you the rich prick looking for an artist or the artist looking for a patron?"

"Neither," Davik said. "I was the idiot at school. I was interesting enough to be around the artists and fuck some of them, but not rich enough to be a patron to any of them. I was supposed to go learn about business management, so I could rescue Kaine Brick before my da managed to run it into the ground."

Talking about Teshii made Lorne burn more. It felt too much like they were dragging Alys into the room and talking about her, too. It all felt entirely too much like Lorne's entire life was in the palm of Davik's hand, and Lorne had only been at the pugilist club a little over a week, and now Davik had him by the veins around his heart, and Lorne knew Davik wasn't going to let go.

"Now *this* story I heard," Rowan said.

"Which story?" Lorne asked.

Davik sighed, spreading his hands on the bar. "I was in Teshii to learn what I needed to save my family's legacy from the Authority— those were the days when the Authority first started hitting tainted-owned business with licensing fees and regulation guidelines. And if they couldn't keep up, the Authority fined 'em even more money. Their goal was to bankrupt the owners and take over the business themselves, and Kaine Brick was easy prey. We were barely keeping up as it was. My grandda worked his fingers to the bone to make Kaine Brick what it was, and my da promptly fucked it all up, and I was supposed to save it. I was ready. I was in love with the most perfect girl I'd ever met, and she loved me, and we'd merge our companies for more stability. Brick and Stone would make each other stronger, and we'd stand against the crushing weight of the Authority, independent businesses employing thousands of tainted between us, keeping them off the foul registry. It was a good dream, once. Didn't happen that way, though."

"This'll be the woman that got away from you, hey?" László asked. "The one who married Bothain Clannaugh—the healer."

"Ffyanwy Rhydderch," Davik said.

He said the name slowly and with perfect care, pronouncing the Lledewydd vowels properly—the h a breathy sound before the r, the double-d like the Dominion's th, the ch making a hard sound at the back of his throat. He said it like a caress, like he could reach through the world and touch her by speaking her name. The simple longing in his voice made Lorne ache. Lorne knew exactly what it was like to love someone that much. Maybe he said Jason's name that same way, like it was the only air he wanted to breathe.

"Why'd she marry Clannaugh?" Rowan asked. "He's a fucking prick. Didn't she care?"

"He was better at hiding it back when we were younger," Davik said. He sipped his beer like he was trying to hide the way his voice had gone thin. "While I was away, he tried to strip apart Rhydderch Stone, the same way he was slowly killing Kaine Brick. But back in those days, he had us convinced all that he wanted to help us. Tainted or no, it didn't make a difference, he said. We were all northern, and he stood together against the hard chains of the Dominion. Ffyanwy was a good soul, and she believed him—couldn't wrap her mind around the idea that someone could lie *so well* because she was honest. So she married him, even though she never wanted to marry. She said it was worth it to save Rhydderch and to keep working as a healer at her hospital. She gave Bothain a son and six years of marriage that he didn't deserve, and he killed her for it."

László drained his pint, resting the empty glass on the bar. "How come no one's ever arrested Clannaugh for murder?"

"You know how it goes," Davik said. "She disappeared one day. Vanished, like she was a dream. Except all of Cruinnich dreamed her and loved her, so no one in Cruinnich ever forgave him. But no one could prove it, either. No blood on his hands. She just disappeared. Who has the power to arrest the Provincial Administrator of the Authority? Certainly not the City Civilian Patrol. Even if he had left her body in the city square, he could have said she had it coming. He's Authority, after all, and she was tainted."

"Fuck the Authority," Rowan said.

Davik shrugged, draining his beer, too, nodding to the bartender for another. "Anyway, nearly went out of my bleedin' mind down in Teshii. Hitting people in my spare hours got me through it. I was good enough, I suppose, but I never had your speed or instinct. You're well past good, laddie. You're great. Give me some time and I'll make you the best."

A shiver of excitement passed through the crowd before Lorne could figure out what to say—Ari came out of the crowd. Davik stood, turning toward him. László elbowed Lorne so hard, Lorne almost fell off his stool. Lorne stood, that too-fast pint draining right down to his feet, making him feel clumsy, too heavy. Davik shook Ari's hand first, and a photographer jostled through the crowd, wrangling her camera into place. Ari's coach elbowed people out of the way to clear the shot. Davik pushed a fresh pint into Lorne's hand, like a prop that was required for the photo. A red ale this time instead of the pale, citrusy lager he had before.

Ari thrust his hand at Lorne next. It was a big hand, bigger than Lorne expected. Rolled up sleeves showed wire-hard muscles of his fore-arms. His hair was still wet and he smelled like soap, making Lorne intensely aware of how sweaty he was. If he took off his coat, he'd prob-ably show wet marks where he was soaking through his shirt.

"I promise I don't bite, Mr. Lightning," Ari said with a grin. "Just want to shake your hand for the cameras."

Lorne looked up at Ari's face, at the charming smile. It was a hand-some face. Lorne hated him. He took the man's hand anyway. It wasn't a shake so much as Ari squeezed Lorne's hand and froze long enough for the camera to pop another bulb.

"We're working on his manners," Rowan quipped. "We found him roaming around the Bay, foaming at the mouth and biting people who tried to feed him, but we're house breaking him well enough."

"Fuck you, Row," Lorne muttered.

László laughed, kissing Lorne on the cheek. "He's still pissing on things, I'm afraid."

Ari grinned, crossing his arms over his chest. His shirt buttons strained. Was he wearing a shirt that was too small on purpose? He wasn't especially broad—he should have been able to fit into things off the rack. "That's fine. I'm used to it, aren't I? There's always boys with something to prove strutting around these pugilist clubs. You don't need to be so surly, Mr. Lightning. I've seen you training, and I'm plenty impressed. You got it in you to be fucking amazing if you keep on track."

"You've been down to the club?" Davik asked.

"Of course I have, Mr. Kaine. The first pugilist club in the Bay? I had to see it."

"You should've let me give you a tour, Mr. Odegaard. We would've been honoured to show off a bit."

Ari grinned again, shrugged. "I know. But I like to see how a place runs when people don't know I'm there. And I'm plenty impressed, Mr. Kaine, don't you worry." He clinked his glass off Davik's. "Would you walk with me? We'll do all the press shit after, I promise, but could I steal a private word with you and the Lightning?"

Davik glanced down at Lorne, and Lorne shrugged. He didn't have any fucking clue. "Sure, Mr. Odegaard. Lead the way."

They left Charlee and Tom behind at the bar and ditched Ari's coach, who kept the reporter busy. László trailed behind Lorne. So close, they could have held hands. Ari grabbed a coat, and then they were out the back door, carrying their pints into a covered courtyard out back. Empty and cold. And quiet, the sound of the city only distant. After all the noise in the club, the courtyard buzzed with its emptiness.

"I heard that you know Tashué Blackwood," Ari said as soon as the door was closed behind them.

Lorne didn't know what he was expecting, but it wasn't *that*. He shrugged, but the air felt too thick all of a sudden. "What's a pugilist want with a tinman?"

"He isn't a tinman anymore, is he?" Ari said. "I know him. He used to fight here."

"Blackwood was a pugilist?" Davik asked, saying Tashué's name like he didn't know the man at all.

"No, a duellist." Ari paused to sip his pint, looking up at the gap between the buildings to get a glimpse at the autumn grey sky. "We hosted sabre duels once a year, and he won every year he fought. All that army training, I figure. It made him tough in a way the other fighters couldn't possibly understand. And he was my wife's tinman. Back when he was actually a tinman and not a wanted fugitive."

"I didn't know you married tainted, Mr. Odegaard," Rowan said. "What makes a perfectly healthy and handsome man like you marry someone like that?"

"You can cut the shit, young Mr. Kaine," Ari said, but the words were delivered gently. "My wife goes down to the Bay. Dragged me with her a few times, too. To listen to people talk, yeah? I'm not threatening you folks or anything—I just have questions about the Red Dawn."

"Ain't no Red Dawn in Yaelsmuir," Davik said. "The Authority says so, and if they say it, it must be true."

"Sure, Mr. Kaine. No problem. There ain't no Red Dawn, and they never meet in the cellar of the *Dripping Bucket* to talk about national revolution. How about Blackwood? Has anyone else around here seen him?"

Davik shrugged. "Don't know him. Never met him."

"I hear he's a real beast of a man, too," László said brightly, grinning into his pint. "Exactly my type. The sort that could wrap his arms right around me and crush me if he had a mind to. I'd remember seeing a beautiful man like that around the club."

"That's why I wanted to ask Mr. Lightning," Ari said, shifting his eyes to Lorne. "You're close to him through his son, aren't you? I remember you, even if you don't remember me. I remember asking Blackwood how he felt about his son fucking some wound-too-tight veteran, drifting through life in Cattle Bone Bay. He said you made Jason happy for the first time in a long time, and that was good enough for him. My coach offered to be the one who broke your kneecaps if ever you turned ugly and hurt Jason."

"Why the fuck are you telling me this?" Lorne scoffed. Every word made his chest too hot, made him feel like he needed to hit something. "Are you threatening me? Over what?"

"I ain't threatening you," Ari said easily. "I'm letting you know that I've got history with the Blackwoods, too. If anyone knows where he is, I'm hoping it's you."

Lorne shrugged, trying to shake off the anxiety crawling through his chest. "He's gone, I guess. Left me to tell Jason that it's all fucked, thank you very much. Or maybe he's dead. Maybe Elsworth got him, and he's lying so no one wonders too hard why he was in the Dunnenbrahl in the first place."

"Papers say Blackwood was trying to escape," Rowan said with a shrug. "Said he hijacked the whole wagon or something."

"How would anyone know that, if all the Patrollers were killed?"

Lorne shot back. Thank fuck Ari had made him angry—made it easier to lie. "Sounds like a fucking pile of shit to me."

"Sure, those are good questions," Ari said. "I've been wondering the same thing. And how about those other bodies in the forest, the ones who weren't Patrollers—who were they?"

"Don't know why you're asking *us*," Davik said, putting an arm around Lorne's shoulder. The measured voice of reason, calming Lorne down. "We're trying to get this boy of ours ready to face you, aren't we? And it's a mighty job, so I don't know when he'd have time to go looking for Blackwood."

Ari shrugged, sipping at his pint and looking at them each, one by one. It was hard to meet his eyes. Clear blue and earnest and friendly and maybe even a little sad. "I'd like to know if he's alive. Heard there's a new man hanging around your club, goes by the name Guinne."

László smiled. He was so fucking good at lying, him and Davik both. "Guinne? He's some northlander, wandered down here looking for Dav."

"Thought I was Red Dawn, didn't he?" Davik said. "Told him my club was open to him any time but had to let him down about all that Army business."

"Sure, Mr. Kaine," Ari said. "Whatever you say. If you see Blackwood, let him know I'm asking for him."

"Sure, I will. If I see him." Davik drained his pint completely, resting it on a window ledge behind him. "What else should I tell him? Why are you looking for him?"

"Tell him that I want to help," Ari said. "If the rumours are true and he's looking for fighters—I'm willing."

"Why?" Rowan asked. "Why would you care about us? You got a career as a pugilist, don't you?"

"Sure I got a career," Ari said. "But I have a conscience, too."

"And a wife, is that it?" Rowan pressed. "A pretty tainted wife, and you look at her and wonder what the Authority might do to her if she were stronger. And you feel a little guilty, do you? A little bit like you shouldn't be so comfortable with your big pugilist club wage and your gambling money and your house-sponsored healer who makes sure your handsome face don't scar too bad. A little bit like you're taking something that don't belong to you every time you benefit from tainted labour. Is that it? So you'll find Blackwood, wherever he is, and play the rebel because you want to feel good about yourself. Trying to make yourself the hero your wife deserves, hey?"

Lorne expected Ari to snap, to growl, to get angry. The accusations were ugly, and Rowan's voice was sharp like he was trying to pick a fight. And North Star help him, if Ari took the bait, Lorne would step in. He didn't care how long Ari had been boxing, and he didn't care if he was some beloved celebrity, if Ari took a single step closer to Rowan, Lorne would tear him apart. There weren't any stupid rules out here in the courtyard. No gloves, no ring, no referee.

"Maybe," Ari said softly. He looked sad instead of angry—his mouth downturned, his eyes relaxed instead of glaring. "Maybe all that and more. Maybe my wife is pregnant now and she spends every day crying because she never wanted to bring a child into this world that treats the Talented worse than hogs for the slaughter. And now that she heard the rumours about what Blackwood said about the children, she's inconsolable. Maybe I feel like I should've done something sooner. Maybe I feel like an idiot for not knowing it was so bad. Is it true, the things they say? About the children?"

"Don't know, Ari," László said. "I'm just a healer, here to take care of the best pugilist Yaelsmuir's ever seen."

Ari looked to Davik like he hoped Davik would say something more, but Davik had fished his cigars out of his pocket and made a show of ignoring the conversation so he could light one. Ari sighed, his shoulders sagging. He drained the last of his pint and scooped Davik's empty glass off the windowsill. "Sure, boys. I know you haven't any reason to trust me. But if any of you see Blackwood, tell him I'm looking for him. He'll know my word is good."

"Will do," László said. "Sorry we couldn't help more."

Ari shrugged. "In case you folks decide you ain't staying, it was nice to meet you now that you're all grown up, Mr. Coswyn. Your left hook is fucking killer. But you're weak on the right. You telegraph it too much, and you don't hit as hard as you could with it. Your shoulder hurt?"

"No," Lorne said. "It's a bad habit I picked up a while back. Broke bones in my hand, and it's like the muscles remember."

"Better break the habit," Ari said. "Trained pugilists will take advantage of it."

"Yeah?" Lorne asked. "Like they'll take advantage of the way you still limp a bit on your left ankle? Is it still sore, or is that a bad habit, too?"

Ari grinned, back in familiar territory. "Yeah, just like that. Look forward to meeting you in the ring."

He turned and headed for the door, but László sighed, pushing both his hands through his hair.

"Mr. Odegaard," László said. "Tell your wife that every child born with Talent is a victory. This is what they want—they want us so afraid to exist that we stop fighting. They want the only Talent to be produced by the Breeding Program so that the rest of us *are* hogs for the slaughter. They want the people who are free to diminish until there aren't enough of us left to fight, and then they'll wipe us out. And maybe it's a ripe pile of shit to put all that on a baby that ain't even born yet, but if we give up living, then they win. But listen—if you tell her all that and she still isn't ready to bring a child into this world for all the reasons you said, she can go to the *Dripping Bucket* and ask for help. They'll know what to do, and they won't judge her for it. Either way, tell her she's welcome in the Bay any time."

"Sure, László," Ari said softly, leaning his back against the door and pushing it open. "I'll tell her that. If she decides that's what she wants to do, should she ask for anyone in particular?"

László shrugged. "Any of the people who work at the *Bucket* will know how to take care of her."

Ari nodded. "You folks coming back in?"

"In a moment, Mr. Odegaard," Davik said. "You've got my boys all wound up, need to give these idiots a while to breathe so they don't pop a fuse at the next fucker who looks at them wrong."

Ari nodded again, stepping out of the way of the door so it swung closed. Once he was gone, the fury and the anxiety ebbed away, leaving room for something that felt like guilt to bleed in to Lorne's veins. Ari wanted to help.

Davik sparked a match on the coarse brick wall beside them, leaning over it to puff on his cigar until the end was glowing. "A couple of days ago, you asked why boxing, yeah?"

Lorne blinked at Davik for a minute, trying to switch tracks again. "What? Yeah."

Davik nodded, flicking the match away. It sizzled out in a puddle between the cobbles. "I don't know what's going to happen after the election. Don't know if we'll make it to tourney season. Maybe we all die, but hey—maybe not. I coulda opened another public house or another brothel, like you said. But those places don't inspire the type of loyalty that I need, yeah? The type of…" He waved his cigar in the air, making a loop of smoke. "Feeling of home. But pugilism? This city loves pugilism.

It's the only sports league we have that runs all year round, gives us a place to be, to meet, to congregate. And this city, they already know you, laddie. They already love you. Lorne the Lledewydd Lightning, the Bay champion. This city respects the Bay, for the first time since... who fucking knows when? Powell Iwan couldn't do that. Ari Odegaard is a fucking hero in Yaelsmuir because of pugilism—hell, all of the Dominion knows his name. He holds two national championships. And he's coming to us, asking to help. And even if I'm killed or arrested or run out of town by fucking Clannaugh, our club will still stand if I'm gone, and *someone* will be left to carry it on after me. And maybe, just maybe, if I can't carry this war to the victory my people deserve? The club I built will give my people a chance." He pointed his cigar toward the door, nodding his head. "That's why, Lorne. That's why boxing."

44

STELLA
DAY 36

Clouds gathered over the sun, and the wagon trundled on. Wind blew warmer than before, melting the snow away, leaving the air wet and resentful, which only made Stella intensely aware of how thirsty she was. Her lips were so dry they were cracking, her throat so parched that it hurt to swallow what little saliva her body made.

A face hovered in the corner of her vision—the one that was becoming familiar, the man stopped Siras from hurting her. He had scratches on his face, beside his eye. Other wounds, too, but they were old and mostly healed. A bump on the bridge of his nose, like it had been broken and was healing with a new kink in the cartilage. Or was it Siras? Dread clawed up her throat—did she see the shine of red hair, mixed with the brown? Siras was lurking everywhere, tricking her again and again.

"I thought the hallucinations were only supposed to last a few hours," he said. He didn't sound like Siras. "Why is she still fucked up? Did we give her too much?"

Someone laughed. "Are you complaining that it's been easy?"

The man with scratches on his face turned away. "I'm asking how come she ain't waking up."

"She showed you she's plenty awake, Hillbraun. Got some nice scratches for your trouble, hey? That's what you get for trying to help a tainted bitch. Ain't a one of them that's much better than a wild animal."

The man who tried to help her was watching her. She squeezed her eyes shut. She wished she could close her ears, too, so she didn't have to hear them talk about her, these words branded on her soul. She'd heard it all before—perhaps none of those men were really here, and it was a new layer to her nightmare, taunting her with words she'd been running from her whole life because she was born with Talent. Rhydderch Stone's legacy was protecting people from words like that, but there was no escaping them, not really.

"Is she like this forever now?" he asked. "Just mute? Did the powder shit break her mind or something? It's been a whole day—aren't you worried?"

A full day—she didn't even remember that much time passing. Fear touched her, but only distantly, like it was a sound from far away, she could make out the shape of it, but she couldn't grasp the full meaning.

"Maybe," someone said. "Didn't Mr. Elsworth say it was developed from the same shit they give the energy units, to make 'em quiet?"

"It's different than what they give the energy units," Siras grunted. So he *was* here—that voice was his for certain. "That's what Bothain told me. He said it attacks the Talent, lives in it forever. The reason she's gone all dumb now is 'cause she's got the Wrath."

"How do you know that?" the man with the scratches on his face asked.

"Can't you feel it?" Siras asked. "Her Talent, oozing out of her like a stench. She's been hiding as a whisperer, and that's the sort of Wrath they get after a while. They shut off from the inside, go a little dead behind the eyes. Haven't you ever seen a whisperer like that? You carried the tin, didn't you?"

"Yeah, I guess I did," the man with the scratches on his face said. "One of my first cases was a whisperer, and by the time I took him over, he already looked empty. The way he looked right through you, it fucked with my head. I didn't have his file for long."

"What happened to him?" someone asked.

"One day, he walked right into the Brightwash. Just up and wandered out of the Facility of Rest and went into the river. Never even tried to swim, people said. Just let the current take him. They said he was muttering something about all the pain in the world, said he said he was tired."

How peaceful that sounded. How merciful an end it must have been. Slipping down into the river and never again having to hear the cruel laughter of people who called them tainted.

The wagon shifted, jostling her enough to make her snap her eyes open. The man had climbed from his horse to the wagon, and the mount was walking along beside Stella with an empty saddle. The man knelt in the wagon beside her, holding out a waterskin. Stella tried to focus on the details of his face, on the shape of his nose and the turn of his mouth—searching for evidence of Siras. How did Siras manage to convince her that he was Tashué? The powder, it must have been, and now she had no way of knowing if she could trust her own eyes anymore.

"Miss Rhydderch." He pronounced her name the way everyone did around here, without the breathy sounds the Lledewyddyd name demanded. "Have a drink of water, at least."

Laughing. Someone called him a taint lover.

"Going in for a second round, Hillbraun?"

"How funny do you think it's gonna be when we have to tell General Clannaugh we let her die of dehydration, hey?" he snapped. "You think he's gonna laugh about it with you? I hear he's got a habit of shooting people who make him angry."

"He only shoots filthy tainted rebels. Ain't that right, Duncreek?"

"Hillbraun's right," Siras said. The voice came from outside the wagon, and it was almost a comfort to know he was indeed here but not in the wagon with her. So long as he kept talking, his foul voice would let her know where he was. "Bothain wanted her back alive. Stop the stupid wagon."

"Best drink up, Miss Rhydderch," the man with the scratches on his face said, pushing the waterskin against her hand. "Then we can keep going."

She didn't want it. She didn't want to keep going, and she didn't want to see Bothain again. She didn't want to look at his blue eyes and see the triumph there. She'd been running from him for so long, but now she couldn't run anymore. She was so tired, so exhausted and cold and empty. Perhaps this was still a dream, and it would pass. Or, if it was reality, the Wrath would take her.

She pushed the waterskin away, and when she did, the realization rolled slowly through her that her hands were tied together. The rope chafed now that she noticed it, and the horror bubbled up through her.

When had they tied her up? How terribly numb was she that she hadn't noticed?

"Miss Rhydderch—" the man said again, sounding desperate. "Please."

The wagon shifted. Siras climbed up, the sun glinting on that copper hair, crushed beneath his bowler. His clothes were travel stained, and blood crusted his whole right side.

"She's always been a stubborn cow," Siras said. "Once she decides she doesn't want something, there's no convincing her, so you have to make her."

"Siras, wait, let me try—"

Siras grabbed her by the arms and hauled her up. Revulsion broke through the numbness, burning the fog away. Stella twisted, pulling her arm out of his grasp—if she could swing at that wound, hit it again, he'd let her go like last time. But he was faster than she expected. He dropped to his knees behind her and grabbed a fistful of her hair. She tried to get away but the pain lanced hot and ugly through her scalp, making her scream, the sound of her own pain rattling through her and shaking the last numbness out of her. *Fight,* her every instinct screamed. *Fight, get away* —but she couldn't. Every time she moved, his hand wrenched her hair, and the pain brought tears to her eyes. His other hand clamped around her jaw, holding her face still, and there was nothing she could do but let her head press against his chest. Her feet were tied together, too.

The man with scratches on his face watched, his hand still clutching the waterskin like he was frozen with the shock. And she wanted to tell him not to be surprised. That this was Siras. This was the heart of him, like all the ugliness of the world had been poured into a man-shape.

She could feel his Talent as sure as she could hear his foul heart beating beside her ear, grubby and vicious, and that always made his cruelty so much worse. It was one thing for Bothain to hate her, for the Authority to sneer at her, for the world to watch her with a suspicious eye even though she used all the strength she had to heal anyone who came beneath her hands—but Siras and his Talent, that rocked the foundation she tried to stand on every time she looked at him. Once, when she was younger, she'd let herself believe that the world was a good place, and the Talented would protect each other no matter what, and together they were strong and proud and safe.

But then she married Bothain, and Siras Duncreek became a permanent fixture in her life, and she learned what a naive, stupid fool she was.

"You said she needs water, Hillbraun!" Siras snapped. "Help her drink."

The man with the scratches on his face shook his head, his mouth moving but no words escaping.

"Fucking hell, what a miserable waste of time," someone else muttered.

The wagon shifted again—another officer climbed up, his bronze badge glinting in the murky daylight. He snatched the waterskin and shoved the man with scratches on his face out of the way, kneeling in front of Stella. She lifted her legs, trying to kick the newcomer away, but he caught the rope between her ankles and forced her legs back down, pressing his knee into her calf and resting all his weight on her to pin both legs down. She cried out again, the pain so sharp and ugly it sent white hot flashes in front of her eyes. She thrashed, swinging an elbow back to try to hit Siras's wound again, but he let go of her hair and wrapped both his arms around her chest, pining her arms to her sides while the second man grabbed her face and poured water at her mouth. It was bitterly cold, and she needed it, but she was halfway through another shout of pain, and the water caught in her windpipe. Choking, gagging, throat raw and angry, more water in her face.

"Stop!" the man with the scratches on his face said. "Stop, fucking stop! You're going to kill her, you fucking idiots!"

"Alright!" Another voice, behind Stella—the driver of the wagon. "Enough! We have to keep moving before the others catch up."

The man tossed the waterskin in Stella's lap, splashing her face, her chest, Siras's arms. The cold of it bit into her clothes—her coat was still open from when Siras pawed at her and it sunk into the wool. He stood, the pressure releasing from her leg. She gasped with relief, but that only set off more coughing, more water catching in her throat.

Now that they had her sitting up, the edges of the wagon no longer restrained her vision. The road and the hills stretched endlessly around her. She felt incredibly small in the scope of all that space. And so terrifyingly alone.

"I'm fucking sick of this shit. I've never had to bring someone back alive before, and it's a fucking waste of time. We should've shot them all, filthy tainted scum."

"Bothain said alive, so we bring her back alive," Siras grunted. He hissed with pain as he stood, shoving Stella aside. "She's all yours, Hillbraun. Why don't you cuddle up to her, see if she'll let you have a squeeze since you've been so considerate. Regular taint-loving hero, you are."

He jumped back out of the wagon and gave a strangled gasp, pressing his hand into his side. Half a dozen men in all. Seven with the driver behind her back.

"You should get that wound looked at, Duncreek," someone said. "Before it rots a hole right through you."

Siras growled, walking back to his horse. "We'll hit that roadhouse tomorrow, and I'll see if they've got a healer around."

"I'm sorry," the man with the scratches on his face whispered. His hands shook when he grabbed his waterskin, pushing the stopper into it even though it must have been empty. "I was trying to help—I didn't sign up for this. I didn't know it was going to be like this, when I took this badge—I thought…"

He shook his head, pushing himself to his feet. He stood a while, his head a penumbra between her and the sun, making his features sink into shadows. She could still tell he was staring at her, though. The badge stared at her, too. And she hated him on principal, hated him for his ability to be surprised by all this cruelty, hated that he was a grown man and still naive enough to think the bronze badge was noble somehow.

The cart started moving again, the suddenness almost knocking the man off his feet. He grabbed the edge of the wagon, bracing himself. He hefted himself up over the side so he could catch the saddle of his horse and hop into it without touching the ground. Stella let herself sag against the wall of the wagon. Sobs bubbled in her throat, fighting against the ache left by all that choking. She didn't dare let them out. She didn't want to give them the entertainment of watching her cry.

45

JASON
DAY 36

Something adjacent to hope lived all day, no matter how hard he tried to reduce expectations. It was so intoxicating, bubbling through Jason's body like that fancy sparkling wine from the southern provinces, rolling in his blood. When was the last time he had hope? He didn't even remember the last time he had something to hang on to like this, something real and promising. Three and a half years, his father had promised to figure 'something' out, but nothing ever came because of course he wasn't willing to actually fight against the Authority. Until he got drunk and held a gun to Rainer's chin, apparently, but that wasn't doing Jason any favours.

But Irén gave him something real. A timeline, a believable way out.

It lasted right up until Verrit cornered Jason in the sleeping hall. Verrit loomed over Jason, catching his arm and breathing hotly in his ear. And everything slid out of Jason's skin, all that bravery and optimism leaving him behind as sure as blood from a severed artery, making him feel cold and empty and stupid.

"I ain't seen you all day," Verrit said. "I hear you have yourself a new friend."

Jason squeezed his eyes shut instead of answering. It wasn't even a question, but he already knew anything he said would lead to something he didn't want. He wished he could sink into the stone and cease to be.

But he only had to survive a few more days, so maybe it was best to let Verrit keep this ugly control.

"Hey," Irén said. Her voice sounded like a nail, driven into the tension in the big hall. And it pierced through Jason's resolve, too, because she sounded so strong and he'd given anything to sound like that again. He used to have a hard voice like that, didn't he? But Verrit and the guards had beaten it out of him. "Fuck off."

Verrit snorted, and it sent a shiver of dread down Jason's spine. "Who the fuck are you, hey?"

"I'm the one who tells you to fuck off," Irén said.

"Irén," Jason whispered. He wasn't even sure she heard him. He wanted to tell her he could handle Verrit for another night or two, and going downstairs gave him a chance to try to connect to the children. But he couldn't say any of those words out loud because they were all dangerous. So he said, "Wait—"

Irén didn't wait. She stepped in front of Jason, but Verrit hadn't let go of Jason's arm, so the three of them were half crushed together. "Go ahead and hit me. Find out how bad this place can be for you."

Verrit laughed, squeezing Jason's arm harder. "You've got everything turned around. I'm the one that makes *your* life hell. This place is mine."

"Verrit."

A guard.

Jason bit his own lip so hard he could taste blood. He hated the way everyone was staring, hated the way the whole sleeping hall seemed to be throbbing with the promise of violence. He should have gone immediately, before Irén had a chance to get involved. Guards were not protectors; they were worse bullies than the proxies in a vicious cycle of shit rolling forever downhill.

"This bitch thinks she can tell me what to do," Verrit said.

"Leave it," the guard said. "It's time to turn in. Make sure everyone is going to bed like they're supposed to."

Verrit looked down at Jason and Irén. The shock and the outrage battled for space in his eyes. When was the last time someone told him no? He probably didn't even remember. He'd been a proxy as long as Jason had been in this place, and he had a small army of inmates who listened to him and made sure this place ran the way he wanted it. But here were Jason and Irén, changing the shape of his life. He squeezed Jason's arm so hard it hurt, so hard Jason's fingers were going numb. Jason wished he could look Verrit in the eye and stand up straight, but he couldn't anymore. He stared down at the floor, wishing it would split open and swallow him so he didn't have to be in this moment. He wanted the freedom everyone kept promising, but it felt more like the people who were supposed to help him were going to get him killed. Just because they won now didn't mean Verrit was going to accept the loss. He was going to come back when there weren't so many guards around and make them both pay for this moment.

"Verrit," the guard said again.

Verrit shoved Jason back. Jason staggered and caught the back of Irén's coat, keeping himself on his feet. Irén stood like a pillar, her feet rooted so firmly that nothing could move her. Rezji came through the crowd, grabbing Jason's arm and pulling him back, away, leaving Irén and Verrit glaring at each other.

"She's going to get us killed," Jason whispered. He hated how much his voice trembled, hated how his eyes clouded with tears. He blinked them away as fast as he could, before anyone could see. "He's not going to take it. He's going to get back at her for that."

"Just come," Rezji whispered. "This is how she handles things. She's always been hard like this. She and her brother had a difficult life."

"Fantastic," Jason gasped, wiping his face. "She and her hard life are going to get me killed."

Rezji pointed Jason toward the bunks. "Gather your things. You sleep with us now."

Breathe. That's what Lorne would tell you. Breathe slow, in and out.

Jason kept breathing through clenched teeth, climbing up to his bunk. He pulled open the plank where he'd hidden his letters from his mother. And the paper he'd gotten from Lorne after his mother died, with the names of his siblings and each of their footprints captured in ink. After Verrit ripped one of the letters to pieces, it felt safer to keep them stashed away. But now, he was either going to get out or die, and he wanted these papers with him. His hands shook as he stuffed everything into his pockets.

He followed Rezji up to the top bunks, where her blankets were set with Irén's. People weren't technically allowed to sleep that close together, but no one listened to that rule. Irén had only been here a day and she was already taking and leaving what she wanted, apparently.

"You're fine, Jason," Rezji whispered. "Everything is good."

Jason shook his head, but he didn't dare speak. People were whispering through the bunks, and Jason could feel the sharpness of it, the anger that simmered. Verrit wasn't going to be happy, and if he couldn't take it out on Jason, he'd take it out on someone else. Whoever got hurt would resent the three of them, making them even more vulnerable.

Irén came climbing up behind Jason, flopping into her blankets. She grunted at the impact her bones made on the wood. She'd forgotten, maybe, that there was no mattress to catch her and cushion her. "Fucking cock," she muttered. "He's not going to give up easy."

"Just forget it," Jason whispered. "Tomorrow I'll go with him and let him do what he wants. It's fine. I'll be fine. I can handle him——"

"I've got it," Irén whispered, catching Jason's hand. "You shouldn't have to do that."

"This is how the world works," Jason scoffed. "We're all meat for someone else to consume, and we decide how many pieces of ourselves we're willing to give away to survive. It's not about what I should and shouldn't have to do—it's the reality here. We shouldn't have to register, either. We shouldn't have to decide between different kinds of torture and enslavement. Compliance is torture, the Rift is torture, a life of running and hiding and lying is torture. This is the world we live in. 'Should' is fucking meaningless."

Rezji grabbed Jason's shoulders from behind, squeezing them. He was being too loud, his voice carrying too far.

"You're right," Irén whispered. "We shouldn't have to. That's what we're fighting for, Jason. You'll see."

Jason shook his head. He wanted to say that whatever Irén convinced herself she was fighting for didn't exist here. Davik Kaine could shuffle his paperwork and throw money at whoever he wanted and build an illusion of control, but this place was still the Rift, packed with people who shouldn't have to be here, people who didn't want to be bad meat but were still meat anyway. But he couldn't say any of those things, because the fear sat too thick in his throat, and he couldn't speak or he'd start sobbing. All the things he shouldn't have to do, or say, or endure would chip pieces out of him, and there wouldn't be anything left.

46

STELLA

DAY 36

"**M**iss Rhydderch? Can you hear me?"

She wanted to tell him to go away. Let her die here in this cursed wagon with her clothes soaked and her toes numb and the wound on her face aching distantly and the blood still crusted on her cheek.

"I don't know if you can hear me—but in case you can, we've stopped at the roadhouse. Means we're only a couple days away from Yaelsmuir. They've got the wagon parked in the barn with the horses and all that. I never got the hang of barns. Fuckin' hate the smell, you know? All that horse shit. This place is *pungent*."

Moldering hay and lingering horse shit and the particular ammonia scent of too much urine built up. The roadhouse didn't clean their barn enough. She must have fallen asleep at some point because she didn't remember arriving here.

Stella peered through the hazy darkness, looking for that golden palomino that had carried her into this mess. She saw it, a flash in the darkness, that lovely blond mane glittering in the light of the moon that came in the window. Had her captors tried to explain the woman in the back of the wagon? Or had they flashed their Authority badges and said she was under arrest. Perhaps that's why the man with the scratches on his face was here. To guard her. Perhaps they'd all take turns guarding her until morning.

"I think you should have a drink of water, but I won't force you."

He rested the waterskin beside Stella's hand, then backed away. He perched himself on the wall of the wagon, the wall that hemmed Stella in, making it hard to see the world when she lay prone. He was as far away as possible, perhaps, without leaving the wagon completely. She tried to flex her fingers toward the waterskin, but they were numb and distant, tingling with discomfort. Was it the Wrath, disconnecting her from her own body?

"My name is Duskan, by the way. Duskan Hillbraun. I don't know why I felt you needed to know that, it's just that I've never been so good at chattering. Feels like I should say something so you know you ain't alone. Mustn't feel like much comfort, the way everyone's been treating you. But, I don't know. I'm trying. This ain't exactly what I imagined when I signed on to hunt a fugitive. They said you were dangerous, that's why they shipped us off with that smoke grenade. I guess it was easy to believe 'cause I figure all the tainted are dangerous, but..." He sighed. "This ain't what I imagined at all."

Stella moved, as slowly and quietly as she could. Just her toes, wiggling slowly in her boots, to make sure she could still feel them. The stiffness of the new riding boots had saved her, apparently—her toes weren't numb like her hands were, so maybe it wasn't the Wrath. Just the rope, tied too tight. But that was scarce comfort. How could she get her hands free if she couldn't feel them?

"I didn't put it together, when Elsworth offered me the bronze." Words tumbled out of him with an air of desperation. Like he couldn't stand the silence. "He said he was terribly sorry about what happened at the station house, and paid for me to see a healer. He made it sound like it was an unfortunate accident, as if I'd slipped and fallen down the stairs. That really made me angry. I figured he was trying to shut me up, since it was his *face of the Authority* who fucked me up like that. Would make the Authority look bad if I pressed charges against Elsworth's star puppet. But he also paid me enough to wipe out all the stupid debts I had at the card houses, and more still. Said I deserved it for my years of service and all that. Hard to stay mad when you've got that many crowns in your pocket, you know? That's when he offered me the bronze and told me about this assignment, hunting someone down for General Clannaugh, a healer missing all these years and hiding in Yaelsmuir as a whisperer. But then you said his name, like you know him. Blackwood, yeah?"

Stella turned. She couldn't help it. His name hooked on to her, tried to spark something like hope. The man—Duskan—wasn't even looking at her. His face was turned toward the nearest window, moonlight painting his features, the scabs turned to dark splotches.

"Duncreek said you'd been fucking some tinman-turned-traitor, so of course it's him. Tashué fucking Blackwood. You know, he beat me 'cause of you and Duncreek. Blackwood said you'd been attacked, passed around a sketch of Duncreek's ugly face, and I said *he's doing us a favour*, and he fucking…" He shook his head. "Never seen a man move like that. I been in fights at the pub, but that day, he woulda killed me if no one had stopped him. Took the whole fucking station house to stop him. Broke my nose and my cheekbones. So some part of me wants to hate you, you know? Wants to blame you for all of it. My whole fucking life, it's sliding off a cliff, 'cause of you and him and Siras. Feels like just my luck." He shook his head, looking down at her finally. He startled a little —his hands went tense, and his eyes went wide, like he was surprised to see her turned toward him. Surprised by her presence and her attention even though he was talking to her. "Can you hear me?"

Tears pricked the corners of her eyes again. Sweet North Star, she was so tired of crying. But the casual cruelty of this man talking about how much he hated Tashué, of him saying *some part of me wants to hate you* as if he expected her to be grateful for the modicum of effort he was putting into seeing her as a real human being, that stung worse than the deep and unforgiving hatred of the other men.

"There was a time in my life when I wanted him to like me," Duskan went on, oblivious to her tears. "Blackwood, I mean. He's a war hero and all that, so I thought maybe I could learn a thing or two from him. But he always had some shit thing to say, like he never thought I'd measure up to him and fucking Mahalouwan 'cause I didn't serve. But I think if I stood aside and let Duncreek do whatever he wanted to you, 'cause you're tainted? Then I would be every bit the slug Blackwood said I was, and let me tell you, I'd rather fucking rot than let that bastard be right about a single fucking thing."

The creak of an open door. A horse snorted, the stamp of hooves in a stall. Stella squeezed her eyes shut. Where was that numbness when she needed it to block all these cursed tears?

"Hillbraun, you gonna come eat or what?"

"I thought I'd see if I could get her to drink."

A huff. "I figured you'd say that. Brought you a bowl. You want a pint, too? It ain't bad. It ain't *good* but it'll do."

"Usually I'd say yes, but fucking hell it stinks in here."

"Then come in, and you don't have to smell the stink."

Duskan Hillbraun shrugged. Whoever had come to see him sighed. Stella opened her eyes again. Straining her ears for any hint that Siras was out there, too. Duskan sat at the very edge of her peripheral vision. A hand stretched over the back of the wagon. A bowl of soup, steaming.

"The sooner you realize they ain't the same as you and me, the easier this job will get. I know you look at her and see a woman, but she ain't. She's rotten from the inside. There's a reason we call 'em tainted, yeah? And if you're tempted to tell me she ain't *like* that 'cause look how quiet she is and look how pretty her bright green eyes are, remember all them bodies we found. The only reason we were able to find 'em is 'cause her and her kind slaughtered a bunch of ours. So she's gonna roll all the way back to Yaelsmuir nice and quiet, instead of using her Talent on us? Count your lucky stars. You should know better—you had the tin all that time, and your face looks like half-chewed shit because of that taint-lover Blackwood. You *know* what these people are capable of. So quit making mooney eyes at her just 'cause she's got a pretty face, and wake up to the reality that she's the enemy."

Stella exhaled slowly, a bit of the pain releasing its grip. This part was easier, its familiarity making it catch on the armour she'd built around her soul so it didn't have the power to wound her the same way.

"If she's the enemy, how come we're following Duncreek, hey?" Duskan asked. "He's tainted—by your logic, he's the enemy, too."

"Course he is. Don't you think for a second that I don't sleep with one eye open, keeping watch for him. The sooner we hand her over to Clannaugh, the better, because then we'll be done with him. I'll even let him take all the credit. But Hillbraun? I'm only gonna tell you this part once. You listenin' close, son?"

"Yes, sir."

"That man, tainted though he is, has been carrying a badge longer than you been pulling pud, and that earns him a measure of respect in my books. Just a half measure, mind. Since he's tainted and all. Your badge is fresh-minted, so I'll give you the benefit of the doubt, especially since you were beat to shit by your own station commander, so maybe you don't know how we hold ranks, us bronzemen. So I'm telling you, good and clear, that if you even put your hands on another bronzeman again without good reason..." The man sucked through his teeth, making an ugly hissing sound for effect. "Now, it's one thing if Duncreek tries to put his hands on a good clean woman, but I'll step in myself if that happens. Can't have the likes of him mingling. He wants to take his due with a tainted cunt, though? You best mind your own fucking business, or else I'll start thinking you aren't cut out for this job. And you don't want me thinking that, do you, son?"

Silence stretched. Stella turned toward Hillbraun, just enough that she could see his face again. The other man wasn't looking at her at all, didn't see her move. But Duskan stared down at her, his teeth clenched so hard, his jaw bulged and shifted beneath his patchy beard. Would he say something? Was there enough steel in his spine that he would counter any of those ugly words?

The wagon thumped from down below the floor, like the other Officer had kicked it from underneath. Duskan jumped so bad, he spilt soup all over his hands, his expression flashing with pain.

"I said, you don't want me thinking that, do you?"

"No, sir," Duskan whispered, his eyes sliding off Stella's face and settling on the empty space between them. "I don't want you thinking I'm not cut out for the job."

"Good answer. Look, I know it ain't easy, the first one? Especially a woman. Would'a been easier if we'd left her dead behind us, cause then you didn't have to look her in the eye so much. That'll be how we usually do things. But Clannaugh and Elsworth said they wanted the bitch back, and they wanted to know how their smoke worked, so here we are. You get through it and it'll be easier after this."

"Yes, sir."

Footsteps and that squeaky hinge and then the barn was dark again. Duskan cursed. And then threw the bowl across the barn, the ceramic shattering against a post.

"This isn't what I signed up for," Duskan whispered into the darkness. "This isn't what I wanted."

How she hated them. Every single one of them. All of the heartbroken compassion she felt when she saw the boy in the cave was burned away by their viciousness. By Duskan Hillbraun's cowardly complicity.

Duskan sank down beside Stella, wiping his hands on his trousers. "This isn't what I signed up for," he said again as if it would protect him from the evil of what was happening.

Stella flexed her hands fingers again, willing them out of their horrible numbness. They moved, closing around the waterskin. She licked her lips with her sandpaper tongue, clearing her throat. It rasped, sore and dry. But she forced the words up anyway.

"I didn't sign up for this either." She tried harder to grasp the water-skin, but she couldn't even feel the texture of it. Fear touched her—how long had her hands been so badly numb? If they were denied blood flow long enough, the tissue could die, causing permanent damage. "I was trying to protect my daughter from people like him."

The light faded—clouds must have slid in front of the moon. Wind howled outside, making the walls of the barn rattle.

"Sounds like another storm's coming," he said, sidestepping the uncomfortable conversation that Stella's word might have inspired. "If it rains again, Officer West will probably want to stay. He wasn't real happy about riding through the rain last time, but he said he needed to gain ground on you."

Stella didn't say anything. What was the point?

"I hope she gets away," Duskan whispered, so softly Stella almost didn't hear him over the ruckus of the rain. His impotent little rebellion, sending those words out into the storm, so quietly that he could deny he'd even said them.

47

LORNE
DAY 37

S weat. Gloves. Weights. The ring. Jogging. Fuck jogging especially. Davik led him on a looping track that meandered through the forest between Cattle Bone Bay and Drystone, then twisted out to the plain that stood in the shadow of the Breeding Program. Davik paused there, every morning. Looked at the high walls and the tiny specks that were the guards on top, his hands on his hips, his breath making plumes in the cold air.

Rain hit them hard on the way back, melting the accumulated snow away, turning the streets to giant puddles as the drains clogged with stubborn ice. Winter, it seemed, hadn't yet secured its hold on the city. But miserable weather was Yaelsmuir's specialty, no matter the season.

A figure waited for them when they got back to the pugilist club. Standing in the rain beneath a black umbrella, his collar turned up around his face. Vasska—he looked so elegant, standing there. The brights were still glowing because the morning was so miserable and dim, their light bleeding down from the tram track overhead, making the misting rain shimmer as it fell around Vasska's umbrella. He'd been coming to the club every day to meet Allie and Ishmael and escort them to wherever they went to work on their print pages. The ones that detailed Tashué's career. Ten years serving in the bloodiest, most harrowing posts of his time. The sort of deployments Lorne used to hear rumours about, the sort of action unseasoned troops talked about with a mixture of awe and terror. Lorne used to wonder what it must be like, to go into carnage like that and come out the other side. And then he walked the Blood Road and survived and wished with all his soul that he could forget.

He didn't know Tashué's career was so ugly at least not until he saw those pages. Everyone talked about the Black Ridge because it was the Black fucking Ridge, but every posting he had before that was a legend maker. When Lorne asked about it as Rowan showed them both the latest page that the printing press had made, Tashué shrugged.

"The Jitabvi are used for the worst shit," he said, as if it was no big deal. "Some of the other Generals called us cannon fodder."

Fucking cannon fodder. That lived in Lorne's mind for a while. He said it so casually, like it was a thing he accepted about himself. Except at some point, he must have rejected it, because he dug in on the Ridge.

"Mr. Kaine," Vasska said, half-shouting over the rain. Why hadn't he gone in to meet Allie and Ishmael? "Your pugilist looks half-drowned."

Davik stopped short of Vasska, running his hands through his hair to shake the water out. "Mr. Czarny. You don't have to stand in the rain—you're welcome inside any time."

Vasska's mouth hooked in a bit of a grin, and he tilted his umbrella closer to Davik and Lorne, inviting them under. Fat load of good it did. Water wasn't landing in Lorne's face anymore, but it ran freely down his back, under the collar of his jacket.

"I thought I would make sure your delivery went smoothly, Mr. Kaine. Since the match is almost here, I thought it would be prudent to make sure you have everything you need."

He tilted his head toward the alley beside the pugilist club. A coal wagon stood in the overhang—the driver had turned his horse team around and backed them into the alley wagon first, so the pair of draft mares were looking out at the street. Rain sluiced down their big bodies in sinuous ribbons, and the driver hunched low beneath a waxed cloak.

"Coal?" Lorne asked. He looked up at Davik. He was missing something, and it made him feel like a fucking idiot. "For the boilers?"

Vasska grinned. "Sure. Coal that needs careful handling."

Davik's face broke into a smile. "Thank you, Mr. Czarny. I appreciate the care." He elbowed Lorne in the side. "Go get everyone."

"For *coal?*" Lorne asked.

Vasska's eyes danced when he smiled again, like he was holding in a laughter. "It's a good thing you're very attractive, Mr. Coswyn. You look very good with your gloves on, and your fighting skills are second to none. You've got an excellent mind for boxing."

Lorne flushed, pushing rainwater out of his face. He grasped for some clever comeback, but his words were failing him. All he could think about was how wet the air was, how tired his muscles were from fucking jogging of all the ridiculous things, how cold and wet and miserable his feet were, how much he wanted to put dry clothes on. And now he felt like shit for the way he talked to Vasska the night everyone told him about energy units. Vasska didn't seem to be holding a grudge, and that made it worse.

"Just go get everyone," Davik huffed. "You'll see."

"Sure, Dav."

Lorne peeled away. Inside, the main hall was chaos. More and more kegs were being rolled in, and they were running new taps to make space for all of them. A delivery of furniture was piling up in the far corner, stacked in wood crates. People from the league had come to inspect the ring and the scale in Davik's office.

Lorne trudged up the stairs, leaving a trail of water behind him as he went. Fucking rain. Up, up. László in the kitchen.

"You look terrible," László laughed. "What did Davik do to you, toss you in the Brightwash for a swim?"

"It's raining," Lorne said.

"No shit it's raining."

Lorne grinned, stalking closer to László. Slow, so László wouldn't know Lorne was coming for him. László wasn't wearing a shirt again, eternally bare chested like clothes were an insult to him. "It's so nice to see you every morning, so cheerful and beautiful. I really appreciate you, László."

László took a step back. "Don't you dare fucking touch me. Get away from me!"

Lorne lunged for him, and there wasn't enough room for him to get away, and Lorne caught ahold of his hand. László squealed, laughed, twisted, trying to get away, but Lorne had him. Lorne wrapped his arms around László's waist and dragged him into a hug, pressing all his damp, cold clothes against László's bare skin. László squealed more, squirming in Lorne's grasp.

"You bastard!" László laughed. "Get off me!"

"Let me show you how much I appreciate you," Lorne said, squeezing László harder. He pressed his face into the hollow beneath

László's jaw. Water dripped from Lorne's hair, trickling down László's chest, making László's skin prickle with gooseflesh. The big alligator tooth on László's necklace dug into Lorne's chest, and he could feel László's heartbeat against his face, strong and steady and pulsing in László's throat. "I've never been important enough to have my own healer before, and lucky me, I get the very best! Why are you making so much noise? What's the problem?"

László laughed, his back thumping against the big counter in the centre of the room. He put his hands on Lorne's chest and gave a half-hearted push. And it felt so good to stand there, their bodies pressed together. It had been a long time since he felt comfortable with another person. László's skin was always so warm, and he always smelled like whatever he was cooking, the scent of garlic permanently ingrained into his fingertips.

"Alright, I give up. I'm soaked now. Thanks so much. Go put real clothes on before I have to heal the chills, on top of everything else."

Lorne gave a long-suffering sigh, letting László go. "Fine. Don't let me appreciate you, then. I see how it is."

"I'll appreciate you more when you're warm and dry, how's that?"

Lorne headed for the hallway, fighting out of his coat. "Dav wants everyone back downstairs. Vasska's brought something, I don't know. They're laughing about coal, but I'm missing something."

"Vasska brought coal?" László asked.

"Yeah, I don't get it."

"You're adorable."

Into his room, stripping the old rags away. He had to admit, there was something nice about putting his new clothes on after they were done jogging every day. It was like he peeled his past away and put on his future. But at some point when he was discarding his old clothes, the guilt crept in. He shouldn't be thinking about how good László's body felt when Jason was still in the Rift. "What's that supposed to mean?"

László grinned at him, leaning on the doorframe to Lorne's bedroom. "It means I like watching you take your clothes off, and I'll do all the thinking for both of us."

More blushing, more guilt. "If you're the one in charge of thinking, we're in deep shit."

48

ISHMAEL
DAY 37

Tashué's hands were warm and surprisingly tender as they slid across Ishmael's leg, like he was memorizing the external texture of Ishmael's muscles before he used his Talent. Except he must have committed the wounds to memory by now—he tended to Ishmael's wounds every morning and every night.

When Tashué's Talent swirled, it was as wide and comfortable as a blanket, draping Ishmael's whole body with familiarity.

"How's it going with Davik?" Ishmael whispered. Buying himself some time before the pain roared through him. The apartment above the pugilist club was quiet for now; Allie had gone ahead to the printing press to make sure the pages from last night were dry and ready to distribute, and Rowan followed. Davik went jogging in the morning, no matter the weather, and now he dragged Lorne with him. László started the day in the kitchen, which was the opposite end of the apartment from the room that Ishmael and Tashué shared because there weren't enough rooms for all of them to have their own.

Tashué shrugged. Sighed. "I don't know. He likes to talk, doesn't he? I draw the floor plan of station houses, I draw what I saw in the Breeding Program. We talk about proof. He says paper isn't enough and we need to get children. I lay down concrete ideas, about the trams, about the factories—and then he goes back to waffling about how we don't need proof. How we should tear it down. I can't tell if he's full of shit or if he just… doesn't trust me."

"A little of both, maybe," Ishmael said.

Tashué's mouth pulled down in the corners, mostly hidden by his beard, his eyes crinkling with his latent frustration. "You think he's afraid of Clannaugh?"

"I think he didn't get to where he is by trusting men that just rolled into the city," Ishmael said. "I think if he is planning something, he's taking all of your suggestions to his people so they can sort it out on their end without you. That way, you can't sabotage it, and you can't sell him up."

Tashué huffed, his teeth flashing in the dim early morning light. More frustration. He looked toward his cavalry sabre, sitting on the mantle like he longed to use it. He'd polished it at some point, probably when he couldn't sleep, the metal and the oil shining with promise. "So then why tell me about a fucking bank robbery?"

"Has László given you any details at all about the bank?"

Tashué shook his head, refocusing on Ishmael. His hands sliding down to Ishmael's ankle. It was so intimate, it burned. The easiest way to deal with all the shit was to lean into a body. Any body. Someone familiar, someone he didn't know. It didn't matter. And here was Tashué, and Ishmael knew what they could do to each other… but Tashué wouldn't. He held Ishmael at a distance. And Ishmael would take it personally, except that he seemed to hold everyone at a distance, now. His eyes always stared off at something only he could see, like he was grappling with something. Stella, maybe, and the wreckage of whatever happened between them. Or maybe it was his Talent, buzzing in his skull. As long as Ishmael had known him, he insisted he didn't have much Talent at all, and now that lie was ripped right open, the evidence left behind in the Dunnenbrahl. The power to explode trees and crush bones. Maybe suddenly being able to break things so horribly would make Ishmael a little distant, too. Was Tashué afraid of hurting people by accident now?

"Sometimes he says something," Tashué said finally, "but I think he's full of shit. László, I mean. He's probably baiting me. To see if I'll back out."

"Or to see if we'll report it back to someone who might try to stop it," Ishmael said. "Wolfe, or Iwan. I don't know who they're most worried about."

Tashué shrugged. "They're right to worry. Aren't they?"

Ishmael huffed, grabbing Tashué's shirtsleeve. The Bellmore clothes fit him fabulously, and helping him button his shirts every morning only made the intimacy worse. "It's not that simple."

"László said Davik thinks we're bait," Tashué said, his voice dropping to a whisper so quiet that Ishmael could barely hear him. "Said Powell sent us down here because he thought Davik would kill us. So, Davik is playing nice, because he figures Powell will come for a fight if we conveniently disappear."

"László told you that, did he?"

Tashué glanced up, his eyes fixing on Ishmael's face for the first time that morning. He looked angry, like he'd been simmering at low heat since they got here, like parts of him were expanding so fast that they pushed at the edges of him. In a strange way, the anger suited him these days. Like he finally had a purpose for all of it. "Is it true? Are we bait so Powell Iwan has his excuse to wage war against Davik?"

Ishmael shook his head. "He wouldn't do that to me."

"Must be nice," Tashué said, his eyes dropping back down as he checked the bottom of Ishmael's feet, touching each place that had been a vicious, angry gash a few days ago. "Having a relationship like that with someone like Powell Iwan. So you know for sure he's not playing games with your life."

"It's all a game, Mr. Guinne," Ishmael said. "A vicious, ugly game, and we're all playing our parts."

"Ishmael—"

"No, I'm serious," Ishmael said. "That's what Deri taught me. It's how we survive. It's all a beautiful, horrible game. There are winners and losers, and you don't want to be a loser. That's it."

Tashué shook his head.

Ishmael huffed. "You're tempted to like László because he's young, and he's charming, and he's smarter than he lets on. And the part of you that's desperate to be a good father has taken a shine to him because he's got that look in his eye that a young man gets when he spent his life growing up with shit. But you should ask him how *his* father died, Tashué. You should ask him how the *Dripping Bucket* got its name. You should find out exactly how much blood that beautiful, brilliant, fucked up boy is willing to shed for Davik Kaine."

"Why would I do that?" Tashué asked. He pressed his thumbs into Ishmael's ankle, testing the joint, making Ishmael wince with too much movement. "Why do you bait Davik and fight with him when we're supposed to be making this work?"

"Because he knows me," Ishmael muttered. "And if I'm suddenly all sweet and friendly and compliant to his whims, he'll know I'm up to something."

"Can't have that," Tashué grunted. "Seeing as we're here to make nice with them so you can kill him."

"This is how it goes," Ishmael whispered. "This is the game you signed up for. For Jason, remember? The first one is always the hardest because you always find yourself sympathizing for the other side. People don't fight for nothing—there's always a good reason for it, and when you spend time with them and you get to know them, you can see their reasons written on their souls. You can't help but wonder if you're doing the right thing. This is why they don't deploy us alone for a while. They send us with someone appropriately cynical, so our handlers can shake us out of it and tell us we're doing this for a reason and that reason is bigger than any individual players."

Tashué shifted, sitting on the edge of the bed and pulling Ishmael's shirt open. His fingers brushed lightly over all the scabs, catching on the stiff twine of each stitch holding the wounds closed. "These are ready to take out."

Ishmael nodded. Tashué stood, walking away. All coiled tension, like a mainspring that would damage everything around it if it fell out of place. He pulled a pair of tweezers and scissors from the desk by the window, where they sat among all the notebooks Lorne had rescued from his apartment.

"So, you're my appropriately cynical handler, is that it?" Tashué asked, sinking back down on the edge of the bed. "Keeping my young and idealistic soul in line with the mission."

"The objective," Ishmael corrected. "We called it the objective."

Tashué grunted in that way he did when he was unimpressed. "Sounds very mysterious and important."

"Yes, that's what the division likes people to think."

It was slow work, cutting the stitches and then pulling them out, since Tashué's right hand struggled with such fine details. The radiator filled the silence, clicking and groaning as the rain pattered on the window. Each stitch caught on the scabs that had formed around it, the twine dragging rough through his skin. The scars would track white lies through the tattoos, once everything was healed, like a fissure through the fine mosaic. Seemed appropriate.

"You never asked about my tattoos," Ishmael said. The silence was going to drive him insane. "We've known each other twelve years, and you never asked."

Tashué cocked his head to one side, turning to Ishmael ever so slightly while also keeping his eyes on his work. "Would you have told me if I had asked?"

"I don't know. Maybe. They aren't all for the division, so I guess I could have told you about some of them. Everybody else asks at some point and it always irritated me. But you never asked, and that felt strange, too."

Tashué shrugged. "Some people get tattoos because they want to talk about them. But those people will open the door to start the conversation. Other people get tattoos for themselves because it's the only way to process the pain. Veterans with tattoos are usually that second kind. I figured if you wanted to tell me, you would. If not?" He shrugged again. "It's not my place."

The last stitch came free, and Tashué used a cloth to wipe away the bit of blood that oozed from the places were the scabs broke. The silence again. The itching, burning, restless silence. Once Tashué was done with the small wounds, he would use his Talent on Ishmael's knee, and then the real pain would burn through him. Ishmael was grateful for it, and he knew he was more mobile than he should have been, but fuck it hurt. He was positive that getting healed by Tashué Blackwood was more painful than any other healing he had ever endured.

"Do you know what ifjahim is?" Ishmael asked. Maybe he was being a coward, buying himself time. Or maybe the truth was that he was that first type of person. The sort that got tattoos and wanted to talk about them, wanted it so badly that sometimes he felt like he was cracking at his seams because the pressure of the truth was so powerful—but he couldn't. Not before. Talking about what he did for the diplomatic division was treason. Except what did treason mean now? "There were a lot of Qasani up in the Black Mountains, so I wonder if you heard the term before while you were serving."

Tashué wiped Ishmael's shoulder again. "It means soldier, I thought."

Ishmael nodded. "It means literally soldier of blood. Elite and all that."

Tashué grinned, just a bit, his amber eyes flicking up to Ishmael's face. "An elite soldier who's a shit shot."

Ishmael laughed. "Well, the word has been around longer than guns have, so being a good shot isn't a requirement."

"What are the requirements?"

Ishmael slid his hand over his shoulder, over the scabs and the tattoos. "We're not a war-driven people like Jitabvi hotbloods. But our culture does make room for people who *need* to fight—to defend the Qasani way of life, to protect their families and their home. A soldier can mean a few different things, it's not only a fighter. An Im-Aqi could technically call themselves a warrior, because they fight hard to keep our culture alive at the temples, especially when we aren't on the mountain anymore. But ifjahim, we kill. Life is sacred, and the gods don't want us to take killing lightly. We mark our bodies with the lives we've taken so we don't forget. The gods will want an accounting of all the lives when we die because life belongs to them, not to us. Bones, blood, and the soul —it all belongs to them, and we're not meant to decide. When we destroy a human life, they'll want to know why."

Tashué's eyes swept across Ishmael's body, across every tattoo. Across the scars that often sat beside the ink. "What happens if the gods think you've killed too many people? Or if some of them weren't for a good enough reason?"

"I don't know," Ishmael admitted. "Some people say Ishka will snuff out your soul if you were too irresponsible. Others say Ishka will hold you for longer, before she sends you back to your next life—to spend some time with you, to teach you how precious it all is. No one really knows for sure, of course. How can they? The will of the gods is not for us to know. We're all trying our best to figure it out and fumble through this life. That's probably a question for my priest. Although I'll bet he doesn't know, either. Humans can't grasp the will of the gods, not really. The best we can do is guess, and try. And pray a lot."

"So it's true?" Tashué asked. "The diplomatic division—they're assassin soldiers?"

It was Ishmael's turn to let the silence stretch. He was supposed to deny this part. But fuck Maes. "That's one of our jobs, yes."

Tashué wiped his hands with a rag, looking toward the window and watching the rain dance a while. Not all that long ago, Ishmael watched the rain dance on Leony's face, the pair of them high and horny for each other and basking in all the possibilities of the future. Tashué's expression was more serious than Leony's had been, his shoulders loose and tired. Ishmael didn't sleep well because of the pain. Which meant he knew Tashué didn't sleep well, either.

Tashué sighed finally, stirring himself out of the stillness. "How does killing for the Dominion Army mean you're protecting the Qasani way of life?"

It was Ishmael's turn to watch the window. More fucking rain. This was a rainy season, even by Yaelsmuir standards. Something cold settled deep in his bones, even though it was always plenty warm in Davik's home. Like his marrow remembered how long he was out in the rain, bleeding and dying as Tashué led that horse through the Dunnenbrahl. "Yaelsmuir has the largest Qasani population of any city outside the borders of the Derccian empire. There was a time when it felt like protecting Dominion interests was protecting them by extension."

"What does it feel like now?"

Ishmael sighed, laying his hand on the mountain tattoo. "I still have to account for the lives, even if I don't know why I fought so long."

Tashué nodded, his eyes sweeping across Ishmael's whole body, studying the ink with this fresh perspective he had. He touched the watch tattoo on Ishmael's forearm, the ink that most people knew about because it showed every time he rolled up his shirtsleeves.

"That one wasn't division related," Ishmael said. The broken watch was the most finely detailed of all his tattoos. "That one is for the men who killed my father."

Tashué nodded. "I'm sorry I didn't ask. I didn't know you wanted me to."

Voices in the kitchen—László and someone else were getting loud, laughing and talking, shattering the illusion that Ishmael and Tashué were alone together. Lorne, probably. Tashué snatched his hand away from Ishmael's arm like they'd been caught doing something, even though no one could see them yet.

"You're healing well," Tashué said, his voice rising to a conversational tone like they hadn't been whispering a moment ago. "Better than I expected. I don't think I need to do anything to the bottoms of your feet anymore. It should take care of itself from here. Unless you want me to? You're taking weight on them well enough."

Ishmael shrugged. "The right side is sore, but I think that's just because my fucking knee hurts and it's messing up the rest of my body."

"Well, maybe you should take it easy for a while," Tashué said. "If you weren't dragging yourself up and down so many stairs every day…"

"Oh yeah, sure, I'll lie here and let you fuck up our lives unsupervised."

"Then I guess you're stuck being sore."

"How are your feet doing?" Ishmael asked.

Tashué shrugged, settling beside Ishmael's knee, resting his hands on it again. His fingers danced over the mountain tattoo, the settled around Ishmael's knee. "Well enough, all things considering. Ready?"

Ishmael groaned. "No."

"We don't have all day, soldier. I have to get back to fucking up our lives."

Ishmael groaned again. The anticipation of the pain made him want to kick Tashué in the face so the big bastard would leave him alone. But he needed to be mobile, needed to be on his feet and involved. Once he didn't need the cane anymore, he'd feel better. At least his job was mostly sedentary for now, helping Allie write articles, helping everyone with the printing press so they could get as many pages out as possible. The hardest part was all the stairs, like Tashué said. So, he resisted the very good excuse to kick Tashué like the bastard deserved, and he grabbed his pillow instead. Pulled it over his face so he could pretend he was coping. Deri would laugh at him, if he were here. But Deri would never face a healer without a shit load of opium in his system first, so for all the laughing, he wasn't any good at dealing with it, either.

Tashué's Talent shifted. Ishmael could feel the change, from a warm blanket to a burning pressure that felt like his knee was going to explode from the inside out. Vicious, burning through every nerve, every sense, until Ishmael couldn't think. Couldn't breathe. Healing with Talent was always shit, but none of the healers he'd seen before made it hurt this much.

He bit the pillow, and he tried not to make any noise, but fuck, it *hurt*.

The door swung open, spilling light from the hallway, and Tashué's Talent relented, leaving Ishmael gasping and half-delirious with the echo of the pain.

"Vasska's got a load of coal or something," Lorne said. "Davik wants us to come down and help. Maybe we're supposed to unload it, I don't know."

49

TASHUÉ
DAY 37

They had to go out in the rain to get into the coal cellar, into the ugly cold. Ishmael walked with a cane, and he was still slow on the stairs, but otherwise he was moving almost normally. It was too easy and too tempting for Tashué to let himself believe they were something like safe here. The raids they expected hadn't come yet, and Ishmael was getting better, and Tashué's Talent was a thing he could almost master. With time and patience, he'd learn to trust it soon. He still had to concentrate to keep it restrained—for all that László offered to teach him things, taking care of Lorne was a full roster of work, so he didn't have time. Or maybe he didn't have the inclination—the boys were almost inseparable, a pair of idiots connected at the hip, their every waking moment dedicated to giving Lorne a half decent chance at surviving his first match.

But of course it was stupid to let himself be comfortable here. Things would get ugly eventually. Like Ishmael said, they were here for a reason.

The driver was unloading the wagon by the time they hit the street, shovelling coal from the back and tossing it into the open cellar door. The rain helped keep the dust down, and when Davik led them to the cellar, another pair of men with shovels were spreading the coal out so it could dry before they piled it in the corner.

"Dav, why are we here to stand around and stare at coal?" Lorne asked. "It's fucking cold out here."

"Take it easy, Mr. Lightning," Davik said. "Don't strain your pretty head, or you'll melt something."

Lorne huffed, moving his body in that anxious shudder of someone to keep his blood moving to stay warm. "How come everyone knows what the fuck we're doing but me?"

"We don't know, either, kid," Ishmael said.

"Thank fuck for that," Lorne muttered.

The wagon driver whistled from the street, and the men put their shovels aside, heading back up into the rain. They were only gone a few moments, and then they climbed back down, carrying a crate between them. The wood was stained back from the coal dust, dripping from the rain. Leather straps on either end of the crate made it easier for them to carry it. They rested it on the floor, far away from the piles.

Davik grabbed a crowbar off the wall, offering it to Tashué. "What say you, Mr. Guinne? You want to do the honours?"

"What am I opening, Davik?" Tashué asked, but he took the crowbar anyway. The iron was cold from being left in the cellar. "Is it going to go boom?"

"You think I'd be standing so close to you if I was setting you up to be blown away?" Davik scoffed. "Just open it, before Mr. Lightning's skin crawls right off him."

Tashué huffed the crowbar in both hands. His heart hammered too fast—whatever it was, it had to be dangerous or at least illegal for Davik and Vasska to be hiding it under so much coal, but at least Davik was still standing close, like he said. He was excited and not afraid. Tashué jammed the end of the crowbar under the lid, throwing his weight down on it to pry the lid up. The exertion pulled the most at the wound on his ribs, but it felt good to move. To do something. So much of his daily life was arguing with Davik and struggling with his Talents.

Nails squealed as they were forced out of the wood. Another wrench down, and the corner was lifted. The exertion felt good, like his muscles were finally coming awake for the first time since the forest, all of the aches and pains settled to the background. A job that he could do with his body and his strength instead of grappling with his Talent so much. The second corner opened faster, and then with two sides up, Davik grabbed the top and twisted it off, leaning it against the wall. The contents were wrapped in waxed canvas, and Tashué pulled the edge back.

Guns.

At first, Tashué thought they were Imburleighs—the oiled barrels and the stunning curly marble stocks were clearly the highest quality. But László grabbed a gun and hefted it out, and Tashué spotted the crest. It wasn't an Imburleigh, that was for sure. But he hadn't seen that crest on any other gun he'd come across in his long years, and he'd thought he'd seen them all—the insignia looked like a donkey.

"Holy shit, Dav, are these the Uhls?" László whispered, his voice gone soft and reverent.

"Aye, laddie, these are the Uhls." Davik grabbed one, too, sliding his thumb over the crest. "First run out of the new factory—they've started production before the whole thing is built to help 'em fund the construction."

"Who makes Uhl rifles?" Tashué asked. "I thought Uhl was the man who invented the rifled barrel, and he sold the patent to Imburleigh. Who's making rifles with his name, and how'd they manage to get the right to use his name for their crest?"

"You know your gun history, Mr. Guinne," László said, his voice breathy and excited, his eyes glittering like those of a predator.

Tashué shrugged. "They made us learn all this shit at the Academy. Said we should know the history of the guns saving our lives, so we'd appreciate them more."

"Mallory Imburleigh is making the Uhls," Ishmael said, his voice low and almost angry. "She's building a factory in Obisza. How'd you get ahold of them, Davik?"

"Did you steal them?" Vasska asked.

"Mr. Czarny, how could you accuse me of such base behaviour?" Davik asked with a grin.

"I'll take that as a yes," Vasska said.

The men came down with a second crate, laying it beside the first.

"You stole rifles from the new Uhl factory?" Ishmael asked. "How? Who were they for—how long before their rightful owner notices they're missing?"

Davik sighed. "Relax, Saeati. You think I don't know how to move weapons? I know you think you're the smartest man in the room all the time, but I've been moving guns a long fucking time, yeah?"

"Why fucking Uhls, though? One of a kind guns, are you serious? Why not get some Imburleighs? They're everywhere, and then they won't be unique to your people."

Davik flashed that charming, knowing, dangerous smile of his, like his favourite thing in the world was baiting Ishmael. "That's the thing. I want them to be unique. I want this city to know it's my people tearing Rainer to pieces. You know what Imburleighs have that Uhls don't have?"

"Anonymity," Ishmael scoffed.

"Serial numbers. Purchase orders. A trackable trail of paperwork. If I buy 'em, I need an account with the Imburleigh factory to get that many guns in one shot—or I gotta pay a middleman who has their own account. And if I steal 'em, the serial numbers link 'em to whoever bought them in the first place. But these? They left the factory clean. They hardly exist. No serial numbers. The only paperwork on them will be that a whole batch of them went out to early investors. Without serial numbers, no one will know which guns I got. An arms dealer's dream come true."

Ishmael shook his head, shifting his weight to his cane. "Someone is going to report them missing, and everyone will know it was you because who the fuck else has brand new Uhl rifles? Then you'll be on the hook for theft of weapons of warfare along with everything else."

"Can't prove I stole 'em if there's no serial numbers," Davik said with a shrug. "Unclench your asshole, Saeati. I know what I'm doing."

Tashué turned away from them, letting the argument wash over him. Ishmael said he argued so Davik wouldn't suspect they were here for Powell, which was probably exactly right. If Ishmael went a single day without snapping and rolling his eyes and generally being impossible, everyone around him would know something was terribly wrong. Tashué went for the second crate instead of listening to any more bickering, prying it open. László's reverence filled the periphery of Tashué's vision, his hands sliding across the barrel, across the wooden stock, his finger tracing the shape of the trigger. He grabbed the bolt action and slid it open with a metallic chink, the sound sending a shiver of terrible pleasure down Tashué's spine.

"They're nice, Dav," László breathed, the reverence making his voice tremble. "Real fucking nice. How many did you get?"

"Plenty."

The men carried a third crate down as the lid came squealing off the second. Lever action, same as the old repeater he gave to Stella. His whole body ached with longing. He'd hoped to see her in his dreams again like the night after his arrest, but she hadn't come to him. If he could actually trust Davik, he might ask about dreams and Talent, and whether or not he'd really seen her that night or if it was a dream, but talking about her—even with the name Stella—was a dangerous game. When she changed her name and ran, she was fleeing Davik at least as much as she was escaping Bothain.

A fourth crate, a fifth. Ishmael stood out of the way, grimacing at the guns like he was personally offended by them.

"We're going to run out of room," Vasska said, his eyes sweeping the floor. "How many crates in all?"

"Ten," Davik said.

"What about bullets?" László asked. "Guns are only as good as the size of your bullet belt."

"They take the same rounds as any Imburleigh of the same calibre," Davik said. "What's your flavour, Mr. Lightning? Lever or bolt?"

"Whichever," Lorne grunted. "What makes them so special? They look like guns."

László sighed, shooting Lorne a disappointed grimace. "Look like guns. Get the fuck out of here."

The men stacked the crates in the corner to make more room and then went back for the rest. The weight of the gun was so perfect it defied logic. The metal was without flaw, without a single crack or seam or any other evidence that might be left by its casting.

"They were crafted by Talent," Tashué said, the realization leaving him in awe.

"That's exactly right, Mr. Guinne," László said brightly. "You can feel it, can you?"

"I can see it," Tashué said, running his finger across the barrel of his lever action he had. "The gunmetal is different, like it's been arranged. There isn't a single flaw or seam in the metal."

"Everything is perfect," László said. "The regular Imburleighs are excellent, but these are fucking perfect. What'd they cost, Dav?"

"Don't worry about what they cost," Davik said. "Just don't fucking lose them."

Tashué racked the lever action even though the gun was empty. The action was perfect, smooth and sturdy. He shifted the weight of the rifle a few times and then wracked it again with one hand, shooting his arm forward and snapping it back so the gun leapt straight up and back down again, the weight of it carrying the lever open and then shut.

"I didn't mark you for the type to know trick shots," László said his voice beaming with joy.

"We learned a bunch of stupid shit for the parades and the competitions," Tashué said. "It was always a good way to make an impression."

"Are you saying you learned trick shots to get tail?" László asked.

"Knowing Tashué," Ishmael muttered, something like good humour creeping into his voice, but his shoulders were still tense. He walked to one of the open boxes and nudged it with the tip of his cane like he wasn't convinced it wouldn't shift into something else. "Yes."

László laughed, sliding the bolt again. "Colour me impressed."

"Let's go, Mr. Lightning," Davik said. "Pick a gun, and then we're putting the rest away. They can't stay here."

Lorne grabbed a rifle from the crate of bolt actions. "What the fuck am I supposed to do with it? Hang it up beside my boxing gloves?"

"How about you shove it up your ass, see if it improves your mood a little?" Davik said. He chucked Lorne on the shoulder, taking the aggression out of his words. "Why so surly, hey? You said anything for Jason, so here it is."

Lorne opened the bolt action, looking into the chamber. "It's been a while since I needed a rifle, is all. Last time I had one, things didn't go so well for me." He slid the bolt action closed. "I thought I was supposed to learn to box."

"Eventually, boxing matches ain't gonna be enough, laddie."

"That's all of them, Dav," one of the men said.

"Great," Davik said, hand plunging into his pocket. "Thanks, boys. Back to the real work now, yeah?"

The men left their shovels in the basement, heading back out to the rain. Tashué wondered what their real work was.

"How about you, Saeati?" Davik asked, putting a foot on the crate of lever-actions and shoving it across the floor to Ishmael. "What's your flavour?"

"I'm a shit shot," Ishmael said.

"Just take one," Tashué said. "If things are bad enough for you to need one, you can club someone with it."

Ishmael snarled, but nodded. "Pass me yours."

Tashué scooped up a second rifle, hooking them both over his shoulder with the leather straps already attached.

"That driver a real coalman, Mr. Czarny, or is he one of yours?" Davik asked.

"He's mine, Mr. Kaine," Vasska said easily. "Are you looking for more work for him?"

"Does he have a covered wagon? Or a carriage?"

Vasska nodded. "Whatever you need."

"You ready to go, László?" Davik asked.

László slid the bolt action a few times, the sound rattling in the cellar, his eyes glittering with such pure excitement that he seemed to vibrate with it. "Tonight? Yeah. We can go tonight."

Davik fished a coin purse out of his pocket, dropping it into Vasska's hand. "I'll make it worth his time if he pulls for us tonight."

"Of course, Mr. Kaine," Vasska said, giving a humble nod. "Whatever you need."

László locked eyes with Tashué. And Tashué knew, without another word, what was happening tonight. "You ready?"

"Sure," Tashué said. "Ready when you are, kid."

50

OZRA
DAY 37

T hey found her gun on the road. Lying in the mud, beside tracks her horse made when it bolted. Kazrani leaned out of the saddle so far it was nothing short of acrobatics, scooping it from the mud and the melted snow. She pulled a rag out of her pocket and used it to clean the gunmetal and the leather strap, her face a twisted mask of pain and fury.

And they rode.

They found the road and followed at their desperate pace, but every footstep felt incredibly slow, taking too long. The pair of them bleeding too much. The horses were so tired and they were so far behind, but Ceridwen kept wishing, and Rhodrishi's Talent dragged strength into them, and they plodded on and on and on.

Ozra fought against his Talent, fought for every breath. Every step. Every beat of his heart. The Wrath was worse than he'd ever felt it, dragging threads through him so fast he couldn't even remember what he'd seen. Just flashes of people's lives. Of pain. Of mountains he didn't know and the furious desert sun and a column of smoke from an endless funeral pyre. A wedding bonfire, the bride with flowers braided into her perfectly black hair, iolite beads strung around her neck, fresh tattoos on her hands. Lovely as she danced, her eyes glittering with joy. Ceridwen and the west coast, so small against the backdrop of all that open space. Laughing at the sheep and the ponies in the fields.

And pain. So fucking much pain. Radiating down his whole arm, making him dizzy, his fingers turning completely numb with it. Every twitch of his fingertips made his shoulder burn. But they kept going. Day and night blended together in a wet and ugly sludge, his every moment a battle between the way the Wrath tried to drag him away, the way the hallucinations crept at the corners of his mind like they would come roaring back at the slightest provocation, and the misery that kept him grounded in his body. Shivering hurt. Breathing hurt. The wound in his shoulder the epicentre of his pain, but it radiated outward to everything.

He could feel Rhodrishi's pain, too. Ugly and terrible, burning through his chest as he battled against the weakening of his own heart. Ceridwen was keeping him alive, and it was a terrible burden to place on her wee shoulders, but they couldn't stop.

To stop was to abandon Stella to whatever cruelty Siras had in store for her. He'd failed so many people he loved in his life—Eilidh, the children, his family. He'd failed to protect Stella. He could see her, in his mind's eye, lying tied in the back of that wagon that carried her back to Yaelsmuir. He could see her fear and her pain, drifting around her like a fog.

The hallucinations had driven sense out of his mind, and his only thought was running from that cave and now—

They couldn't stop.

The roadhouse almost blended into the wilderness, the wood walls and the thatched roof washing it in hues of brown that blended with the autumn foliage. Rain pelted the building and everything around it, turning everything to mud. They rode up on it so suddenly that the appearance of it ahead of them took them by surprise, like it had materialized out of the horrible weather. Relief hit first—they'd caught up. Exhaustion next—they'd caught up, but they were so wet and so tired and drawn so thin that Ozra couldn't even begin to fathom how they would help. They had to pull back, to go back the way they'd come so the whole damned roadhouse didn't see them. There was no cover out here, far from the borders of the young forest to the east of the city. At least the rain was letting up.

"How many?" Mahalouwan asked. Too tired to make full sentences.

Her eyes stared distantly, like she wasn't really looking at anything but her own exhaustion.

"One guarding inside the barn. The rest are inside the inn proper."

"But how many?"

"Seven, I think. Including Siras, and the one guarding."

"You think?" Mahalouwan asked, her eyes flicking to Ozra's face. "Seems like time to know for sure, doesn't it?"

"Sure thing, Lieutenant," Ozra snapped. "Let me ride up and count 'em, how's that? I'll step right inside the dining hall and ask how many bronzemen are hanging around, let them do a roll call."

"You don't have to be a fucking ass about it," Mahalouwan snapped back, a little bit of her old temper dragging her up out of her exhaustion. "I am aware that it's all a few tonnes of shit. But there are only two of us capable of fighting, and I'd like to know how many guns I'm facing. And how many innocent people there are down there."

Ozra shook his head. "Ain't no travellers but the bronzemen, I don't think. Everyone else is staff of the roadhouse."

"That doesn't make them any less innocent, Ozra!"

"I fucking know that!"

"But Mam's down there?" Ceridwen asked.

Ozra looked down. Sweet North Star, he was so tired. He hadn't even heard her come up. They'd sent her away with Rhodrishi, looking for shelter, so they could try to come up with a plan without her having to listen to how impossible it all was. And now she stood between their horses, her own pony left behind, looking half-child and half-mud-fae, soaked to the bone and filthy and slumped with her exhaustion.

"Ceridwen," Mahalouwan said. "You shouldn't be here."

Ceridwen blinked away the rain, turning her big eyes on Mahalouwan like she was trying to reach for something like fury, but heaven help her, she was so young and so small. With all the rain, it was impossible to tell if the wetness on her face was tears or not, but it was likely. She hadn't ever stopped crying the whole time they were chasing her mother.

"But she's down there?" she pressed. "She's at the roadhouse?"

"Aye, she's sheltered in the barn. Safe for now." He didn't know if that was a lie or not, not with Siras in charge. He hadn't seen anything, but he didn't know if that was simply because he had no grip on reality, no focus and a spotty memory because the pain and the Wrath made him drift so much. "We're going to figure it out, Ceridwen. We need a moment to think."

"What is there to think about?" Ceridwen asked, her voice rising. "We go and get Mam. That's what you said we were going to do. You said we were going to find her and get her back. You promised!"

"We are," Mahalouwan said. "I swear to you, we will. But it's not as simple as riding back down the hill and walking into the barn. We're outgunned, and if we start shooting, we risk getting your mam killed, as well as anyone else who works at the roadhouse. We have to think. Go back to Rhodrishi, girl. We're going to get her."

"But—"

"Ceridwen," Mahalouwan snapped. "No more arguing. Go back to Rhodrishi, and let us figure it out."

Ceridwen clamped her mouth shut, looking up at Mahalouwan with a heart-shattering mix of fury and pain. Ozra wished with every shred of energy he had left that he could go backward and change this moment, so she didn't have to face this. Even if they were able to save Stella from this, Ceridwen would never be the same. The scars it would leave would last her whole life. Did that make her glass, like Blackwood apparently told her? Or did it make her fragile, leaving fissures across the surface of her? She shouldn't have to be glass—being Talented shouldn't preclude her from having a decent childhood.

"Yes, Lieutenant Mahalouwan," Ceridwen barked, such incredible scorn in her voice that it made her sound older. Older than she should have needed to be.

She spun on her heel and stalked off, around the bend in the trail they had used to get away from the road.

"She's got some steel in her, that girl," Mahalouwan said. "She'll be ferocious one day."

Ozra reached up, pushing a hand through his hair. The rain had eased to a fine mist. Talent—Ceridwen's and Rhodrishi's, certainly, because his was next to useless—protected him from the cold, dragging heat from somewhere in the world and storing it in his core so that only the surface of his skin felt the wet and frigid air.

"We'll wait for nightfall, I think. If there's only the one guarding her, maybe we can kill them quiet, slip her out."

"And then what?" Ozra asked.

Mahalouwan shrugged. Her horse shifted beneath her, stamping its feet to show its impatience. She winced, twisting so her weight balanced on one leg instead of sitting evenly. "Maybe we'll make a mad run back to the city. How long can they keep this up, do you think? Rhodrishi and Ceridwen, I mean. Would've been nice to have Talent driving us on a few forced marches, back in the day."

"Lieutenant Mahalouwan, are you thankful for Talent? Mark the bloody calendar. It's a miracle."

Mahalouwan scowled. "It's been a helpful tool in a trying time. Do you think we could keep pushing like this, make it back to Yaelsmuir?"

"I thought the whole fucking point of this was to get away from Yaelsmuir."

"Sure, and look how well that's been going for us, hey?"

Ozra shrugged—and regretted it. His shoulder, fuck, the pain was ferocious. She was right. They couldn't travel much farther, and there was no where safe to lay low this close to Yaelsmuir. They could cross into the Dunnenbrahl, but now they were closer to the city than they were to the mill town, so maybe their best route was south.

"If we can kill Siras, maybe it's worth it. We can stop in the Bay, with the Red Dawn—Davik keeps healers around, and we'll head into the Dunnenbrahl after a day or two's rest."

Mahalouwan nodded, settling properly in her saddle again and turning her horse around. "Let's go find Rhodrishi, see if he's found shelter."

Ozra kicked Caraid after Mahalouwan's stolen Authority mount. The old gelding was so tired that his hooves dragged in the mud, each footstep slow and reluctant. Ozra shifted, dropping out of the saddle as carefully as he could, but hitting the ground still sent a shock of pain through his body so vicious he couldn't see. Couldn't think. There was only the white-hot agony, the fracture in his bone resentful. If he were smarter he might have tied his arm in a sling, but hell, none of them had been smart. They chased after Stella, as fast as they could.

Rhodrishi came to them out of the haze of precipitation. Of them all, he looked the worst. His pallor was terrifying, like they were watching him die in slow motion, day by day. He looked at them a long time, eyes sliding back and forth between Mahalouwan and Ozra like he was searching for something.

"Where's Ceridwen?" he asked.

A jolt of fear burned away Ozra's pain. "What do you mean? We sent her back to you."

Rhodrishi shook his head. "She didn't come back. She came to find you, and I wasn't fast enough to stop her."

51

STELLA
DAY 37

The storm was vicious through the night, into the morning, lashing the barn with so much noise it was impossible to have a conversation. Not that Stella was particularly inclined to chatting with Duskan. Sitting together through the storm was better than listening to him tell stories about how much he hated Tashué, or listening to him congratulate himself for realizing she was human.

It was impossible to tell when night shifted to day—the barn was so dark, the storm blocking so much light, that it seemed night stretched forever. Duskan tried to urge her to drink, pushing his waterskin against her fingers, but her hands were useless. And then the rain eased, the sound dying to a dull hum.

"I can't feel my fingers," she said.

He blinked at her a few times, surprised by the way her voice rasped out of her. "What?"

"I can't feel my fingers," she said again. "I'd drink, but I can't hold the skin. The rope is too tight."

Duskan stared down at her hands. There must have been some daylight that let her see the shape of his face. Those half-healed wounds were terrible, and it didn't surprise her at all that Tashué was capable of such violence. He'd killed that man, Hale. The one who killed the children. Was that before or after he beat Duskan Hillbraun?

"I shouldn't touch the rope," Duskan said finally, and Stella's heart sank. She wasn't surprised. Siras was terrifying, and the steady, calm threat from the other bronzeman probably lived in Duskan's head all night. But it still sent a hollow, empty feeling through her. "If you sit up, I can hold the skin for you, yeah? And then I can see about getting you something to eat. Maybe breakfast. Hell, maybe lunch. Depends on how long this rainstorm lasts, hey?"

Stella nodded. She'd try again about her hands when he came back with food. Perhaps if she explained how dire it was, how the damage could be permanent, the ugliness of it would convince him to loosen the ropes. And then…

What?

What could she possibly do?

Run?

The idea was so absurd it almost made her laugh. She had no supplies, and she didn't know how far she was from anything. She didn't remember this roadhouse at all—was it close to Yaelsmuir? A few days away? Was there a forest nearby she could disappear into? Could she get back to Ozra and Kazrani?

She didn't know.

Perhaps her best chance of survival was waiting until they brought her back to the city. If she escaped the wagon while they were on the streets, she could run. Disappear into the mass of people there. It wasn't ideal, but it was better than running down the road. All she had to do was survive long enough to get to Yaelsmuir and get away from these men before they brought her to Bothain.

Getting upright was a challenge with her hands and her feet tied, but she fumbled and struggled. Duskan's hand hovered close to her like he wanted to help but didn't dare touch her. He grabbed the waterskin instead, pulling the cork and waiting for her to get herself sat up. Getting upright sent dizziness through her, making her stomach lurch, but it was so empty that the threat of nausea was meaningless. Moving seemed to wake her system enough for it to tell her how hungry she was, so empty it was like she'd become a cavernous pit. Duskan held the waterskin to her lips, and drinking with someone else holding the skin was an effort in frustration. Water hit her lips and spilled down her chin. She turned her head away before he half-drowned her, swallowing the water she had in her mouth carefully so she didn't choke on it. Her throat was so dry that swallowing hurt.

"I'm sorry," Duskan said, trying to brush the water off the front of her coat. "You should have some more. We'll try again when you're ready."

Stella shook her head, lifting her arms to press her face into her coat sleeve, drying the water off it. "A little at a time," she said. She could explain that the body could only process small amounts of water at a time, and that the urge to gulp water when the body was dehydrated was wasteful at best and dangerous at worst. "I'll have more later."

Duskan nodded, pushing the cork back into place and resting the skin beside Stella's leg. "I'll leave that there in case you want to try on your own. And I'll go find something to eat, hey?"

He pulled himself over the edge of the wagon, dropping down to the barn floor. Was he really going to leave her alone? Was no one else guarding the barn?

Bitterness sat thick in her throat. No one was guarding her—they didn't think she was capable of escape and didn't think anyone was coming for her. They assumed she was so helpless and so numb that she would lie in the wagon all day, unattended. Or Duskan was her only guard—and his slip in judgement was her chance.

The door stuck in its frame when he dragged it open, and he had to yank it hard. All the damp air had warped it, no doubt. He walked out of the barn. And left the door open behind him.

Outside, the rain had subsided to a thick mist, and the sun struggled through the storm, but after all the darkness of the barn, her eyes perceived the door as a beacon of light.

She looked around slowly, trying to swallow the way her heart hammered. Not numb anymore. Tired, dizzy. But she was in a barn. With horses. The big, lively palomino was in a stable, stripped of its tack. She didn't have to run—she could ride. Did she had time to get the tack on the horse, saddle up? Probably not. But she could ride bareback if she had to. She wasn't especially good at it, but she'd done it enough times that she could do it if that's what it took to survive.

She had to get the ropes off. Off her wrists, off her ankles. And then she'd take the horse, and go. Hang on for dear life. There had to be something sharp enough to cut rope.

She moved her legs, flexed her toes. Her ankles, her hips. Her body hurt so much, like it was atrophying from lying in this cart so long. How many days since Siras had caught her? She wasn't sure. Two, maybe three. Surely not more than that. There were so many stretches she didn't remember because the smoke and the powder tore her away into all those horrible nightmares, but now she was awake. Alive.

Her hands hurt when she put weight on them, the ropes digging into skin, flaring hot pain every time she moved. She winced—but pain was good. Pain said the numbness wasn't a sign of nerve death. She didn't dare reach for her Talent, lest the nightmare hallucinations come back—or worse, the numbness that stole her will to live.

She hooked her elbows over the edge of the cart, using her arms to drag herself up enough to get both feet under her. It wasn't that high of a wagon. She sat on the edge and dropped, her feet landing in the horrible slushy mixture of straw and manure and water that ran into the barn from the door and the cracks in the stone foundation. The smell her boots kicked up made her gag. She tried to take a step, but sweet North Star, she'd miscalculated this. Her boots were tied together, and she couldn't move them independently of each other. This was stupid—this was why they'd left her, because even alone for a time, she couldn't possibly escape. She hooked one elbow over the side of the wagon beside her, hopping along the floor. If she fell, she'd be caked in the foul-smelling water. If she could get to the tack room, there would be plenty of sharp things there—tools for grooming the horses, for fixing things around the barn.

A shadow in front of the door.

Stella's whole body went tense.

But the shape wasn't big enough to be a man. A child. Stella couldn't see any details, the way the light lit the child from behind, the way the darkness swallowed her face. The child stepped inside, moving in that slow, unsure way someone did when their eyes were adjusting to darkness. Stella's heart leapt to her throat. She would know that silhouette anywhere.

"Ceridwen!" Emotion hit Stella so hard, she couldn't breathe. Hope—and then terror. She tried to take a step but her legs—she'd fall. "Ceridwen, you shouldn't be here!"

"Mam, I came to save you! Lieutenant Mahalouwan and Ozra and Rhodrishi, they're all here. We followed you all night and all day. If we run now, we'll run all the way up the road and back to them."

"I can't," Stella said. Some ugly doubt wormed its way through her elation—what if this wasn't Ceridwen? What if the hallucination was back and this was some trick of her mind? "My hands and feet—Ceridwen, you have to cut the rope, and then we'll go. Close the door so they can't hear us, and come help me with these ropes."

Ceridwen threw her whole body against the door, pushing it closed. She came fast, her boots splashing in the water, her body colliding with Stella so hard it almost knocked them both down. Stella looped her arms around Ceridwen's body, pushing her face into her soaking wet hair. And her fear melted away. Even soaking wet, it smelled like Ceridwen, like her travel-worn clothes and the very particular scent of her sweat and the way she always smelled a little bit like campfire and garlic these days.

"I wished," Ceridwen said. "I wished that everyone would be warm and strong, and I wished that our horses would survive, and we rode all this way without stopping to sleep. We had to come back, to find you. I'm sorry we lost you, Mam, I'm so sorry—I had my eyes closed because I was scared, and I didn't notice!"

"Thank you, Pigeon," Stella said. "It's alright. I was scared, too. I'm sorry I fell behind. I wish I could have brought you somewhere safe, and warm, so you could have a family and learn your Talent like you deserve." She lifted her hands over Ceridwen's head, standing up straighter. "I need you to cut the rope and then we'll go."

Ceridwen nodded, grasping for the belt knife she'd worn all along. The blade flashed as she drew it, catching a bit of light from the window, filling Stella with hope. Sweet North Star, if this wasn't real, if this was some terrible trick of her mind—was this to be her life now? Doubting everything she saw lest it be the hallucinations creeping back?

A shadow passed in front of the window—such an insignificant window, letting only the tiniest sliver of light, but there was so little daylight in here to begin with, every sliver counted for something. Stella's breath caught in her throat, and she held it, straining her ears. Ceridwen slid the knife against the rope, but it didn't do enough. Did Stella hear footsteps outside, squelching in the mud?

"Ceridwen, hide," Stella whispered.

"But you said—"

"Shh! Hide. Right now. In the stall, or somewhere—leave me the knife, and go!"

Ceridwen pushed the hilt of her knife into Stella's hand and Stella tried to grasp it, but her useless fingers flexed and then did nothing. The knife fell. Ceridwen bent to pick it up, but someone on the other side of the door used the handle, making the metal jiggle. Stella pushed Ceridwen away, toward the nearest stall. Ceridwen staggered, feet splashing in the mud. The door opened, just an inch, but squealed as it caught in the frame and jammed. Ceridwen grabbed the wall of the stable and jumped, tumbling over the edge, disappearing as the door squealed again and opened. Stella put her boot over the knife. If it was Duskan, maybe she could tell him some lie about needing to empty her bladder, and it would buy her time to pick the knife up.

But no, of course she wasn't that lucky. It was Siras.

He had a bottle of cheap whisky in his hand and he came halfway into the barn before he noticed that Stella wasn't in the wagon anymore.

"Well, look at you," he said, his voice thick and too smug. It sent a shiver down Stella's spine. "You're up. Where's your guard?"

Stella shrugged. "He left to get something to eat. I didn't know I needed a guard."

"Well, clearly you do, since you're sneaking around the moment he leaves you. Guess you're not as lost as you wanted us to think, hey?"

"I needed to urinate, Siras," Stella snapped, letting her revulsion and her desperation come up through her voice. "I don't know how long I've been sitting in that wagon, but I needed to get up and relieve myself. Or was I supposed to piss my pants?"

Siras shrugged. "Go ahead then."

Stella huffed, flexing her fingers. "I can't. I can't get my trousers down with my coat on, and I can't get my coat off with my hands tied together."

Siras tilted his head to one side, tapping the bottle of whisky against his leg. "Last time we let you go, we took your whole coat off. You don't remember?"

"No," Stella breathed, holding her hands out to Siras. Praying with everything she had that Ceridwen would stay hidden while Stella tried to figure out what to do. "Please, Siras. I really need to go."

"I don't think you've ever asked me *please* for anything before," Siras said. He tapped the whisky bottle again, making a slow rhythm of tapping and sloshing. "It was always orders with you, like you owned me and it was my job to hop to. I like hearing you ask nicely."

Stella tried not to scowl even though the words made her feel ill. "Please, Siras?"

He grinned, pushing his coat open and pulling a knife from his belt. Longer than the one Ceridwen carried, and curved—a vicious looking hunting knife. He came closer, each step agonizingly slow, that knife glinting in the same beam of light that glowed on Ceridwen's knife, still hidden beneath Stella's boot. Sweet North Star, she had to hide it somehow, had to kick it away or Siras might see it.

He leaned close. He smelled of whisky and sweat and that terrible, pungent scent of a bad wound. And those eyes, those hateful green eyes, they tore into her. "If I help you, you'll do something for me."

She squeezed her eyes shut, turning her face away from him so she didn't have to smell his breath or feel it on her face.

"Say it. Say you'll help me, or you can piss yourself for all I care."

Stella shook her head, keeping her eyes shut. Ceridwen's knife, below her boot, was so far away. So close, but so unhelpful. "I don't know what you expect me to do."

"You're a healer, aren't you? They don't have any clue how to help me, and I'm fucking rotting because of you. Seems right that you should fix the mess you made, hey? So, I help you get your clothes off, and then you help me so I don't die of gangrene."

Stella nodded, keeping her eyes closed. *Please, Ceridwen, stay where you are.* "I'll see what I can do."

Something pulled on her suspenders. Stella opened her eyes in time to see that he'd slid the knife under the suspender, and he was pulling it hard. The knife was so razor sharp that the suspender frayed, and then the tension pulled it apart. She couldn't step back, or she'd fall. She had to stand and let Siras cut the other suspender, so the front of her trousers sagged down where the buttons were still open.

"There," Siras said, bright and cheerful. "Now you can pull 'em down no problem."

"Except I can't use my hands or move my feet."

"How'd you get this far, then?" Siras asked. "What were you going to do?"

"I wasn't thinking," Stella said, shaking her head. "I just needed to go."

A shadow across the door, again—Duskan, with a bowl of food and a mug of coffee. He froze when he set eyes on Stella.

"What are you doing?" Duskan demanded.

Siras turned, spreading his hands. The knife still in one hand, the bottle still in the other. "You left the prisoner unattended, idiot. She was either trying to escape, or she needed to piss. Why don't you cut the ropes off her legs, see if she tries to make a run for it. Go ahead, Ffyanwy, I'll even give you a head start if you like, make it sporting."

"Fuck off, Siras," Duskan muttered.

"You going to let this poor woman piss her pants, Hillbraun? Inconsiderate of you."

Stella shook her head. Gods, how had Siras turned even this into some miserable torture? "Never mind. I can't, not with everyone here."

"Don't be difficult, Ffyanwy. Get it over with," Siras said with a laugh. He stepped around Stella, placing the whisky bottle on the edge of the wagon. "Quick now."

He kept his back to her, pushing his knife back into the sheath on his belt. There was a bit of a shake in his hands. She hadn't noticed it before because she was so busy trying not to look at him. But he shrugged slowly out of his coat, his movements sluggish and struggling. He was in a lot of pain. Feverish, probably, because of the infection. She almost reached for her Talent, just to touch him. Just to see it. To know what damage he was carrying, to know if she could use it to her advantage, but even at the thought of using her Talent sent a shiver of dread through her. Would the numbness come back? Would the hallucinations?

"It's a good sign, isn't it?" Duskan asked, stepping a little closer. "You needing to piss, I mean. It's good, right? Not too dehydrated after all."

"Yeah," Stella said softly. "I suppose."

Duskan nodded. He rested his bowl and his coffee on one of the stalls—the same wall that Ceridwen had climbed over. If she was even real. What if Stella had dreamed her? That would be best. Then Ceridwen didn't have to listen to any of this or be in the middle of this. Stella shifted her weight a bit. There was definitely something beneath her boot.

"I can't do anything with my feet tied together, Duskan," Stella whispered. "And my hands, too…"

"You don't need your hands to piss, Ffyanwy."

"But I do need them to help you with your wound," Stella snapped. "And they're so numb right now that they're useless, so if you loosen them, I can help you."

She didn't even see the hit coming. Her face burned, and she fell, and she didn't have any way to catch herself, so her whole body hit the side of the wagon. She went down into the sludge, the whole horrible mess of it splashing around her face, soaking into her coat.

"What the hell did you do that for?" Duskan yelped.

"Fucking bitch doesn't get to talk to me like that," Siras muttered.

Stella gasped, gagged—the shit-mud sludge spread cold on her face, in her hair. And her face burned with the hit, the scab from the last hit broken open and bleeding again. The casual viciousness of it, the fierce impact. She looked past Siras, standing over her now, to Duskan. For a moment, a long, tenuous, terrible moment, it looked like he was going to do something. His fingers twitched toward his gun belt, and his face lit with fury.

But then Siras turned his back on Duskan, totally unafraid. Because he judged already that Duskan wouldn't do anything to stop him, and he was right. Siras was down to his shirtsleeves, and he'd bled through his shirt again, the infected wound leaving a ring of wetness around the brown-pink bloodstain. And the holster for his gun, strapped around his body on the opposite side as the wound, the grip pointing outward. If she could get ahold of it—

He reached down before she could finish the thought, grabbing her by the rope between her hands and hauling her up. He winced, and groaned, his whole body tensing as he tried to protect his wounded side. And Stella didn't struggle because she was so relieved to be up off the filthy floor, water running in cold rivulets down her back once she was upright.

"Help me put her back in the wagon," Siras grunted.

Duskan came forward slowly, and he couldn't look at Stella again. He looked at the floor instead, climbing up on the wagon and grabbing Stella under the arms to drag her up. Fury clogged in her throat. Rage burned in her whole body. So much for the things he said about not being a slug, so much for convincing himself that she was human. All it took was Siras growling at him once, and he was helping. She twisted, trying to get away from him, but his hands were stronger than she expected and he had her up in no time. If she screamed, would anyone in the roadhouse hear her? Would they even care?

Siras climbed up after Duskan, breathing slow and heavy, his hand cupping his side. "You're going to fix this, bitch. It's getting worse, no matter what I do. You're going to fix the problems you caused."

"I can't," Stella said, shaking her head. She tried to push herself back, away from Siras, but there wasn't room to get far. The knife, she'd left the knife behind. If it was even real. Had she seen Ceridwen at all? "Siras, I can't help you like this. I'm filthy, I'll make the infection worse— and my hands, I can't feel my hands. Untie my hands, and let me clean up, and after I'll do whatever I have to."

Duskan jumped down from the wagon, leaving her with Siras. Curse him. She hated him worse than Siras. Siras's cruelty was honest, at least, but him, he'd tried so hard to convince himself he wasn't the same, and then he walked away.

Siras grabbed her by the trouser leg, dragging her closer, and as loose as they were, the hem rode down. She twisted, trying to get away from him, but he laughed. Grabbed her by the shirt next. His hand was so hot —feverish. The wound was killing him slowly, but heaven help her, it wasn't enough to save her from him.

"Siras, don't," Stella said. If he kept laughing at her, maybe she could think of something. She twisted away, backing up until she was sitting, wedging herself in the corner like she could sink right through the wood and shield himself from Siras from the other side. "I'm filthy—covered in horseshit. We'll both wind up sick. Just let me get cleaned up, and then I'll help you. I promise. It's badly infected, but I can still help you!"

Duskan walked away, all the way to the door, shaking his head like he hated it but didn't want to watch.

"He was right!" Stella shouted after him. She flexed her fingers, but she still couldn't feel them. If she used her Talent, could she *make* them move? "He was right about you. A slug! Lower than dirt! Walking away and letting it happen—everything he said about you was right!"

Duskan stopped, halfway to the door. Turned. But then his eyes slid down to the floor, and he sneered. "Siras, the bitch had a knife. She was trying to hide it by standing on it."

Siras laughed, grabbing Stella's ankles. "A knife, hey? Where'd you get it, Ffyanwy?"

Stella lunged for Siras's gun. She threw her Talent at her hands, at ligament and muscle and nerve, dragging energy through them, trying to banish the numbness, forcing them out of their horrible stillness. Pain seared through the nerves so hot and bright it made her shout, but they were moving—she could feel the gun in her hand, the cold wooden grip, the weight of it, her hand straining to lift it.

Siras grabbed her wrist. The gun fell, striking the side of the wagon and bouncing off. Siras's Talent twisted out, too, laying like a blanket across Stella's body, and through it, she could feel his incredible pain. The fever made his joints ache, made his head throb, and his side radiated agony every time he moved. And he was desperate. Desperate for her to fix him, because he didn't know how to heal himself, and he didn't want to die.

A gunshot.

Duskan's chest, obliterated. He fell.

Siras spun toward the door of the barn, hand grasping for the grip of his gun, but it wasn't there.

Clatter of metal on the floor—the cup of coffee, the bowl of food, it had fallen from the stable wall, the bowl rolling on one side through the sludge. Because Ceridwen had climbed over the stable wall and she dove for Siras's gun, picking it up out of all that filthy water on the barn floor.

A shadow across the door again.

Ceridwen lifted the gun and pulled the trigger, and the gunpowder roared. The bullet took Siras in the chin first and then ripped its way up, exploding out the top of his skull. His head snapped back, and he hung in place for a fraction of a second, long enough for Stella to see the wreckage that used to be his face. His Talent lived a moment, their minds connected, and she could feel every moment of it. The buzzing, roaring, vicious impact. And then nothing. For a horrible moment she didn't know if she was the one shot. He listed to the side, his body hitting the side of the wagon, which held him up. Tears turned Stella's vision blurry, mercifully obscuring the details. She lifted both feet and kicked him in the chest to knock him away from her and he fell back with a heavy thump.

She couldn't breathe. She reached up, touching her own face to convince herself that she was fine. Her jaw was still there, her skin swollen and wet and filthy but still there.

She hooked her elbow on the side of the wagon and dragged herself up. All she wanted to do was get away. Didn't matter where. Just away. She dragged herself all the way up to the seat of the wagon, where the driver would sit. Siras's blood was all over her, soaking into the front of her clothes, hot and stinging on her face like acid. She half expected him to get up again, to keep coming. Her fear of him made an undead monster of him, her mind's eye imagining him rising up with half a face because at some point in her life she had accepted that Siras would never stop hunting her.

But he was dead.

"Mam!"

Ceridwen scrabbled up the wagon, up to the driver's seat, throwing herself against Stella even though Stella was covered in gore. Stella dropped her arms around Ceridwen's head again to hug her, dragging them together. Ceridwen trembled in Stella's arms, and her sleeves were wet with the awful sludge from the floor, but Stella didn't care. She clung to Ceridwen, the pair of them trembling.

"I tried to help by wishing, but it was scary!" Ceridwen gasped. "It made the nightmare vision come back, and it didn't stop that other man last time so I had to do something. I'm sorry it took me so long!"

"Stella." Kazrani's voice. "Let's go. We need to get out of here, fast, before—"

Gunshots next door, at the roadhouse. They clapped through the barn like distant thunder.

52

OZRA
DAY 37

It was a shit plan, but it was all they had.

Mahalouwan would go to the barn and get Stella and—hopefully—Ceridwen, since there were only two men there. Siras and one other. And they would take the horses and go. Go as fast as they could, in whatever direction Stella wanted.

Ozra and Rhodrishi would hold up the rest of the bronzemen at the roadhouse as long as they could. Whatever it took for Stella and Ceridwen and Mahalouwan to get away.

And it was real shit because Ozra only had one good arm so he was stuck using one revolver instead of both of them, or his rifle, and Rhodrishi's complexion had gone so grey that he looked dead already, but they looked each other in the eye and silently, without needing to think too hard about it, agreed that it was worth it. Ozra had always known the Authority would be the death of him, so why not stand while Stella took her girl and got away? Maybe then he'd rest with Eilidh and his children in the fabric of Talent and he could tell her he finally stood for something. For a child who deserved a chance.

They went in quiet. Ozra held his revolver in his good hand, and the second was holstered and ready for when the first ran out of bullets. Twelve shots in total, that's what he had before he had to figure out how he was going to reload with one good hand, but frankly if he lived long enough to need to reload, he would be damned surprised. Rhodrishi behind him, so tired his feet dragged, but he held that massive .45 of his anyway, held it across his chest and pointed up at the ceiling so they wouldn't accidentally kill anyone who didn't deserve killing.

The Enquiry Officers were sat down for their lunch, scattered across a couple of tables. The dining hall was big enough to sit fifty people, leaving a lot of empty tables with only the Officers using a pair of tables. Ozra's eyes swept the gathering quickly—shit. There should have been five Officers, but there was only four. And a young man. A boy with bright, frightened eyes, his hands already shaking when Ozra stepped in, like things had been going bad before they even got there.

And the rest of the roadhouse staff, clustered at the far end of the hall, near the bar and the kitchen. Three in all, one of them a child not much older than Ceridwen. She was trying to pull a line of fresh pints, but the keg must have been almost empty because it was draining foam into the glass.

"No one move," Ozra said. "Stay right where you are, and no one needs to get hurt."

The boy at the table put his hands up immediately, and the girl pulling pints gave a fearful, exhausted wail and dropped the glass in her hand to cover her face.

One of the bronzemen put a hand to his hip and started to rise out of his seat, his chair scraping against the uneven planks of the wood floor. "Fucking—"

Ozra stepped to him, putting his gun right to the man's skull, pressing it hard and forcing him back down into his chair. "I said don't *fucking* move, or I'll paint the floor with your rotted Authority brains."

"We haven't got much money, not this time of year," the roadhouse keeper said. She looked to Ozra with tired eyes, her face lined with age and worry. "Isn't much business with all the cold and the rain. We've got their copper, and you can have it. Just take it and go."

"We aren't here for money. We're here for the woman they arrested," Rhodrishi said. "An innocent woman, and they've tied her in the back of a wagon and beaten her into submission. Our people are taking her out of the barn, and once she's a safe distance away, we'll leave you folks alone. We don't want any bloodshed—we want her."

"An innocent woman my left nut," one of the bronzemen spat. "A filthy tainted bitch. We've arrested her because she's dangerous, just like the lot of you."

Ozra glanced at the boy, the one with the wide eyes and the shaking hands. "You go on down to the floor, boy. Nice and slow. On your hands and knees, you crawl back to your family. I don't want you to get hurt if lead starts flying, yeah?"

The boy's mouth opened, closed. Tears streaked his face, danced in the peach fuzz beard he was trying to grow.

"Go on now," Ozra said. "I told you, none of you folk need to get hurt."

The boy slithered down to the floor, but he couldn't seem to summon the coordination or the courage to move. He crawled beneath a table and stayed there.

"You think you'll get away with this?" the bronzeman hissed, leaning against Ozra's gun like he was daring Ozra to pull the trigger. "You think we'll let you walk away? We'll hunt you down, tainted filth. We'll find you again like last time. And then we'll drag you behind the wagon, all the way back to Yaelsmuir, so Bothain Clannaugh can make you watch as he exterminates every tainted in Yaelsmuir. That city is infested with your kind, like a plague run rampant. And he's going to burn those streets and give 'em back to good, clean people who deserve a better life."

Ozra thumbed the hammer back, leaning over the man, pushing the barrel harder against the man's skull. The man's face spasmed with the pain he was trying to hide. If Ozra could move his other arm, he'd take the fucker's gun, but even twitching his fingers hurt so bad he couldn't see. "You should'a killed me when you had the chance. 'Cause now you get to spend your last miserable moments on this side of your Keeper's Gate looking at my face. And then when I blow your brains out, you'll go to that Gate knowing the tainted aren't ever going to quit. You can't get rid of us. You've got your Breeding Program and your energy units, trying to make us obsolete so the world won't notice when you try to exterminate us, but you know what? You're the one who's obsolete. You're the one who's inferior. You think your cruelty makes you special? I see the core of you. You ain't special, or brave. Deep inside, you're terrified that you're nothing, and you spent your whole life trying to prove that you ain't scared, but now here you are, sweating. Because the people who made your personality around hating have caught up to you to hand out retribution for your life of mediocre savagery. You call us filthy? You kidnapped a woman and degraded her to prove you're some kind of man. You feel like a man now?"

"So fucking do it," the bronzeman spat. "Kill me."

"Conn," the owner said. "Come over now, Conn. Get out of the way."

The boy under the table pulled himself half a foot along the floor.

Rhodrishi moved slowly through the open space, his rifle pointed at the bronzemen at the table. Toward the family, clustered together, getting the boy, Conn, in his line of sight before the shooting started. "Where's the fifth?"

"You can't kill me, can you?" the bronzeman said, his mouth twisting in an ugly, vicious grin. "'Cause there aren't enough of you here. Two guns against five, and you with nowhere to hide once there's lead in the air. The minute you pull your trigger, my men won't have a reason to sit still anymore, and then you're done."

"Maybe, but it ain't enough to save you, is it?" Ozra asked. "You'll still be fucking dead."

"Where's the fifth?" Rhodrishi asked again. His footsteps clapped loud on the floor as he entered the open space between the tables and the bar. "There's a fifth officer, where is he?"

"He's upstairs!" Conn shouted, his face pressed so hard against the floor that the words were muffled. "He went upstairs!"

A gunshot—not in the roadhouse, but outside, in the barn. Sweet North Star, let it be Mahalouwan. Let Siras be the recipient of that bullet. A second shot. And then silence.

"Good now," Ozra said. "You hear that? That's two of yours gone to the Keeper. You sit real quiet now, and you don't have to follow."

The creak of a footstep on wood. Out of the corner of his eye, Ozra saw the last bronzeman, coming down the stairs, drawing his gun out of his hip holster. Rhodrishi swung his whole body and his rifle roared and the bronzeman fell instantly, blood painting the walls of the stairwell. The leader, under Ozra's revolver, went for his own gun. Ozra pulled his trigger, and the big .45 slug obliterated his skull. He fell hard, and Ozra thumbed back the hammer again, turning to the nearest man, but he was too slow. He could see it, every second stretching around him. Too slow. The man already had his gun out, and the vicious barrel of it was pointed at Ozra's face and Ozra couldn't pivot fast enough. But another gunshot from up by the bar ripped open his throat in a bright spray, and he went down. His revolver fired up at the ceiling, spraying Ozra's shoulders with splinters. Ozra swung his arm to point his revolver at the next closest man, but the last two hadn't moved. They had their arms right up in the air, as far as they could stretch.

Ozra took a step back from the dead leader, risking a glance toward Rhodrishi and the bar at the far end. The owner, she had a gun out, the point still curling spent cordite smoke as she stalked across the open space.

"Conn," she said again, racking the action of her rifle so it spit out the empty shell. "Up now, son. Behind me."

Conn scrabbled to his feet, all gangly, clumsy limbs. He ran toward the owner of the roadhouse, skidding and tripping over his own feet, and then he was behind her. He went to his hands and knees and vomited, spilling so much beer the poor boy had to be drunk. No wonder he couldn't summon the coordination to crawl away.

"We don't want any trouble," one of the last bronzemen said. "Just take your tainted cow and go."

The woman stalked closer, three more steps, and then she pulled the trigger. The man's face disappeared, and his body toppled against the last bronzemen. The last one tried to stand, hands still up.

"Wait!"

Ozra shot him in the chest. He folded around the impact, red spilling out of him. And then he went down, too.

The woman swung her rifle on Ozra, her chest heaving, her eyes wild with her fury. Ozra let go of the handle of his revolver, balancing it on his finger with the trigger guard and holding it toward her so she could take it if she wanted.

"We don't want no trouble with your folk, ma'am," he said. "We wanted Miss Whiterock, like I said."

"Whiterock," the woman echoed. "That's the woman in the wagon?"

Ozra nodded. "Her and her girl, we were trying to take them away from here, and then these foul bastards caught up to us. We'll take her and go."

The woman nodded. Her eyes tracked Ozra, up and down. The fury was fading, leaving shock in its place, draining all the colour out of her face. "You're bleeding."

"Aye, they shot me a few days back."

"You should go see if she's alright," the woman said, nodding toward the door. She pointed her rifle down at the bodies, like she half expected one of them to get up again, even though the only movement in any of them was the nerve-numb twitching of a body that didn't know it was dead yet. "And then you can bring her back in here, and we'll see what we can do about those wounds."

Ozra nodded. "Thank you."

The woman nodded back. "They were scum. Every last one of them. It ain't right, what they talked about doing to that woman. Go see if she's alright."

"Yes ma'am."

53

STELLA

DAY 37

Her hands hurt when the blood flow returned. She moved her fingers and tried to get the process going, but there was no rushing it. She tried to tell herself that the pain was good. Pain meant she was still alive. But the pain and the surprising kindness on the face of the woman who cut the ropes away shook Stella out of her shock and made her weep again.

She wept silently as the owner of the roadhouse helped her out of her clothes, tossing them all into one of the giant cauldrons they used to cook for the huge functions they hosted sometimes in the summer. She'd do her best to boil the stains right out, she said. She didn't have anything spare to send Stella off with, she said, or else she'd just as well burn everything. The boiling would have to do. They brought out their big copper wash tub, setting it in the kitchen because the roadhouse only had one tap, so they had to fill cauldrons with water and boil them on the massive stove and then dump them into the tub one at a time. The men were banished from the kitchen—Rhodrishi and Ozra, and the boy, and the house owner's brother, told they could clean themselves upstairs and out of the way. Kazrani stripped down, too, and the roadhouse owner restitched the terrible wound that had torn its stitches on their desperate ride to chase after Stella. Stella leaned her head out the roadhouse window, pouring water over her own head to wash all the filth out of her hair before she retreated to the bath.

"I shoulda done something sooner," the woman whispered as Stella lowered herself into the tub. The water was so hot that her skin tingled, the heat making her itchy all over after the long, lonely cold. "But I've only got the one gun, and there was so many of them—I didn't know what else to do but play by their rules. But then your friends came, so I had to do what was right."

Stella wanted to tell the woman that was how the Authority worked. They came to a place and acted with such impunity that it convinced everyone they were helpless. They called themselves the *Authority*, like it was their right to walk through the entire world like they owned it, and said it was a thing they did to protect people. But she couldn't summon the energy to speak. She sank down beneath the surface of the water and let it hold her a while. Hold her in silence and stillness so that for a moment, she could pretend this had never happened. For a moment, she was suspended in water with her eyes closed, the copper walls of the tub all around her, hemming her in. Protecting her from everything.

She stayed under until her lungs ached. Until they screamed. Until her own instincts made it impossible to hold her breath anymore. And then stayed under a moment longer, exhaling through her nose and sending bubbles of air twisting up away from her. And then she followed them up, breaking the surface and sucking in a deep, desperate breath of air.

"I promised Conn's mam I'd take care of him," the woman said. She was talking to Kazrani, or maybe to herself. "I swore he wouldn't want for nothing, and we'd always have a place for him here. But those bastards, they made sport out of picking on him—I should've done something sooner."

"It's easy to tell yourself what you should have done," Kazrani said. She sounded so exhausted, so bone-weary that it almost made Stella weep again. "But it's useless. We can't change what happened. All we can do is keep going forward."

"You're tainted?" the girl asked. She looked so terribly young, not much older than Ceridwen. "That's why they had you, right—because you're tainted?"

"Talented," Ceridwen said. "We aren't tainted. There's nothing wrong with us. It's Talent."

"I'm sorry," the girl said quickly. "I didn't mean—"

"Were you folks running from the trouble in the city?" the older woman asked. She wiped the blood off her hands with a ragged old piece of cloth, looking up at Kazrani. "They say it's going to be bad."

"What trouble in the city?" Stella asked.

The woman shrugged. "It's hard to tell heads from tails from it all, but the papers make it sound like there's going to be riots in the streets. They say the army of the Red Dawn is making problems for Yaelsmuir, like they did up in Cruinnich, and they say some general's there to bring peace, but I ain't ever seen an army bring *peace*."

"Did you serve?" Kazrani asked.

The woman nodded. "Too long, and then a few more years after. And then Conn's mam—well. I promised her I'd keep him safe, and now they're saying it's going to be bad down there. And I wonder if I should be moving on."

"Mam, no," the girl said. "We built this place back up from a falling down ruin—we can't quit now."

"Hush, girl," the woman snapped. "You don't know. You haven't seen what it's like."

"They can't run us off after how hard we've worked!"

The woman shook her head, looking up at Kazrani. "Did you come from the city? Do you know what's happening?"

Kazrani looked to Stella. "No. We left a while back." She laughed. "Well. Ten days ago. Before it started, whatever it is. They were going to bring her back, I think."

"General Clannaugh wanted her, they said," the woman whispered, like she didn't want Stella to hear, except the kitchen wasn't that big, and there wasn't any other noise to drown her out. "I don't see why he's down in Yaelsmuir, making trouble. Fist of the North and all that—I thought he was from Cruinnich. They didn't say what for. Just that he wanted her back alive."

"He's my husband," Stella said. "I suppose he wants to look me in the eye, gloat that I couldn't ever get away."

"I thought the Fist of the North was married to the healer woman," the owner said. "The one from the stonesmith family."

Stella looked the woman in the eye and nodded. "Yes. Ffyanwy Rhydderch."

The understanding came over her face slowly, and she nodded. "Right then. You should come on out of the tub, Miss. Let your wee one clean up, too. And then you folks can have a meal—"

"You don't have to feed us," Stella interrupted. "We can get out of your way as soon as we're dressed again. I never meant for anyone else to get involved. I'm sorry we brought this to you."

"Well, it'll be a while before you can go anyway, since I'm boiling the shit out of your clothes. And I'd appreciate the help, getting the bodies buried. The ground ain't frozen yet, so if we get to work quick, they'll be well hidden and then the snow'll cover their grave. We don't get a lot of visitors around here this time of year, but I'd like 'em out of my mess hall before they stink up the place. You're excused, Lieutenant, given the state of your ass. Shot clear through it, hey?"

Kazrani laughed. "Aye, clear through. My Captain won't ever let me live it down once he hears about it. I've some experience getting rid of bodies, from my time serving. So if you don't mind me sharing my professional opinion, it's easier to burn them than to bury them. Burn them, and then take the ashes away from here and scatter them."

"Even with the rain?"

Kazrani shrugged. "A bit of cooking grease can get the fire going."

Footsteps rang across the empty mess hall, echoing into the kitchen. Stella sank low into the tub, and the woman stood, taking a deep breath like she would give their intruder an earful. Kazrani reached for her gun.

"Stella." It was Ozra—he'd stopped short of the kitchen to give them privacy. "You should come as soon as you can."

"What's wrong?" Stella asked, pushing herself up. "Ozra, what is it?"

The floorboards creaked a few times and Stella could almost imagine Ozra shifting from one foot to the other. "You should come. Quickly."

The roadhouse owner gave Stella a woollen nightgown, almost warm enough to shield her skin from the chill in the air, and she ran up the stairs barefoot, clutching Ceridwen's hand every step. The floorboards were cold and uneven beneath the soles of her feet, but Ozra's urgency filled her with a sense of looming panic. Up, up, three floors to one of the family suites. The boy sat in the stairwell, slumped against the wall and looking miserable. The roadhouse owner's brother, hovering in the doorway like he was keeping it open for their arrival.

Rhodrishi in a bed. He still had all his travelling clothes on and his boots were leaving mud stains on the bedclothes. Asleep. Or something like it.

"What happened?" Stella asked.

"He dropped," Ozra said. He was stripped down to his bare chest, and they'd bandaged his arm and tied it across his body in a sling. "We were each telling the boy about the first time we were drunk, and he went down. His heart—it's been bad since the cave."

"The first time you were drunk, Ozra?" Stella scoffed.

Ozra gave a helpless, lop-sided shrug with one shoulder. "The fucking bronzemen, they were forcing him to drink. Thought it was funny, were making bets on whether he'd pass out or throw up. We were trying to make it funny for him so he didn't feel so fucking miserable. And then Rhodrishi went down."

Stella went to the bed, pressing her hands against his face. She sank her Talent into him immediately, listening to his heart. His skin was cold and clammy beneath her hands, his pulse thready and struggling in her ears. But even as she did such simple, easy things, she could feel the ugly, fermenting dread bubbling to life in her chest, choking her like bile. Healer's heart. She could see the strain, some places too thick with scarring, other places too thin.

Fix it, you bitch, fix the damage you caused!

Stella's snapped her eyes open. Siras stood in the corner of the room, his head blown apart and his fingers twitching, reaching for her. She opened her mouth to scream, but no sound came—she released her Talent and the image of Siras disappeared as suddenly as it had materialized in the room. She pushed herself to her feet, moving away from the bed, her whole body trembling with the desire to bolt out the door, to run out to the road and never stop running to get away from Siras's corpse.

"Mam, what's wrong with him?" Ceridwen asked. She sank onto the edge of the bed, grabbing Rhodrishi's hand and squeezing it hard. "Rhodrishi! Can you hear me? Rhodrishi!"

"It's his heart, Ceridwen," Ozra said, pushing her hands into the mess of Ceridwen's hair, wet from the rain but drying in the warmth of the roadhouse. "He told us he was struggling with it, and now it's going to fail."

"No!" Ceridwen wailed. "No, it can't! He can't die, Mam! Please! You're a healer, aren't you? That's what you said—you were a healer before, and you know how to help people, don't you?"

Stella shook her head. The hallucinations lived as a threat in the edge of her awareness, waiting for her to use her Talent. But if it could help Rhodrishi, it was worth it. But she couldn't find words.

"If I wish, will it help?" Ceridwen asked. "If I wish for him to be healthy, will he come back?"

"Ceridwen," Ozra said, but he wasn't fast enough to speak, either.

"I wish his heart gets better!" Ceridwen cried. "I wish his heart gets better and he wakes up and he's fine."

Her Talent was immense, filling the room, cradling Rhodrishi's heart. She could see it beating, each contraction guided by Ceridwen's incredible willpower. But Ceridwen's face split with fear, with agony. She squeezed her eyes shut and folded both her hands over her face, curling inward like she was hiding.

Ozra acted before Stella could, going to the bed and sinking down on his knees in front of Ceridwen. He swept his good arm around her, dragging her into a hug. "Alright, wee girl, alright. We'll do our best, won't we? We'll make him comfortable and help him out as best we can. Your mam can tell me what to do and we'll try our best."

Ceridwen nodded, but her eyes were still squeezed shut. "He helped us save Mam," she whispered. "The least we can do is save him, too, even if the nightmares are scary."

She had the hallucinations, too—of course she did. They said it lived in Talent, and she'd inhaled the smoke in the cave, the same as everyone else.

Stella squeezed her eyes shut. If she kept her eyes shut, she wouldn't see Siras. It didn't matter what she heard, she wouldn't open her eyes.

She sank into Rhodrishi's heart and listened to the laboured rhythm of it, feeling the heat of Ceridwen's Talent that nursed it to live, cradled it on. If there was any saving him, they would save him together.

54

TASHUÉ

DAY 37

Each Uhl rifle took fifteen bullets.

It had been a long time since Tashué had handled rifles so often. He kept his old Imburleigh clean, and it had been in good working order when he loaded it and handed it to Stella, but it occurred to him that he couldn't actually remember the last time he'd fired it. The only thing he could remember with any clarity was putting it into Jason's hands in the field outside the city and pointing toward the target Tashué had set up fifty yards away. And Jason was an excellent shot in that way that sometimes he was good at something but didn't seem to understand how impressive it was. How long ago was that? Before Jason ran away for that short time and then turned up again with a young veteran in tow. They'd spent less time together after that, like Tashué had failed some test, and so Jason kept his distance.

With time offering so much perspective, it was easier to grasp what drove Jason away—his Talent. It must have been quickening, and Jason must have been trying to figure out what to do. Who to trust. Where to turn. And then time ran out, and Tashué's own colleagues came for Jason because one of them must have noticed, even as Tashué remained willfully blind.

The last time he fired any gun was to kill Hale. One bullet, right through his skull, turning him into an empty shell. And lighting something in Tashué that hadn't gone out.

The wagon had room for half a dozen people, but there were only three of them. László, Rowan, Tashué. Fifteen rounds in each of their guns. Forty-five large calibre bullets, capable of destroying people. Ripping them apart until they were nothing but piles of too-wet gore, like the Patrollers in the wagon that night Tashué was arrested. Every shred of Tashué ached with the hope, the prayer, the desperate plea to fate and the North Star that things wouldn't go that badly. *Anything for Jason* was easy enough to say, but the death of innocent people—

"What's the plan?" Tashué asked. He couldn't let himself spiral into useless thoughts. Better to know what was coming and be prepared for it.

László didn't look stressed at all. He lay on his bench like he was having a break, his rifle cradled on his chest. "The plan is you listen to me and don't cause any problems." He shuffled through his pockets, pulling out a small leather case. Chewing tobacco, Tashué thought at first, but no—when he fished a few leaves out of the bag, they weren't the right colour to be tobacco. Khat. It had been a long time since Tashué chewed khat, but he'd recognize that leaf anywhere. "You'll be fine, Mr. Guinne. Relax."

"You can't be serious," Tashué muttered. "You can't honestly tell me that we're going to pull this off without a reasonable plan. Tell me you know what you're doing, László. Tell me you've actually thought this whole thing out, and spent some time in the bank, watching the rhythm of how people work, and tell me that you actually know where the money is instead of hoping they'll hand it over the second you start waving your gun in their faces."

"You sound like you've got some experience with bank robberies," László said, teeth gnashing on the leaf to get the astringent juice flowing. "I'm glad I brought you along."

The gun felt too heavy. How many people would be in there? Maybe it was closed—maybe the reason was because he knew the place would be empty, and he was jerking Tashué around. But if that was true, why bring guns? László had a rifle and a revolver, fully loaded and ready to shed a torrent of blood. The revolver was smaller calibre, the sort of gun that was plenty deadly but quieter because it didn't pack as much of a gunpowder load. And that fucking khat to work himself up, too.

"No, but I have experience with dangerous operations," Tashué said slowly. Keep his reins on his temper, don't give László an excuse to go off before they even got there. "If this goes bad, it'll be on you because you didn't prepare and because you got high on khat on the way in."

"Holy fuck, would you relax?" László said. He sat up and pushed his hand through his hair, which somehow only managed to make it look messier. "Just because I haven't told you what the plan is doesn't mean there isn't a fucking plan, alright? Maybe I want you to shut the fuck up and learn to listen, hey? Maybe I want to know that you're here to do what you're told instead of fucking us over at the first chance you get because that's what tinmen *do*. They make promises, and then when the Authority tells 'em to hop-to, they rip you apart for the fun of it. So excuse me if I don't trust you yet, *Commander*."

Tashué bit down hard on the inside of his lip, fighting to swallow all the fury. He might have let himself argue, except László was right. He'd carried the tin for nineteen years, and before everything imploded, he'd taken the brass badge of a station house commander. It never felt right that these people trusted him. In the pugilist club in front of everyone, László acted all buttery sweet in a way that set Tashué's skin crawling because it didn't sit right with Tashué that Davik and his people trusted him so much already. It was a bit of a relief that László was being honest and had given up the act. "I'm done with the Authority."

"So you say," László said, lying back down. "I guess we'll see."

"How many people have you arrested, do you think?" Rowan asked. There wasn't any resentment in the question, just young and earnest curiosity, like he'd never actually spoken to a tinman before. "Over the course of your career—how many people have you put in the Rift?"

"I don't know," Tashué admitted. "Too many."

Rowan cocked his head to one side. He looked so much like his father when he did that. "How many people have you killed?"

"What do you want me to say, Rowan?" Tashué asked. "Too many. Every single one of them is *too many*. I shouldn't have carried that badge, and I shouldn't have let the Authority turn me into a weapon against their enemies, but I did. I can't make it make sense, and I won't insult your intelligence by trying to justify it."

"That's the most sense you've made in days," László muttered.

"But why'd you take the badge in the first place?" Rowan pressed. "You're tainted, your son is tainted—how did they convince you to hate yourself so much?"

Tashué sighed, closing his hands around the wooden stock of his rifle, the maple warm beneath his palms already. "I never hated myself, or anyone with Talent. I was just... afraid." If he let himself think too much at any given moment, he could feel it again—the rhythm of that woman's beating heart before he made it explode in her chest, the feeling of turning bone into dust. The awareness that he could reach into anyone's body and do that again. It made the weight of his own temper all the more terrifying. "I was afraid that the only thing I was good at was killing. Death and destruction for Crowne and country. I wanted to stop. To get away and come home to my son. I thought the law of the Authority was there to protect people. I thought taking the badge would let me build a life helping people."

"Helping people?" Rowan echoed. He looked Tashué in the eye when he said it, but he didn't look angry or sad. He looked tired, which was worse. He was too young to look that jaded and exhausted. "My mother was killed by the Authority. I don't remember her. Da's always telling stories about her and Ffyanwy and how much he loved them. Ffyanwy especially, but my mother, too. I always wonder what life might have been like if the Authority hadn't taken them both, like maybe Da wouldn't have been so fucking angry all the time, you know? I know it was complicated, between the three of them, but they loved each other. At least that's what he says. Maybe we never would have come down here if they were both still alive. But he says that my mother would have liked it down here in Yaelsmuir. She was Pashibé, so her family had roots down this way. You know, before."

Ffyanwy—Stella. What would she think of Rowan Kaine?

"My mother was Pashibé, too," Tashué said softly instead of thinking about Stella. "Through my grandmother."

Rowan cocked his head to the side again, his little tell that Tashué had taken him by surprise. "You don't have ishani tattoos."

Tashué flexed his hands. The absence of ink left an emptiness, like his skin knew what it should feel like. "No, I don't. My grandmother, she didn't teach us any of the traditions. She thought it would keep us safe from the Authority, if we could blend in. But no one with Talent is safe at all, are they?"

Rowan shook his head, looking down at his hands, too. "Da said next summer we'd go up to Cruinnich so I could get mine. Said he's been gone long enough now and Bothain Clannaugh ain't in Cruinnich anymore, so we should be able to sneak up there, find my grandmother and her family. Said I should get them from family, even if I haven't been able to see them much. But now Bothain Clannaugh is *here*, so I don't think Da will want to leave until this is all settled."

The wagon stopped before Tashué could think of an answer. László sat up, swinging his legs off the bench. Tashué's heart seized, paused, clenching so hard it felt like his chest was collapsing inward on itself. And then it beat double-time, racing its way up his throat so he couldn't breathe for a moment. North Star guide him, he prayed that no one would die.

"Ready?" László asked.

Rowan nodded. "Ready."

László swung his eyes on Tashué, staring into him, daring Tashué to balk, to refuse, to back out. "Commander?"

Tashué nodded. "Ready."

László kicked the back door open and jumped down, swinging his rifle over his shoulder. He spat the khat into a gutter. The wagon had stopped in a Drystone alley—wide and well paved, the buildings around it with sloping overhangs that kept the alley half covered. The bank felt enormous, looming beside the wagon with its white sandstone walls and not a single window facing the alley. The nearby street was lit by brights, the light of them making long shadows across the cobbles.

László led them around the side of the building, into another alley. Narrow, the building beside the bank so close Tashué could stand between the stone and touch both buildings with his elbows. There was hardly any light in the smaller alley and it took Tashué's eyes a long moment to adjust. László marched down the alley to a door in the side of the bank. He stopped and knocked. Fucking knocked—no wonder he wasn't worried about the robbery. He must have arranged it with someone who worked for the bank.

The door creaked open. It bled the faintest touch of light into the alley, illuminating the silhouette of whoever opened the door. László grinned wide at the pair of spectacles that peered out at them.

"Good evening, Mr. Riley," László said brightly. "Have you got everything ready?"

"Yes, yes, of course," the man said. He opened the door a little farther to let László in. Rowan followed, and Tashué behind him. The hallway that stretched in front of them was narrow and only lit by a distant gaslight giving off a soft glow. But after the darkness of the alley, the hallway seemed bright. The man who let them in was almost as tall as Tashué, but rail thin, the glass and metal of his spectacles glinting in the light. "Close the door, please."

Tashué pressed the door closed behind him, the whole thing moving only reluctantly on its old hinges, the stone incredibly heavy. Once it was closed, the silence was strange. Stretching. Thick and fuzzy in Tashué's ears. The city was always so loud, existing in a dull roar in the background of everything, but the windowless walls of the bank blocked it out.

"I got your telegram," the man whispered, leading them down the hallway. Their footsteps echoed with incredible volume on the backdrop of all that silence. "Everything's unlocked and ready."

"Fantastic," László said. "Hopefully you've destroyed the telegram already?"

"Of course, Mr. Dargis."

"How's your wife?" László asked. "Has the babe come yet?"

"Not yet. A couple of weeks, still. But her health is much better now. We're optimistic."

Around the corner, and the vault door was open. Metal several inches thick, the holes for the deadbolt set at least five feet deep into the stone wall. And then, on the other side, the bags. Somehow it was fewer bags than Tashué expected, sitting rather unimpressive and lonely in the middle of the vault room.

"Thank you, Mr. Riley. That's perfect." László elbowed Rowan in the side, pointing back down the hall. "Have the wagon back right up to the alley, and we'll have Mr. Guinne start with all the heavy lifting."

"I'm going to leave," the banker whispered. Tashué couldn't figure out why the man was whispering—the bank was clearly empty, and there was no fathomable way anyone outside could hear them. "If you could damage the locking mechanism, it would help give the impression you broke in."

László nodded, gave another of his youthful, charming grins. "Will do."

"Thank you, Mr. Dargis," the banker whispered. "I appreciate this."

"Trust me, Mr. Riley," László's voice had turned too fast and too sharp, and his hands twitched like they were desperate to move, "the pleasure is all mine."

The banker led Rowan back down the hallway, leaving Tashué and László in the vault alone. László was completely unable to stand still. Tashué recognized the way khat burned him into motion. Hell, he'd felt it before. His company used to chew khat before battle, before duels, in the midst of the kind of all-night parties they organized with bonfires and all kinds of intoxicants because hotblood Jitabvi were firm believers in living life in the moment. He knew first-hand how it honed the killing instinct. Something buzzed in Tashué's ears, something angry, something too wound up. László adjusted the strap of his Uhl so it lay across his chest, freeing both his hands.

"We'll carry everything to the door, and then load them all up at the same time," László said. "You think you can carry two at once? They're heavier than they look."

"László, what the fuck is this?" Tashué asked.

László went still. He looked up at Tashué with his big warm brown eyes, too wide and filled with too much energy. "Don't tell me you're *disappointed* that it's going to be easy. What's the matter, big man? You want to shoot somebody? All wound up now and nothing fun to do with your new gun, hey?"

Tashué shook his head. "Why did you let me think it was going to be a fucking robbery when it's—what? What are we doing here?"

"Insurance fraud," László said brightly. He grabbed one of the bags by the leather handle and hauled it up until he held it across his chest with both hands. He grunted as he threw it, the bag coming fast toward Tashué, but it was too heavy for the toss, and it landed at Tashué's feet with an impressive thump. Bank notes, maybe, instead of coins. "Mr. Riley's been skimming, hasn't he? Can't blame him. I think anyone would go a little insane, walking into a room like this and seeing all this *money* sitting here. But he skimmed too much, and now the bank is short, so here we are. We'll take what we can load into the wagon, and he'll file an insurance claim saying we took way more than was actually here, and the insurance will cover the loss, and everyone is happy! And no one gets hurt! Why do you look so fucking angry about it?" He laughed, hooking his thumbs in his trousers. "All that *poor me* talk about how you didn't want to hurt anyone, and now you're pissed that I'm getting Dav's money without putting anyone in danger. You really have yourself believing your own bullshit, don't you?"

"I'm angry because you fucking lied to me about a bank robbery!" Tashué snapped. The buzzing silence in his ears made it feel like they were stuffed with cotton, and all the anticipation of what he was preparing to do turned to acid in his veins. "I'm here to help my son, and you're wasting my time with fucking *games*. Why didn't you tell me what we were doing here? Did you think it was funny, telling me we were robbing the place? Letting me sweat it out, wondering what the fuck was going to happen? I'm not interested in letting you people waste my fucking time!"

László's eyes went hard and a little bit empty, his head craning back and his mouth twisting into a vicious, dangerous smile. "You people?"

"Yes, you people," Tashué said, even as his last shred of good sense was screaming at him to stop talking. Stop making it worse. All they had to do was take the money and go, but his heart was beating so hard, his chest hurt and he had to let that fury out before he exploded. "You Red Dawn people, living down in the Bay like it's a fucking party. You think this is funny? Do you have any idea how bad it's going to get once the Bay implodes? How many people are going to die?"

László laughed and rolled his eyes and lifted another bag. He threw it at Tashué, and the strength of his anger carried it farther, so that Tashué had to step back out of its path. This one moved with the loud chink of coins, the metal inside tinkling like musical instruments gone discordant. "Fuck off. First you're pissed that we're going to do something violent here, and now you accuse me of playing games because I'm smart enough to come up with money without anyone getting hurt. Get over yourself, Mr. *Guinne*. Put all that energy of yours to good use, and start carrying shit down the hallway."

"You fucking lied to me," Tashué said. "How am I supposed to help and trust you people if you lie to me?"

"What the fuck makes you think I give a shit if you trust me or not?" László snapped. He came closer, stalking through the big empty room, around the bags. "You come down to the Bay after nineteen fucking years serving my enemy, and you talk to me like you think I owe you something? Go fuck yourself. Dav said we were going to test you, so I tested you to see if you were sending word to General Wolfe or maybe Powell Iwan. So far so good, hey? Looks like you and Saeati kept your mouths shut, colour me surprised!"

Tashué sighed. Stupid to argue with the kid when he was high on khat. Stupid to argue about the fact that no one was going to get hurt here. This was good. Mr. Riley was long gone, and they would empty the place out and no one else needed to get involved. This was what he wanted, damnit—no one was going to get hurt. "I don't want to do this, László. I don't want to spend all my energy fighting with you or trying to figure out what new game you're playing. I'm here for my son. I'll do whatever it takes to get him out. Do you know what that's like? Do you know what it's like to know with certainty that you'd give anything for someone you love more than you love yourself?"

"Great," László said. He reached into his coat and pulled out a revolver, thumbing back the hammer and pointing it right at Tashué's face. "You're done playing? Well, so am I. What if I decide the best way to make this look like a proper robbery is with a body, hey? Then Dav doesn't have to sweat about you anymore, and we don't have to spend another thought wondering when the Authority is going to come for you and fuck us all over. I don't have to lie to you or play games with your delicate fucking ego. Maybe the only thing I owe you is lead, tinman. I'll put a hole in your skull and carry the money out myself and tell your son his daddy died a hero. And it'll look good for the insurance company, won't it? Nothing like a body to make a robbery look *real*."

Tashué sighed, all the fury bleeding out of him. "Sure, László. In the head sounds good." He stepped forward, over the heavy bags, looking past the revolver and right at László. "Or right through my heart, bleed me out as fast as possible. Nice big mess that way."

László sneered, resting the point of his revolver right on Tashué's chest, just to the left of Tashué's sternum. Aiming for the heart, like Tashué told him to. "You don't know what the Authority has done to my family. You want your son, I get it. Lucky for you, he's still alive. I lost my brother, my mother, my stepmother, my father. I lost my friends, my home. I lost the life I should have had, miles away from this shit-smelling city. I don't belong here. I belong down on the lake, where the world actually makes sense, but instead I'm fucking *here* and I wouldn't be here if it weren't for the Authority. My sister is in the Rift to help your son, so don't you ever question my dedication for this cause again, you hear me?"

"László," Rowan whispered, standing in the door of the vault. "What the fuck?"

"Mr. Guinne thinks we're down here playing games," László laughed. "What do you think, Row? You think we should show him how serious we are?"

"I think we can't afford the war with Powell Iwan," Rowan said. He came into the vault slowly, circling around behind László to get ahold of the back of László's coat. "Like Da said, remember? It's not a good time to piss the old bastard off."

"So that, at least, was the truth," Tashué said. "The reason Davik hasn't killed me yet is because he doesn't want to break whatever cease-fire treaty he has with Powell."

László shifted his arm ever so slightly and pulled the trigger. The gunshot was deafening, echoing inside the vault, the puff of spent gunpowder rising in Tashué's face. The bullet chipped into the stone and went skittering away into the hall.

László grinned wider than before. "Well, shit. You didn't even flinch, did you?"

"Not my first time having a kid wave a gun in my face," Tashué muttered. "Are we done?"

"I don't know," László said brightly. "Did I get my point across?"

"Sure, László." Tashué hooked the rifle over his shoulder and turned his back on László, leaning down to pick up the bag. It was about as heavy as he expected, the coins inside shifting as he lifted it, jangling together. "Let's get moving so we can leave."

Voices.

The sound made Tashué's chest seize again. Mr. Riley was supposed to leave, but two voices echoed down the hall, fast and urgent and quiet.

"Shit," Rowan breathed.

"Eryn, please, don't—whatever they're after, it's not worth it. They have *guns*! Just let them take what they want—we're not supposed to be here!"

"Fuck," László said. He didn't sound particularly upset or stressed at all, like it was a minor inconvenience.

Tashué turned first, getting out of the vault faster than László. Mr. Riley and the woman with him had stalled halfway down the long hallway, lit from behind by gas lamps in the main lobby of the bank. They both froze completely when Tashué stepped into the hallway in front of them, their words dying half-spoken.

"Stay right there," Tashué said. He pointed the Uhl at the floor in front of their feet, his finger on the trigger guard. "No one needs to get hurt. We'll take the bank notes, and we'll go, and then you can go back to your life like you never saw us here."

"How did you get in here?" the woman asked. Eryn. With curly hair and an elegant trouser suit that made it look like she was headed somewhere for drinks after this. What was she doing here so late at night? "Who are you?"

"None of that matters," Tashué said, keeping his voice as calm and even as he possibly could, even as the inclination to violence made his trigger finger ache. Fuck, László was right—he was so wound up for a fight that it woke all the sharp parts of him, all the things that kept him alive during deployment and action against enemy armies, and it was hard to shake that instinct off. "Stay right where you are, and we'll be out of here as soon as we're loaded."

"No, we should go," Mr. Riley whined, grabbing Eryn's arm and tugging her backward. "Let's go, Eryn. We'll do like he said and pretend we weren't here. We aren't even supposed to be here this late at night. Please!"

"You're not going anywhere until we're done and gone." Tashué's Talent twitched, a living blood-thirsty consciousness that lived in him. The easiest thing would be to kill these people. Crush their bones and pop their hearts like he did to the Enquiry Officers. The instinct sent cold shame down his gut, making him feel heavy. It shouldn't be this easy to consider killing two people who weren't a threat at all. "Lie down," he forced himself to say instead. "Right where you are. Flat on your stomach, with your hands stretched out in front of you."

"Mr. Riley." László's sing-song voice echoed in the hall from behind Tashué's shoulder, menacing and amused and tight and light, all at once, freezing Riley and Eryn before they could obey Tashué's instructions. "You told me no one would be here."

"I forgot to file my slips," Eryn said softly. "I came back to—Mr. Riley, what did you do?"

"I didn't—"

"You let them in!"

"Eryn, please, not now!"

"You let them in, and you opened the vault so they could help themselves? What did you do? Why would you—"

László's revolver barked before Tashué could tell Eryn and Riley to shut up. The smaller calibre didn't give as ferocious a roar as the rifles would, but the silence of the hallway made it echo again and again like he was firing more than once. Tashué's ears rang, his eyes dancing with the spots of light left by the muzzle flash. For a moment, just a moment, it looked like László had fired another warning shot; Riley and Eryn stood side by side, frozen in the middle of a flinch like they didn't know how to react. Riley pressed both his hands into his chest, searching for wounds.

Eryn took a half step back. And then her knees buckled. She fell hard, her hands catching her, blood streaming from her chest in a dark rope; it hadn't shown in her clothes because of all the layers of dark wool she wore and how the gas lamps in the hallway lit her from behind and left her face in total shadow, but once she was on the sandstone floor, all that blood poured out of her, spreading in a puddle around her hands. There was something easy and familiar about casual violence. Something in the quiet and the blood that made the world make sense. Everyone died eventually, and Tashué had spent twenty years trying to pretend he wasn't at peace with that. Trying to convince himself that killing wasn't easy. But it was.

"What did you do?" Riley wailed, snapping out of the long moment of shock. He pushed his hands into his hair. "What did you do—Eryn, no—what did you do?"

He reached for her.

"László, don't—" Rowan gasped.

The revolver barked again and caught the top of Riley's skull. The small calibre didn't have enough power to punch through bone twice; it hit his head and went in, but never came out again. The hole it made turned into a geyser as all that pressure escaped, spraying brain matter and blood in a vicious, ugly arc as Riley fell.

Eryn screamed. She screamed at the floor and at Riley's corpse and the way his skull sprayed blood at her. She tried to stand, but her movements were wobbly and uncoordinated, her legs refusing to take her weight no matter how hard she tried to stand. Tashué's Talent bled into her before he could stop it. He could *help* her, he could stem the flow of blood. The bullet had clipped her spine, and that was why her legs wouldn't work, but the wound was survivable if he stopped the bleeding—

Except he knew with sharp and terrible certainty that László was right. The money was going to the Army of the Red Dawn for the revolution, and if the Patrollers who would inevitably come found out who was responsible, they would come tear the Bay apart before the revolution could even start. They didn't have time for anything else, because the whole city was holding its breath and waiting for the first person to flinch and start the violence, and every day Bothain spent waiting gave them more time to get traction. To find proof, to get Jason out, to rip apart the Authority.

"Put her out of her misery, would you?" László huffed, elbowing Tashué in the side.

"Please," she whimpered. "Please—I don't—please!"

"For fuck's sake, László," Rowan gasped.

"Don't get squeamish on me now, Commander!"

"She didn't *do* anything!" Tashué said, the instinct to say the words mechanical even though László was right. She didn't do anything, and she was completely innocent, but if they let her live, she would explain to the Patrollers what had happened.

She tried to stand again. Almost made it, but then her legs gave out on her again, and she hit the wall with her shoulder. The pain must have broken through the shock, and she screamed. She sobbed. She coughed and choked and went down to the floor, trying to drag herself away.

North Star preserve his soul, how had his life come to this? The shame rose like bile in his throat. This was worse than what his Talent did to the Enquiry Officers, because at least the Enquiry Officers were trying to kill him and Ishmael.

"Anything for Jason except the dirty work, is that it?" László snapped. "I have to do that part because you still need to convince yourself you're the hero. Fuck you."

Tashué moved his finger to the trigger of his rifle. Better to do it with a bullet instead of Talent. The Uhl had a stiff trigger, and he really had to pull. The hammer dropped and the charge exploded and the short range turned her chest into so much paint, splattered over the floor like gruesome art. An offering to the darkest parts of Tashué's soul, dragging all those horrible pieces out of the box he'd tried to keep them in for nineteen years since he left the military.

"Well, shit," László said, bright and happy. "I didn't think you'd actually do it."

Tashué racked the lever action. The spent shell catapulted out, bouncing off the wall beside him and landing in the blood. "Let's get the fucking bags loaded already."

55

ISHMAEL

DAY 37

A llie frowned when she worked, her mouth turning down sharply at the corners, her brow knitting together tightly as her fingers moved. The big composite came together with an agonizing lack of speed. They had to build each word on the plate backward, one infuriating letter or space at a time. Somehow, even though she wasn't the one running the second-hand press, and even though she only ever touched the clean metal, not yet used, she still had ink on her fingers and a smudge of it on her jaw below her ear. Like it was drawn to her, splattering on her skin simply by being in the same room as her.

"Spelling mistake," Ishmael said, earning a scowl.

"Where?" Allie scoffed.

Ishmael touched the composite halfway up the work they'd already done. The plate was enormous to run a full newsprint-sized article, and they'd been working on it a day and a half already. The Rhydderch article. "One of us left letters out of *thoroughly*."

"Dammit," Allie hissed. She touched the word, sliding her finger across the whole line of set type. "Dammit. That line *barely* fits—if I add the missing letters in, it will knock the word *shine* off the end of the line and into the next one, and then I have to reset the whole chunk of text below it. We have to get this one out at the boxing match."

Ishmael winced. "Well. We're publishing to the Bay. Maybe they won't notice. Over in the Commonwealth, printers have been dropping letters out of words on purpose to cut down on all this fiddly shit. Commas, too."

Allie sighed, sitting up straighter and rubbing her eyes. The ink on her fingers left black smudges on her cheekbones, making her look like a racoon. A coal miner. She stared up at the ceiling a while, and the way she craned her neck back gave Ishmael full view of the last shapes of the faded bruise. Every time he saw it, the guilt opened up like a wound that refused to heal. Tashué had asked him to help her before everything collapsed in on them. And he'd been such a mess from killing Losek for Powell that he hadn't listened. He was too busy being angry at Tashué for stupid things, and angry at Deri for being dead, and angry at himself for being a fucking mess all the time. But Allie wasn't interested in his guilt or his apologies. And she never tried to cover the bruise. She let everyone watch it heal. He tried to apologize since they met, but she wouldn't have it.

"Don't do that," she'd told him when he tried. "Don't sit around and feel guilty for what happened. Don't make it my job to tell you it wasn't your fault."

The guilt didn't go anywhere, though. But he swallowed it, and kept it off her plate so it wasn't her job to make him feel better, like she said.

He turned away from her on his chair, eyes scanning the massive table of type in front of him. The tiny metal letters made his eyes ache. Davik relented, giving them the cellar beneath the Dripping Bucket, and Wolfe had sent a press and paper and stacks and stacks of boxes of letters. So he and Allie hunched over plates and set letters together to make the pages, while Vasska helped with the printing press, stamping each page with the articles Ishmael and Allie built, and employees from the *Bucket*—who didn't mind losing wages for a few hours to come downstairs and help—hung the papers up in the impossibly long hallway beneath the street to let the ink dry. Writing the articles turned out to be the easiest and least time consuming part of the process.

Ishmael picked up a line of type, one of the White Shield slugs they'd made with the massive Linotype machine. They mentioned Tashué's White Shield as often as humanly possible. Ishmael's career was harder to publish, so they talked endlessly about the watch shop and the Saeati name and the Qasani community, which made Ishmael ache. Thank the gods his parents weren't alive to see this mess. It would break their hearts.

Allie's attention had wandered off the ceiling and over toward the press. Ishmael glanced over her shoulder, following her eyes. Vasska had his back to them, and over by the fire it was warm enough that he'd stripped down to his shirt sleeves. He had ink on him, too, black stains on his hands, on his sleeves, in his bright blond hair.

"So, what are we doing, boss?" Ishmael asked, tapping the line of type on his palm. The lead was cold. The whole basement was cold. They kept the ink close to the fire so it didn't freeze, but the corner where they could fit the typesetting table was too far from the flames to catch the warmth. Ishmael would have used gloves, but that made the letters too hard to handle. "Are we fixing the type or are you day dreaming about Vasska Czarny's lips for the rest of the night?"

"What?" Allie asked, turning sharply, a blush climbing up her cheeks.

Ishmael chuckled. "I don't know what you're waiting for. He would drop everything for you if ever you invited him for a drink. Or a smoke. Or whatever it is you need to get in the mood."

The blush got deeper, and Allie leaned forward, snatching the missing letters from the boxes to start fixing *thoroughly*. "It's stupid. I don't have time for this. We're trying to start a revolution, and I'm not getting emotionally tangled up with the man who's set to inherit the Bay. It's frivolous and ridiculous."

"I'm not talking about emotions, Miss Tei," Ishmael laughed. "I'm talking about a good, relaxing, invigorating fuck. If you don't want to, I won't mention it again. But if you want to? If you look at him and wonder what his hands feel like on your body and what his lips taste like? It's not frivolous. We could all die tonight. Or tomorrow. Or at any point from here on. Bothain Clannaugh could knock down that door right now and gun us all down, or we could we could get shot at the boxing match by some trigger-happy Patroller who's on riot patrol. But right now, in this moment? You're young and you're beautiful and maybe a little horny, and so is Vasska. There's nothing frivolous about being *alive* while you have the chance because you never know when the chance will disappear."

"Spoken like a true hedonist," Allie muttered.

Ishmael shrugged. "Spoken like someone who's only wish is that they had a little bit more time with the people I loved. Spoken like someone's who's deepest regrets are all the things I left unsaid and all the chances I didn't take."

Allie shook her head again, beginning the slow and miserable job of sliding all the words around on the composite. "You say that like all the people you love are behind you now. Like there's no one else."

"Not all of them." He shuffled through his pockets, finding the bag of raisins he'd taken from Davik's larder. He wasn't able to keep snacks anymore since he had to be mindful of how often he was out in public. Everything he had was at the *Bucket* or in Davik's kitchen—and it was slowly driving him out of his mind. "But enough of them that I've noticed the pattern."

"What do you think is taking so long?" Allie asked.

"Vasska? He's waiting for you to say something, I think."

"No, not Vasska," Allie huffed, rolling her eyes at Ishmael. "General Clannaugh. We're fighting a revolution, not planning my sex life."

Ishmael grimaced, shaking his head. "I don't know what's taking so long. I thought he'd make a move by now. He's waiting for us, maybe. Letting us hang ourselves in the court of public opinion. If he doesn't start the fight, it's harder for us to say we're defending ourselves."

Footsteps down the stairs—one of the bartenders made her way down, hovering in the doorway. "Mr. Saeati? Dav is asking for you."

Ishmael sighed, gathering up his cane. The fucking stairs were the worst part of his life these days, but thank fuck for Tashué's Talent and how quickly he was able to push the healing along. "What now?"

"Miss Redbone is here, sir. Dav said you needed to hear what she and Miss Winter have to say."

Something cold rolled through Ishmael's body, and the tension made his knee ache anew. It was one thing for Eirdis Redbone to come talk politics with Davik—her boxing match was tomorrow, after all. But Illea? And Davik had apparently decided that hearing what they had to say was worth admitting to Eirdis that Ishmael was indeed alive and hiding in the Bay, which didn't feel promising at all.

"Sure," he said. "Tell them I'm coming."

The bartender led Ishmael to one of the private rooms on the second floor of the *Bucket*, over the kitchen and incredibly hot. Which, after freezing his fingers over their composite, felt like heaven. There was a dining table set in case they wanted to eat. An assortment of breads and jams sat as offering, but there were no servants around to distribute the food. Everyone had settled on the other side of the room, on a selection of sofas and soft chairs. Davik had an incredible eye for comfortable furniture; maybe having a whorehouse made you an expert in what shape of chaise lounge made people want to sit in place forever and never want to leave.

Mallory's eyes lit up when she saw him, and she pushed herself to her feet. "Ishmael! You're alive, thank the North Star. What happened to your leg?"

Ishmael let himself limp into the room, eyes scanning the faces watching him. Eirdis, Illea, Mallory, Davik. Mallory was a surprise. Illea and Eirdis looked plenty comfortable, though, like they knew this room and had met Davik here before. If that was the case, it wasn't really a shock that Illea and Eirdis had come down to the Bay to scheme with Davik; after all, the Bay was more important to the Yaelsmuir economy than rich people liked to admit, and neither Eirdis nor Illea were the type to leave things to chance when it came to control.

"A young man named Matt dislocated it," Ishmael grunted. He made his way to the closest soft piece of furniture and rested the cane on the arm of it so he could strip out of his coat.

"Why?" Mallory scoffed.

Ishmael shrugged, casting a longing glance over that table. He wanted to go see what was on offer, but fuck his leg hurt. "He wanted Captain Blackwood to tell him how much he knew about the Authority's secrets. Captain Blackwood declined."

"Matt had a bronze badge, didn't he?" Davik asked, even though he knew the answer.

"He did indeed, Mr. Kaine." Ishmael sank down into the sofa, breathing a sigh of relief as he came off his leg. "He is no longer serving the Authority."

Illea's colour went a little pale and a little grey, but she lifted her chin and took a slow breath. Strange, that. It wasn't like her to be squeamish. She glanced toward the table and the bread like she was considering getting up and snatching something for herself, but something stopped her. Manners, maybe.

"General Wolfe sends his regards," Eirdis said. "He thought we might see you if we came down here, which he only admitted with great reluctance. He would have come himself, but he's currently under house arrest."

"House arrest?" Ishmael echoed. "Under whose jurisdiction?"

"Guess, Ishmael," Eirdis said. "It can't be that much of a mystery."

Ishmael snarled, clenching a fist around the head of his cane. "Fucking Clannaugh."

"Fucking Clannaugh indeed," Davik said slowly. "Fucking Clannaugh is the reason I called you here, Saeati. Our esteemed Miss Redbone has a few things to say about this whole mess, and I would appreciate your insight."

Davik was angry. The thought struck Ishmael only as Davik's emphasis fell strangely on the word *insight* and the way he sat so stiffly in his chair. He spoke slowly so he could keep control of his words. Ishmael's eyes swept over everyone's faces again, trying to gauge what had sparked such low-simmering fury from Davik. Eirdis, maybe. Eirdis and her angry eyes and the firm set to her jaw that she got when she was arguing with people and thought she was right.

"Sure," Ishmael said. "My insight."

"I take it Captain Blackwood is alive as well," Eirdis said. "And hiding somewhere in the Bay."

"I can neither confirm nor deny Captain Blackwood's whereabouts," Ishmael said. "Although rumour has it the Authority killed him."

"Ishmael, don't," Eirdis said.

"What are we supposed to do, Miss Redbone?" Davik asked, spreading his hands. "Lie to you? I know he's a valuable man these days, but I can't make him appear out of thin air for you. Wherever he went, I had no part in it."

"But you've taken in Ishmael Saeati?" Eirdis asked, turning her pale, angry eyes on Davik. "I'm to believe you found the one and not the other?"

"Aye, Miss Redbone. Mr. Saeati looked so pathetic, limping his way around the Bay. Like a mangy, injured dog. I expect Blackwood left him behind. If the big bastard is smart, he left the city entirely."

"That's what Bothain thinks you've done," Illea said. "He thinks you left to find Deri's allies and hide with them. Apparently Maes is hoping for it, so he can track those people down."

Fury clawed its way up Ishmael's throat, but he fought to keep his features impassive. Hopefully his general bad mood would cover the fresh layer of outrage he felt at Maes's name. But Mallory was watching him in that silent, intent way she did, so maybe he wasn't fooling her at all. Not after she saw Clannaugh had Ishmael the letter from Deri and say *if I hadn't seen your file myself.*

"You're on a first name basis with General Clannaugh, are you?"

Illea rolled her eyes at him. "Don't you start with me, Ishmael. My first name basis with him is helping you, isn't it? Because now I'm here to warn you that Maes doesn't feel like things are settled even though Deri is dead, and all of this is an excuse for him to stick his nose into Yaelsmuir business."

"Isn't Maes some politician in White Crown?" Davik asked. "What's he care about Yaelsmuir?"

"Maes cares about power," Ishmael said. "And he'll take it however he can get it. Yaelsmuir may not be as opulent as White Crown, and we haven't any royalty up here, but we have industry, and this city has money. And Rainer Elsworth wants to build a police force. That's more than enough to draw Maes's interest."

"We're going to prevent the police force," Eirdis cut in. "This is going to stop, and we'll run this election properly, and the people of this city will vote Myron out once and for all. The only reason his career has survived this long is because Miss Winter hasn't openly opposed him in the past. But Illea has kindly thrown her public support behind the Redbone campaign. We're finally ahead in all the polls. Every single one, Ishmael. You know how valuable that is. But the vote isn't won yet. Civil unrest could still derail us. If people start to wonder if maybe the police force is necessary after all, then I lose. It's that simple. And I'm not interested in losing."

"What civil unrest?" Ishmael asked. "Haven't you noticed how quiet the Bay is these days? It's rather relaxing down here."

"And it's going to stay that way," Eirdis said. "At least until after the vote. Stay gone, Ishmael. Disappear fully. Stop running these inflammatory papers, and find somewhere else to hide. For your sake, and for the city. And Mr. Kaine, if you would be so kind as to produce Captain Blackwood for a peaceful surrender to the Patrollers, and we will figure out what other measures need to be taken to maintain an air of control. I suspect it will be a round of arrests, and I come to you out of courtesy. Perhaps you could give us a list of people who could be arrested without interrupting the flow of your business too much."

Well, shit. No wonder Davik was angry.

"Courtesy, is it?" Davik asked slowly. "Leave it to a politician to think that coming into my quarter and demanding the right to arrest my people is a courtesy."

"Your quarter?" Eirdis echoed. "I was under the impression that the Bay belongs to Powell Iwan and you were but a house guest. If you prefer, I could go to him and ask for a list of people. I'm sure he will give me plenty of names of Red Dawn soldiers."

Davik tilted his head to one side. And smiled. A slow, poisonous, vicious smile, that reminded Ishmael of a big cat yawning to show its massive teeth. "Your courtesy is startlingly short lived, Miss Redbone."

"Eirdis, you can't be serious," Ishmael said. "There's a reason we're pushing this hard. It goes beyond the election."

"I know, damnit," Eirdis snapped. "You think I don't know? General Wolfe explained everything to me, and Rainer's actions are deplorable. Obscene. Which is exactly why everything hinges on this election. If Myron is Governor again, it gives Rainer the latitude to protect himself, and we can't have that."

"It won't matter who's Governor if the people of Yaelsmuir revolt," Ishmael said. "We'll drag Rainer through the streets and have him drawn and quartered, so we can hang the bits of him all around the city so the world knows the Authority is a bloated corpse."

"Ishmael," Mallory gasped.

"What?" Ishmael snapped, turning his gaze on her. "I don't expect you to judge me for knowing what's necessary, *General* Imburleigh. You know what war looks like."

"Isn't it possible that knowing what war looks like is exactly why I don't want to see it here?" Mallory asked.

"Perhaps you should explain why Mr. Saeati's position is so dire, Illea," Eirdis said. "So that he knows exactly what's at stake if he doesn't cooperate."

Illea sighed, looking between Davik and Ishmael. "Bothain has been gathering up all the evidence you have been so generously supplying. The pile of illegal media, the massive shipment of guns that came down the river—he's sending it all down to White Crown, over the telegraph wire and in the mail, so General Maes can show the Queen exactly what Mr. Kaine is up to."

"How does Clannaugh know about the guns?" Ishmael asked, turning to Davik. Even though he knew the answer. Nothing passed through the Hive without Powell Iwan knowing about it. He was getting ready to make his move. "You only just got them today."

"I don't know," Davik said slowly, his voice gone so sharp it could cut through bone, so cold it left ice in the air. "How *does* he know?"

"It wasn't me," Ishmael said, meeting his eye.

"What concerns me is what he's doing with the news, Mr. Kaine," Eirdis cut in.

The realization hit Ishmael so suddenly that he could almost feel the gears in his head meeting, and starting to spin, setting off the long line of thoughts. "He'll have the Army of the Red Dawn declared anti-Crowne militia so he can march his precious 12th up here to bathe the city in blood instead of waiting for the Queen's Council to vote on the police force."

"You need to stop," Eirdis said again. "You need to put an end to this before it gets out of hand. Bothain Clannaugh and Eduart Maes are formidable enemies, and I won't be inviting their wholesale slaughter into Yaelsmuir."

"But you'll step aside and let Rainer Elsworth get away with mutilating children?" Ishmael asked. "That's what we're fighting against down here. Talented children, bred by the Authority like prize beef, and then turned into *energy units* to power industry."

"I'm not letting him get away with anything," Eirdis snapped.

Illea reached out, putting a hand very delicately on Eirdis's wrist. She'd been strangely quiet, but that disinterested look she wore gave her away. Ishmael had long since learnt that the only time Illea looked bored was when she was paying the most attention. A clever ruse that he'd adopted himself, and he wasn't even sure if she was aware of the habit or not. Maybe she wasn't used to sitting with Davik Kaine after all—maybe his company, in his pub, kept her on her guard, stemming the flow of whatever advice she wanted to give. Or maybe she was playing Eirdis and she'd chosen to stand with Clannaugh—he was exactly the type she liked to use, and his connection to Maes made him the most powerful man in Yaelsmuir.

And then there was the matter of her pregnancy—the thought struck him hard. He watched her a while, letting her feel the weight of his attention. The memory of that last time they spoke crawled out from under everything else that had happened since. She was pregnant and desperate to get rid of Myron. What an incredible gift this chaos must have seemed.

"After the election, we'll bring him to account for everything," Eirdis continued, calmer than before. It was a surprise Illea had tried to restrain her since her passion was as practiced and purposeful as the rest of her appearance. It was why the Bay loved her, all that fire and rhetoric that was deemed unseemly by Highview and their ilk. But maybe Illea could see that it was wasted on Davik, especially given the topic of conversation. "But I can't do that if Myron wins. We're talking about innocent people. Who knows how many hundreds of people will die if you let Clannaugh get a foothold in the Bay? Consider the cost, Ishmael—"

"You're right, Miss Redbone," Davik interrupted. "You're absolutely right. I have no interest in fighting a war with Bothain Clannaugh over Tashué Blackwood. I don't know the man. I don't care for him much. He brought a lot of aggravation to my door, didn't he? If I see him down here, I'll send for your Patrollers. I don't know about the arrests, though. My people won't like it."

"My advice would be to let the Patrollers arrest people at the boxing match," Illea said. "Things will get rowdy after the fight, as they often do at sporting events. Let the Patrollers charge a slew of people with the usual drunken party charges, break up a number of fights."

"Can we even run the boxing match with all the unrest?" Eirdis asked, glancing at Illea. "Won't it be dangerous?"

"With all due respect, Miss Redbone, I won't be calling off the match the day before it's supposed to run," Davik said stiffly. "The people of this quarter have been working hard to make this match happen. We built the club ourselves, and Mr. Coswyn is a rising star in the Bay. If we cancel the match, you'll get your rioting, except they'll blame you. Whether or not you show up to your own fundraiser is your business, I suppose. If you're afraid, you don't have to come. But if you cancel it, the Bay will never forgive you."

Eirdis opened her mouth as if to argue, but Illea squeezed her hand.

"He's right, Eirdis," Illea said. "You can't cancel. And you *must* be there. The Bay is your largest and most loyal voting base. If you insult them now, your career in public office is over. You have to show your face. If you're feeling especially bold, you can get arrested."

"Illea, be serious," Eirdis scoffed.

"I am being serious," Illea said. "If you're arrested in the Bay for standing with the people here? Your career in this quarter would be untouchable."

Eirdis went quiet as she considered it. The tilt of her head and the way her eyes flicked between Davik and Ishmael said she was thinking about it. It was so incredibly exhausting. He shouldn't be surprised. He'd had this conversation a dozen times over, and it all seemed so petty when he was helping people manipulate *their* politics, *their* people, *their* voting base. It was his job. But now that it was his city, his home, his streets, now that it was people he knew, people he loved, and it was all on behalf of children who deserved more from the world, it was infuriating. Enraging. Exhausting.

"I want you to produce Captain Blackwood, Mr. Kaine," Eirdis said. "Before the election. I will turn him over to General Clannaugh, and they can hang him or whatever they want, and it will pull the wind out of Maes's sails before the Queen gives him the move he wants."

"Of course, Miss Redbone," Davik said. "Anything to protect my quarter. We'll be seeing you at the match, then?"

"Yes, Mr. Kaine," Eirdis said, pushing herself to her feet. "I think I will."

"Ishmael," Mallory said. She'd been even quieter than Illea, her eyes guarded and her mouth drawn into a hard line. "Would you walk with me for a moment?"

"Walking isn't exactly my favourite hobby these days, Mallory," Ishmael said, tapping the cane on the floor. "Why?"

Mallory sighed slowly, glancing between everyone in the room one by one. "Is there anywhere private we can talk?"

"You can have the room, General Imburleigh," Davik said, pushing himself to his feet. "I should get back to the club. You should come by, Miss Redbone. I know my folks would be honoured to have the opportunity to show off their hard work, and you could come meet young Mr. Coswyn."

"I best be getting back to Brickheart," Eirdis said. She *had* to know how insulting that was, and she didn't seem to care. "I've too much to do before the match. You'll catch up, Mallory?"

Mallory nodded. "I can make my own way, Eirdis."

56

LORNE
DAY 37

Training without Davik or László or Rowan felt an awful lot like drifting through the water without a rudder to guide him, but he didn't have time to feel lost, so he worked anyway. He threw punches until his body screamed, and then watched other people spar while he ate a pile of food that László left for him. And then trained some more, even though it was late, because he couldn't go upstairs to the apartment. The emptiness of it made him cagey, anxious. The quiet felt unnatural.

Rowan came back first. He didn't have his fancy Uhl rifle with him when he walked through the club and he didn't have any blood on his clothes, either. The relief at seeing him again was so powerful it made Lorne feel ill. It had to be a good sign that he'd come back relatively quickly with clean hands. Right?

"Where's Da?"

"Over at the *Bucket*," Lorne said.

Rowen sent someone across the street and then retreated out of the crowd of the pugilist club.

"Everyone's back?" Lorne asked. "Everyone's safe?"

Rowan shrugged and turned away. Didn't want to talk about it out in the open, maybe. Lorne's bones quivered as he followed Rowan to Davik's office. Exhaustion and excitement were a strange combination, fuelling him on even when he wanted to collapse into a sweaty heap, but he couldn't rest now. László was back. László was safe. He hadn't been arrested. Tashué too—Lorne chose to believe everything was fine because Rowan didn't look panicked, and there wasn't any blood on his clothes, and he didn't smell like gunpowder.

László sat on the edge of Davik's desk, half a dozen canvas bags on the floor at his feet. His body vibrated, buzzed, the excitement in him so big that it couldn't be contained by the outline of him. He laughed when Lorne stepped in, kicking one of the bags, but it was so heavy that it didn't move much, sagging to the left and hitting the leg of Davik's desk.

"You did it," Lorne breathed. His voice was a hot metal rasp through his throat, fighting through disbelief, through tension, through excitement. "László, you actually fucking did it."

"Of course I fucking did it," László laughed. "Have a little faith in me, Mr. Lightning. We've been working on this a long time."

"Come here."

László stood up straighter, the grin wide and wild across his face, his beautiful brown eyes shining. He had to step over bags to get to Lorne, clumsy, gangly, moving too fast for his limbs to keep up. He threw himself against Lorne's body, so hard they almost fell over. Lorne caught him, wrapped his arms around László, barely keeping them both up. László pushed his face into Lorne's neck, giving a deep, rumbling sound that almost sounded like a purr. It felt so good to hold László, to feel that rumble of László's voice against his skin. So good he felt ashamed. He *wasn't* falling for László Dargis. It was just that he was so fucking comfortable here, and living with László and Davik was the first time he'd actually liked Yaelsmuir, and so his stupid emotions were all muddled together in his head. Convincing him he had feelings for László when it was just that he had finally found a place that felt like home, and it gave him a clarity he'd been looking for his whole life. And tomorrow, Jason would get out, and he'd get the chance to hold the right person in his arms. Finally.

"You're so fucking sweaty." László's husky bedroom voice melted Lorne's skin. "I love it."

László kissed him. Slow but rough, teeth scraping Lorne's lip in a threat, a promise that things could get wild in an instant. Lorne groaned against László's mouth, his heart pounding so hard it was rattling his rib cage. He wanted it. He wanted it so bad he could hardly breathe.

Wanted it so bad it made him hate himself. Their tongues danced together, and their bodies vibrated at a shared frequency exclusive to them, shaking away Lorne's twisting thoughts. László's mouth tasted strange, something sweet and astringent on his tongue.

"What is that?" Lorne asked. He caught László's lips between his teeth, sucking the flavour off him. "What did you eat?"

"You want some?" László asked, grinning.

"What is it?" Lorne asked again.

"Just a leaf," László said. "Just a little leaf that kicks you in the heart and makes everything feel sharper. You should have some with me. We should feel this good together."

"Yeah," Lorne said. Stupid answer, and he knew it immediately, but László was intoxicating. "Sure."

László pulled a leaf out from somewhere, rolling it into a tight ball before putting it in Lorne's mouth. "Chew it slowly. Hold it between your teeth and don't swallow the leaf."

He did as László said, pressing the leaf between his teeth, that same flavour spilling over his tongue, making him salivate, which only pulled more flavour from it.

The door swung open, and Tashué came in, Rowan trailing behind him. Rowan only carried one bag, but Tashué had two—one on each shoulder like bags of potatoes, keeping them steady with his big hands. He paused a moment when he saw Lorne and László tangled together. Lorne let go of László, taking a big step back, his whole body burning with shame. And then Tashué walked into the centre of Davik's office, shrugging his shoulders to drop the bags at Lorne's feet.

"Where's Davik?" Tashué grunted.

"Ah—he's coming," Lorne said.

"Maybe you could help us unload," Tashué said. "There's still a lot left."

Lorne staggered down the hall in Tashué's shadow. Rowan was coming in again with a new bag. He had started crying at some point, his face wet with tears, eyes wide and red. Why was he crying?

Tashué stomped past Rowan, out the door. Lorne realized too late he wasn't wearing a shirt. It was fucking cold outside, so cold it hurt. The rain had stopped, but the wind was still howling and wet like it would blow the storm right back. Tashué walked to the back of the wagon and leaned in, dragging a bag out and shoving it into Lorne's arms. His muscles vibrated, exhausted but fuelled by the stupid leaf.

"How'd it go?" Lorne asked.

Tashué shook his head, dragging two more bags to the back of the carriage. "Fucking great. Two people died."

"Who?" Lorne asked. "Who died?"

"Two employees at the bank, dead because of us." He rested his hands on the bags, looking Lorne in the eye. There was something about his hot amber gaze that made Lorne feel incredibly small. "When I said I was here for Jason and I was willing to do anything for him, I meant it. Who are you here for, Lorne? László? Your boxing gloves?"

Lorne opened his mouth to answer—to say something half decent that might explain how the boxing gloves were for Jason, that the match was for Jason, that Lorne's heart beat for Jason, but he knew how stupid it would all sound because Tashué had walked in on Lorne and László tangled all together.

"Fuck you, Tashué," Lorne said, instead of saying any of the perfectly good words that were flitting through his head. "You don't know me."

"I do, actually," Tashué laughed. "You're not that mysterious. Three and a half years is a long time to be alone. And maybe you can convince yourself you're fine for a while, but there's only so many times you can polish your own wood before you start wishing for someone else, right?"

"Right!" Lorne snapped, tension flowing from the leaf and straight into his chest. "And that's between me and Jason, isn't it? Because we're fucking adults, and we talked about it, and we made a deal over shit like this. Which I would have told you if you'd asked me instead of throwing your bullshit accusations at me!"

"A deal," Tashué echoed.

"Yes, a fucking deal!" The bag was heavier than he'd expected, dragging at his exhausted arms, and his jaw felt half locked around the leaf, but words came out of him in a hot, furious rush. "No one important. And it was the easiest thing I've ever agreed to in my life because no one in the world could ever be more important than him!"

Tashué rolled his eyes, grabbing one bag in each massive hand and lifting them like they were nothing. "Yeah, Lorne, sure. I bet that deal didn't see László Dargis coming, did it?"

Lorne opened his mouth to deny it, but Tashué didn't wait for an answer. He stalked back to the door and threw his big shoulder against it to force it open, sending it swinging too hard on its hinges so it hit the wall behind it with a bang so loud Lorne felt it in his gut. Lorne scrambled to keep up with him, but he couldn't seem to move fast enough even though his heart was racing a million beats a minute, and his hands were so filled with energy they shook as he hefted the bag of money up to his shoulder. Time moved faster and he had to drag himself through it to keep up. The leaf, it must be the leaf. And the fact that he'd let himself think that things were going to be fine, but two people had died, but Tashué wanted to argue about László.

Davik was in the office by the time Lorne got back. He laughed at the bags of money. He stood at the centre of them and turned in a circle once, twice, like he couldn't quite believe what he was seeing. Lorne dropped his bag at Davik's feet, and Davik laughed again. He sounded like László, laughing that much.

"Do you want to see, Dav?" László asked.

László didn't wait for an answer, either. He unbuckled the top flap of the bag, dragging it open and upending it. Tightly bundled stacks of paper spilled across Davik's desk. Davik grabbed a stack, and then another, piling them in an orderly tower, like he couldn't bear the mess on his desk, but he was also laughing at each bundle, stacking them higher and higher.

They did it. They'd robbed the *fucking* bank. Lorne's heart beat faster, faster. His arteries vibrated. Stolen bank notes for the revolution. There wasn't any blood on the money but there were two bodies tied to it. What happened? The questions were fucking endless—who killed those people? Why? Had they put up a fight? Had they left Tashué, Rowan, and László no other choice? Or was it easy? Rowan was crying, and Tashué's whole body boiled with his fury, but László was so fucking happy that it sent Lorne spinning. Had he killed both people?

"I didn't just get notes," László said, grabbing another bag. "I got crowns, too. I thought we could use the crowns first, because other banks'll be suspicious about notes for a while. Copper and silver and gold."

He lifted the second bag, and that one gave the clink, metal coins inside shifting. Coins spilt everywhere, a cascade of glittering, shining gold that rolled like a wave across Davik's desk, knocking the pile of banknotes over, pouring down onto the floor, clattering, spinning, leaping through the air. And Lorne's jaw was flexed too hard, clamping the leaf between his teeth so his whole face ached with the pressure. The sound of the gold clattered in his skull over and over again, the coins bouncing off the floor. Moments passed in snatches, faster than Lorne could grasp. László threw his arms around Davik's shoulders. Davik hugged him so hard László's feet left the floor. He spun László around, and they were both laughing. Surrounded in money. Laughing too much.

It was all suddenly and inescapably real. There was no stopping it all, not now. They were a tram without brakes, and they were heading down-hill, hurtling toward the inevitable end. Except Lorne didn't know what that end would be. And he couldn't move. He was rooted in place, watching, his mind over-saturated with the sound of all that glittering gold and the taste of the khat leaf. László leaned across the desk, sweeping his arm through coins and notes, sending them tumbling and rolling and twisting in the air, a waterfall of sparkling wealth.

Lorne dropped to his knees beside the pile of money on the floor, picking up gold coins and shoving them back into the empty bag. Just to do something. He had to move or the fucking leaf would burn him alive, but he couldn't think of anything helpful to do except cleaning up the mess László made with all that stolen money. The gold was warm and heavier than he expected, and the paper was thick and soft like fabric.

Tashué dropped another bag in the pile, on top of half the gold that had fallen on the floor. "Did you tell him?"

"Tell him what?" László scoffed.

"Fuck's sake, László," Rowan gasped. "What, did you forget?"

"Tell me what?" Davik echoed.

"Two people died," Tashué said. "Two bank employees. I take it no one was supposed to be there, but sometimes life tells you to go fuck yourself. I figure we have until someone tries to open the bank, before anyone knows."

"It was supposed to be easy, László," Davik said. "You said no one was going to be there."

"The manager said he wanted to let us in," László said with an exag-gerated shrug. "So he let us in. The woman wasn't supposed to be there. She said something about filing something, I don't know. So we shot them both."

"You didn't have to shoot them," Rowan said, shaking his head. "You didn't have to. We could have had them sit down and shut up, and then they could have walked away when we were done."

"I know what I *could* have done, and I know what *would* have happened if we had," László said, throwing up his hands. "The woman had figured it out, and she would have told the Patrollers what she knew. The Patrollers would have leaned on Riley for details, and then he would have sold us up the river. And once I killed her, I had to kill him too, because he didn't have the spine to keep his mouth shut about murder. He would have sent the Patrollers our way in an instant, and that would have been the end of it. So I shut them both up and now we're fine."

Rowan shook his head, hands swiping angrily at the tears in his eyes. "Innocent people—"

"Oh Rowan, shut the *fuck* up," László laughed. "You're all fired up when you talk about us against them, but now that it's time to fight, suddenly they're innocent people? Grow up. No one is innocent. This whole fucking city has blood on their hands. You knew that yesterday, when you were mouthy with Ari about his tainted wife. Are you going to cry about every single one of our enemies that we kill? Next time we're under threat, are you going to pull the trigger, or are you going to stand around and think about how cute and innocent they are, even though they'd let the Authority kill us all because we're *tainted?*"

"Fuck you, László," Rowan gasped, swiping at the tears in his eyes. "It's not a character flaw to not be a blood-thirsty lunatic!"

László lunged at Rowan, but Tashué was between them faster than Davik, before László could put his hands on Rowan. He held up an arm, the flat of it hitting László's chest and stopping him dead.

"You don't get to come at him for struggling with it," Tashué said, his voice gone flat and cold. "Maybe it comes easy to you, and maybe you're right that we didn't have a choice, but he gets to feel it. What we did was fucking horrible, and it takes time to come to terms with the way the world shifts when you see something like that. So take a walk and let him process it. Let him figure out who he wants to be when everything goes to shit."

"Fuck you, Mr. *Guinne*," László scoffed, spitting the fake name out like it tasted bitter in his mouth. "You don't give orders around here."

"László, he's right," Davik said. "Take a fucking walk."

"Dav," László scoffed.

"Here," Davik said, hefting one of the bags. "Give the copper away. Pass it out. Give it to everyone here for all the hard work they're doing."

"Yeah," László laughed, the sound skittering over Lorne's brain. The anger was gone in an instant. "Yeah, you're right. Yeah. Folks'll like that. I'll tell 'em it's from you, hey?"

"Yeah, you do that, László," Davik said. "Fucking good job."

László lifted one of the bags, tossing it at Lorne, and Lorne had to move fast to catch it so it didn't hit him in the face, and all the weight of coin shifted in his arms like something liquid and hard at once. László grabbed the other bag, heading for the door. "Let's go, Mr. Lightning. Let's fucking go. Your fans are waiting."

57

ISHMAEL
DAY 37

"There are guards at the factory now," Mallory whispered, once everyone was gone. She moved to the chair closest to Ishmael so she could lean in. "I asked who hired them and what exactly they're guarding, but no one on the board seems to know. Or they're pretending they don't know. They are generally averse to answering my questions these days, never mind in the middle of all this."

All this. Ishmael sighed, shuffling through his pockets, but there was nothing in there for him. He'd left the damned raisins on the table beside Allie's elbow. "Haven't there always been guards at the factory? To keep people away from the guns."

Mallory rolled her eyes, shooting Ishmael a weary glare. Sweat beaded on her temple, down her jaw, kissing the collar of her bodice. She always wore such high collars, no matter how low hemlines were plunging in the name of shifting fashion. Gods, he needed something to eat to hold his attention, or he was going to get himself in trouble, watching the lines the sweat made on Mallory's skin. "I am aware, thank you. I meant *more* guards than there used to be—and they're guarding the buildings that have furnaces."

"Ah—they're guarding the place where the children are working," Ishmael said softly, all thoughts of Mallory's sweat evaporating from his mind.

She nodded. "Exactly."

"Are they Authority?"

"I don't know," Mallory admitted, her eyes going distant and a little hard around the edges. "I thought it wouldn't look good if I asked too many questions this time. The board is generally annoyed with me as it is since I've been fighting with them over Mairead's seat. If they are Authority, I don't want them to report back to Rainer that I'm asking so many questions."

Ishmael sighed, shuffling through his pockets again. "Do you smoke anymore?"

"Only occasionally, when I'm especially stressed."

Ishmael nodded, pulling his cigarette case from his pocket and flicking it open. "Seems like a good occasion, then."

Mallory sighed, wiping her eyes as Ishmael pulled a pair of cigarettes from the case. "So long as it's only tobacco."

"Please, Mallory," Ishmael scoffed. "You're much too uptight for anything more fun than tobacco. I've learnt my lesson."

Mallory rolled her eyes, snatching the cigarette from Ishmael's fingers. "We're fighting a war against everything our society is built on, and yet you still manage to find time and energy to be petty and insulting. Truly you are a work of art, Ishmael Saeati."

"Pettiness is my armour against the insanity of it all," Ishmael said, sparking a match and holding the flame out to her so she could light her cigarette. "If I don't casually insult people I deeply care about at regular intervals, I might actually go out of my mind. Again."

"When's the last time you were out of your mind?" Mallory asked, exhaling the first cloud of smoke. "This morning?"

Ishmael forced a smile, lighting his cigarette quickly as the flame crawled down the matchstick, getting perilously close to his fingertips. "It's been a while. I think you were still hiding in Cruinnich in those days."

Mallory grimaced and looked away, like she was trying to hide the pain he'd caused. She exhaled slowly, blowing a line of smoke over toward the hearth. "I won't apologize for doing what I had to do to save my marriage."

"I wasn't asking for an apology," Ishmael muttered. "I was making a joke."

"You still haven't learnt the difference between a joke and being cruel with a smile on your face." She looked back at Ishmael and there was a bit of a tremble in her hand when she lifted her cigarette to her mouth again. "I'm not doing this with you. This infantile bickering, back and forth. I don't know what it is about you that always makes me want to pull out my own hair so I have something long enough to *strangle* you with. Honestly, Ishmael, why are you smiling? Like you're still a smug, self-satisfied child."

Ishmael tiled his head enough to blow the smoke over Mallory's head. It billowed up toward the ceiling, dancing among the old, exposed floor joists. "I was going to apologize, actually."

"You were not," Mallory scoffed.

"I swear I was. You're right. This isn't the time for me to make jokes. But I have to admit, it's nice to know I can still get such a passionate response out of you, Mallory Imburleigh."

She shook her head, looking away again. At another time in their lives, Ishmael would have reached out to her. He would have touched her hair and kissed her neck and teased the high collar of her bodice down, unwrapping her like she was the finest gift there was. And she would pretend to stay angry with him the entire time, but she would still let him kiss her, touch her. They were young when they learnt together that they liked to fuck angry, that there was incredible power and release in riling each other up, tearing each other apart, and making each other orgasm. But they were too young and inexperienced to know how to clear the tension it left behind, and all their anger festered between them like unclean wounds, until nothing could have saved them.

"Mairead does this, too," Mallory said. "She's weaponized apologies and humour against her... against Alistair."

"It's fine," Ishmael said. "Alistair is her father. He's done everything for her."

Mallory turned to Ishmael, her deep thinking face returning. "Maybe you have grown. There was a time not all that long ago when you weren't so understanding."

Ishmael shrugged, plucking a shred of tobacco off his tongue. "How many guards in total? How big of a building are we talking about?"

Mallory sighed, shifting to reach a nearby ashtray. "We have two furnace operations. One to smelt the iron ore and turn it into ingots, and another to melt the ingots and make them into gun barrels. Most of the smaller pieces are made from steel, but those pieces aren't made at the compound—we've outsourced them to a plant outside of Lida. The contract with the Authority was simply for Talent to fire the furnaces to keep the temperature consistent and precise. The contracts cost considerably less than the amount of coal it would take to achieve the same heat." The words caught in her throat, and she turned her face away from Ishmael, pressing her hand to her mouth. Tears glistened against her eyelashes, and she blinked them away quickly. "Children. I should have known something was wrong when the directed work programs for the Uhl factory were so much more expensive. But the Uhl factory pays a living wage to an adult, and the Authority enslaves children."

Ishmael caught Mallory's hand, squeezing it gently. "You didn't know because the Authority made sure you didn't know. But now we see them, and we're going to fight it."

"You're not going to stop?" Mallory asked.

"Absolutely not," Ishmael snorted. "I'll tell Davik to hold distribution of the next paper until tomorrow so Eirdis shows up like she promised. And then we keep going."

Mallory sighed, looking up at the ceiling. "So many innocent people."

"How many innocent children, Mallory?"

Mallory's eyes snapped down to Ishmael, her mouth pulling into a furious sneer. "I know, Ishmael. I know it's necessary. I can know that, but I can still have a moment or two to feel the weight of what's going to happen. And I can curse Rainer Elsworth for making us all complicit in his evil." Her gaze trailed down to Ishmael's knee. Her fingers twitched like she wanted to touch it. "Is it really dislocated?"

"Yes, it was *really* dislocated," Ishmael muttered. "You think I'm hobbling around for sympathy?"

"Well," Malory said, her mouth pulling in a bit of a smile, "it wouldn't be the worst thing you've done for attention."

Ishmael laughed. "That's true, but it's actually dislocated. An Enquiry Officer actually popped it on purpose while his colleagues actually tried to hang Captain Blackwood from a tree."

Mallory shook her head. "Did he survive it? The hanging."

Ishmael pushed himself to his feet. Slowly, carefully, shifting his weight between his good leg and his cane until he was up out of the chair. All of the leaning on the cane made his shoulder ache, but it was better than trying to make his way without it. At least the bottoms of his feet were mostly healed. He was doing well, considering it had only been a few days. He clung to that, telling himself over and over that it was getting better, instead of letting himself panic about whether or not this cane and this pain were his reality now. Taking on Maes with his mobility compromised—what if it never went away, like Wolfe's leg?

Stop. Don't lose focus.

Over on the table, there were a few ashtrays. He rested the half-smoked cigarillo on the edge of the ashtray and went for the bread, plucking up a roll that was studded with dry fruit and swirls of cinnamon and clove, the top glistening with sugar.

"How big is the factory building," he asked, instead of answering, "and how many guards?"

Mallory nodded, satisfied with his non-answer. "The two buildings cover a span of about two hectares at the rear of the whole compound. It's all stretched out and the buildings are open on the sides to keep ventilation, or else the heat would be lethal. You can't get to it without going through the main hallways of the building, where I encountered the guards. There were six for one hallway. There must be some kind of system to let the employees through—there's a large workforce who handle everything except the firing of the furnaces."

"Would these people have access to the children?" Ishmael asked, sitting on the edge of the table so he could rest his cane beside him and use both hands to tear the roll open. Even though talk of the children— he had to call them children, because calling them energy units felt too much like accepting they couldn't be saved—turned his gut to stone. "Has the labour force seen the children at all?"

Mallory shook her head. She pushed herself to her feet, and Ishmael envied the ease with which she stood. She came to the table, gaze sweeping across the tray of offerings, but nothing enticed her enough. She leaned beside him, looking down at the ember of her cigarette. "No, the Authority employees handle them. There are workrooms in the cellar, where we stored the coal back before we had the Authority contracts. The Authority officers are tasked with managing the... the children. They had to pass security clearance and sign a mess of contracts to have that much access to Imburleigh grounds. One man retired recently, and it took months to replace him."

"So we wouldn't get in by force, not without high casualties," Ishmael said. "We'd have to smuggle people past the guards, under the guise of being an employee."

Mallory grimaced, and Ishmael could see her thinking, calculating. She frowned when her thoughts turned inward like that, a crease forming between her brows. "You want to take the children?"

Ishmael nodded. "That's what it will take to counter Clannaugh and Maes. Davik's trying to find a way, but…" But Davik wouldn't be alive much longer if Powell had his way. "I don't know. We need results. We have to go around them, straight to the Queen. If they're telling her we're moving against the Crowne, we can show her the truth of what we're really fighting for."

"How do you know she'll listen to you?"

Ishmael shrugged. "The last time I answered a question like that about the Queen, I got a lot of scowling from you for my honest answer."

Mallory scowled again, taking half a step back. "I thought you were being a pig."

Ishmael rolled his eyes at her. "It's been a long time since I've owed you any explanation about my sex life, Mallory, and yet you keep asking about it."

Mallory shook her head, and something had changed in the air. Something charged and angry, something that hadn't ever had the chance to heal. "I can try to get paperwork, but that's not usually my job. It would probably be easier to work on forgeries, but even that will be a challenge. The employee paperwork is complicated by design."

Ishmael grimaced. "We don't have a lot of time, not if Illea is telling the truth about Bothain. See what you can start, but it might be easier to find some other children somewhere else." He needed more assets, more people who knew the inner workings of things, needed information from the inside. He wished for a moment that Stella was still here—if only he'd gotten the chance to talk to her before she left, maybe she could answer some of these questions if she knew how Clannaugh did things. He plucked a bowl of honey from the table and dipped his bread, buying himself time to think. All the sugar and honey was cloying on his tongue, but there was enough spice in the bread to give it depth. "What's her angle, do you think?"

"Who, Illea?"

Ishmael nodded, sucking honey off his fingertips. "First name basis with the Fist of the North."

Mallory sighed. "I don't know. She says cooperating with him is in our best interest. She says he'll get what he wants, one way or another, and it's good for us if he considers us allies. But there are things she's not telling me. Or perhaps it's things she's not telling Eirdis. I haven't had the time to see her alone."

"Is he staying with her?"

Mallory nodded. "In her house."

Ishmael sighed, tearing off another piece of bread and swiping it through the honey. "What about Wolfe? Have you seen him?"

She nodded at that. "Illea said it's for his own good. She seemed to imply there was some rivalry between him and Maes, and whatever happened here could have grave repercussions on him."

The relief that rolled through Ishmael's chest was deep and almost terrifying. If something happened to Wolfe in the midst of all this—

He stuffed the bread into his mouth to have something else to focus on. "She isn't far wrong." He had to pause to suck honey off the roof of his mouth. "That will come from Clannaugh—which means the pair of them probably are communicating quite openly."

"Is that good for us or bad for us?"

"I don't know. Depends what Illea wants. Tell me about the Uhl factory—tell me about the first production run of those rifles."

"Why?" Mallory asked. The change in subject left her blinking at him a bit, like the switch had taken her by surprise. "What do they have to do with anything?"

Ishmael sucked more honey off his fingertips, leaning closer to Mallory so he could drop his voice. "How might Davik Kaine have gotten his hands on ten crates of them?"

All the colour drained out of Mallory's cheeks, her eyes scanning his face. She came closer, stood taller, all the defeat and hopelessness snapped right out of her. "The large shipment of guns—those were Uhls? Davik Kaine has Uhl rifles?"

"I take it Clannaugh didn't mention that?"

Mallory shook her head. "Not to me—or at least, all I have is what Illea's told me, and she never gave any indication..."

Ishmael nodded. "And judging by your reaction, you didn't knowingly sell your new experimental guns to him on purpose."

"No, Ishmael, I did not knowingly sell guns to the man who bombed Cruinnich. You find yourself with dangerous allies, these days."

Ishmael shrugged. "It's necessary and temporary."

"You weren't there!" Mallory snapped. "You didn't see the devastation. He said he did it for Ffyanwy, but then he filled her hospital to bursting. She would have been devastated by all the bloodshed. We wrote to the King and begged for military support to put an end to it, but the

King's health was ailing at the time. Do you remember that? Were you even in the Dominion?"

"I wasn't," Ishmael admitted. In spite of Mallory's animation, he kept his voice as quiet as he could, glancing pointedly toward the door. Hopefully it was enough to remind her they were in Davik's whorehouse. He tore another piece of bread off the roll, but his appetite had gone dry again—thinking about Deri was going to be the death of him. "We heard about it over the news wire while we were deployed. We also heard that Bothain Clannaugh was lining people up in the streets and shooting them for nothing more than the suspicion they had connections to rebels. Which, as you know, *General* Imburleigh, is a war crime. Not all the violence can be laid at Davik Kaine's feet. Some of it was someone else's fault."

Mallory shook her head, unmoved by the shared culpability. "And yet, when Davik Kaine was run out of town by the Army of the Red Dawn, the violence ended," she said, her voice only a low rumble even though her whole body was animated with her outrage. At least she'd taken the hint about being quiet. "And the King died, and Queen Leony took the Crowne, and her first act as Regent was to send healers up to help us. A whole regiment of army healers, just to try to stop the deaths."

"Listen to me," Ishmael whispered, dropping the roll down to the plate. "I know. My allegiance to Davik Kaine is temporary. For the children, Mallory."

"You can stop patronizing me about the children," Mallory hissed, her whole body going ugly tense like she was honestly thinking about hitting him. "I know, damnit! I can still wish there was a simpler way—"

"You think I don't wish for something better, too?" Ishmael asked. "You think I wouldn't take the first alternative that came in front of me? It's too far gone for that. Captain Blackwood kicked something into motion with his fucking stunt, and now we're all scrambling. But Maes didn't send Clannaugh up here to get the police force peacefully. If he wanted that, he would have sent a politician. But he sent the Fist of the North, with all his fancy 12th medals, because he knows what Clannaugh does best: spills blood and makes the nation think he's right to do it."

Mallory sighed, the tension draining back out of her again, making her shoulders slump. She crushed out her cigarette beside Ishmael's, which still twisted smoke, burning uselessly in the ashtray. She reached into the pocket of her skirts, pulling out a letter. Something stuttered in his chest, like his heart forgot how to hold its own rhythm.

"This came for you," she said, turning it toward him. His name, but no address, was written on the front in perfectly precise handwriting, a flourish on the S that matched the logo for his watch brand. "I don't remember when. It may have only been a few days, but everything…" She shrugged. "I lost track. I didn't open it—I never do. I believe in your right to privacy in the things the two of you. But I know she's going to tell you that she's coming here. She's already in Obisza. She told me she wants to come down to Yaelsmuir before the winter, if the weather holds the way it has been. If not, she'll be here with the spring thaw. She would have written this before everything started. The news will be spreading through the country. It will reach her any day now. Ishmael, what do I tell her?"

"Mallory," Ishmael snapped, the panic and the frustration carrying him away before he could calm himself. "What the fuck do you mean? Tell her not to come. That's the only answer—tell her she *can't* come."

"She might not listen to me," Mallory said. "She's twenty now—a woman grown. And once she hears that Rainer Elsworth apparently had you murdered, I don't think anyone could keep her away."

Ishmael groaned, pushing his hand over his face. "If you don't think she'll listen to you, send a telegram to Alistair and tell him to put her under house arrest. Tell him to lock her in her room if he has to—you're the one who went on and on about all the innocent people that are going to die, and you have the slightest suspicion that she'll come here in the middle of it all? You're her mother, aren't you? So fucking *parent*."

The slap came so fast he couldn't avoid it—she swung and clapped him right on the side of the face so hard he saw stars. He braced himself on the table, his hand clipping the tray of bread and catapulting rolls across the table.

"You haven't the right to tell me how to parent," Mallory hissed. "You wouldn't know the first thing about taking responsibility for another life, Ishmael—you don't even take responsibility for yourself!"

"How could I know, when you took my child from me before I even knew she existed?" Ishmael snapped. "You didn't even give me the chance to try!"

"No, I'm not doing this with you," Mallory said, shaking her head and taking a step back. "You love to rewrite history and make yourself into some helpless victim, but we both know you would have made a terrible father. I had a duty to my child and to my family, and you were gone. In jail, I might remind you, because even at the Officer's Academy, you couldn't quite get over your own ego long enough to follow basic rules like not murdering fellow classmates!"

"It was self-defence—"

"Ishmael!" Mallory snapped, her hands turning to fists, her face clouding completely. "Shut *up*! You killed a man and the Academy put you in jail for it. I thought they were going to hang you—and even if they didn't, what life would she have had if I told the Imburleigh board who her father was? They would have stripped her of everything to keep you out of Imburleigh affairs. Your name would have doomed her before she was even born. And then, when you didn't get the hanging you deserved, you were gone. Just gone. I had a choice to make, and I won't apologize to you for picking up the pieces of the things you destroyed with your childishness. She has a real future now, no thanks to you."

"She won't have anything if she comes down here and gets killed in the rioting," Ishmael hissed. Never mind all the things that Mallory said that weren't true—his daughter *needed* to stay in Obisza. "And if that happens, it'll be on you. You can still stop her from throwing her life away—that life that you so desperately clung to, because you couldn't imagine a future for yourself where you weren't the favourite Imburleigh child."

Her shoulders tensed, her hand twitching like she was going to wind up and clobber him again.

"You got one free hit, Mallory," Ishmael snapped. "Touch me again, I dare you."

She laughed, shaking her head. "Are you threatening me, Ishmael? What are you going to do, send my head to Bothain, too?"

"Not at all, General Imburleigh," Ishmael said, letting his voice go syrupy sweet, tilting his head back and giving his best charming smile. "But you and I both know that pain is my favourite foreplay, and if you let yourself get that wound up, you might do something you regret. Again."

It worked to diffuse the violence, at least—she sneered, taking another step back. She tossed Ishmael's letter to the table with a scornful flick of her wrist. "You really are a pig. I guess I should thank you for consistently confirming that I was right not to trust you enough to try to raise a child with you. Thank you for reminding me, over and over again, how blessed I am to have married Alistair."

Ishmael grit his teeth on all the retorts that burned on his tongue. Better to let her have the last word. If he spoke again they would kick up *every* old fight, the same one they had over and over again when they let themselves remember what had happened between them over the years. And he didn't have time for this petty back-and-forth, this self-harm with words, dredging up each other's flaws and throwing them at each other's feet. She took her last word and her moral high ground with her like a trophy, slamming the door behind her so hard it rattled the whole fucking room.

Ishmael snatched his cigarette from the ashtray, taking a drag, but the smoke did nothing to calm all his furious nerves. He hooked his hand under the half-empty tray of bread and threw it across the room, the metal clattering against the wall. He slid off the table, taking his weight on both legs, but the spasm of pain only stoked his fury hotter. He swept his arm through the whole spread, sending jars of jam and the bowl of honey crashing to the floor, shattering glass and spraying half the room with sticky-sweet fruit preserve.

The letter—if this miserable fucking week had taught him anything, it was that he should read the letter now before some new disaster hit. He snatched it off the table next, clamping his cigarillo between his teeth so he could puff on the last of the smoke as he tore the letter open. The way his daughter put the beautiful flourish on the S made his chest ache. It meant she practiced the Saeati logo enough to do the calligraphy herself.

There was a photograph inside, along with the letter. Mairead Imburleigh was so beautiful and it stole the fury shield from him. Thick black hair and the straight nose that reminded Ishmael of his mother and eyes that *glowed* with confidence and determination. He had so many pictures of her through the years, from infancy to now—twenty, or near enough to it—and her eyes had not changed. Neither had the expression her eyebrows made, the arc of them, like she knew she was meant to be composed and still for photographs but couldn't *quite* master that blank and neutral face. But she looked like Mallory, too, with the shape of her mouth. She was tall like Ishmael's family, long limbed—and it was funny how much she also kind of resembled Alistair Imburleigh. He was tall and dark-haired, too. One wouldn't necessarily know that Alistair had no relation to Mairead at all.

For a moment, he thought his daughter was sitting with Stella White-rock. Curly hair—lightly coloured, blond or brown or red, the sepia tones washed the exact details out—and the dimple in her chin, the freckles all over her face was uncannily Stella. But of course that wasn't possible.

The letter was in Mairead's elegant script, but it was more brief than usual.

Mr. Saeati,

I write to you in the hopes that I will see you soon, so I will save all my best gossip for when we sit down with a drink or two. I hope the weather serves me well and I am able to get to Yaelsmuir post haste—I understand you just got home from deployment, and so I'd like to take the chance to catch you in the city.

If the weather betrays me and I am delayed too long, I will write you a longer letter. Mother wishes me to stay in Yaelsmuir for a while, in order to take my seat on the Imburleigh board of investors. Hopefully that will give us plenty of time to get to know each other properly. Finally.

Don't tell Mother—but were it not for your presence in Yaelsmuir, I'd much rather stay in Obisza and watch the factory come to life. It's stunning, the things Miss Rhydderch can do with stone and her Talent. She says that anyone can learn to use Talent if they try hard enough. I may be tempted enough to ask her to teach me, but alas, I am meant to be a Proper Imburleigh and sit on the board instead.

I enclosed a picture of myself with Miss Rhydderch. She is everything I hope to be as I take my role as a true and proper businesswoman of the Dominion. Caring, focused, driven, fiercely intelligent. I hope she will join me in Yaelsmuir in the summer, if only for a short time. I would love for you to meet her. I have told her all about you, and we have spent many a night staying up far too late and talking about life. I find her to be very wise, even though she is only a few years older than me. I hope you like her.

If it is agreeable with you, and if Mother thinks it appropriate, I would very much like to see your father's watch store after I arrive. Miss Rhydderch showed me a train that you made, some time ago. Apparently it belonged to her sister, Ffyanwy. Their father commissioned it from you directly, and Miss Rhydderch said you made it with your own hands. You truly are an incredible craftsman. I hope you will teach me a little of your skills.

One last thing before I go—did you know there is a Qasani temple here in Obisza? I have very much enjoyed going there and speaking to the community leaders. They say much the same sort of things that you have told me in the past, and it makes me feel more connected to you. So, if I must stay in Obisza through the winter, at least I have good company here.

I hope I can make the journey sooner rather than later, though. I hope by the time you receive this letter, I am already on my way down the road to see you. I hope you are still there when I arrive.

634 | LEGACY OF BRICK & BONE

Yours in anticipation and excitement,
Mairead

Miss Rhydderch—it had to be Aelwyd, the younger Rhydderch. Ishmael scanned the date of the letter, trying to remember how the weather was back when she wrote it. It had been raining so much, would she still be in Obisza? Gods, how many days did it take if she was on the road already?

He didn't have time for this. This was exactly why the diplomatic division took great pains not to deploy their diplomats to work with people they had a chance of knowing. Nowhere with family ties, nowhere with business investments. The personal stakes made all the necessary work so much harder, made even the obvious decisions feel more complicated.

Nothing here was complicated, it was simple. Clannaugh was going to kill people, and Ishmael was going to kill people, too, and they would fight over the Queen's attention.

But gods save him, there were so many people here he cared about, so many people he wanted to protect even though he knew he couldn't. If it weren't for the fact Davik kept promising to get Jason out, he would have insisted they do something by now. All the waiting felt too much like giving Elsworth time to cover up his crimes, but moving before Jason was out felt like throwing his life away. Once the unrest started, the Rift would lockdown so hard, no one would come out, certainly. Deri would be disgusted with him for the hesitation, but he couldn't look Tashué in the eye and convince him that sacrificing his son was the right choice— nor could he make the choice behind Tashué's back and try to force Davik's hand.

And now, and the possibility of one more set something frantic and wild in his chest that made it hard to breathe. Gods, his daughter, he couldn't protect her in the middle of *this*.

The door creaked open behind him. Ishmael spun—and regretted it. His knee flexed too much and a fresh spasm of pain shot up and down his leg, stealing the air out of his lungs. For a horrible moment, as he was moving, it felt like the kneecap was going to leap out of place again. But he froze, his hand moving to the joint like he could hold it still

Tashué closed the door behind him slowly, his eyes taking in the mess Ishmael had made with slow regard, like it didn't fully surprise him.

"I just told Mallory Imburleigh that I don't know where you are," Ishmael said. "Plausible deniability."

Tashué's face wrinkled in an unamused smirk. "I'm not a fucking idiot, Ishmael. I waited until she stormed out. She didn't see me. You really get under her skin, don't you?" His eyes swept pointedly over the mess again. "But I guess the feeling is mutual."

Ishmael grunted, backing up to rest his weight on the edge of the table again, breathing slow through the pain. For all that it was getting better, it seemed like the kneecap would never forgive him. Like once it had been taught how to slip out of place, it was always in imminent danger of jumping out again.

Tashué walked past him, trailing the smell of cordite through the air behind him. He pushed a boot through the wreckage of Ishmael's temper, glass crunching beneath his weight. He kicked a few rolls out of the way and bent down, retrieving a jar of fruit preserve that hadn't shattered. Honey and blueberry jam dripped off the outside, but the glass and the lid were in tact, so Tashué grabbed the corner of the tablecloth to wipe the jar clean.

"So, Mr. Appropriately Cynical Handler," Tashué said. His hands flexed once, and the lid came open easily under his strength. "What is the operating procedure when you do something that was fucking shit, and you feel like a giant mound of shit because you know you *should* feel worse than you do, but you don't because this is the price you're willing to pay for the mission?"

"The objective," Ishmael corrected.

"Right," Tashué grunted. He found a spoon in the mess next, plucking it up and wiping it on the tablecloth to clean it of spilled food and floor dirt and broken glass. He spit on it and cleaned it again. "The objective."

Ishmael sighed, dropping the letter and the photograph on the empty table beside him, letting the image of Mairead stare up at the ceiling. "Well, usually I find a bottle of brandy and something good to smoke, and then go hunting for someone who likes to fuck rough. That's what I liked about you. You always knew how to hurt me without actually, you know, causing any damage. Does your whisperer fuck rough?"

"Don't," Tashué said, the one word loaded with so much cold threat that Ishmael knew Tashué would hit him again if he pushed this one. The thing about knowing someone could take a punch was that it got harder to keep your fists to yourself.

"Yeah, fine," Ishmael muttered, crossing his arms over his chest. "You asked me."

Tashué breathed slow, in and out, like he was trying to chase the fight instincts away with his veneer of calm. He scooped out a spoonful of preserve and sucked the sticky, gooey mass off the spoon. That silence again, that terrible, loaded silence that made creases in his face like he was concentrating.

"You smell like gunpowder," Ishmael said.

Tashué nodded. "Someone let us in—it was all set up to look like insurance fraud. We take the money, he says the bank was robbed, the insurance company pays more than what we took. Easy."

"But?"

Tashué shrugged. "But someone else was there. So we killed them both."

"And you're upset that you're not upset enough? About the killing."

Tashué nodded, scooping up another spoonful of preserve. It looked like cherries and blackberries, swimming in their own tart juices.

Ishmael sighed, snatching the jar out of Tashué's hand. "That's usually a sign that we're losing it, and it's time to think about retiring."

Tashué laughed, handing the spoon over and crossing his arms over his chest. "I can't retire now. We're just getting started."

"Welcome to the diplomatic division, kid." A spoonful of jam—sweet and spiced heavily, the tart cherries like little red gems of flavour. "It's shit all the way down."

His eyes tracked slowly over the mess Ishmael had made, and then down to the table. The photograph. His head tilted to one side, and Ishmael could *see* the shock rolling through him. He reached out in that way that people did when they weren't even thinking, his fingers brushing over the tumble of curls captured by the photographer.

"Why do you have...?"

Ishmael dropped the spoon into the jar so he could scoop the photograph off the table, holding it up. "That's Aelwyd Rhydderch. I don't usually pay attention to gossip from up north because it's all been boring since Davik was run out of town, but she's quite a few years younger than her sister. Maisie says they're only a few years apart, the pair of them, so she must be mid twenties now at most. She's got big shoes to fill, the younger Rhydderch girl. But that family has always been a legend-maker."

Tashué turned to Ishmael, amber eyes studying the side of Ishmael's face. "Who's Maisie?"

Bastard. Sometimes he was too sharp. "Mairead Imburleigh."

Tashué took the photograph out of Ishmael's hand, studying it again with new eyes. "Why is the eldest Imburleigh heir sending you photographs?"

"It's all we have… She grew up in Cruinnich mostly, and I was always away. And Mallory married Alistair, a lesser Rhydderch cousin, which was a much better family line than anything I could offer. My father was getting started in those days, hadn't broken out of Yaelsmuir yet." Ishmael shrugged. "What do you want me to say?"

Tashué shook his head, snatching the jar of preserve back and handing Ishmael the photograph. "I've known you twelve years, and yet I didn't know you at all."

"Oh, fuck off," Ishmael snapped. "You think just because we were fucking, I owed you something? A sob story about my whole life because your big arms were so sweet and comfortable? Get the fuck out of here. I didn't keep secrets *from* you. There were just things that I couldn't ever talk about to anyone."

"So why are you telling me now?"

Ishmael shot Tashué a scowl. "Maybe I fucking hated keeping secrets all that time. Maybe I've resented them all my life. Maybe if I could talk about the shit that mattered to me, I wouldn't have spent so much time drinking and smoking."

"And maybe we're going to die." He said it casually, scooping up more preserve and sucking it off the spoon. "So what does it matter, anyway?"

"Exactly." Ishmael sighed, looking down at the photograph. At Aelwyd and all those curls and those eyes that were exactly the same shape as her sister's. "I wish I could have talked to her."

"Mairead?"

"No." Ishmael leaned closer to Tashué so he could still be heard when he dropped his voice. They were in Davik's club, after all, and Ishmael had no idea what Davik would do if he found out that the pair of them knew the woman he called Ffyanwy. "Aelwyd's sister."

Tashué's face spasmed with pain, the first thing that really broke through that hard shell that had formed around him since the day they were both arrested. He had another spoon loaded up with jam, but he stared at it a while like his appetite had disappeared. He thrust the spoon back into the jar, resting it on the table.

"You have anything to smoke?"

"Just tobacco."

638 | LEGACY OF BRICK & BONE

"That's what I meant."

Ishmael nodded, handing over his cigarette case and his match. "It's going to come down to our word against the Authority. Clannaugh is going to insist we're anti-Crowne militia and all that. Rebels. But if we can convince the Queen that we aren't fighting against Crowne sovereignty—if we can show her we're standing against the Authority specifically and there's a good reason for it, maybe she'll grind it all to a halt. Clannaugh can't slaughter us if he and Elsworth are arrested for their crimes. I should go down to White Crown myself, try to get a secret audience with her."

Tashué lit himself a cigarette before answering, shaking out the match and flicking it down into the mess Ishmael had made. "What's Stella have to do with any of it?"

"Who better to testify against Bothain Clannaugh for his crimes than his wife?"

That pain again, tearing so deep through Tashué's expression that guilt flared in Ishmael's chest. "She was running for a reason, Ishmael. It's not just about her and Clannaugh. There's a child to consider—and who knows how Davik will react?"

"As your appropriately cynical handler, that's my cue to remind you that we're doing this for a reason, and that reason is bigger than any individual players. You're fine with murdering two people at a bank for the notes, but suddenly with the Whiterocks, you've turned soft again?"

Tashué leaned back, exhaling a cloud of smoke at the rafters. "I don't even know where she is. She could be halfway up the mountains by now."

"Sure, fine." Ishmael lay the photograph on top of the letter again, and then eased them both back into the envelope. If he went down to White Crown and left Tashué unsupervised, would the big bastard make it worse? Or could he drag Tashué down the river with him, maybe? If Jason was getting out tomorrow, maybe. "I didn't ask you to produce her, I wished I could have talked to her before she left. Help me hobble down the stairs. Davik's staff can clean up this mess, and we can raid his larder for real food instead of you surviving on sugar and tobacco."

Tashué sighed. "What if it was a mistake to let her go?"

"Oh sure, when I say it, I'm the asshole, but when you say it, you're the long suffering hero who misses the other half of his soul," Ishmael muttered. "Very romantic, Captain. Let's go. I'm hungry."

58

ILLEA
DAY 37

Illea had been sneaking onto the Wolfe property since she was a child. She'd never been forbidden from coming here; their parents were close and Elysia had always been considered good company for Illea. But there was a time in her life when permission made a thing less desirable, and so she invented reasons to be stealthy, snatching pieces of freedom from her father's firm control because the thrill of excitement she got from it was intoxicating. And when her father started frowning at the idea of her growing close to Amias, she pursued him with more and more hunger, finding places to hide as they learned to worship each other's bodies until there was no untangling them. Until Amias was ready and willing to retire from the military so Illea's father would give them permission to marry.

After the meeting in the Bay, she disembarked the carriage at Mallory's house and went into her home. From there, it was a simple walk along the edge of the Dunnenbrahl. The night meant she didn't have to retreat to the other side of the trees to avoid being seen; she could take the path along the edge of the forest instead, so worn and so familiar that she didn't need to see in order to keep to it. And then, into the kennels— one side of that building was hidden from view from the inside of the manor by the looming walls of the stable. The dogs rose a ruckus at her arrival, but the dogs were always raising a ruckus. The kennel hands looked surprised at her arrival, but when she said she wanted to see the

General, they understood. One of them headed into the house, and Illea settled in to wait.

The musky scent of the dogs was almost comforting, if only because Amias loved his breeding line so completely. These animals were all the descendants of his original breeding pair, and the quality of the breeding line was growing to international acclaim under Nathaniel's management. A little piece of his dreams for the future lived on through them.

Patience had long been one of Illea's strengths. The patience to let people make mistakes so she could benefit from the wreckage. The patience to let investments mature slowly. The patience to watch the world shift and know that her time would rise. Lately, her patience was failing her. Restlessness, anxiety, frustration—it all simmered in her until she felt as if she could hear one of Ishmael's watches ticking at all times, counting every second until—

Until this child grew enough that others knew her body was changing, or until gossip spread out of her control.

Until this election, which suddenly didn't matter at all, and mattered more than anything.

Until someone finally gave her a solution she could use again Myron.

Until some concrete news of Ishmael. That, at least, had happy news: he was alive, if a little worse for wear.

Waiting for Nathaniel was harder than she expected it to be. The kennel hands kept their distance, but their whispering to each other marked the time passing. Passing. Stretching. Most of the dogs settled into the beds, but some paced at the walls of their enclosures like they were infected with her impatience.

A shadow danced outside the window finally—two shadows, or was it even more than that? Illea stepped back, folding herself into darkness so no one outside could see her. The dogs started their ruckus again, barking and whining, excited for their master, and Nathaniel's voice came firmly to each of them over the sound of his cane tapping on the floor, commanding them to hush. Some listened, some didn't. Let them bark. If there was an Officer outside the window, let the dogs drive him half out of his mind so he didn't try to hear what was going on inside.

"Illea," Nathaniel whispered when he saw her. "What are you—"

"I met with Ishmael," Illea cut in. It was getting late and she needed to get back to her own home before Bothain wondered why she was lingering at Mallory's so long. "He's alive."

Nathaniel's relief wasn't as palpable as Illea would expect—he must have known already. "He's down in the Bay?"

Illea nodded. "With Davik Kaine."

"Illea," Nathaniel said, stepping closer. "What are you doing? Someone said Clannaugh is staying with you—is the bastard holding you against your will—"

"General," Illea interrupted again. "We don't have time to argue about Bothain Clannaugh. I invited him to stay. He was going to stay with Rainer, but his intentions have pivoted since everything. He is an ally for now, and we should welcome him as such."

"Bothain Clannaugh is no one's ally," Nathaniel said with a sharp shake of his head. He stood ramrod straight, his hand around the head of his cane so tight that he looked like he was trying to crush the silver back into an ingot. "What have you done?"

"I'm not a youth to be scolded for stealing a boiled sweet," Illea snapped. Her eyes flicked to the far away window. Quietly, she had to be quiet, no matter how annoyed she was at Nathaniel's paternal tone. One of the dogs gave a piercing whine and another started pawing at the gate. "All these years, we've been trying to maneuver quietly against Myron and Rainer, and nothing has worked. Now Bothain will hand me the results I need, and I'm to turn away from him, simply because you disapprove of his character? Whether he does it out of loyalty to me, or loyalty to himself, it doesn't matter. I need Myron out. He can't claim my child from a jail cell for national crimes."

Nathaniel sighed, his shoulders sagging. He came closer to Illea, pulling open a door—a small sitting room, with a wood stove and a few chairs scattered near the heat the stove made. Sometimes, when the females were whelping, they needed round-the-clock care, so there were plenty of comfortable places for the kennel hands to hunker down. He limped to the closest chair and sank down into it, rubbing his leg. It was getting worse lately, and this wet, miserable weather must have been making it ache more. He shifted to the edge of his chair, dragging the door of the wood stove open and tossing a few chunks of wood into the flames to bank them up.

"How's Ishmael?" he asked.

Illea moved to the chair closest to him, sweeping her skirts out of the way to sit on the edge. The warmth of the fire kissed her face, chasing the chill out of her skin. "Alive and furious, it seems. With a limp that matches yours, now."

Nathaniel nodded. "His knee looked terrible."

"So they did come here that night," Illea said. "They came here from the forest. And you sent them down to the Bay?"

Nathaniel nodded. "I knew I couldn't protect them. And I was right. Prisoner in my own home. They've trashed everything. Poor Hattie spends her days wandering around the house sobbing, trying to sort out what she can fix. Slashed paintings, smashed furniture—they turned Amias's room upside down, said they were looking for hidden evidence."

A pang of old grief rippled through Illea's chest—Amias's room had been held in a sort of stasis since he died. His things gave them something to touch and hold when they missed him most keenly. Sometimes, she half convinced herself that his clothes still smelled like him, but maybe they smelled like the house. Like Hattie's laundry soap and the ever present scent of smoke and horses and the acrid burn of gunpowder. Was it all destroyed?

"Ishmael said he didn't know where Blackwood was," Illea said rather than think about Amias's belongings. "Kaine said that he'd taken Ishmael in alone."

Nathaniel shrugged. "I've been here, Illea. I don't know."

"Are you worried I'll tell Bothain where to find him?" Illea asked. "What is it about him that inspires such loyalty from you?"

"If I have to explain my loyalty to Ishmael, then you aren't the person I thought you were."

"I meant Blackwood," Illea snapped. "Don't take that tone with me, Nathaniel Wolfe. I know you're angry about everything, but this isn't my doing. I didn't invite this into the city, and I didn't devise the idea for energy units. I'm only trying to catch the tide so I'm not swept under by it all. We're trying to protect *you*, you stubborn old fool. Bothain said Maes hates you—wants an excuse to have you brought up for charges. If you stay here in your house, then it can't be said that you helped the rebels."

Nathaniel shook his head, but he didn't look at her. The realization that he hadn't looked her in the eye at all since she arrived was a cold feeling, settling below the surface of her skin, out of reach from the warmth of the wood stove. She watched his face for a while, only his profile, his eyes staring into the flames and stubbornly avoiding her.

"I wanted things to be done civilly," he said finally. He sounded tired, defeated, like he was already mourning the violence that hadn't happened yet. "Before I knew, I wanted the politics of it all to be dealt with the right way. Trusting the voters, building a future. I wanted to believe that problems could be so easily solved. And then after—I told Captain Blackwood that we don't solve problems in this country by killing people. I made him walk away because I wanted to see Elsworth charged for everything he did. If Captain Blackwood blew a hole in his skull, the man would never face justice for what he turned us into. This entire nation turned evil, because none of us thought to ask questions. And now, here's Bothain Clannaugh, with all his regimental medals, proving that we do in fact solve problems by slaughter. A national hero for lining people in the streets of Cruinnich and shooting them with no cause. An economy built on slave children, and the wars of other countries." He sighed, looking down at the floor. He tapped the end of his cane on the floor boards a few times, shook his head. He seemed a husk of himself, slowly being crushed by all he was trying to carry. "I was so determined to believe in my own altruism that I invented a country that doesn't exist and imagined solutions that will never work. Because we aren't a civil nation. We are a nation forged in blood."

Perhaps not angry at her, then. Angry with the whole world, but not her specifically. There was relief in that.

"If they get the police force, there'll be no stopping Clannaugh." Nathaniel finally turned to Illea, his eyes searching her face, but somehow he still avoided her gaze. Beseeching her, his features drawn and pinched with his rising agitation. "Tell me you understand that, Illea. Tell me that you know he'll burn this city down to advance his career. We can argue in circles about what it takes to get rid of Myron later, but at least admit that you've unleashed a power that will cause incredible suffering on our streets."

"I haven't unleashed him. I did not invite him here. This end was coming to us one way or another, and Rainer set it in motion it the moment he started campaigning for his provincial police force. He drew Maes's eyes to our streets and Maes sent Bothain to snatch power for him. At least I can leverage my position with him to protect those I care about. If Bothain sinks himself comfortably into my bed while he's here to do someone else's bidding, I can direct him. Not much—he's not especially malleable. But a little. Enough to protect myself and my future. To protect you. With a bit of luck, to protect Ishmael, but I don't know. Ishmael's fate isn't in Bothain's hands, I don't think. Even if he survives this, Maes will want him. There's something unresolved between Maes and Deri, and Ishmael is a pawn caught between them all." Illea shrugged, turning her face toward the fire. All the bluster had fallen out of her, leaving her vulnerable to the exhaustion that ate at the corners of her awareness day and night. A normal symptom at this stage of pregnancy, Tilde assured her, but no less frustrating. "I've never been so unsure of the results of an election. I can't tell which way the city will lean once things start in earnest. Eirdis is ahead in the polls for now, but I suspect that's because nothing terrible has happened yet. The city thinks things are going to resolve peacefully. But Bothain is waiting for Kaine to act first. And if Kaine doesn't do something soon, Bothain will force his hand."

"So what are you hoping for, Illea?" Nathaniel sighed. "Why did you come here?"

"If Myron gets elected, Rainer will try to bury all the terrible things he's responsible for," Illea said. "Bothain says Maes will engineer Rainer's fall, but to what end? He'll take the Authority over himself, I imagine, and our city is even more vulnerable to his whims. If Eirdis wins? I'm not sure the outcome will be entirely different. So long as she's Governor, what does she care about Rainer's fate? She'll hand the problem to Bothain and let him do whatever he pleases while she builds her career on the back of civil unrest. Ishmael told Mallory he wanted to go around Yaelsmuir politics and go straight to the Queen. Bring his proof down to her and lay it all out before her. If he succeeds, it could be the end of Myron and Rainer. With luck, it will also stall Bothain's march to power for a while. If we destroy the credibility of the police force, maybe it buys us time to understand the scope of what game Maes is playing on our streets, and out maneuver him."

Something wistful crossed Nathaniel's features and he finally met Illea's eye. "Sometimes I'm tempted to say you sound like Amias, but then I wonder if he sounded like you. Perhaps he caught the little pieces of wisdom you said so casually even back then and regurgitated them as if they were his own."

Illea smiled. "That seems like something he would do. I like to think I sound like my father. I try to imagine what advice he would give in a situation like this."

Nathaniel nodded. "Nikos would say: if we don't like the terms of the game, add new terms."

Illea could almost hear her father's voice, drifting into the room through the long years of his absence. "Exactly. If we don't like either candidate for the Governor's office, we need another candidate."

"So close to the election?" Nathaniel sighed again, turning his attention back to the fire. "This cycle has been going so badly because Eirdis was unprepared. So, who could possibly organize a decent campaign now? Won't a third party simply dilute the vote so far that the outcome will be too muddy to make an impact?"

Illea shrugged slowly but even so, her heart started beating faster. The weight of her words pressed in on her ribcage before they even said them. "Rainer always tells me that most people voting for Myron are voting for the name Winter. That's why he's always needling me to play along. So what if the *Vote Winter* slogans suddenly had new meaning?"

Nathaniel's attention snapped back to Illea's face. "You'll run against Myron? And put yourself in direct opposition with Clannaugh?"

"Opposition? Whyever would we be in opposition? We're cooperating with each other, General Wolfe," Illea said sweetly, folding her hands in her lap. "General Clannaugh and I are building a path to the same future. He can chase Davik Kaine around the Bay, and our side can play by the rules he wrote. Sending letters to White Crown about the terrible violence. Sending photographs of the most shocking depravity. Ishmael can leverage his relationship with the Queen, and through him, we can paint a fuller picture with Myron and Rainer out of the way, and by the end of it, we have what we want. Protecting the city from Maes and his cronies, punishing Rainer for his crimes, and no more Myron in my house."

Nathaniel shook his head. "It won't be that easy, Illea. Clannaugh and Maes make formidable adversaries. Ask Davik Kaine. I'd tell you to ask Gwilym Deri, but he's dead."

"I never said it would be easy. Nothing worth fighting for was ever easily attained. I'm running out of time. I need results."

Nathaniel's face spasmed with pain and he glanced down at her lap, the same meaningless instinct that made her touch her navel. Perhaps she was imagining her belly, turned plump by the life growing inside it. Or the child she would have this time next year, cradled in her arms and filled with their shared hopes and dreams.

"I'm sorry we couldn't manage something sooner," he said softly. "I wanted…"

"A civil solution," Illea said. "I know. If we drove him to leave of his own volition, we could congratulate ourselves about how elevated we were. How very enlightened, settling things peacefully. But you're right that this nation was forged in bloodshed. This city doubly so."

Nathaniel nodded. "Well—what if you ran *instead* of Myron? Once the violence starts, this city will want someone to blame. What if he buckled under all that pressure, leaving a gap for you to stand in?"

The silence that stretched after those questions was deafening. Bile rose in Illea's throat, sour and apprehensive. And yet also filled with potential. With surety. Was he thinking about what Ishmael said, before everything went so gloriously awry?

You could always kill him.

Nathaniel leaned forward, pushing the door to the wood stove closed. "I should go. There's only so long my guards will leave me in peace out here. You should wait a while before you leave, though. They didn't seem especially convinced that I was here to tend to the dogs. They might decide to keep an eye out."

Illea nodded. "I can slip into the stable and then around the back."

"I'll get word to you somehow," Nathaniel promised. "Don't announce your candidacy until the violence starts."

"Agreed."

59

LORNE
DAY 37

The leaf kept spilling the juice across his tongue, so bitter, making his heart beat faster, faster, faster, until he couldn't distinguish between one beat and the next. It was a giant thrumming in his chest, a single note of life that was going to swallow him whole.

He threw the bag over his shoulder anyway, following László down the hall. There weren't as many people in the club as there was most other nights. The day before the match, all the casual observers had been kicked out so Davik's people could finish whatever needed to be done. People unpacked crates of furniture to dedicate one corner to lounging, and Charlee pulled pints from the taps to test them. The noise of the crowd roared in his ears like it was ten times bigger, the leaf making everything sharper, bigger, closer. László led him through the people, to the ring. Lorne's throne, that's what Davik called it. László tossed his bag up, over the ropes.

"You alright?" László asked.

"This fucking leaf," Lorne breathed, his voice passing through him too fast.

"Spit it out," László said, grabbing the bag from Lorne's hands and tossing it into the ring beside the first bag. It landed with a thump that made the whole stage jump, the sound rolling thunder, looming chaos. "If it's too much, just spit it out."

Lorne spat the leaf on the floor and climbed up onto the stage after

László. Not that it did any good. The effects were already pulsing through him with every beat of his too-fast heart.

"Good evening, beautiful people," László called, even louder than all the noise the crowd made. "You've all been so loyal, and you've worked so fucking hard and none of this would be here without you. You built this place, and we love you for it. You built it! So, we have a gift for you. A gift, because Dav appreciates you all so fucking much—come here!"

"What is it, László?" Tom called.

László laughed. "Come closer." He grabbed one of the bags, shoving it into Lorne's arms, hands fast and nimble to unbuckle the top and wrench open the drawstring. He climbed up on the ropes, bracing himself on the post at the corner, up over Lorne so Lorne leaned into his hip to keep him steady up there. "Ready? Catch."

László pushed a hand into the crowns, dragging them out and tossing them into a wide, high arc over the crowd. A glittering copper rain, falling—hands shot up from the crowd, people plucked the copper out of the air. It fell on their shoulders, in their hair, clattered on the floorboards. László grabbed another fistful, another, another, tossing them in every direction, so that everyone in the crowd had the chance to catch some, the bag lighter with each fistful László dragged out. And Lorne watched each glittering arc, half expecting each coin to turn into a drop of blood. Two people died for this money.

Still, what László said felt right. Us against them.

The bag was empty. Lorne dropped it and fought with the second bag. He plunged his fingers into the crowns to feel that much money. The copper wasn't warm like the gold was, and it didn't flow through his fingers like blood. The coins were new and bright, stamped with the outline of the Crowne on one side, Queen Leony's portrait on the other. László hefted the bag up, resuming his position on the middle rope. More coins, flying. Raining copper. And the crowd churning. Roaring. A surge of humanity, scrabbling for coins, gathering them up. Lorne wondered how many coins there were in each bag, how many people there were in this place. Were there enough to go around? Enough to go around more than once? Enough to go around a hundred times?

He held László by the hips, holding him steady on the ropes. Held him by the thighs. Slid his hands up and down, feeling the wool of László's trousers too acutely beneath his palms, feeling the heat of him. He pressed his face into the small of László's back, into the linen of his shirt. László never wore a shirt. It wasn't natural. Lorne wanted to drag László's shirt up out of his trousers and feel his skin and taste his sweat.

And then the bag was empty, and László turned in Lorne's arms. Hands were in Lorne's hair, and they were kissing again. Sharing breath. Sharing a heartbeat.

László broke the kiss, slipping out of Lorne's grasp again like his body was water that couldn't be contained by any human arms. He jumped down from the ring, and someone caught him, lifted him, carried him. He was laughing again. Maybe it was the leaf that made him laugh, maybe it was the robbery. And then László wasn't laughing anymore because he was kissing someone else. Celebrating, alive, overflowing with joy.

Even though two people were dead. The fact buzzed back into Lorne's skull, circling around like it was going to try to make contact again. Try to make him feel it. Sharp and dull at the same time. Two innocent people. Maybe because he hadn't seen it, it was harder to grasp. But how many innocent people had Lorne seen destroyed by the Dominion's wars? Everyone was *innocent*. All the ridiculous things the Dominion fought over were meaningless. Everyone who died on the Blood Road died for an ally that stood against the Dominion now, died for territory the Dominion didn't hold anymore. Those kids, most of them as young as Rowan, were innocent even though they were in uniform. So what the fuck did innocent even mean?

But this meant something. For Jason. For the children in the Breeding Program. For the Talented who had been so horribly used. What was two people against all of that? Us against them. So maybe two people was the entrance fee to revolution.

"Where'd the money come from?"

Lorne turned to the familiar voice. Vasska and Allie—they'd come back from wherever they went to print their pages. They both had ink on their faces, and they were holding hands. Of all the stupid things to notice, it was the hand-holding that drew Lorne's eye. Their fingers fit so nicely together, and László was in the crowd kissing whoever he wanted, and Lorne was standing in his ring, on his throne, alone.

He jumped down, heading for the bar.

"Lorne," Vasska pressed. He followed through the crowd, which had gathered on one side of the ring because that's where the crowns were. That's where László was. "Where'd the crowns come from?"

"It's from Dav." He couldn't tell if he was speaking too fast or if time was passing quicker than before, and he grabbed one of the water jugs the bar kept for him, trying to anchor himself in a recognizable moment. Who knew about the bank robbery? How much could he even say? "To show his appreciation for everyone's hard work."

"Sure," Vasska said, settling at the bar, on a stool, like he half expected to be served. "But where'd it come from?"

Lorne shrugged. Too hot, he was too hot. He poured the water over his head. Wash the feeling away, cool down. It didn't help. Water ran down his chest, cutting cold trails across his body, sharp as razor blades tracing lines over each curve his muscles made. He shook his head, spraying water out of his hair, listening to the chink the droplets made when they hit the shelf of glasses behind him.

"Ask Dav," he said. "He told us to give it away."

"Are you alright?" Allie asked. She grabbed a cloth from behind the bar and scrubbed at the ink on her hands.

"Sure," Lorne said. "No. I don't know. László gave me some fucking leaf. I think my heart is going to explode."

"Sounds like khat," Vasska said. "You just have to ride it out. Use the energy."

Lorne pushed his hands through his hair, feeling the tracks his fingers made against his own scalp, feeling every *fucking* hair move. "I hate it."

Vasska laughed, the sound dancing across Lorne's senses. "Somehow I'm not surprised. You don't seem like the type to need more energy."

"How long does it last?" Lorne asked.

Vasska shrugged. "I don't know. I generally stay away from it because I don't like how it makes me feel. A while, I guess."

"Fuck me."

Lorne grabbed a bottle of gin from under the bar, cracking the green wax seal. Juniper gin, his distillery. He wondered how many bottles Davik bought. Wondered if Davik knew that Lorne had Juniper shares. Stupid question. Of course he knew. Davik Kaine knew fucking everything. Lorne thought he had secrets, but instead his life was written out on his skin for everyone powerful to read over and decide his worth. Lorne pulled the cork, releasing the warm scent of botanicals. He didn't know fucking well anything about how to make gin, but he knew what he liked when he drank it, and Juniper was the best he'd come across. The Bay evidently agreed—of all his investments, the gin distillery was making the second-best return, trailing only behind the crematorium.

Lorne took slow sips from the bottle, letting the gin burn away the taste of the fucking leaf. Watching László. The crowd had him and he was their star, his smile glowing brighter than anything Lorne had ever seen.

László spotted Lorne watching him, and he grinned. He left his crowd behind to come to the bar, snatching a cigarette from someone's hand as he passed. He floated on the laughter that lived in the centre of him, dancing ever so slightly, making the charms on his necklace sway as he moved to music only he could hear. Smoke trailed after him, the thin white paper burning slow, releasing the smell of tobacco and hashish in a billowing off-white cloud. And Lorne was rooted in place by the sight of him, frozen in a moment that was neither too fast nor too slow. László draped his arm around Vasska's shoulders, taking the cigarette out of his mouth long enough to plant a kiss on Vasska's cheek.

"The three of you look too fucking grim over here," he said. "I hate it. Don't you know how to have a good time? Have you ever tried it before?"

Lorne shrugged. "You're better at it than I am."

"Good news, I'm willing to teach you." László stretched the cigarette out to Lorne and winked. "Step one, smoke with me. Step two, come let your fans adore you."

The smell of hashish was familiar, and he hated it, but Lorne smoked it anyway. Smoked it because László had smoked it first. What was it about László? About this place? Lorne couldn't break away, couldn't lean out of the wild skid they were all doing, couldn't even say no when he was offered things he hadn't touched in years. He hated most of the things that made smoke. Things that made you slow and stupid, things that rotted the soul right out of you. And now he hated khat, too, because his heart was crawling between his ribcage, trying to escape his chest.

Jason was in the Rift, and Lorne was smoking hashish in a pugilist club, surrounded by people he didn't know. People he would fight and die for when not all that long ago, he'd sworn he was done being a soldier. He didn't know who he was anymore.

Maybe that was a lie. Maybe he'd been this person all along. Learning to fight and loving it. Unpacking guns in cellars. Maybe he was built for this, assembled with the right measures of anger and stupidity and hunger so he always came back to fighting in one form or another. On Powell Iwan's stage, in Davik Kaine's ring, in Yaelsmuir's streets. He was born to be a soldier, and the boxing gloves were his uniform. And maybe he'd been lying to Jason and himself for five fucking years, pretending to be a better man than he was.

"What about you, Miss Tei?" László asked, leaning his elbows on the bar so the charms of his necklace swung in the air toward Lorne, and he couldn't help but watch them, couldn't help but lean closer to them. He wanted to catch them and hold them in his hand and ask László what each of them were, if there was a story behind any of them. The tooth especially. A bullet casing, a piece of metal that look like the sight of a rifle. "Do you know how to have fun?"

Allie gave a nervous laugh, but she took the cigarette when Lorne offered it to her. "The last time I smoked hashish, I was with my brother."

"Oh yeah?" László asked. "Where's he? Maybe you should invite him over so I can have more entertaining company."

Allie exhaled smoke through her nose. "He's dead." She delivered the words with such matter-of-fact flatness that it knocked the smile off László's face. "The Authority killed him in the riots at Station House 4."

László cocked his head to the side, reaching across the bar to take his cigarette back. "I didn't know your family was tainted."

Allie gave a small shrug, but she wasn't making eye contact with any of them anymore. "We aren't. But my brother was in love, and he was always especially stupid when he thought he was being romantic."

"Well, shit," László said, grabbing the bottle of gin and exhaling another cloud of smoke. He lifted the bottle, offering it up to the sky and looking directly at Lorne. "Here's to idiots in love who fight for us and die for us when they don't have to." He took a long pull from it. Handed it to Allie, who drank in slower, smaller sips.

"Khat, gin, and hashish?" Vasska asked. "Aren't you a healer?"

"What, because I know how a body works, that means I have to be boring?" László laughed. "Maybe my Talent allows me to know *exactly* what I can handle so I can have a really fucking good time. I didn't expect to be judged by you, Mr. Czarny. The heir to the empire built out of everything fun in the Bay."

"Just because my grandfather made his business selling bodies and drugs doesn't mean I have much interest in those things," Vasska said, and he was blushing again, unable to look Allie in the eye. Like he knew exactly how he wanted to have fun, and he was afraid she would see it flash through his mind.

"I might be high, but I can still smell bullshit," László laughed. "I know you know how to have fun. I've seen it."

Vasska was blushing so bad, he looked like he was going to burst a blood vessel. "Doesn't your pugilist have a match tomorrow?"

László shrugged. "He does. So?"

"Shouldn't he be resting?"

"What do you say, Mr. Lightning," László asked, turning that grin on Lorne. "Do you want to go rest, or do you want one really good party before everything changes?"

Lorne shrugged. Fucking too late now to ask him if he wanted to rest. His skin was going to split open and crawl away. He had to get the energy out, that's what Vasska said. He wanted to rest, and he wanted to win against Ari tomorrow. But neither of those things were possible anyway, so fuck it. "Maybe resting is a waste of time when we have no idea what happens next."

"That's what Ishmael said," Allie said.

Vasska laughed, finally looking at her. "Well, if Ishmael Saeati said it, it must be good advice."

"It must be," Allie said.

She leaned across the gap keeping her and Vasska apart and kissed him. Vasska froze for a second, but then he melted into her, dragging her against him until there was no room between their bodies at all, that desperate, hungry kiss of people who had been thinking about this kiss since the first moment they laid eyes on each other.

And it made Lorne feel terribly alone, standing on the wrong side of the bar. Alone and intrusive.

He swept up the bottle of gin and wandered away again, toward the crowd. Gin and hashish and khat battled in his body. His heart was still wild, racing, but every step took too long, every joint taking its time to bend. He was too aware of muscles flexing through his whole body every time he lifted his leg, every time he shifted his weight, every time his foot hit the floor. His feet dragged. Swept through the copper crowns still scattered on the floor, winking at him as they made their way across the cavernous space. Who was going to clean all the copper up?

Someone was shaking Lorne's hand. Smiling. Laughing. Everyone here laughed so much. Excited for the match tomorrow, Mr. Lightning. Thank you for the copper. Proud to have you fighting for the Bay, son. Sweat. Hands. People he didn't know, so happy to touch him. They'd built this place for him, but he was trying to get his body ready for a match he didn't feel qualified for and a war he was prepared to die for. He searched the crowd for a familiar face, but he couldn't find any. Everything blurred together in a hazy mass. If he was a better person, maybe he would recognize more of these faces.

The crowd around him pulsed, moved, evolved into a being with its own energy, its own heartbeat. A riptide, dragging him deeper. Someone kissed him. And maybe this was what he needed. Better to kiss someone he didn't know, wouldn't remember. Because the only reason he was thinking about kissing *anyone* was because he desperately wanted Jason again, wanted to hold him and kiss his tears and make everything alright for both of them. When was the last time he was intimate with someone? In the summer, maybe. The night he slept with the girl who played piano at the Songbird—the songhouse that rented space from the distillery that made Juniper gin. The pair of them plied a silk-clad man from Highview with more rum than he could handle. And when the man passed out drunk in one of the private rooms above the songhouse, the girl took every coin he had left in his pockets—one of the hazards rich people had to accept when they came to the Bay to drink and fuck—and she paid for a different room, letting Lorne sleep in the bed with her. Letting Lorne kiss her and hold her, letting him seek comfort in the smell of her hair and the taste of her skin, because it was easier for both of them to fall into each other than it was to admit they were lost and alone.

And now, the crowd had him. It was easy to believe he'd never be alone again. He was here, with them. Alive. Each moment stretched like a rubber band, threatening to snap back at him. So many bodies, so many people, so many sweeping muscles and powerful limbs and the curve of hips and chests, and so many hands, reaching, caressing, holding. The smell of sweat and the smell of beer and the smell of wool, dragging him deeper. Someone slid their hands up his back, fingers tangling in his hair. His mouth dragged across someone's bare shoulder. His hands touched skin and sweat. If he closed his eyes, he could just about convince himself it was Jason. Jason's mouth and Jason's soft skin and Jason's slim shoulders and Jason's hands, undoing the buttons on the front of his trousers. Only a heartbeat passed, and he had his hands in someone's hair. Another beat and pleasure rolled through his whole body because someone was sucking his cock, and it felt so good he couldn't breathe. His heart hammered and he missed it, somehow, missed the moment of his own release, and he was left in the slow, contented buzz of after. Walking through the club again because the khat made him restless even as everything else made him too slow.

He slid off the face of the world. Falling. On the floor, dizzy. Staring up at the ceiling, which spun further and further away. When did he get down on the floor? He rested his hands on his own chest to make sure he was still in his body. Rested his palms over his heart and felt the gunshot power of each beat. László laughed. Where had László come from?

"What are you doing on the floor?"

Lorne slid his hands back up, pushing his fingers over his face, into his hair. It was a good question. "I don't know."

"You're going to get stepped on."

Vasska's hand, on his arm, pulling him up. "Why don't we go upstairs before you get trampled?"

On his feet, but only because Vasska and László were dragging him up. The gin and the hashish were fighting against the khat, trying to make him tired even though he couldn't stop moving. How long had he been on the floor? Allie and Vasska and László, walking with him. Bare feet pressing over the copper crowns, the metal cold after lying forgotten for so long. Still winking like copper stars, shimmering, dancing. When had he taken off his boots? He went back down to the floor slowly, on his hands and knees, feeling each copper press into his skin in round points, marking him with their shape. Warm and glittering copper stars, scattered everywhere.

"You're on the floor again," László laughed. "We're supposed to go upstairs!"

"I wanted to see them," Lorne said, pushing his hand through the crowns, feeling them slide across the wood floor, catching on the seams between the planks of the hardwood. Everything was getting slower. Slower. Dragging further. "They look like stars."

László grinned, and it was perfect. He came down to the floor with Lorne, lying beside him. Lorne grabbed as many copper crowns as he could with one sweep of his hand, lifting them up over his chest. If they were stars, they were supposed to be above him instead of below him. But they weren't stars, they were copper. Copper that László stole.

Lorne let the crowns go. They fell toward his chest—but didn't hit him. They stopped falling too soon, spinning in place above him. Spinning, tumbling, but never going anywhere. Time had stopped moving too fast, maybe. It was frozen now.

Copper spun, and one of them hovered so close to his chest that he could feel the air it moved with every rotation, sliding over his skin like a kiss.

And then there was more copper in the air, jumping up from the floor like it all forgot it wasn't a star, rising up around him. Spinning, catching the light until they *were* stars. Maybe Lorne was losing his mind. But it was beautiful, so maybe it didn't matter. He flicked one, and it spun away, higher, higher, until it hit the ceiling and bounced off.

"Are you doing that with Talent?" Lorne asked. "Did you make them into stars?"

"Yeah," László said. "It's easy. You just kind of... pick it up."

Lorne wrapped his arm around László's shoulders, dragging him closer. "It's beautiful. You're beautiful."

László smiled. And the coins spun faster, shining over their heads like fireflies in the summer. He kissed Lorne on the throat, on the chin, on the lips. All the charms of László's necklace rested on Lorne's throat, cold and heavy with the weight of László's life. The copper coins fell out of the air, drumming against the floor with musical percussion, chinking and dancing and bouncing all around them. Copper rain that didn't touch them.

Back up to his feet, even though the fast feeling was falling out of him. He was tired. But László led him up the stairs, back to the apartment where everything was warm and safe and quiet. Into his bed and László followed, their bodies pressing together, tired and thousands of years away.

The long moments finally snapped and let go, sending Lorne plunging down into sleep.

Didn't last long.

Or it lasted forever.

He floated in that dark, empty place. Never alone again. Alone so completely, he didn't remember his own name.

60

JASON
DAY 38

Even in the Rift, they heard about the boxing match in Cattle Bone Bay. A few guards followed pugilism. Shifts were traded, and arrangements were made so that those who wanted to be there could make their way down. Inmates wagered meals and blankets and good work orders on the outcome of the match, which they wouldn't hear about until morning shift change, but that didn't dim the fervour of the betting. Most bet on Ari Odegaard.

The name sent an old echo of longing through Jason's chest—he had good memories of the pugilist club in Brickheart. He liked to sit at the bar with his father and watch people. It was the one thing they did together that let Jason forget his father carried that fucking tin badge. Kazrani liked it there, too—and once, when her son Tevir was visiting, Tashué let the pair of them go off together because Tevir was old enough. Tevir nicked a half-empty bottle of bison grass vodka, and they went up to the roof and they stayed up there all night. Jason confessed to Tevir that his Talent was quickening slowly, and he didn't know what to do. And Tevir whispered, *yes you do*.

Ari found them up there after dawn and fed them breakfast before sending them home to Tashué's apartment, ignoring the empty bottle of vodka that sat between them.

Ari Odegaard was the safe bet for the match in the Bay, of course. The city's beloved hero. His skill and his career gave him an easy advantage. But no one betting knew Lorne, so maybe they were all betting wrong.

"Today's the day," Irén whispered to him in the morning, the quiet, slow hours before everyone climbed down from their bunks.

Today's the day. She'd only been here a short time, but 'the day' had already arrived.

He half expected to be moved out of the routine immediately. Every now and then, someone was transferred from the main population before breakfast. But Irén and Jason were herded down into the mess hall with everyone else.

The anxiety clawed at Jason immediately. It got worse when he realized Verrit was nowhere to be seen. And then everyone started walking to their morning chores, and Jason knew things had gone wrong. They made it all the way to the gardens. The moment they stepped through the door, Jason knew he was going to die in the Rift.

There weren't any gardeners outside. No guards, either. Just a dozen proxies, clustered together like they were trying to hide from the cold.

Jason tried to turn and open the door, but someone pushed it shut from inside, and the sound of the metal lock thunked through the wood so loud that Jason could feel it echoing in his marrow. And he wanted to tell Irén that she brought this on them, that this was their consequence for standing up to Verrit, but there wasn't time to speak before the proxies swarmed them.

"Fucking hell," was all Irén had time to say.

Irén stepped in front of Jason, pressing him back against the door. But fuck that. When she stepped to meet them, Jason followed her, taking the first swing. Knuckles hit face, and he was rewarded with a hot rush of someone's blood, but then the chaos had him. It didn't matter how much he swung, didn't matter how hard he hit, there were too many people. He was flat on the ground, and he didn't even know how he got there. The path was hard and cold, a bit of ice clinging to the stone pavers, gathering in the shadows. Someone kicked him, and then Irén was over him, kneeling beside him because there wasn't enough space for her to get up, but she kept swinging anyway. Someone fell, and their thrashing got in the way—it was enough time for Jason and Irén to stand. Someone grabbed Jason by the waist, dragging him away. Someone hit Jason in the face, and his legs went out beneath him. His vision tilted off to one side, spinning away.

His Talent was nothing but a headache that lived in his skull, and this island prison stripped away everything good and human from the world, turning them into animals that devoured each other for survival.

He missed Lorne and he missed his father and he was going to die without seeing either of them again. Or maybe he would see his father, maybe they'd stand together in front of the Keeper of the Keys because apparently his father was a rebel now, and Jason was willing to bet that rebels had a short lifespan.

Fuck the Authority. Jason spat blood and rage at the sky and thought it again, letting the words hold him in life. Fuck the Authority.

Fuck every single one of them, every guard, every officer, every paperwork creator, every administrator. Fuck the Rift and everyone who ran it.

The door opened. The squealing of those old rusted hinges was loud enough that it sliced through Jason's disorientation.

He was lying on his back, staring up at the slate grey sky, bodies around him, but they had stopped assaulting him. Backing away, giving him space to lie and bleed and shiver in the cold.

The proxies scattered. Out of the corner of his eye, Jason saw one hit the ground, a guard's boot on the back of his head, holding him down.

Verrit loomed over Jason, hands on his hips, his coat turned up around his cheeks. "Got yourself into trouble, hey Blackwood? Good thing I told the guards to come look for you, isn't it?"

Jason squeezed his eyes shut, letting himself focus on all the pain in his body. All the vicious, burning, aching places that made it hard to breathe. It was better to focus on that than to look up at Verrit's smug face. He'd set Irén and Jason up to get jumped and then brought the guards in to stop it so he could deny his involvement. Fuck him especially.

"Up you get, now," Verrit said. "You're alright. Walk it off."

So long as Jason stayed on the ground, lying on the stone with his eyes closed, he could convince himself that this was just a dream, and none of it was real. He was in Brickheart, where he belonged, and the Rift was a terrible nightmare. Any minute now, he'd wake up and see Lorne and kiss his serious mouth, and he'd fight with his father about something stupid like their laundry. That was the way his life was supposed to be. He wasn't really here.

Verrit grabbed Jason by the arm, dragging him up so fast it made Jason's head spin. "Let's go, Blackwood. Up."

Jason forced his eyes open, and even the weak sunlight seared through his vision, too hot and too bright. His stomach clenched, and his knees buckled down again. On his hands and knees, he vomited onto the path, his thin gruel breakfast coming up without much resistance at all. Rain pelted the mess he'd made, driving it into the cracks between the stones. When had it started raining? He wished he would do the same. Wished he would melt into the ground and cease to be.

"Let's get you down to the infirmary, get your head looked at," Verrit said, grabbing Jason again. "I'll walk you."

Irén sat with her head in her hands, rain sluicing down her face, her blood running from a wound Jason couldn't see. Dripping between her fingers, mixing with the rain. Had to be a lot of blood for it to run like that.

"Leave him alone," she said. She tried to rise to her feet, and when she pulled her hands away from her face, Jason could see the gash half-hidden by her hairline, where all the blood was coming from. "Jason—"

"He needs to go the infirmary," the guard grunted, shoving Irén back down. "Sit down before you fall over."

"Get the fuck off me," Irén snarled, shoving the hands away. "If he dies, I'll have your fucking balls, you hear me?"

"I know!" the guard snapped, shoving her down again. "I fucking *know*, alright? That's why he's going to the infirmary. Make sure his skull isn't split 'cause of the trouble *you* caused. Sit down, and let him get looked at."

Jason looked down at his feet so he could watch them shuffle on the ground. He had to concentrate that hard to keep them going. Left right, left right, left right. Keep moving. Every time his foot hit the ground, it sent another bolt of pain through his skull. They passed into the looming darkness of the Rift and the darkness of the long hallways welcomed him like an embrace.

You belong here, the darkness said. *You don't fit anywhere else.*

61

TASHUÉ

DAY 38

He dreamt of a wedding.

A man and a woman, sitting with their fingers laced together, their palms turned to the sky. Needle and ink slowly built their tattoos, lines and shapes that spread from one hand to the other, the story of them folding into their skin. The couple spoke their vows into the wind, so the land could hear their promise to each other. So the mountains would echo with their hope for the future. Tashué didn't understand the words, but somehow he knew what was being said.

Drawn together by life, each a piece made whole, soul and blood. We carry the past in our hearts and we carry the future in our hands, with love and hope for tomorrow.

Tashué sat close to them, a guest at the wedding, his back to a bonfire where the feast was slowly roasting underground. But his own dreams seeped in, putting people he knew around the fire. His soldiers. They had discarded most of their uniforms and they were down to trousers and bare feet, or just a shirt, or just their drawers. Or nothing. Dancing and drinking and kissing each other. None of them had braids in their hair. They were a flurry of limbs and loose hair and skin mottled with ink and scars. Pleasure and intoxication and kiss-bruised lips. He looked for Kazrani among the bodies, searching for her familiar tattoos, but she wasn't there. The more he looked, the more he realized who was missing.

It wasn't his whole company. It was only the people who had died. The soldiers he had lost in his time as the company's Captain.

Even as they danced, Tashué's soldiers seemed to be watching the bride and the groom, like they were aware of the dream, the same as he was aware of them. The groom was so much younger than Tashué ever knew him, his face not yet marked by the long years between now and this memory, but Tashué recognized him anyway.

Rhodrishi.

He turned away from his bride as she spoke her vows, looking directly at Tashué. "You're alive."

The relief in his voice made Tashué feel terribly guilty. He looked up at the sky. The summer sun was setting behind distant mountains, spreading dusk shadow across the clouds. Summer humidity hung in the air so thick he could taste it, even in the dream. Tashué shivered anyway, pulling his coat around his body—his dreams put him in his filthy dress greens, even though Wolfe's staff had fed the uniform to the fire days ago. His coat wasn't enough to keep him warm, nor was the fire behind him, and it didn't matter how he buried his face in his collar, he was still cold. Winter's cold, wet chill chewing at the edges of him.

Rhodrishi stood—his face aged as he rose, lines like canyons across his features, grey hairs threading through the pure, inky black. Once he was on his feet, his younger-self still sat sitting in the grass, leaning closer to his wife to rest his forehead against hers as the tattoo artist continued her work.

Rhodrishi came to Tashué, looking up at him. The light of the fire behind them cast a warm and loving glow across Rhodrishi's profile.

"How are you adjusting to your Talent?"

Tashué focused on Rhodrishi's face again. "How did you know I've been using my Talent?"

Rhodrishi shrugged, gesturing to his younger-self. "You've walked the dreampath to me. It's a pretty strong clue."

"This is real?"

Rhodrishi nodded. "In a sense. It's 'really' my dream, and you've 'really' wandered into it. I always imagined I would get the chance to teach you about Talent, but of course things never go the way we imagine. So—how is it?"

Guilt rolled through Tashué again. It would have been nice to learn from Rhodrishi, but his own stubborn refusal to even contemplate who he was kept a wedge between them. And now... "I can't control it. I'm aware of everything, all the time. I have to wrestle it into my own skull, or I can't think because there's so much... noise. It feels like I'm sharing myself with another being... like it's another version of myself. Something dark and ugly."

"Tashué Blackwood," Rhodrishi said slowly. "After your career, you think there's some *darker* version of yourself?"

Tashué grimaced, looking down at his hands. He half expected to see blood on them from the bank employees, but they were clean. "I don't know. Maybe I thought I had made myself better after all these years. But now it feels like the worst parts were lying in wait."

Rhodrishi gave another shrug. "That's more accurate than blaming your Talent. Your capacity for brutality is yours alone. Not your Talent's fault. It's true that it can feel like a separate force—it can come to have a mind of its own. But only because we teach it who we are and what we need."

Tashué clenched his hands into fists to feel the flex of his muscles and the shift of his tendons. The words dragged a flash of anger through his chest but he couldn't grasp why. Maybe it was that tin badge he used to wear, trying to tell him he was tainted and not to be trusted. "The last time we spoke to each other, you said it was like a muscle. We shape it as we use it."

Rhodrishi sighed, turning away from the wedding and toward the bonfire. He walked slowly through the grass, like he was pulled toward the chaos of Tashué's soldiers as they danced. "Talent is, in theory, a blank slate, but it doesn't stay that way for long. It's the ability to shape the world, yes, but how we interact with things is different from one person to the other. Our personalities shape it, and in turn our Talent shapes us, bit by bit, until it's impossible to tell which thing began to change first. If you spend thirty-some years teaching your Talent that it's a thing not to be trusted, it becomes hyper vigilant to threats. Often, after someone grapples with their Talent as long as you did, it will turn against itself. It will take some time for you and your Talent to become accustomed to each other."

"Davik says I might never get used to it," Tashué said. "He worries I suppressed it too long."

"It's possible," Rhodrishi said with a shrug. "It depends on how long you live, I suppose."

Tashué laughed. "Now that's some good old-fashioned army optimism."

"You should count yourself lucky," Rhodrishi said. "Your quickening was violent and ugly—it could have killed you."

"You felt it?" Tashué asked. "The moment I quickened?"

Rhodrishi nodded. A cold wind blew through the dream, like a winter draft cutting through the hot summer air. Tashué pulled his coat tighter around his chest, for all the good it did him. Somewhere in the distance, the creaking of trees even though there were none to be seen. And then the horrible percussion blast that changed everything, rolling up toward them from memory.

"There's a line between us, drawing us together," Rhodrishi said. He walked right into the crowd of soldiers until they danced around him, a storm that didn't touch him. "So, yes, I felt it when it finally broke through. There's another line between you and her. She felt it, too."

The figure of Stella, over near the flames, but she shimmered, the outline of her indistinct. Like she was trying to step into the dream but wasn't fully asleep. Tashué tried to reach for her, but someone stepped in the way, and the image of her disappeared. She was nothing but a cloud of smoke and his own longing.

"I shared a dream with her," Tashué said. "After. Was it real, too?"

"I can't speak to a dream I wasn't a part of. But it's likely. We were all worried about you."

Tashué shook his head. "I never should have let her go."

Those words again. They came unbidden, just like when he said it to Ishmael. He didn't even know what he meant, just that the separation was an open wound, hemorrhaging something out of him.

"That's part of it," Rhodrishi said. "That's what I mean. Loving her has become who you are, and so it is a part of your Talent, too."

"Is that what you mean by there being a line between us?" Tashué asked. "Me and her—and me and you?"

Rhodrishi nodded. "You remind me of my boys."

Tashué looked toward the younger-Rhodrishi, still kneeling in the grass, far from the soldiers. The tattoo artist packed away her tools, using a cloth to wipe away blood and excess ink. Rhodrishi's wife leaned forward, kissing his face, his lips, his hair. She had flowers in her hair and a string of iolite beads around her neck, the indigo blue stones catching the light of the fire. Her ishani tattoos were intricate across the backs of her hands. Dream-Rhodrishi stood with his wife, and he kissed her cheek.

"Was it like that for you and her?" Tashué asked. "You never talked about her."

Rhodrishi sighed, looking down at his hands. The tattoos were faded and worn, scars cutting through the ink lines. "The best thing about a joyful moment is the ability to share it with someone. When your wife turns to you and says, *remember that day in the raspberry thicket, when the storm came on us so fast we couldn't possibly get home soon enough, so we picked raspberries in the rain?* And then you nod, and say, *and we tried to make love, but I thought it was a terrible idea because the raspberry canes were so sharp. And it was all horribly embarrassing when we got home soaking wet, with scratches on our faces because we'd tried to lie down in a raspberry thicket like a pair of fools. Who tries to make love in raspberries?* And then she laughs, and kisses you, and says, *you were always so serious, about everything. I told you that you'd have frown lines before long—and I was right.*" He closed his hands on the tattoos, looking at the dream of his wife, watching the tattoo artist pluck more flowers from the field and braid them into his wife's hair. "She was always so much more passionate than I am. It was that passion that drew me to her. It kept me warm, like sitting beside a bonfire. But it was that passion that took her from me, too. And now, when I remember the day in the raspberry thicket, all I can think is how I wish I appreciated her wild spirit more when I still had her, instead of being embarrassed by the scratches on my face."

One soldier knelt beside Tashué, in front of a massive drum, pounding a furious rhythm for the other soldiers. Those tattoos, that face —an old spasm of regret and grief crossed through Tashué's whole being. The Ridge and everyone he lost up there lived forever in his nightmares, along with almost every other posting, but it had all become a formless mass of suffering, time chipping away the old details. But now, this memory-dream reminded him of their individuality. Their faces, their voices. How they lived, how they died. They all danced so close to the fire that it had to hurt—except they were dead. Their bodies already knew the flames. Maybe that was why they were drawn so close to it.

"I remember him," Rhodrishi said, giving a sad and distant smile to the soldier at the big drum. "He was one of the soldiers who helped carry you into my tent, that first time. I ordered them both out, and of course Lieutenant Mahalouwan followed orders. But he wouldn't leave your side. I remember because it was unusual for the Jitabvi soldiers to be so attached to their Captain. I thought you must have made quite an impression on your company and it made me wonder about you. He slept under your cot so he wouldn't take up any room. And then, when the restlessness drove him out of his mind, he roamed around, trying to find ways to help, but he made such an awkward pest of himself that we sent him to chop wood to get him out of the way."

Tashué laughed. "Yes, that sounds like Qirin. I don't remember him being there."

Rhodrishi smiled. "Once you were out of the delirium and I was confident you'd survive, he went back to Iris Company to tell everyone you were coming back to them. You lost him at the Ridge?"

Tashué nodded, looking toward the bonfire again. Qirin was still kneeling in front of the drum, but someone was braiding his hair for battle. And Tashué wanted to tell them not to go. "At the Ridge. He led a charge down even after I gave the order to dig in. Not a single soldier came back up from that charge."

Rhodrishi put a hand to his chest, his breathing going thick and slow, his eyes drifting closed. Tashué touched his shoulder, but he didn't know what to say. He didn't need to ask if the older man was alright. The pain was etched clear on his face. When it was over, Rhodrishi sank down. Sitting in the swaying grass, among the forest of bodies, within reach of the drum. He breathed slow, resting his hand on the side of the drum to keep himself steady. His younger-self and the dream of his wife came to the soldiers. His wife folded into the dancers like she knew them, and his younger-self watched with open, glowing adoration. And Qirin kept drumming, sweat beading on his body, dancing over the horse tattoo on his chest.

"Sometimes, when my heart stutters like that, I swear I can hear her whispering to me," Rhodrishi said softly. "Telling me to come. I resisted so long. I kept thinking I had more to do. I wanted to accomplish more, wanted to see the revolution my son keeps ranting about. His mother would have been so proud of what became of his career. She wasn't ever sure of the boys going to the Academy, but she allowed it because they learned things from the military that they could use to help on the smugglers' road, or in the legacy territory. But Eilas? That boy is going to change the world." A bit of a smile pulled at Rhodrishi's mouth, and he looked up at Tashué again. "I suppose he hasn't been a boy in a very long time. He's a few years older than you. He's down in White Crown now, or he was the last time I walked to his dreams... Everything I've wished for all my life is here, and I think I'm going to die before it unfolds."

Shock rolled through Tashué slowly, distantly, like the dream kept it from hooking him fully. "Why?" He crouched beside Rhodrishi, putting a hand on the older man's shoulder. "What can I do to help you?"

Rhodrishi shook his head. "Stella and Ceridwen are doing everything they can. But I pushed too hard, tracking her down. It was worth it. She's had a rough run of it."

Panic. Just like when Ishmael withed to talk to Stella, ripping through all the numbness, lighting him on fire. "What do you mean, a rough run? Rhodrishi, what happened?"

Rhodrishi shook his head. "The Authority happened. What else? She survived it, but I can't speak to what she endured. If you see her again, she can tell you. I hope you see her again. I think she's going to change her mind and go back to you."

Tashué squeezed Rhodrishi's arm harder, clinging to him desperately like he could hold the older man in life. "Rhodrishi, please, tell me how to help you. Where are you? I can figure out how to send someone—do you need a healer? Is she safe?"

Rhodrishi turned his gaze on Tashué, lifting his chin and taking a slow breath, a little of his fury unfolding, a little of that terrible anger blooming. Tashué had only seen that anger twice before, once when they sat in Tashué's office at the station house and talked about what *home* meant, and again at the hospital the day Stella left Yaelsmuir when Rhodrishi asked Tashué what kind of man he was going to be. And both times, Tashué felt he had failed some test, like Rhodrishi had been disappointed in his answer.

A new figure wandered into the crowd—not a soldier this time. Gianna Tarbrook, the healer Tashué killed. She had oak leaves and moss caught in her hair, and her clothes dripped with all the blood she'd lost. Blood he lay his hands in as he tried to save her life.

"Your name means One Who Sees," Rhodrishi said, watching her walk around the edge of the fire. Aimless, lost. Searching for someone or something.

"I know," Tashué said. Desperation made it hard to breathe. Why wasn't Rhodrishi answering about Stella—and why did it feel like he was being tested again? "You told me at the Imburleigh factory, the day I got this."

He reached into his pocket, where all his medals jangled together. He offered Rhodrishi the stupid medal Myron had given him, obnoxiously heavy and overly ornate. Rhodrishi closed his hand around it, like he was trying to hide the gold from Tashué's soldiers. Or maybe he was trying to hide it from Gianna. She died the day after he accepted that fucking medal.

"You asked me how my mother would feel about that stupid brass badge I took," Tashué went on. "She's the one who taught me to be afraid of the whole system, but I still think she would have been terribly sad to see me with that badge in my hand. She told me to follow the laws, not to uphold them. She wanted me to keep myself safe, and instead I traded my soul."

Rhodrishi nodded, a bit of the exhaustion falling from his face, like the years were melting away, and he was invigorated with new life. "Do you see now?"

"Yes." The word dragged right out of his gut, tearing him apart from within. How could he not see, with Gianna standing right there? "It's rotten from the core. It was never meant to protect anyone, except people with the money and power to benefit from our suffering. I took that badge and ate up their lies like a starving dog taking scraps from the master's table, and they taught me to snap and snarl at all the other dogs. They convinced me it was what I had to do in order to survive. They keep the dogs hungry and snarling and fighting each other because they know if the dogs ever got wise and stood together, we'd eat them alive, wouldn't we?"

Rhodrishi nodded, and his eyes softened. Tears brimmed, but he didn't wipe them away or try to hide them. "You'll stand."

"Yes," Tashué said again, and it came easier this time. "I'll stand."

Rhodrishi nodded again, turning his eyes back to the younger version of himself and his wife. She laced her fingers together with one of Tashué's soldiers, and they danced together, the pair of them so graceful and strong at once. Aya, Tashué remembered. Kazrani's lover for so many years. Qirin's half-sister.

And Stella again, walking beside the flames, shifting and indistinct. Mud and blood caked into her clothes, her eyes searching the crowd for Tashué.

"Rhodrishi, tell her I'm sorry."

Rhodrishi cocked his head at Tashué, one eyebrow raising. "What for?"

"I told her I would fight for her after all the things she told me, but I haven't. Everything is a fucking mess. I haven't done anything."

"Do you mean to tell me that you haven't successfully executed an entire revolution in two weeks?" Rhodrishi asked, tossing the medal to the ground in front of Qirin's drum. "I'm disappointed in you, Captain. Here I thought you were a soldier of the Dominion army."

"Here in the Dominion Foreign Deployment, we are purveyors of promises that are impossible to keep," Tashué said. A reflex. He didn't know how many times he'd said those words. How many times he'd heard them. The unofficial slogan of the Officer's Academy. "Fuck, it's been a long time since I've said that."

Rhodrishi elbowed Tashué, giving a bit of a smile. "It's the only way to commit to a mission. Promise more than you can deliver, and survive anyway. You're consistent."

Tashué laughed. The soldiers at the bonfire were dressed again, ready for war. Milling around the flames, waiting to be told to mount up. They clustered in knots, leaving Gianna alone in the field. The good humour drained out of him, the guilt sliding back in. "She said I could move mountains. And every day, I feel like I'm letting her down."

Rhodrishi turned to look at the mountains, distant in his dream. To the west, past the bonfire, hiding in long night shadows. The line of them blocked out the stars, hid half the full moon. Tashué's grandmother called the full moon this time of year a raspberry moon because it always came full around the same time the raspberry canes were coming ripe.

"That's the difference between Skairn folk like her people and Pashibé. Skairn will look at the mountains and wonder if they can be moved by men. Legends say Skairn folk taught us how to move them with Talent in the days of the Godking. They're stubborn, and it's beautiful. It's what kept them independent from the Godking all those years ago. It's that stubbornness that gave this country the North Star. Together, we inched that mountain border west, to give ourselves a bit more room to breathe here on the legacy side. It never occurred to us to try, until they taught us, because we Pashibé look at the mountains and let ourselves be moved by the majesty of them. And you, a son of both. Pashibé from your mother, Skairn from your father." He looked up at Tashué, giving a tired smile. "Are you sure they need to be moved?"

Tashué opened his mouth to answer, but he didn't know how to respond. Before he could find any words, Rhodrishi put his hand to his chest again, the painful expression spasming worse than before. Tashué sat beside him, but there was nothing he could do but hold the older man. For a moment, the solidness of him shifted, faded, like he was about to disappear.

I wish your heart gets better.

The voice sent a shiver down his spine—Ceridwen. That was Ceridwen. Her Talent had quickened, and she was keeping Rhodrishi alive.

"If you see my son, tell him I'm proud of him," Rhodrishi said, his voice strained with pain, but he forced the words out in a rush. "He's with his General. They've decided to stand, too, the pair of them. I think they're coming to Yaelsmuir, but I don't know. Tell him you're the one I used to write about. Tell him I'm sorry I couldn't hang on."

"Rhodrishi..."

Rhodrishi shook his head, clutching Tashué's filthy sleeve. "Please. I've taken care of the people you love because I love you like a son of my own. Because they deserve it. But if you see him, tell him—"

"Alright," Tashué interrupted. Rhodrishi's desperation made Tashué's throat feel too tight, and he had to wrestle the words out. "I'll tell him. If I survive all this, I'll find him, and I'll tell him."

Rhodrishi nodded, squeezing his eyes shut. "She's waiting for me. I can't wait to tell her that I was right about you. It took you long enough to prove it. I almost didn't get to see it."

Tashué laughed again, even though it hurt. Even though Rhodrishi was fading again, even though all the soldiers behind him were beating the war drums. "I'm sorry it took me so long to see."

Horses milled around, churning up the field. The Jitabvi ponies knew those drums, and it always got them excited. Qirin dropped his drumsticks in the grass, scooping the gold medal up and holding it out. Tashué took it from his hand and tossed it into the flames. Fuck Myron and his stupid rose gold. Gianna's eyes followed the medal to the fire and she watched it melt.

Rhodrishi slipped out of Tashué's grasp. For a moment, the younger image of him lingered. So young, so in love, his eyes brimming with hope. His new wife took him by the hand and drew him to his feet. They kissed, and she dragged him into the mess of soldiers to dance. And Stella, almost solid. Maybe the reason she looked distant was because she wasn't fully asleep yet. Maybe she hovered in that almost-dream place, where she could still hear the room around her. And if he waited, she could fall asleep completely, and she would come to him.

"Stella," he said, reaching for her.

But the dream of the wedding disappeared, leaving Tashué alone with his soldiers and his filthy uniform and the drums of war.

And then they were all gone, too, because Tashué was awake in the small room he shared with Ishmael. Another storm rattled on the window, another horrible, rainy day. It sounded heavier this time, like maybe there was a bit of ice. A bit of sleet.

He never should have let her go.

He rolled slowly from the bed, listening to the rain a while. Ishmael groaned in his sleep and shifted. It sounded like he'd wake up, but then he wrapped an arm around one of the down-stuffed pillows and settled again.

Restlessness drove Tashué out of the bedroom, even though he was tired. Even though a miserable ache had settled between his shoulders, because he went through life tense and ready for a fight in a way he hadn't in a long time. If he was a better man, maybe he would have nightmares about the woman he'd killed yesterday instead of dreams of Rhodrishi and Stella. He wanted those deaths to matter more than they did. They should have mattered as much as Gianna. But maybe it was a kind of numbness, something that drifted through him untethered for now, something that would settle into his chest later.

Davik was in the kitchen already, soaking wet from jogging in the rain, but he crouched in front of the wood stove to feed logs into the firebox.

"You didn't drag Lorne out with you?" Tashué asked.

Davik shook his head, feeding one last log into the flames and leaving his hands stretched out to catch the heat. "Didn't want him twisting his ankle on the ice before the fight. Besides, I thought he could use the sleep after last night."

Tashué pulled one of the water jugs off the counter, drinking slowly to wash the taste of his sleep out of his mouth. City water wasn't usually safe, but the whole club put great effort into having endless gallons of boiled, clean water available for Lorne during his training. Davik rose to his feet, the wood stove door squealing shut on its old hinges, the latch thumping closed.

"Jason's getting out today?" Tashué asked. "That's what Lorne said. The boxing match is a distraction for something."

"Yeah," Davik said, brushing sawdust and bark off his hands. "That's the plan."

He walked away, like he was trying to get out of the moment. Or maybe it was nothing, maybe he was anxious to get out of his wet clothes. Tashué should let him go, because wet clothes were real shit, but the dream lingered in his head. He'd only quickened a few days ago and there was never enough time to talk to anyone about Talent, making him feel like he was wrestling with this incredible thing along.

"Davik," he called. If he didn't ask now, Davik would be busy getting Lorne out of bed and ready for the fight. Ready for the long day of political speeches and photographers, ready to face the club filled to bursting with people.

Davik paused in the hallway, looking back over his shoulder at Tashué, still in the kitchen.

"Do you ever have dreams that are so vivid and so complete that they feel more like memories?" Tashué asked. "Like you're sharing with someone else."

Davik relaxed, his shoulders going soft. "Aye, of course." He pushed his hands over his face, through his hair, shaking water away. "It's called walking the dreampath. At least, that's what Rowan's mam called it. She taught me and Ffyanwy how to do it, so we could stay connected when she was running the smugglers' road. Talent is like…" He flexed his fingers like he was grasping for words. "It's not just a thing that we do. It's shaped by who we are. And it shapes us in return. Some Kaadayri nations have laws against using Talent to kill because it changes you. Not that it matters, hey? Killing with your bare hands changes you, too."

"Yeah," Tashué said. "It sure fucking does."

Davik looked up at Tashué for a while, sitting in the weight of the silence. The fire crackled, and the apartment was peaceful. Waiting for the day. "Who are you dreaming about?"

Tashué shrugged. There was so much he couldn't say. He looked down at the jug of water in his hand instead of looking Davik in the eye. It was stupid to ask Davik of all people when every second thought in Tashué's head was for Stella. If he said the wrong thing, might he slide off into saying things that would give her away? "People I love. People I lost. I wish I could get them back, but… I don't know."

"Sometimes that feeling means they're close. Like you can almost touch them if only you could reach far enough? Your Talent knows where they are and it's trying to pull them to you. Although I may in fact be full of shite, because I've been feeling like that about Ffyanwy for years, and she's long gone."

Tashué clenched his fist instead of saying anything. How *gone* was she?

If the dream was real, did that mean Rhodrishi was dying somewhere in the wilderness? Did it mean Stella was thinking about coming back, like Rhodrishi said?

"I heard Miss Tei and Saeati put together a long article about her," Davik said. "Ffyanwy, I mean. Dragging up all them old rumours about the things Clannaugh did to her. Apparently Saeati said they wanted people to remember who we were fighting against. Fist of the North, wife beater."

Tashué nodded. "They're ugly accusations."

"I still remember the first time I saw her with a bruise," Davik said. Tashué had come to recognize a particular tone of voice Davik had when he talked about Ffyanwy, soft and wistful, like recalling a fairy tale or a miracle. His voice was a bit harder this time, but that longing was still there. That pain. "She tried so hard to hide it. He didn't hit her face often, but if he did, she'd stop coming to the hospital, send word that she was ill or whatever excuse. I don't know how it was while their son was still alive, but after he died, that's when it got real ugly. He blamed her. The boy was tainted 'cause of her, after all." Davik shrugged, like he realized he was babbling. Standing in his kitchen, dripping wet, but lost in years gone by. "I shoulda killed him when I had the chance. There was a moment, before it all went real fucking ugly, that I had a gun in my hand and a clear shot at his back, but I let Rowan's mam stop me. *Think of your son*, she said. Rowan was just wee, and things were almost peaceful in the city at the time. I shouldn't have listened to her. She'd still be alive if I'd pulled the trigger."

"You don't know that," Tashué said. He set aside the jug, looking up at the cupboards for something easy to eat. But he wanted a smoke. He hadn't rolled any cigarillos since before the arrest and the tobacco cravings sat in his chest, ugly and insistent, day and night. A sure sign he needed to quit. "Isn't it equally possible that killing Clannaugh in that moment would have made things worse? That more people would have died in Cruinnich if the Red Dawn was responsible for an assassination of their Provincial Administrator?"

Davik shrugged.

"No, don't shrug at me," Tashué grunted. "You want to play *if only* and paint some bright and shining possibility. If only you'd shot Clannaugh in the back, then your son's mother would still be here. And Ffyanwy would be here, too, and you'd have them both, lucky bastard. And you'd be the hero of Cruinnich because you brought an end to Clannaugh's reign of terror before it got really bad. Maybe you'd be

Mayor of Cruinnich by now, and Rowan would have a bunch of adorable red-headed half siblings because you and Ffyanwy were so hopelessly in love. Right?"

Davik shrugged again, but he met Tashué's eye. A bit of a smile pulled at his mouth under his beard. "Well. I've never been one for politics. The rest sounds good, though. Sounds like you've had some practice with the *if only* game."

"Of course I do," Tashué muttered. "If only I had retired after they flogged me, then Keoh never would have taken Jason and run. If only I had dug in sooner, half my company would still be alive. If only I stayed on the Hadia after I retired, then Jason could have had a better life, surrounded by people as wild as him. He would have liked it out there. But then I have to be honest instead of selling myself this dream life where Jason and I are magically happier. Out on the Hadia, they're afraid of Talent, too. They don't trust it, and the army has strict regulations for how it's dealt with. Can't serve in the regular forces if you're tainted. So, maybe he would have been just as miserable. And, more to the point, I didn't stay on the Hadia, and you didn't shoot Clannaugh in the back, and so here we are, with this particular pile of shit. Wishing for something different doesn't help us survive today. It only distracts us from what we're up against."

Davik pushed both his hands through his beard, ringing water out of the thick hair. "You ain't exactly what I expected, Mr. Guinne."

Tashué spread his hands. "Neither are you, Mr. Kaine."

"Fair enough. You'll help the kids down at the printing press today?"

Tashué nodded. "Ishmael wants to distribute the Rhydderch article at the match, so it's a good way to keep busy and out of sight. Vasska has a speech about the Authority."

Davik laughed at that, turning and heading down the hallway again. "Redbone won't be happy!"

"Fuck Redbone," Tashué called after him. "Ishmael told me what she said, about the whole thing serving her campaign."

"I told you!" Davik shouted, his voice echoing all the way to the kitchen as he headed further down the hall. "I told you people wouldn't give a ripe shite. We been beggin' 'em to see us for years. Decades. They don't want to see, because it's a bit inconvenient, innit?"

Tashué sighed. He didn't like to admit it, but Davik was right.

But maybe Ishmael was right, too. Maybe what they needed was someone who knew how dirty Clannaugh was. If they could make it about more than just the Talented and the Authority—make it about the incredible scale of greed that fuelled Clannaugh, if they convince the city that Clannaugh was no hero and anyone who trusted him was looking for blood, maybe it would be enough to draw all of Yaelsmuir into the fight. What he said to Rhodrishi in the dream stuck in his head, rattling around his skull.

They keep the dogs hungry and snarling and fighting each other because they know if the dogs ever got wise and stood together, we'd eat them alive, wouldn't we?

If the city thought it was only about the Talented against the Authority, nothing would ever change.

But if they could see that the whole system was rotten, could see men like Rainer Elsworth and Bothain Clannaugh as symptoms of it, maybe it would shake them out of their complacency.

"Fuck," he muttered to let some of the frustration out. Some of the guilt. Some of the old, sour rage.

He stepped out into the hall in time to see Davik heading to Lorne's room. He'd changed into dry clothes, pushed a comb through his hair to slick it back out of his face. But he paused when he saw Tashué again, like he could feel the purpose sitting on Tashué's shoulders.

"What if I could find her?"

Davik froze so completely it was like looking at a photograph. The glow of his gaslights lit his expression, caught in a moment that looked like panic. Like hope, half-born but held in check because hoping was terrifying. "That isn't funny."

"I'm not joking," Tashué said. And it felt like a betrayal. Stella was running from this man, too. But Ishmael was right when he said it was about more than any specific person. The individual lives were only tiny pieces. "I could stay here and fight on the streets. But anyone can do that, and you aren't listening to my advice anyway. We need the whole city to hate Clannaugh as much as we do, right? So all the violence seems justified. We can't let him look like a hero. People still talk about what happened in Cruinnich between you and him, but everyone tells each other you deserved it. But if we make this about him, about how all of this is a game to him—maybe then people would stand with us. Not just the tainted, but everyone. She could end the fight before it even starts."

"How do you know where she is?" Davik breathed. "How could you possibly know?"

"It feels like I could reach out and touch her," Tashué said. "Like if I could just stretch my hand far enough, she would reach back. You said that means she's close."

Davik broke out of his stillness in an instant, coming fast at Tashué, both his hands hitting Tashué's bare chest and shoving him back. "How long have you known? I took you into my fucking home, and you listened to me talk about her, and you fucking lied to me by pretending you had no idea!"

Tashué shoved Davik back. "Explain to me when I started owing you anything, Davik! Why the fuck would I trust you when I didn't know you?"

Davik came again, grabbing Tashué's arms, his hands shaking as they clenched hard around Tashué's biceps. "Tell me where she is. Tell me how to find her."

Tashué grabbed Davik by the front of his shirt, fabric bunching in his fists. "No. Listen to me, and think. You can't go after her. You made a deal with Iwan—you're getting Jason out. Today, right? That's what the match is for. You'll get Jason out today, and the match will keep people here, and then tonight I'll go. I'll find her and—"

And what?

Beg her to come back to face Bothain Clannaugh and Davik Kaine at once. It seemed so cruel now that he was saying it out loud. The way her voice trembled when she spoke to Allie about everything she was running from.

What if she didn't want to come back?

Davik laughed, letting go of Tashué's arms to push his hands through his hair again, his eyes lit with something wild and hungry and sad. That hope again, gaining ground, stripping all the practiced cynicism out of his features. "You strike a hell of a deal. Jason for Ffyanwy, is that what you're saying?"

"I'm not giving her to you, Davik," Tashué said, pushing Davik away. "She's not a bargaining chip for me to throw down. If she decides she doesn't want to see you, I'll protect her from you without question."

"Protect her from me?" Davik breathed. "What the fuck is that supposed to mean?"

"You'll get my son out," Tashué said. "Tell me you'll get my son out, and I'll go tonight. As soon as he's safe, I'll go."

"What do you need?" Davik asked. "How far do you need to go?"

"I don't know," Tashué said. "I hope you're right, about our Talent drawing us together. I have that horse, the one I took from the Enquiry Officer. I need supplies for the road."

Davik shook his head, fumbling in his pocket for his timepiece. "I have to go. I have to get the idiot ready for his weigh-in, or they'll pull us out of the match."

"Go," Tashué said. "I'll go find what I need."

Davik pushed past Tashué, trailing his hand on the wall as he walked like he was dizzy and he had to keep himself up. "All this time, I thought I was going out of my bloody mind. Like I'd spent so long wishing I could see her again that I convinced myself she was close. She was here? In this city?"

"You've got a weigh-in to get to, Davik."

Davik shot a glare over his shoulder, so filled with rage and loathing that Tashué could almost feel the air boiling with heat. But then it dissolved so fast, Tashué wondered if he'd imagined it. Invented animosity when Davik was simmering with his complicated relief. "Not what I expected at all, Mr. Guinne."

62

OZRA

DAY 38

The sun rose sluggish and reluctant, another day dawning with a storm threatening. Smoke from the bonfire lingered in the air, the smell of charred wood and charred flesh permeating the walls of the big room. Ozra sat by the window, near the head of the bed, all night, watching the flames dance. Mahalouwan helped drag all the bodies out, offering every last bronzeman to the flames. Especially Siras fucking Duncreek.

Ozra thought about going down to the bonfire to help, or at least to watch, but every time he rose out of his chair, a terrible sense of dread dragged him back down. Stella had fallen asleep, half in a chair, half sprawled across the foot of Rhodrishi's bed, but Ceridwen kept vigil, even though the hallucinations made her weep all night. It wasn't right to leave her to carry this burden alone. Didn't feel right to try to convince her to stop, either. So he sat. And waited. And stewed in the exhausted melancholy. Felt strange, the way he was almost disappointed to have survived. He'd been so sure that he would catch a bullet in the midst of his stupid, hare-brained plan, but he hadn't counted on the people at the roadhouse hating the bronzemen almost as much as he did. And not a one of them had Talent—they were just people, protecting their own, doing the right thing. How long had it been since Ozra had lost faith in people being willing to do something foolish and dangerous and brave when it was right? He trusted the logging camps with all his heart and soul, but that was only because most of them were running from something and they had no choice but to protect their camp in that forest. He hadn't trusted people on this side of the river in… years. Maybe not ever.

But he was still alive, even though he hadn't thought it possible. And maybe a bit disappointed over it. He hadn't seen Eilidh since the hallucinations on the road, and pieces of him missed her so bad that he was ready to lie down and die to be able to touch her again. To hear her voice saying his name. He would have traded places with Rhodrishi in an instant, but it wasn't his time. And Ceridwen and Stella needed a shoulder to lean on through this, especially since Mahalouwan faced the fear of loss by running from it, apparently.

"Ceridwen," Ozra whispered as the sun cast a few beams in the window beside his head. The night had passed, and he was so tired it felt like parts of him was dissolving. "Come on over here, and have a rest. He's fine for now."

Ceridwen stood from her dead-eyed slump that she had adopted, sitting at Rhodrishi's head and resting most of her weight on the headboard. At some point in the night, Stella had teased all the knots out of her hair, but she hadn't put any new plaits in, so it flowed loose down her back, drying into curls and strawberry blond waves, but they seemed to annoy her. She spent the rest of the night constantly pushing her hair out of her face or twisting it over one shoulder to try to keep it contained. He would have braided it for her, but he only had the one good arm. She came slowly to Ozra's chair, her feet scraping the floorboards, too heavy for her to lift them all the way. She climbed up into Ozra's lap, settling carefully to avoid his bad arm, resting her head on his other shoulder. He wrapped an arm around her and pulled her close, but she didn't close her eyes. She stared out the window, at the smouldering bonfire pit where the remains of the dead bronzemen were covered in ash and coals.

"How come he isn't waking up?" she whispered. "I keep wishing, but he isn't waking up."

"Ah, girl," Ozra said softly. "Not even Talent can keep death away forever. Eventually, the body has to let go."

Ceridwen blinked away her tears, something dark and angry passing in front of her face. "What's the point of wishing? Nothing I wish for ever happens."

"Using your Talent is brand new, Ceridwen," Ozra said. "With time, you'll learn how to use it more effectively."

"What's the point?" Ceridwen spat. She pushed her hair back from her face again, gathering it all in one hand like she meant to tie it, but she had nothing to tie it with. "Whenever I wish, I see the terrible things. And wishing never got me anything, anyway. I wished for a da all year, and then we left Mr. Blackwood behind. I wished for that boy to leave us alone, but it didn't work, and Rhodrishi had to shoot him. I wished for Siras to leave Mam alone, too, but that didn't work either, so I shot him. I wished for Rhodrishi to get better, and he's not waking up!"

Ozra sighed. "Talent can't change everything. It can't build a father for you out of nothing. And it can't change the heart of a man like Siras Duncreek. Wishing has helped, though, hasn't it? You wished to be warm at night, and you were. You wished for me to come out of the Wrath after I was shot, and your wishing pulled me back. You wished us strong enough to survive so we could save your mam, and it worked. We wouldn't have caught up to her without your Talent keeping us going. You did that, girl. You saved her. And you saved her again by shooting your enemy. If you were Kishoan, your family would give you your warrior tattoos for that. Up north, we call it hunting bronze, and you'd keep his badge as a trophy. My uncle had a hundred badges, last I saw him. I hope he's got a hundred more."

"How come it won't save Rhodrishi, though?" Ceridwen pressed. "How come he hasn't woken up?"

"His body is very tired," Ozra said. He didn't have the courage to tell her that this was the end. The exhaustion made it hard to keep his eyes open, and the pain in his shoulder hooked on every thought, making it harder to find words anymore. She needed her mam to guide her through this, but Stella was sleeping, as she was right to. Ozra couldn't imagine the exhaustion and the pain in her soul—as bad as his shoulder throbbed, he knew her time with Siras was worse, whether it left marks on her body or not. "Even if it weren't for his heart, we pushed hard to catch up to your mam. Maybe he needs the rest."

Ceridwen nodded. "You think so?"

"I don't know." He couldn't lie, though he wanted to. "We'll see."

Rhodrishi twitched in his sleep, giving a bit of a groan. Ceridwen slithered down off Ozra's lap, returning to his side and grabbing his hand with both of hers.

"Don't die, Rhodrishi," she begged. "I don't want you to die. I wish your heart gets better."

The sunlight danced in Ceridwen's hair, illuminating the mud stains that had dried to a crust on her clothes. And something dark on the back of her neck—more mud? No, it didn't seem to be the right shape for mud. The lines were so fine, so delicate, black faded to something almost blue. It looked like... a tattoo.

A tattoo.

Ozra's heart skipped a beat. Sadness and joy vied for his attention. Ceridwen was a Breeding Program child, then. Sweet North Star, that explained so much, how a child her age could be so incredibly strong. Authority made. Bless Stella for saving her, for taking her away from that vile place. She'd succeeded in exactly the thing Ozra had desperately wanted to do but completely failed—she'd saved a child from the Authority. That's why she was running so hard and so long. She wasn't running *for* herself, or at least that wasn't the whole story. She was running to protect this girl. But Ffyanwy Rhydderch was never in the Breeding Program, so Ceridwen's mother was... someone else.

Did Ceridwen even know she bore such a mark? She'd never mentioned it—but then, what would she even say? He wondered where Stella had found Ceridwen. Wondered who made the precious girl. If she was from Cruinnich, he might well know the numbers she had. Felt invasive to wonder, though.

Rhodrishi groaned again, his fingers twitching between Ceridwen's hands. His eyes flickered open, turning toward the sunlight that came in the window like he was watching the dust motes dance. His attention settled on Ceridwen's face, and he smiled.

"Rhodrishi, can you hear me?" Ceridwen asked softly.

"I hear you, sweet child. I've heard you all along, wishing me to stay."

"It worked?" Ceridwen breathed.

Rhodrishi nodded, trying to shift, but something must have hurt—he winced, gave another groan, the fingers of his other hand twitching. Ozra pushed himself to his weary, half-numb feet, crossing to the bed.

"Let me help you," he said. "Do you want to sit up?"

Rhodrishi shook his head. "I'm tired, Ozra."

"Aye, you and me both." He sank down on the edge of the bed, leaning against the headboard with his good shoulder. "You gave us a bit of a scare."

Rhodrishi's eyes drifted closed again. Ceridwen made a small whimpering sound in the back of her throat. She crawled onto the mattress and stretched out against Rhodrishi's chest, pushing her face into his shoulder. Rhodrishi moved enough to put his arm around her shoulders, tilting his face down to her hair. That tattoo—Ozra's eyes were drawn to it again, even though he told himself not to look. It wasn't his business. If Stella wanted him to know, she'd tell him. But he was close enough now that he could make out the numbers if he pushed her hair out of the way.

"Ceridwen," Rhodrishi said, saying the name like a precious blessing, saying each syllable with as much love as her mam did. "You can let me go, sweet girl. You don't have to fight for me."

Ceridwen whimpered, pressing her face harder into Rhodrishi's chest. "But I don't want you to die!"

"I know. But no one lives forever, and I'm so tired. Let me go."

"Rhodrishi, no—please!"

Rhodrishi sighed, letting his eyes drift closed again. Ozra stood again, even though he was so tired that dizziness made his head too light. Around the bed, to Stella. He lay his hand on her shoulder, giving it a squeeze.

"Stella," he said. "Stella, wake up. Your girl needs you."

Stella lifted her head, half-rising before she was even fully awake. "Ceridwen?"

"He said he's ready to go, but she can't bring herself to let him."

Stella nodded, pushing her own hair out of her face. She went around the bed, kneeling beside Ceridwen and stroking the girl's hair, fingers sliding tenderly over all those curls. "I'm sorry, Ceridwen. I wish we could give him more time, but it isn't right to force him to stay with us. It's the hardest part of being a healer—knowing you could help, but choosing not to because someone is done fighting. We all go eventually."

"Will the Keeper of the Keys take him?" Ceridwen asked. "Let him into heaven?"

"No, Pigeon. He's Pashibé. His people believe in the memory of Talent, and when his body dies, he'll sink back down into it. And one day, that energy will be reborn into a new person, and his Talent will live on. So it's not the end for him. His body will return to the earth, and his soul will know peace. And we'll miss him terribly—" Her breath hitched, and her eyes filled with tears. She pressed her fingers to her lips, trying to shake it off. "We barely know him, but he's as good as family, isn't he?"

Ceridwen nodded. "I've always wanted a big family. It's not fair that we keep losing the people who love us!"

"You haven't lost them, Ceridwen," Ozra said, even though his heart shattered with the same pain. "Their love lives on in us our whole lives. Talent holds memory, and so do we. We were blessed to have him for the time we did, and him dying doesn't make that love stop."

Rhodrishi's arm twitched again, pulling Ceridwen even tighter to his chest. And the poor girl sobbed, so hard and so earnestly that it shattered pieces of Ozra's soul. And she let go of her Talent—the thickness of it in the air dissolved, leaving Ozra's ears buzzing like silence that was too complete to be comfortable. Stella wept again, too, resting her head on the mattress behind Ceridwen's back, taking Rhodrishi's hand.

And Ozra stood, frozen. He didn't know where to go. If he should try to find Lieutenant Mahalouwan so she could come, too, or if he should go to Stella to offer her some comfort. Or if he should stand back and bear witness. He couldn't remember how long he knew Rhodrishi. They'd only encountered each other a few times, but there was something about meeting people on the smugglers' road that let you *know* them to a depth that couldn't be accounted for by the short time they spent together. They didn't need to explain their lives to each other. The road exposed everything, and surviving it with another person tied you together.

The dizziness didn't let go—if he kept standing around, he'd likely faint. He went back to his chair, but that tattoo. North Star preserve him, he couldn't resist looking at it each time it caught his eye. And this time, when he passed it, he could see the numbers.

Like plunging into the frigid river, that shock. Except it was worse than the river. It was bigger. Big as the ocean. The cold of the shock swallowed him whole, and even though he knew he should breathe, he couldn't. He could do nothing but stare. And not breathe. And feel the pain, the pain of suffocating, the pain of memory assaulting every part of his mind at once. He had to sit because he was going to faint for sure. He had to make himself breathe before the world went black.

He staggered to the chair and sank gracelessly into it, and the pain of jostling his arm that much roared through him, forcing half a shred of sense into him.

Ceridwen's sobbing went quiet—she'd cried herself to sleep in Rhodrishi's arms. And her wishing had mended his heart enough that it was still beating even though she'd let go. It wouldn't last long, but at least she could sleep a while in his arms. At least he could go holding the sweet wee girl who'd drawn them all together.

Stella pushed herself to her feet, wiping her eyes and turning to

Ozra. He looked up at her, trying to find some gentle way to tell her that he knew, trying to find a good way to ask all the thousands of questions that flitted through his head. But it had been a long night, and exhaustion turned his brain half-wool.

"That's my number," he blurted, instead of saying something gently. "0579—that's me. I burned that number off my chest because I never wanted to see it again."

Stella froze. Blinked away tears. "Ozra—"

"She's got Eilidh's number, too. 1232—that's our girl, the first one who died. Lioslaith. How—"

Fear flashed over Stella's face, her hands turning to fists. "Ozra, I can explain—"

Ozra shook his head. He didn't need her to explain. He didn't want her to look at him with that fear, either. His mind twisted over everything, snatching at random words that Ceridwen had said in the short time they knew each other. "She wished for me. She wished for a da for a whole year, that's what she said. It wasn't Eilidh I was seeing—it was her. Her Talent found me and pulled me to her, because she was wishing for her da—wishing for *me*."

Stella took a step back, putting her body between Ozra and the bed, like she half expected Ozra to stand and snatch Ceridwen and take her away. "I'm sorry. I didn't know—not until you said the thing about your tattoo. I didn't—if I'd known who you were or how to find you, I never would have kept her from you. I've always wondered who her parents were, doomed to make her and lose her. But Ozra, please—she came to me when I was so broken that I thought I would die. I was a million tiny pieces, but finding her put me back together again. She gave me a reason to live, to run, to survive. Please don't take her from me."

"How did you do it?" Ozra asked. "I felt her die."

"I knotted up her Talent." Her words came in a hot, desperate rush, her hands still in fists. Her bare feet on the floor, her nightgown, and all that untamed curly hair—she reminded him of Eilidh. "Kona taught me how. She and I used to do it together, to help people run from the Authority. So I did it to her and to myself so we could hide and the Authority wouldn't feel how strong we were. I was going to settle out west, but Bothain sent Siras after me."

"Bless you," Ozra breathed. He reached through the terrible gap between them, a gap only a small amount of space but turned into a yawning chasm with the fear painted so clearly on Stella's face. He rested his fingers on her wrist. He would have taken her hand, but he didn't want her to feel trapped. "She's the only one left. All the others have died. I couldn't save any of them, but you—bless you, Stella. Bless you for being a better parent to her than I could ever be."

She shook her head and pressed both her hands over her face like she was trying to stuff her grief back in, but it broke out anyway. Her head bowed, and her shoulders slumped and she wept again, biting her own lip to weep quietly like she was afraid of waking Ceridwen. Ozra struggled back up to his feet and wrapped his good arm around her, and she melted into him completely, sobbing against his shoulder.

"Why Pigeon?" Ozra blurted. "Why do you call her Pigeon?"

Stella laughed, lifting her head off his shoulder and wiping her eyes with her sleeves. "She was such a fat wee baby, wasn't she? The people that helped me travel west used to pinch her cheeks and joke that she was so fat that she would be delicious in pigeon pie. And so I called her my pigeon pie for a while—then just Pigeon."

Ozra laughed with her, looking down at Ceridwen again, sleeping gently in Rhodrishi's arms. "Not so fat anymore, hey? She's growing into those cheeks."

Stella nodded. "She'll grow to be a lovely young woman, sooner than I'd like. Seems like just yesterday, she was learning to walk, tripping over that blanket."

That blanket. The blanket that Eilidh made and sent away with her. So that thread he saw was right, and real, and not a figment of his confused drifting.

"What do we do now?" Ozra whispered.

Stella sighed softly, sinking down onto the edge of the bed and wiping her face. "We wait. She'll make a good healer one day. If she can escape the hallucinations. His heart is doing well for now, all things considering. But he's ready to go, so... we wait."

63

LORNE
DAY 38

Maybe it was the headache making him feel especially surly, or maybe it was nerves, but Lorne still didn't like the look of the scale.

"Let's go, Mr. Lightning," Davik said, giving Lorne a bit of a push. His voice had the same edge of impatience it had when he dragged Lorne out of bed. Late. "Get your shit off, and get up on the scale."

Lorne fumbled with his clothes. He'd only had time to get half his clothes on anyway. Trousers, shirt, socks, boots. Someone had brought them up and dumped them on his bedroom floor at some point while Lorne was sleeping.

Up on the scale and Miss Brady fiddled with the slide adjustment. The clanging metal hit Lorne's skull like fucking drills, cutting his headache open wider. The scale revealed he was 136 pounds.

"Two fucking pounds," Lorne muttered.

"Two pounds," Davik agreed, clapping Lorne on the shoulder.

The scale jumped with the impact, climbing up to a more impressive number, but then sank right back down to 136. Miss Brady fiddled with it a bit more to make sure it was right and then wrote it in her notebook. 136, in slow, elegant handwriting, a little embellishment on the 3 that almost made it look like a respectable number, but then Lorne saw Ari's weight: 159.

And everything pounding in his skull felt worse.

"What the hell was all that eating for?" Lorne muttered, as Davik dragged him off the scale. Lorne wanted to stay until the scale said something better than 136. "All that money, all that food—what the hell, Dav?"

"Hey, relax," Davik said, patting Lorne's shoulders again. "It's hard to put on weight while you're still movin' around, and you've been working hard, yeah? And it's only been a matter of days. But now we know you can put *some* weight on, even with all that moving. We'll get more on you after this fight, since the tournaments don't start 'til spring."

"Two pounds is excellent in such a short timeframe, Mr. Coswyn," Miss Brady said brightly. "Your shoulders look bigger than the last time I saw you—if you stand there for me, I'll take your final measurements."

Everyone watched as she used her tape to measure his arms, his shoulders, his fists again. As if his hands could have grown. His chest, his waist, the circumference of his thighs. They were all a bit bigger, the muscles cutting lines through his skin when he flexed. But he still looked skinny, his wrists and his knees still pushing too insistently at his skin. He'd eaten so fucking much because he was supposed to put weight on, get heavier, because that's what boxers did, but now it felt like a miserable waste. He could have fed a whole fucking family with all the food he'd eaten since he got here. 136 was a shit number. He'd met Ari already, seen the way his 159 pressed at the seams of his shirt, straining the buttons when he crossed his arms over his chest. He'd seen Ari with his gloves on, those muscles carrying every punch perfectly, the tattoo on his back flexing. Lorne was going to step up into that ring at his pathetic 136.

"Looks great, Mr. Coswyn," Miss Brady said. "You've been working very hard to get into condition, and it shows."

"Does that mean his odds go up?" Davik asked with a bit of a grin.

"We'll announce his odds at ten this morning," Miss Brady said. "Leaves people plenty of time to bet until this evening, doesn't it?"

She packed up her things and made her way out, and Davik's office was still too full with that stupid scale and all of Lorne's frustration, grinding against the underside of his skin.

"All of that for two fucking pounds," Lorne said.

"Two pounds is a good thing," Davik said. "Trust me, laddie, you did good. Hey. Look at me."

Lorne didn't know what to do with his hands, with his feet. With his whole body. There was so much tension in him, and he didn't know how to let it go. There was nothing for him to do but wait.

"It's just a fight, yeah? Just like all your other fights before."

"Nothing mattered when I was fighting before."

Davik put his hands on Lorne's shoulders, warm and firm, pressing down like he wanted to force Lorne to be still. "Listen to me. No matter how this fight goes, you've done your job here. You're going to get up in that ring and get enough experience to know what it feels like to be a proper pugilists. And then in a few months, the tourneys seasons starts, and you'll know what you can do, and you'll wallop all the other fighters."

The words landed dead and hollow at Lorne's feet, and he realized why his skin was crawling off him. "Do you really think we're all still going to be here by the time tourney season starts?"

Davik nodded slowly, patting Lorne's shoulders. "We'll see, won't we? Something you learn as you get older is it don't matter how bad things get, how much blood there is in the streets, people still demand to be entertained. So, let me tell you, if this pugilist club is still standing, we'll run fights out of it, and that's the end of it. And if it ain't standing? Maybe that means we've changed something, and maybe that means we don't have to hide anymore. So, today we're going to do our best to make it look legitimate, aren't we?"

Lorne sucked in a deep breath, letting the words roll through him. There was something simple about it when Davik put it like that. Either they were alive to fight in the spring, or they weren't.

"And Jason?" Lorne asked. "László said—"

"I know," Davik interrupted. "We're doing what we can. Go get dressed even though you feel like ripe shite. Really let loose last night, hey?"

Lorne flushed, and it made his head pound fucking harder. "He gave me that khat, and then the whole world started going too fast."

Davik shrugged. "If we make it to tourney season, no more fucking around like that the night before your match, yeah? Save it for the night after. Go get dressed. The real nice suit, the one with the pinstripes."

Lorne shifted. "The one with the pinstripes is a little... loud. Isn't it?"

"Of course it's loud. It's an exhibition match, laddie. Be an exhibition. You'll be eating with Ari and Redbone for the press."

"Why am I eating with my opponent?" Lorne asked. "Aren't we supposed to hurt each other?"

"Aye, you will, but you'll come out of it respecting each other, too. It ain't the same as having an enemy. You're in this sport together, and it carries the pair of you. You'll understand when it's over, trust me. Go, I'll meet you out there when you're dressed."

"Where's... Mr. Guinne?"

Davik gave a bit of a shrug. "He can't be here when it's busy. You know that. Someone might recognize him, especially with all these Brickheart folks around."

"I know, but..."

But he loved Tashué like a father, and part of him hoped to see Tashué at some point today. He wanted someone from his life before to be here to see him now.

L ászló helped him dress in the blue pinstripe suit. He paired it with a deep, plum-coloured shirt and a silk brocade waistcoat, and it was all too much. All that food for two pounds, and all the money spent on clothes for him, and he didn't deserve it.

"You look real sharp, Mr. Lightning," László said with a grin, smoothing out the front of Lorne's waistcoat. He looked tired, his eyes more than a little distant, but he smiled at Lorne anyway and picked a hair off Lorne's sleeve. He's slept in Lorne's bed after they dragged themselves upstairs. Had anything happened between them through the night? He couldn't remember. "Real fucking sharp. A proper celebrity."

"I look ridiculous," Lorne muttered. László had put a collar on the shirt, and the tight, stiff linen chaffed under Lorne's chin, around his throat. He didn't even remember the last time he wore a shirt with a collar. "I look like those idiots who come down to the Bay from Highview to chase tail."

"Shut up," László said, giving Lorne a bit of a shove. "You don't have to like it, you have to wear it and let people take photographs."

Lorne shrugged, trying to get used to the way the waistcoat and the jacket sat so heavily on his shoulders. "They're getting Jason out today, right?"

László nodded. "That's the plan. Later in the day, I think. I'm sure Dav will let you know."

"He won't say anything," Lorne said, pulling at the front of the waistcoat. Was it too tight, or was he not used to clothes that fit him? When was the last time he wore a waistcoat? In the military, maybe. "I asked, and he changed the subject."

"Of course he did," László muttered. "Did you expect him to give you details of his illegal raid on Authority property?"

"He had us give away two bank bags filled with copper crowns last night," Lorne muttered back. "I don't think he's too concerned about legality."

"That's because no one was here except us last night," László said. "Today is a different story. People from all over the city, the press. The Patrollers will be here by now for riot control. So be patient, yeah? When it's safe, I'm sure he'll tell you."

"Sure," Lorne said. And he needed the words to be true so badly he could almost feel them in his hands, like precious gems he could grasp and hold close to his heart. Jason, today. All Lorne had to do was fight. "How long do I have to wear the suit?"

László laughed, stepping away and heading for the door. "Until the match. Let's go. Your fans are waiting."

———

Breakfast—a small mound of pancakes slathered in butter, and slabs of peameal bacon, and a bubbling cauldron of molasses baked beans—was set up at the bar, the smell of it all making Lorne's mouth water. It was past lunchtime by the time Lorne was dressed, and Ari turned up with his coach and an entourage of people from Brickheart. Ari's suit was as colourful and obnoxious as Lorne's, which made him feel a bit better. Brick red and a silk waistcoat that looked like spun gold, his watch chain glittering in the light of all the brights. The photographers organized them just right, so when Ari and Lorne stood shaking hands with Eirdis at Lorne's elbow, the photographs caught the boxing ring behind their shoulders. Flashbulbs popped a dozen times, leaving Lorne half-blind.

"You get used to all the photographs eventually," Ari said, settling on the edge of his stool. "And the press, for that matter. I don't think you ever get used to the fans, though. At least I haven't. It feels strange, the way you carry so much for them. You tell yourself it's just pugilism, but the stories they share about how having something to look forward to pulled them through their own darkness—well. I think if ever I got used to that, I wouldn't like myself very much."

Damn the bastard for being so likeable. Made it harder for Lorne to convince himself he hated Ari instead of accepting he was intimidated as fuck by the man's hard-won skill.

The food, though indulgent and delicious, tasted like ash in Lorne's mouth. Nothing felt right. He wanted to see Jason. Wanted Davik and László to give him a straight answer. He wanted to hate Ari, and he wanted to get the fight over with instead of all the photographs and talking. At least he didn't have the rot gut feeling he usually got from too much gin. He must not have drunk much. The misery was all in his skull, an echo left over from all that too-fast time, but even that was starting to fade.

"What happens with the leftovers?" Lorne asked. "They don't expect us to eat everything, do they?"

"They'll make more and feed the crowd after Eirdis's speech," Ari said. "You get used to this part, too. All the waiting before the match."

"Do you get used to your opponent being a smug, condescending asshole?" Lorne muttered.

Ari only laughed at that. "Sure. Just like you get used to the new kids coming up through the ranks, snarling at everything because they're scared shitless and don't know how to be vulnerable to a process they don't understand yet."

"Mr. Coswyn!"

The sound stopped Lorne's temper dead in its tracks—a child's voice, calling for his attention. Lorne turned in time to see the kid pushing through the crowd. Ten at most, a face full of freckles, his hair a wild mess. He had something in his hand, and he offered it to Lorne—a wooden carving of the sea drake from the Lledewydd provincial flag, the emblem of the west coast, its sinuous body twisted over itself.

"My mam wanted you to have it," the boy said. "Said she was proud it was a Lledewyddyd boy in Dav's ring. Said you'd do the west right."

"Thank you," Lorne said, closing his hand around the wood. It killed some of the pressure in his chest, some of the fury. "Tell your mam I said thank you. Where is she?"

"She couldn't come out. She ain't been well, but she wanted you to have this. She made it herself."

"Let me buy this from your mam, then." Lorne pushed his hand into his pocket, pulling out coins. He still had the handful he'd brought with him upstairs. He dropped a few coppers into the boy's hand, wishing he could give the boy gold instead. "She did an amazing job on it. She shouldn't have to part with it for free. Tell her thank you, tell her I said I hope she feels better soon."

The boy stared down at the crowns like he wasn't sure what to do with them. Coins that flew a few hours ago, shimmering in the air because of László's Talent, coins that László and Tashué stole. Even though the boy couldn't possibly know all of those incredible things, simply having them in his hand struck him still with awe.

"Best put them away, son," Eirdis said. "Before they sprout wings and fly off."

The boy gave a wild, happy laugh and shoved the coins into his pocket before melting back into the crowd.

Ari leaned closer. "That's the part we don't get used to. What is it?"

"A draig y môr," Lorne said. "The dragon of the western sea. Sailors say it's good luck to see a draig y môr."

"Good luck to see a dragon?" Ari asked. "I would think they're dangerous."

Lorne shook his head, setting the wooden toy on the bar beside his plate. "If they want to cause trouble, you don't see them first. They just take you. But if you see them swimming in the ocean, it means they've taken mercy on you, and they won't sink you."

Ari laughed. "That's the bleakest lucky charm I've ever heard of."

Lorne shrugged. "That's the sea. Beautiful and dangerous at once. You love it and you hate it. It gives us everything we need to survive, and it swallows us whole."

"And it takes everything back eventually," Eirdis said. "That's what they say out west, right?"

Lorne nodded. "Exactly."

Eirdis checked her watch a few times before she apparently decided she was tired of waiting for Lorne and Ari to finish eating. She plunged through the crowd toward the ring, letting people stop her every few steps. She shook hands and laughed at whatever stories people told her.

"Eat faster," Ari said. "She'll be calling us up after the speech and then no more food until after the match. Maybe not until tomorrow, depending how you feel after."

Lorne lifted another piece of peameal bacon off his plate, folding it in half and biting off a chunk. The pork was deliciously salty, making his mouth water. It was, he had to admit, a perk.

Eirdis finally made it to the boxing ring, and climbed through the ropes. She looked taller up there, somehow. Like maybe she stood straighter, as if standing above a crowd filled her with extra stature.

She lifted her hands above her head. The warehouse went quiet.

"Friends!" she called. "Thank you all so much for coming today to help contribute to the campaign and help us celebrate Cattle Bone Bay's very first pugilist club!"

Someone in the crowd whistled, the sound piercing and shrill, setting off the first round of applause. Eirdis grinned, waiting for the cheering to die, her hands on her hips, her smile infectious.

"We've a good fight for you tonight, my friends," she went on. "But before we get started, indulge me in a moment of gratitude. We wouldn't be here without all your hard work. Thank you for everything you've done to make this possible. I've arranged for everyone to be fed this afternoon, while we wait for this historic fight. I offer the food free of charge, but if you've a few crowns to spare, the Sisters of the North Star are taking donations. Everything will go back to the Bay, especially as another terrible winter is upon us."

People hooted at Eirdis's pun, and she grinned widely, spreading her hands like it was an unintentional slip.

"With winter comes the vote," Eirdis said, her voice gone appropriately grim as she folded her strong hands over her chest. "And a vote for Winter is a poor vote indeed."

"Down with the police force!" someone shouted in the crowd.

"Yes, sir!" Eirdis shouted back, stirring herself out of her grimness. "A vote for Winter is a vote for the Provincial Police Force!"

The crowd roared and booed, and Eirdis nodded.

"Who here wants a damned police force?" she demanded.

The crowd booed again, and Lorne thought that if anyone dared suggest they were for the force, they would be ripped apart by this seething mass. The crowd wasn't exclusively Bay—there were people from every quarter, come for the match. Come to see Lorne the Lledewydd Lightning, against Ari Odegaard, the Brickheart darling whose career made the league accessible to everyone. He wondered what those folks thought of a whole warehouse full of people booing the police force.

"Who here wants Winter's cronies peaking in your windows and spying on you in the night?"

Another roar sent a shiver down Lorne's spine.

"Who here wants Winter's men to control this city? Who here wants Winter's men to have the power to stop us from enjoying fine evenings like this? Mr. Kaine and Mr. Iwan have gone through great trouble to organize this club, for you, my friends. For the Bay. For Yaelsmuir! Some people might call them thugs, criminals, but you know what I call them? Fucking brilliant! Hard working! Unyielding! The city sneers at us, down here in the Bay. Winter and his cronies, they say we live in the shit down here, don't they? Like we're not good enough to even be a part of Yaelsmuir! Is that who you want for your Governor? A man who would sooner spit on you than shake your hand?"

An outraged roar, and Eirdis paused to give it time to roll through the crowd.

"Isn't it time for a Governor that hasn't forgotten you, friends?" Eirdis asked. "A Governor who isn't ashamed of you? Who respects you? Who knows that you are the spine and the beating heart of this beautiful city? Don't you deserve a Governor who comes to you in your home and celebrates victories with you? Someone who will speak for you when the Bay needs protection from Rainer Elsworth's power-hungry legislation or Myron Winter's greed. They'd like to bleed you for every copper coin and every freedom you have left. You deserve better than that, my friends!"

She paused again to let the crowd cheer. Smiled and basked. She looked so comfortable, when the thought of going up there with her set Lorne's heart hammering in his throat, making it hard to breathe. All the food turned into a cannonball in his gut. Someone started chanting, Cattle Bone Bay, again and again, and the whole warehouse took it up until it shook the very air, made the walls rattle.

Eirdis lifted her hands again, and the chant died. "We wouldn't be here at all if it weren't for Powell Iwan, who keeps the Bay safe for the likes of us. We refuse, not welcome anywhere else in this city. Powell Iwan takes care of us! He told me he wanted to be here, but his health won't allow it. So he sent his grandson instead to speak for him. Would you do be the honour of joining me, Mr. Czarny?"

Vasska moved slowly through the crowd, people stopping him to hug him, to shake his hand. He almost looked comfortable in the midst of the ritual, like speaking to the people of the Bay was what he did most naturally. He finally climbed up, and the crowd cheered for him. If he was feeling any ill effects of last night, he wasn't showing it. But then, he hadn't chewed any khat, just smoked a bit and kissed Allie Tei.

"Thank you," Vasska said, his voice soft. People went silent to hear him. "Thank you for coming here tonight. We gather here to celebrate the victories of the Bay, but also to take a stand. Something is happening in this city, something vile and filthy, something that none of us should be allowing. I want to extend my deepest gratitude to Miss Redbone for coming here tonight even though there's been rumours of Rainer Elsworth coming to the Bay to punish us for *his* crimes."

A whisper passed through the crowd, and a shiver ran through Lorne's whole body, making his spine feel too tight. He hadn't expected Vasska to get up there and talk about the Authority, but his heart surged with pride. Vasska was going to make his stand for the children.

"We've all heard the things Rainer Elsworth has been accused of," Vasska went on. "The crimes he commits against the bodies of children. He wants us to believe that they deserve it because they're tainted, but when I look at the faces all around me, I see disgust at the very mention of Elsworth's name. I'm so proud of all of you. We see Rainer Elsworth for who he really is. Just like Tashué Blackwood and Ishmael Saeati saw him, and he killed them for it. Rainer Elsworth is a slug, a vile and tiny man who takes power from the bodies of *children*. We won't let him get away with this, will we?"

How many people in this club were Talented? Davik's army, Davik's quarter. How many had come from other quarters? Lorne's eyes drifted over the crowd, taking in all the faces. People he recognized. More people he didn't. Where was Davik? Was he getting Jason out, somehow?

Allie and László and a knot of people from the *Dripping Bucket* bled through the crowd, passing out pamphlets they'd printed. And people were getting angry, agitated, working themselves up into righteous fury.

"I asked you a question, my friends," Vasska said softly. "We won't let him get away with this, *will we?*"

The crowd roared. The sound split Lorne in half. They stomped their feet, and the vibration of that much rage passed up through Lorne's body, washing away his exhaustion, filling him with their energy.

"Fuck the Authority!" someone yelled.

And the crowd took up the chant, stomping in time with their words until the whole building was rattling with rage. And the pride turned rabid in Lorne's chest. He wasn't even from here, but the Bay had claimed him, had put its mark on him, like a criminal's brand, an army tattoo. Except the Bay branded you on the bone instead of the skin, left its mark that only other Bay people could see, somewhere behind your eyes. It didn't matter if you were a new arrival, and it didn't matter if you left and stayed away for the rest of your life, once your eyes said *Bay*, that mark never went away. And Lorne used to hate that about this quarter except now he knew it was home. Home he'd always been searching for, home he'd always have even if he left. It was good to belong to the Bay, good to feel it close around him so he had no choice but to stand up straighter.

Vasska held up his hands, and the crowd went silent again. He pitched his voice lower than before, forcing everyone to hold their breath so they could catch every word. "I urge you, my friends, to remember that I asked you to stand. When Rainer Elsworth comes to our streets, looking for a fight, remember that I asked you not to submit. Rainer Elsworth thinks he can come down here and bloody us up a bit and call himself some kind of hero. He's got his friend with him, General Clannaugh. Fist of the North, they call him. Because he pummelled the people of Cruinnich into submission and then got bored and wandered off to buy himself a military career. And now he thinks he can come *here*, to the Bay, and rough us up for his own ego? He doesn't know who he's picking a fight with, does he?"

Another angry roar. Eirdis was sweating—even from this distance, Lorne could see the shine of it on her face. Was she swept up in the anger, or was she afraid of it?

Allie pushed a paper into Lorne's hands, like she was so submerged in the crowd, in her job, that she didn't even know who she was standing with anymore.

What Happened To Ffyanwy Rhydderch? The headline screamed the words in thick black ink. The whole page shouted a lot of angry things about Bothain Clannaugh and his bloody reputation, but it focused mostly on Ffyanwy and the reputation of the stone company and the hospital they built up north.

"Vote Redbone!" Vasska called. "A vote for Redbone is a vote for peace!"

Eirdis lifted her hands again, but her smile looked panicked and a little wild. "Thank you, my friends! Thank you. Let's get the afternoon started, shall we? Mr. Czarny, if you'll announce the fighters for us."

"First man up is from Brickheart," Vasska said. "I know we're all rooting for our very first Bay pugilist, but I would like to extend my deepest gratitude to Mr. Odegaard for participating in this event later tonight. We can't have a boxing match without a pair of pugilists, and Ari Odegaard has proven himself to be the very best the city has to offer, so please give him the warm welcome he deserves."

Ari slid off his stool as the club started chanting his name. He shook hands as he walked through, his suit cut perfectly to show the lean lines of his shoulders, the shape of his biceps when they flexed. 159 pounds of professional pugilist form. Totally unfazed by what he'd witnessed, by the whole place roaring their outrage at Rainer Elsworth. Or maybe he was swept up in it, too. Maybe he was proud. He shook Eirdis's hand first, and then Vasska's, leaning closer and whispering something in Vasska's ear. Something buzzed through Lorne's skull. All the agitation and fury that wanted to unleash itself at Ari, his opponent, his enemy. But Davik said it wasn't the same as having an enemy. And Lorne understood it already, because Ari made it impossible to hate him. Lorne couldn't help but remember how sad he looked, standing in the empty courtyard behind the club in Brickheart, speaking in a soft voice about his wife and all the ways the world was still letting them both down.

"And of course, Cattle Bone Bay's very first pugilist champion— Lorne the Lledewydd Lightning!"

The roar of the crowd was a primal, seething, boiling thing. Lorne had to force himself to walk. To push through the freezing feeling in his limbs, like he was turning to ice. To stone. Walk, one step at a time, all the way to the ring. It didn't matter. None of it mattered. This wasn't a real tournament, and it didn't matter how much anyone weighed. He'd been fighting men bigger than him for years. It was just like fighting in the Hive. The club would take a profit for this fight, whether he won or not, and a portion of those profits paid his wages, and he'd send every crown to Alys, and Davik would get Jason. Later today. Maybe now. Thanks to Lorne fighting, providing a distraction to the whole city. The outcome of the fight didn't matter.

Eirdis shook Lorne's hand, patting him on the shoulder. Vasska next. And then Ari. They shook again, and the photographers popped more photos.

"How long does it take before I get used to the flashbulbs?" Lorne asked instead of screaming.

"Takes a while, I'll admit," Ari laughed.

Lorne turned, looking out across the crowd. Eirdis was shouting again, but he couldn't hear her for all the buzzing in his ears. In the middle of the crowd, he could only *feel* how big it was by the presence of it, by how hard it was to move through the club. But up here, he could see the spread of it, sprawling in every direction around the stage. People were still coming in, dripping from the storm that raged outside.

So many fucking people, here to see him fight in a few hours.

He couldn't possibly convince himself the match didn't matter.

64

JASON
DAY 38

I t was ugly cold in the infirmary. Jason was already cold and wet from the rain that caught them after the fight, already shivering and miserable. But the healer expected him to strip down anyway, standing and watching him with distant, glazed eyes that stared off at something else. A guard stood nearby. With a gun. There weren't many guns in the Rift. The presence of it took up physical space in the air.

Everything hurt. Peeling off his clothes required him to use muscles and joints that were bruised and inflamed and bleeding. Bending down made his skull feel like it was actively trying to burst. It hadn't stopped hurting since the children lashed out at him, and now it was so much worse. But he did it. Every layer. He couldn't remember the last time he was fully naked. Bathing was a precious privilege in the Rift, one he wasn't graced with often since the guards never liked him much. And then his father got banned, and Jason lost the steady stream of coin to bribe the guards for comforts.

Every shred of clothes turned into a heap on the floor. Jason stared down at his own body, at the scars this place had left him with. The tattoos he'd gotten since coming here because a needle and ink made of ashes and the way his skin looked were the only things he had any control over. He slid his hand over the most recent one, the death prayer he'd written into his skin for his mother. It was finally healed, all the dead skin flaked away, all the redness gone. He'd done that tattoo himself because he didn't trust someone who didn't speak Sittami to get the shapes of the letters right.

The guard kicked the clothes aside and pushed his hand into Jason's hair, like he was looking for hidden weapons. Pain—the guard's fingers came away red with blood.

"Fucking hell," the guard grunted, grabbing Jason's shirt from the pile and wiping his fingers on it. "Go."

The infirmary was big enough to care for dozens of people, in theory, but mostly the infirmary turned inmates away. Sleep it off, tough it out, you're fine, go back to work. If you could convince them you deserved to be saved, they sent you to see a registered healer with Talent—the healer on duty led Jason into the small room where a gap was left in the suppression. There was nothing in the room except a table bolted to the floor, and the door was only bars, the gaps between them wide enough to shoot through if the inmate inside tried anything.

Stepping into the room was such perfect relief that Jason wept. It burst from him before he could stop it, even though it made his wounds hurt more. His head, his ribs, his shoulders—it all ached. But the vise on his Talent was completely gone. His Talent swirled through his body like a cleansing wash. It hadn't been this unrestrained since he broke the suppression. Even in his little hidden spot in the cellar, the suppression sat on some of him, preventing his Talent from fully suffusing his body. But now, he was free. He could see his wounds in his mind's eye, the damaged cells, the pooling blood, the torn skin. He could feel the eddies of his own willpower, focusing on those spots without him even trying, energy welling beneath each wound and starting the healing process like his Talent knew what to do without his conscious decision.

"Stop that," the healer grunted. "You're not supposed to, and if you have a concussion, you'll make it worse."

Jason forced his eyes open, meeting the healer's gaze through the blurry mess of his tears and the pain that throbbed in his temples. He could feel the healer's Talent spilling out of him in uneven jerks, as choppy as the ocean in a storm. Hesitation, maybe. A lack of focus. Or maybe he hated this job and never liked the moment when his Talent touched someone else's, when all the borders and boundaries that kept people apart and individual faded away and they blended into one person for a little while.

The healer's Talent and consciousness hit Jason like a bag of bricks. Loathing and resentment and fear and pain—he couldn't tell who all those emotions were directed at, if the healer hated Jason specifically or if he hated the guards and the Rift or maybe he hated himself for being here. Maybe all of those things, bundled together.

He felt the healer touch little bits of who Jason was, all the fear and the anger that battled in the centre of him all day, every day. All the longing, all the aching loneliness. He felt so exposed, worse than his nakedness. The healer was looking into him, and those feelings of resentment didn't go away—so maybe the healer *did* hate Jason, simply because Jason was an inmate in this place. Maybe the healer thought Jason deserved this treatment.

Tears dripped from Jason's chin, landing on the top of his feet. He didn't dare reach up and wipe them away. He didn't want to give the healer any reason to flinch or the guard any reason to shoot him. Although he didn't really know why. Maybe it was time to give up. Maybe death was better than this existence. They were supposed to get out. Transfer to the Breeding Program, a dangerous and uncertain journey through the Bay. That's when Davik would save him. Allegedly. It was supposed to be today, but now it looked like he'd been right to doubt. It was getting harder and harder to believe in a world outside the Rift. Maybe the world had ceased to exist and it wasn't possible to leave this place.

The healer's Talent retreated. "Some fractured ribs and a mild concussion, but nothing too bad. Don't need to do anything about it this time. He should be written out of his work duty for a bit. He'll need stitches in a few places, but I can do that without Talent."

The guard didn't move, his hand hovering over the grip of his gun. "What about his head?"

The healer shrugged. "It's a cut. People bleed when you beat them, if you hadn't noticed."

The guard scowled. "Isn't it faster if you seal shit up?"

"Isn't it faster if you let me do my job without asking stupid fucking questions?" the healer snapped. "I don't use Talent unless I have to—that's the policy, and I don't break policy so you can go back to scratching your balls and watching the inmates murder each other."

The guard sneered, but he unlocked the door anyway. "Out."

Jason closed his eyes, pausing for a moment. Just a moment. Just a beautiful, simple moment where he could feel the power of his own Talent and the potential it represented. He let himself daydream a future for himself where he broke out of here with his own power. Extended the fury of his Talent and broke every wall down.

Except his Talent wouldn't leave this room, so it wouldn't happen like that. The moment he flexed his Talent, the healer would say something, and then the guard would shoot him, and it would all be over. So, he shuffled slowly out of the room and the vise-headache came back as soon as he stepped through the doorway.

The healer made the guard pump water into a basin, and then the healer handed Jason a rag. The water was viciously cold, as cold as the rain that pelted him outside as he lay in his daze, but scrubbing blood and grime off his skin was almost worth the miserable shivering that wracked his whole body.

"Put your drawers on and sit down."

Bending over almost made Jason vomit again, but he swallowed hard against it and fumbled into his drawers. It wasn't nearly enough to warm him or cover him in any significant way. The shivering only got stronger as the water from the basin cooled his skin even more, water draining from his hair.

A gash on the back of his head below his hairline. Another on his shoulder. Two stitches in his lip to keep the split closed. It all took long enough that Jason wondered where Irén was. She was bleeding bad enough to need stitches, but she wasn't here.

The hope that felt so good yesterday had sloughed out of him like so much dead skin. It was stupid to think she could do anything. Irén Dargis had overestimated the power of Davik's protection. The guards had killed her. It wouldn't be the first time someone came in here, thinking they were top shit, only for them to die in less than a week. Irén's demise may have been record time, but it wasn't surprising. Jason was stupid to let Irén's confidence infect him. But now reality was sitting in the room with him again, and he had no fight left. Why bother?

Another guard came, speaking in a low voice to the guard who had his eye on Jason. Jason didn't hear what they said to each other, and he didn't care anyway. The healer was at Jason's side again, pushing something into Jason's hand. Little tablets, like candies but smaller and pressed hard.

"Morphine," the healer whispered, using a rag to wipe tracks of dried blood off the back of Jason's neck. The gentle compassion in his voice sliced Jason wide open. He didn't realize how terribly the resentment burned him until that softness sat like a caress on his soul. Maybe the healer hated the Rift and kept himself guarded in front of the inmates so the guards left him be. "It'll take the edge off the pain a while."

Jason closed his hand around the tablets, squeezing his eyes shut. "What happens if I take them all at once?"

"It's not enough to kill you, even with how skinny you are," the healer grunted. "You'll ride the high a while. Probably sleep through it. Better to take them one at a time, to stretch it out." He stepped away quickly, kicking Jason's clothes over to him. "Get dressed. Get off my table."

Jason pushed himself to his feet, letting the shivering and his stiff limbs hide how clumsy his hand was with the tablets stashed in his palm. Morphine. That came from opium, didn't it? The same terrible thing that stole his mother away from him. Her letters tracked the unwinding of her mind as she started smoking again. She used to write such long letters, talking to Jason about things his grandparents tried to teach him before they died: pieces of their culture that his father didn't know enough to teach. But then she started smoking again, and her letters got shorter, drifting away into ramblings Jason could barely track.

But maybe he understood it now. It was easy to imagine the desire to turn into something numb and oblivious when life felt like *this* every day. When there was nowhere for him to go that was even remotely safe from torment, when every day brought fresh wounds and more pain and the unrelenting headache that made him feel only halfway alive.

He wondered how long he'd sleep with the three tablets of morphine.

Wondered if all the letters from his mother and the paper with the names of his siblings were ruined, soaked by the rain. He should have left them in the bunk he shared with Irén and Rezji. He should have known he wasn't getting out of this place alive.

"We're going to put you downstairs for a while until we sort this shit out," the guard muttered. "The warden says you're going to the Breeding Program eventually. It was supposed to be today but the paperwork didn't come through. I don't know why you didn't register sooner, save us all the fucking trouble. You must really love all the chaos, hey? You people must feed on it like fucking leeches. I'm not losing my fucking job because you get some kind of thrill out of causing problems."

The guard shoved Jason in through the open door, into the cell. Jason staggered, catching himself on the wall, the pain and the anger shaking him up, out of his despondency, dragging him up into the person who had survived three and half years of this *shit*. He spun around even though it hurt to move that fast, facing the guard.

"Hey, *fuck* you," Jason said. "I did what I had to do to survive. I'd like to see you get through this place without your fancy uniform and your big gun. I bet that thing makes you feel *real* brave, doesn't it? Makes you feel like you can say whatever you want to people. But I see you, and I see who you are, even though you've got that extra cock on your hip to wave in people's faces. You're a fucking coward, just like Verrit."

The guard snorted, swinging the door of the small cell closed. The latch echoed in the long hall. The rain hissed in the small slit of a window, cold and miserable, and the guard stood on the other side of the doorway a while, looking in.

"I'll let Verrit know you're nice and safe," the guard said. "It was good of him to make sure you and the new bitch got out of the garden, wasn't it? It's important for you people to look out for each other."

"Fuck you," Jason spat.

"You said that already, Blackwood," the guard laughed, stepping away. "I'll give you some time to yourself to see if you can think of something cleverer than that. Maybe when I come back, you can suck on my extra cock and see if it puts you in a better mood."

He walked away down the hall before Jason could respond, his footsteps fading as he rounded the corner and headed back upstairs. The anger died away as quickly as it came, leaving Jason alone with his pain. He sank down on the floor in the far corner, his legs quivering. The morphine suddenly felt so fucking heavy in his hand, so hot, so full of promise. He'd never gotten morphine from the infirmary before. He wondered what it felt like. Wondered how much of his pain it would take out of him, wondered how much of the despair it would kill.

Just one. He took one out of the three to see what it felt like.

65

LORNE
DAY 38

"Where's Dav?"

Rowan shrugged. "Ain't seen him since this morning. He didn't say where he was going, last you saw him?"

Lorne shook his head. "You think it's something to do with Jason?"

László's turn to shrug and he glanced toward the door. They were in Lorne's dressing room and the door was closed, but the noise of the crowd bled in. "Ari's still a little weak on that left leg. I tried to keep an eye on it today, and I think he's still favouring it, like you said."

Lorne nodded, looking down at his gloves. He wasn't wearing them yet—he held them in his lap. Davik was supposed to come put them on. All the people he wanted for this moment were somewhere else. Davik, no one knew where. Tashué, under the *Dripping Bucket* with Allie and Ishmael, working on their next pages. Jason, still in the Rift. At least László was here. He hadn't left Lorne's side all day.

"Keep him moving," László went on. "He might not really be ready to come back. If you make him take weight on that left leg, it might keep him off balance enough that you can get in past his defences."

Lorne nodded again. "He's so fast, though."

"Yeah, he is," László agreed. "But you're faster. If you hit fast and hard enough, maybe you can end the match quick before his technical skill can get the better of you."

"I wonder if he talked to his wife," Lorne said softly. The weight of it all was off-kilter in his chest. He was fighting for everyone and everything, fighting for those children in creche, fighting for Jason and Valen, but somehow all that fight had turned into this boxing match and it didn't fit together right. "I wonder what they decided to do."

Rowan sat quietly, watching the door. Something was different in him since the bank robbery, like the loud parts of him had fractured off and rotted away to nothing. Lorne had seen it before, all through his life, but most often and most poignantly in the military. There was something about being fifteen that made most people so sure of who they were, and who they wanted to be—and how they'd respond to their first fight. At that age, it was so easy to convince themselves they were as tough as their heroes. Tougher, even. And then first contact with the enemy came and they had to confront how much blood there was in a person, or how fragile the human body was, and even though they survived the fight, suddenly they were aware of of how impermanent it all was. How stupid and naive they'd been for being so sure.

The referee knocked and stepped in, casting his eyes around the room once before furrowing his brow. "Time to glove, kid. Where's your coach?"

"I don't know," Lorne breathed. It surprised him how much those words hurt, coming out, like he was breathing crushed glass. "He hasn't been here since the weigh-in."

"I know how to wrap his hands," László said, standing. "I can do it."

The referee shook his head, pulling his watch out of his pocket and frowning at the time. "Needs to be the registered coach."

"Are you kidding me?" László snapped, stepping closer to the referee. "That's ridiculous. What do we do if something's happened? Cancel the match?"

"The league has rules for a reason, Mr. Dargis," the referee huffed. "The coach is responsible for gloves to prevent cheating."

"Oh," László said, his voice gone cold and sharp. "Got it. I'm tainted, so I can't be trusted not to cheat."

"That's not what I said—"

"Just go do Ari first," Lorne interrupted. "Dav will be here. He's not going to miss this."

Another sigh, a long stare at his watch. "Fine."

László opened his mouth to argue more, but the referee stepped out again, pulling the door shut behind him.

All the waiting and anticipation crawled through Lorne's body, making his tendons ache, making the cartilage between his bones sore. He bounced his legs so he could move something and let some of the energy out, but somehow it only wound him up more. He glanced at Rowan. At the far away eyes and the way his mouth structured itself into a permanent frown. That, at least, had been there before. Lorne wanted to say something helpful about how it was fine to be unsure. It was normal to need time to figure out who he wanted to be after the surety died.

"You're going to be amazing," László said, sinking back down beside Lorne. "Dav's going to be here, and you're going to thrash Ari, and then we'll have a nice smoke after to celebrate."

Lorne sighed, tapping his gloves together a few times, listening to the leather. Imagining how it sounded when it hit skin. Different than bare knuckles on skin. Funny, considering leather was just skin anyway. But maybe all the stuffing in the gloves is what changed the sound. He wanted to ask about Jason again, but what was the point? "Ari weighs 159, did you know that? I weigh 136. I never knew how much I weighed before, so I've never thought about it. But that doesn't sound like enough, does it? Twenty-three pounds sounds like a really big difference, at least for something like this."

László shrugged. "Athletes come in all shapes and sizes. Eating every day is doing you good."

Lorne rested his gloves on Davik's chair and leaned forward, elbows on his knees, chin on his knuckles. Where the fuck was he? "How tall is he, you think?"

"Ari?" László asked. "About the same height as you. Maybe an inch taller, but I doubt it's that much. Why does this matter?"

"I don't know. I've never thought about any of this shit before. No one ever weighed us when we fought in the Hive. We just fought. Now it's all I can think about. How much do you weight? About the same as me, I guess. But you're taller, so maybe a little more. I'll bet Tashué weighs a lot. More than Ari. But I don't know how to even guess something like that. I wonder how much Ijaz weighed."

"Hey," László said, squeezing Lorne's shoulder, stemming the flow of words. "It doesn't matter. It's just a number because the boxing league likes to keep track of things. It gives people something to talk about when they're arguing about who's going to win. But none of it matters, not really. Ijaz was probably twice your weight and you still beat him."

Lorne pushed his hands through his hair and leaned back against the wall. The energy was building, building, until he started tapping both heels, drumming on the floor in an alternating rhythm. It was going to be strange to fight in shoes. Strange not to feel the wet-slap of his knuckles on skin. Or maybe not—he'd been learning reasonably well. Faster than he expected. So, maybe he'd figure this shit out, too, just like he figured out how to survive in Gaffryn and how to survive everything else.

"I heard the league is talking about breaking the fights down into weight classes," Rowan said. "Lightweight, heavyweight. I don't remember all the terms they were using. That way there can be more division in the league. More championship fights, more titles."

"There you go," László said, like that decided anything. "This may be your only chance to trash Ari Odegaard, hey? Prove the weight is just a number, and it's all down to how stubborn your thick skull is."

Lorne nodded. "Sure."

The door opened.

Davik came in like a winter storm, wriggling out of his coat as fast as he could, shaking water from his hair.

"Where the hell have you been?" Lorne asked, pushing himself to his feet.

Davik shook his head, tossing his coat at the bench. "It's nothing, Mr. Lightning. Unexpected business, is all. It's time to fight, yeah?"

"Yeah, and we almost fucking missed it," László snapped. "All that work and they were gonna pull the match out from under us because you weren't here."

Davik grabbed Lorne's shoulders, squeezing so hard it hurt. And his hands were ugly cold, still wet from the rain. His whole body wound as tight as Lorne felt, his hair hanging limp and wet around his face. "I'm sorry. I'll explain it to you boys after, I promise. But for now, we got a match. You all set?"

"Yeah, Dav." Lorne shrugged Davik's hands off his shoulders. "I guess I am."

"I'll go get the referee," László said, pushing himself to his feet. "Row, go get Dav new clothes before he freezes his balls off. He deserves it, but we need to make a good showing for the match, don't we? He should at least be dressed well for it."

Davik turned back to Lorne and gave his best, widest grin, the one that shone like a lamp, the one that seemed to animate his whole body. "I'm proud of you, boy. So fucking proud. Let's get this done, hey?"

Lorne nodded and his chest filled and his eyes threatened to betray him by doing something stupid like getting weepy because he'd never been the kind of man people were *proud* of. The last time someone said they were *proud* was Rhion Coswyn. He wanted to catch this moment and hold it forever, frozen in time.

Davik grabbed a towel off the shelf, scrubbing water out of his hair, out of his beard. He wriggled out of his soaked layers, down to his shirt sleeves.

"Is it Jason?" Lorne asked. "Did something happen with Jason?"

"No, laddie," Davik said. "Nothing happened with Jason. I'll explain it to you tonight, after the fight. After you thrash Ari."

Lorne opened his mouth to press harder, but the door opened again, and László followed the referee back in.

"Mr. Kaine! Did you forget you had an appointment with the league tonight?"

"Sorry," Davik said, tossing his shirt into the pile of soaked, discarded clothes. The *Kaine* tattoo on his chest took up so much weight in the room, with this whole city convinced he was some other Davik Kaine. "Some urgent business needed my attention."

"You're very wet."

Davik barked a laugh, shooting something like a glare at the referee. "Got caught in the storm, didn't I? My son'll be back down with a change of clothes for me, and then we're good to go."

The referee shifted in his spot, adjusting the front of his waistcoat like he was loaded with as much nervous energy as everyone else. Was he afraid of Davik? Or wound up for the match. "The league doesn't like to run late, Mr. Kaine. Especially when it comes to the tourney season."

"Yes, sir," Davik said, wiping his hands on his towel. "Won't happen again, sir."

He grabbed the cotton wrapping for Lorne's hands, passing them to the referee. The referee unwound all that cotton, holding it up to the light to see through the fabric before winding them back up again and handing them back to Davik. Lorne wondered how many times Davik had done this for other people. He was so good at it. Tug, wrap, tuck, done. Lorne watched his hands, studying the movements he made. Was this his future? Davik wrapping his hands, Lorne wrapping someone else's. When he was done fighting, maybe he'd teach other kids how to fight, he'd take them mean and wiry off the streets and put gloves on them and make them use all that anger in a way that might save their lives. Or kill them. Shit. Was there any way to save people? The world took everyone, eventually.

But that could only be his future if he lived that long.

Davik leaned back, and the referee ran his hands over the wraps, between Lorne's fingers, around his wrists. Satisfied, he rolled a rubber stamp over the back of Lorne's hands, leaving an ink logo on the cotton.

"What's the stamp for?" Lorne asked.

"Proves that I watched your coach wrap your hands," the referee said. "Few years ago, we had fighters sewing weights into their wraps so they'd hit harder."

Gloves next. The referee weighed them first, and then gave them to Davik. Lorne leaned hard to get his hands in place, and then Davik's nimble fingers pulled the ties to perfect tension. Lorne flexed his fingers as much as the gloves would allow. The blood stains from his practice fights danced. The referee offered Davik some paperwork to sign.

"Thank you, Mr. Kaine. See you in the ring. Good luck, Mr. Coswyn. The league is happy to have you."

Davik exhaled slowly, and Lorne could feel all the tension sitting in the room. Maybe Davik had half-convinced himself to believe in the future of this club, too. Even though he insisted it wasn't important. He'd built this place, after all. Turned it from another Bay warehouse into something beautiful and warm. Or maybe he didn't give a shit about the fight, and he was wound up from whatever the hell he was doing before.

Rowan came back, carrying fresh clothes for Davik. Davik changed into dry trousers, a fresh shirt. He didn't bother tucking it in, didn't bother buttoning it up. It was warm enough in here, he could get away with it, and he could show off that Kaine tattoo all night.

"Dav," Lorne said. The silence was going to split his skull open. "Jason?"

"We can't do this right now, laddie," Davik said, pulling the suspenders up over his shoulders. "There's too many people here, and you've got a fight. You ready?"

"Yeah, Dav," Lorne breathed. *We can't do this right now* sounded too much like the sort of thing that came before bad news. "I'm ready."

László grabbed Lorne's coat off the hook. "I'll be right there, keeping an eye on you. I'm not allowed to help you until the match is over, but when it's done, I have you."

Lorne nodded. He couldn't get his hands through the sleeves with his gloves on so László draped it over Lorne's shoulders, letting it hang across Lorne's body like a cape.

Davik opened the door to the hall and all the noise in Lorne's head stopped. He walked, but it was without thought, without intention. It was mechanical and instinctual. The crowd roared, seething, bursting at the seams. Like the western sea in a hurricane, waves cresting and crashing against each other, their voices the howling wind, but somehow none of the sound reached him. Lorne stepped into the ocean of bodies and it parted for him. Davik walked beside him, guarding him—someone lurched from the crowd and hit Lorne with his whole body, sending Lorne staggering. Fight-hot instincts made him lift a fist to fucking swing, but Davik burst into motion, shoving the spectator away. The crowd devoured him, whoever he was, pulling him back in. Davik put a hand on Lorne's back and they walked on.

"There it is, laddie," Davik said, low over Lorne's shoulder as they headed for the ring. "Your throne. I built it for you. Make that fucker bleed all over it."

Shivers, across his whole body. He felt like he should say something, but his teeth were clenched together so hard his jaw ached like when László gave him that fucking khat but better because he was actually going to *use* this energy. It had a purpose this time. He knew what to do with it.

László reached the ring first. He climbed up, stretching the ropes open with his feet and his hands. Lorne climbed up after him. László made a big show of sliding his hands across Lorne's chest and then slowly peeling his coat off, and the crowd cheered and howled so loud the sound hit him like a physical force, sliding over his skin, filling every hollow, empty place in his chest that had never felt full before. Until now. László kissed Lorne once on the lips, throwing the coat over his shoulder to free up his hands enough to grab a pen and another piece of paper from the referee. He laughed as he read it, leaning closer to Lorne.

"This form wants to know if you're sober," he shouted, his voice straining over all that noise, "of sound mind and body, and consenting to this pugilist match on this fine evening."

"Yeah," Lorne said. Could László even hear him? "Sure."

László grinned, turning Lorne around and putting the paper on Lorne's back. László signed it, the pen making a fast scratch between Lorne's shoulder-blades, and the paper was half damp with sweat when

László handed it back to the referee, who sighed at László. Davik came up next, bringing a wooden stool with him and resting it in the corner.

Lorne swept his eyes over the crowd. So many people. They didn't even look like individuals anymore. Just a bobbing ocean of excitement.

Davik grabbed Lorne by the arm, pushing him down onto the stool. "Don't worry about the crowd, laddie."

Breathe. Don't get lost in the excitement.

Ari bounced in his corner, twisting his body every time he came up. His arms loose, his knees springing. Up, up, up, up. He kept is back to Lorne, talking to his coach, who nodded at everything Ari said. Best boxer in the city. His ankle didn't look sore. He was taking his weight on both feet evenly. Lorne hadn't thought to look at how he walked throughout the day, even though they spent all that time together. But it mustn't have been a significant limp, or else Lorne would have noticed.

"Don't look at him either," Davik said. "Look at me."

Lorne took a deep breath, shifting his eyes to Davik. Davik rested his hands on Lorne's shoulders, leaning in close. He was always so close. Like he wanted to take up the entire field of Lorne's vision, like he wanted the pair of them to share the same space.

"It's just a fight," Davik said. "Two men with gloves on, knocking the shite out of each other. Yeah? Keep your feet down, keep moving, don't let him get you. Keep him dancing with you. You're younger than he is and faster than he is. Maybe those young legs of yours can wear the old man out, hey?"

Lorne nodded. "For Jason. Right?"

"That's right, laddie."

The referee called them into the middle of the stage to shout the rules at them. "No biting, no elbows, no knees, no feet, no grappling, no head-butting."

Fists only.

Ari reached out with one glove, and Lorne reached back. Leather tapped together in some replacement for a handshake. Fuck this guy for being so damned polite and charming all the time.

The referee backed away. Ari bounced a few more times and then dropped his shoulders and brought his gloves near his face.

Breathe. Don't forget to breathe.

The bell rang.

In the Hive, one of them would have charged in because it made the crowd happy, and even though you were fighting for your life up there, you did what you could to make the crowd happy because that made Powell Iwan like you.

Ari didn't charge. He edged forward, half a step at a time, and Lorne kept to his left. Like László said. Left, left, closer. Ari kept his weight balanced, waiting for Lorne to step into his big reach, pivoting on his left foot that was supposed to be fucked up, but it didn't look like it hurt him at all.

Ari feinted with his left, and Lorne stepped away from it, and Ari's other fist met Lorne in the middle. Smashed against Lorne's side, into the ribs, but even as the pain burst through Lorne's chest, he snapped one fist forward and caught Ari right in the mouth. Ari stepped in closer anyway, crowding Lorne, hit him in the body again and again, left and right, and Lorne couldn't step or twist or slip fast enough. Lorne lifted a leg to kick him away—*shit, feet down.*

His back hit the ropes, rough jute rubbing hard on his skin. Lorne snapped a fist up. Chin. Another. Jaw. Another. Clapping against Ari's ear. Ari staggered, coming down hard on that left leg, and Lorne saw it, the wince, the grimace, the shaky leg that almost dumped him. Swing again, hit the shoulder, again, in the face, *don't fucking kick him in the ankle don't fucking kick him in the ankle don't fucking kick him in the ankle.* Lorne shoved Ari back, trying to get himself some space. Some room to swing, to breathe.

Ari stepped in again and Lorne swung for his face. Leather on skin. Ari staggered back. Lorne stepped off the ropes, closer, closer, trying to catch his breath, but his whole fucking body hurt, every muscle, every organ.

Ari spat on the canvas, blood running from his mouth, dripping from his chin. And the chemical fight lust fuelled Lorne on, burning him alive.

Ari's eyes were cold and hard as they locked on Lorne over those red gloves, waiting for Lorne to come back within his reach again. Lorne edged in, closer, closer, forcing Ari to turn on that left foot, taking his weight on it too much, waiting for him to wince again, waiting for that flash of pain across his face. Ari's lips opened, his teeth red with his own blood, and Lorne rushed in—

The bell rang.

The referee stepped between them, shoving Lorne back.

Davik grabbed him by the arm, pulling him away, to the corner, pushing him down into the stool. Lorne sank back against the wooden post sucking in deep breaths, trying not to wince at the pain in his ribs, in his sides. Was something broken?

"You're doing good, laddie, you're doing fine." Davik poured water across Lorne's head, soaking him down, washing the sweat away, cold on his hot skin. "Drink a bit."

Lorne grabbed the jug, clumsy with his gloves on, taking a slow drink. Pushed the jug against Davik's chest. And there was blood on his gloves, white leather taking on the red, Ari's mouth giving Lorne more stains.

"Don't let him crowd you like that," Davik went on. "Don't be afraid of him. He tries to push you, you push back. Aye, he's fast, but I still say you're faster. Just don't fucking kick him, yeah? I saw that leg go up. You can't do that shit in league fights. Don't kick him or they'll never stop calling us dirty."

Lorne shook his head, spraying water from his hair. Davik pushed Lorne's hair out of his face, running his fingers through it until the water kept it almost slicked back.

"We'll get you a haircut after this, so you look a little less like a drowned rat."

"Let them think I'm a fucking rat," Lorne muttered. "Fuck them."

"That's the spirit," Davik laughed. "Up you get, then, go show him how hard it is to catch a Bay rat."

Lorne pushed himself to his feet, and Davik stepped out of the way. Ari was still sitting. His coach was still trying to mop away the blood. Ari leaned over and spat blood into a bucket and his coach dumped water over his head, too. He shook his head and sprayed water and blood and squeezed his eyes shut but the referee was in the centre of the stage, counting down the last seconds of the single minute they had between rounds. Ari stayed in his stool as long as he could, rising to his feet as the bell rang for the second round. Lorne put his fists up and let Ari come to him, let him shuffle and bounce forward on that fucked ankle.

Closer, closer, don't fucking kick him.

Ari swung first, and Lorne twisted to the left, catching Ari low in the gut. Ari took the hit, swung, down onto Lorne's shoulder. Swung again, into Lorne's chest again, and Lorne staggered away on shaky legs, trying to catch his breath. He turned to face Ari, and Ari wasn't following. Ari took a step back, getting his fists up. He shook his head again, the blood still running from his mouth.

In, again. Swing. Ari moved like smoke, like liquid.

Lorne's knees hit canvas, the rough texture tearing his knees all to shit even through his trousers. He could feel the hot burn, feel the blood. He didn't know how he got down there, except that his head was fucking spinning. Tilting, swaying. The pain was distant, far away, like his own mind was dodging it.

Get up, they don't count in the league, you have to just get up.

Up.

Shake it off.

Ari swung as soon as Lorne was up, but Lorne slipped enough, and the swing grazed his shoulder. Lorne surged in even though his ears were ringing and he couldn't really think. Didn't need to think anyway. In, closer, faster, hit him again.

The referee was between them, shouting, shoving, cursing, shoving. Lorne staggered back. Davik had him again, dragging him, away, away. Ears ringing so fucking much.

"You can't fucking hit him after the bell rings, you shite," Davik shouted, shoving him down into the stool again. "You're lucky that didn't land. You have to stop when the bell rings."

"I didn't hear it. Fucking everything's ringing."

Water, on his head. Washing over his ears, but not washing all the noise away.

Lorne tilted his head back, closing his eyes. More water, on his face. He opened his mouth, and Davik poured some water in. Lorne swished it. Spat it out. Must have bit his lip or his tongue because he couldn't remember Ari hitting him in the mouth, but the copper taste of blood was there.

"Don't let him hit your shoulders," Davik said. "He's trying to make it harder for you to hit him."

"Yeah, Dav," Lorne breathed, spitting out more blood. "I get it. If only he'd quit hitting me, I could hit him better."

"Don't be a cunt about it."

Lorne focused on Davik's face, on those dark eyes that bore into Lorne's soul. "I don't know why that's an insult."

Davik blinked at him. "What?"

"The way you chase skirts around, I would assume you like a good cunt. So I don't see why you say it like it's a bad thing."

Davik grinned. "Yeah, sure. Sweet like a cunt, you are, and I want to eat you up."

"Next you'll call me a cocksucker like it's supposed to offend me."

Davik laughed at that, rising to his feet. "I'm game if you're offering, but you're a bit busy right now, hey?"

"Yeah," Lorne said, focusing across the ring at Ari, who was still spitting blood, still trying to look like he wasn't in pain. Lorne grinned at him. Ari grinned back. "A little busy, I guess."

Up. Bell clanging.

Ari kept his arms down at first. Down, loose. Old man, that's what Davik called him. Didn't look like a fucking old man. But his arms must be getting tired for him to keep his guard dropped like that.

Lorne stepped in.

Ari's hands came up, but he was starting to lag. Starting to falter. Lorne swung for his body, muscles, ribs. Forced him back on his back ankle, *don't fucking kick him.* Ari gave a shout—maybe he was hurting, fucking good—surged in fast anyway. Hard. Swinging. Forcing Lorne back, back, back to the ropes again, and Lorne took the hits even though everything fucking hurt, took the hits on his body until Ari was over committed, arms too low, head too far down, and Lorne brought his arms up high hitting Ari in the shoulders, in the face, in the head. A hard right took Ari in the ear and spun him. Staggered him. Ari stepped away, shoulder hitting the wood post that held the ropes, but then he lunged again and hit Lorne under the chin. Lorne staggered.

The bell rang.

Lorne almost tripped over his own feet as Davik guided him to the stool. He listed to one side, his shoulder pressing into the rope beside him, Davik's hands dragging him up straight.

"Stop letting him get you cornered."

"Stop giving me shit advice," Lorne snapped, spitting blood with every word. "I know, fuck! He doesn't want to fucking quit, does he?"

"You're doing good, laddie, you're doing fine. Six rounds now, hey? That's pretty fucking good against a champion like him. You're almost done."

"Six?" Lorne closed his eyes, wishing the ring would stop spinning. "I thought it was three."

"Naw, laddie, six rounds now. You alright? Hey, look at me. Open up those pretty blues of yours, and look at me."

Lorne dragged his eyes open and Davik was leaning in close again, so close their foreheads touched, that intimacy that felt so strange in this place, with this man, this man he had expected to hate except Lorne didn't hate him at all. Lorne loved him.

"You alright?"

"Yeah," Lorne said. "Head hurts. Like someone hit me or something."

"That's not funny. You need me to call it, get László in here to look at your thick skull?"

"No," Lorne said, pushing Davik away, hooking his arms over the ropes to drag himself up. "I'm fine. I was joking. Let me finish."

"Sit, sit, you've still a few seconds, yeah? Sit. Have a drink."

Water, on his face. Drink a little. Spit water, spit blood. Was the bell ringing, or was that his ears? His head, maybe. His whole fucking body, ringing with purpose.

"You sure you want to keep going? Six rounds against a champion is good, laddie, no shame in calling it."

"Let me fight, Dav. This is what I do. Let me do it."

"Fine. Don't let him crowd you anymore, keep moving."

Keep moving.

Bell.

Ari stepped in first, swinging hard, Lorne twisted to meet him. Miss, swinging through the air, heavy glove pulling him off balance. Twist, swing again, use that momentum. Miss. Fucking Ari, moving too fast now, or Lorne moving too slow. Swing again, his shoulder hurt when he missed, muscles swollen and tired, hard to take a deep breath, but Ari wasn't swinging either. Just slipping, stepping fast, wincing when his ankle hurt. Lorne swung again and again, didn't matter that it missed because Ari could only back up so far. His body touched the rope, but he gave another of his angry, spiteful shouts and surged in and Lorne was spinning again, staggering away, no pain, just a lurching, dancing, roaring world, *don't fall, they don't count here, you go down too much and you're done.*

Ari stepped in, swung again. Lorne twisted to face him, his arm coming up, tangled with Ari's arm, putting pressure on the elbow, pinning Ari's arm so Ari couldn't fucking swing anymore, and Lorne hit him hard in the chest, holding him, hard in the gut, hard in the shoulder, and Ari tried to twist away but he couldn't because Lorne had him. Hit him again, folding him in half.

Referee. Bell.

"Shite, laddie, you've really done it now. Sit down, fuck. Sit!"

Davik pushed him into his seat but didn't crouch down to talk. He stood in front of Lorne and watched Ari. The referee was over there, talking to Ari, and Ari was nodding and shaking his head.

Lorne reached up to grab Davik's hand, but the gloves wouldn't let him grab things so he smeared Ari's blood on Davik's shirt. "What are they saying?"

Ari's coach shouted across the ring, but Lorne couldn't quite hear him, or his mind couldn't quite grasp the words. And Davik stepped into the middle of the ring, leaving a footprint in the blood on the canvas. Ari's coach charged Davik but Davik didn't flinch. Leaned in like he was perfectly happy to take a hit. Like they were up next. Ari sat up straighter and called his coach back.

"Dav, what's going on?"

Davik came back, dropping to one knee. "No grappling, remember? Not supposed to hold him like that. The referee is leaving it up to Mr. 159 if he wants to disqualify you for that or if he wants to keep going. Only one more round—I can't tell which way he'll go."

"Oh fuck, I'm sorry."

"Naw, laddie, don't be sorry. You haven't been training long enough to change your habits, hey? Don't worry about it. We shoulda had you here months ago to get you ready. Drink up. Not too much, in case he still wants to go."

"Dav, I'm sorry."

"It's fine. Drink."

Water in, spit it out to get rid of the blood taste. More water.

Davik stood and turned. Hands on his hips. The blood on his shirt was going dark and dry. Lorne looked down at the jug, at his gloves. At all of Ari's blood on the white leather. Shit, it was a good idea, the white leather. Lorne wondered if Ari could see where Lorne's blood was, or if those splatters were hidden by the red-brown dye.

Across the ring, Ari wasn't looking at his gloves. He was looking at Lorne. Breathing hard nodding at the referee. What did the nod mean? 'Fuck this kid, I'm finished' or 'Yes, I'm sure I want to keep going.'

Another head shake, another nod. The referee stepped away. Ari's coach poured water on his head, washing some of the blood away, but it kept coming, kept oozing. Lorne could see it now, the spot under his lip that was ripped open, maybe his tooth had punched right through, the blood dark and thick and always coming no matter how much his coach mopped him up.

"He wants to keep going," Davik said, patting Lorne's shoulders, taking the water away. "No more trying to give him a kiss, hey? Fists only."

Lorne nodded. "Fists only."

"On your feet, then."

Up. Ari sat a little longer, pushed his coach away again. Sat until the referee turned to him. Sat right until the bell rang. Up. And the world moved so slow. It was perfect. All of it. Lorne's whole body buzzed with pain and the fury of a fucking good fight. And watching Ari move was exactly as beautiful as he expected it to be. Those blue eyes lit with something primal, ascending to some holy place. The pair of them, bleeding because they wanted to. Because it summoned something ancient into this warehouse, something they both worshipped with their gloves on.

Ari came across the ring. His ankle didn't want to hold him. He flinched, his knee giving out for a second. Just a tiny moment where his foundation was less than perfect. Took a breath. Balanced himself again. Fists up.

Lorne let him come. Let him shuffle. Let him lunge first, but even as he swung, Lorne could see the pain in Ari's face. Lorne twisted, to the left. Left, always to the left, and Ari tried to turn without putting so much weight on his ankle, but it was getting clumsy. Lorne charged and Ari staggered to find his footing again and twisted and his fist came up in Lorne caught it right in the shoulder but he still swung and hit Ari in the chest, even though his shoulder was screaming with pain. Ari staggered, onto his bad ankle. Bore his teeth as his leg tried to dump him. Lorne swung again. Ari twisted, swung back. Lorne didn't let up, swinging, swinging, forcing Ari back on that bad ankle again, again, again.

Ari hit the ropes, and Lorne was on him. Their bodies pressed together. Lorne wasn't totally sure he was standing, but he was most certainly swinging and Ari tucked his head behind his gloves and curled himself down to try to protect his body, but there was only so much he could guard when Lorne was right on top of him. Lorne hit and hit and hit without even knowing what he was swinging for, just meat and bone, again, again, again.

Bell.

Davik had him again, dragging him back. Back, back, until Lorne was in his seat again. Dumping water again, more this time, a great shower of cold water, drenching his whole body, dripping across his eyes, running down his shoulders, soaking into his trousers.

"You did good. I'm proud of you. I didn't think you'd last that long, but you got some fucking grit in you, hey? You did so good."

"I've got him now," Lorne said, looking across the ring at Ari, watching him lean to one side, both his gloves pressing into his knee like it was the part that hurt him the most, but Lorne could tell by the way he held his foot up off the stage that it was that ankle that was doing him in. Finally. Doesn't matter how much technical skill you've got, if you can't stand, you can't hit. "His ankle's still fucked like I thought."

"Ah, the judges will call him the winner," Davik muttered. "Here, spit, let's see what bits of you need to be stitched up."

"No, I'm not done," Lorne said. He pushed himself up to his feet and grabbed the rope so he wouldn't sink back down. "I'm still standing. I can still fight. I fucking have him, Dav!"

"You won't get any argument from me on that, but the fight's over," Davik said. "Eight rounds. That's what we signed. Eight rounds or knock-out, and that big stubborn head of yours didn't let you fall, so it goes to the judges now. It's fine, laddie, it's good. Sit, let László look at you."

Lorne's legs felt rubbery and too far away as he sank back into his seat. How could it be over? It didn't make sense. They could still stand. If they were still standing, they should be still fighting. Nothing about fucking boxing made sense.

Ari brought his leg up higher, and his coach pulled off his boot, his sock. Pushed Ari's trouser leg up and wrapped Ari's ankle up tight in bandages. And Ari leaned to one side and spat more blood, more blood, and someone gave him a wet towel that he held to his face until the blood soaked through the cloth, dripped onto his legs and down onto the canvas between his feet. The person took the towel away and threw stitches into Ari's lip above his chin, where the hole punched right through.

László's face, hovering in front of Lorne's, blocking his view of Ari. "Open up your mouth, let me see what's bleeding in there."

Lorne opened his mouth wide, but his jaw ached. When he tilted his head back, he could feel his blood going down his throat. It almost choked him. László nodded and leaned back, pushing Lorne's hair out of his face.

"Looks like your cheek, I think. We'll get you some more water in a minute so you can rinse your mouth. I'll seal everything up in the dressing room."

The referee waved Lorne over and he pushed himself to shaky legs. The pain was threatening to catch up. Everything hurt. Ari got up, too, shuffle-limping, putting his weight carefully on his ankle as he came to the centre of the ring, his coach beside him. Davik walked with Lorne, one hand on Lorne's arm like he was ready to drag Lorne back if Lorne so much as breathed too hard. He could feel it, maybe, how Lorne wasn't done. The fight couldn't be over like that. Not when they were both still standing.

The referee stood between them and took their wrists in one hand each and said a lot of shit about the rules and the scores, and then he lifted Ari's arm high up over both of their heads.

And Lorne forced himself to breathe, to stay still. Forced himself to look at the crowd instead of looking at Ari. Forced himself not to think about how his 136 looked like such a shit number next to 159, except he *was* thinking about it, about the flourish Miss Brady added to the 3 because otherwise it lacked the presence Ari's numbers had. If only Lorne was heavier, he could have hit Ari with more weight, hit him with those big sledge-hammer hits that Ari had, could have knocked Ari flat before so many fucking rounds got away from him.

Ari turned to him and held out a glove like before the fight, but this time his glove was wet and bloody like even the leather was sweating and bleeding. Lorne grit his teeth and swung, maybe a little too hard, maybe a little too much fucking attitude, hitting Ari's glove and knocking his arm down, but Ari stepped closer and grinned at him—fuck him, he *grinned*, his blond beard turned red, the black stitches standing stark against all that pale hair.

"You did good, kid." But the words were thick and ugly because his mouth was fucked. "You're going places."

Lorne bit his own tongue instead of telling Ari to go fuck himself and Davik dragged him back again. Steered him away, dragged apart the ropes so Lorne could climb down. László hooked his arm in Lorne's and Lorne was leaking blood all over both of them, water and sweat dripping from his hair, but László obviously didn't care. And the crowd pressed in, jostling, slapping his back, people leaning in to shout at him over the chaos, over all the noise, but Lorne couldn't hear anything with all the roaring and ringing in his head. There was too much tension in his shoulders. He wasn't finished swinging.

Tashué sat on the bench in Lorne's change room, and he pushed himself to his feet when Davik led Lorne in. He was dressed for the ugly weather, a heavy coat and a scarf hanging loose, gloves sticking out of his pocket like he was getting ready to go somewhere. And everything in Lorne's body buzzed brighter than before.

"Hey," he said. "Good to see you still on your feet."

Something unknotted in Lorne's chest, something hot with relief. The last time he saw Tashué, they fought about Jason and the bank, and some part of Lorne wondered if Tashué would ever look him in the eye again, but here he was. As if to say they'd figure out the shit they were fighting about some other time, and for now Tashué was glad Lorne survived the fight.

"I lost." Stupid thing to say, but Lorne couldn't think of anything better. He tried to wipe his face with his arm but it wasn't any use. "I should've hit him harder so I could finish it properly."

"Next time," Tashué said.

"Yeah," Lorne agreed. "Next time."

"Sit down, laddie, let's get those gloves off, get some ice on your face afore it gets real ugly."

Lorne sank down. Davik sat in his stool and turned Lorne's hands over and started pulling on the laces, but Lorne wanted to tell him to leave it, leave the gloves on, because Lorne wasn't fucking done fighting yet, maybe he'd hit a bag a few times to let all the pressure out of his shoulders, but his shoulder fucking hurt and his chest hurt and his head was still ringing.

Davik dragged the gloves off his hands, and they felt strange with the release of pressure. A sharp set of shears cut the cotton wraps away and they fell to the floor, decorated with the ink from the stamp. Davik pushed a towel into Lorne's hair, and Lorne used the corner to wipe sweat out of his eyes.

"How's his head looking?" Davik asked. "I don't like that he can't remember a couple rounds."

"A concussion for sure," László said. "It isn't too bad. I'll keep an eye on him for the night but I think he'll be fine."

"I've been taking shots to the head my whole life. None of them killed me yet."

"Your whole life, is it?" Davik asked.

Lorne nodded. "My mother hit me with a frying pan when I was eight or so. Don't remember the hit. She used to threaten me with it when I was getting mouthy. I remember being a shit, and then I remember waking up with a headache, and my mother was crying and saying she was sorry for hitting me."

"Well, fuck. No wonder you're so bleedin' pleasant."

Lorne shrugged. "Opium's shit."

"This is going to hurt, but it's to help you," László said.

Pain. Tearing through Lorne's whole body. Hot and ripping, dragging—he wanted to shout, but he couldn't breathe enough to make words. Davik pushed a bag of ice against Lorne's face, and the shock of the cold hitting him made him dizzy. And then the pressure of László's Talent let go, and Lorne could breathe again.

"I'm sorry," László said, pushing his hands into Lorne's hair, holding the bag of ice. "That ties everything up, makes sure nothing is bleeding too bad. Takes some of the swelling out of your face so your eyes don't close up. You don't have any broken ribs. All your organs look alright. I think you're going to be fine."

"Here, laddie, spit the blood out."

Lorne leaned forward, spitting more blood out of his mouth. His jaw ached, his teeth ached.

The door swung open. "Mr. Iwan's sent for you, Da," Rowan said. "You and Mr. Guinne and he's asking for Mr. Saeati, too."

"Shit," Davik breathed. "What does he want?"

"Dunno," Rowan said with a shrug. "Didn't say. Just that he wanted to see you."

Davik scowled, looking up at Tashué. Then back at Rowan. "Go tell Saeati to meet us at Iwan's. Where's Czarny?"

"Last I saw him, he was heading upstairs with Allie Tei," Tashué said.

"You want me to get him, too?" Rowan asked.

"No," Davik said quickly. "No, let him stay here. Just in case it's trouble."

"What kind of trouble are you expecting?" Tashué asked.

Davik grimaced again. "The bank, maybe. We'll grab some bank notes, as many stacks as you can stuff into your pockets, so he can't say we ain't paying our tithes."

"Dav," Lorne said. "What about Jason? Any word?"

"I have to go, laddie," Davik said, catching Lorne's hand. "Can't keep him waiting, can we? We'll be back. You stay here, and László's going to take care of your thick head. We don't take head injuries lightly around here."

Tashué and Davik left the change room, leaving Lorne buzzing with the quiet. Was Jason out, somewhere in the city? When would he find out?

"You want a smoke?" László asked. "To take the edge off the pain, wind down a bit?"

"Yeah," Lorne said. "To take the edge off."

66

TASHUÉ

DAY 38

They stopped in Davik's office so Davik could pull stacks of bank notes out of hiding places—a floorboard that lifted out of place, a hidden cabinet behind a shelf, a false bottom to a desk drawer. He stacked them all on his desk, and Tashué stuffed them into his pockets. The paper was waxy, tightly bound so it felt like a small brick, a portrait of the Queen inked on each one. Each note worth ten gold crowns, or ten silver crowns, depending on the stack. How many notes were in each stack? He couldn't even tell. He couldn't wrap his head around the wealth. It felt immeasurable. So vast he couldn't even comprehend the total of it.

He'd give it all to get Jason.

"Is it still storming out there?" Davik asked.

"Yeah, Davik," Tashué muttered. "It's still fucking storming."

"Well shit. It's gonna be a long walk, hey?"

For the first time since Tashué lived in Yaelsmuir, there were carriages for hire in the Bay. They'd come from other quarters to serve the attendees of the match. Tashué flagged one down so they didn't have to walk to the dry-docks in the storm and tied the reins of his stolen horse to the back of the carriage so she would follow. He hoped to leave the city as soon as they were done talking to Powell.

Except maybe Powell was looking for trouble, like Davik said. So maybe everything was fucked.

"Do you feel it, when you're close to the forest?" Tashué asked. Before the silence had the chance to breed too much doubt.

Davik looked up at him for a while, like he was surprised Tashué was talking. "Feel what?"

"I don't know," Tashué said. The carriage rattled them bad as it bounced over the uneven Bay cobbles, the ugly rain loud as it pummelled the carriage roof. The poor driver must have been fucking miserable out there. Tashué was tempted to peel off a bank note or two and leave them on the bench as a nice tip. "I felt it after I quickened. I'm still struggling to pull myself back constantly, or my Talent bleeds everywhere and I can't think. But the forest, it's different. It feels bigger somehow. Older. Aware."

"Aye," Davik said. Almost shouting over the din the storm made. "That's Myfawnwy. That's the story, anyway. There was a kingdom in the forest, once. A great wooden hall in the centre, and clustered villages hiding in the trees. And Myfawnwy, she was their princess. West-coast born, but the people of the Dunnenbrahl loved her plenty, and she loved them back. And then the Godking burned her hall and the whole fucking forest because they dared defy him. Myfawnwy's ghost has been living in that forest ever since. You never heard the stories?"

"The Wraith of the Dunnenbrahl," Tashué said. "They say she rose up out of the forest and destroyed a whole branch of the Godking's army. I always thought that was a legend. She's real?"

Davik shrugged. "Don't know, I never went in the forest to ask around, did I? But I do know that plenty people say there's more wild Talent in that forest than anywhere else in the Dominion. Like the forest knows you're there. Folks step careful in that forest. They say it has a habit of taking people who get too greedy."

A shiver passed down Tashué's spine, filling his chest with something cold. Something tired. If he remembered his history lessons right, the Godking was the one who started the hatred against Talent. Or maybe he fed it most viciously, directed the nation's hate onto the Talented, using it to build his own momentum to power. Swallowing the individual countries and city states that scattered across the continent to make one unified kingdom, holding it for generations. And his own bloodline turned on him, Voth the Liberator raising an army to back the North Star and the Ash Child—but that legacy of distrust for Talent lived on and on. Until now, how many hundreds of years later, they were still fighting. Children were being made into energy units because this world still refused to believe they were worthy of being considered human. He'd been alive forty-two years, aware of his Talent for... thirty? And this world had made him so afraid of himself that he'd never asked anyone to explain his own abilities to him.

Would it ever stop?

The time to think about it ran out—the carriage dropped them at the dry-docks. He untied his horse's reins from the carriage and led her into the warehouse. The place was filled with planks of wood and the smell of sealing tar, but no one was working. The quiet was invasive, the stillness making Tashué's shoulders itch. They were next door to the office where Tashué and Ishmael and Allie had slept for a few hours after arriving in the Bay. So little time had passed since then, but so fucking much had changed. Some part of him was exhausted by it all, exhausted and frustrated and fed up. He missed Stella, and he wanted his son, and there wasn't a single day that passed that he didn't rot in his own guilt for how bad everything had gotten on his watch.

They rang the bell over the locked door that guarded the only stairwell up and waited in the cold. The storm outside kept howling, ice bouncing off the city, the sound rattling through the warehouse. It was cold enough to turn to snow soon. Winter had arrived.

Adley let them in. Up the stairs, a full three stories. It was warmer and quieter than the rooms Powell kept above the Hive, the one where Tashué sat with the old crime lord and made a deal over an empty bullet casing. A proper kitchen, some dark bedrooms, and a lot of wood stoves and fireplaces. The furniture was simple and sturdy and decades behind fashion—it all reminded Tashué of things that his grandmother used to have in her single, rented room.

"Good evening, gentlemen," Powell said. He sat at the dining table, hunched low over a bowl of soup that twisted its steam into his face. It smelled of garlic and onion and mushroom, making Tashué's mouth water. He'd only eaten a few scavenged things as he worked with everyone under the *Bucket*. The Ffyanwy Rhydderch article they'd sent out in time for the political speeches had dried up his appetite. How long ago was that? What time was it? Almost midnight now? "Have a seat. Where's Saeati? I thought you were looking after him, Mr. Blackwood."

728 | LEGACY OF BRICK & BONE

"He's looking after himself these days, Mr. Iwan," Tashué said. Powell sat at the head of his table, so Tashué picked a chair near the middle, one that gave him a view of the door and the window over Powell's shoulder and a view of Adley, who hovered between Powell and the kitchen. And Davik, who settled at the opposite end of the table, putting his back against the wall so he could face Powell with his whole body. "His knee is getting better, so he keeps his own company."

Powell nodded, his eyes flicking to Davik. "How's our boy doing, Mr. Kaine? I suppose he didn't die in his match, else I would have heard about it by now."

"The Lledewydd Lightning did very well, Mr. Iwan," Davik said graciously. "He was a little rough when you sent him to us, but László took good care of him. He went all eight rounds against Odegaard, lost by judges' decision. But that's better than I expected considering how little time we had to train him."

"I'm glad of it, Mr. Kaine. He's a good boy, that one. Thick and stubborn and more than his fair share of angry, but it's those things that's kept him alive so long, isn't it? And they make him perfect for living down there in that club with you."

"Aye, Mr. Iwan," Davik said. "I like folks who are thick and stubborn. Turns 'em into survivors, like you said."

Powell nodded. "I've a few things for you, Mr. Blackwood. I hear they're yours, and you've been missing them since the day you were so dramatically arrested."

Powell flicked his fingers at Adley, who disappeared into the kitchen and came back with a small crate. Tashué fought the urge to stand, keeping himself seated as Adley approached. There was something tense in this apartment, something ugly and filled with hidden violence—he couldn't help but remember the things László said about Tashué being bait, about Powell throwing Tashué into Davik's hands to see what Davik would do. But when Adley rested the crate on the table, Tashué caught the sight of copper gleaming in the darkness. An urn. It emptied him. Poured him out as surely as he'd given the ashes from that urn into the Brightwash.

Adley pulled the urn out of the box and set it in the middle of the table. Keoh's urn. Tashué had thought it lost, but somehow Powell had tracked it down in this massive city with all the mudlarks and riverbank trawlers who picked valuable things from the river to make ends meet.

"Cost me a pretty penny, it did, buying it back from the tinker who had it," Powell said. "But I thought you should get it back. The ashes were gone when my people tracked it down, but at least your boy could have his mother's urn."

Tashué cleared his throat, reaching out to touch Keoh's name again. Her number, the one tattooed on Lizanne's neck. "I put her ashes in the river before I was arrested. It's what she wanted. That's why I was down there when the Patrollers found me."

"Ah, that's a bit of a relief then," Powell said with some false fondness that made Tashué's skin crawl. What the fuck did Powell Iwan care about Keoh Gian Ly's ashes? "It's good that she went where she wanted to go."

"Thank you, Mr. Iwan," Tashué said. "I'm sure Jason will appreciate it if he ever gets out."

Davik winced.

Powell nodded, his lips pulling into a snarl-smile. "Aye, you tell him old man Iwan takes care when he can, won't you?"

"Of course, Mr. Iwan," Tashué said, even though it set his teeth on edge.

Adley's hand went back into the crate, and he pulled out Tashué's cavalry knife. Rested it on the table in front of the urn.

"Found all your lost things, didn't we?" Powell said. "Because old man Iwan takes care when he makes a deal."

Tashué's gun. Adley laid it in front of Tashué, the weight of it so familiar that Tashué could almost feel it in his hand. It had been cleaned and oiled so that it gleamed in the dim lamplight. The chamber was empty.

"Have we got any bullets that might fit into that big old gun, Adley?" Powell asked. "It was empty when we bought it back, Mr. Blackwood, but maybe we can send you off fully loaded, hey?"

"I think so, Mr. Iwan," Adley said. "I'll be right back."

"Thank you," Tashué said again. "I appreciate it."

"We've something for you in return, don't we?" Davik said. His voice was so tight, it reminded Tashué of a rubber band, stretched to the very limit of itself before it was about to snap. "Why don't you hand it all over, Mr. Blackwood? Show Mr. Iwan how much we appreciate him."

Tashué stifled a sigh, pushing himself to his feet. He wished Ishmael was here. Ishmael was supposed to handle shit like this so Tashué didn't have to, because it was all fucking exhausting. He was tired of sitting between powerful people who were busy waving their egos around while the fate of everyone with Talent was hanging in the balance. Tired of fucking around, trying to claw one more ounce of power out of the city at the expense of everyone. Playing the exact game that people like Clannaugh wanted them to play. Starving dogs devouring each other over scraps of the Bay, like Tashué said in his dream. There had to be a way out of the bloody cycle, a way to cut through the shit and stand up. But maybe killing Davik was the easiest way, because then Powell had no more reason to play games. With Davik out of the way, Powell could hold the Bay. Would he keep Clannaugh out of it?

Maybe he was keeping Clannaugh out. Tashué had expected raids on the Bay by now. Five days since his arrest, and the whole city was holding its breath.

Tashué emptied his pockets, one stack of bank notes at a time, piling them on the table in front of Powell. It was a fraction of what he and László and Rowan had taken, but it was still enough to buy half of Yaelsmuir, or at least it seemed like it. Such a tiny stack of paper, worth so fucking much gold.

"From the bank you blagged, hey?" Powell asked.

"Yes sir, Mr. Iwan," Davik said. "We ain't had the chance to count it all yet, but that'll be your tithe for the trouble."

"For the trouble?" Powell echoed.

"The bank wasn't in the Bay, Mr. Iwan," Davik said. "We didn't ask permission, I know, but it was all rather by the seat of our pants, wasn't it?"

Why lie? It wasn't by the seat of anyone's pants—László had planned it with poor, doomed Mr. Riley for weeks, apparently. Maybe even months.

"Aye, sure, the bank was in Drystone, but you're supposed to ask my permission any time you get into big business that fucks with Bay business, aren't you? So imagine my confusion when I hear that two bank managers were found dead in their own bank when customers queued up outside the door. Imagine my fury when I get word from the Patrollers that they would like to question me about this bank I've never heard of. Imagine the bloodshed that'll come to this quarter once Bothain Clannaugh decides he's had enough. I don't like sitting down with men who have that much ego, Mr. Kaine. But I hadn't any choice but to sit and talk with him, did I? He wants to make arrests and I don't like the idea of letting his tinmen come through the Bay, scooping whoever they see fit."

"There's no way to tie that bank to the Bay," Davik said. "We were discreet. If he really had proof it was us, he would've come for us at the boxing match, wouldn't he?"

"Pull the fucking whisky corks out of your ears and fucking listen to me, you smug shitheel," Powell snapped. "It don't matter how discreet you were. It don't matter if you got the money by fucking magic, and it don't matter if you pay me so much tithe that you haven't two coppers left to rub together—two people died in a Drystone bank when Bothain fucking Clannaugh is here, looking for any excuse to rip open *my* quarter to come looking for *you*. He don't need to prove it was us. He don't need a single scrap of evidence. All he needs to do is loudly declare that the Bay is being held by the Army of the Red Dawn, and they're stockpiling weapons and murdering innocent people for bank notes, and then he gets to roll his pretty little division right through us. And you, you fucking idiot, you invited him in with this shit."

Powell swept his hand through the pile of bank notes, sending them tumbling across the table, spilling onto the floor. One of them slid over the wooden tabletop to thump against the base of Keoh's urn. It was strange to see the money beside Keoh's name. She would have been so impressed with it. Tashué could almost see her—the younger version of her, the woman he loved once, before the opium ate the best parts of her away—grabbing the stack and cutting the paper band open so she could spread the notes out between both her hands like she was fanning out a deck of cards. He could hear her laughing like that time he brought khat home from the Hadia, and they brewed tea with it because it was dried leaves instead of fresh. He hadn't thought about that day in a long time, but everything lately kicked so many memories out of the dusty corners of his mind. How long ago was that? Before the Ridge. Before Jason.

"Why didn't he come down to the pugilist club, Mr. Iwan?" Tashué asked. "If he thought it was enough to get him in the Bay, why didn't he come for Davik while everyone was at the match?"

Powell shrugged slowly, looking at Tashué. "Why do you think, Mr. Blackwood?"

"Because you got your chance to make a deal with him," Tashué said.

"What the fuck kind of deal did you make?" Davik breathed.

Adley came back into the dining room, walking right through the tension and ignoring the bank notes on the floor. He set a box of ammunition on the table, right in front of Keoh's urn. "There you are, Mr. Blackwood. Those should fit that old cavalry cannon of yours."

Tashué sighed, pulling the box closer to him. The bullets rattled in the cardboard box, clinking together. The .45 long were harder to find on the civilian market since the military was the biggest purchaser of them. They packed a mean punch, though, as Edgar Hale's skull demonstrated not all that long ago. He rolled open the chamber, looking down the barrel to make sure it was clear all the way through, to make sure there wasn't any river sand left. The gun was immaculate.

Ishmael was supposed to kill Davik. But Ishmael wasn't here yet, so apparently Powell was just as happy for Tashué to make it happen.

"Who went on the merry little bank robbery?" Powell asked.

"Does it matter?" Davik asked.

Powell knocked his knuckles on the table a few times. "Don't test me, Mr. Kaine. Who's responsible?"

"Me," Tashué said. He loaded his gun slowly. The sound was so familiar and so violent, charging the air with such potential for death and destruction. "I went, Mr. Iwan. Me and László Dargis."

He wasn't sure why he left Rowan out, except that he knew that Powell was looking for someone to hold accountable, and he couldn't offer up a child. A fifteen year old boy who was in over his head and cried over innocent people. And maybe Rowan would be offended that Tashué considered him a child, just like Tashué would have been furious at the same age, but he couldn't help but be intensely aware of how short a life fifteen years was when the whole world was sliding off its axis.

Powell snorted. "László Dargis is your discreet bank robber? Now you're taking the piss, Mr. Kaine."

"It was supposed to be—"

"Don't tell me any more supposed tos," Powell snapped. "László Dargis will be arrested, and Clannaugh can charge him with whatever crimes he wants to charge him with."

"László is the healer for the club—"

"I don't give a shit," Powell snapped. "I don't care about your club, and I don't care about what you think you need for it. You've fucked me real ugly this time, and you'll pay to balance the scales. Peace isn't pretty, Mr. Kaine. Peace is brutal, and it takes a lot of suffering. But you know what causes a lot more suffering than making peace?"

Davik didn't say anything. He pressed his lips together so hard that they disappeared beneath the thick brown of his beard. His eyes flicked back and forth between Tashué and his gun and Powell's furious face and a little bit of sweat beaded on his temples. Tashué filled all six chambers and flicked it shut, resting the gun on the table.

"I asked you a question, Mr. Kaine. What causes a lot more suffering than making peace?"

"What causes more suffering, Mr. Iwan?" Tashué supplied.

"War," Powell said. "War and the fury of General Clannaugh. You of all people should know what war with the Fist of the North looks like, so you can imagine why I won't have it on my streets. Don't look so angry, Mr. Kaine. László Dargis gets to die a hero, which is a better fate than that mess of a boy is destined for. Have you still got that bullet casing, Mr. Blackwood? The one you put in my hand when you made me a promise."

"I do, Mr. Iwan." Tashué shifted enough to reach into his pocket again. He had all his medals in there because he didn't know what the hell else to do with them, and he pulled the whole handful out. He dropped them on the table, the tangled mess making a massive clank. The White Shield fell halfway out of the scrap of cloth he'd wrapped it in, the enamel catching the low light from the oil lanterns. The rose gold from Myron Winter—the sight of it surprised him. The dream of throwing it into the bonfire was so vivid, it felt like a memory. He spread all the medals out, but the casing wasn't there. Back into his pocket—the smaller things had settled at the bottom: a few crowns, a stray match, a scrap of cloth from the medal he got for the wound that brought him under Rhodrishi's hands. And the casing, finally. It was cold and light, but all the weight of Hale's body was still attached to it. All the weight of Davik's body, too. He rested it on the table, open side up, like a tiny shot glass that he could pour all his fury into. "I haven't forgotten."

"I wondered how Bothain Clannaugh knew about the guns," Davik said slowly. So slowly. Each word dragged through the air like a razor over stubble, scraping everything, threatening to cut. "At first I thought it was Saeati who sold me out, but you know, I've learned how to spot it when he's being a lying shite. He gets all syrupy and charming, makes me want to knock his fucking teeth into the back of his throat. But he said he didn't, and I believed him because he looked as angry as I was." He clenched both his fists and then unclenched them, pressing them into the top of the table, spreading his fingers out and looking down at the scars and the tattoos. "So, what's this deal exactly? You must have made it before the bank robbery, because he knew about the guns before I even had them. I didn't take the bait with Coswyn or with Blackwood, so you skipped all the waiting and sold me to Clannaugh the day he got here."

"Don't sound so surprised," Powell muttered. "You would have done the same if you *could* make a deal with Clannaugh, but he wants your head so bad he won't meet with you, will he? So you tried to make your deals with Redbone instead, but she doesn't have the same weight in this country, does she? And she doesn't make deals for blood like Bothain Clannaugh does."

"You wanted the Blackwood boy out," Davik said. His eyes flicked to Tashué when he said it, a last desperate prayer in a room that was about to be his coffin. "I'm the only one who has all the pieces, and I'm the only one who can make it happen."

"You're a fucking liar," Powell grunted. "If you could have gotten that boy out, you would have done it by now. You think I'm stupid? You think I got to be the ripe old age of eighty-seven in *this* fucking quarter by being the sort of man who buys a load of cowshit for the price of diamonds? If you had any intention of getting that boy out, you would have made it happen. But instead, you're stringing me along with a promise you never intended to keep because you thought it would keep you alive longer, didn't you?"

"And I was right, wasn't I?" Davik snapped. "You left me alive this long to see if I'd really do it, to see if I would make it happen. You got Saeati involved to let me know you were watching, and then you sent me Coswyn and then Blackwood to let me know you were running out of patience."

"You said you were going to get him out tonight," Tashué said.

"You think I would have sent Irén in if I was just playing games?" Davik scoffed. "The Dargis twins are my fucking family. Aunt and uncle to my youngest children. I don't throw my family away for nothing."

"So where's my son?" Tashué snapped. "Why isn't he out yet?"

"I cancelled it," Davik said, the truth spilling out fast and desperate. "I sent her in to help him, but the next day, Vasska brought me you and Saeati. I knew, I fucking *knew* that one of you were going to off me the moment that boy set foot in the Bay. So I held the transfer until I could figure out what the fuck to do to save my own hide. And I was right, wasn't I? Why else would Iwan send me the man who killed Hale unless he wanted me to know that my time was running out? And now, here we are, the pair of you—what? Threatening me? Get him out or my head goes to Clannaugh? Fuck you. What do you want me to promise, hey? What can I say that buys me my life back from Clannaugh?"

Tashué had to admire the defiance in him. The fury, the spine it took to look Powell Iwan in the eye and tell him to fuck off.

"I'm well past threatening you now, Mr. Kaine," Powell said. "I'm just waiting for my delivery boy to show up so we can finish this."

"If you kill me," Davik said, looking Tashué in the eye, "what happens to the children? You think he's going to fight for them? Or is he going to sell me to Clannaugh and wash his hands of this whole mess? And when that ain't enough to call Clannaugh off, what's to stop him from selling you, too?"

Good fucking question. "You said you cancelled the transfer yourself," Tashué said. The weight of his gun had felt so right when it was in his hand. Felt like solutions. Fuck all these games. He needed to move, to go after Stella. But he was playing games with Davik, too, promising him Ffyanwy when Tashué knew Stella probably didn't want to see Davik even if she did come back. Didn't matter. He needed Jason. "You made me a deal, Davik. Jason for Ffyanwy."

"You're right," Davik said, forcing the words out in a rush. "I didn't know if I could trust you at all, but then you said the thing about Ffyanwy and I thought, fuck it. The big bastard is in this for real. So I tried to get everything going again, but the Authority won't sign the transfer order now. They said it's too dangerous with all the rumours about you and Saeati stirring up trouble in the Bay. I told them there isn't any trouble, but they said no. Not worth the risk of getting caught in the middle of riots. They're holding him and Irén in the Rift for now until things settle. But I'm going to figure something else out, I swear to you. That boy of yours knows how to break the suppression, and I want him to teach my people so we can get into the Breeding Program next. You and him and me, we can save those children together. Did you know that one of Keoh Gian Ly's children is still in creche? His name is Valen Gian Ly and his number is 1693-0239-8983."

Valen—the name bled Tashué empty again. One of Keoh's children. "Why didn't you tell me sooner?"

Davik shook his head. "That tin badge. I didn't know if I could trust you."

Fair.

The sound of Powell's doorbell made Davik flinch. All the colour drained out of his face.

"That'll be Saeati in time to help," Powell said, cocking his head toward the hallway. "Go let him in, would you?"

"Yes sir, Mr. Iwan," Adley said.

He opened the door to the hallway that led up the stairs, the hinges creaking as he pulled it closed behind him, the treads creaking even more as he made his slow way down.

"I made you a deal, Mr. Iwan," Tashué said, glancing at Powell. "I told you I would stand in Davik's gap when you had him killed, but I wanted my son. What plan do you have to get him out? I've wasted three and a half years waiting for something to happen, and I need to know my wait is over."

"Fucking backstabbing bastard," Davik hissed. "I let you into my *home*. I put you up with my family. I protected you when no one else would have you. You said you were fighting for the children, and I believed you."

Powell flicked his fingers at Tashué. "We'll deal with it later."

"No sir," Tashué said. "We'll deal with it now. What are you offering me?"

Powell huffed, throwing up a hand. "We'll make a deal with Clannaugh, then. Davik's head for the boy, and then the pair of you can fuck off out of this city for all the trouble you've caused me."

Tashué sighed. "I'm tired of making deals and playing games, Mr. Iwan. I just want my son."

"Good. Get rid of Kaine and then you'll have him."

"I can get him out tomorrow!" Davik shouted, slapping both hands on the table, standing up. "You hear me? Irén can get him out tomorrow, all I have to do is give the word."

Davik's Talent twisted through the air, one last desperate attempt to defend himself now that Adley wasn't in the room anymore.

Tashué picked up his gun, this weapon he'd carried for so long. It had so many bodies on it, so much death, but he knew with perfect clarity that this was the only death that meant anything.

Pulling the trigger was the easiest thing he'd ever done in his life. For Jason.

The gun bucked in his hand, and the bullet he fired took Powell Iwan in the chest and tore him wide open. He stood before his body knew it was dead, his chair falling back. Blood painted the wall behind him, the floor, the back of the chair—which had a hole blown through it where the bullet exited Powell's back and kept going. A step toward the door.

Another. And then he fell, face first toward the door, hands and feet twitching in that terrible death spasm.

Davik exhaled slowly, looking down at Powell's body. "Well, fuck."

Tashué sucked in a deep breath, watching all the wild layers of shock and victory flash across Davik's face. "I want my son, Davik."

A clatter on the stairs before Davik could answer—the sound like someone falling. And then a voice. Adley, maybe, bellowing with rage.

Tashué shot to his feet.

67

ISHMAEL

DAY 38

Don't do anything stupid.

That's what he wished he could tell Tashué as soon as he heard that Davik and Tashué had gone to see Powell. Don't do *anything* stupid.

Ishmael said the words again and again in his mind, like a prayer, an incantation, willing half a shred of sense through the universe so it would bury itself into Tashué's skull. And he sat in the back of the hired carriage, thanking the gods there was so many carriages in the Bay, while also wishing it would go faster. If Ishmael's knee wasn't so fucked, he would have run instead, all the way there in some miserable marathon across the quarter through the storm, but it wasn't possible. All he could do was sit and let the carriage rattle over the cobbles. And pray Tashué didn't do anything stupid this time.

The carriage let him off as close to the dry-docks as it could get; the only road wide enough was closed to public access to keep it free for deliveries. Ishmael pushed himself hard through the narrow alley, even though it hurt. His boots slithered on the cobbles, slick with water and ice, his knee giving a warning howl of pain each time, but he had to keep moving. Toward the eerie glow of it. The dry-docks, the warehouses around it, and the Hive were the only places in the Bay that had Talent-powered brights because the boosted productivity was worth it. Powell Iwan let the Authority set up exactly one station house in the Bay, let one single tinman come in to manage everyone who worked the Hive and the docks.

He wished he knew how long Tashué and Davik had been ahead of him. How long they'd been sitting in Powell's home. Maybe, if he was uncommonly fortunate, Davik and Tashué had taken forever to get across the city, too, and nothing had happened yet.

That fucking horse again—the one he rode out of the Dunnenbrahl. She was standing hobbled in one corner of the warehouse, saddle bags packed. One of the shiny Uhls sat in the scabbard hanging from the saddle horn, and Tashué's cavalry sabre hung down the other side. Was Tashué leaving? Where the fuck was he going?

Didn't matter—didn't have time to think about it, not now.

The door at the bottom of the stairs was locked, and he pulled hard on the bell cord to set it ringing as loudly as he could. This was the worst possible time to have a fucked knee. If he could scale the building, he would—climb right up to a window and let himself in so he didn't have to miss a single extra moment. What did Powell want? He was angry about the bank, maybe. Was Jason out yet? That was supposed to happen today—fuck. Ishmael needed to be there immediately, and every moment he stood in front of the locked door made his heart feel like it was going to burst. He should have brought his lock picking set to let himself in. How angry would Powell be if Ishmael broke down the door?

Footsteps on the stairs—thank fuck. He knew those heavy footsteps. Adley was coming down to let him in, which had to mean Powell was comfortable enough in the meeting to let Adley walk away. Hopefully that was a good sign. Gods, let it be a good sign.

Adley dragged the door open and stepped aside. "How's your leg?"

"It's shit," Ishmael muttered, shuffling into the narrow hallway. Stairs stretched in front of him, and he was tired just from looking up at them all—the inside of the warehouse was three stories, making for a long and miserable climb up. Not as long as miserable as it would have been to climb up the Hive. Small mercies or something. "What's the meeting?"

"Mr. Iwan is furious," Adley grunted. He hooked his arm in Ishmael's, helping him up the stairs. "The fucking bank. Clannaugh came himself to ask what happened."

Shit. That was exactly what Ishmael didn't want to hear.

Up, one step at a time. He could conquer three stories so long as he didn't let himself think about how many steps there were between him and the door at the top of the flight. There was only ever one at a time.

"Clannaugh was here?" Ishmael asked.

"Aye, this afternoon. He was going to have Patrollers sweep the Bay, but Mr. Iwan promised to deliver whoever was responsible. Guess you'll be putting his head in that box, hey?"

"That doesn't make sense," Ishmael said. "He's been waiting for an excuse to come bloody us up. Why walk away after he thinks we robbed a bank?"

The single gunshot clapped down through the hallway. Adley froze. One foot on the step above Ishmael. The scrape of chair legs on the floor above. A thump.

Adley's Talent spilt into the hallway, a storm rolling in so suddenly Ishmael could taste it in the air. His fist closed around Ishmael's arm so hard it sent a jolt of pain, so hard it was going to leave a bruise for sure.

"What did you do?" Adley snarled. "You planned this with Black-wood and Kaine?"

Ishmael shook his head. "Planned *what?*"

Adley's Talent pushed into Ishmael's chest, a pressure that made it impossible to breathe. Burning in his very sinew like a virus that made him feverish and nauseated. "You traitorous piece of shit, you took Kaine's side after everything Mr. Iwan did for you?"

Instinct made him move faster than he could think—best way to kill someone with Talent was to drop them so fast they didn't have the chance to use their abilities. His hand went for his stiletto—skinny and almost delicate and deadly sharp. He flicked the sheath away and swung up in a death arc that ran the viciously sharp point of the blade across Adley's throat. Blood came in a hot, sticky spray, splattering Ishmael's face. Adley made that gurgling, wet bellow as air whistled through the blood spilling into his trachea.

Adley's hands went to his throat. Talent swirled so thick in the air Ishmael could taste it even over the iron tang of blood. His hands grasped, twitching, clinging to life. His knees went weak, and he grabbed Ishmael's arm. Adley fell. Ishmael tried to catch himself, but as soon as his weight hit his bad leg, the awkward angle saw his kneecap pop out of place like it kept threatening. Ishmael gave a strangled gasp-shout, and he went down with Adley, the pair of them tumbling down the stairs in a vicious tangle of limbs. Each step tried to catch Ishmael but failed, and so the wooden tread slammed into him, grinding against bone and the soft places, pain flaring everywhere. And Adley's blood, spilling all over him, hot as it soaked into Ishmael's clothes. But there wasn't enough of it. Ishmael had opened enough throats in his life to know the bastard wasn't bleeding fast enough.

They hit the bottom, tumbled into the hallway, and Adley still had him. His hands spasmed on Ishmael's clothes. Adley was still breathing, still moving. Ishmael shoved him away, dragging himself across the floor —the stiletto was at the end of the hallway, gleaming in the faint light that came in the crack under the door. He tried to get up on his hands and knees, but his fucking knee—the pain robbed the air right out of his lungs and he collapsed back down, push-dragging himself with his good leg and both hands. Adley, behind him, breathing, coughing, wheezing, a bellow of rage building with every breath he took. Ishmael's fingers touched the leather of the stiletto's hilt—so close—Adley grabbed him by the foot and dragged him back. The pressure made Ishmael's kneecap jump back into its proper place, the strange sensation of pain and relief dragging some mix of laughter and a shout out of him. He twisted to face Adley, swinging up with a fist, knuckles catching Adley's jaw. Blood and spit leaked out of Adley's mouth, teeth red as fury made him bite the air. His throat wasn't even fucking bleeding anymore—the line had healed, pulling closed enough to make a line of crusty scab and angry pink scar tissue under all that blood.

Adley's big fist came down, crashing against the side of Ishmael's head, sending his senses swimming. He tried to twist away, but Adley's knees pinned him in place, and Adley hit him again. So hard Ishmael's head crashed against the wall. And that vicious ugly Talent was back, squeezing Ishmael's whole body, the pressure so heavy his bones screamed. He was going to fucking die even though he'd cut Adley's throat. He twisted again, trying to throw Adley off him, but Adley's weight wouldn't budge. Adley's fist came down again and the whole world melted. Hard to grasp.

Ishmael reached up, fight or die. The almost-scar was weak from the fast healing. Ishmael dragged his nails across it, ripping, tearing. Blood came again, slow at first. A trickle. Harder, fight harder or die—fingers probing, tearing, ripping at scar tissue, hot and slick beneath his fingers. Adley tried to grab for Ishmael's hands, but his fingers were slick with his own blood, and they spasmed on Ishmael's wrists like he couldn't quite control them.

Flesh parted finally and Ishmael could feel hard cartilage beneath his fingertips. Adley screamed, the sound like thunder rolling across Ishmael's senses, the vibration rattling his throat. Ishmael's fingers slid through muscle, reopening the wound, tearing at the seam the scar made until he found the artery and that tissue was as delicate as everything else Adley had healed and it opened beneath Ishmael's nails and released a downpour.

Blood hit Ishmael's face, his eyes—he couldn't see. He didn't need to see. He kept clawing at Adley's throat. He could feel the skin trying to knit even as his fingers tore new things open. He could feel the desperate swirl of Adley's Talent, hotter than the blood, trying to close it up again. But Ishmael's hands kept scrabbling, ripping, even though his brain was sending white bolts across the back of his eyelids because he still couldn't breathe. He was going to pass out. Adley's Talent was going to crush his bones like Tashué had done to those Regulation Officers. Blood in his mouth and in his eyes. They were going to die together, Ishmael coated in Adley's blood but his body destroyed under all that Talent. Something snapped, somewhere in Ishmael's chest—a rib, the pain so vicious it made him gag, but the spasm of his muscles made the pain flare hotter.

The door at the top of the stairs swung open, spilling light down the steps. Enough light to show Adley listing to one side, bleeding faster than he could close the wound. Footsteps on the stairs. Adley's mouth moved, ever so slightly, his jaw working like he was still chewing on his lingering rage, his fingers reaching for his throat again.

The vicious roar of gunfire. Just one shot, the light of it flashing in the stairwell like lightning. Adley's head popped, splattering the hallway with bone and gore.

Adley's Talent finally let go, but his body slumped down onto Ishmael, all that weight landing on Ishmael's chest. The pain made him want to scream, but his lungs were too empty, too angry, too frozen.

Tashué, on the stairs. He came down fast, grabbing Adley by the coat and shoving the corpse off Ishmael. He grabbed Ishmael's arm, trying to pull him up. Breathe. One breath and then another, even though it hurt so fucking much. But at least he could fucking breathe—and choke on Adley's blood, and gag on the taste of it, so much of it, hot in his mouth. He spat. Pain ripped through his chest. He tried to stand as Tashué pulled him up, but his knee refused to take his weight. He fell. Tashué caught him by both arms, before he hit the stairs. Tashué sank down to the steps, sitting so Ishmael could go down gently. Tashué's Talent swirled between them, familiar and soothing, rolling through Ishmael, searching. A big hand swiped over Ishmael's face to clean some of the blood away.

"Is any of it yours?"

Ishmael shook his head, but the movement sent dizziness sweeping through him. He was falling again, but there was nowhere for him to fall —nausea ate through him fast, and he gagged again, gagged and choked on the scream that tried to rattle its way up his throat because his ribs hurt so much.

A shadow at the top of the stairs, the figure of a person spilling down the treads. Footsteps, coming down. Powell wouldn't come to look at violence. He wouldn't care.

"Well, shit," Davik said. "Made another mess, hey?"

If it weren't for the fact that Ishmael couldn't speak, that his whole body was spasming with too much pain for him to even process it all, that he was choking on his twisting dizziness, that all he wanted to do was close his eyes and sleep away this moment until he was healed again, even if that took weeks, he would have called Tashué a fucking idiot.

"What are we going to do about Adley?" Davik asked, easing down the stairs, the treads creaking with each step.

"Make sure the door is locked. I don't fucking know. Here." Tashué held up his revolver as Davik passed them. "I'll get Ishmael upstairs, get him sorted enough to walk, and then we'll get out of here. If anyone comes to ask too many questions, shoot them in the face."

"Sure thing, General Guinne."

"That's what you're calling me, now?" Tashué grunted. He levered himself to his feet and dragged Ishmael up. "General?"

"Aye, well, if you kill the most powerful crime lord in the city for me, I think that earns you a battlefield promotion. How many bullets in this cannon of yours?"

"Six," Tashué said. "You've got four left."

"Great. Make it fast, hey?"

What the fuck did you do? What the fuck did you do? Ishmael willed the words through his head over and over again, hoping Tashué's Talent would let him see the words like a brand across his mind. *What the* fuck *did you do?*

Blood dripped from the top step, a soft *patpatpat* that Ishmael could only hear as the panic subsided. His heart hammered in time with the drip, the sticky mess. Up to the top of the stairs, and the lights inside the apartment shone on Powell's body. The old man had taken the bullet to the chest, and it ripped him open. He must have stood, tried to step away, before he fell again—his chair was tipped over, and his body pointed away from the table, like he'd been trying to run for the door.

"He wanted me to kill Davik," Tashué said. He dragged a chair from the table and guided Ishmael toward it so Ishmael could sink down into it. "Like I owe him anything when all he's done is make me empty promises."

"Fuck," Ishmael breathed. It hurt to talk, like the word rattled around his injuries. "Tashué—fuck."

"Davik said he can get Jason out," Tashué said. He dropped to his knees in front of Ishmael, and his Talent pressed against everything, like a crushing hug that Ishmael could feel in the core of him. He pushed Ishmael's trouser leg up like he was trying to see Ishmael's knee, but the wool was too tight, too soggy with blood. "And the children, Ishmael. Powell didn't care. So, I made a choice. Davik is going to get Jason, and I'm going to get Stella back so we can get around Clannaugh."

Ishmael caught Tashué's hands, holding him still. "We don't have time." Fuck, it hurt to talk. He swallowed, but the pressure lingered, like Adley's hands were still there. "I told Illea to be ready for a head. I thought it was going to be Davik, but—" He was falling again. So dizzy that the whole world was trying to throw him off.

Tashué grabbed him by the shoulders, holding him in his chair. "We're going to make time. You're not dying on me, not now."

"No, listen—we have to take his head."

Tashué shook his head slowly. Not a denial, judging by the look on his face, just bafflement. "Why his head?"

"So we can blame Clannaugh. We have to make it look like he came at us first and anything that happens next is us defending ourselves. Make it look like retribution for the Rhydderch article."

Tashué turned to look at Powell, at his staring eyes, frozen by death in a moment of abject panic and pain, at his stiff, curled hands and the gaping maw where his back used to be, gone now because the large calibre bullet ripped him to shreds on the way out. "Sure. But I'm helping you, first."

Ishmael tried to shake his head, but that dragged the nausea back up. He leaned over, and his stomach clenched and this time the vomit came, thick and sludgy with blood he'd swallowed, or was that his blood? He couldn't even tell—gods, it hurt so fucking much. But Tashué had him, held him, kept him in the chair so he didn't fall into his own vomit. And then when the heaving passed, Tashué's Talent rolled through him, comforting at first and then pain so vicious and ugly that Ishmael saw white.

And then black—

And then nothing.

———

P owell's body was a dark shadow in the corner of Ishmael's vision. Tashué's face, hovering over him.

"We're going," Tashué said. His voice came to Ishmael distantly, like Ishmael's ears were stuffed with cotton. Or maybe his whole head was buzzing, drowning out the sound of Tashué's voice. "Are you ready?"

Ishmael groaned, blinking a few times to try to clear his eyes of the haze. Things were blurry—or as that because it was dark? He tried to turn his head to see Powell, but pain flared in his neck, in his shoulders. Fucking everything hurt. "The head—did you get the head?"

"You were serious," Tashué said, the words escaping with a bit of a laugh. The words were so light, dancing in the air, like it was all a big joke.

"Yes I was fucking serious," Ishmael breathed, fury jumping to life, burning over the pain. "I told you, we need it—"

"Yeah, sure, I got it," Tashué said. Why did he sound relieved? "Davik's going to bring it out, because I need my hands to carry *you*. I'm glad you weren't joking."

"Tashué, what the fuck? Why the fuck would I joke about you cutting off someone's head?"

"I don't know," Tashué said, and he was laughing again. He put his hands on Ishmael's shoulders and helped Ishmael shift slowly. "It's been a weird fucking week, alright? Let's go, soldier, on your feet."

Down the stairs. Gods it was ugly, the pain pushing him down into the haze again, threatening to make him pass out. It would be easier if he passed out. Nausea and blood and dizziness and that horrible smell of death. He didn't dare put any weight on his bad leg, so he braced himself against the wall with one hand and held on to Tashué with the other and hopped down one step at a time. And then Davik behind them, carrying a crate with an urn in it, and the vague shape of what could have been a head, wrapped in a pillow case.

"That fucking urn again," Ishmael muttered.

"Yeah," Tashué said. "Keoh's. Powell found it, apparently. Gave it back to me."

"I'm starting to think Keoh's urn is bad luck."

Tashué shrugged. "She might agree with you. Or maybe I'm bad luck."

"Yeah," Ishmael gasped, hopping down another step, "no shit."

Davik squeezed past them, half-leaping over Adley's body. Tashué stepped right on Adley's back, lifting Ishmael over so Ishmael didn't slip in all the gore on the wood floor. Davik kicked the door open, and then they were out into the open warehouse. Davik shifted his grip on the crate so that he held it with one hand, then ducked his shoulder under Ishmael's other arm to help take his weight. They made better time like that, moving at a fast clip, Ishmael hanging on to both of them. And the pressure on his ribs was agony, but it didn't matter, they had to keep moving.

"I gotta get across the river," Ishmael breathed. "I gotta get the head to Wolfe, tell him to deliver it to Clannaugh tomorrow—"

"Are you out of your mind?" Davik interrupted. "You can't go to Highfield—do I need to remind you that you're a wanted fucking man, Saeati?"

Ishmael shook his head. He wished he could shake the thick cotton feeling right out of his skull, but moving that much made his head spin. He was going to be sick again. "I gotta get the head across the river. You and Vasska—you have to hold the Bay together. Vasska has to think it was Clannaugh, or he'll try to move against you—you can't kill him, Davik."

"Right, sure, I won't touch Vasska Czarny," Davik said.

"No, you're not listening," Ishmael snapped. Made his head *throb*, raising his voice like that, but Davik had to listen. "If he thinks you did it, we're fucked. I have to get it across the river, to Wolfe." But fuck, Wolfe was under house arrest, that's what Eirdis said—did that mean Clannaugh had guards inside the house, or just outside? Fuck—they were almost out of the warehouse, but he stopped trying to keep up, letting his good leg slide across the floor. "Wait, I can't—put me down a second let me figure out—I need to think—"

"Alright, Ishmael," Tashué said. At least he wasn't laughing anymore. For a moment, Ishmael thought he'd snapped, and he didn't want to imagine what Tashué would be like if all that restraint in him shattered. "Just a second and then we need to go."

Tashué maneuvered Ishmael over to a pile of boxes, and Ishmael sagged against them. His heart hammered with the exhaustion, the wild fear, the agony—he had to fight for each breath, filling his lungs as slow as possible or he'd start hyperventilating with all the pain. He pressed his hands against his ribcage, the side that hurt the most, the side where he thought he heard something snap, like Adley's Talent had started to crush him. His mouth was sour with blood and vomit, making breathing even harder. He tried not to think about all the ways a broken rib could really fuck him—sometimes they popped lungs, punctured organs—but if it was that bad, surely he'd know it? Or at least Tashué would, if he'd tried to help. He didn't have time to worry about himself. He was conscious. It had to be a good sign. So he had to *think*. But thinking made the dizziness worse.

"I can't go to Wolfe's because Clannaugh put him under house arrest —fuck," he said, pushing the words out. If he started talking, maybe it would help him focus. "We need to get the head across the river— someone needs to put it in Clannaugh's hands—we need people see him get it so he can't deny it."

"Why don't we send it with a courier?" Davik asked. "Wrap it all up in packing paper, pay someone to deliver it."

Ishmael laughed, and it made the pain flare. He then groaned, pressing his hands harder against his chest, wishing the pressure would make it hurt less. Gods, he should have let Deri's healer teach him how to use Talent. He could have really used the ability to see his own wounds right now, to at least know if he was dying or not. "Great minds think alike, but no—I told Mallory and Illea to expect your head. They need to know it's going to be Powell. I need them to help make it worse, need them to blame Myron and Rainer—Illea. We'll take it to Illea. She needs to sell it as Clannaugh's idea."

"So you were really going to kill me, hey?" Davik asked.

Ishmael looked up at him, at the long shadows around his head. The bright glowed softly. Did that mean there was a brightman around some-where? That someone was coming? "Yeah, Davik. Of course I was. I was going to let Powell Iwan try to negotiate a peace with Clannaugh over your head, and while Clannaugh was arguing with Powell, I was going to rip him apart. But Tashué doesn't *fucking* listen to me when I tell him not to do anything stupid, and it saved your life. So now we're all stuck on the same fucking side. You wanna argue about it, or do you want me to cover your ass so you can keep up the good fight. For the children, remember?"

"Are you really going to cover my ass, or are you going to sell me to Clannaugh?" Davik asked. "Is that why you're so anxious to get to the rich side? So you can tell him where I am?"

Ishmael shook his head. The world tilted. "I can't sell you to Clannaugh, not now. Vasska can't hold the Bay alone."

He wasn't even sure if he said the words out loud or if he only thought them. His ears buzzed. Thick and high pitched. Was anyone speaking? Or had the whole city gone still and silent?

"No more arguing," Tashué said. Hearing his voice was a relief. "We need to get you back to the club. Your head's getting worse."

"Vasska's at the club," Davik said. "Isn't that what you said? He's with Tei—do we want him to see us now?"

"We'll tell him what happened, except we'll say we arrived too late. Tell him we found Ishmael and Adley at the bottom of the stairs, left for dead. So we brought Ishmael back."

Davik didn't answer. The moment stretched. Ishmael's pulse pounded in his ears, his skull aching with every beat.

"Davik, if I let him kill you, I can't get Jason," Tashué said. "That's all I want. I want my son and then I'll go. Besides, he's in shit shape. What's he going to do?"

"Right," Davik said. He pushed the crate into Tashué's hand. "I'll get a carriage. Wait here, General."

"Stop calling me General," Tashué muttered.

"It's my Army," Davik said. "I get to promote you as I see fit."

"It's not a fucking joke, Davik."

"Trust me, I am intimately aware how extremely unfunny this whole fucking situation is," Davik snapped, but his voice dropped to a whisper-hiss that drilled into Ishmael's aching skull. "But you picked a side, and now you're delivering a fucking war trophy to Bothain Clannaugh. I remember *vividly* how bad my life got the last time Bothain Clannaugh had a reason to start shooting people, so I say we're a real fucking army now. And you're the one I've got with the Academy education, so you're my General now."

"Wait," Ishmael said. "We can't bring the head to the club if Vasska's there."

"We'll drop it off at the *Bucket*, then. They'll help."

Maisie's letter was ruined. Thank the gods he'd read it this time. It seemed so innocent, incongruous with Powell's head in his lap, stuffed in a pillow case—except half the reason it was ruined was because it was drenched with Adley's blood so maybe not so innocent at all. So, he could understand why Tashué had been laughing before. It was all so fucking absurd that it hardly seemed real. Ishmael turned the letter toward the light, trying to peel the paper off the photograph, but it was tearing, sticky and tacky with blood. He could just about see the details in his mind's eye. His daughter. And Aelwyd Rhydderch. What secrets did Aelwyd know about her sister's husband?

"I wish I could have talked to her," Ishmael said. "Anyone from the Rhydderch family. I bet they all have plenty to say about Bothain fucking Clannaugh. I need to go to White Crown. I should have gone yesterday, as soon as I heard Clannaugh was sending shit to the Queen. Where's Stella, Tashué? Where did she go? Could you reach her in a few days? Convince her to come back?"

"I'm going to find her," Tashué said. "You were right. We're all just pieces of it, fighting for something bigger. But first, you need to see a healer. We'll go from there."

Ishmael nodded—and regretted it. Gods save him, he was going to be sick again.

Davik came back into the warehouse, wet with the rain.

"He's getting worse," Tashué said. "It's getting bad fast."

"Aye," Davik said. "All the more reason to hurry."

Tashué led his horse out, and Davik helped Ishmael limp toward the carriage. For the first time in his memory, Ishmael was grateful for the shit weather. With all the rain and sleet, Ishmael probably looked like he was staggering around the city drunk after the boxing match.

The nausea clawed its way up his throat, and he squeezed his eyes shut. As if that would help. Why did it feel like his head was getting worse? The rattle of the carriage, maybe. The way it shook him so it felt like he was spinning faster and faster. When had they started moving?

"Ishmael," Tashué said. "Can you hear me?"

Ishmael grunted. "You're as loud as ever, Captain."

"We're taking you to the hospital," Davik said. "Your head is proper fucked, isn't it? Worse than László can handle."

"We can deliver the head to any of them," Ishmael said. "Rainer,

Myron, Clannaugh—it doesn't matter who. So long as people see them opening it. Vasska can't think it was us, or we're fucked."

"Sure, Ishmael. We've got it. You're not allowed to die, you hear me?" Tashué's voice was strained. And far away. Like Ishmael was under water. But when he opened his eyes, he was still sitting up in the carriage. "Don't do anything stupid like you keep telling me."

Even as he tried to curse Tashué for everything that had become of them since the day they were arrested, he also knew half the blame lay at his feet. People tried to tell him. People tried to warn him that a storm was coming, but he was so busy feeling sorry for himself that he'd missed his chance to manage the chaos.

The carriage driver dropped them behind the hospital. In the same courtyard where all those carriages milled around the day of the hospital opening. The day Bothain arrived and put Deri's letter in Ishmael's hand. The day Tashué fucked everything. Ishmael tried to follow Tashué, but something tilted inside his skull, the dizziness roaring back as soon as he stood. Tilted and then he was falling. Tashué caught him before he hit the ground. His chest seized and tried to vomit, but there was nothing left in his stomach but stringy blood and bile.

"Lie down," Tashué said. "Ishmael, just lie down."

Ishmael shook his head. He wanted to say there was no where to lie down—if he went down in the street, he'd never get back up again. Everything hurt so fucking much, and the rain was so ugly. But there was a bench. Why was there a bench in the street?

"He must be in a bad way," Davik said. "He hasn't said something obnoxious for a whole half hour."

"He's doing it for the sympathy," Tashué said, but his voice was strained with worry. "He loved all the attention last time, so he's going in for a second act."

"He would."

He blinked a few times—fire. No, light. Glowing brights and a long ward and hospital beds with crisp white linens, waiting for him. Fuck—how much time had he lost? Somehow Tashué had gotten him up to Wolfe's hospital but he didn't remember it.

"Hey," Tashué said. "They're going to give you some morphine. It's going to ease the pain and then they're going to help you."

Tashué's face, hovering in front of Ishmael's vision. There was blood in his beard. Ishmael hadn't noticed it before. He wondered if it was

Powell's blood or Adley's—or someone else's. So many chunks he didn't remember.

"Sir," someone said. "Can you hear me?"

"No," Ishmael said. He lifted a hand, resting it on Tashué's shoulder. Tried to push him away, but Ishmael couldn't muster the coordination. "No morphine. I need to see the Queen—I need to tell her—"

He tried to push the morphine away—he hated morphine. The needle was big and unforgiving, and the effects were so strong. It wasn't like riding the smoke. He had something to say except he couldn't remember what. Something important. He needed to see the Queen, except he couldn't remember why.

Someone grabbed Ishmael's arm so hard it hurt. Pinned it against the mattress, put so much pressure on the joint that the pain rattled all the way up to Ishmael's rib. A sound, like an animal caught in a trap—it was him.

The needle broke skin. The hot rush of morphine flooded his whole body.

He couldn't grasp the moments tightly enough. Just when he knew what was happening, the world seemed to shift and melt into a new reality and he couldn't remember the time between.

Water, over his face. Washing blood from his hair, splattering on the floor. He pressed his hands against the firm mattress below him, clinging to the sheets because if he let go, he was sure he would fall. Fall right down into the centre of the world and never come back up.

After everything he did for you—

He wanted to turn to Tashué and... He didn't know what. Screaming felt too passionate. He wasn't exactly close to Powell. It wasn't like family, like Wolfe or the people who worked at his watch shop, people he loved but didn't know how to talk to them, so he avoided them. Powell took care of him only because Powell could use him.

But when he opened his eyes, Tashué was gone. Faces he didn't know gathered around him.

"Just relax, sir. We're going to help."

"I need to see the Queen," Ishmael said.

If only he could remember why.

68

JASON
DAY 39

The morphine came through him slowly, unfolding so gently he didn't notice right away. It chipped the edges off his pain, so none of it held him so sharply or so intently. It rippled through his anxiety, breaking it into smaller pieces that were easier to ignore. Even the ache in the bone started to drift away. He was aware of it, but it was strangely distant. Like shadows, sitting in the fibre that made him.

If this was what opium felt like, it was no wonder his mother couldn't stop smoking.

He was lucid enough to know the thought *should* have made him sad and angry, but the morphine kept the knowledge from connecting to the shape of any emotions. It was just a thing that drifted to his mind, weightless.

He sat on the floor because there was nowhere else to sit. The cell was so narrow he could touch both walls at once. An oil lamp spat foul smelling smoke and inconsistent light down the hallway. None of it mattered. They were flat, uninteresting facts.

He stared down at the other two tablets for a while, small and white in his palm. He was tempted to take them both. If one tablet made him feel light and far away from his pain, maybe the other two would make him feel something like good. Maybe he would float up so high from all the things that were trying to crush him. A few hours of perfect escape.

It didn't seem right that the healer had given him enough morphine to get high but not enough to die if he wanted to. Forcing him to stay alive when there was nothing for him was a fresh layer of cruelty. One more thing he didn't have any control over.

He sighed, reaching into his pockets. His mother's letters were ruined, like he'd worried. He wasn't out in that rain long, but it was the hard kind of rain that soaked you to the bone in moments. The ink was running into the paper, and the paper itself was trying to disintegrate— especially the older ones he'd been hanging on to for a while. The smell of her was gone. He wondered what that smell was that made him think so clearly of her. Was it opium? Sweet and a little smoky, sunk into her identity. Changing her layer by layer. The story his father told him rattled around his skull—she broke a man's arm with her Talent, crushing the bone for money to buy more opium. The letters told a different story of their time in Roa, painted a vision of peace and comfort and belonging. Which version was true? His father's version or his mother's?

Was it possible for both things to be true?

Maybe she felt loved there in a way she never had before, but maybe the opium ate into her soul because she was trying to escape the things she was running from when she took Jason and left Yaelsmuir.

Rattle of metal bars—Jason dragged his eyes open against all the weight of the morphine. Irén, down the hall, in another cell. When had she arrived? How long had he been down here? He wasn't sure. She stood with her hands on the bars of her cell, shaking them. Making that rattle. And there was so much blood, all over her, matted in her hair and pooled in the seams of her clothes. Settled in the chips on her shoulders like it would fill in those gaps and make her more compliant.

"It was supposed to be today," she said. Wild and desperate and angry. How did she have so much energy left? "They were supposed to move us out of here fucking *today*. What the fuck happened?"

"I told you," Jason grunted. "I told you it's all shit. Davik Kaine is nobody here. Maybe he can get away with shit in the Bay, but this is the Rift. It's a different fucking world."

"No, it's fine," Irén said. "We can get out. All we have to do is get to the boat, and then I can get us across the river."

"How are we supposed to get out?" Jason asked. "You have a key?"

"That's not fucking helpful!" Irén snapped.

Jason shifted slowly, rolling away from her. He almost felt sorry for her and the way the panic had to be setting in. The realization that Davik Kaine's word meant fucking nothing in here. The confidence crumbling away like mortar between the bricks of her identity until parts of her were at risk of tumbling out of place. Except he was too tired and too sore and too sick of it all to spare her that much emotion. Maybe later, when the morphine wore off, he'd resent her for the mess she'd made. But for now, drifting. A little bit like freedom. If his body was forever stuck in the Rift, at least his mind could float away. All the resentment and anger and pain they imposed on him couldn't reach him through his morphine shield.

Rattling bars again—Irén couldn't be still. She held both bars so hard she looked like she was honestly trying to rip her cell door right out of the wall. But it was useless.

"When do you admit that this is your fault?" Jason asked.

Irén laughed, but it was a hard, angry sound. "What the fuck is that supposed to mean?"

"I told you," Jason said. "I told you things work a certain way around here. We don't fuck with the proxies because they get to kill us. It's that simple. If you didn't pick a fight with Verrit, we would still be in the regular room and maybe we could figure out a way out of here, but no. You couldn't let me handle it, and now we're locked up here."

"Blaming me because I stood up for you sure is a funny way around blaming the actual people responsible," Irén scoffed. "You know, all the people who stand on our necks because we have Talent. The guards. The proxies. The fucking Authority for putting us in here in the first place."

"Don't worry, I'm still plenty fucking angry at them," Jason muttered. But he didn't feel angry. It was a strange, unexpected gift from the morphine. No anger, just a distant awareness of it. No fear of death or the pain of it. Simply an existence. "But we didn't have to get the shit kicked out of us, and we didn't have to get locked down here. If you'd listened to me—"

"No!" Irén snapped. "Fuck you! Dav sent me in here to help you because you're special or something. He's got it in his head that you're going to help us fight, like you're the North Star risen again! He thought since you broke suppression, you must be something incredible—so imagine my disappointment when you're another whipped dog, skulking around here with your tail between your legs, snivelling and grovelling for the Authority. And then you blame *me* when I tried to help you stand up for yourself? I don't fucking think so."

Jason laughed. The sound bubbled up out of him like water from a spring, dragging the silt of his own emotions into the current. "I don't need your help to stand up for myself, Irén. I've been standing up to these people for three and a half years, and it got me nothing. Fucking nothing but broken bones. Tell me what is so heroic about standing when they keep chipping parts away? What's the point?"

"The point is we fight until there's nothing left to hope for, and then we keep fighting anyway," Irén said. "Because if we lie down and let them walk across our backs, they win. They crush out everything, one piece at a time, and then it's like we never existed at all. Where's your anger? Where's your fury? Jason, for fuck's sake, why are you giving up!"

Jason rose to his knees, putting his hands on the bars. The cold iron dragged something hot out of him, cut through the morphine. Or had he been down here long enough that it was wearing off? "It must be really nice to go through life so convinced in your own superiority that you get to turn up your nose at people who are *only* surviving. As if that makes me less than you. Let me tell you, it's easy to stand when there's people around you to hold you up. It's easy to be ferocious when you can count on Davik Kaine and his giant fucking ego. But in here, there's no one but me. I'm fucking alone. I stood *alone* and they pulled little pieces off me, layer by layer. So yeah, I gave up. I let Verrit take what he wanted because I didn't want to die in here when I thought the Authority had killed my father, just like they killed my mother. I didn't think I could survive another beating, but I got one anyway thanks to you. You can't help me, so you don't get to judge me. Not when you wouldn't survive a week in here."

"But you did survive," Irén said. "And you aren't alone. You weren't before, and you aren't now. You're in a prison with hundreds of people. If ever the lot of us stopped letting them make us smaller, we would take this place over in a single night. We outnumber them so badly, they had to turn us against each other. Choosing the cruelest, most vicious proxies they could find and giving them power over us—that's how they win. They turn us against our own people and we're so convinced that we're alone and worthless that they keep stuffing more and more of us into prisons or into compliance. That's what I've been trying to tell you. We aren't alone, Jason. We're an army. We need to fight together!"

"How?" Jason snapped again. He hit his palms against the bars and the door gave a more satisfying rattle than when he kicked it. "How, Irén? How do we fight when we're locked up?"

"You broke suppression once," Irén said. "Can't you do it again?"

Jason shook his head. Made him spin a little, off to one side. He rested his cheek against the cold stone and let his eyes close again. "I can't."

"Yes, you can. Jason!"

"No, you don't understand—I *can't*. They're children. That's what I was trying to tell you. They're children, and it hurt them when I broke through. One of them is dying. I wanted to get to them and help them somehow, but then you started the fucking fight with Verrit, and I couldn't get to them anymore."

"So you'll let us rot down here because you don't want to fight anymore?"

Jason dragged his eyes open, glaring at her across the hall. "I'm sorry, are you saying that I should hurt children to save us? Tainted children, who didn't ask to be here? Fuck them, right, so long as we can keep fighting?"

She hit her bars again, making the door rattle. "I didn't say that!"

"Then what did you say? Explain it to me like I'm a fucking idiot!"

Irén shook her head, taking a step back from the bars. Once she was deeper in her cell, he couldn't see her anymore, but her boots clunked on her floor as she paced. In circles, probably, because he caught sight of her shoulder passing near her door and then it was gone. Again, again, again. And then she was back, hands gripping the iron. "How did you find out about them? The children. Did you see them?"

"I heard them. I was downstairs in the food cellar, and they spoke to me through Talent. They asked for my help. One of them is sick—her Talent is killing her because it's too strong, and she doesn't know how to stop. I wanted to find them but..."

"Yeah, but I fucked up, and now we're here," Irén huffed. "I got it. How did you speak to them?"

"They connected to me with Talent. I can't connect to them while I have the headache. I can't feel them at all."

"Why could you feel your Talent in the basement but not here?"

"There was a gap down there," Jason said. "Where the one section was shrinking so it didn't touch the other section. That's what they call each other—Section One, Section Two, Section Three, Section Four."

Irén sighed, and her pacing went quiet. "Fuck this place."

"Yeah," Jason said. "That's what I've been saying."

He closed his eyes, resting his forehead against the bars. The morphine was definitely wearing off—the pains came rolling back, building into a steady ache. He'd lost track of the morphine tablets. They weren't in his hand anymore. Where had he put them?

He dragged his eyes open, looking down at the floor. There, with his mother's ruined letters, the two white tablets sat in the centre of his cell. But now that he was angry again, the idea of giving that emotion up to the void of numbness scared him. The anger was all he had.

"Do you feel that?" Irén asked.

Jason turned to Irén, leaning against his bars to see her. "Feel what?"

"The suppression—it's fading."

Jason shook his head, shooting to his feet. "No! I wanted to help her!"

You said you would come back.

The words were so quiet he could barely grasp them, and yet the familiarity of them rent his chest open with fresh pain. Fresh guilt.

"I'm sorry! I couldn't go downstairs—I'm sorry."

I'm scared.

"Yeah," Jason breathed. "I'm scared, too."

"Are you talking to the child?" Irén asked.

Section Three says we never should have trusted you. But I don't want to die. I'm scared.

Jason tried to reach for his Talent, to summon the strength he knew he had. But it caught in that vise, making his headache sear harder, meaner.

You can't use your Talent, or they'll know we broke again.

"Then how am I supposed to help you? Let me help you!"

The vise eased, just a little. The pain in his skull, ever present, faded to a thin screen, letting a bit of his Talent leak through. He put his hand on the lock on his cell door, and he could see it, all the internal pieces. Simple, really, the way it worked. A few things that moved and the bolt that held it in place. It only took a casual flex of his abilities, and he could feel the whole thing move, even though the concentration made his head hurt.

The suppression flared back to life.

But his lock was open.

He pushed on his door, and the hinges squealed and he could step out into the hall like the door was no boundary at all. This was why the Authority was so desperate to convince everyone that Talent was a filthy, dangerous thing, that tainted people couldn't be trusted. Because the

whole world sat in the palm of their hands. Walls and locks and founda-
tions were but slim suggestions to him. The illusion of a boundary.

I'm scared, the child said again. *I was here when the old Section One died. I
felt it. It's terrible. I don't want to die!*

"I'm coming," Jason said. "I'm going to find you, and then I'm taking
you out of here."

He stopped to grab his mother's letters. Stupid, maybe, but it was all
he had of her. The paper crumpled too easily in his hands, and he
stuffed it in his pockets anyway. Maybe later, if he got out of this safely,
he could dry them out and preserve some of her words. The morphine
tablets, too. He grabbed them by some instinct because they were on the
floor with the letters. Out into the hall. The morphine must have had
him a little because his feet felt so far away, dragging even though he was
trying to hurry. Hard to control. Not nearly as fast as he wished they
would move. Or maybe that was the pain from the beating, grinding in
his joints. It was hard to walk. His feet felt so heavy. The toe of his boot
caught a seam in the stone floor. He staggered, falling again—he caught
himself on the wall, his hands stinging at the impact.

Nausea rolled through him again. Maybe the rush of fear and hope
were at war in his stomach. But his stomach was empty—he'd puked up
his breakfast and he hadn't eaten since. What time was it now? Was it
even the same day? The night after? He couldn't tell. It was so dark
down here, he couldn't tell how much time had passed. Maybe the
morphine was still echoing through his body, making him dizzy and dull
and too clumsy to walk. Stupid, this was stupid.

Footsteps in the hallway.

"Shit!" Irén breathed. "Jason, get me out too!"

Jason stopped at Irén's door. She smelled like blood and rain and
stale sweat, and her eyes glittered in the bad lamp light. He put his hand
on the lock again but his Talent caught on the horrible suppression, the
vise squeezing.

"Let me go," Jason said. His voice echoed, thin and desperate, in the
empty hall. He hated how small he sounded, how scared. All he ever
wanted was to be mountainous like his father, an immovable force. But
instead, he was small and scared and tired. "Let me use my Talent so we
can help you!"

I can't let go, or they'll know—

Verrit rounded the corner, his hulking figure filling the narrow hallway. Jason fought hard to drag his own Talent through the suppression,

but the vise was tight enough to catch it. Pressure swirled in the base of his skull like steam gathering in a sealed pot. Like fluid, pushing his cartilage out from between his joints. He clutched his own head, squeezing the sides of his skull, his mouth open and trying to scream. But even that was stuck, too. The shadow of Verrit came through the darkness, closer, closer, his low chuckle rolling through the hallway.

"How'd you get out, you little fucking rat?" Verrit asked. "Did you squeeze between the bars?"

Irén gave an inarticulate bellow of rage, shaking the bars again. Jason took a step back. Going forward meant colliding with Verrit. There was no getting past him, not in the narrow hallway. Jason moved back, as fast as he could. All the way back to his cell, grabbing the door and dragging it closed in front of him. The hinges gave their squeal again—too slow—Verrit was fast. Got his arm in the door before Jason could pull it closed. He took a step into the cell, looming in the doorway, his big shoulders blocking out the light from the lamps.

"Where are you going, Jason? Don't you like having a private place?"

Jason clenched his hands into fists, reaching for that old fury. Not all that long ago, he was so filled with it that it sustained him for three and a half years. He didn't need to break the suppression, he needed to move his Talent through it and then—something. Maybe he could save himself for once. "Leave me alone you fucking slug."

Verrit laughed, shoving Jason against the wall. "Didn't you learn your lesson this morning? You're mine, Jason. You always have been, and you always will be. Your piece of shit father put me in this place, and one day I'll be out of here and I'll get to look him in the eye and tell him how much I enjoyed your company. Just so he can know a fraction of how bad it is in here."

"Fuck you, Verrit," Jason gasped. "You're never getting out of here. This place is going to keep you until you bones are rotted into dust."

"He wants to help you!" Irén shouted, rattling the door again. "He wants to help you and you're going to let him die? Do something, fuck!"

The vise let go. So completely that Jason's Talent suffused his whole body. But Verrit's Talent spilled around them, too, a cruel and vicious force that filled Jason's tiny cell with pressure. Verrit groaned, the slimy feeling of his pleasure invading Jason's consciousness.

"Holy fuck," Verrit gasped. "I forgot how good that feels."

Jason fought with his own Talent, struggling to release it. But it was still stuck, like the morphine had tangled it into a knot that he couldn't pick loose. The pressure built, and built, searing through his nerves, lighting his whole body on fire with pain. Someone was yelling, so loud it made his ears rattle—him, it was him, that was his voice, ripping its way out of him, shredding him from the inside out, and still his Talent was stuck.

He was on his back.

Staring up at the dark ceiling.

It wasn't the morphine; it was Verrit, blocking Jason from his own strength. And Verrit was laughing, the sound almost as loud as Jason's screaming. Verrit put his foot on Jason's chest, pinning him to the ground.

"What's the matter, Jason?" Verrit asked, shouting over Jason's screams. "Is something hurting you? Fuck, you squeal a lot, hey?"

Verrit kicked Jason in the side, punching the air out of his lungs. The pain burned, hot and wild, knocking Jason out of his own consciousness for a moment. All he saw was white-hot pain, searing across his ribs. Verrit still held him in stasis, like stepping on a water hose. Verrit grabbed him by the hair and dragged him up into a sitting position, against the wall. Jason caught Verrit's hand, trying to haul himself up. Kicking, the heels of his boots sliding on the floor, looking for purchase. Pain. So much pain.

The squeal of another cell door—footsteps.

Irén.

Verrit turned, facing the door. Irén. "Fuck you, bitch. You want some, too?"

Jason could *feel* Irén fighting to bring her Talent to bear, but Verrit blocked her, too, with all the efficiency of the children. Maybe he used to do this same job, working suppression somewhere else in the city, until he was non-compliant.

"Come face me, you snivelling piece of shit coward. It's the two of us this time. No guards to save you, no proxies to back you up."

The pressure. Sweet North Star, the pressure was going to kill him. His own Talent left splinters in his own bones, tore the tissue of his muscles and sinew. He was screaming again, somehow, even though it felt like he couldn't breathe. He rolled toward Verrit—if he could release the pressure—

He grabbed Verrit's leg, squeezing as hard as he could, focusing all that strength and pressure on everything beneath his hand. He could see

Verrit's skin, the capillaries beneath it, the fatty layer and then muscle. Bone.

The pressure popped through something in Jason, and poured into Verrit and the bone shattered.

The little pieces that made Verrit's ankle, the big, round section at the base of the leg—dust.

Verrit screamed, his weight shifting, falling. He caught himself on the wall. Jason tried to push himself out of the way, but Verrit fell fast. Jason couldn't stop pouring that pressure, up through Verrit's body. He could hear it, the crunch, fractures running up the bone, pieces disintegrating away becoming calcium pulp that shredded his muscles. Blood—the bone shards had nicked a vein. Knee, femur, pelvis. More pressure, more destruction, every bone that Jason could find. Spine, ribs, shoulders, the thrashing stopped. The screaming winked out. Jason must have crushed his heart with all that pressure or maybe popped his lungs. Blood seeped out of Verrit's body, but Jason couldn't tell where it was coming from. It was dark, and hot, and wet, spreading across the floor, soaking into Jason's clothes.

Irén grabbed the back of Verrit's coat, hauling his body off Jason. "Holy fuck."

Jason tried to suck in a deep breath, but it hurt too fucking much. He could only inhale in tiny increments, his breath catching. But his Talent was swirling already, the release of pressure giving it room to move through him, pooling like a balm in all the wounded places. But even that hurt, the healing touch making his nerves scream their protest.

"Time to get up," Irén said. "We need to get the fuck out of here."

"We have to help her," Jason breathed. Irén grabbed his arm, dragging him up, even though it hurt so fucking much. "We have to find her!"

Jason shoved Irén out of the way, stepping over the bleeding, twitching corpse.

Into the hall and around the corner. He could see the closet in his mind's eye, the memory lodged there like a stone. Two floors up and down a hallway, right above where they were now. If he could get there—

"I'm coming," he told her.

But there was nothing.

There was no feeling of that child, nothing lingering in the air. Just silence. Stillness.

He reached his Talent through the hallway, looking for the barrier that the other sections would make. Section One, Section Three. But even as he touched those walls, they dissolved like crepe paper in a storm. Talent popped to life in the Rift. Jason could almost see the bunk hall, roaring awake, Talent pouring out of each person in a terrible, vengeful wave.

"They're dead," Irén said.

"No—that doesn't make sense. Only the one was dying—the others were fine. We have to find them!"

"Jason," Irén said, catching Jason's arm. "They're dead. They're all dead. Can't you feel it? They're gone!"

"No! We can't leave them!" Jason tried to reach for them, searching desperately for their Talent. Where had they gone? She had to be wrong. She hadn't even known about them before he told her, how did she know they were dead? "Where are they? We have to find them. Irén please—wait—let me find them!"

Jason shoved her away, even though it made his body scream with pain. Through the halls, as fast as he could. If he could find one of those closets, he could bring the children out into the world. Carry their precious little bodies out into the streets so the whole city could see what the Authority did.

Into the cellar. He must have gotten turned around. Or maybe this was the only way out—maybe the stairs he used to get down to the food cellar was the only way back up. The sour onion smell was familiar. Almost comforting except he hated it here. He hated the walls and he hated the dust in the air and he hated that smell.

He could almost feel the girl's Talent in the air, swirling motes that would settle after a while. And above Jason's head, the carnage. He could feel the pain and the fear and the incredible power. An entire wall collapsed, reshaped by someone's Talent so the prisoners could run out into the horrible storm. Guns and blood and dying guards. Maybe that was why he couldn't feel the children anymore. Maybe there was too much Talent in this place, muddying the air, turning it into a hurricane of violence and vengeance.

"Please Irén," Jason whimpered. "Please. We have to find them. They're just children! They asked for my help. Please!"

"They're gone, Jason," Irén said. "We can't help them because they're already dead."

Jason sobbed, pushing his hands into his face. But he let Irén drag him away. Up the stairs and out into the storm.

69

TASHUÉ

DAY 39

"**D**o you know his name?" the healer asked.

Tashué shook his head, looking down at the blood on his hands. It was a mix of Powell's and Ishmael's and Adley's, in all likelihood. The rain had washed some of it away, but he clung to the creases in his hands and the rough skin of his calluses. "No," he lied, even though he hated himself for it. This was Ishmael's best chance at survival. "We found him like that, out in the street. There wasn't anything in his pockets. Probably got rolled for whatever coin he had."

All of Ishmael's belongings were in Tashué's pockets, along with Tashué's medals and they empty bullet casings. Felt like another betrayal. He wanted to call himself someone who cared about Ishmael, but here he was, handing him over to the hospital instead of saving him. Just like he was about to go racing after Stella instead of letting her go. Bargaining with Jason's life instead of doing something to get him out.

The healer looked Tashué in the eye. Could the man feel Tashué's Talent? Could he taste the lie, sitting in the air?

"So you were out past midnight, the pair of you," the healer said. "Walking through the storm. And you found him, where? In the middle of the street? And you picked him up and dragged him here, is that it?"

"We should go," Davik said. "We don't want to get involved with the Patrollers. We don't want any trouble. We didn't want the poor sod to die out there in the storm."

"He may still die," the healer said sharply, unimpressed by the pair of them. "The concussion is severe, and there's only so much that Talent can do for him. We can't make the swelling stop, nor can we evacuate the blood pooling between the skull and the brain matter. We'll help him as best we can, but he made require trepanation."

"What the fuck is trepanation?" Tashué asked, though he thought he knew. Fuck, Ishmael—

"A piece of the skull is cut and removed," the healer said. "It lets the pressure out so the swelling and the buildup of blood doesn't cause irreparable damage. But it's an unreliable procedure and the survival rates... They're not good. It's a last desperate act, one that we will try to avoid, but... If needs must, we have a few surgeons on staff who have been experimenting with the technique. A few have experience with patients who have survived."

"You'll have a meat monger cut out a chunk of his skull?" Davik scoffed. "Fuck's sake, that's grim."

"If he survives it, he'll be missing a part of his skull?" Tashué asked.

The healer shrugged. "If we do nothing and he dies, his skull isn't much use to him, is it? I only tell you this because I hope you could give us some clue as to who he is. If he's going to die tonight, it would be good for his loved ones to be notified, wouldn't it?"

"We don't know anything," Davik said again. "We found him. Let's go, Mr. Guinne. We don't need this mess after everything."

"Send a runner to Davik Kaine's pugilist club," Tashué said before he could stop himself. "Have them find Allie Tei. She knows him. His last name is Kol Khara. Tell her to come and bring someone with a camera."

"Right, enough," Davik said, catching Tashué's arm and dragging him toward the door. "We're fucking leaving."

Tashué shoved Davik off him. But he walked. North Star preserve him, he walked out of the hospital and into the rain. He turned his face to the downpour and let it pummel him, so cold it hurt. Shards of ice hit his hair and his growing beard and it clotted in his clothes.

"If they figure out who he is, we may as well have handed him to Clannaugh," Tashué said.

"Sure, and if we'd brought him back to the club, he'd be dead by morning," Davik said. "I told you, László can't help him. You heard them. The last shot he's got is if they can take off a fucking piece of his skull and someone prays he survives it."

Tashué pushed his hands over his face, for all the good it did him. The storm kept howling, kept beating him down like it was trying to defeat him. He didn't even know who he was anymore. Two people died at the bank, and he'd let László convince him it was right because he wanted it to be that easy. He killed two more men tonight, cut off a fucking head. And it was easy. It was the easiest thing he'd ever done because it was for Jason. For Lizanne. For Stella and Ceridwen.

But would any of them be able to look him in they eye if they knew what he'd done for them?

"Hey," Davik said, grabbing Tashué's arm again. "Don't fucking freeze up on me now. We can't stay here, big man. If they send for Patrollers and one of them recognizes you, we're fucked."

Tashué dragged his arm out of Davik's grasp again, marching down the stairs. These same stairs he'd carried Stella up. It was raining that night, too, but not this badly. He'd sent the people he loved most in the world out into this miserable weather and he told himself that he was here for Jason, but then he got lost. Lost in his own self-pity and the layers of confused rage. He was going to make it right.

The big dapple-grey mare was as miserable in the rain and the sleet as everyone else stupid enough to be out tonight. She stood with her head bowed, her eyes closed. The stolen saddle bags were crammed with as much dried beef and hard tack as he could find on short notice, wrapped tight to protect it against weather like this, but he had no way of knowing if it would even be enough. In theory, she'd been travelling for twelve days, which should have been enough time to carry her and Ceridwen to the mountains. But the weather—and what Rhodrishi said —maybe she was close.

"I'm getting my son, Davik," Tashué said. "I'm done playing fucking games, waiting for you to sneak him out or whatever you were planning. I'm getting him out tonight."

"What the fuck are you going to do?" Davik asked with a sharp-edged laugh. "Charge up the bridge, break the door down?"

"I'll figure it out when I get there," Tashué said. He pulled himself up into the saddle, settling into it with perfect familiarity. "He broke suppression, didn't he? So I can do it. I'll break suppression, and then it's over. No more fucking around. I didn't do it sooner because I thought there was still some quiet, safe way out of this, but there's nowhere safe for us, is there? So, fuck it. I'll get my son, and then we'll find proof. The trams—there's children in every fucking tram in this city. All we have to do is take them out of the jobs the Authority assigned them to, and then no one can look away. No one can accuse us of being bloodthirsty rebels, not when they see what we're fighting for."

Davik caught the reins before Tashué could gather them up, holding them in his fist and blinking up at Tashué through the rain. "You're going to get yourself fucking killed, trying to pull shit like that!"

"What do you care, Davik?" Tashué snapped. "You said yourself, you never had reason to trust me. Nineteen years with that badge, maybe this is my penance for it."

"What about Ffyanwy?" Davik snapped back. "You said you know where she is—you said she's close. If you charge at the gates of the Rift because it's easier to die a tragic hero than it is to fight ugly, what happens to her? Where is she, Tashué? At least tell me that before you throw your fucking life away!"

Something rolled through Tashué's Talent, something vicious and hot and enormous. Like the ripple of pain that didn't belong to him, a shout of rage rising on a hundred voices. It pulled Tashué's Talent into the hot centre, filled his ears with things he couldn't possibly hear from where he was. Gunshots and the grind of stone as it changed shape. Davik felt it, too. He turned to face the Rift.

70

JASON
DAY 39

"Wait here."

Sure. Wait here. As if Jason would go anywhere else.

Irén ran back into the storm, and Jason sat in the boat. Shivering. They'd dragged it out of the river to dump all the water out of the bottom, then slid it back down the bank. His whole body was soaked by the storm, lit with pain. He couldn't make it heal too fast. He didn't know much about healing, but he knew that from somewhere— maybe it was a thing everyone knew, or maybe it was an understanding that lived in his Talent. If you forced it along too fast, it made things brittle, and the pain could last forever.

He closed his eyes instead of bothering trying to see anything. Flashes of light lived and died on the island. People trying to escape, no doubt. Trying to see their way through the night. Guards took up a stand on the bridge, blocking as many people as they could. Pops of gunfire, the ignition of all that gunpowder. So much blood and pain.

His Talent was like a raw open wound, exposed to everything. It hadn't been like this before he was arrested—he'd figured out how to pull his Talent close to his body, keeping it to himself so he could hide it from most people. But now he couldn't remember how he'd done that. Now it was an exposed nerve, another sense that he couldn't turn off.

But he couldn't find the children. They were gone.

He squeezed his eyes shut and sank his Talent back into the Rift, searching for the rooms where they were hidden. Every hallway, every corridor, until he found the little closets where he'd seen the children the first time he'd connected to them. Like wandering through the halls himself with his Talent instead of his body. But the rooms were empty.

No, not completely empty.

There were *things* left behind, the chairs the children sat in, their life maintained with feeding tubes and catheters. But the children were gone. A vial of liquid morphine lay on the floor in each room—more than enough to kill, it had to be.

Irén was right. They were dead. Section Two failed and some inmates started moving their Talent, so their keeper killed the others. Why? It didn't make sense. Why not use the remaining children to control the inmates? They had to know that inmates could get out once they could use their Talent. Maybe they were afraid the children would be found. They were meant to be a secret, after all. Not that anyone was looking for them. Everyone was taking care of themselves because they didn't know the energy units were children. Escaping, getting away. Killing. Killing every guard, killing the proxies. So much blood, running those halls red. A storm of ice and death.

Jason reached into his pocket. If the letters might have been salvaged before, they were ruined now. The rain was relentless. And the morphine tablets. They were still intact, held together by their own pressure, but starting to crumble away into powder. Jason pulled them out, holding them a while. He could still hear the sound of Verrit's bones cracking, shattering, the feeling of it rippling through his own body like an echo of that pain.

The morphine he'd taken had finally worked its way out of his system. The healer said it wasn't enough to kill him, but it almost had— his own horrifying inability to act in a reasonable amount of time had almost been the end of him. And now he had the memory of Verrit's bones disintegrating under his willpower, and that feeling built nausea in his gut like a new foundation.

"Get in," Irén said, the suddenness of her voice across his senses making him jump. "Slow and careful, so you don't tip it right over."

Glaen and Rezji—she's gone back for Rezji, and Glaen had tagged along. It was a bit of a relief, feeling Glaen climb into the boat. He was such a gentle, quiet man. It would be nice to have the company of someone who didn't know the weight of violence. Glaen sank down beside Jason, his hands fumbling with something—a blanket. He wrapped it around both of them, drawing Jason into a hug.

"Are you alright?" Glaen whispered.

The boat rocked as Rezji climbed aboard, and Irén shoved it out into the water, jumping in.

"Fine," Jason breathed. He couldn't bring himself to explain the feeling of broken bones. Couldn't speak about the children because if he did, he would start sobbing. They'd asked him for help, and they were all dead. He didn't deserve to be sitting here in this boat, in the midst of an escape. "Just cold."

Irén kicked the boat off the shoreline, and her Talent unfolded, so powerful it drove them north, against the raging, vicious current.

"Glaen," Irén said. "I want you to check her wound. I can't do it and move the boat at the same time."

"I haven't any skills with wounds," Glaen said, shifting away from Jason. "I wouldn't know what—"

"You don't need to know anything," Irén snapped. "Just look at it, and tell me what you see."

"What wound?" Jason asked. But his voice was too soft. They didn't hear him.

"With my Talent?"

"With light, if that's easier. If you can make the light small."

Glaen's Talent was a small and gentle thing, making a little ball of light. No bigger than a marble, glowing in the palm of his hand. Enough to light his features: the downturn of his mouth, the wild look in his eye. "Where are you hit?"

"In my ass," Rezji grunted.

"Oh dear—I'm sorry."

It was so absurd that Jason almost laughed, but the sound caught in his throat and tried to turn into a sob. He bit down on it, squeezing the morphine tablets harder. He could feel them start to disintegrate in his hand. If he was going to take them, he needed to do it soon, before they ran through his fingers in the rain. His chest hurt so fucking much. Worse, the pain of knowing he'd almost convinced them to trust him, but he failed.

Children.

He just wanted to help them.

"It's hard to make Talent do something new," Rezji grunted.

The light showed all the blood on Rezji's trouser leg. Jason squeezed his eyes shut rather than watch. He didn't want to be involved in any of it. He didn't want his Talent to touch anyone else. He didn't want them to feel his panic, his revulsion, like he felt the healer's emotions.

"I think it's stopped bleeding now," Glaen said.

"Not much blood in the ass," Rezji grunted.

"Is there an exit wound?" Irén asked. "Somewhere the bullet came out?"

"I don't think so," Glaen said. "Only the one hole."

Irén cursed under her breath, a long string of words in a language Jason didn't understand, but there was something about cursing that was universal. The weight of it hit the same, no matter what the syllables were. "Does your leg hurt?"

"My ass hurts."

"What can I do?" Glaen asked. "Tell me what to do."

"You need to use your Talent to look into the wound," Irén said. "The same way you looked at the ground. You let your Talent bleed into the wound, find the path it takes."

"It's fine," Rezji said. "It hasn't hit the bone. I can see it—it's not lead, like a bullet. It's a piece of stone. Deep, but not on the bone. I'm fine."

"A ricochet?" Irén asked.

"If that's what it's called—yes. A piece of broken stone. It's fine."

"You should still see a healer," Glaen said. "Wounds like that are filthy. You don't want to get gangrene."

Rezji nodded. "On shore."

Glaen shifted back, moving slowly through the boat and edging closer to Jason, pulling the blanket back over his shoulders. Fat load of good the blanket was doing. With all the rain, it was soaked through, which only seemed to press the cold closer to Jason's skin. But then Glaen's Talent flexed again, heat crawling through the blanket fibres, growing in intensity until it made the blanket steam. Warm and wet was a slight improvement over cold and wet, but Jason was still shivering, even as that warmth sank deep into his core. The shock, the grief, the weight of his own Talent that he didn't dare trust. And on the island, people were still dying.

"Are you sure you're alright?" Glaen asked, pressing his hand against Jason's forehead. "Are you ill?"

"No," Jason said, shaking his head. Ill? He felt like he was going out of his mind. "I just—I've never killed anyone before."

"Who did you kill?"

"Verrit."

"He deserved it," Irén said. "You get used to it, killing people who deserve it."

Jason flinched, the words stabbing through him. He didn't ever want to feel like this again, but he didn't want to get used to it, either. He stretched his arm out over the river, feeling the spray of it as their boat moved against the furious current. The morphine tablets disintegrated, sliding out of his palm and into the Brightwash. "I hope not."

I rén drove their little boat right up to the Market Wharf. Only the barest structure stood—the Wharf and dozens of buildings had been burned away by a fire. Jason remembered the days and days of smoke that hung in the Rift, blown across the river by the drifting winds. Remembered the rumours of how it started. A brightman, the Army of the Red Dawn, a chemical explosion. A thousand different stories. He couldn't even remember them all.

The storm had blown itself out for now, the air thick and wet with winter cold. Glaen kept their clothes warmer than the temperature of the air, at least, so they could all stop bleeding their precious body heat into the night. Climbing up the ladder structure that had been hastily tied to the stone piles driven into the bottom of the river was agony. Jason's ribs screamed their protest, his whole body trembling with the ugly intensity of it. But he couldn't stay and hide in the little skiff, so he grit his teeth and climbed anyway. Up into the light. The Market Quarter had brights to light the streets, and Jason felt terribly exposed. At least in the darkness of the river, no one could see them, but here—when would the city know what had happened on the island?

As he stood out in the open, he realized how long it had been since he stood in a city street. Three and a half years, and the only time he'd been outside was in the garden, with its cramped paths and its raised beds and the high fence that kept everyone in. Now, space stretched around him, the river at his back and the city sprawled out in front of him. He could *walk* in any direction. No one would stop him. The possibilities were endless, overwhelming. Maybe it was the pain or maybe it was shock rolling through him, making him too tired to process it all, but he didn't like the space. He felt too small and too exposed.

"Why are we in the Market?" Jason asked, pulling the warmed blanket tighter about his body. "Shouldn't we go to the Bay?"

Irén shook her head. "Everyone will be going to the Bay. Besides, I told my brother to meet us here, in the Market. He'll come as soon as he knows there's been a breakout."

"I'm sorry," Jason gasped. Stupid thing to say. He didn't even know why he said it, or what he was sorry for. Maybe he needed the words out. Apologizing to the children.

"Don't be," Irén said quickly. "He deserved it."

Jason shook his head again, but no words came. He wanted to say that no one deserved to die like Verrit had. Jason didn't even know if he *was* dead. Maybe he was still lying there in that cell, all his bones pulverized, his heart still beating. His mind still screaming with that pain.

"We should find some shelter," Glaen whispered, dragging Jason closer. "Somewhere warm and dry."

"No, we should stay here," Irén said. "I need to be here, to keep watch for my brother. It won't be long now."

"How do you know?" Jason asked. Panic gnawed at the edges of his mind. He hated it here, hated standing in the street, waiting for someone to notice they didn't belong. It didn't matter how hard he tried to hide, he'd always have the tattoo that marked him as property of the Rift. He'd have to find someone willing and able to cover it with a new tattoo, maybe.

"I'm sure word of the breakout will spread fast," Irén said, "and he'll know to come."

"So will Regulation Officers," Jason said. "They'll be combing the city for us. They won't let everyone walk away—they'll never stop looking for everyone they lost. They'll hunt us until they've tracked every one of us down. We can't stand around and wait for them to come find us—"

"Hey," Irén said, her voice cutting over Jason, firm and commanding. "This isn't the time to panic. We're out. It's not the way we intended, but here we are. I told my brother to meet us here if anything happened. He left the boat for us, right? So he'll do it. He'll meet us here, and then we'll find a place to lay low for a while. It won't take long—the whole city will go to shit soon, and then we'll go back to the Bay."

"I thought I was supposed to meet someone," Glaen said. "For Davik."

"Yes," Rezji said. "We're early. We'll wait here. He'll meet us in the Market."

"Who are you meeting for Davik?" Jason asked.

Irén held up a hand, shushing them all. Whistling. Someone was whistling, almost like a bird but not quite.

"My brother," Irén said. She turned to Rezji. "You're not coming?"

Rezji shrugged. "I stay with him. I'll meet you later. In the Bay. Take care of Jason, yes? I like him. He's a good boy."

"I can take care of myself," Jason gasped. But he couldn't take care of himself. He was falling apart, disintegrating like the morphine tablets had, and soon he would cease to be a person anymore. He'd be Talent, bleeding everywhere.

"You sure can," Irén said. "You proved that tonight. But it's time to go, yeah? We'll spend some time on my brother's riverboat until the city settles. He's a bit of an ass, but he's cute, kinda like you."

The whistling again, louder, and Irén started to lead Jason away. Rezji caught her hand, dragging her back—Irén came swiftly, throwing her arms around Rezji's neck, the pair of them kissing each other so deeply and so hard they looked like they were going to topple over.

It stole the breath out of Jason. The shivering returned in force, making his teeth chatter. If Irén's brother was coming, did that mean Lorne was coming, too? Three and a half years—could he *finally* kiss Lorne again?

Rezji broke away from Irén first, wincing, her hand going to her bloody, open wound.

"You need to see a healer," Irén said. "Tonight. Find one tonight."

"I will," Rezji said.

Irén nodded, stepping away. "Take care of yourself."

She took Jason's hand and led him back to the Wharf. It felt like such a terribly long walk, the street stretching out around him, the openness making him dizzy. Making him feel like he was sliding out of existence. He was trembling so bad he could barely walk anymore.

"It's alright, Jason," Irén whispered, pulling him along. "My brother is a healer. He can help. And then we'll find Davik and tell him every-thing—Davik is trying to help the other children, the ones at the Breeding Program. We'll make it right."

Another boat bobbed down in the river, bigger than the skiff that carried them off the island. A wild spill of Talent kept it under the piles even as the river tried to drive the boat back down toward the Bay. The skiff broke away from where Irén tied it to the Wharf, the little boat that carried them across the river dancing backward downstream. The skiff hit a stone and spun around, bobbing, leaping, like it was happy to be free.

Irén started the climb down first. Jason stood on the catwalk, shivering. Trying to summon the energy to climb again. He was so sore. So tired. And even though he was afraid of the wide open spaces of the Market, he didn't think he had the strength to climb down that ladder. Climbing up had been hard enough, but now that he faced going back down, the exhaustion gnawed at his joints. Rotted his bones. Throbbed through his whole chest.

"Irén," he breathed. "I can't."

"You can," Irén said from below him. "You can, Jason. We have to climb down, and then you can rest, and László will look at your wounds. He'll know how to help you. I know the theory behind healing, but I've never been good at it like he is. Come down and I'll guide your feet, and then you can rest. We're so close."

Footsteps rattled over the catwalk, sending the vibration into Jason's bones. Irén cursed, climbing back up as fast as she could.

Jason turned, the dread leaking out of him, leaving only quiet resignation. This was it, the moment his luck ran out. And maybe it wasn't so bad, after everything. At least he'd die free.

Hands on his shoulders, the form of a body, silhouetted by the nearby light. Lifting him up, pulling him along the catwalk.

Into a crushing hug.

The strongest, most perfect hug he'd felt in his entire life.

His father's Talent swirled around him both, probing into the wounds, soothing Jason's pain. The relief broke him out of the fear, out of the numb inaction, and Jason dissolved into sobs. He pressed his face into his father's chest and poured all his grief into the soggy wet wool of his father's coat, into the heat of his father's body and the way it encircled him, protecting him from even the weather. Jason's knees gave out, and he couldn't hold his own weight anymore, but it didn't matter. His father held him up.

"I have you," Tashué whispered, pushing his hand into Jason's hair. "It's alright, Jason. I have you."

"They died," Jason gasped. "The children in the Rift—all four of them—they asked for my help, but I couldn't—they died. I think the bastards killed them."

"Who?" Tashué asked. "The prisoners?"

"No—the one in charge of them. They called him the Keeper."

"Jason, I'm sorry," Tashué said. He squeezed Jason harder, and it should have hurt but it didn't, as if Tashué had taken Jason's pain. Just like the morphine had, but gentler. "We're going to make them pay for it. We'll rip it all apart. I'm sorry, Jason. I'm sorry I didn't listen to you sooner. You were right, all these years, and I couldn't hear you. I didn't want to believe it—I'm sorry I didn't trust you."

How long had he *wished* to hear those words? And now they were rattling through him, but so was the sound of Verrit's bones, cracking against his eardrums, living in the shape of his own Talent. He could feel his father's bones. His father's heartbeat. And his Talent had perfect awareness of how easy it would be to destroy those things that kept his father alive, as if his own strength was hungry for more death even though he never wanted to feel that sensation again.

"I'm just like her," Jason said, the words spilling out even as his chest spasmed. "I crushed his bones just like she did."

"Like who did?" Tashué asked.

"Mother. You told me that story—she broke someone's arm with her Talent. I did it, too, when Verrit came for me. Crushed every bone he had."

"Yeah," Tashué said. "I did it, too. When they came to arrest me—I didn't have time to think. I crushed them like they were paper and twigs."

"It's common for people who have big tempers and a lot of Talent," someone said. Standing behind Tashué, soaked from the rain. "You've got all that willpower and no training yet, and so you just..." He lifted a hand and turned it into a mean fist, his knuckles wet and shining, the tattoo on his fingers dancing when he moved. "We'll hone that into something special."

There was something comforting in knowing that the destructive power was hereditary. All these years, he'd wanted to be as big and confident as his father, and now the pair of them had killing Talent that mirrored each other, like they were two halves of the same whole. Jason was the same shape of his father after all, if not in physical body, then in sheer force of willpower. And the shape of his mother, too—big temper and a lot of Talent, that was her exactly.

And yet he didn't want this to be his legacy. He didn't want to be a man who could kill so casually.

"Dav," Irén said. "What are we doing? We should go, right?"

"Who's got the boat?" Davik Kaine asked. Standing behind Tashué with those tattoos on his hands, the darkness and his facial hair obscuring most of the details of his face. Jason tried to figure out what he expected from this name he heard so much. "László?"

"Yeah, Dav!" a voice called from below. "We gotta get back. I think things are going sideways."

"Where's my idiot pugilist?"

A rattle on the catwalk—whoever was in the boat was climbing up. László. Irén's brother, Lorne's healer. "Back at the club. I slipped out as soon as I heard. I left him at the bar. Figured the state he was in, he was better off staying there. But when I was coming to the docks, I passed Patrollers in the streets. I don't know—I think they're searching the Bay for escapees already."

"I knew it," Irén said. "We should head up river a few days, lay low until things settle."

"What?" László scoffed. "Lay low, are you fucking serious? Everything we've been working for, everything we've been trying to do—it's happening right now. Right fucking now, Irén, this is our chance. And you want to fuck off and lay low?"

"Jason," Tashué said, stepping back. Off the catwalk and onto the street, pulling Jason with him. "Listen to me. I have to go."

Rage replaced all the fatigue, burning hot through Jason's veins, making his body tense. "Go? Go where?!"

"There's someone who can help," Tashué said, sounding calm in that way he so rarely did. When there was no changing his mind, no riling him up for a fight. "László's right—everything is falling apart, and the city is going to eat itself alive. The only way through this is if we convince people to stand with us instead of letting the army slaughter us, and I know someone who can help pull us together. I have to go get her."

Jason shook his head, trying to grasp the words. He'd been waiting to get out for three and a half years, and now his father was leaving? "Everything's falling apart—how could you—"

"I'm coming back," Tashué interrupted, giving Jason another squeeze. "You were right, all these years. I'm sorry I didn't listen to you, Jason. You were so right about all of it. I swear to you, I'm coming back to fight this with you. If I thought for a second that you'd come with me so I could keep you safe, I would ask you. I would go down on my knees and beg you to come with me. We'd only be gone a few days and then once I find her, we'd be back here to fight. But it won't matter what I say, will it? You won't come. You have to stay."

Jason opened his mouth to argue by some stupid habit. Just to be contrarian, to berate his father for presuming to know him so well. But the bastard was right. For all that he said he was tired a moment ago, something in László Dargis's voice hooked in him, and he could almost see it. The freedom, the change. And Lorne—he needed to find Lorne. He needed to get to the Breeding Program, see if he could find his way in. Find his brother.

"Tell me what to do," Jason said. "If you're leaving—what should I do?"

"The children," Tashué said. "The Authority calls them energy units."

Jason nodded. "They were in charge of the suppression in the Rift, but someone killed them and took them away."

"So that we couldn't find them and use them as proof," Tashué said. "But they can't get rid of all of them, can they? They're all over this city. In station houses, in trams, in the factories. You need to find them and flood the city with proof. We have to show the whole world we're fighting for a *reason*."

It wasn't raining anymore, so Jason could look up at his father's face. He'd changed so much. The last Jason saw him, he was wild and desperate and a bit broken, pieces of him splintering away as his world dissolved around the lies the Authority sold him for so long. But now, he was hard again. Harder than Jason had ever seen him. His eyes glittered with something like anger, but that word was too small, too messy, too inexact.

"What are we doing, General?" Davik asked. "We can't stand around here all fucking night."

"Dav," Tashué said, still holding Jason's shoulders. "Do you trust me?"

Davik laughed. The sound was bright, infectious. Unhinged. "Do I trust you? I don't fucking know. Do I have a choice?"

"You should go back to the Bay," Tashué said. "Find Vasska, make sure he's willing to stand with you. Make whatever deals you have to. Nothing matters except standing and keeping Clannaugh out of the Bay. Ishmael said Clannaugh's going to march troops through the city, and we can't let them come into the Bay and start shooting people. Blockade the bridges, the streets—any way into the Bay, seal it off. Dig in. Resist."

"That's not enough," László scoffed. "Everything we've been working for, and now you want us to, what? Hide in the Bay? I thought you were serious about changing things."

"I am," Tashué said with such perfect certainty that it sent a shiver down Jason's spine. He imagined this was how his father sounded, all those years ago, when he was Captain of Iris Company, tearing through whatever distant wars kept the Dominion Foreign Deployment Army busy. "That's why I'm going to go find Ffyanwy Rhydderch. But whatever she has to say isn't any good if Clannaugh slaughters everyone."

"I'm not *fucking* hiding anymore!" László snapped.

"I know!" Tashué roared. "Shut up a second and listen. I'm not asking you to hide. We were tiptoeing around before, waiting. But now? The Rift is fucked, Powell is dead—there's no more laws to worry about. There's no peaceful way to end this. So, you need to find the children. As many of them as you can. Whatever happens in Yaelsmuir, it has to matter enough that the rest of the country can't look away. They can't shrug this off as something we deserved." He pulled something out of his pocket, pushed it into Jason's hand. One of his sketchpads, the cover battered and the spine cracking. "Get as many photographs as you can and send them everywhere, out of the city. Down to White Crown. See if you can get people to bring prints down to White Crown on barges, in case no newsprints are willing to publish them."

"I'm barricading the Bay, but I'm sending boats out?" Davik asked.

Tashué nodded. "That's why we need Vasska. He holds the Hive."

"Does that mean we're going to the Breeding Program?" László asked. "That's why we did all this for Jason. Because he broke suppression."

"I can't break it like that again," Jason said. "They're children. It hurt them when I did that—I think that's the reason one of them died. I broke them, and it hurt the one so bad she couldn't recover."

"László," Tashué said. "Did you keep any guns?"

"'Course I did," László laughed. "You think I'd let beauties like those Uhls get away? I nicked as many as I could from those crates before Davik hid them."

"Good. Jason needs one, and so does your sister," Tashué said. "All the plans are here. The trams will be easiest, I think."

"What about Lorne?" Jason breathed. And something like shame bubbled in him. All of this was happening, all these things he wanted, but he wanted to see Lorne. Three and a half years, he'd been waiting for this, and now Lorne wasn't here.

"I'll find him," Davik grunted. "Make sure he isn't getting his fool head kicked in by those Patrollers. Vasska was at the club anyway, so they're probably together."

Jason sucked in a deep breath. Sucked it in so long and hard that his lungs ached. His ribs ached. But the pain seemed so small in the shadow of his father's strength. Maybe the bones weren't broken after all, or maybe his father had healed him when their Talents bled together—or maybe he'd become separated from pain, elevated above it. Something like anger settled in him, except it was purer than any anger he'd ever felt in his life, just like the look he'd seen on his father's face. Energy units, all over this city. He could almost hear his father's thoughts. The children, everywhere. The factories. The station houses. The trams, sliding around the city, round and round and round in circles.

"Fuck's sake," Irén muttered. "You really got us into the shit this time, didn't you?"

"Fuck you, Irén, this is what we wanted," László snapped. "We been in this stupid city for a fucking decade, *wishing* we could change something. Praying for someone with big enough balls to actually fucking do something. And now it's happening. It's here. You don't get to turn coward on me now."

Irén swung, hitting László in the chest with a clenched fist. "I didn't say I was turning coward, you ass! I need a fucking second to hate everything!"

"László," Tashué said. "Go get the guns."

"What about my barge?" László said. "I'm just leaving it?"

"I'll take it back to the Bay," Davik said.

"If you crash it, Dav, I swear to everything holy—"

"László!" Tashué said again, harder this time. "Go get the fucking guns."

László threw up his hands, turning and heading back to the catwalk. "Yeah, sure, fine. Fuck's sake. You don't have to be a dickhead about it."

Tashué exhaled slowly, shaking his head and looking up at the sky. The wind hadn't quit even though the rain had stopped.

"That's it then?" Davik asked. "You're going."

Tashué nodded, letting go of Jason and holding out a hand. Davik shook it. It was strange, seeing Tashué and Davik Kaine shaking hands. For so long, Jason's idea of Davik embodied everything Jason wanted to believe in. Someone who stood against the Authority, someone who protected the tainted. He'd gone searching for Davik years ago, praying for safety. But he'd left the Bay without finding him, convinced Davik Kaine was a myth. Knowing in his bones that there was no such thing as safety for the tainted. There was no port to protect them from the storm.

Davik was supposed to save Jason from the Rift, and Jason had let himself believe it was possible, but Davik had failed to deliver. Were it not for the child dying, Jason would be dead. Verrit would have killed him.

So, maybe Davik was a myth. Maybe he was a man cloaked in lies.

All that time, Tashué had carried that tin badge. Another lie, that stupid badge. Follow the laws and you'll stay safe. What a load of shit that was. The laws were there to control people so someone with more power could take what they wanted.

And now, apparently, Tashué and Davik were on the same side. Something had happened since Jason had last seen his father. Had he given up one set of lies for another?

Jason shuddered at the thought.

"You better come back, General Guinne," Davik said. "I'm putting a lot of faith in you."

"You better fight," Tashué said. "All the posturing and talking is over. There's nothing left but to fight."

Davik didn't say anything to that. He turned and headed back to the catwalk as Irén and László were coming back. The rain had washed all the blood off Irén, leaving the line of stitches on her brow below her hairline. Another in her eyebrow. That's where all the blood had come from. The face bled so fucking much.

They had guns, big rifles with bolt action, the malevolent barrels pointing up at the sky. László handed one to Jason, just like that. Like it was nothing. Like they knew each other already. Jason took it out of some instinct—something came toward his hand, so he took it. But even as the weight of it strained at his tired arms, he hated it. He hated the wood, and he hated the metal, and he hated the potential for brutality it represented.

"It's nice to meet you, Jason Blackwood," László said. "I've heard a lot about you."

"It's nice to meet you, too, László Dargis," Jason said softly. "Thanks for taking care of Lorne for me."

"We'll catch up to him soon," László said, but a little bit of the bluster had fallen out of his voice. He sounded… worried. "He's tough. Doesn't have any quit in him, does he?"

"Yeah. He's been like that as long as I've known him."

"Let's go."

Tashué led them away, turning into an alley where he stopped beside a massive horse. Her reins were tied to a post, and Tashué's fingers picked the knot free.

"When did you get a horse?" Jason asked. It all felt so distant, so surreal.

Tashué took the reins in his hand, leading them back toward Brickheart. "She belonged to one of the Enquiry Officers I killed."

The fact was sobering, stripping away the heady relief. Reality hit hard. No matter how much Jason had thought about this moment, no matter how much he fantasized about making the world a place where the Talented were safer, where they had more freedom, where the Authority was toppled, it didn't prepare him for this, not really. It had always ever been a transient dream, half formed without any details. A lie. Something impossible to attain.

But now it was forming real weight in the pit of his stomach, a truth that he couldn't escape. He was free from the Rift and he had a gun in his hand and they were finally fighting.

It was going to be ugly.

71

LORNE
DAY 39

There were so many people in the club.

More than before—had to be. Or maybe now that Lorne was riding the smoke of László's hashish, it took him longer to wade through the chaos.

He was fighting, and he didn't know why. Didn't matter why. Fighting and swinging, and his knuckles hit flesh and the pain was delicious. This was who he was made to be. Just a body, swinging, hitting, colliding with the whole fucking world, muscle and bone and pain and anger, spilling out of him. Swinging again and someone was bleeding and the crowd shifted and flowed, a riptide carrying him away.

Someone else grabbed him.

"Fuck's sake!" Rowan said, grabbing Lorne by the arm and dragging him out of the riptide of bodies. "I leave you alone for half an hour, and you're already fighting again?"

Lorne laughed. "It's a political rally. What good is a political rally without a few fist fights?"

"László said your fists are retired for the night. He told me to look out for your stupid thick head, because the concussion can get worse if you get hit again. Would you make both our lives easier and sit the fuck down?"

"Where's László?" Lorne asked.

"Don't know. He didn't say where he was going. He just left in a hurry."

Stool.

Bar.

Water.

Drink.

Floating.

Beer, frothy and cold.

He wanted to ask about Jason again but Davik was already gone. Left with Tashué a while ago. Where'd László go?

He was dreaming but he was awake.

Dreams lived in the smoke with him, penetrated his bones. He could see the club and all the people in it, but he could also see the ocean. It didn't matter where he went in the world, didn't matter what he did or what drugs he took or how hard he buried himself in violence, he could always see the ocean at the edge of his vision. Taunting him.

The cliff a few miles from Gaffryn. When he was a young child, he'd go there with other children during the day to climb down the rocks into the little sheltered bay, to pluck mussels off the rocks. Some kids sold them for a few copper crowns to buy something else, but Lorne brought them home to eat because when his mother was chasing poppy dreams, she forgot to buy food.

He could see his sister, and her ocean-grey eyes, and her hunger squall, the sound of it rattling the little cottage they lived in on the edge of town. And his mother, slipping down into the smoke, complaining that Alys was too loud. He could see himself tying baby Alys to his back and going down into town to beg or steal—whatever it took to keep feeding her.

The day his mother died, he stood at the top of that cliff in the rain, looking out at the raging sea. He could remember, with too fucking much clarity, the thought that he should throw himself and Alys both right off that cliff so that the sea could have them—the sea took everything good— and neither of them would have to live another day in hunger or in pain. He didn't remember what it was that made him walk away. Maybe it was that Alys was so small and so warm, and he couldn't bear the thought of the water turning her body into a cold, empty shell, like it had her father.

The wooden dragon, in his hand. The one the boy gave him before the match. For good luck. Except he'd lost the match, and no one would give him a straight answer about Jason. It was supposed to be tonight, so where was Jason? So much for good luck.

A jug of water in his other hand.

He poured it over his head, wishing it would wash the heat away. Wash the memories away. Cold downpour over through his hair, into his coat, clinging to the fleece, beading on the surface of the leather. Would Alys want to come here and live with him? Could he give her a good life in this city, finally?

The crowd roared around him, louder than the memories. Someone else was fighting, over near the stage. There was beer everywhere, all over the floor, and broken glass glittered, and someone was bleeding, their face a curtain of red.

It made Lorne laugh. There was so fucking much blood in the world.

"Nicely done tonight, Mr. Lightning," the bartender said. "Showed 'em all how tough a Bay boy is, hey?"

Lorne squeezed the draig y môr, feeling the details press hard into his palm. "I lost."

"Hey, we all lose some of our fights in life, don't we? But eight rounds against a champion like Ari—that was special. You need another beer?"

"Sure," Lorne said, dropping a few coins on the bar.

"Oh, no, sir, you don't pay for beer in your own club," the bartender said.

"Put it in the tip jar, then."

"Yes, sir. Thank you, sir."

Lorne didn't smash the glass like he was half tempted to, drinking half of it in one go instead.

"Easy, champ." Ari settled into the barstool beside Lorne, nodding at the bartender. "I hit you a few times in the head tonight. All that alcohol will thin the blood, make you more likely to bleed even after your healer looked at you."

"Fuck you," Lorne muttered. "You're my opponent, not my coach, or my healer, or my mother."

"Where are all those people?" Ari asked. "*Someone* should be looking after you. I thought I saw László leaving as I was coming in."

"I don't know. László said Rowan's taking care of me tonight." Where *had* László gone? He sucked back more beer. "And my mother is dead. I don't need them. I can take care of myself."

Ari waved to the bartender. "How about some water for our Mr. Lightning?"

"What exactly do you want? Where's *your* coach, hey? Where's your wife? Are you hanging around, looking for a rematch? I won't go easy on you this time. There's no rules at the bar."

"I'm not looking to pick a fight, son," Ari said. "I want to talk. I was supposed to go home and make love to my wife. She worries about these fights. I don't blame her. Doesn't matter how good I am, I take one bad hit and that's it. But that's life, isn't it? I was halfway home, and I started thinking about you, about this place that Dav built. I have to admit, I'm impressed. So I came back like a fucking idiot. Are you always so sunny and pleasant, or is this my special treatment because I beat you?"

"Go fuck yourself," Lorne snapped, spinning to Ari. "You think you know something about fighting? You think you got some skills because you stand in a ring and hit one guy with fucking pillows on your fists? If you need a fucking scorecard to know who won, it's not fighting."

"I know that," Ari scoffed. "Trust me, kid, you made that plenty clear tonight. I've never seen a man move quite like that. Like you don't quite live in the same reality as the rest of us. You also made it clear that I was an idiot to try to come back. Mover like you? If you'd known what you were doing, you would've had me. My ankle really started hurting in the second round, but you didn't know how to use it, did you? Haven't had the chance to train enough, change your own instincts. I'm impressed. And relieved. I'm going to retire proper now, and I'll know that I got out before the Lightning came up, and I didn't get my teeth handed to me on those big white gloves. Nice touch, the white."

"That was Dav's idea."

"Of course it was. Ever the showman, Davik Kaine. Have a drink of water, kid. It's good for you after a fight, helps you piss out any blood in case I hit you in the kidneys."

Lorne picked up the whole jug the bartender gave him, drinking deep. The water was cool inside his mouth, washing a bit of the blood taste away.

"If you think so little of boxing and the 'pillows' we wear on our fists, why are you doing it?"

"Because Powell Iwan told me to," Lorne muttered, setting the jug down beside his pint. "And if Powell Iwan says, 'you're a boxer now,' then I guess I'm a fucking boxer, aren't I?"

"That's it?" Ari asked. "Because Powell Iwan said so?"

"You ever look that old man in the eye? Try it sometime. Try looking at him and all the emptiness that lives behind his eyes, and see if you can tell him 'no.'"

Ari shook his head slowly. Or maybe the whole world had slowed down. "That's bullshit. The kid I fought tonight wasn't there because someone told him he had to be. The kid I fought was there because he loved it. Because it made him feel real and whole. Made him feel like it was the only place in the world where he actually belonged. So, maybe you need to lie to yourself and say you hate fighting and you hate hurting people, but the thing about the ring is you can't hide from the man you're up against. He can see you clearer than anyone else in this fucking world. You don't hate fighting. You hate that you love it. You hate that you're good at it. You think that's something to be ashamed of for some reason."

Lorne grabbed the glass of water in front of him, the condensation cold beneath his hand, giving something to focus on other than the way the hashish and the pride and the anger all battled each other for supremacy. "What makes you think you know me so well?"

Ari shrugged. He slid his thumb through the condensation of his pint glass, frowning at it. "I used to try to convince myself I hated it, too. Retired from the military before the honourable five was up, but then I think I lost something. I don't know. Not fighting made me uglier than I was before. I started following league matches, and I thought that would be a better way. With pillows on my fists so the fight doesn't kill the stupid kid who doesn't want to admit that fighting is all we have."

It sucked all the anger out of Lorne. He looked at Ari, at the bruises on his face, at the black stitches half-hidden in his beard. Ari's sadness sank between them, drowning out all the noise in Lorne's head, all the disjointed thoughts that flitted around.

Ari drained the water in his glass and snarled at it like he wished it was beer. "I can tell Dav boxed, once. Not since coming to Yaelsmuir, or else I would have heard about it. Those sharp brows of his, he must've bled from them a lot. I almost missed the scars at first, because the thick eyebrows hide them. I'm sure he's a good coach because he knows you—shit he got you through eight rounds, didn't he? After less than two weeks training? But I was thinking about you and him and this place. I think I can teach you better. If you'll have me. That's why I came back, instead of going home to my wife. I wanted to offer to coach you before good sense changed my mind."

"Why would you do that for me?" Lorne asked, even though he thought he knew the answer.

Ari shrugged again. Worse than Jason, with all his shrugging. "That way I can retire from fighting and still pull a wage from a pugilist club."

"Why not coach at your own fucking club, then? The one in Brickheart that everyone says you built."

"Because there aren't any fighters I can work with down there. None of them have anything worth writing home over, you know? Worse, the lot of them figure they've got something to prove. Makes a fighter hard to teach. But you, you don't need to prove anything, do you? You know who you are. And you're fucking *good*. If I could put some time into you, reform those Hive habits 'til you're used to following league rules, I could take you from good to excellent. And then when you're the champion of Yaelsmuir and you start touring other cities for nationals, I can tell people 'I trained that boy when he was nobody, and now look at him.' But you have to get some discipline in you. You have to take it seriously."

"I am taking it seriously," Lorne scoffed.

"Oh yeah?" Ari laughed. He nodded at the bartender, and the man started pulling a pint. "That why you stayed up all night getting high and fucking around? Gossip spreads fast, Mr. Lightning, especially when you have group sex in public places, even if it's your own club."

Lorne shrugged, chewing on all the things he wanted to say but couldn't. He couldn't explain that he did that because László robbed a bank and gave Lorne khat, and it felt like the whole city was tilting toward war and he wanted to feel less alone before it all fell apart.

"Don't go all quiet on me," Ari said, elbowing Lorne and giving him a grin, as much as the stitches in his lip would allow. "I'm not judging. How old are you? Twenty-three?"

Lorne pushed his hands over his face, trying to scrub away the sluggish feeling that was sinking into him. "Twenty-two. I guess I'll be twenty-three soon."

"You guess?"

"Yeah, I think so. I'm pretty sure I was fourteen when I signed for the military. I know some kids that young lie about their ages when they sign because you get a better wage at fifteen, but I don't think I knew that when I signed. So when I said fourteen to the recruitment officer, I'm pretty sure that was right."

Ari nodded. "Almost twenty-three, more or less. Probably. So I understand it. A pugilist club feels a little bit magic, with everyone going out of their way to take care of you and beautiful people wanting to fuck you because you're important all of a sudden. But if you want to be excellent, you have to set some boundaries, follow some routines. And if you don't want to burn yourself down, you have to ground yourself in something internal so you don't get so swept away in everything happening around you. Anyway, I'll teach you all this if you'll have me."

"Davik's my coach," Lorne said. "I'm not replacing him. He built this place. He built *me*."

"I know that," Ari said with a nod. "I wouldn't try to replace him. I'd work beside him. It's his club, and I'll let him set the pace. I want to help. However I can. I guess I can understand why no one trusts me enough to pull me into the Red Dawn, so I was thinking about how else I might contribute. This place, it must be a front for all that underground shit, right? That's why Dav pours so much time and money into this place, and that's why he had his people pass these out." He pushed one of the pamphlets across the bar. That headline again, the biggest letters they'd used since they'd started printing. *What Happened To Ffyanwy Rhydderch?* "Is it true he's the same Davik Kaine that fucked up Cruinnich, or are those rumours?"

"I don't know about any of that," Lorne muttered, pushing the pamphlet away. "I'm just a pugilist."

Ari grunted. "Sure, just a pugilist. So am I."

Lorne shook his head, trying to organize his thoughts. How had he gotten here? He'd been nobody for so damned many years, and now people knew his name. They gave him gifts simply for existing, wanted to buy him drinks, wanted to train him.

He reached into his pocket, finding the draig y môr. He set it on the bar beside his glass, the dragon coiling on the wooden bar top, mouth open like it was going to eat the pint glass whole.

"Why didn't you disqualify me? Dav said the referee left it up to you whether you wanted to disqualify me or not, after I got you by the arm."

"Ego," Ari snorted. "I didn't want people to say I took the easy way out 'cause I was afraid of you. I didn't think you'd take me with one round left. You came pretty fucking close, though. I won't admit that to anyone but you, my wife, and my coach, but there it is. You almost had me."

Lorne wanted to ask about Ari's wife, and her pregnancy, and what they'd decided to do about it, but maybe it wasn't any of his business.

He liked the feeling of the hashish. The khat was too fucking much, but the mellow roll of the hashish, slicing him away from all the big chains of anger, that was pretty good. He could rest his head on the bar and drift a while, or maybe he'd sleep. And the chaos of the club would be his blanket, protecting him from the world. But where was everyone? László, Davik—he expected to see them around, at least.

No, Davik was gone. He was supposed to talk to Powell Iwan or something.

Lorne pushed himself up out of his stool slowly, and his legs wobbled like they weren't sure about taking his weight.

"Hey, take it easy," Ari said. "You alright?"

"I'm fine," Lorne said with a shrug, except the shrug rolled weird through him. The hashish, the beer, the shots to the head, all building layers. "László must be upstairs. I should go find him."

"That's a good idea," Ari said, standing too. "Get some sleep, hey? We'll talk about it in a couple of days once you can think without getting a headache. Don't forget your dragon."

Lorne grabbed the wooden carving, trying to put it in his pocket, except he couldn't muster that much coordination. He tightened his fist around it so he wouldn't drop it and headed for the stairs. Ari's hand closed around his arm, helping him through the crowd. Someone grabbed the front of Lorne's coat, and he was falling, pulled off balance. Spinning. Someone laughing. So much laughing. Was it László? He reached, but his hands caught nothing but air.

"Off," Ari said. "Get the fuck off him. Mr. Lightning is done for the night. He's going to bed. Get out of the way before I start swinging!"

Walking. Maybe he hadn't fallen after all. It's just that the hashish had him hard now that he was standing. He hadn't noticed how much the world spun when he was sitting.

"When I see Dav again, I'll have a chunk out of his hide for leaving you unattended," Ari said. He held Lorne and walked with him. The hallway opened up in front of them and there weren't so many people there. "Where the fuck is he?"

"Don't know," Lorne said. They passed Davik's office, the place that had all the money in it after László robbed the bank. The place with the scale that made Lorne feel like meat, except he was an insufficient amount of meat. He didn't punch heavy enough, and he lost the match. "Rowan's supposed to be in charge. Where's László?"

"Well find him, kid, don't you worry. We'll get you upstairs, and you'll sleep it off, yeah?"

Stairs. Fuck stairs. A torture device. Davik said they were supposed to make him springy but he hated them. There were so many of them. Up and up and up, it felt like they stretched up forever. Like he was trapped in a corridor, always climbing, reaching for something he couldn't get to. He was tired of reaching, tired of climbing. Tired of being trapped, hemmed in.

A door creaked on its hinges. It was dark upstairs, the lamps spilling only the vaguest light. The kitchen was empty. The place was quiet. Almost. Someone was having sex down the hall—the creaks, the groans, those sounds were unmistakable. Was it Davik, celebrating with the bookie again? No—Davik was gone, and he was usually louder than that.

"Nice place Dav's got up here," Ari said, guiding Lorne down the hall. "Which room is yours?"

The place was too empty. Too still. Lorne walked down the hall, his feet dragging. The quiet of it all drilling into his ears. He pushed the door to László's room open. László wasn't there. His coat was gone. Which was strange, because László hardly ever wore it. He spent so much time here, in the club or the apartment, where it was so warm that he could walk around shirtless all the time. But he wasn't here because he wouldn't need his coat unless he left.

"Where'd he go?" Lorne asked.

"Don't worry about it," Ari said. "Go lay down a bit, and I'll figure it out for you. I'll go find Rowan, have him look at your head again, make sure everything's fine up there."

Alone. He was alone in the room. Standing near the bed, the floor tilting. Or was he tilting? The hashish maybe, making him float a little bit above the floor, and that's why it felt like everything was tilting even though the room was standing still.

He hated how empty the room was without anyone in it but him. Hated how much space there was around him, how empty the bed looked. How strange László's wardrobe looked without his coat hanging from the door.

Back out into the hallway, he went to the room Tashué and Ishmael were sharing. Maybe one of them would be home. It was late at night, wasn't it? So they should be here, because they came here at the end of every day, and Tashué did what he could to heal Ishmael's knee. But their room was empty, too.

Tashué's sabre was gone. Lorne remembered carrying it here himself, remembered the way the blade rattled in the metal scabbard as the carriage bounced down the street. The driver hadn't been willing to carry Lorne and László into the Bay, so he dropped them off in front of the tram tracks, and they had to walk the rest of the way, lugging all of Tashué's shit across the quarter, Lorne half numb with grief and fear and shock because he thought Tashué was dead.

He could still hear that stupid sabre rattling, even though it was gone. Everyone was gone.

No—it wasn't the sound of the sabre rattling. Someone was knocking on the door. Banging. Urgent.

He turned again and went back down the hall. What time was it? Who the fuck was knocking—was it László? *No, that's stupid, László wouldn't knock, he'd just come in—fuck, where's László?*

Lorne pulled the door open, praying it was someone he knew. A face he recognized. Fucking anyone, so long as he wasn't alone anymore. But it was some kid. Sopping wet from the rain and standing in front of the door, looking up at Lorne with wide, desperate eyes. Her mouth moved but she talked so fast, all Lorne could hear was a rush of sound. Buzzing.

"What?"

"I'm looking for Allie Tei. Is she here? I need to see Allie Tei. I have a message for her, from the hospital in Brickheart. Someone said she was up here. Is she here?"

Lorne blinked. He didn't know. He didn't know where anyone was.

Footsteps in the hallway. He looked over his shoulder to see Allie, scrambling into trousers. They weren't hers. Vasska's trousers? Sure. Why not. Everyone had someone but him.

"From Brickheart?" Allie asked, shoving past Lorne. "What's happened in Brickheart?"

"Mr. Kol Khara was delivered to the hospital," the child said. "The people who dropped him off said you knew him. Said you should come. Bring your camera."

Allie shook her head, pulling all her hair out of her face. "I don't have a camera... Who? Who's at the hospital?"

"Mr. Kol Khara," the child said again. "He's in a bad way, the healers said he might die. Thought someone who knew him should be there."

"Who is Kol Khara?" Vasska asked. Standing in his drawers down the hallway.

"Oh no," Allie said. "Ishmael—"

She spun on her heel so fast it made Lorne dizzy, running back down the hall.

"How do you know it's Ishmael?" Vasska asked, trying to catch her as she passed him.

"Do you want me to waste time explaining or can you help me find my clothes?"

Lorne looked down at the child. Still looking up at him. Waiting for her tip for delivering the message. Lorne fumbled in his pocket. Something fell out of his hand. The draig y môr, on the ground. He dug through his pocket and found more copper crowns. Brand new because László stole them from the bank. He dropped a few into the girl's hands, and the girl turned, sprinting back down the stairs. Job done.

"Hey," Vasska said, catching Lorne's arm. "Are you alright?"

"Sure," Lorne said. "Where's László?"

Vasska shrugged. "I thought he was with you."

There was so much noise downstairs. A roar, vicious, angry, seething. The crowd had turned into something ugly down there, but Lorne couldn't imagine why. Everyone was so happy when he was last down there.

Something pulled at him. Curiosity, anxiety, itching in his chest, dragging him down. His boot knocked the draig y môr into the stairwell.

"Hey," Vasska said. "Lorne, wait—"

The draig y môr went tumbling down the stairs, the wooden statue bouncing off each tread, tumbling end over end until it hit the floor of the hall and spun away, out of sight. Lorne followed it down. Stupid, maybe. Stupid to follow a dragon into that much chaos. Ari wanted him to be upstairs, to go to bed, to wait for László, but László was gone.

Patrollers were guarding the back door. Four of them, standing shoulder to shoulder. The draig y môr lay in the empty space between them and the club patrons, standing in the hall. Milling around, buzzing with something anxious.

"You can't just keep us in here!"

"What gives you the right?"

Allie pushed past Lorne, dressed in her own clothes, but she skidded to a stop when she saw the Patrollers at the door and the malevolent crowd. One of the Patrollers turned to face Allie, pointing his gun right at her face, the double-barrel shot gun turning everything cold and quiet.

"Go back upstairs," the Patroller said.

"Why?" Allie gasped. "You can't keep me here. I have to go—I have to go to the hospital—"

"Any medical triage required will be dealt with in the morning," the Patroller said. "Go back upstairs or I'll arrest you."

"Hey," Vasska said again. "Ari's right. Let's go back upstairs before things get ugly, and I'll find out what happened."

"I need to go, Vasska," Allie said, her desperation making Lorne's skull itch with sympathetic agitation. "Sir, please, I'm a reporter for the Highview Times. I have a lead about something at the hospital in Brick-heart, and I need to go."

"No one leaves until the Bay is secured," the Patroller said. "No one in or out until we have orders otherwise."

"Lorne," Ari said, coming out of the crowd. Into the open space. He stopped right beside the wooden dragon, like it was a checkpoint. He moved with his hands up, palms facing the Patrollers, but he looked at Lorne. Lorne couldn't meet his eye for long, his heavy head always sliding down, leading his eyes to the dragon on the floor. They were supposed to be good luck. "It's fine. Go back upstairs, kid. I'm sure it's all a misunderstanding, isn't that right, Patroller? We don't want any trouble here. These people weren't involved in whatever happened in the Rift. They were here for the match, yeah? So we can all relax."

Lorne shook his head, his eyes making their slow way back up Ari. Long legs and that same tight shirt, and the stitches in his bottom lip to close the wound that bled so fucking much during the match. There was blood all over Lorne's ring, the canvas soaking it up like the thirsty earth. So much blood in the world, an ocean of it, ready to drown them at any moment.

"Mr. Lightning," Ari said, speaking so slow it felt like he was stuck on something. "Go back upstairs. Lock the door behind you."

"What happened at the Rift?" Lorne asked.

Something clicked in the room, like a bone breaking. Or maybe it was in Lorne's brain. Something switched on, filling him with panic. Frantic, ugly fear that built pressure in his chest and made him feel like he was going to vomit, except it was stuck there. Halfway up.

"Go back upstairs," Ari said again.

"What happened at the Rift? Ari, what happened at the Rift?" Why the fuck was he asking Ari? "Is it Jason—did something happen to Jason? Where is he?"

Ari wouldn't know anything. Lorne *knew* that. But the words tumbled out of his mouth anyway because the desperation pushed them out. He turned to the Patrollers and he looked past that shotgun. Who brought a fucking shotgun to a place like this? If it had buckshot in it, it would take out half the crowd when it threw its vicious lead pellets everywhere.

"Back up!" the Patroller snapped.

"I'm going to get him," Ari said. "He's just a pugilist, yeah? He's had a long night. I punched him in the face a few too many times cause he's stubborn, but he's fine. Just let me get him back upstairs, and then every-thing is fine. Right? We don't want any trouble here, kid. Don't care about the Rift or whatever's happened. We were all here for a nice night for Miss Redbone, weren't we? And now Mr. Lightning here is going back upstairs, and he'll sleep off the beer and the smoke, yeah? None of us want any trouble. Let me get him back upstairs? Please?"

The Patroller nodded. It all happened so slow. Little moments drag-ging on forever. Stretching on and on until Lorne didn't remember who was talking. Him, or Ari, or the Patroller with the shotgun.

Ari stepped forward. He kicked the dragon, and the wooden statue went spinning across the floor again, hitting the toe of Lorne's boot. Ari's hand hit Lorne's collar, getting ahold of the soft fleece. Lorne shook his head again, taking a step back.

"What happened at the Rift?" he asked again.

He felt each word leave his mouth with perfect clarity because the question was burning him alive.

And then chaos.

He didn't know if Ari pushed him or if he fell or maybe he'd pushed Ari like an idiot, and he was the one who lost his balance because the whole world wouldn't stop tilting. But he hit the ground so hard it made his teeth rattle. The impact punched the air out of his lungs. He wanted to scream but he couldn't. He wanted to move, to get back up, but he couldn't. Hands on his shoulders, a knee on his leg, a fist coming down toward his face.

Pain.

Spots in front of his eyes. Blood in his mouth. Twisting, tumbling, falling. No, not falling. He was face first on the floor. His blood pooled under his mouth. He wanted to scream in rage and pain but he still couldn't because he couldn't breathe in. Someone on top of him, crushing him.

"Get the fuck off him!" Ari shouted. "Get off him! You can't hold him down like that, you'll fucking kill him! Get off him!"

Feet on the floor around him, the crowd was coming closer. Shouting. Calling his name. A body of rage, filling the hallway, coming closer. Coming to save him, maybe, except they couldn't possibly save anyone because that fucking shotgun still loomed over Lorne's head. The black barrel in the corner of his eye, promising so much death. The crowd closing in on Ari and someone screaming *get back, get back*, except the crowd didn't give a shit.

Ari staggered, coming too close to the gun.

Flash, bang—Lorne couldn't hear.

He blinked the tracers out of his vision and saw red.

Ari's chest was a curtain of red.

Ari fell hard, hands on his throat, back into the crowd. Except his throat wasn't fucking there anymore because the shotgun ripped it to nothing. Someone screamed. Someone else fell on top of Ari. Lorne twisted, thrashing his whole body, and it was enough to get his chest off the ground. Suck in a deep breath, fill his lungs. The door opened behind him, blasting his whole body with cold air. The storm outside was screaming, and he was screaming, too. The Patrollers dragged him over the floor, leaving a streak of his blood behind. Another gunshot and a Patroller fell beside him. So much screaming, he didn't know who was responsible for all of it. Maybe it was him, just him, screaming loud enough to be ten people because everything hurt, and something had happened to Jason in the Rift, and Ari was dead. Ripped open. Bleeding all over the hallway, Lorne's home.

The Patrollers dragged him right out the back door. He rolled as he fell over the threshold. His shoulder hit the street. Leather and fleece dragged rough over the cobbles. Rain pelted him, stinging and vicious cold. The door swung shut, blocking out the light, the sound, cutting it all off in an instant. Lorne listed in the silence. Alone again. Or unconscious? No—if he was unconscious, he wouldn't be wondering about it.

He moved as much as he could, pushing himself up. On his hands and knees first. And then higher, so he was kneeling in the street, staring at the back door and the Patrollers leaning on it, two of them holding it shut as the crowd pounded on it from inside. The shotgun popped open, and the Patroller holding it pulled the empty shells out, tossing them into a puddle.

"What the fuck are we doing?" one of them asked. "We were supposed to hold the crowd!"

"You can't fucking hold a crowd that big, not from inside," the man with the shotgun said. "Fucking stupidest order I've ever gotten in my life. We need more men here, to surround the building, guard the doors."

"So what are we doing with him?"

"That's the Lightning," the Patroller said. "Davik Kaine's pugilist. We'll hand him over to Clannaugh, maybe he can use him. I don't fucking know, alright! But I'm not dying in there!"

Lorne groaned, the sound coming out of his chest like panting. "You killed him. You killed Ari."

"Shut up!" the Patroller snapped. "If you hadn't fought, this wouldn't have happened!"

Lorne shook his head. He didn't remember fighting, not until they had him on the ground and he couldn't breathe. The puddle under his knees was so cold. Ice shone on the cobbles, on the threshold to the back door, on the handle. The whole door rattled. Gunshots inside, clapping distant and weak. They probably didn't sound weak in there.

"Put some manacles on him or something before he tries to run," the Patroller said. "We'll turn him in to Clannaugh at least, save our asses. This fuckup isn't our fault. We never should have been in there!"

Lorne laughed. Stupid to laugh. Nothing was funny, and these people had guns. But he laughed anyway, and he spat water and blood out of his mouth, blinked against the ice pummelling his face. "You're fucking right, you never should have been here. The Bay is going to eat you alive."

He saw the shotgun coming, but he couldn't move in time. The wooden butt hit him in the face and knocked the whole world right out from under him.

72

TASHUÉ

DAY 39

The courtyard behind the *Pint Under the Rails* set a familiar ache in Tashué's bones. The last time he was here was less than a week ago. He'd bought the bottle from Pallwyth, walked down to the river with Ishmael, put Keoh's ashes into the Brightwash. And now Ishmael was probably dying because of the choices Tashué made that day. If he let himself think about that too long, he'd ride back to that hospital and take up vigil at Ishmael's bedside. Or carry his remains down to the Qasani temple, so his priest could rally the community around him. He had to go. He had to find Stella. Because Ishmael, his appropriately cynical handler, would tell him that they're fighting for more than any individual person.

He tied the horse's reins to the support post of the tram line to search for the spare key Pallwyth kept. Hidden away in a crevice between bricks in the wall, the spare key was offered as safe haven to Pallwyth's most loyal customers. *Just in case*, he said when he showed Tashué and Kazrani the key. *This world, you never know.*

"Go sit down under the bar," Tashué whispered, pushing Jason into the pub ahead of him. "No one will be able to see you down there."

Jason went to the bar, sinking down onto the floor with his back against the wood, giving a sigh so long and slow that Tashué could almost see the tension unfolding from his body. He cradled the Uhl rifle across his lap, pointing it up at the ceiling. Irén sank down beside Jason, pressing her back against the bar. "Your old man sure is something, hey?"

"Yeah," Jason said. "I'd say you get used to it, but I never did."

"Why are we stopping at a pub?" László whispered, stepping behind the bar. "Gonna grab a pint before we fuck the Authority?"

"Jason needs to sit for a bit. So do you, for that matter. No one can take photos until the sun's up anyway."

"Damn," László said, giving his wild grin. "I was hoping for a pint."

"Just sit your ass down, would you?" Tashué grunted. "It'll do you good to stop moving for a whole hour."

Footsteps creaked on the stairs, and László spun, lifting his rifle, the butt snapping up to his shoulder with perfect precision and his whole body folding to sight along the barrel and brace for the .45 mule kick. Tashué reached out, resting a hand on his arm, gently easing it down.

"It's me, Pallwyth," Tashué said. "I'm only staying a short time, and then I'll be out of your hair. And if there's any trouble before that, I promise we'll go. The kids needed a moment to catch their breath."

"Mr. Blackwood?" Pallwyth asked, easing down the steps. The darkness inside the pub was thick and heavy, and Tashué could only see the vague form of Pallwyth's body on the stairs behind the bar. "Rumour has it you're dead, sir."

"Can't trust rumours, can you?" Tashué asked. "I'll pay for anything we take."

"That's alright, sir," Pallwyth said. "As I see it, I still owe you a drink or two after you paid me a whole silver for a shit bottle of blended whisky. Help yourself to whatever you need."

"Put the gun down, László," Tashué said. "Just relax."

László sucked in a deep breath, pointing the barrel of the rifle at the floor. Pallwyth made his way down slowly, the stairs creaking.

"Shall I light a lamp, sir?"

"No, leave it," Tashué said. "It's best that it looks like no one's here."

László breathed slow again, his hands gripping his rifle too tight, like he was coiled with tension that he couldn't release.

"László," Irén said, kicking László's boot. "Just come sit down before you blow the poor publican's head off."

"Yeah, sure," László said, sinking down beside Irén. "Sorry, sir. It ain't personal. Just been a wild night is all."

"Sure, son," Pallwyth said. "You kids come up from the Bay?"

"Yeah," László said, resting the butt of his rifle on the floor so the end pointed straight up at the ceiling, his hand still around the barrel like he'd bring it back to his shoulder to shoot something at the slightest provocation. "From the Bay."

"You should go back upstairs, Pallwyth. I don't want you to get dragged into the trouble. If anyone comes looking say you never heard us come in."

Pallwyth didn't go. "You still take the copper whisky early in the morning?"

"Ah, no," Tashué said. He stretched out his hand, offering Pallwyth the key back. "Last time, things went a little out of control for me. And I'm not staying."

Pallwyth came close enough to pull the key from Tashué's hand, closing his fist around it. "You mind if I have a dram?"

Tashué shrugged. "It's your pub."

There was enough light for Tashué to see Pallwyth leave the key on the counter and grab a bottle and a glass from the bar. The cork squealed as it popped out of the neck, and Pallwyth poured himself rather more than a dram, the cup shaking in his hand.

"Is it true? The things people heard you say at Mayor Wolfe's hospital?"

"Yes," Tashué said softly. Hopefully Jason could find the proof, and then no one would ask if it was true anymore. "It's true. I'm trying to prove it. I don't mean to bring trouble to your door, but the kids are tired, and they needed a place to sit a while. Just until morning, and then they were never here."

"Aye, I think I can hear one of them snoring," Pallwyth whispered. "Who are they? How'd you fall in with Bay kids at your age?"

"One of them is my son," Tashué said.

"Jason?" Pallwyth asked, looking toward the end of the bar, but of course he couldn't see any of them from where they stood. "I didn't recognize him."

"In your defence, it's dark in here, and it's been a while."

"It sure has, hasn't it?" Pallwyth took a long swallow of the whisky. "So, it's true, then, that they broke down the Rift? Someone went up this whole street, knocked on every door to tell us to stay inside. But then, instead of guarding these streets, they went down to the Bay. Don't know why they went to the Bay. Seems to me they should have guarded the roads closest to the bridge to the Rift, stopped people from even getting to the Bay in the first place."

Tashué nodded. "They've been spoiling for a fight with the Bay. This was the excuse they needed."

A pause, and then the sound of more whisky in the glass. "Well. It's going to be an interesting day, isn't it?"

"It is."

Tashué pulled his timepiece out by habit, but it didn't help. It was still broken because things didn't magically get better. All the kids were asleep —he could hear the three of them, one of them definitely snoring, the other two breathing heavily. Hopefully Lorne was fine, back at the club. Hopefully the three of them—Lorne, Jason, László—would live long enough to sort through whatever mess they'd gotten themselves into. They should be allowed the time and space to have twenty-something-year-old problems of having too much love to give instead of their lives revolving around war. But if Tashué remembered being twenty-some-thing, they'd probably find time to angst about their feelings whether there was a war in the streets or not.

"I need to go," Tashué said, tucking the broken watch away. "What-ever happens today, you should stay home. It's going to be ugly."

"Right," Pallwyth said, dragging the bottle off the counter. "Sure. Be careful, Mr. Blackwood. It would be nice to see you again when it's over, so we can have a dram and you can tell me what really happened."

The little publican retreated to the stairs. Tashué stepped to the end of the bar again. László was the one snoring, slumped against his sister's shoulder. She was so much smaller than him, maybe half a foot shorter. They were both whip thin, though, both a little wild around the edges. Irén wasn't sleeping like Tashué thought, wedged between Jason and László. The stitches on her face gave a harshness to her expression. Her hair still dripped water onto her shoulders.

"Are you sure about all this?" Irén asked.

Tashué shrugged. "I'm not sure about anything, Miss Dargis. But I know war."

"Ten years, hey? That's what László said while we were walking down this way. He sounds like he likes you."

Tashué shrugged. "Here I thought he hated me."

"That's the Dargis attitude. If he actually hated you, you wouldn't wonder. He said the papers down in the Bay were publishing the things about your career. Ten years serving, five with the Jitabvi."

Tashué nodded. "Doesn't sound like a lot, but when you're living it, it stretches on forever. I have to go."

Irén elbowed Jason. Just enough to make him sit up straighter, his eyes flaring open and his whole body going tense. Tashué crouched down, reaching out and squeezing Jason's hand.

"You sure I can't convince you to come with me?"

Jason wiped his eyes, looking around the pub. But then he shook his head. "I can't go now. I want to help the children. Find my brother. I have to stay."

Tashué nodded. "Then I have to go before I change my mind. You'd better be alive when I get back."

Jason came up as fast as he could, throwing his arms around Tashué's neck. Tashué caught himself on the bar or else Jason would have pulled him right over.

Tashué pulled Jason against his chest, holding him tight. He smelled like blood and sweat, his clothes musky in spite of how long he'd spent out in the rain. And maybe if Tashué was a good father, he'd let Jason go somewhere peacefully. Maybe he should have taken Jason somewhere, to an inn or something, where he could bathe and get new clothes and put a decent meal into his system. Recover a bit. Or he'd drag Jason out of the city kicking and screaming so he could keep Jason safe out on the road.

But he wasn't a good father. He'd proved that time and time again. Failing every test, every measurement. His son tried to tell him the whole system was broken, and he didn't listen for years. And then his son paid the price for his willful blindness, rotting in a prison for three and a half years.

He was, however, a soldier.

Like he told Irén, he knew war.

"You'd fucking well better come back," Jason whispered.

And with that, Jason was choosing to fight. Tashué respected that. Understood it. Jason wasn't a child anymore, and he could make this choice.

Maybe it isn't your job to save him, Stella had said. *Maybe it's your job to bear witness when he saves himself.*

Maybe it was his job to let Jason be the hero Tashué couldn't be.

Tashué closed his eyes and squeezed Jason even tighter. Both arms, all the way around him. Sweet North Star, it felt so good to hug him again. All these years, all he wanted was to hug his son. Whatever happened, he'd carry this feeling for the rest of his life.

"I'll be back in a few days. If I can't find her, I'll come back."

Jason nodded. "Good luck."

He had to let go.

It was snowing when he stepped out into the courtyard. Of course. It came softly, the ferocity draining out of the storm. It drifted down between the ties on the tram track above the courtyard, piled itself in delicate mounds on the courtyard walls. The big mare flicked her ears toward Tashué, lifting her head. Her tail swished against her flanks, brushing snow off her fur. He pulled his scarf tighter around his face and untied the knot of her reins.

"Let's go, big girl. See how much ground we can cover before the snow really fucks us."

She snorted at him. He led her out of the courtyard, and she danced as she walked, pushing her chest against his back like she was trying to rush him. Young and eager, hungry for movement and action. He climbed up into the saddle again, the familiar creak of leather like a forgotten song to his soul. His sabre rattled as the big mare made her way through the alley, her head high. He had to drag hard on the reins to keep her moving slow. As soon as a clear, straight stretch of road opened in front of them, he slapped her flanks with the long reins and she took off like a shot, muscles bunching, stretching, the air around him whipping through his hair, pulling at his clothes. Carrying him out of Yaelsmuir.

73

ILLEA
DAY 39

Sleep was scarce at best, but lately it had become a rare beast. The pregnancy brought exhaustion that dragged through every day, but all night, Illea lay in her big wide bed and watched the long shadows flicker in her bedroom. There were too many things to do, too many thoughts demanding her attention, no matter how tired she was. The shifting of an empire was a heavy thing. Inviting Bothain to her bed had helped. His hunger was aggressive and energetic, tiring her out enough that she could rest a while. But he hadn't returned since yesterday. All the things he wanted to accomplish kept him somewhere else. In the Bay, perhaps.

Getting up in the morning was a slow ritual now, which was endlessly frustrating. She wanted to get up and start occupying her mind, but if she got out of bed too fast, the nausea caught her. She ate some of the things Beatrice left for her, which helped considerably. At least Myron was staying at Rainer's house. Winter manor finally felt like her home without him.

Soon, she wouldn't need to think of him at all.

Restlessness drove Illea down to her kitchens. The whole kitchen was beautifully chaotic as it came to life, each person knowing their job, directed by Savvas with his iron rule. Savvas himself moved with perfect confidence, like he was built for this purpose, like he knew the stove and the fire and the simmering pots as well as he knew the beating of his own heart. Long, strong arms reached into the massive ovens without fear, callused hands handled stockpots half as tall as he was. Watching him work was comforting. He'd been in this kitchen… as long as Illea could remember. No matter what chaos was happening in the city, in her businesses, or in her personal life, Savvas was always here, cooking meals to serve her considerable staff, prepping for whatever she was hosting next.

He paused when he noticed Illea standing in the doorway, his big face lighting with his toothy, charming smile. But he didn't pause for long. He reached out to the sweet cream that simmered away on one of the smaller burners, stirring it so it didn't turn lumpy while the starch in it cooked. There was nothing worse than lumpy sweet cream. If it weren't for Tilde's insistence that Illea keep her diet varied for the sake of the pregnancy and her overall health, she wouldn't eat anything except sweet cream and fig pudding.

"It's horrifically early, Mistress," Savvas said. "Can I get you something?"

"No, I'm fine for now," Illea said. "I'm watching a moment. Ordering my thoughts."

"It's just breakfast, Mistress. I needn't any supervision. No need to worry."

"Of course, Savvas," Illea said. Just breakfast. Except nothing was simple these days. Nothing was *just* anything. If Bothain had his way, the city would be burning before the new year. And Illea had to catch her own rise through the political field, or Bothain would leave her behind. Of that, she had no doubt. A man did not come to be one of General Maes's favourites by being sentimental about allies if they turned into dead weight, no matter how much he enjoyed Illea's bed.

But if she was Governor, that would secure her place for a while.

"Would you like to come in and sit," Savvas asked, "or are you intending to hover anxiously until you think of something better to do with your energy?"

Illea lifted her chin, squaring her shoulders. "I am never anxious, Savvas. I'm only watching."

"Yes, Mistress," Savvas said, handing the spoon to one of the other cooks so they could take over stirring. "Would you like some tea while you're not-anxiously watching?"

"You're incorrigible," Illea said, but she smiled in spite of herself.

"The gall of you, honestly. I've given you too much freedom around here. You don't know your place."

Savvas grinned even wider, turning to drag the massive door open. "I would be happy for you to show me my place, Mistress! If you'll give me a moment, I need to get the tarts out of the oven before they burn, and you can show me my place any way you like."

Illea laughed, shaking her head. "Stay focused on your work, you scoundrel."

"Yes, Mistress." He pulled a tray of butter tarts out of the oven, resting them on the counter. The tops were almost burnt, giving them the perfect caramel scent.

Illea watched the steam curl off of them, the smell making her mouth water. "When will the sweet cream be ready?"

"A while still, Mistress. But there's still some in the larder from yesterday. Shall I fetch it for you?"

Illea nodded. Savvas set aside the tea towel he'd used to carry the hot tray. He emptied the jar of yesterday's sweet cream into a bowl and grated some cinnamon over the pillowy whiteness of it. He offered it to Illea with a deep courtly bow, and kissed her on the cheek when she took the bowl from his hand.

"Get back to work, you miscreant," Illea said, giving him a smile to soften the weight of the scolding.

"My pleasure, Mistress."

The sweet cream was indulgently thick and sugary and warmed a little by the flavour of the cinnamon. She headed back down the hallway, eating as she went. She'd only slept with Savvas once—or was it twice?—in the dark and chaotic days after Amias had died and before the marriage contract with Myron was finalized. Her father was so ill in those days, his liver failing no matter what the healers did to try to revive it. Illea was a ghost of herself, and Savvas's big arms and charming smile offered a refuge from all the darkness. Savvas brought all the care and vigour to sex that he always had in the kitchen, but what Illea liked most about him was that things hadn't changed at all between them after. It was just a thing they had done together, a thing that kept Illea from being alone in her bed with her monumental grief for one night. He went back to normal like it had never happened, and their usual flirting continued.

"Mistress," Beatrice said, catching up to Illea halfway down the hall. "A telegram for General Clannaugh."

Illea handed Beatrice the half-eaten bowl of sweet cream, plucking the telegram envelope from her hand. Addressed to Bothain, care of Illea's address. Such a little thing, a telegram card. It couldn't be any more than a few grams worth of paper, and yet it had incredible weight.

She slid her fingernail under the seam of the envelope, tearing it open. Bothain said she could. The missive was brief and to the point—the Queen had granted his request for martial support, deployed under peacetime laws that only allowed one-tenth muster of the division. She wouldn't declare the situation in Yaelsmuir a civil emergency, not yet. The guns and the bank robbery had apparently swayed her some, but not enough, which was about what they expected. If Bothain was smart, he would have the city in chaos by nightfall and then Leony would have no choice but to send the full division.

But was that what Illea wanted?

"I should bring this to him as soon as possible," Illea said. "Did he leave word where he'd be today? Did he get anything from the boxing match?"

"Yes, Mistress," Beatrice said. "He sent word a few hours ago—Cattle Bone Bay is rioting."

Illea nodded. "Good. He'll be down there already, I imagine. Any word on whether or not Eirdis got herself arrested? Did the riots start at the boxing match?"

"I'm not sure," Beatrice said, shaking her head. "News is limited. The Authority has asked that residents stay home—something's happened at the Rift as well. There's been some violence or a breakout. They're trying to search the city to catch whoever escaped. The telegram delivery had to be given special dispensation to even leave the telegram office, he said."

Something at the Rift—they'd discussed the Rift as a potential chaos point if she recalled correctly, but Bothain hadn't given her details of which actions he'd chosen to pursue.

A knock on the door rang through the whole house. Someone was out front, using the heavy door knocker to make as much noise as possible. Beatrice turned immediately, heading toward the sound, but another servant beat her to the front foyer and dragged the door open. A pair of Patrollers stood on the front steps, snow swirling behind their heads.

"Miss Winter?" one of the Patrollers said, looking past the servant at the door and straight at Illea, like a man who had never called on a wealthy home before. The eye contact while she stood in her home, in little else but her dressing gown and the thin shift she wore beneath, felt horribly invasive. For a moment, Illea imagined the Patrollers stepping into her house, tearing things apart like the Authority did at Nathaniel's house a few days ago.

"This is Miss Winter's house," Beatrice said, stepping in front of Illea to block any more eye contact. "How can I help you, Patroller?"

"General Clannaugh sent us to escort Miss Winter to Park Island as soon as possible."

"Why Park Island?" Illea asked.

"I don't know, Miss Winter," the Patroller said. "He only asked me to escort you there. He said it was urgent."

S now twisted down in gentle spirals, laying peaceful on every surface, turning to sludge on the roads, turning the sky murky grey. The brights were still glowing even though it was well after dawn by the time Illea made her way out of Highfield, the glow of them shining on the snow and the ice. Now and then the wind gusted through the streets, rising to a vicious howl, making it difficult to tell how much snow was falling from the sky and how much was swept along in the draft.

It was a relatively short journey to Park Island. The bridge from Highview down to Highfield stopped at the large island, where the bones of an old fortress had been converted to an amphitheatre. Carriages were gathered in the field already, the drivers clustered around a brazier that glowed with coals. Illea's escort marched around her carriage the whole way there, and then the young man who came to her door offered a hand to help her down once her driver parked near the other carriages.

"Miss Winter," another Patrollers said. "General Clannaugh asked that you come inside right away."

Into the amphitheatre, then. Illea had dressed in plenty of layers, at least, and she wore a walking skirt with a short hem, so she didn't have to hold it up as she picked her way through the swirling motes of snow. Through the door that led into the seating area. Some seats were carved from stone, but others had been built in the remodelling, with iron scaffolding and wooden seats that seemed flimsy, especially when the theatre was packed to capacity, and sometimes looked like they were swaying if the spectators on the wooden seats got especially animated. The walls of the amphitheatre blocked out most of the gusting wind, but the open structure let the snow tumble in, a cold and brittle blanket across every seat and turning the stage as white as old bone. The Patrollers led her around the curve of the stage, to some of the wooden steps. People stood underneath, another coal brazier giving off a line of smoke that signalled the gathering place.

Illea rounded the corner, pausing to take in the moment. The strange assembly. Bothain of course was to be expected, but not Myron and Rainer. Illea had imagined that Bothain's scorn of Myron's campaign had been obvious enough to make Rainer distrustful of him, but apparently not. Nathaniel Wolfe was also a surprise—for a man under house arrest, he was a little way from home. He must have slipped his guard when news of the riots broke. And Vasska Czarny.

Of them all, young Mr. Czarny was in the worst shape. He had blood on his clothes and on his face, and when he stretched out his hands to the fire crackling in the brazier, there was blood worn into the creases and the nail beds. If he was the one bleeding, it was hard to tell—he stood relatively straight, his chin lifted in quiet defiance. His eyes were deeply lined with rings of exhaustion, but they were hard. They swept over Illea like he was annoyed by her presence, though she couldn't imagine why. She'd dealt with Powell Iwan's grandson before, and all her dealings with him had been good for both of them.

"Illea," Nathaniel said. He shuffled closer to her, leaning heavily on his cane in that way he did when he was furious, like the pain was tied directly to his anger. "You shouldn't be here. Go home."

"Excuse me," Illea scoffed. "You'll not dismiss me like I'm a meddling child, no matter how much I love you like a father. Bothain sent for me, and I'm here."

Nathaniel's mouth turned to a hard line and Bothain stepped past him, catching Illea's arm and leaning down to kiss her on the cheek. Myron's face turned deep red, like he still imagined himself to have some possession over her, when she'd been going out of her way lately to show him he had nothing. No single part of her belonged to him except her name, and she would take that back soon. A matter of days, ideally.

"Thank you for coming so quickly, Miss Winter," Bothain said. "Did you, by chance, receive any mail for me last night?"

"I did," Illea said. She retrieved the telegram from her pocket, handing it over. "You said I could open it."

Bothain nodded. "Thank you."

"Is that why you had us stand around in the cold for over an hour, General Clannaugh?" Vasska scoffed. "So that you could receive your mail? Well, we're all very impressed by the size of your ego, I assure you. Could we perhaps get on with negotiations now?"

"We should arrest him," Myron said quickly. "Him and Wolfe both, for harbouring enemies of the Crowne and the Authority. Isn't Wolfe meant to be under house arrest?"

"Go ahead and arrest your own Mayor," Illea scoffed. "I would love to see how you explain that to the press, Myron. House arrest is one thing, but throw him in the city jail, see how far the riots spread then."

"I suppose there's nothing to stop you from arresting me if you'd like to wave your cock around, Mr. Governor," Vasska said, so coolly and filled with scorn that Illea couldn't help but like him. He'd always been a shrewd and vicious businessman, hiding his razor-sharp mind behind his spoilt, rich grandson act. "But if I'm not back in the Bay by noon, my people will execute the hostages we have and hang them from the Hive so you can see the lives you threw away for *your* ego."

"Before you so casually mention executing hostages," Bothain cut in, "perhaps you should ask why I so desperately wanted my mail."

Nathaniel huffed, snatching the telegram card out of Bothain's hand.

"The Queen has granted his request for martial support," Illea said. "One tenth muster for peacetime actions. That was granted on the grounds that Davik Kaine has been assembling weaponry for a militia, and there was reason enough to believe that the Red Dawn was responsible for that bank robbery. Mr. Czarny, if there's been trouble in the Bay and you execute hostages, that will be enough to turn her hand, I think. She'll have no choice but to declare a civil emergency and send the full division."

Nathaniel handed the telegram card to Vasska, his other hand gripping the head of his cane so hard it turned his knuckles white. "You've done it now, Myron. There's no peaceful way out of this for you."

"For me?" Myron scoffed. "You're the one who's sided with the rebels tearing this city apart. You're the one who encouraged Eirdis Redbone to stand with criminals!"

"Careful, Mr. Keene," Vasska said, using Myron's family name with such weight it sounded like a threat, and Myron spluttered deliciously. "One of the criminals is standing in front of you, waiting for an answer about whether or not you want your hostages back."

"How many?" Bothain asked.

"Four were taken alive," Vasska said. "The rest were killed by the crowd after Ari Odegaard was brutally murdered by the riot patrol you sent. I ask that the barricade be safely opened between Cattle Bone Bay and Brickheart so Mr. Odegaard's remains can be returned to his coach and his wife, both of whom are waiting by the tram tracks to receive him. I also ask that our pugilist, Lorne Coswyn, be released from custody. And if you've murdered him, too, I ask his body be returned to us so he can be given the hero's funeral he deserves."

"And Eirdis," Nathaniel added. "You can't hold your campaign opponent under arrest."

"We want Blackwood and Saeati," Rainer said. "And Davik Kaine. Produce them all for arrest and you'll have your murderous little pugilist back."

"That's not possible," Vasska said. He flicked his wrist, casting the telegram card into the fire. The paper curled in the flames, turning black and then white, ash crumbling away.

"I thought you were here to negotiate, Mr. Czarny," Rainer said haughtily. "If you strong-arm us, how are we supposed to believe that you're here in good faith?"

"I'm not here in good faith, Mr. Elsworth," Vasska said, smiling. "I'm here with full intention of watching you burn your own career to the ground. There is no good-faith agreement that can be made with a man who breeds and mutilates children to be used as power. I'm hoping that General Clannaugh and Miss Winter will invite the Queen to Yaelsmuir, so she can be here when you're arrested for your crimes against humanity. I am, however, willing to haggle with you for Lorne Coswyn. He's the Bay champion, after all, and my people are rather fond of him. I'm hoping that seeing him returned safe to the quarter that is so devoted to him will help pacify the streets. I think it's in everyone's best interest not to give General Clannaugh an excuse to wander through the Bay shooting people like he did up in Cruinnich."

Rainer's eyes bulged, and Myron made a small squealing sound. Nathaniel put his hand on Vasska's shoulder, like he was coaching the young man to some restraint, but Vasska clearly didn't need the guidance.

Bothain smiled. "So, Mr. Czarny, let's haggle. We'll take Blackwood, Saeati, Kaine, and you'll let the Authority into the Bay to search for Rift escapees."

"What happened at the Rift?" Illea asked.

Nathaniel glanced at her, then glared at Bothain. "Someone seems to have killed the children that were tasked with keeping the suppression on the building. Without the children—sorry, the energy units—to separate the inmates from their Talent, the inmates broke out easily. Slaughtered the guards and left."

"I wonder who might have done that," Vasska said.

"I wonder indeed," Bothain said. "Sounds like something Davik Kaine might do. I want him, Mr. Czarny, and then you'll have your peace."

"I very much doubt that, General Clannaugh," Vasska said. "You're hoping I'll walk away without a deal, which is why you're giving me such impossible requests. I don't know where Davik Kaine is. I can't make the quarter stand aside quietly while you raid and arrest whoever you want. I haven't seen Captain Blackwood since before he was arrested—I heard Rainer Elsworth had him killed. And Ishmael Saeati is dead. He died last night."

"No," Illea said, the word rolling right out of her before she could stop it. "You're bluffing."

Vasska shrugged, pulling a photograph out of his pocket and handing it over. Illea reached for it. Nathaniel reached faster, snatching it out of Vasska's hand.

"You don't need to see it, Illea," Nathaniel said. "Not again."

Not again was exactly right. *Not again* rolled through her bones, her joints, echoed in her marrow. In her soul. Not again—a man she loved like family, stolen from her. Not again—it must have been terribly bloody for Nathaniel to try to protect her from it. Must have been an ocean of blood, just like her beautiful Amias, bleeding all over her lap on the forest floor, olive skin turned to ash in the bright summer sun.

"What happened?" Illea gasped.

"I want to see the body," Bothain said. "I want to be sure it's him."

"Of course, you do," Vasska sighed. "He was turned over to the hospital in Brickheart. You can go bully them for the corpse as soon as we're done haggling here. Although, as you can see from the photograph, his body is in rough shape."

"Ah, but he's got all those tattoos, hasn't he?" Bothain said, snatching the photograph from Nathaniel's hand. "How did he die?"

"A number of wounds were assessed by the healer, but ultimately it was massive head trauma," Vasska said. "The last anyone saw him, he was going to meet my grandfather. Now, I know you haven't any history in this city, so I'll fill you in. Ishmael Saeati was Bay-born, and that's enough to make him like family for our citizens. More than that, his family name is responsible for a large number of jobs that are ever so precious in the Bay, and the Qasani temple he donates to regularly has a number of outreach programs that helps to feed and clothe the people of this city regardless of their creed or their background. I know everyone on the civilized side of the river thinks of him as a drunk, but down on our streets, he's a hero. So is Mr. Odegaard for that matter—the man who brought pugilism to the common quarters. And I think your people killed Ishmael, just like they killed my grandfather."

"Your grandfather," Rainer spluttered, genuinely surprised. "What happened?"

"I'm not entirely sure what happened," Vasska said. "But he's dead, murdered in his own apartment. Why don't you ask General Clannaugh? I think he knows. He was seen leaving the apartment a few hours before it all happened."

"I assure you, Mr. Czarny, I do not," Bothain said. "I made a deal with your grandfather for Davik Kaine's head. I'm assuming the man responsible for your grandfather's death is the very man he was supposed to sell to me."

"Spare me," Vasska snapped. "I've had a long night, General. Watching good people die hasn't put me in the mood for games. The Bay doesn't know yet. They're angry enough already, but they still don't know about Ishmael Saeati and their beloved patriarch, Powell Iwan. Until they know, you have a bit of time to decide how you want this to go. If I can give them their pugilist champion back, at least, maybe it will pacify them some."

Illea shook her head, turning away from them. She couldn't listen. She'd never in her life walked away from business or politics, but she couldn't stand and listen to them squabble. Ishmael. *Not again* rolled down her spine. *Not again* wouldn't let her think. It twisted through her mind over and over. One by one, she lost the people she loved the most in this world and was left with tiny men with tiny minds instead. Myron Keene and Rainer Elsworth were scum on the bottom of Illea's shoe, but she was stuck with them. Even Bothain was a poor consolation prize compared to Ishmael, whom she'd known so long. Who understood how terrible a hole Amias had left.

The cold got ahold of her as she walked; the farther away from the fire, the more vicious the chill that gripped her. She hadn't realized how ugly the wind was, not when she was standing so close to the flames. It felt like a metaphor for something, except Illea couldn't wrap her mind around what exactly. Was Bothain the fire? Or was he the cold?

Nathaniel's cane tapped its way after her. He caught her arm and pulled her against his chest. He smelled like blood. The iron tang of it was thick in Illea's mouth—was it real, or her imagination? There wasn't any blood on his clothes, not that she saw. Perhaps it was her memory, dragging that horrible smell up from the forest floor and taunting her with it.

"What happened?" Illea asked. "Did you see it? Were you there?"

"I'm sorry, Illea," Nathaniel whispered, crushing Illea tighter against him. She hadn't gotten far away from the brazier. The men gathered around were probably still within earshot. "I'm sorry. I told you not to stay. I didn't want you to find out, not like this."

Illea groaned, pushing Nathaniel away. "I need to go to Brickheart. I need to see him. What if it's not him? Couldn't it be someone else?"

"General Clannaugh?"

Illea spun to the new voice. A courier had arrived, walking hesitantly through the amphitheatre seating. He had a box with him.

Everyone froze. Illea took a step back, further away. Nathaniel took a step closer, like he'd throw himself at that box if he had to. Vasska stepped back, away from the brazier, putting more distance between himself and the boy.

"General Clannaugh," the courier said again. "I was told you were expecting me, sir. I tried you at Mr. Elsworth's house, but the servants told me you were here. The shipper wanted me to ensure I put the parcel directly in your hands."

Bothain pulled his gun from its holster, pointing it at the ground in front of the courier's feet. "Don't come any closer. Who let you in here?"

"Sir?" the courier asked. His whole body froze mid-step, his eyes flicking to the gun in Bothain's hand. "The Patrollers let me in, sir. I was told you were waiting for this. They let me through when I showed them the shipping label."

"Illea, go," Bothain said. "Go right now."

"Oh for fuck's sake!" Myron huffed. "Enough of the damned dramatics, Bothain. We all know you're very surly and brutish, but there's no need for a whole production, is there?"

"Myron, don't!" Nathaniel barked.

It was too late. Myron was already marching up to the courier. He snatched the box out of the boy's hands—the boy gave a yelp and tried to hang on to it, but Myron caught him off guard enough to get it from his grasp. A hat box, the ribbon tied, the tag hanging from one side.

"To General Clannaugh," Myron read. "The gift you asked for. What fresh hell is this then?"

"Don't fucking open it, you idiot," Bothain snapped. "It could be a bomb for all we know! Did you plan this, Mr. Czarny? Lure us all here under the pretence of negotiations, and then get your vengeance with a bomb?"

All the colour drained out of Myron's face as he finally grasped what he'd done. "A bomb?"

"We should leave him there holding the cursed thing," Vasska laughed. "That'll solve at least half my problems."

"No," Myron said. "No, that can't be right. Who would send a bomb? It can't be a bomb, that's absurd. This is Yaelsmuir, not a bloody war zone."

"Illea," Nathaniel said, turning to her. "Walk away."

"No!" Myron howled.

He dropped the box. He bolted.

It fell for a terribly long time. Hung in the air like one of the swirling snowflakes, except it was a hat box. Illea couldn't think clearly enough to move, to react, to even conceive of all the reactions she saw around her. People were moving as the box fell, scattering, trying to get away as fast as possible. Nathaniel grabbed her, pulled her. The box hit the ground first, and then Illea's knees did, the layers of her skirts only softening the blow a little bit. Her hands hit next, burying cold into the snow and hitting the stone so hard her palms were numb a moment before the pain hit.

Nothing happened after that. It was only stillness and quiet. Illea pushed Nathaniel away, looking toward the box. The top had tumbled off, half-revealing the contents. A bit of white fluff, like sparse fur, or stylized silk. Maybe it was a hat, some horrible joke.

Bothain moved half a step closer, nudging the box with the toe of his boot. Vasska laughed. It was a heart-wrenching sound, wild and manic, a horrible, broken, half-sob of a laugh.

"Oh dear god," Rainer said, "whose head is that?"

"I believe our negotiations are over, General Clannaugh," Vasska said. "It seems to me, you weren't here to negotiate in good faith, either. I was right to think you had my grandfather killed, wasn't I? What was your intention for his head? Will you send it to the Queen?"

The head belonged to Powell Iwan. The white fluff was his hair. His skin was so grey he almost blended into the stone below the wooden seats.

"Illea," Nathaniel said again, his voice gone quiet and hard. "I think it's time for you to go."

"Yes," Illea breathed, wiping the snow off her hands. "I think you're right."

H er hands were still bleeding when she climbed into her carriage. She left a smear of it on her driver's glove when he helped her up, left another smear on her skirts. Tilde grabbed her hands and dabbed them with a cloth.

"What happened?" Tilde whispered.

"They said Ishmael's dead," Illea whispered. "I don't know what happened. We're going to Brickheart. If he's dead, I want to see his body."

"Are you sure—"

"I wouldn't say it unless I was sure!" Illea snapped. "Tell the driver. To Brickheart."

"Yes Mistress."

Tilde opened the door enough to poke her head out to speak to the driver, giving Illea enough of a view of the other milling carriages. Vasska Czarny had walked away from the negotiations, too, but it looked like Nathaniel, Bothain, and Rainer had stayed to talk. Myron was at his carriage, sitting with the driver and drinking from a flask with trembling hands.

If Illea had a gun, she'd shoot him. End it herself.

Curse him, and Rainer too—they brought this ruination to Ishmael. Had Bothain really organized that head? It was hard to tell, sometimes, the difference between his surprise and his smugness. Bothain said Kaine was ferocious when backed into a corner, so it was possible that Kaine had caught Bothain off guard with the ferocity of Kaine's retaliation. Or he really had done this, and he'd blame it on Kaine to get his civil emergency. Was Ishmael's death intentional or collateral damage?

"Tilde," Illea whispered. "Leave the Patrollers behind. We don't need them to escort us."

Tilde nodded, passing the message to the driver.

The cart rattled after the driver flicked the reins, the horse team leaning into their traces. The Patrollers marched around the carriage, ahead of the horses, leading the way across the field. It was slow going, the wheels in the snow, but they hit the road leading to the bridge, and the carriage rolled easier over the hard packed earth. The driver flicked the reins again, and the horses broke into a fast trot, heading along the straight stretch at a clip the Patrollers couldn't keep up with. The ramp up to the bridge was a long, slow slope, curving around, and the horses trotted all the way up, the carriage rattling Illea miserably, but it was worth it. Once the carriage was up to the bridge, the driver tugged the horses back down to a walk.

"Which way, Mistress?" the driver called.

"Where's Vasska Czarny?" Illea asked. "Did he pull ahead of us?"

"I think so, Illea," Tilde said. "What are you planning?"

Illea shrugged. "Is he ahead of us or behind us?"

Tilde opened the door again, letting the cold blast of air in. "He's just behind us, Mistress."

"Follow him off the bridge, and then offer him a ride."

Tilde sighed. But she passed the word to the driver. Illea plucked the rag from Tilde's hand, pressing it against her own palms to seep up the blood. The wounds had turned hot and stinging, especially the deep spot on the meaty part below her thumb. She should have been wearing gloves with how cold it was out there, but she'd left them behind in the carriage.

Easier to think about gloves and the sore spots on her hands than about Ishmael. Better to think of these little things than let herself get completely lost in Amias. *Not again* tried to creep its way back into her mind, but she didn't have time. She wasn't the young woman she was back then. Twelve years ago. That day, and all the long, lonely years since, had taught her too many terrible lessons. And a few good ones. Best not let herself get lost in the act of wishing for things that weren't possible, or else she'd miss her chance to make her own future. If Ishmael was dead, she'd deal with that grief after she spoke to Vasska.

The sound of the other carriage passing hers sent her heart hammering again. The bomb scare had happened so fast, she almost hadn't had time to taste the fear. It was just a moment, a moment of terrible potential that didn't happen. But now, something had started trembling in her chest, down in her gut, crawling beneath the surface of her skin. The lingering fear, maybe, finally getting ahold of her. Mixed with the terrible fury.

Down the bridge and into Highview. Her driver sped up again, and then both carriages stopped. The streets of Highview were wide enough for them to stop side by side, and Tilde opened the door again in time for Illea to see Vasska open his door as well.

"Miss Winter wonders if you'd like a ride, Mr. Czarny."

Vasska sat still at first, his eyes fixing on Illea as he considered her. Measuring his possibilities, assessing his risk. Perhaps remembering the sight of his grandfather's severed head and wondering if Illea had a hand in it. Finally, he sighed. He climbed out of his carriage and into Illea's, settling on the bench opposite hers.

"Most generous of you, Miss Winter," he said stiffly, like he knew he owed some pleasantry. "Are your hands alright?"

"Fine," Illea said, closing both her hands around the cloth. "It seems Cattle Bone Bay is in quite a bit of turmoil, Mr. Czarny."

"Indeed," Vasska said. "The riots started late last night. Things are quiet for now, but that's because we chased all the Patrollers and tinmen out of the Bay."

"And captured a few before they could get away?"

Vasska shrugged. "Like I said, my people will execute the hostages unless I'm back soon."

Illea nodded. "Of course. I won't keep you long. I heard about the Rift, about Ishmael, about your grandfather—is there anything I'm missing?"

Vasska sighed, spreading his hands and looking toward the window. The cart rattled on. "Last night, I was at a pugilist match for Eirdis Redbone's campaign. This morning, people I care about are dead, missing, or arrested. I'm certain there are things I'm missing. I can't help but wonder what hand you had in any of it, Miss Winter. You certainly made no effort to hide your allegiance to Bothain Clannaugh, who seems to be the source of a rather large number of my problems."

"Are you sure it was Bothain?" Illea asked. "And not Davik Kaine?"

"Sure? No. But the General is still my enemy. He said as much himself. He'll write to the Queen about the suffering he wrought, and then march his Army through the Bay, slaughtering whoever stands in his way. As I see it, I have a few days to fortify my quarter, and then I'll be under siege."

"Perhaps I could be of some assistance," Illea said.

"Is this where you offer to try to talk some sense into him?" Vasska muttered. "Try to temper his hand or some such?"

"No. I haven't that much control over Bothain. He marches to Maes's orders, not mine. But Rainer and Myron are going to steal this election unless we do something quickly."

"Eirdis was polling favourably, Miss Winter. A bit of time in the city jail won't be enough to deter the Bay from voting for her. If anything, it will make their support stronger. And Ari Odegaard's death will galvanize Brickheart." His eyes wandered down to his own hands and he stretched them out in his lap, like he was studying the bloodstains. "He was innocent in all this. He was only trying to save Mr. Coswyn from the Patrollers."

"Yes, yes, I'm sure you and Eirdis will whip the whole city into a terrible fury over what happened last night," Illea said. "That's why Rainer is going to *steal* it. He'll use the unrest as an excuse to refuse to deploy voting stations in the Bay, or he'll have the election postponed. They did it in Cruinnich a few times while the fighting was at its peak, and they did it in Dür when the Authority swept over the lake, arresting all the tainted who were living in the floating villages. You and I both know that Rainer is the sort to resort to *any* tactic to keep his grip on his power, so we need to anticipate how to undercut him when he inevitably resorts to dirty tactics."

Vasska's head cocked to one side, a little bit of his practiced rage draining out of him and showing the cool, fierce young man he was beneath. "I'm listening."

"For years, Rainer refused to even contemplate moving against your grandfather because he feared retribution from the Bay."

Vasska snarled. "Yes, Miss Winter. I'm aware. Which is why I'm sure Rainer and Myron, at least, aren't the ones responsible for what happened. Was the head your idea? To help boost Clannaugh's position with the Queen?"

"It wasn't," Illea said. "I would not have chosen to be there if I knew it was going to be delivered."

Vasska tilted his head again, watching Illea's face. "So, what are you offering?"

"I think it would be in our best interest for you to tell Cattle Bone Bay that Rainer and Myron were the ones responsible. And I think it would be in our best interest for Myron to catch the full weight of that retribution."

"Oh really?" Vasska scoffed. "And why is it in *our* best interest to blame Myron when I'm far more interested in blaming Clannaugh?"

Illea handed the cloth to Tilde, looking down at her hands. There was a blood blister close to the centre of her palm, tucked against one of the creases. "Do you know who General Maes is?"

Vasska gave a bit of a nod. "He's on the Queen's Voting Council, most famous for his feuding with the late General Deri. A vicious Crowne loyalist, vehemently opposed to provincial autonomy."

Illea nodded slowly. "If Bothain dies here, Maes will burn this city to the ground. If Myron dies? I might find myself in a position to speak directly to the Queen."

"Aren't you already in a position to speak directly to the Queen? She stayed at your house, after all."

"My position needs strengthening, especially when this city faces such terrible unrest."

Vasska tilted his head back to look up at the ceiling, sighing so long and slow that he seemed to be deflating. "Ah. I see. If I were so inclined to get rid of your husband for you, you might be likewise inclined to beg the Queen for mercy on Cattle Bone Bay's behalf. But I'm not to touch Clannaugh because you've still a few deals with him that you'd like resolved. You'll play the both of us, and then sell whichever one of us fails to entertain you sufficiently. You'll excuse me, Miss Winter, if I worry about my chances when playing for your attention against General Clannaugh. I hear he's been rather attentive of your needs since arriving in the city."

Illea fought the urge to roll her eyes, but the resentment turned sour in her mouth in an instant. "You're very young still, Mr. Czarny, so I'll forgive you your assumptions that I can't separate sex from opportunity. Perhaps you haven't had enough of it yet at your age to know the differ-ence, but once you're a haggard old slut like I am, you realize that an orgasm is rather a mundane thing. Fun, but if you're desperate, you can have a few in your own company without needing anyone else involved."

Vasska laughed at that, shifting on his bench to sit up a little bit straighter. "How young do you think I am?"

"If that's the part you want to talk about, perhaps I've made a mistake in assuming you're clever enough to give me what I want," Illea said. "Shall I have my driver drop you off so you can walk back to the Bay?"

"Maybe not just yet," Vasska said, folding his hands in his lap. Cool again. Good. "What can you promise me, Miss Winter? So that I know the value of this opportunity before I say anything else embarrassing."

"I can promise you that I won't let Bothain come for your head next," Illea said with a shrug.

"Does that mean he's really the one responsible for my grandfather?"

"Honestly? I don't know. But he'll benefit from it either way. "You'll have to produce someone we can arrest to appease him. Kaine or Blackwood."

"What if I don't know where they are?"

"You'd best find out in a hurry."

"So, I kill Myron and produce at least one decent arrest. That's my side of the bargain?"

Illea shook her head. "You don't have to kill him. I can find someone else, since I imagine you'll be rather busy down in Cattle Bone Bay for the foreseeable future. All I need from you is to tell people he's the one who asked for your grandfather's head. Let the public cheer his death, so when it comes, they aren't inclined to ask too many questions. And, yes, I need Blackwood or Kaine, for bargaining. Either one will do."

"And you're offering what, exactly?"

Illea shrugged. "My ever lasting gratitude. My glowing endorsement. My considerable business flow, which will be interrupted as long as there's chaos in the Bay. I expect the Hive is shut down in light of the riots. That won't do, Mr. Czarny. I need my barges passing through this city uninterrupted."

"No, that won't do," Vasska muttered. "Heaven forbid you should be short on profits this business quarter."

"You can pretend to be a bleeding-heart moralist as much as you like, Mr. Czarny, but you and I both know the Hive is the centre of this city. We need to get back to business as soon as possible. Rainer knows it, too. He's going to run Myron's campaign by turning this city against you, quarter by quarter, until you're so villainous to the people of this city that they're cheering for *your* demise. By the time he's finished, he'll install one of his cronies as head of the Hive."

"Are you trying to imply that Clannaugh will treat with me in a way that Elsworth won't?"

Illea nodded. "He promised me Rainer's destruction. We'll get it one way or another. Not before untold violence, though, so the question remains: are you interested in working together so you can survive the storm with the Hive? Or should I find some other way clear of my husband once he and Rainer have destroyed your birthright?"

Vasska shrugged, picking lint off his trousers and flicking it at the floor. His face settled into something tired, something sad. For all that Illea called him young, he looked worn all of a sudden, his mouth turning down like he was battling hard against emotion. It surprised her. Which part of this was upsetting him? The blood on his hands, perhaps —he'd mentioned Ari Odegaard, the pugilist. What had happened at that club?

"Can you get Mr. Coswyn out of jail?" he finally asked, his eyes on the backs of his hands again. "If he's alive."

Illea nodded. "I'll try."

"Then you have a deal."

Illea knocked on the wall behind her. The driver pulled the horses to a stop, and Tilde opened the door again.

"Oh—I suppose you'll be wanting to go to the hospital in Brick-heart," Vasska said, pausing halfway out the door. "You'll have to go around the long way. No one is letting traffic through the Bay. But it won't be worth it. We took our photographs of Mr. Saeati, and the hospital cremated his remains. He hadn't any family here in Yaelsmuir, and the hospital needed the room. With the riots, there's going to be a lot of people in need of healers, especially if you let Clannaugh make things worse. I didn't bother telling Clannaugh since the idea of him wasting half the day chasing after Mr. Saeati's remains entertained me, but... well. There's nothing in Brickheart for you, Miss Winter."

A lump clogged Illea's throat in an instant, taking her by surprise. She sucked in a deep breath, but it wheezed through her. "The Qasani tradition is for the remains to be given to his priest."

"I know," Vasska said. "I'm sorry. I brought his ashes to the Qasani temple this morning."

"How did you get them if you were trapped in the Bay?"

"General Wolfe brought them to us. One of the healers guessed Ishmael's identity and sent for the General last night to confirm."

Illea shook her head, but she couldn't speak. She didn't dare. All the grief had caught up to her, slicing through her heart so it felt like she was bleeding under her own skin. She pressed a hand to her mouth, but her fingers trembled. Vasska cast her one last sad glance, and the genuine grief in his eyes undid her. There was no more room for business or politics or cursed Myron. She bowed her head and wept for another friend lost, for all the things she could have said to Ishmael but never did, for all the things she'd lost because he was gone. Just gone.

74

TASHUÉ

DAY 41

It was quiet, out on the road.

The swirl of snow deadened all the usual sounds, and all the open space around the city gave Tashué's Talent room to wander without the awareness of so many people grinding against his mind. He could hear life; creatures of all sizes hid in the snow, defying the illusion of stillness. But none of it demanded his attention as insistently as the city. The only thing he could think about was Stella, and surviving the cold.

Thoughts of what he'd done chewed at the edges of him, but only distantly. He could blame his Talent for the people he killed in the forest all he wanted, but he'd shot the woman in the bank and Powell Iwan with nothing but his hands and a gun. He'd found a knife and cut Powell's head off at Ishmael's bidding, taking him at his word that it was necessary. He could try to convince himself he didn't know who he was anymore, but that was a lie, too. He'd carried that badge for nineteen years to hide himself. Because if he had laws behind him, holding him in, guardrails on his darkest instincts, he could pretend he was a decent man. But the laws were shit, so fuck it all.

Ride. He hoped his Talent knew where she was, like Davik said, because there was an undeniable feeling in his chest dragging him north, north, north, making it hard to sleep at night. North. Go north. She's *right* there.

Out here, it was easy to follow the road—it was a straight shot for quite a few miles, and when it meandered this way or that, it was flanked by undulous foothills that guarded it like sentries all the way—even though the snow piled up steadily until he couldn't see the packed earth anymore. The snow fell slowly, peacefully, but the unrelenting twist of it came and went the whole time Tashué was travelling, so that by the time the roadhouse rose out of the distance, everything lay in a blanket of pure white. At first, when his Talent started to hear the sounds of people, he thought he was imagining it. How could there be people out here in the endless stretch of snow, in the half-buried wild grass, in the rolling hills. But there was a roadhouse, up ahead—the roof and the barn were so layered in patches of white that it looked like another hillock except for the line of smoke that twisted up from the chimney. He hadn't realized it was there until he was only a few yards away.

And the noise. The heartbeats that tugged at his awareness, the footsteps that came to him over the distance as clearly as if he stood in the main hall himself. The clatter of pots in a kitchen he hadn't reached yet, the crackling of a fire he couldn't see, running water.

He had to pull his Talent back again—after a couple of days on the road alone, he'd stopped trying. Picture his Talent like it was blood from an open wound, imagine the pressure that kept it under control. Bit by bit, the awareness fell away, until all he could hear was snow. The crunch-squeal of it beneath his horse's hooves as she slogged through it, her heavy breathing that sent plumes of condensation from her nose, his own breathing. Quiet.

A figure stepped out of the barn. Small, a smudge of colour against all the white. A child. A shock of strawberry blond hair without a hat, and heavy winter clothes.

Ceridwen.

His heart skipped a beat.

Ceridwen made a sound like a laugh and a sob, her whole body leaning forward to run through the snow. Except her legs were short and the drifts around the barn were all the way up to her knees, and once she left the path from the barn to the roadhouse, she fell.

Tashué kicked the mare forward, but she was tired. Her feet dragged through the gathering drift, and though she lifted her head like she wanted to try to go faster, she only walked. Fuck it, he slid down from the saddle and ran. But his running wasn't much faster, the snow eating up his boots, clinging to his stride. His legs were sore, his body exhausted from the ride. He hadn't been in the saddle that long in fucking decades, and now that he was moving, everything screamed at him. Didn't matter.

Ceridwen pushed herself up out of the snow only to fall again and she laughed, the sound lilting and pure, making Tashué's body soar with the joy.

She pushed herself to her feet and took three steps, enough to close the gap between them. She leapt toward him, hitting his chest so hard it almost knocked him over, but he caught her. He lifted her right up off the ground, but the weight threw him off balance, and the snow was thick around his feet so he couldn't shift fast enough, and he fell, too. Went down to his knees. Ceridwen buried her face into Tashué's coat, and her laughter dissolved into sobbing, the sound bubbling through her, making her whole body tremble. And Tashué held her, because he understood it. The relief and the joy were tangled with melancholy, with regret. He rubbed her back and squeezed her as tight as her body could bear and knelt in the snow. He never should have let them go.

Movement caught his eye—someone stepped out of the barn. A man Tashué didn't know, his coat on him awkwardly because one arm was in a sling against his chest. The other hand held a revolver, but he held it only loosely, his finger away from the trigger, the barrel pointed at the ground.

Ceridwen leaned away from Tashué finally, resting both her hands on his cheeks like she couldn't quite believe what she was seeing. Her hands were warm, so warm it almost hurt after so long out in the cold. Her face was bright red and streaked with tears, her gaze studying every inch of his face.

"Are you real?" she gasped.

"Yes, little warrior," Tashué said. "I'm real."

"Ceridwen," the man said. His voice rolled over her name easily. "Go inside, fetch your mam."

Ceridwen wriggled out of Tashué's arms, pushing herself to her feet. It was a slog through the snow, but once she hit the beaten path, she ran, her boots throwing up clods of snow and mud from the path. She hit the door to the roadhouse, dragged it open, disappeared inside.

Tashué pushed himself to his feet, brushing the snow off his trousers. At least he was wearing his cavalry boots—he had them on when he was arrested, and it was the only article of clothing worth keeping after he washed the blood and gore off them.

"You must be Blackwood," the man said. He had a round burr like

Davik, but his felt more honest somehow. More natural. "I'd offer to take your horse in for you, but I ain't so good with just one arm."

"And you are?" Tashué asked.

Maybe he shouldn't have been so gruff about it. Maybe he should have said something that sounded more like a greeting and less like an accusation. The man, whoever he was, was familiar enough with Ceridwen to give her instructions, and she listened immediately. And he was wounded, so maybe he *earned* that familiarity. But Tashué was tired. And sore. And shame cut the life out of his joy. He'd left Jason and Ishmael behind, and he didn't know how they were coping back in the city. Maybe they were both dead.

"Ozra Sgèin," the man said. If he was bothered by Tashué's curt tone, he didn't show it. He put his gun away, holstering it on his chest in the cavalry draw position that let him draw with either hand. He had a pair of revolvers. "I've heard a lot about you, Captain Blackwood."

Tashué shrugged instead of following the impulse to say that anything Stella said was kinder than Tashué deserved. He wasn't the man Stella wanted him to be. The mare had followed him through the tracks he'd made, and she nudged his shoulder when she caught up to him.

"She's probably tired," he said. "Could use a meal."

"Aye, and I'm sure the same could be said for you, hey? Come round back." He retreated into the barn. "I'll open the big door for you."

Tashué slogged through the snow to the back of the barn. He must have passed beside the kitchen, because the smell of sizzling meat wafted on the breeze, making his mouth water. Only two days on plug jerky and hard tack had already made him ravenous for a real meal.

The barn door squealed when Ozra pushed it open, and Tashué led his mare inside. There were half a dozen horses inside already and a big wagon parked in the centre. The floor had been freshly swept, and the air inside was warm from all the bodies of the horses. One of the horses popped its head up to the edge of its stall and gave a squeal of welcome; the mare flicked her ears toward the other horse, stretching out her nose to him as Tashué led her past.

"You hush," Ozra said. "Enough of your flirting. You're too fucking loud."

Ozra pointed to a stall on the other side of the aisle from the friendly horse, and Tashué led her in. Stripping the tack off the mare was an old, familiar echo of who he used to be. He hadn't stripped her down fully while he was travelling, because he never camped anywhere properly. But horse care was something he learned in the military, something he perfected in his time with his Jitabvi company, and the motions came back as if he'd never stopped. He brushed the snow off her coat and she whickered softly at him. Her head bowed, her eyes closed. She needed the rest of the day to recover from the hard slog before he turned around and started heading back. And the exhaustion caught up to him, too. The dark of the barn, the warmth, the repetitive action of the brushing. It cut all the tension out of him, made his limbs feel so heavy he could sleep standing up with her, his face propped against her shoulder and breathing in the scent of her sweat.

Ozra packed the feeder on the side of the stall with hay, the smell of it rich and clean. The mare lifted her head, chewing gratefully.

"She won't come in here," Ozra said. "Best go out to meet her before she freezes herself in the bloody snowbank."

Tashué looked up at Ozra, his thoughts moving too slow to grasp what the other man was saying. He felt like he'd missed part of the conversation. Had he actually fallen asleep? "Who?"

Ozra tilted his head toward the smaller door, the one Ceridwen had come through. The snow swirled over the threshold, the light invading the murky, dusty darkness in a sharp beam that made Tashué squint. He couldn't see anything beyond the intensity of that light.

No, that wasn't true. A figure stood outside the door, blocking some of the beam. The sun glinted on copper hair.

Tashué moved slow out of the stall, pulling the door closed behind him, making sure the latch caught. He wanted to run again, but the wagon was in the way. The back of the wagon was empty, but the wood was stained with blood—the red-brown patches caught his eye as he squeezed past it. His boots scraped in the snow, over the footprints Ceridwen left, and then he stood in the doorway, blinking and half blind as his eyes fought to adjust to the brightness outside. The sun had pierced the clouds, and it glowed on all the white snow.

And Stella, in front of him. She had pulled her coat on over her clothes, but she wasn't wearing a hat either and all her hair was wild in the wind even though she'd tried to restrain it in a plait. She stood in the snow like she was only half-awake, staring at Tashué as the wind pulled on her. Her hair, her clothes, it all danced. He couldn't breathe, looking at her. He didn't feel like he needed to. She was the air, she was the beating of his heart, she was everything. Standing near her made him whole again.

"Say something," she whispered.

He blinked against the power of all the sun, the details of her face coming only slowly. The wound from that day in the Market—when everything was burning and the man attacked her—had healed to a thin scar, but it was almost hidden by the big, mean bruise on the side of her face. The other cheek had a fresh gash, crusty and dark with scabs. He didn't know what to say. He should apologize, maybe. Apologize for being an idiot, for wasting so much time, for letting her go when they should have stood together. For the way he drank after she left, for the way he turned ugly while she was gone.

"Say something," she said again, desperation and panic rising in her voice. "So I know you're real."

"Stella," he said, because he couldn't think of anything else to say. Maybe she could hear how much he loved her in the way he said her name.

She took a step closer. Just one. He reached for her hair first, of all things, pushing his fingers into the tangles and the curls, to hell with how the curls trapped him. She tilted her face up to him, and tears glittered in her eyes, but when he leaned over her, she stood on her tiptoes and kissed him. And it was perfect. Her lips were warm, another reminder of how cold he'd been since he left Yaelsmuir. How empty he'd been since she left him. A few days, two weeks at the most, and yet so much had happened, ripping him in a thousand directions, into a million shards.

But he was being rebuilt.

Holding Jason again, even for a moment, had begun the process of cobbling him back together.

Kissing Stella wrapped purpose around him.

Stella broke the kiss first, leaning back so she could look him in the eye. She touched his beard with trembling fingers, sliding over the hairs like she was memorizing the new length of them. "You're letting it grow out."

Tashué shrugged, easing his fingers out of her hair so she could step back if she wanted to. "I haven't had time to shave. I don't attend as many fancy banquets as I used to."

Stella laughed, tilting her head back toward the sky. And then the tears came, rolling slow down her cheeks. He wrapped his arms around her and hugged her against his chest. "You should come inside. I'm sorry —we can't save him. But perhaps it's good you're here now, in the end."

———

He walked through a mess hall with blood stains on the floor, past people he didn't know. They had all the tables and chairs pushed into one corner and were making slow work sanding the floor down to get rid of the blood. He could feel them watching him as he passed, but they didn't say anything. The kitchen radiated the smell of meat and bread, making his stomach gurgle with hunger, but Stella had him by the hand and led him up the stairs. More blood on the treads, sunk into the grain, and a chunk of the wall chipped away from a bullet. Eventually, he would ask what happened, where all the fresh blood came from. But for now, he followed her up. His legs ached with every tread they climbed, screaming their fatigue, their anger. Two days in the saddle, and now four stories of stairs, all after he'd been up all night, dealing with Powell Iwan and Jason and Davik and Ishmael.

Sweet North Star, he hoped Ishmael was still alive. Hoped Jason was fighting as ferociously as Tashué thought he could.

The room was quiet and warm, the hearth glowing with a fire. Kazrani was stretched out on the floor, in a pile of blankets and pillows that she must have dragged in from another room. Her hair hung in the single mourning plait of someone holding death vigil.

They'd dragged the bed—overly large, the kind rented to a whole family—away from the wall so it faced the single window. The sun came in and lay across Rhodrishi, but it didn't give any life to his features. He was so motionless that Tashué thought the older man had already died until Stella sat on the edge and Rhodrishi's fingers twitched. Just a little. Just enough that it seemed like he was acknowledging her, even though his eyes were still closed.

Tashué walked as softly as he could, the heels of his cavalry boots clunking on the floor. Kazrani didn't stir. He sank down beside Stella, reaching for Rhodrishi's hand. His skin was cold.

"I saw him in my dream," Tashué said. "He came to me... a few days ago. Before I left the city."

Stella nodded. "He's been wandering a lot—I can feel it. I wonder if he's found his family, scattered as they are across the Dominion. I hope so. I hope they all get the chance to say goodbye."

"Walking the dreampath," Tashué said. "That's what Davik called it."

Stella tilted her head toward him, something dying out of her expression. Something hard and distant stripped the intimacy from her, like she was on guard. "You walked to me. Do you remember?"

Tashué nodded. "I saw you in your house. With your son."

"And I told you not to trust Davik Kaine. I told you—one day you just would, and you wouldn't even remember how you got to trusting him. It would be your new reality. I warned you."

He couldn't look her in the eye anymore. He turned back to Rhodrishi, watching him. Holding his cold, still hand, straining his ears to hear if Rhodrishi was breathing. She was right. She was right, and the shame that burned through him was so vicious, he couldn't breathe again. Except instead of feeling whole and complete, it was a great black swathe of failure. Of foolishness. How could he ask her to go back, after everything?

"He said his wife was waiting for him," Tashué said. And he understood now how pure that joy was. How deep a love it must have been for her to pull on him the way she did, even after she was long gone. "Said he was looking forward to seeing her again."

Stella nodded, turning her face away from Tashué to look out the window. "Kona always said that we sink back into Talent when we die. It holds us and our memories. A little bit of our essence lives on, one way or another. That part is universally understood among all the Kaadayri nations I've ever known. What happens after is up for debate. Rebirth, or some afterlife, or maybe just nothing."

Ceridwen came into the room before Tashué could think of something to say. She had a badge in her hand, and Tashué knew that shape immediately. Enquiry.

"Ozra says I'm Kishoan," Ceridwen whispered, padding across the room so carefully her footsteps were almost silent, like a cat drifting over the floor. "He says if I was up north with his family—with our family—they would give me my warrior tattoos. He can't do it himself, with his arm broken. He says maybe when it's better, if Mam thinks it's the right thing to do, he'll do it."

"Your warrior tattoos?" Tashué asked. He turned to Ceridwen, and she sank down on the bed beside him, leaning against his chest. "How do you know you're Kishoan?"

"Ozra is my da," Ceridwen said. "I wished for him, and he came for me. I pulled him to me. He was hiding in the Dunnenbrahl, he said, wishing to die because he thought all his children were gone, but then he started coming this way, and he didn't know why."

Tashué looked to Stella, and she nodded. She wiped her cheeks again, and she still wouldn't look Tashué in the eye, but there was a peace about Stella's face that Tashué had never seen before.

"I killed Siras," Ceridwen said, offering the badge to Tashué like it was proof. "I tried to wish to make him stop, but it didn't work. Ozra said that Talent can't change the heart of a man, so that's why the wishing didn't work. So, I shot him with his gun. That's why Mam won't go in the barn. She said it feels like her death in there."

Tashué turned to Stella again, watching the fresh but exhausted pain bloom across her features. She lifted her chin and stared at the ceiling. He put a hand on her back and she closed her eyes, leaning against him. Accepting the comfort he was offering.

"She tried to help with the horse chores," Ceridwen went on, "but it made her cry, so Ozra said we would do it. I'm glass, like you said. But Ozra said I'm also a warrior now. Maybe I'll also learn to be a healer, like Mam, if we can figure out how to use our Talent again without seeing all the nightmares."

"Slow down, Pigeon," Stella said, dragging her eyes open and forcing a smile. "Poor Mr. Blackwood doesn't know anything about what happened. We'll explain it to him bit by bit."

Tashué reached slowly into his pocket, pulling out the badge he'd kept from the day they arrested him. A week ago. The whole world had changed in a week. Or maybe it hadn't changed at all—maybe it's that he finally saw it, like waking up from a long, ignorant sleep.

"I killed an Enquiry Officer, too," Tashué said, showing her the badge. "Three of them, when they tried to arrest me and Ishmael."

Ceridwen nodded sagely, squeezing her badge tighter. "Ozra calls it hunting bronze. He has two. He shot a hole right through one of them. Miss Mahalouwan has some, too, but they make her sad."

"Go eat, Pigeon," Stella said. "You've worked hard all day, helping with the barn and sanding the floor. You've earned it."

Ceridwen shot to her feet, but something made her pause. Her eyes searched Tashué's face. She looked so much older than when he last saw her, and it was a shame. She'd lost something, some precious, irreplaceable innocence chipped out of her. She should have still been a child, but now she was a warrior, old enough to get tattoos. Did she know about the tattoo she already had? Maybe that was how she knew Ozra was her father. "I missed you. I wished for you, too."

"I missed you too, little warrior."

Ceridwen nodded, pocketing her badge. "Are we going back to Yaelsmuir now?"

"Let me talk to your mam," Tashué said.

Ceridwen nodded and headed out. She didn't skip anymore. She stomped. In the silence left behind her, Tashué could finally hear Rhodrishi's breathing. Laboured, slow. But still there. For now.

Stella gave a long, slow sigh. "It was all for nothing."

Tashué reached for her, but she turned her face away from his hand. "Stella—"

"No," she breathed. "I took her and ran to protect her, but all I did was run in a horrible circle. I never had a chance of getting away, not this time. I didn't protect her from anything. She had to protect *me*. What kind of mother needs her own child to protect her? She killed a man because I couldn't—and Rhodrishi is dying now because of me, because I couldn't fight for myself—and Kaz, and Ozra—but it was all for nothing. Because you're here to ask me to go back. He's dying for nothing and it's my fault."

"Stella," Tashué said again, but he didn't try to touch her this time. "It's not your fault. It's Siras Duncreek's fault. Bothain Clannaugh's fault. The Authority's fault. Hell, it's my fault. If I'd listened sooner, maybe I could have..." He clenched his fists, biting off the thought before he could fall down the same spiral. It wasn't her job to comfort him after he'd made so many mistakes. "I wish I had something wise to say, something deep and helpful, but I don't know. When I shared the dream with him—he told me he was dying. He told me he'd seen his son in his dreams. War is coming. I promised him I'd stand. I promised him I would find his son and fight. He also said it was worth it, Stella. It was worth it to save you."

Her composure crumbled again and she pressed her face into her hands, folding over double. She wept quietly, gasping, her shoulders shaking as she fought for each breath. Tashué reached for her again, touching her shoulder as gently as he could. If she flinched away from him again, he'd leave her be.

But she didn't.

She turned to him and let herself fall against his chest. He wrapped his arms around her again, dragging her in as close as two people could get. He wished he could take this pain from her and carry it himself, but he couldn't. All he could do was hold her.

"I'm sorry, Stella," he said. "I'm so sorry. I'm sorry for everything."

She wept until she was too tired to sit anymore, and then she rested her head in his lap. He turned, resting his back against the headboard. She followed him, lying beside Rhodrishi with her head in Tashué's lap, and he stroked her hair. Carefully, letting his fingers pass over the curls instead of getting tangled in them this time. The cold from outside was trapped in his clothes, the snow on his knees from falling to the ground soaking into his trousers and making his legs cold. But once she cried herself out, Tashué didn't dare move again. Without the sound of Stella crying, he could hear Rhodrishi breathing again. Still so slow, the moment between each breath stretching longer and longer. Moving felt too much like it would risk missing the moment Rhodrishi passed. He couldn't explain why it mattered that he was here, just that it did. Rhodrishi had thought himself dying days ago, when Tashué had seen him in the dream. But for whatever reason, he'd hung on this long. Maybe he was waiting for Tashué to come. Did he know Tashué was here? Would it matter to him?

He sat. He waited. Once he moved, he would have to contemplate going back to Yaelsmuir. With or without Stella. He would respect her decision, but he had to go back. He couldn't leave Jason holding all the weight of the war. He had to find out if Ishmael survived. Had to see it through to the inevitable, bloody end. Even if he was sure a part of him would go dark if he had to leave Stella behind.

Rhodrishi's breathing slowed even more, stretching impossibly, the silence in the space between breath so long that it made Tashué's chest hurt. He held his breath each time, straining his ears to hear. Rhodrishi took one breath, louder than the others, like a gasp. Stella sat up, reaching for him. But there were no more breaths after that. He was still.

"Oh, Rhodrishi," Stella whispered, taking his hand again. "Thank you for everything. I'm sorry I didn't get to know you longer."

75

STELLA
DAY 41

Rhodrishi's funeral pyre was already built by the time Tashué arrived. Ozra had made it himself, one log at a time, refusing to be still. At least he wore the sling, keeping his arm still enough to heal. He wanted to help wrap Rhodrishi in the shroud—improvised, out of bed linen—but he couldn't. So he and Stella talked Tashué and Kazrani through it. Though neither Stella nor Ozra were Pashibé, they'd both witnessed the funeral rituals enough times they could cobble together what was proper. Mostly.

It seemed right that Tashué was the one to do it, at least. He'd arrived in time for that.

Kazrani was quiet throughout. Quiet and as tired as everyone else, still limping on her bad leg.

Rhodrishi had set aside the few things he wanted passed down to his kin, wrapped in a swatch of cloth he'd cut from his own clothes. And everything else he had went into the funeral shroud with him to be burned.

By the time Tashué carried Rhodrishi's body out, the sun hung low on the horizon, turning the hills into impossibly long shadows. Tashué placed Rhodrishi carefully on the pyre, even though the man was beyond any suffering now. His body was empty, and judging from how easily Tashué carried him, terribly light. Ozra brushed snow off the pyre and used a log he'd pulled from the hearth in Rhodrishi's room to start the flames. And though the loss left a shard of pain in Stella's heart, she didn't weep anymore, and neither did Ceridwen. They'd wept so much for Rhodrishi already, and now that they gave him to the flames it felt like a release he had earned. Something he wanted, something he asked for. Ceridwen held Ozra's hand and watched the flames dance, her eyes a little bit distant. Staring off into nothing as the sun sank lower still.

"Is it true Bothain is in Yaelsmuir?" Stella whispered once the sun went down. Once the stillness drove her out of her melancholy, wearing her fear away. Once the flames warmed her face so much it felt like they were giving her life again. "That's what the Enquiry Officers said. They were bringing me back for him."

"It's true," Tashué said. "Apparently he retired from the Authority and went to the Academy for his General's stars. He's taken the 12ᵗʰ, and he's in Yaelsmuir looking for a fight. Davik and I are going to give him one. But Ishmael is hoping he can go down to White Crown and tell the Queen everything he knows. Everything about the Authority, the children—all of it. I'm hoping you'll go with him."

"To White Crown?" Stella asked.

"Yes," Tashué said. "To tell her what you know. That's what Ishmael wanted. And if he's dead, then we'll find a way to get you down there anyway. I don't know. But it's what he wanted—he said the only way for us to have a shot is if the Queen pulls support from Clannaugh, which she might do if she understands why we're fighting."

Stella looked up at Tashué, watching his profile as the flames danced on his features. He looked different. He'd always looked a little bit angry, a little bit lost, but now there was something cold in his eyes. It had never been there before, at least not that she noticed. He'd always been so hot, like he was burning from the inside out, and that burning saved her from her own cold, distant numbness. Where had the cold come from? What is the way he guarded his grief? Or was it his soldier's face. He was a leader of warriors, once. It sounded like he was getting ready to be a leader of warriors again.

"Ishmael asked you to come?"

Tashué sighed, turning his face away from the fire for the first time since it was lit. He slid the back of one knuckle across Stella's cheek, touching the spot bruised by Siras's hand with such tenderness it almost made her start weeping again, but she was tired of tears. She was empty of them. There were none left for her to shed.

"He hoped you would know things that could help us. About the

Authority. Even if you told the Queen the same things you told me, it would mean more coming from you. You were there in Cruinnich."

"Ishmael asked you?" Stella repeated. "Not Davik?"

"No, not Davik," Tashué said. But he dropped his hand, looking down at the space between their feet. "I told him who I was looking for, Stella. I told him I was coming out here to find you. But I said I wasn't sure where you were, so I'll go back one way or another. If you don't want to come, I'll tell him I was wrong about you being close. I'll tell him I don't know where you are, and you can go."

"Mam, I want to go back," Ceridwen said. "Please? He came all this way—you're the one that said we never should have left Mr. Blackwood!"

"Just wait, Ceridwen," Ozra said. "It's for your mam to decide. It won't be safe there, not for you or for her. We may still make our way to the forest."

"I don't *want* to go to the logging camp," Ceridwen whined. "I want to go back to Yaelsmuir. You're the one who said nowhere is safe for the likes of us. So why not go back? And fight?"

"Ceridwen," Kazrani said, her first words since waking. "Give your mam time to think."

Ceridwen gave a dramatic huff, stuffing her hand into her pocket again. Reaching for that badge. Siras's badge. She kept it like a token, a trophy. It made Stella sick to the stomach every time she saw it, but it wasn't for her to forbid Ceridwen from keeping it. She'd kept Ceridwen away from who she was long enough—knotting up her Talent, running across the world when her own birth father was still looking for her, in his way. Now it was time to let her be.

That decision didn't make it any easier to contemplate going back, though. Bothain was in Yaelsmuir. And Davik. Siras was dead, maybe, but he'd only ever been an extension of Bothain. A tool for Bothain to exert his cruelty and control over her before his own hands turned on her, too. Before Davik dismantled her sense of self enough that for a few horrible weeks, she agreed with him when he said they had to do something to *the energy units* to force people to see the horrible reality of the Authority. It was an easy thing to wish to go back when it wasn't really an option. In the long, lonely nights in her bedroll. After Siras caught up to her. Going back was a wish for a thing that wasn't possible at that time, a wish for a part of her life before it was all so complicated. When she wished to go back, she imagined herself before Siras found her, before Tashué knew about Ceridwen and Bothain and Davik, when she was

Stella Whiterock, a whisperer at the Facility of Rest. And Tashué Black-wood was the neighbour who taught her how to be passionate again. But there was no going back to that delicate, beautiful moment. It was behind them, come and gone in what seemed like a few heartbeats. The weight of reality hit them before they even had the chance to know how precious their innocent tryst was going to feel in a few days.

Except it wasn't innocent. In remembering, she'd washed the moment of the dark pieces that were inconvenient to that feeling of nostalgia. The first night she went with him to his bed, he had blood on his shirt from Gianna Tarbrook, the healer who died on his watch, and he carried a badge for the Authority. And she surrendered to him because she thought it was temporary. She was already planning to leave.

So, she couldn't even go back in the way she imagined, because the version of that memory that she'd idealized since leaving Yaelsmuir didn't even exist.

She reached out to Tashué slowly, letting her fingers slide along his wrist. He had high quality clothes again, and the sleeve was actually the right length. He looked down at her hand like he couldn't quite believe she was touching him, flexing his fingers only slowly. The scar on the side of his hand, the one from the day they pulled that boy out of the wreckage of the Market fire, was still struggling to heal fully, half a bright pink line of fresh skin, half new scabs as if he kept ripping the wound open. She twined her fingers in his and leaned closer, resting her fore-head on his shoulder. Sweet North Star, it felt so good to lean on him again. Some part of her still expected him to dissolve and become Siras, like a fever dream she'd never fully wake from, but for now, it was utterly, convincingly him. The timber of his voice and the smell of his sweat and the details of his scars, they were all him. The way he called Ceridwen little warrior, as if he'd known, even before all of this happened, how ferocious Ceridwen would need to be one day.

"Tell me what happened," Stella said. "Tell me everything."

Tashué sighed, squeezing her hand. He glanced at Ceridwen. "Maybe she doesn't need to hear…"

"She's earned the right to be included," Stella said. "To know what we're going back to."

He unwound the whole story, laying the words down next to the fire. He couldn't look her in the eye again, watching the flames instead, watching the snow melt around the pyre. Watching the shadows and the light dance on the toes of their boots as they stood side by side. From the day he was arrested for threatening Rainer in a drunken rage, to the days he spent with Davik, to Powell Iwan's death and Jason finally coming out of the Rift because the children there died. And perhaps Stella was too tired to be surprised by anything anymore, but the words rolled through her without shocking her as much as they ought to. Nothing about Davik surprised her anymore.

"You were right when you warned me I would trust him," Tashué said. "I killed for him. But I don't think I had any other choice. Trust him or not, he's the one holding the Bay. He's the one with the Army to stand against Clannaugh."

Stella shook her head. "That's Davik for you. He's very good at convincing you there's no other choice but to do what he wants."

"I'm sorry, Stella." He finally turned to her, his eyes searching her face. "I shouldn't have told him you were out here."

"No," Stella said, meeting his gaze. "You shouldn't have. But he would have found out one way or another."

"Because you'll come back?"

Stella nodded. "In the morning. It's too late to travel now."

"We're going back?" Ceridwen gasped.

Stella bit her lip. She should send Ceridwen to the logging camp anyway. Ozra could take her, and maybe Kazrani too—they could hide with her in the Dunnenbrahl, at least until spring. But the thought of leaving Ceridwen behind filled Stella with panic. Which was worse? Bringing her to Yaelsmuir and risking that she'd die in the violence there? Or sending her away and risking that no one could protect her anywhere?

Kazrani sighed, stepping closer to the flames. She pulled the ribbon out of her hair, the one that kept the single braid in place, and cast it into the fire. She shook the plait loose, letting her hair fall down her back in a crimped black wave.

"Stella—would you let me braid your hair?" Kazrani asked. "Before we go?"

"Braid my hair?" Stella echoed.

Kazrani nodded. "Back home, there are a lot of words for family. It's a complicated idea on the grass. There's the family we choose, the family that made us, the family ties of the people we love. It's why the mishrakha army thinks we're all incestuous—they only have one word for family, so things don't translate well. Anyway, we took Tashué as ashurin—no blood ties to any of us, but we chose him. Before we shipped out to the Ridge, his hair was long enough for Qirin to give him ashurin braids. You remember that, Captain?"

Tashué nodded. "Of course. And I remember the army cutting the braids off me after I was arrested. Said they weren't approved uniform for someone of my rank."

Kazrani grimaced. "Fuck them. You were family. Still are. And so are you, Stella. I'd like to give you the same braids, if you're comfortable with it. There's the practical reasons for it of course—keeps your hair well protected, one less thing to worry about."

Stella smiled. "Are you saying that you've chosen me to be your family?"

Kazrani shrugged and nodded at once. "We haven't known each other long, but I respect you and all that you've survived. For that girl, for yourself. It's so easy to think of strength as a violent thing because that's the sort of strength we can see most clearly, but you... If you were Jitabvi, you would be coldblood, I think. And for all that we celebrate the hotbloods and their prowess in battle, we all know that none of it would be worth anything without the coldbloods. The future of our people is what we're all fighting for, and there's no future without all the things the coldbloods build. It's our honour and our purpose to protect them."

"I would be honoured," Stella said. "Thank you, Kazrani."

Kazrani nodded and fished a comb from the pocket of her heavy coat. She caught Stella by the hand, pulling her closer to the fire. Stella stripped out of her coat, the heat of the fire warming her skin until it ached. Kazrani stood behind her, shaking loose the simple plait Stella had been doing herself, using the comb to pick out the tangles in the curls.

"Which name should I say?" Kazrani asked. "While I braid, there's a song to sing that welcomes you to the ashrab—the family. Should I welcome you as Stella, or...?"

Stella closed her eyes, drawing a long, deep breath, until her lungs felt so full they could burst. Tashué had asked her this question a few times already—once in his apartment, where she told him to call her Stella, and once in the dream they shared, where she didn't answer at all. But Stella's life was defined by running, by hiding, by knotting up her own Talent so she could avoid being seen, by making herself smaller so she could survive.

But this decision—going back to Yaelsmuir, even though it meant facing Bothain—wasn't about being small or hidden. It wasn't about survival anymore. It was about tearing apart something big, about standing even though it might kill her. About standing in the centre of it all and yelling everything she knew at the top of her lungs so no one could look away.

She released the breath in slow increments, feeling the protective layers of *Stella* fall away. "Call me Ffyanwy."

76

ISHMAEL
DAY 41

P ain.
   Screaming.
   The pain tore the scream out of him, but even the screaming hurt. The thrashing hurt. The way he grasped the air, reaching, clawing, trying to drag himself out of the darkness and the sludge and the agony. Hurt. But he couldn't stop because the pain drove him out of his mind, out of himself, out of any sense of reason or control. Burned away everything except the pain and the need to get away from it.

Someone grabbed his hand. His wrist. Held his arm still.

"Ishmael," said a voice. He knew that voice. But even the act of moving his eyes and trying to find the face that went with the voice was agony. "We're going to give you more morphine. Just until I'm finished. A little bit longer and then it's over. The pain is good. It means you survived."

The morphine didn't hurt, but hit his vein like cleansing fire all the same, burning into the core of him, scorching parts of him away. Dragging him back down into the nothingness that had him before the pain found him.

An eternity of nothing.

Stretching him out until he was paper thin. Until he was wrapped around all the empty space between being awake and being dead. Sleeping, but not really. Aware, but not really.

Retching—foul bile, crawling up his throat, burning his nose and making it hard to breathe. Hands in his hair. A voice in his ear. Choking on the bile, because it was the only thing left in his system, no matter how much his body tried to purge him clean. Morphine sick.

"You're so dramatic, Ishmael."

That voice again. He knew that voice. Why did it feel so strange to hear that voice? He knew it was out of place. But he didn't know anything else. He tried to look—turning his head made him dizzy.

"You're finished now, finally? Good. Lay down. Rest."

He tried to open his eyes, but the world was blurry and too bright, and it seared all the way into his skull. Hands on his shoulder, pushing him until he was back down. Head sinking into something soft—a pillow —and the world went a little fuzzy again. So tired. Still in pain, but the edges of it weren't so violent anymore.

He tried to ask for water, but his voice only made a horrible whimpering sound.

Rest.

Not sleep exactly.

He was still aware of sounds around him, of people moving. The mattress shifted a few times. Someone spoke in low tones. About him. His head.

He floated.

The pain broke apart into smaller pieces, until he could tell the difference between each one. His knee hurt—that pain was deep and round. Last he remembered, his knee was getting better. Why did it hurt so viciously again? His chest hurt—tight, like pressure, making it hard to take a deep breath. His arm hurt—his forearm, the pain in the skin, pulling, sharper. His head hurt the most. Hot and sharp and consuming, throbbing in time with the beating of his too-fast heart, tightened around his skull, squeezed the nerves of his eyes.

Gods, he was so tired. Sleep danced around the corners of his mind without claiming him. Left him in his own consciousness long enough to start wondering things.

How long had he been floating in nothing?

Where was he now?

The last thing he remembered... he wasn't sure. Allie, maybe. The Rhydderch article. Tashué's voice. Nothing that explained the pain.

"Ishmael?"

Who's voice was that? Soft, sad.

"Ishmael, can you hear me?"

He tried to say something, but it took so much concentration. His mouth moved but no sound came out. Try again—this time, sound came, but his mouth didn't move enough to form words. He grunted. A little better than the whimpers from earlier, at least.

"I think he's waking up! Ishmael, can you hear me?" The shouting seared through the pain, like the words were hitting him with brute force.

He tried again. His voice scraped up his throat, catching on his tongue that was too thick with dehydration. Lips so dry, they were cracking. Again. Almost a word.

"Can I get you something? Some water? You should drink."

"Loud," he said. He opened his eyes. Allie stood beside him, her face framed by too bright sunlight. "You're loud."

She laughed. It hurt. She lay her hands on his face and that hurt too. He closed his eyes but leaned into her hands. Even though it hurt, it felt good to be touched by someone he knew. Something other than confusion and pain.

"Sorry," she said, her voice softer. But giddy, energetic. "You had us scared for a while."

He groaned. But he reached for her because it felt so good to know who was touching him. Felt good to know he wasn't alone in the nothingness and the pain hadn't driven him out of his mind. She squeezed his hand back, and that didn't hurt. Felt good to do something that didn't hurt.

"What happened?" Allie asked. "Do you remember?"

Ishmael tried. The headline of the Rhydderch Article flashed through his mind's eye, those big bold letters, as big as they could go. Taking up fully a quarter of the page. *What Happened To Ffyanwy Rhydderch?* Talking to Tashué about her. Ishmael saying, *I wish I could have talked to her. Anyone from the Rhydderch family.* Tashué's whole face spasming with pain. But nothing else. Like reaching for a shadow and closing a hand in the darkness, but of course there was nothing to catch.

Newsprint, on the bed with him.

"What happened?" Ishmael asked, reaching for the nearest page.

"Don't worry about that right now," Allie said, pulling the paper out of Ishmael's hand. Gathering up the whole stack and taking it out of reach. "We'll explain it later. You're supposed to rest. Your head was bad."

Ishmael grunted, fingers twitching. "What does it say? I need to know—"

"That's enough badgering my patient, Miss Tei." That voice again. Ishmael opened his eyes, and this time they focused. Eilas Kheir, Deri's most trusted healer. He stood in the beam of sunlight from the window, the light laying on his features so clearly that there was no mistaking him for anyone else. That sardonic smile, those thick black eyebrows that tried to make his face seem friendly and soft, except the way his intelligent amber gaze ripped into a person was intimidating and he knew it. "He needs to rest."

"He's badgering me, Mr. Kheir," Allie said. She stepped back from the bed, out of reach, tucking the newsprint under her arm.

"Eilas," Ishmael said. He wanted to say more. To ask why Eilas was here, to ask about Deri, to say something—something important. He needed to go to White Crown. The feeling came so urgently, carrying so much anxiety that Ishmael tried to push himself from the bed. He needed to go to White Crown. Moving that much brought the nausea back.

"Stop," Eilas said, pushing Ishmael back down with strong hands. Ishmael couldn't fight it, even though he wanted to. "You need to rest. Your head injury was very severe. I consider it good news—turns out you have a brain and you use it, despite overwhelming evidence to the contrary. You'll heal, but you need time."

Ishmael sank back down. Eilas's Talent unfolded like a warm blanket, and Ishmael spun off into sleep.

It was quiet when he woke again. Quiet and mostly dark. A lamp glowed somewhere far away. Newsprint scattered over the bed again. Some attempt at organization had been made, but Ishmael must have moved, spilling the pages across his blankets. Weight, on his legs. Gods, he hadn't noticed that before. Was there something wrong with both his legs? He flexed his toes, but it made his knee scream at him. He groaned, looking down at his feet. It wasn't his bad leg that felt heavy, it was the other one—

A head, on his lap. Someone had pulled up a chair to his bed and had fallen asleep with their head against his leg. That posture, those shoulders, it was all so familiar that it washed the pain out of him. Salt-and-pepper hair that he saw in his dreams.

It couldn't be—

He reached down to all that thick hair, his fingers sliding through the mix of black and grey. It couldn't be. He was dreaming. Hallucinating. The morphine was giving him some equivalent of an opium dream but more powerful. Or maybe he was dead, and this was what his soul saw while he was waiting to be reunited with the gods. Ishka, goddess of the soul, had given him this one gift before she wiped his soul clean to send him back to a new life. Letting him see the one person he loved most, one more time.

He tried to speak again, but gods, his throat was so dry. A pitcher of water sat beside the bed. They must have helped him drink at some point, but it wasn't enough. He was back to making inarticulate sounds instead of forming words.

The head popped up out of sleep and turned to face him.

Deri.

A new sound gurgled out of Ishmael's throat. Some mix of a laugh, a sob, a groan. He reached for Deri's face, this man he'd been mourning for two years. It couldn't be. But he felt skin below his hand, and the rough stubble of a few days' past shaving. Deri turned his mouth toward Ishmael's palm and his hot breath danced across Ishmael's skin. He lay a kiss on Ishmael's fingers so it felt like Ishmael could catch it and hold it.

"You're dead," Ishmael breathed.

Deri chuckled. "I sent you a letter. I thought you'd figure it out, but I guess your communication skills are more lacking than I thought."

"I didn't get it," Ishmael said. The words came out slow, clumsy.

"You didn't get it?" Deri echoed.

Ishmael shook his head. Pain lanced down through his neck. He closed his eyes, keeping himself still until the pain rolled back out of him.

"Fuck's sake. I knew something had gone wrong. I waited as long as I could—but then I had to leave. Next time I fake my death, I'll make sure I hire a private mail carrier. Can't trust the Royal Mail these days."

Deri's voice sounded so good that Ishmael wanted to grab him and kiss him, but moving still hurt. He wanted to hit Deri, to pummel his fists against skin and bone, wanted to scream and cry, letting out all the grief that had been trapped since the day he heard Deri was dead. But that much emotion made his head hurt. He kept his eyes shut and focused on breathing, but it didn't help. The whine was coming out of him again, ripping up through him, making his head hurt more. Deri pushed himself to his feet, the chair scraping on the floor. Ishmael's eyes flared open, hands reaching —*don't go* he wanted to say, but his mouth wasn't working. He couldn't muster the concentration for words when his head hurt so fucking much.

"Just relax," Deri said, sitting beside Ishmael's pillow. The shift of the mattress made Ishmael sag toward Deri's legs. Deri took him by the shoulders and pulled him up, so that his head rested in Deri's lap. "Relax. I'll get in trouble if I let you get too riled up. Eilas isn't happy about coming out of retirement. He made some vague threats about not letting you think too much or else he'd come for my balls. Again. Breathe. Nice and slow."

Breathe. In and out. Breathe through the panic and the pain.

"You're dead, too, for whatever it's worth. Do you want to see the photographs? It's fantastically gruesome. It might not be enough to shake Maes off for good, since we couldn't let Clannaugh see your body. He'd probably cut your heart out to make sure you were really dead. Even Eilas couldn't have fixed that. The big bastard made a mess of the hospital, hoping to find you, but they handed him one of your tattoos and sent him on his way. Wonderful staff at that hospital. Wolfe has a good eye for people who couldn't give half a fuck, doesn't he? Here. Eilas said you should drink when you woke up."

Deri took him by the arms and helped him sit, pushing the cup into his hand. Ishmael had to focus so hard on gripping the cup that it made his hand tremble. The skin of his arm felt too tight, like it was pulling. A bandage covered his forearm, and a bit of blood seeped through in a dry red-brown line. Deri helped him lift the cup to his mouth, helped him drink. The water was cool, and his throat was so dry it hurt to swallow, but it helped. Deri took the cup away after only a few sips, setting it on the table. Ishmael sank back down, his head resting on Deri's chest. Deri's heart beat slow and familiar. The heart that allegedly stopped two years ago. Eilas lied to the Queen so Deri could get out of White Crown, but Deri wrote that letter to Ishmael and Maes read it—

"He knows you're not dead." Talking was easier when he was calm, but his words still sounded slow and clumsy. Too heavy on his tongue.

His brain couldn't process talking and emotions at the same time. One or the other.

"Who?" Deri asked.

"Maes." Ishmael spat the name like venom, but he had to breathe again, had to calm himself back down or he wouldn't be able to say anything else. "He read the letter. I didn't get it, but he did."

"We'll deal with it later," Deri said softly. "You need to sleep."

Ishmael reached for the closest newsprint, but Deri snatched it out of his hand.

"Stubborn shithead," Deri said, the curse spoken like a loving pet name. "Sleep. That's an order, diplomat."

Too tired to argue—Ishmael closed his eyes. The darkness was inviting, dragging him down again. But he had things to say. Important things. He didn't have time to sleep. How long had he been here, in this bed? He needed to go to White Crown. He caught Deri's hand, clinging to wakefulness. Clinging to Deri, in case it was a dream. His hands weren't as big as Tashué's, but they were plenty strong, familiar scars settling against Ishmael's palm. They fit together, him and Deri. There was a time that he imagined retiring and settling out west, on Deri's poppy farm, the pair of them fitted together for the rest of their lives. But then Deri died and everything fell apart—and that was a lie. A painful lie, covering a beautiful, merciful truth.

And Yaelsmuir was falling apart, too, but no one would tell him how bad it was.

———

The sun made the room glow. Made the stone around him warm. He didn't know where he was, but it was quiet here. Deri slept behind him, his arm around Ishmael's chest to pull them together, his face pressed against Ishmael's back. Snoring softly. Ishmael lay still a while, listening to the snoring, watching the dust motes swirl in the beams of sun. Everything still hurt, but at least he could think.

What happened? He tried to remember, reaching slowly through his mind. The Rhydderch article—Tashué's face when Ishmael wished to talk to Stella. The sound of smashing plates—no, that was the day before the Rhydderch article, after he fought with Mallory about Mairead.

Rowan, soaked by the rain—*Da sent me to get you. Said Mr. Iwan wants to see you.*

Blood. And then what?

A stack of newsprint on the table, beside the jug of water. He reached for them slowly, but his arm hurt. Pulled. The bandage was stuck to his skin, the blood that seeped through was dry and caught in whatever wound the bandage was covering. He teased the knot open, challenging though it was with one trembling hand. Unwound the cotton. The bandage tugged on the stitches as he peeled it away. It didn't matter how carefully he tugged at it, it had caught on the scabs between the stitches, and the only way to get it off was to rip the scabs away with the bandage. It hurt, but not nearly as much as some of the other wounds. Not nearly as much as the pain in his chest at what he saw.

His tattoo of the watch had been peeled off him. A skin graft covered the big open wound it would have left behind, the stitches holding the transplanted skin in place. Two neat strips, cobbled together. Old loss rolled through him, burning with fresh edges. That tattoo was perhaps the one that said the most—the tattoo he got for the men who killed his father. He dropped the bandages to the floor, watching the fresh blood seep out from the suture line. Watching the vivid redness become little jewels before running down his skin.

"General Wolfe's idea. Said that's the one you're most known for, so Maes might appreciate it as a trophy. We took some skin off your ass to cover it up again so it heals faster. One strip off each cheek. Good thing you've always had a big ass."

Ishmael turned slowly. Eilas stood at the end of the bed, a cup in his hand that gave off fragrant steam. It twisted through the sunlight.

"Canny old soldier, Wolfe," Eilas said. "I can see why you and Deri like him so much. He hides a lot of anger under all that talk of civility and diplomacy and provincial rights, doesn't he?"

Ishmael nodded. "I think he does it to try to balance the scales. Figures he owes the universe something for all the ugly battles he's directed."

Eilas grunted, walking around the bed to sit in the chair that Deri previously occupied. He swept all the newsprint up with one hand, clearing enough space to put the cup down. "We'll let that cool some and then I expect you to drink all of it. You lost a lot of blood."

Ishmael watched the stack of newsprint, his fingers twitching with the desire to reach out and grab them from Eilas's hand. There was no way he could move that fast, but he wanted to know. Eilas must have spotted him watching, because he held the whole stack up.

"You can look, but as soon as you feel dizzy or nauseated, you have to give them back. Go slow. Don't try too hard to read. I spent a lot of time saving that slab of opium-smoked fat you call a brain, and I won't have you fucking it up. I'm supposed to be retired, for fuck's sake, not looking after you *again*."

Ishmael nodded. Eilas's eyes fixed on Ishmael's face, his chin dipping down, the intensity of him sizzling. Waiting, stretching, like he expected Ishmael to argue.

"As soon as I feel dizzy," Ishmael said, stretching out a hand. "Please?"

Eilas handed the whole stack over. Ishmael let it rest on the bed in front of him, spreading them out. The smell and the powdery feeling of fresh news print was familiar now after spending days churning them out under the *Dripping Bucket*. The Rhydderch article was in the stack. He tried to read the headlines, but his eyes slid off them too fast. Hard to focus. If he let his eyes drift, then it didn't make his head hurt. He absorbed the words slowly, one at a time, the headlines only.

Bay Justice For Powell Iwan over a photograph of the Hive, bodies tied by their ankles and hanging upside down, every one of them headless and naked. A letter carved into each of their chests to make those two words again. *Bay Justice*.

Ishmael Saeati Murdered By Authority? And the photographs were harrowing. Him—allegedly—in a hospital bed. The photograph was offset so it was only the edge of the bed, and one arm hanging out, and the side of his face. He was still enough to be captured in perfect detail, but the healers around him were a blur. So much blood the sheets were dripping with it. So much blood it pooled on the ground around him. Could that really all be his?

"They were accommodating enough to place you on a bed a previous patient had occupied," Eilas said. "The poor sod bled everywhere rather photogenically."

Ishmael pushed the page away. Another, bloodier, of the inside of Davik's pugilist club. Bodies stacked in the ring, blood running down from the raised platform in dark sepia toned ropes. Blood on the floor, with footprints smudged through it. The whole fucking city was bleeding, hemorrhaging life through Clannaugh's hands. *Ari Odegaard Dead—Wife Speaks Out*.

There were more pages, but the ache settled right behind his eyes. He couldn't focus. He pushed them away, squeezing his eyes shut again. Just until the spinning stopped, until his stomach relaxed again.

"Miss Tei has been busy," Eilas said. "She churns these out faster than anyone can print them. She's taken to badgering papers all over the city to take her articles. She's a good find, that one. If I had any respect for the Dominion military left, I'd send her up for the press corps. But I wouldn't wish a military career on my worst enemy. Where'd you find her?"

"Captain Blackwood found her," Ishmael grunted. "Where is he? Did he get himself killed?"

"If he did, there aren't any photographs of it," Eilas said. "Miss Tei seems to think he's the one who brought you to the hospital, but no one's seen him since before Iwan died. The old man's head was a nice touch. Was that really Clannaugh's idea, or did you do it?"

Blood—the memory flashed through Ishmael's head. Blood and Powell Iwan's chest blown open. His own pain making him sick. Adley dead on the floor. Did he arrive and find it already done, or did he do it? But focusing on the memories only made them harder to grasp, made his head hurt again. "Don't remember."

"It may come back," Eilas said, his tone softening some. "It may not."

"Don't start feeling sorry for me," Ishmael grunted. "Then I'll be worried I might actually die."

"I think you're through it now, unless you do something especially stupid. You need to give your skull time to heal. I've done what I can to get the process started, and I'll keep helping it along, but I don't dare push it too quickly. You don't want brittle bone in your skull, of all places, thick though yours may be."

"My skull was fractured?" Ishmael asked.

"No, we had a surgeon cut a piece away to let the blood out. We were able to get rid of the clot that was causing most of the pressure and replace the bone in time for the healing to take. These things have to move quickly, or else the shard of bone dies, and it won't rejoin the skull. You were exceptionally lucky. The healers at the hospital—hard-working though they are—didn't have the skill required, but the General wanted to come up the river to find you, so here we are. He'll probably ask you to leave once you're well enough, but you won't. Will you?"

"When can I travel?" Ishmael asked. He touched his head, searching.

He found a patch where they'd shorn his hair away, where stitches jutted up like rough sentries guarding the wound. "Soon?"

Eilas's eyebrows rose. "You'll leave Yaelsmuir?"

"I have to," Ishmael said. He reached for the newsprint again, laying his hand on the stack. Ink representing the ocean of blood, spilling in the streets. "It's only going to get worse. I need to go down to White Crown —I need to tell the Queen everything. I need to tell her what the Authority's done."

Eilas looked down at Ishmael's hand. He was silent so long, it made Ishmael's heart beat faster. That had to be bad. If whatever Eilas wanted to say was so heavy that he had trouble finding the words, it had to be terrible. Deri's arm tightened around Ishmael's chest, like he was pulling Ishmael closer. He wasn't snoring anymore—he must have woken up at some point.

"Do you want to tell him?" Eilas asked. "Or are you going to make me do it?"

Deri sighed. "If you tell him, maybe he'll be angry with you instead of me."

"Tell me what?" Ishmael asked. "Eilas—what?"

Eilas drummed his fingers on the arm of his chair. "Any day now, our Queen will have a King."

Ishmael's heart leapt. Soared. Beat in double time, so hard it choked him. "Raheem."

"She told you?"

Ishmael nodded. "Last time she was here."

"Yaelsmuir's uprising was deemed a fortuitous opportunity," Eilas said, drumming his fingers again. The sound hit Ishmael's skull like rapid-fire gunshots, sending tension down his spine. "Maes and Clannaugh are focused on the Army of the Red Dawn, chasing rumours of Davik Kaine, building their provincial police force on the backs of the rebels. And in the meantime, Leony and Raheem will marry, sign a few treaties, and assemble Raheem's division to move against Maes. If we're especially lucky, they'll get the better of him soon."

"Good," Ishmael breathed. "We'll go down to White Crown, tell her what we know about the Authority. She can add Rainer Elsworth and Bothain Clannaugh to the list of arrestees."

"Ishmael," Deri said. That tone of his that was half-worried, half-annoyed, like he knew there was going to be a fight, but he was compelled to speak anyway. "She knows."

"How?" Ishmael asked, turning to Deri. But he turned too fast and the dizziness had him, sliding him off into a spinning oblivion. Acid climbed up the back of his throat, threatening to make him vomit again. He squeezed his eyes shut, clenched his teeth. Waited an eternity for it to pass. "How does she know?"

"Eilas told her," Deri said simply. "He's been gathering evidence for years."

"I was hoping this day would come," Eilas said. "And when it did, I vowed I would be ready."

"That's good," Ishmael said. "She'll have no choice but to do something. She'll have to rein Clannaugh in—she won't let him paint us as lawless criminals if she understands what we're fighting for."

Silence again. Stretching so long it seemed as if time stopped. The world ceased turning for a moment, leaving Ishmael spiralling alone through fresh layers of panic. He grabbed the news pages again to touch something familiar, just to know he was still real, still capable of movement. Listened to the paper as it crumpled in his hands, powdery ink smearing across his palms. All that blood turned to black ink on white pulp. The whole city was bleeding and no one was going to stop it.

"It was decided that the marriage was worth it," Eilas said. "A Crowne-Deri alliance opens up avenues for retribution—"

"We wouldn't have to *get* retribution if we stopped Clannaugh before he torched the whole fucking city," Ishmael snapped. It hurt. Gods, it hurt. His head pounded, seared, shredded, like his skull was cracking open under the pressure of his fury, his betrayal, his preemptive grief. "She could arrest him and Rainer both and stop it—"

"She'll come," Deri said. "Ishmael, listen. She'll come when she can. When she's got herself well insulated against Maes's fury."

"How long will that take?" Ishmael asked. "How many people are going to die while we wait? Innocent fucking people, fighting to protect children!"

"Everyone's innocent," Deri said. "And no one is innocent. That's what I taught you, Ishmael. For the objective, anyone is fair game, so long as it gets us what we want."

"You'll let a whole fucking city burn so your son will take the Crowne?" Ishmael asked, pushing Deri away. He had to get out of here. He had to go find someone. Davik. Tashué. Vasska. Fucking anyone, anyone who could do something. But moving so much hurt his knee.

Made his head hurt so much he couldn't see anymore. He floated in a white cloud of rage. "You greedy fucking coward!"

Hands on his shoulders. Weight shifting. Was he falling? Or just dizzy? Was he screaming again, or did he *want* to scream, want to rip his own hair out just to do something with all this rage, want to peel the rest of his own tattoos off because everything he'd ever done for Deri and the Dominion was a fucking waste, a lie, a crime.

"Stop!" Deri's voice cut through the roaring in Ishmael's ears. "Stop —you're going to tear your stitches again, for fuck's sake!"

"Move," Eilas said, his voice even more commanding than Deri's. "Hold his arm."

The morphine burn was familiar now. It sliced away the fury, silenced the screaming in his chest. He drifted down into nothingness like so much nighttime snow.

"I never said you had to give up," Deri said. His voice led Ishmael up out of the dark places, out of the restless morphine dreams that chewed on him with anxious teeth. He sat in his chair again, turned toward the window so the evening light danced in his salt-and-pepper hair. He looked good, the bastard. Two years, Ishmael had been grieving. Two years, he'd been wandering somewhere between wanting to live and heal and wanting to die to get away from the stretching, aching, endless loneliness. And Deri had the fucking cheek to come around here, looking well rested and well fed. "I never said the city wasn't worth fighting for. I torched my whole career to come and fight for those children. Torched my whole fucking life. I wanted to bring you with me and tell you everything, but Maes sent you back to the Commonwealth, and then it was too late. I had to go."

Ishmael lay still a while, watching shadows climb over the stone walls as dusk settled again. The morphine must still be sitting in his veins. The pain was distant. His thoughts were calm, removed from the wild anxiety that made his head hurt so fucking much. How long had he been here in this cursed bed? Where *was* this cursed bed? The room was so big, and the windows were double-paned glass, definitely too luxurious for anywhere in the Bay. A wood stove in the corner simmered a pot of broth. A fresh pitcher of water sat on the table. All of the news pages were gone. That privilege was apparently revoked.

"How long have you known?" Ishmael asked.

"A while," Deri said softly. "Since Obisza. I wanted to tell you——"

Ishmael grunted, turning away from him. He watched the pot for a while, watched the steam swirl up. Every now and then, a few droplets of water jumped up out of the pot and landed on the surface of the stove, sizzling away in an instant.

"Don't be a fucking cock about it."

"Lick my fat ass."

"I would, but you haven't bathed in a while. You're getting rather pungent."

Ishmael bit the inside of his lip so he wouldn't laugh. He wouldn't give Deri the satisfaction. Bastard.

"You were right when you said Rainer's never been smart enough to pull all this together," Deri said. "He's a middling politician, a mediocre businessman, but his hunger for credit and notoriety is what pushes him on. He never thought to ask why Clannaugh let him take the credit for all these programs. Breeding Program, Enquiry, the energy units. They set our economy leaps and bounds ahead of other countries, and Rainer gets to be the one with his hand on the rudder for it all, like he's responsible. But he isn't."

"Clannaugh and Maes have been feeding him ideas," Ishmael said. "Letting him build it all, letting him take the credit. So they could let him take the fall if ever it was challenged."

Deri only grunted his confirmation.

"If we tear down the Authority here in Yaelsmuir, let it all fall on Rainer, Maes will rebuild it with someone else as a figurehead. The Queen has to take Maes down, too, or it's all for nothing."

Deri sighed, rising up out of the chair. He came to the bed, settling on the edge. He lay behind Ishmael again, kissing the side of Ishmael's neck. "I'll help them fight. Hold the city as long as we can. Keep pumping proof out to the whole country. To buy the Queen as much time as she needs. She'll come when she can."

The morphine kept the despair at bay for now. "Yaelsmuir has to burn."

Deri nodded, his face brushing against Ishmael's back. "Yaelsmuir has to burn."

ABOUT THE AUTHOR

Krystle Matar has been writing for a long time, but things got serious when Tashué Blackwood walked into her life, an amber-eyed whirlwind. Her debut, Legacy of the Brightwash, is a SPFBO Finalist, an r/Fantasy nominee for Best Debut and Best Indie.

When she isn't arguing with Tashué or any of his friends, she parents full time. She has a lot of children, too many hobbies, and one very excellent husband.

She is currently working on lots of stories set in the Dominion, is 1/4 of the Swords & Corsets Podcast, and is probably obsessively rewatching BBC's Ripper Street and/or anything that Dennis Lehane worked on like Apple TV's Blackbird.

Check out krystlematar.com for publishing news. You can also join the newsletter mailing list, which will have deleted scenes, extra stories, publishing news, and more!

Printed in the USA
CPSIA information can be obtained
at www.ICGtesting.com
LVHW091039011023
759814LV00023B/1303/J